Anelisha Knight In

The Legacy of Dragons

Book 2

JULIA T. LYE

ANELISHA KNIGHT IN THE LEGACY OF DRAGONS

For information contact :

Front cover design by Diana Buidoso

ISBN: 9781896794556

First Edition: October, 2021

10 9 8 7 6 5 4 3 2 1

Also by Julia Lye

Anelisha Knight

The Yarns Of Gods

Magikier Chronicles

The Olde: Volume I
The Olde: Volume II
The Olde: Volume III
The Olde: Lost Fables
Left Behind
The Anelein
A Cention's Tale
The Magisterium
A Lockewood Gathering
The Great End Saga

Other

Outcast
The Travellers
Relics of a Lost World
Rothell Manor
The Stranger Side of Tomorrow
What Lies in Wait

Dedicated to Cecilia.
Distance has nothing on us.

1

Starting Fresh

Date Unknown

THERE WEREN'T ENOUGH MEDICS. OF ALL OF US WHO ESCAPED THE chaos and culling of Valencia's enacted plans, only a handful possessed the kind of magic we needed most at present. My sister counted among them, which was telling enough of our sorry circumstances. I pitied the wounded refugees sedated under her hands.

Oh, right, I was one of them.

The moment my brain finally processed that I had escaped likely doom, my injuries flared up with mind-consuming agony, like fire up my arms, and I dissolved into it. The intense pain came out of nowhere and hit all the harder for it. In the blink of an eye, there was only torment, and in some distant sector of my besieged mind, I heard my own wet sobbing, cracking voice, and cries for help more than I felt them. I think it was then that Faith saw fit to put me under.

Hers had to be my least favourite magic of all. Not that I knew much about magic, having only stumbled upon my own in a fit of panic, then scraped by on adrenaline alone. Me, the Champion of Blackano – just something I had heard on whispered voices while my friends rushed me to whatever healer they could find.

Then, blackout.

Faith's doing, I assumed, by the feel of her hand on my head. Her magic was like when dentists freeze half your face for a filling, except one touch was enough to numb the entire body, and when your mind finally cleared of the insipid haze that came with it, all your joints were locked up and stiff. Really, just the worst.

I woke up to find the lacerations trailing up my arms were sutured and painless. Considering the enduring hubbub of the infirmary around me – looking like a circus tent in an empty field, although the screams were hardly joyous – I doubted I was out for much longer than a day.

I still faced the threat of reopening my wounds, but at least some of my strength had returned. Surely, the fact I hadn't died was owed to healing magic, but the enduring pain all throughout my body just went to show how much we lacked, a stark contrast coming off the generous utilities and ample magikiers of Blackano.

For many, the help they needed just wasn't available, limited to the specializations of healing magic our handful of healers were practiced in. A simple glance sideways showed me as much.

Branching, bloodred patterns over Lin's skin from the perfect circle in the middle of her forehead – like tattoos, really – had already become permanent scars. Her perpetually bloodshot eyes, mixing red and black in the sclera, had her avoiding eye contact with the rest of us. If there were healers who could get rid of these grim markings, we certainly didn't have any at our disposal.

She was only fourteen years old, but from now on, her reflection would be a constant reminder of the kirranite parasite she almost didn't escape. When I looked at her, all I could see was the cold-blooded cruelty Valencia Lupei was capable of.

2

So, This Is Cellana

Day 2

A DAY OF TENDING TO THE WOUNDED PASSED BEFORE WE REFUGEES OF Blackano set out to find the City of Gates where magikiers who had chosen this life were meant to go. After all, this country, Arillia, was the entry point for fresh meat to finally enlist in service to the centions. Every magikier was required to serve a minimum of fifteen years on Cellana, shortened only by death, but we didn't talk about that part so much. And I was under the impression our situation complicated matters some.

By the first night, we came to the conclusion nine thousand of us had escaped Blackano, a great deal of us having suffered injury. Among the majority of Blackano citizens left behind were Roxy and Alfred. We couldn't know if they'd even survived, or if they ended up like Dahlia, killed in cold blood; or like Key-Keeper Anticus, overtaken by the kirranite parasite. Although the thought weighed heavily on everyone, we couldn't bring ourselves to speak their names. The friends we'd failed.

We appointed a commander, Seth Knox – and truly, he was the only leader among us by whom I would abide. He had sent our slinky, little dragon mascot ahead to the City of Gates to return with emergency services, but we couldn't wait any longer without food or water.

There would be provisions at the City of Gates, and enough for all of us. So, at dawn on the second day, volunteers with enough strength towed the injured on hastily made stretchers, and those of us too weak to be any help paved the way with weapons drawn and offensive magic on stand-by.

The thing about magikiers was, we weren't all created equal. The only help I could offer was to refuse a stretcher, myself.

An overexertion of magic had cut my arms into ribbons, but my legs, at least, could support my own weight. Faith and Kev were some of the lucky ones, having been mended to full health back in the bunker where we had more healers at our disposal.

A well-worn road of cobblestone and grime led from the field where the gateway spat us out. It looked like summer here, but this was an alien planet after all, so who was to say.

The air was brisk and dry, raising goosebumps along my arms where the bandages didn't cover. Huddled together like marching penguins, I walked among my friends with healers and stretchers bustling all around, but my eyes were wide on our surroundings. Our slow-moving convoy followed the cobblestones into a forest of cloud-brushing trees whose leaves were pleated and yellow, and the bark a chalky grey which, when touched, left a fine powder on my hands. But of course, I had to brush past the trunks as we walked, my nose following the faint scent of freshly peeled citrus fruit, somewhere between lime and orange hanging with tangy bitterness in the air. After all, these were-

"Alien trees!" I burst, eyes wide on the ashen powder. I sniffed the dust on my palm, only to jerk back upon catching a whiff of the sickly-sweet stench of blood stained into my bandages. Right, I probably should've seen that coming. Nevertheless, I continued, "These are alien trees! Guys, we're all seriously underreacting to the fact we're on an alien planet!" Somehow, the radiant rings making up a good portion of the sky hadn't driven the point home. "Or... Hm, does this make us the aliens?"

My friends all shared a concerned look no matter that I, the subject of their concern, strode along between them. With Brett still resting atop a stretcher Kev and Lin carried, and Faith attending to him as our resident nurse, it wasn't exactly inconspicuous, but I wasn't unfamiliar with their exasperated concern.

Shrugging, Lin noted, "Wasn't the first magikier made on Cellana?"

A quiet gasp escaped me. "So you're saying the Knox's were the aliens all along? That Seth's part-alien?"

She shared another look with Faith. "Sure."

"Oh my god!" I failed to stifle my half-hearted chuckling upon noticing the ashy powder caking my bandages. "I'm gonna forget we ever had this conversation, thank you very much." As I spoke, I dusted my palms off on my sweater, only for the sutures quilting my skin beneath to tug on a patch of dried blood making stiff the once-soft material. I sucked back breath between gritted teeth, clenching my fists at my sides to fend off the slight sting of a suture pulled taut.

Faith raised an eyebrow at me, catching my reaction. "Why don't you try walking like a zombie?" She mimed her meaning with two arms stuck out ahead of her, and for the added dramatic effect, lolled her head on her shoulders. The ghost of a smirk played behind her weary eyes. "Before you shred all the hard work of our healers." She nodded down to the fresh red blotches flowering across my bandages.

"I doubt that's very practical," I mused, mocking her typical tone. It was a pitiful imitation of her, so much so, I doubted she would've known I was imitating her at all if she wasn't my sister.

She bumped my side, shaking her head in exasperation, but her movement only drew my gaze to Brett on his stretcher, falling into view just over her shoulder. The smile slipped from my face.

"Speaking of practical, have you heard anything from Briar?" Lin asked in her flat voice, although I could hear her effort to sound upbeat. For the nth time, I wracked my brain for any hint of the telepathic dragon's voice, but the connection between our minds was down. My friends watched me, a glimmer of hope in their eyes, but only until I shook my head, mouth a tight line.

"We're on Cellana for one day and she's already gone AWOL," Brett grumbled.

I shot him a sideways glance. "Give her a little credit, the sassy reptile has *some* integrity."

Faith shook her head. "It's not a question of integrity, Annie. We all know what the centions did to dragons. He's only saying, well, she'd have to be some sort of emotional masochist to stick around." My sister's gaze flicked up to the swarm of darkness hovering high overhead. "Especially now that Dyval's been keeping a close eye on us, glory to her."

The dark cloud which moved like a swarm of too many birds had been shadowing us refugees since our arrival on Cellana, the saving force that got us through the gateway in the first place. This was the god-like Dyval, the first cention to show magikiers any sympathy in... I wasn't even sure how long, if ever. See, I was still new to all this, with only four months of the mandatory two years' training under my belt. Too many of us hadn't finished our studies, but the military police who had defended us in Blackano's bunkers now defended us here. I only hoped they were enough for all I'd heard of Cellana's dangers.

"Even more reason to hurry back..." I muttered with downturned gaze. Briar couldn't risk crossing the centions, not now that she'd sacrificed some secret thing to protect me from their wrath. After all, I was the one who manipulated them. I was the one who stole the power of a shonte for myself. And she leapt in to defend my actions. But considering I was the one Valencia most wanted to kill, I felt that I deserved a better chance at beating her, at least in the name of self defense.

"So what's taking her so long?" Kev asked with a harshness to his tone I assumed stemmed from our whole messed up situation, but the answer came unspoken, provided by the sight ahead.

Our convoy of refugees slowed to a halt on the outskirts of the City of Gates low in the valley where the forest thinned and the fields burned. Among the caravan of stretchers, my friends and I were stuck behind too many people to see anything clearly, only the black plumes of smoke billowing from rubble and ruin, carrying a stench of death and an eerie silence on the calm breeze. The buzz of too many voices met a new hum nestled in my head at the sight of this smoke.

"No..." The whisper stowed away on my breath, a thought. Over the heads of hundreds, beyond the toppled walls of the city, there lay only devastation. My heart skipped a beat, lightning shooting through my veins. "Briar's down *there*?"

I shot off before my friends could stop me, squeezing between the frozen bodies of the hopeless. I heard them calling out after me, but my feet only hit the cobblestones harder. I pushed my way through the convoy, ducking past the military police making up the front lines, but a hand caught my arm just as I breached the sea of lost souls. His grasp squeezed fire into my arm where my cuts were sewn shut, but just as quickly as he had taken my arm, he released me.

Wincing against the fleeting pain, I rounded on whoever had grabbed me, only to find the blue eyes of Seth Knox. He searched my golden-brown ones for whatever reason would have me sprinting headlong toward potential danger. Didn't he know this was my M.O.? His mouth quirked up in one corner, as if to say he should've expected rash action from the likes of me.

"That's probably not the best idea," he noted with a nod toward the ruined city over my shoulder. "Looks like there was a recent attack." The smile slipped away to melancholy; his eyes engrossed on the scene beyond me. "Or an extermination."

"Briar should've been back by now. Has she said anything to you?"

He glanced up toward Dyval's presence, the dark cloud casting a yet darker shadow over the convoy. "She's scouting the area, but now I see why. We need food, shelter, water… and our only hope for that is the city, even in ruins. If we can, we'll need to take it. But until Briar reports back, we can't make a move." He must have noticed the despair seeping off me, for his eyes found mine again, soft with the echo of a smile. "Until then, we're safe under Dyval's protection. That is, as long as we stay together. She pledged her protection to the refugees, glory to her, not to each of us individually."

My sister's dragging feet and jaded groans introduced her only moments before she shoved through the loitering military police awaiting Seth's command. "Why do you do this?" she panted, stomping up to me.

Tearing my eyes from Seth's, as deep and as blue as the ocean, I muttered for Faith, "I thought I could do… *something.*" At my words, her eyebrows crawled high on her forehead, and she made an exasperated motion to the bandaging all up my arms. Yeah, okay, so that kind of thinking was what got me into this cut-up mess, but what else could I do? Nothing? Rolling my eyes, my gaze landed once again on Seth's steady regard, so honest and full. Only to him did I concede, "But you have a point. About sticking together. I just wish Briar would talk to me."

"From what I can tell, she only wants to give you a break." His tone was gentle.

"I don't think I'll be getting a break, whether she keeps me in the loop or not." I gestured out to the ruined city, dark with soot and stretching far to the horizon beneath bright clouds. Although the city was sparse and obscured by smoke, it was sprawling. From here, I noticed a dried-up moat surrounded the city walls, and atop the walls lay the remains of destroyed turrets.

Faith glibly deduced, "If that's not it, then she's using her brain and keeping *you* from throwing yourself at whatever danger might be out there; your favourite pastime."

I opened my mouth with index finger raised, about to make a counterpoint, but hesitated on the notion that she was probably right. My finger wilted with the thought, joined by my scowl. "Ah… That does sound like something she'd do."

"With good reason. This new power only enables you to act *more* recklessly," Faith pointed out, but the real betrayal came with Seth's sage nod in agreement. Taken aback, I gave a dramatic gasp, making a spectacle of my played-up reaction.

Briar hardly gave me a moment's warning before her voice bombarded my head, opening the telepathic connection I'd awaited all day. "*Truly, your actions only prove their point. In order to act selflessly, you must be selfish. Your untimely death would only bring success to our enemies. So I ask, now that you've arrived on a world hellbent on your destruction, please do make yourself aware of what dangers are posed to you, and act selfishly to avoid them. Do that, and you'll save countless more lives than those lost defending you.*"

Oh, right, in all my fretting over Briar's silence, I forgot her tendency to lecture me. My shoulders slumped and I crossed my arms over my chest. My thoughts echoed with my response, "*Selfless selfishness? Now that's what I call counterintuitive.*"

I could just about feel her rolling those reptilian eyes of hers, forcing the ghost of a smile over my lips. Faith caught the shift in my expression, a light dawning in her eyes.

"She's in your head?"

Before I could answer, Briar's voice returned, but this time not just in my mind. Seth and Faith started in alarm – neither of them as familiar with Briar's surprise telepathy as I had come to be – when she relayed, "*The City of Gates is devoid of life. Long dead magikiers litter the ground, but hardly enough to represent how many must have lived here prior to the attack. As for said attackers, they've vacated the area. Whatever reason they had to destroy the city; it was certainly not to take it for themselves.*"

"A massacre..." Seth breathed, eyes narrowed on the ravaged City of Gates, landmark of the magikier presence on Cellana. And we magikiers, the favoured creations of centions in modern times, were enemies to all cention-created beings prior. He didn't open his mouth, but I heard his voice over the connection Briar forged between our four minds asking, "*What about the smoke?*"

"There's no evidence of recent life in this city, but you know as well as I, the embers of a magikier aren't easily snuffed out, except by magic of a similar kind. I would imagine, whoever cast the flames fell to their enemies before extinguishing their fury and no magikier remained to temper the blaze. So it simmers and chars, a moment from ash, but cannot be dowsed except by those among you."

"Is the city safe?" Faith asked, "Is there food? Clean water?"

"The keep's reserves are well-stocked with preservatives, granting the impression the attack came swiftly and ended just so. As for the well, I should think its water can be purified of the blood and corpse which taint it with some help from your elementally gifted brethren. No?"

Deliberation drew a crease between Seth's eyebrows as he pressed his knuckles to pursed lips. "I'll assemble those of us equipped with the necessary magic. What about heating? Electricity? Arillian nights are notorious for their cold snaps."

"A consequence of the north, I should think. The city's heating systems appear to be out of order, however repairable. Until then, you have my fire."

"*Thank you, Briar.*" He glanced to me, eyes lighting up with an idea. "Your friend, Mister Song, he's an ecological empath, isn't he?"

"You mean Brett?" I asked, earning Seth's nod. "And ecological empathy is…?" I winced, suddenly very aware that I'd forgotten the magical capability of my ex. That was probably something I should've retained, considering we'd recently worked things out as friends since our lives had become inextricably intwined through the tragedies beset upon us all.

Faith explained, "His magic lets him observe past events in his environment," and turned to Seth, answering, "That ecological empathy?" He met her response with an appreciative smile.

"Exactly. Could you send him to me once we're all settled?"

"He was injured in the escape, leaving his heart weak." Faith's voice came brisk as the biting breeze.

A glint of indignation blazed behind her composed façade, flashing the memory of their almost-fight behind my eyes, way back when Faith and Seth first met. She hadn't liked him then, either, and that was when he was only the bearer of bad news.

She continued, "The healers are worried too much stress could send him into shock. Even cardiac arrest."

"Too many of us barely escaped with our lives. It would be our downfall to bench each and every one of the wounded," Seth grimly noted, passing a glance up my arms in a moment so fleeting, it couldn't have meant anything real. Even so, I shivered under his regard in stark contrast to the warmth that seared across my skin. "Mister Song's rare magic might lend us a glimpse into the past, so we can prepare for the future. As unfair as it may seem, his rare usefulness denies him the luxury of sitting things out. Please, once he's had time to rest, his help will go a long way."

Narrowing her eyes, it was a moment before she nodded in resignation. Looking to me, she tilted her head back toward our friends, long ribbons of ginger hair falling over her shoulders. I doubted we would find them again amongst all the rest. So I lingered, caught between wanting somehow to help

Seth and fleeing before either of them could realize just how ineffectual I was.

"*You need not feel so useless, Anelisha,*" Briar spoke in my mind, washing my face with the warmth of my blush. I was taken aback to hear her use my name. She'd taken to calling me magikier or nothing in Blackano, but I supposed, I was no longer just a magikier anymore, was I? By the lack of reactions from Faith and Seth, I gladly assumed I was her only recipient.

"*Uh-huh,*" I answered for lack of a voice to give to all that stewed within me. Still, the golden dragon was in my head. She knew all the miserable thoughts I couldn't bring myself to face. But I would pretend they didn't exist.

"*See how long that lasts you,*" Briar warned, and the connection between our minds dropped with a snap of clarity that no longer had my thoughts echoing inside my head.

Before the convoy got going again, Seth had his military police escort those capable of fire manipulation – I assumed including Kev – into the city, where they were tasked with eliminating the fires. Only then did Seth direct a second taskforce capable of earth manipulation – again, I could only assume Lin was counted among them – to stabilize any buildings at risk of collapse. He kept up like this for some time, bringing Faith and I to wander in search of Brett for hours only to finally give up and sit among the thousands simply waiting. This was why I was happy to follow Seth, he who had his nose stuck in Blackano's archives for years and now knew just how to delegate tasks to magikiers with the relevant magic. He who would've been Key-Keeper, the head of Blackano's government.

As dusk painted the sky a brilliant gradient of reds and purples around the luminous, white rings which cut from east to west, he finally made the call to move the convoy in. There were only three entrances to the City of Gates, portcullis gateways. The cobblestone road led right up to the nearest of these, where the heavy, metal grating had been melted away to allow free entrance.

Inside the city, Faith and I shared a surprised look to find ourselves walking a road lined with funny-looking cars somewhere between new and old-fashioned, unlit neon signs, solar panels, electrical cables strung up between buildings, and other modern luxuries, juxtaposed with things like raggedy market stalls, old-timey tramways, carriages that looked like they were supposed to be pulled by horses, and the kinds of too-wide roads that hadn't yet been narrowed by renovated shops and houses on either side. Squat little buildings speckled the urban landscape surrounding the city center where soaring skyscrapers seemed to balance the sky on their pointed tips. Elevated train tracks wove between these tall buildings, only to break off at random points where the metal had been warped or fractured. The City of Gates was a place out of time; I could only assume other magikier cities shared such innovations.

Even with half the buildings collapsed to rubble, the haze of dissipating smoke, and the charred discolouration that diminished this once-vibrant city, there was still so much life in our surroundings. It wasn't that the advancement of technology halted at any one outdated point in time, but rather, that technology's advancement took several left turns where Earth turned right, only to be called back to the familiar with every new generation of magikiers brought in from Blackano. And now, the City of Gates was bereft of its people. We trudged through the city en masse, silent as the dead strewn across the streets.

As we approached the city center, Dyval's protective force encircled the keep – an arena-sized, walled-in building of blood-red stone, manicured and reinforced as if a baroque castle had a one-night stand with brutalist architecture – where our sizable force made camp, spilling out around the titanic and honestly, quite jarring building under tarps and tents. We distributed canned food from the stores, cooked up a mass dinner of preserved rations in the kitchens to fill over nine thousand bellies, shovelled food into our mouths, and established an infirmary in the main hall, just outside the command room where Seth and his elite got down to business.

Faith and I were passing the command room on our way to the basement where the uninjured were to sleep when I caught a glimpse of the elite huddled around a fat, box-shaped television and a radio transponder. They tinkered with the machines in hopes of contacting other cities, but static signals droned on unbroken. It didn't look like anyone was within reach of the radio's signal.

Dawn shone in from teeny-tiny windows near the mural-decorated ceiling before I collapsed next to Faith on the cold marble of the arena-sized underground. There, we shared a blanket and settled in to sleep among a legion of lost souls. I'd never felt so much like an ant.

3

Guess I Won't Be Getting Settled

Day 3

I COULDN'T SLEEP, COULDN'T EVEN CLOSE MY EYES WITHOUT FINDING myself transported back to where it all went wrong. My mind did find trouble pinning this ultimate disaster to just one moment, blurring the distinction between my mercy and what followed. I could practically feel the grip of the sabre rubbing callouses into my too-tight grasp again, the thrumming of my heart high in my throat, and the reluctance to spill another's blood burning behind my closed eyelids.

Biting my lip, I opened my eyes only to find the barbed shells of kirranite faces snarling down at me from the darkness, where my vision superimposed imagination on mere memory. The logic of it did nothing to help the momentary terror bursting in my head like white fire. Even so, I think I preferred this to the guilt. Without sleeping fears, I was treated only to mournful tears.

The hours ticked by under this canvas of pitch-black darkness, teeming with sleepless hallucinations, while Faith tossed and turned beside me. I dug my nails into my palms to fend off the bad dreams lurking just below the surface of my subconscious mind, occupying myself with thoughts of how best to lend a helping hand around the keep. Such plans only fended off the darker thoughts for so long, but after what felt like the longest night I'd ever endured, morning finally came.

And as it turned out, such plans weren't up to me. With morning came the distribution of jobs to every last one of us, as governed by Seth and his advisors – who couldn't have slept a wink for all the work they must have put into this – and as implemented by his elite. Faith, of course, was assigned to the infirmary. Day shifts, just her luck.

She sent me a look of encouragement over her shoulder as I stepped up to state my name and magic. Although both officers seemed to recognize me immediately, I found myself rambling, "My magikier class is divine, with the whole looping back around on the centions' magical feed to manipulate their power thing. I know, unusable. But I'm the shonte so… Give me something good?"

Searching a long list of names, all the tired officer had to say to me was, "Training." The officer next to him had a little more life in her as she offered me a set of clothes to replace my bloody wardrobe. This new set must have been pilfered from the city's abandoned abodes, and from the stock of clothes I could see behind them, Arillians really had a thing for blue-themed outfits. On top of my folded clothes, I noticed a metal chain and metal tags, engraved with the words,

Knight, Anelisha.
Tier 1 Carmavi.

My hands automatically took the offered outfit, but my eyes fixed to the first officer. "Just training? You've got to be kidding me."

"Special orders. Carry on." He waved me forward to address the next person in line, but the woman officer made a face like she agreed with me.

"I don't see a weapon with all this," I noted, lifting the folded outfit in my arms for show.

"You weren't assigned one," she answered, and although a keen glint entered her eyes as if to say more, she merely motioned me forward in keeping with her partner.

I left the keep's commodious basement in a daze. For its brutalist exterior, the interior was surprisingly flouncy and artistic, with bas-reliefs and frescoes adorning the walls, and wiry metal sculptures interwoven with iron banisters. Faith met me at the top of the marble stairs, eager to hear what job I'd been tasked with, but I was speechless. Here I thought all my training was over, at least since leaving Blackano. That was certainly the treatment everyone else seemed to be getting. But lo and behold, I was *still* in training!

"So?" my sister asked.

"Can I go with you to the infirmary? Just for now." Just while I figured out what to say to Seth, who would've assigned my task.

She raised an eyebrow but shrugged her indifference, happy to have me around if a little longer. We ducked into a side room off the main hall to change out of our nasty, battle-weathered clothes – which was to say, stiffly uncomfortable with sweat and blood – and into the fresh outfits allotted to us by the officers. I'd been given one of the smaller sizes to fit my 5' height – kids' clothes, probably – but Faith had a more ill-fitting outfit, just slightly too small for her. The girl was built like a barstool, always the leggy one out of the two of us. After all, she took after Mom. I wouldn't know if I took after Dad, considering I hardly even remembered what he looked like, and the fact that my body was technically a reincarnation born from magic muddled the specifics of my genetics yet further. But that was just another thing I chose not to think about, at least not until I had to.

I had never worn anything quite so heavy – beginning with romper undergarments, then paper-thin pantaloons under the heavy folds of deep blue harem pants tucked into knee-high combat boots, and a billowy white top to fend off chafing from a studded leather tabard snug around my middle, topped with a cropped leather jacket that buttoned up to my chin, with spacious, blue-dyed, wool sleeves tucked into elbow-length gloves which doubled as bracers and tripled in use with weights sewn into the knuckles – and even so, I couldn't complain about the surprising weight of my new wardrobe after the biting cold chills of last night, instead thankful for the extra layers. Not to mention the surprising style inherent to the blue, white, and black themed outfit. I never would've guessed a culture cultivated by war cared so much for appearances.

For now, I stowed my new gloves in the belt pouch of my tabard, wary to don them over my shredded flesh, and rolled my sleeves up over my elbows.

Faith was happy to shower me with compliments, probably expecting some in return, but I felt like a child in knight's armour. She, meanwhile, sported a comfortable-looking gambeson and a fancy, solid red strip of cloth as a belt around her waist, the only non-blue colour upon either of our persons, with knee-high combat boots – sheathing a boot knife each – and spacious pants like mine.

"Why do you get the cool boot knives?" I whined, drawing my foot up as close to my face as I could get it in search of my own. Nothing, nada, not a boot knife in sight, just boot.

"Good question. I've been assigned to the infirmary, so I doubt I'll be doing much fighting except in defense of my patients." Distraction had entered her tone as she checked herself out in the sheen of the marble flooring.

"And they expect you to do that with a few well-placed kicks? They might be overestimating their staff," I mocked, "But at least you have a weapon! I've got nothing, besides these." I raised my fists, although the effect diminished in the absence of my gloves' brass knuckles. At my stance, Faith burst into another bout of laughter and my face settled into a frown.

"They won't send you out to fight. You're too important," she attempted to reassure me, much to the opposite effect as I was reminded of my true *calling*. Training, not fighting; that's what this was for.

Before she could realize the ill effect her words had on me, I let loose a theatrical groan and marched us off toward her new workplace.

The infirmary was bustling when we arrived. We were lucky to find Brett among the masses, asleep on the very same stretcher-turned-cot he was likely carried in on. Like bees floating between flowers, the small number of healers jumped from one patient to the next, lingering only as long as was necessary. They all wore a similar red strip of cloth around their waists like Faith's, signalling their duty. I vaguely remembered someone saying the injured outnumbered the healers twenty to one.

Some of the healers recognized Faith as we entered under the tarp of the infirmary, sheltered within the main hall of the keep. They were on her in an instant, drawing her away to business with the uprooting force of a tornado, and just as much gusto. I, meanwhile, plopped myself down next to the snoozing Brett and leaned my head back against the support beam by which he lay.

As I expected, Kev and Lin were off providing their help toward jobs my shonte magic should've easily accomplished... if not for my injuries. But I refrained from these thoughts. Instead, I grumbled under my breath about training. Who here would even know how to train a shonte? I was the second one in existence, and the first one died back when dragons could be counted among Cellana's native fauna.

"Annie?" Brett groggily said, making me jump as he pushed up on both elbows.

Tucking an errant tress behind my ear, I turned to face him. "I'm sorry, did I wake you?"

"I thought you were talking to me."

"Nope, just myself, like a crazy person," I chuckled.

Noticing something, or perhaps a lack of something on my shoulders, he glanced around the busy infirmary. "Where's Briar?"

"Scouting, I think." At the flippancy of my tone, he sat up properly, watching me as if he meant to decipher some hidden message. "What?" I asked.

"You okay?" Oh boy, it must've been painted across my face if *Brett* could gauge my troubles.

"You're the one in hospital," I pointed out, "Which is, by the way, a nicer set-up than the basement."

"Is that why you're here?" He was never one to waste a smile, but I could hear the ghost of one on his voice. I scoffed, giving a care-free wave of my hand.

"I'll have you know it's only a matter of shirking my responsibilities." Before the disapproval in his eyes could reach his tongue, I chirped, "For other more interesting responsibilities! Seth wanted to see you. Something about your magic." I hesitated, looking him over as he lay sprawled on the stretcher. "Can you do it? Use your magic when you're like this?"

"It's not like your shonte magic. I'm not exactly using up my own resources when I tap into it, just siphoning whatever the centions prepared for me," he explained, somehow managing to teach me what four months of training in Blackano had failed to, "Knox of all people knows the cap on any magikier's ability. I can manage whatever he wants."

"Right…" I muttered, staring hard at my hands and the bandages that covered them.

Out of the corner of my eye, I noticed Brett do a double take. "What are you wearing?"

A smirk drew up the corner of my mouth. "Let's just say it's part of the reason I want to have a word with Seth." I clambered to a stand, stopping myself a moment from dusting off the filth of the floor. I really needed to start catering to my injuries.

Too late, I noticed Brett struggling to get his feet under him, meaning to join me.

Throwing out my hands, I quickly interjected, "Whoa, hold your horses, pal. I don't think I need to remind you that you *literally* died. Your heart stopped beating. Like, three days ago. I'll bring him to you."

"He's busy enough putting a harness on this dumpster fire. I'm not about to be the guy who pulls him away from helping everyone else." He wobbled to a stand, but I held my arms out, ready to steady him if he lost his strength.

Careful around my own pains, I drew his arm across my shoulders. My stomach fluttered with old emotions, but I told myself I was just supporting his weight. Even so, my abdomen quivered and the soreness in my muscles complained against any manner of physical exertion. He wasn't the only one in need of rest.

"Can I just say, this is ill-advised," came the voice of my sister as Brett and I began our slow traipse out of the tented area, followed by the tap of her toes in a perfect imitation of our mother. "Where do you think you're taking my patient?"

Brett sent her a small wave which Faith kindly returned while holding her stern glower for me. The busy traffic in the main hall met us at the edge of the tent, but I stopped, glancing back toward Faith.

"Only where our great leader asked," I answered over my shoulder. She huffed, blowing a lock of ginger hair out of her eyes. With a dry chuckle, I touched two fingers to my forehead and out in a casual farewell, calling, "I'll have him back before dark!"

In the main hall of the keep, high window frames had been sculpted in the aspect of beastly mouths, pouring beams of daylight into the room and over the heads of the busy crowd. Grand marble bas-reliefs in the guise of monstrous faces surrounded these nearly ceiling-level windows, reminding me once again of the dangers this world posed. I averted my gaze, unable to meet the wild eyes of the high sculptures.

Brett hardly noticed this momentary shift in me, stifling his scoff in response to my words and shaking his head in amusement as I walked him toward the command room. "You haven't changed one bit."

"We only stopped talking for a month, a week, and two days. Not that I… not that I was counting." I attempted a playful tone, but a heavy silence descended in the wake of my words. What was a month of heartbreak to just two days of terror, slaughter, and chaos at the hands of someone I once considered like a sister? In an instant, my gaze turned stonily to the floor, my mouth a thin, white line. No, nope. That above all else was the truth I wouldn't confront.

"Annie…" Brett began.

Before he could continue, I warned, "I'm taking a page out of your book, Brett. I'm not about to spill the beans on my feelings. I really just… can't." He gazed at me, tilting his head, with confusion in his turquoise eyes.

"I was only going to say you look like you're struggling," he noted in a jaded voice. My face warmed with blush as I noticed my own heavy breathing, a testament to how unfit I'd become since the advent of shonte magic in my life.

Huffily, I grumbled, "Are you aware you're uncannily difficult to read? Because it haunts me."

"My superpower," he mocked in an equally flat voice. A laugh bubbled up in my chest, reminiscent of the old days, but faded before reaching my lips.

At last, through the hubbub of the main hall, we reached the door to the command room. A dim glow of generator-powered lamps filled the stone chamber, slipping out through the cracks between metal door and metal frame. A shadow paced back and forth in the light shining out from beneath, but only one. Seth Knox. I wondered if he'd spent the whole night pacing.

First, I pulled my elbow-high gloves over the ends of my sleeves, wincing as the thick leather snaked over my lacerated flesh. Seth didn't need to see more of my bandages.

I raised my hand to knock on the wrought iron door, but stopped at Briar's mental intrusion, beckoning me, "*Enter. I've informed this one of your arrival.*" I assumed by "this one" she meant Seth.

"*Cutting out the middleman, I see,*" I answered. Going for the handle, my palm lit up with pain as I pushed the evidently pull door and proceeded to walk right into it with a loud thud. Brett failed to contain his surprise, crinkling his nose and snorting a laugh, having narrowly avoided being guided into the door by my supporting arm. "It's a pull," I groaned with a hand cupping my face as heat bloomed up my neck.

My nasally words had Brett struggling to compose himself with both hands pressed to his mouth. "You're ridiculous," he stated like it was a general fact.

Only then did the door swing out before us, and I attempted a smile through the pain. The opening force was none other than Seth Knox, wearing a perturbed expression. My blush deepened, steaming hot across my face.

A funny mix of concern and relief entered those sapphire blues. "Are you okay?"

"Okay? *Sure.* Incompetent? Without a doubt," I groaned into my cupped hand. "But I brought Brett. Like you asked."

"Thank you," he said, nodding to Brett in acknowledgment.

He motioned us inside, holding the door open to avoid another mishap. Somehow, it was always doors that consistently made a fool of me. Why even have an all-powerful domenth and her dubiously alive sister for archnemeses when doors posed such a threat?

Seth busied himself in the room, muttering over his shoulder, "I'll only be a moment. Come in, I just need to leave instructions should anyone come looking for me… grab a couple things to keep a record…"

He carried on speaking to himself as he bustled around the room, collecting a notebook, files, pens and other little things into a satchel on his hip. He must have sent his elite out to gather whatever data resources had been archived in the city. Knowing his librarian spirit, I wasn't surprised. It seemed his elite had spent the night gathering everything they could possibly find.

Like me, Seth had on a new outfit pilfered from this fallen city, except *he* looked good. He wore a long coat befitting of an army general with silver buttons all down the front and up the arms, around which he had wound black ribbons in a criss-cross pattern over the lower half of his sleeves. Silver-embroidered designs adorned the lapels, and the centions' crest sung his allegiance over his left breast. He wore this dashing coat open over a white shirt bloused over a pair of navy blue, form-fitting pants, tucked into calf-hugging, knee-high combat boots with decorative, silver buttons up the shins and a silver plate over the toes which glimmered in the lantern light. A decorated sabre was sheathed on his left hip, and a book carrier on his right.

A lock of ebony hair fell over his eyes as he rushed around the room, the back of his coat billowing out behind him. There was no question, Seth Knox could pull off any outfit and boy did I wish he would pull off mine.

Catching myself on that last thought, my eyes flicked guiltily to Brett, then to Briar who could easily have been eavesdropping on my embarrassing nature. She lay coiled around herself atop a war table where little figurines marked camps across a map I would never have recognized if not for my four months' studies in Blackano. It was a map of Arillia, the country in which we currently found ourselves. And she had her little, lizardly head in the palm of her semi-bovine hand, neck coiled over her too-long body so many times just for her arm to reach – the epitome of a jaded disposition. Yep, she definitely heard me.

"*I need not listen to know your awkward nature,*" she mused in my head, "*But I do believe the state of things might find him too busy to live out your fantasies–*"

"*Stop! It was an intrusive thought! Let it die,*" I pleaded her.

Whether or not she would have, Seth resurfaced from behind his antique desk at that moment with his satchel full to bursting. Although his eyes were distant with distraction, he kept on task. "If you'll follow me…" He motioned us forward with a wave of his hand, punctuated by Briar's assault on my person as she leapt from the war table to perch herself comfortably across my shoulders.

Brett barely had time to remove his arm from across my shoulders before she planted herself there, and I caught him with a hand on his waist. Taking no notice, Briar coiled herself comfortably around my collarbones. She was like my very own, live feather boa, except she was heavy like an actual boa and her rough hide was clammy to the touch. So nothing like a feather boa.

Seth moved slowly to accommodate Brett's physical exhaustion as he met a pair of officers at the gate. The armed military police made up the rear as Seth led us out of the keep and into the rubble, making sure to cater our pace to Brett, for which I was thankful. I was sure Brett would have pushed himself to match any speed.

Outside the walls surrounding the keep, we clambered up and over what was once a building with the ease of climbing a hill, Seth offering a hand to both me and Brett as we went and the officers keeping an eye on our surroundings. I was glad for my new get-up as bitter breezes tousled my already unruly hair into an aspect of live flames, cold only on my face. Our silence grew heavier the further we walked.

In stark contrast to the colourful interior of the keep, a grey film of ash coated everything, darkened only by blood stains and black char. We hadn't come this way yesterday. An area the size of a baseball field had been completely levelled, seemingly in the dead center of the city where everything had been incinerated to dust and ash. This was ground zero.

It was a moment before I noticed the taut wire in me, spooled up tight around my lungs. It was another moment before I noticed my hand firmly clamped on Brett's waist. I loosened my hold on him, worried I was only weighing him down. The residual odour of smoke had my head spinning, or was it doing that on its own?

"I feel a bit jetlagged," I mumbled through the silence of soft winds kicking up the ash, "Do you feel jetlagged?" Unthinkable things crunched under our feet.

Seth considered it, "Hmm, well…"

Glancing up at him, I found a tired, sunken quality around his eyes, so brilliantly blue in contrast to his dark skin tone I might not have noticed if not for the breathy exhaustion in his voice.

"Have you even slept?" My voice was soft.

"I had planned on it, but they needed me to…" He patted his satchel as if in explanation, and with that, glanced around. We had come to the very middle of the dead zone, leveled by whatever catastrophe had emptied this city of its entire population. "We're here." I wondered if he'd slept at all since escaping Blackano but assured myself even Seth Knox had to run out of steam sometimes.

I met Brett's eyes, shooting him an encouraging smile, and released my support of him. To my surprise, I teetered on my feet when I broke from him, but Briar shifted her weight on my shoulders as a counterbalance. The pair of officers hung back, their focus on the distant buildings where snipers could have lain in wait. Vaguely, I wondered if there was anything the pair could do if that was the case.

"*Sit,*" Briar commanded, "*Looking back so far into this environment's past will take some time. Especially for a magikier.*"

She didn't have to tell me twice. My knees buckled, and I crossed my legs under me, sitting in the blanketing ash. Seth was reading off his notes to try to guide Brett's search as Brett sat across from me with his palms flat on the ground. He closed his eyes, eyelids twitching, and drew his mouth in a pensive expression. I had never seen him use his magic before. He looked so… serene, contemplative, connected to something beyond what I could sense. Beads of sweat broke over his brow.

Snapping his notebook shut, Seth dropped down next to me with a huff, mushrooming soot out around him as he propped his elbows up on bent knees. "Now all that's left is to wait." His eyes flicked restlessly back to the keep, to his people, to his work.

Tentatively, I rested a hand on his shoulder, feeling the taut muscle jump under my touch. "You could use a moment's rest."

His eyes met mine, striking a match in my chest, and he caved with a humble smile. Giving a gentle exhale, he let his tired eyelids lower like a contented cat and pressed a hand over mine on his shoulder, careful not to apply too much pressure to my wounds. "I suppose so."

Even back in Blackano, I would either find him hard at work or asleep at his desk, but at least back then he shared the workload with Levi Videl… who had turned out to be Valencia's second-in-command. That was just another dark cloud hanging over Seth's head, but I dared not bring it up.

Now, I imagined him resting his chin on his forearms, eyes fluttering closed, and my fingers combing through his hair until his breathing deepened and slowed. His black locks looked soft, uncharacteristically dishevelled sure, but luxuriant and glossy all the same. My fingers twitched up toward the natural wave brushing the tip of his ear.

"*Am I to assume you still want my report?*" Briar interrupted, as only Briar would. So much for a moment's rest.

Seth snapped back to attention, removing his hand from mine to flip to an empty page of his notebook and pull out a pen. "Of course," he said, a look of relief in his tired eyes to have something to work on.

I dropped my hand from his shoulder, still warm from his touch, and slumped under Briar's weight. Maybe it wasn't so absurd to think he hadn't slept a wink since arriving on Cellana.

"*I only felt the information somewhat dire.*" Sarcasm laced her tone and made hyperbole of her words with what followed. "*Sizable enemy camps lie hidden in the crags on the outskirts of our boundaries, blending in with the northern vales. Remnants of the city's assailants, I imagine. It was an entire ordeal burning a party of scouts sneaking away from the City of Gates early this morning. Awfully fire-resistant, those pora.*"

"Pora?" I echoed as Seth jotted everything down in his notebook. My mind wandered back to Blackano's lecture halls.

Diseases in and of themselves, pora infected magical beings in order to spread their kind with any exchange of bodily fluids. They didn't have the kirranite hivemind, but a pora's rabid hankering for any and all magical blood was terrifying in its own right and didn't exactly help to keep their contagion in check.

"They know we're here..." Seth murmured, bringing one of the officers to glance warily over her shoulder. Of course they did, we'd extinguished fires only a magikier could put out like some sort of reverse smoke signal to our enemies. He swore under his breath, having come to the same conclusion. "How many would you estimate?"

"*Enough to lay siege and triumph again,*" Briar considered, "*Or rather, that would be the case if we did not possess the protection of a cention. I believe they've held off for that reason alone, seeking some plan to elude her. No force of pora could hope to harm a cention on their own. Of course, Dyval cannot be expected to barricade an entire horde and prevent every last one from entry, let alone withstand the dirty tactics to which they'll undoubtedly resort should you choose to disappear behind her defense.*"

"One stray pora could be all it takes," he mused. Infectious buggers.

I glanced at Briar, whose long neck drooped low off my shoulder and coiled back around to peer directly at Seth. The perfectly round eyes on either side of her small head didn't blink, molten gold irises and black slit pupils fixed on him. "*What will you do?*" she asked.

"I can't do anything until I speak with my advisors." His eyes shifted to Brett. "We need to know how the city fell in the first place. I'll work from there."

"*Then you had better work fast,*" Briar advised. I shot her a sharp look.

"*Maybe don't add another layer of stress to a hundred-layer cake.*" The thought echoed in my head by accident, but I was glad to find she hadn't included Seth in the reception. If there was anyone who could handle what he was up against, yeah, it was Seth Knox, it had to be, but that didn't mean I wanted any of this for him.

"*While it is advisable to avoid suffocation beneath stressors, I would have thought you'd learned better than to ignore the situation entirely,*" she sent my way. Without a hitch, she held Seth's gaze and rerouted back to her initial point, "*Once you've dealt with the pora threat, or the threat has dealt with you, what are your intentions? What is there for you on Cellana, when the greatest threat to magikierkind will chase your shonte until one or the other falls?*"

"*Now you're talking about me like I'm not even here,*" came my grumbling thoughts. She ignored me, intent only on Seth. So, I pointedly said, "Shouldn't we take things one step at a time?"

Seth caught me up in a sidelong glance, drawing warmth across my face. "We can't let Valencia sneak up on us, even if the pora are our most immediate threat. Sooner or later, she'll find her way to Cellana." Concern drew a line between his brows as he met my eyes. "And to you. We can't hope to match her forces if they get through. We aren't enough to protect you."

And if I kicked the bucket, then Valencia could bring her evil, domenth sister back into this reincarnated body of mine – hers? – ours. And if Valencia teamed up with said evil sister, then they could take on the centions. And if Valencia and Evelyn *killed* the centions… Well, that would be something like the end of magic, wouldn't it? No magikier was self-sustainable, not like a shonte. But Valencia was a domenth, and she offered herself as a power source to any magikier who claimed loyalty to her, in return for equal access to their magic. Then there were pora and kirranites – the monsters magikiers had been created to fight. Their magic was disease and decay, made sustainable by leeching magic and devouring life. They would only keep consuming. They would be without equals. Oh boy, now that was a dark vision of the future if I ever heard one. And I wouldn't even be alive to see it.

I shook my head, shaking out the horrible images unfolding in my mind. "This is why I leave the future to the future. How can we plan for this? We don't even know what we're doing right now besides surviving. And how good are we at that, really?" My eyes flicked to Brett, still in a trance-like state. Even now, I noted the welts on his wrist where the bolt of lightning which stopped his heart had struck him.

Seth frowned, extending a hand as if to pat my knee and comfort me, but stopped himself. And goddamn, he was doing something with his mouth while his eyes roved over me. What I wouldn't have given to know what was going on inside his head. "We can warn the Empress."

I raised my eyebrows high on my forehead. "Hold on. There's an Empress now?"

He took a moment to look confused. "There's always been an Empress." Seeming to realize I wasn't the good student he'd assumed, he explained, "She presides over the three clans of magikiers on Cellana from the First Great City." Even this was news to me. "The clan leaders of Arillia, Schevon, and Loruna swear fealty to the Empress and don't act in matters of war without her say-so."

"Hold up, you're telling me an actual magikier is running the magikier world on Cellana? Why does that strike me as unlikely?" I sarcastically noted.

"She was hand-picked by the centions, glory to them, but the Empress' position makes it so they don't have their foot in the door of magikier politics on Cellana. Not like they did in Blackano."

"Seriously? The *one* time..." I shook my head against potential heresy I would be unwise to let slip, releasing a sigh. "So, it's up to us to warn this Empress about Valencia? About everything?"

He took his hand away to jot down his ideas. As he did, he looked to Briar. "But to do that, we'll need an audience with her. And some sway, if it's war we're asking for."

"Can't we ask Dyval to speak to her? She'd still have to listen to a cention, right?"

"*And you would see how stubborn a cention's knee is to bend,*" Briar chortled, "*Dyval will not gladly be reduced to a messenger.*"

"I thought we were past that?" I groaned, "You know, when I gave her a big ol' lecture in the void between worlds? And she called me every variation of a minor nuisance?"

Hesitating in his notetaking, Seth quirked an eyebrow at me. I supposed this was the first he'd heard of it.

Sending him an exaggerated wink, I boasted, "I convinced her not to tear me limb from limb for accidentally using my magikier ability to take power. Pretty rad, I know. Not to toot my own horn, but I think that's why she stuck around." One of the officers made a noise like a snort before composing himself, reminding me we weren't exactly alone. Heat rose up my neck to colour my face red.

"That's-" Seth was saying, looking more lost than ever and even more impressed, but Briar cut him off in both our minds.

"*I've spoken to Dyval.*"

"Well that was quick," I noted.

"*Her answer was predetermined, for her promise was to aid you, not to act on behalf of you. Ongoing skirmishes and invasions from more ancient enemies on this world urge her not to divert the Empress' attention from where it's most needed. Indeed, this world the centions shaped needs not thinkers, only mulch. While Valencia is our greatest threat, a passing comet indifferent to all that she scorches, she is not the only threat to magikiers, nor is she the only threat to Dyval and the centions if magikiers should fall. The centions would rather not offer an opening to the beast Valencia released upon this world ages ago.*"

Oh, right, the Kaipracan. The centions' age-old nemesis who took all pora and kirranites under his wing when they were abandoned by their original creators. The whole reason magikiers were sent to Cellana at all. Weird how immediate danger makes you forget these things.

"Not to be *that* person, but the Empress still needs to be warned," I muttered, "We can't let the centions sweep Valencia under the rug again."

"Even more than that, we'll need her support to keep you safe from Valencia." Giving a reluctant nod, stiff and small as if to go unnoticed, Seth decided, "We'll just have to make the case ourselves."

"*And how do you expect to stand in the court of an Empress half a world away? Without Dyval's sway, I'm afraid any attempt to influence the Empress will require a formal council.*"

"Well, that's annoying," I huffed, "Why can't you just open a mind link with her?"

"*I am not Dyval. My voice is bereft of authority, and in this world of malice and distrust, I would not even be granted the opening. Do you truly believe one of her stature would be left defenseless on a front such as this, so intimate and vulnerable? No, I cannot reach her mind, for the barricades put up in front of it, wrought by centuries of old magic layered like bricks atop her throne.*" Her forked tongue flicked bitterly at us, tasting the sooty air.

Seth furrowed his brows, illustrating an inwardly turned frustration. "I won't undermine a cention's command, but this calls for an Inquisition."

The officers met each other's eyes, quite obviously eavesdropping at this point.

Even Briar ruffled at the word, her notched scutes spiking out the same way a cat might fluff up in alarm, jabbing me through my leathers. "*I would hesitate to name it such just yet. You've hardly left the starting gate.*"

"And if we continue to hide in the City of Gates, we'll remain toothless," he mused, "Dyval has allowed me the privilege of leading her people without the overbearing bureaucratic practices that halted Key-Keeper Anticus at every legislative turn, but this has also caused her to take a step back."

Wincing, I fixed my gaze on my hands. The ultimatum I brought up to her was likely the only reason she offered us her protection; our loyalty came at a cost, and considering my new standing as a shonte, this matter of loyalty was a pressing issue for the centions.

"With her attention so diverted and no hope of reinforcement, we'll lose too many in the effort to make the City of Gates our permanent home. Which is, itself, a misstep if Valencia finds a way to Cellana."

"*Allow me to ground you in reality once more. To reach the City of Gold in the heart of the Loruna clan, greatest of them all, you would need to travel west across the Pam Sea with ships from Schevon. Or travel the perilous land bridge of Trime between Schevon and Loruna. There is no leisurely footpath to the First City. And yet, whichever you choose, the fact doesn't change that the first leg of your journey, Arillia's trains, are compromised.*" Oh goodie, more obstacles.

"We're at a standstill, then," Seth mused, "For as long as Arillia remains overrun."

"Overrun? This is only one city," I pointed out.

He glanced down at his notebook, wearing a contrite expression, as if any answers it held were written in invisible ink. "I can't imagine the City of Gates would have fallen and remained unoccupied if the Arillia clan itself wasn't compromised."

Just like that, my mind snapped back from this distant goal with the Empress, planting me right behind all the obstacles that stood in our way. The first among them: a legion of pora waiting just outside our safe zone. How the hell did Seth keep up with this 24/7? How could he possibly remain sane, let alone level-headed about it all?

Brett gasped across from us where he sat in the middle of the dead zone, startling me nearly out of my skin. For a moment there, I had forgotten why we were here.

"Breathe," Seth advised him, extending a hand to clasp his shoulder. Brett blanched, drained of his usual olive tone as if he'd seen a ghost. "Take your time. Find your bearings."

I had only seen Brett tremble and heave with shaky breath once before, just days ago as he recounted the death of Dahlia. Now, his angular eyes opened wide as he raked a panicky stare over the leveled area, expecting enemies from all directions. He gulped back short breaths, working to calm himself, and I rested a hand on his knee, catching his startled eyes on mine.

"You're safe," I reminded him, my own breath catching in my throat as I shoved doubt from my mind. He *was* safe. I would never let anything happen to him. And just to drive the point home, I gestured between the pair of officers. "Whatever you saw, it's over now." He nodded, holding my gaze like it was his last lifeline.

He still needed a moment, just to process whatever it was his magic had shown him. Briar sank on my shoulders, and I saw Brett settle across from us, releasing the tension in his muscles. She must have pushed a sense of calm into his mind as she had sometimes done with me, a suggestion of tranquility rather than a mind-numbing force like Faith's magic.

"It was pora." He paused, as if anticipating our surprise, but with a raised eyebrow, continued, "Once they were inside the city walls, it was ruin and blood. But they couldn't get in on their own. The graduating class-" His words came out shaky, strained. He glanced up at Seth, pain behind his eyes. "Thousands of magikiers came by the cobblestone road, just like us. They were welcomed into the City of Gates, and they coordinated an attack with our enemies. *Magikiers from Blackano* coordinated the attack. The survivors were intentionally infected and taken prisoner, and the magikiers who betrayed them... it looked like they led the pora."

"Magikiers and pora don't just work together," Seth hissed, his lip curling in disgust, "To what end?"

My heart plummeted low in my stomach. "The Liberation Front has taken its next step. We were surprised when so many chose Cellana at last semester's graduation, but it was just part of their plan." My head spun. "Enemy of my enemy is my friend, right? The centions are their common enemy. Valencia's followers, no, her *army* is already here."

4

Definitely Handling the Shonte Thing

SETH AND I PRACTICALLY CARRIED BRETT BACK TO THE KEEP AS SETH implored details in a gentle tone. Brett described the city's ruin in immaculate detail. I could feel him working himself up under my supporting hands. Even I was getting worked up, but only until I tuned them out, a monotonous buzz muffling my headspace. Instead, I stared sightlessly at the back of the officer heading our group.

"*How can pora work with magikiers?*" My thoughts echoed in my head, alerting me to Briar's eavesdropping.

"*You said it yourself; a common goal,*" she mused.

"*No, I mean, I thought pora were supposed to be all bloodlust-y and unconscionable. I thought the mere smell of magic was supposed to drive them up the wall. But here they are, making friends with a whole revolution's worth of 'em.*"

She paused, weighing her response. "*Remind yourself who it was spreading such information.*"

"*Well goddamn, was anything I learned in Blackano grounded in fact?*" I caught myself on an audible groan, stifling the sound before I could alert Brett and Seth to my inattention.

"*I should hope your botanical knowledge stands,*" Briar pondered, "*Lest you find yourself picking poisonous berries.*"

I winced, mentally sifting through the little I'd retained regarding Cellana's flora. "*I spent most of my training on the edge of tears, so pardon me if I've accidentally repressed some of it.*"

"*Only the parts that matter, it would seem.*"

"Brett?" came a familiar voice, calling me back out of my head.

We had arrived on the grounds of the keep without my noticing, the officers having returned once again to their posts at the gate. From the hub-bub of magikiers going about their tasks, Kev rushed over to meet us like a traipsing bigfoot on his long, wiry legs. After what looked like a laborious day heating metals for the metalworkers, his maroon tunic was grimy, soot-strained, and damp with sweat, especially around his thick, leather utility belt. Even so, he wasn't lacking in energy.

I shook off my distraction as Kev took Seth's place to help support his brother. He peered between me and Seth, trying to hide the accusatory look in his eyes. "What's he doing out of the infirmary?"

Brett waved him off, although he had no choice but to accept his support. "I'm fine, Kev. Just doing my part."

"Oh, your civic duty to stop your own heart?" Kev mocked, but real concern lay beneath the jest. He glanced to Seth. "Was it important?"

"Undoubtedly," he answered with a dour look about him. No longer supporting Brett, he clapped his hands, rubbing warmth into his palms. "Now, I'll need to get back to my advisors, I'm afraid." He met each of our eyes. "Is there anything else, before I go?"

"Oh, I have something," I quickly interjected, and gestured down to my outfit. "My training..."

He smiled. "Right. Being that there's only one among us who's even tenuously equipped to train a shonte, I've assigned Briar as your mentor. Nothing is more important than your adjustment to these new abilities."

"Briar?" I repeated, and the little dragon curled her long tail around my waist, giving an encouraging squeeze. "And I'm unarmed because...?"

"Briar hoped it would dissuade you from leaping into battle," he chuckled, as if the idea was nonetheless preposterous. He certainly knew me...

Toward the little dragon clinging to my person, I thought, "*Okay, baby-proofing aside, you made it pretty clear you don't know the inner-workings of a shonte.*"

"*That may be true, but my guesses are better informed than those of meagre magikiers. What's more, I would not trust your training or your magic in others' hands,*" she returned. I supposed it made sense, considering she was around when the first shonte was still kicking. I dipped my chin in a compliant nod.

"Good luck, Anelisha." Seth passed one final, polite smile over us, bidding, "Song brothers," and headed into the keep following a troop of his elite, returning once again to his command room. When he was gone, Kev turned a stern look on we who remained, but before he had the chance to as much as open his mouth, Briar was back in my head.

"*We would be wise to begin immediately,*" she noted. By the startled expression on Kev's face and the flit of Brett's eyes to her lanky body, I assumed I wasn't her only recipient.

Patting my back, Kev encouraged, "Go ahead, I can walk Brett back."

"You're really treating me like I'm not right here?" Brett huffed.

"Acknowledgement is for people who care about their physical well-being," Kev snidely retorted, drawing the corner of my mouth into a smirk.

Briar hastened to interject, "*Linger longer. I had hoped the pair of you would be of use to me.*" Judging by her attempt at a well-mannered tone, I doubted it was her intention to sound so entirely cryptic.

Brett spoke before Kev could do so for him. "I've got nothing better to do. Lead the way." Kev sent him a disdaining look, and when Brett flat out ignored this, he flicked his eyes to me, pleading that I intervene.

Unsurely, I touched a hand to Brett's chest with my other still wrapped around his middle, asking, "Are you sure you don't need a break? I mean, after everything your magic showed you..."

He shook his head, meeting my eyes with determined regard. "I'm with you, Annie. Whatever you need. I'm yours." At his words, a constrictive pain entered my chest, too tight for the familiar squeeze he had often impressed upon my heart while we dated. The once-usual fluttery sensation in my gut became something queasy, nauseous. Plugged up like this, loving him only hurt.

"Ow, my sentimental heart," I wheezed, clapping a hand to my chest to overplay the genuine pain there. This earned a roll of his eyes, but the decisiveness of his proclamation killed any objections to his coming along and Kev's shoulders slumped in surrender.

We were off, following Briar's mental mapping to a vacant section of the keep's outer court in the shadow of the surrounding walls.

She sent Kev off to gather a bucket of water from the well – something to do with my training, I supposed – and allowed Brett and I a moment's rest as we awaited his return. As Briar picked strange fruits from the boughs of a nearby tree, Brett and I sat together on the grass, although to call this world's fine, golden threads grass marked a slight against their wonder. But, for lack of a better word, grass was what I would call it.

"*You recall, Anelisha, how it was desperation which bled the magic from your heart?*" Briar was saying as I lolled my head back on my shoulders, trying to memorize the radiant rings in the sky. "*In turn, you bled from the expulsion of your energy, and so continue to bleed?*"

"*Well, yeah,*" I hummed absent-mindedly.

"*My will is to teach you a means of accessing your elemental connection without relying solely upon emotional anguish and passionate outbursts. As long as you continue to do that, the power will only be available to you in all its glory, or none at all. Nothing in between. One way or the other, it will be your downfall.*"

"But emotional anguish and passionate outbursts are, like, who I am," I teased, not even bothering to contain our conversation to thought. Brett leaned back against the wall, crossing his arms behind his head as he gazed unbothered between me and Briar. He might have been zoning out, himself, for all the interest he showed.

"*At least you seem to be self-aware,*" Briar groused, and flung a fruit at my stomach. I barely managed to catch it, only to rake in breath between gritted teeth at the pain of doing so. Sinking my teeth into the mango-like fruit with skin like a plum, I found it was surprisingly juicy, so much so that purple juices squirted out the side of my mouth like a burst tomato. "*But this must change. Are you not always the one in search of a middle ground?*"

"But you're looking for subtlety," I said around the food in my mouth. Brett winced, watching me like I was an embarrassment. He wasn't wrong.

Swooping down from the tree to land in coils by my knee, she answered, "*A shrewd observation. I ask you now to push your magic into the earth beneath you. Dig its hooks in deep and probe the connection between yourself and the natural world. Become acquainted with it, let it speak to you, and take control.*"

"You want me to make small talk with the dirt?" I muttered, unsure what she meant. Brett glanced between us, finally bringing me to wonder if Briar had included him in her side of the conversation. If all he had to go off of were my one-sided responses, he was likely having a hard time keeping up.

Briar huffed, flicking her tail in frustration. "*You could at the very least make an attempt. This is the foundation of all magic training, not just restricted to shonte magic. There will be no progress until you've mastered this most basic connection to the power sheathed within you.*"

"Mm," I grumbled, and lay back on the grass. Closing my eyes, I slowed my breathing and tried to feel the world under me, the grass poking up through my sprawling red mane, the rock jabbing uncomfortably in my lower back, the unnerving thought of bugs – alien bugs, at that – crawling on me. I shifted my position.

"*You're not focusing, Anelisha,*" Briar grumbled in my head. "*And you will never focus yourself as long as you concern yourself with what you should be doing and not what you* are *doing.*"

"*You know, I'm starting to think I'm the last person the power of a shonte should've been given to.*"

"*Truly, but it was not given to you, was it? You took it, out of necessity and the desire to protect your loved ones. If that is not motivation enough, I cannot say what is.*"

I grumbled under my breath, shifting my position on the ground as if moving my arm several degrees outwards would mend all my problems.

Briar heaved a sigh in my mind. "*As I see it, your struggle with this magic is a blessing in disguise. Allow your findings to fix you, and you may discover more in yourself than just the capability to use it.*"

"*Yeah, yeah...*"

"You look like you're trying to take a nap when you're three coffees in," Brett noted, and I heard him move closer. Peeking through a squinted eye, I found him sitting cross-legged next to me. "When I first tried to connect to my magic, it was like trying to flex a muscle I wasn't aware of. It was a workout, still is, but I've gotten better at it. Because I treated it like a muscle."

"Of course you did," I chuckled, eyeing his athletic physique, only to catch myself acting not enough like the ex-girlfriend I was – after so long spent unlearning every fractal of him I'd fallen for, it turned out loving him was just like riding a bike.

Just as quickly as I caught myself falling back into familiar thought patterns, I found myself imagining Val's advice if she were here. She would have said something along the lines of, "*You need a rebound, stat,*" and would have set about finding me one. But she wasn't here, and after everything that had happened, she wouldn't have done a single thing for me. Not anymore.

Shunning all thought of her from my mind, I knotted my fists in the grass and tried to focus.

Taking myself back to the bunker where I had first tapped into my power as a shonte, I remembered the feeling of pushing my energy into the stone wall, plucking the strings within me attaching my will to fire, and the sense that the prime elements of the natural world were extensions of myself.

But I had a goal when I made that connection. If I hadn't done what I had, people would've gotten hurt or died… the people I loved…

"*You're working yourself up for another outburst,*" Briar interrupted, "*But I am not asking you to* do, *Anelisha. Only feel.*" Her voice was barely a breath in my mind.

Fine. I threw out the jarring memories I had so easily summoned. Instead, I imagined my magic probing out and reaching the earth under me. But no matter how hard I tried, that's all it was; imagination. With it, flashes of memories returned to me, leaking through the floodgates. The soul-draining exhaustion of raising a tidal wave of stone. The horrible, smoky feeling clouding up my insides as my fires ate at Clayton's back. A whining screech peeled between my ears, like metal on metal. My arms burned under my sleeves, recalling the pain of accessing my magic. Dizziness swathed my head.

"*Stop,*" Briar cut in, a powerful command. The memories slipped away. "*I would advise you disentangle your power from thoughts of destruction.*"

I snapped back to the present, the sounds of people going about their tasks around the keep filtering into my ears. No one had noticed how close I'd come to – to what? *Destruction.* But all it seemed was a dismal reminder that I was out here, failing even to meditate, while everyone else did their part.

I sat up, startling Brett. "I don't feel anything!" I burst, throwing out my hands in frustration. "I don't even know what I'm doing wrong." The ground came alive beneath my hands, bucking to the sound of my frustrated sigh and shaking a bushel of fruits from the boughs above. One of them struck my shoulder, but that wasn't the reason I flinched. "Did I do that?"

"*As I said, you've worked yourself up. Relax.*"

"How can I when I'm the most useless person in this entire city? At least I finally did something!"

"No, Annie, you're not-" Brett began, but cut himself off as he faltered for words. I didn't want to hear it anyway. I hadn't meant to speak so candidly.

"Never mind," I grumbled, crossing my arms and pressing the fresh cuts under the pads of my fingers to suffocate the slight pain. Anything to distract from the gory images slipping once again into my mind. No longer memories, but projections of what could have been.

In my mind's eye, I saw Lin, lifeless on the ground behind a monstrous kirranite, my sister's last line of defense beaten down until only the pastel pink of her hair, matted and bloody, was recognizable. Faith, her ankle bent at an inhuman angle, her face wet with tears, contorted into agony and terror in the shadow of the kirranite. And what followed... If I couldn't control this magic, these dark fantasies would only come to life in fresh and unimaginable ways.

"*Might I suggest you refrain from fabricating scenes you most wish to avoid, lest you summon them to reality?*" Briar warned, but her mental feelers were gentle as she nudged these notions from the center stage of my mind. "*I thought you knew better than to expend yourself on terrors beyond your control.*"

"I... I need a break." Pushing up to a stand, I paced back and forth before Brett and Briar with hands clamped on my hips. Rounding back on them, I demanded, "Can't you just tell me what I'm messing up?"

Briar huffed a sigh, shaking her head despondently. "*Just because this is new to you does not mean you'll never attain the skill. And I don't refer only to its violent potential. You're aware this magic can also be used to heal, are you not?*" I perked up at that, back straightening in my surprise, but she continued, "*Give it time-*" She cut herself off, bolting up like a meerkat with head raised high on a tall neck. It was a moment before Brett and I heard what she had. "*You've been noticed.*"

A distant wail, then sobbing. A woman's voice called out for help. Brett looked to me as if he meant to stop me, knowing my disposition in these situations, but my hesitancy matched his. The screaming resounded from beyond the walls of the keep, bouncing off the stone from the danger zone.

"Please! *Please!* Can anyone hear me? I need help!" the distant voice sobbed, thick with emotion and breaking terribly around tears. My heart leapt to my throat. The emotion in her voice was the last straw, moving me without any input from my perturbed mind.

Brett was too slow to stop me. My hasty feet clambered up the stone steps alongside the wall, mounting the rampart on the edge of Dyval's protection. Brett tailed close behind, and only at the top did he finally catch my arm.

"Annie, think about this. What's she doing out there?" He spoke these harsh words into my ear, but I hardly heard him over the pounding of my blood. My hammering heartbeat shook my whole body.

"*I can help...*" My own thoughts echoed in my mind, alerting me to Briar's presence.

"*You would not first assess the situation?*" she prodded.

"*I think it's pretty obvious she needs help.*"

"*And it must come from you?*"

"*This is a waste of time-*" I moved to vault the banister and make a break for the wall's opening, but Briar's slinky tail caught my waist, her talons digging into the ramparts. "*What?*"

"*Your eagerness to get involved inspires the carelessness of others,*" she growled, although for the life of me, I couldn't understand her disdaining tone.

It was at the sight of Kev, sprinting out beyond the walls to the fallen figure in the middle of the barren road, that Brett's energy renewed and he hurdled the steps back the way we had come, shooting after his brother with a rasping shout of, "What are you doing!" I moved to follow, but Briar coiled herself tighter around my waist, anchoring me to the parapet.

"*The woman to whom they run is no magikier of ours,*" she hissed in my mind, "*She's bait.*"

My heart plummeted. Of course...

"Kev!" I screamed into whipping winds, but if he could hear me, he didn't show it. This sudden gale could have been manifested to carry the call for help and stifle any warnings thrown from the keep. Part of the trap.

"Why didn't you warn me?" I loudly burst, sending Briar a glare.

"*I did. And allow me to digress, but I fear this may be a trap set explicitly for you – the ever-selfless shonte. If indeed these are liberation front magikiers, I have no doubt they've been made aware of you.*"

A frustrated groan clawed up my throat. "Okay, then I guess the better question is why do you have to be so goddamned cryptic?"

From here, all I had was a view of the unfolding scene and no way to help. Just as Kev reached the woman, he stopped dead in his tracks as if having heard something, glancing back toward Briar and me. Briar nodded her small head in his direction, and in turn, his eyes hardened with something like bold determination.

He had a flame in his hand before the bait could move, summoned from a lighter he carried. From here, I watched him warn her against trying anything, their voices carrying easily in my direction on the winds, but within that same instant, two others leapt out of hiding from the demolished buildings.

They were unlike anyone I had ever seen, even from this meagre distance of at most thirty feet. With a waxen sheen of glimmering sweat, it looked as though all the blood had rushed to the surface of their skin and hung there for far too long, purplish and bloated. The whites of their eyes were a yellowy brown and speckled with red, their irises either beetle black or their pupils inflated to consume all colour, the sockets sunken and dark with palpable exhaustion. The teeth they bared would fit better on a wolf and their nails had become like blackened talons or had fallen off completely. They looked like disease, two steps beyond the grotesquerie I had imagined pora to be. And I knew, these were pora. They weren't robust and bristly like kirranites; they were slippery, sinuous and agile with tough-looking skin.

Kev grew the fire in his palm, whipping it around to keep the pora from him, but something interfered. I couldn't make out what it was that changed, but without warning, the fire lashed out in a wild dance and turned back on him with purple discolouration. He barely leapt out of the way in time, forcing the fire to extinguish itself, when Brett leapt into the fray in defense of him. Except, he was unarmed, and his magic wasn't exactly offensive. Still, he met her in hand-to-hand combat.

Briar launched from my person, catching the wind on her wings, and rained fire down over the pair of pora. I hurried down the stairs, running to help Brett as Briar chased her victims through the streets. Their haste to flee – together in one direction – lent the disconcerting impression they were happy to lead her away.

"*Worry not for me. I'll rip the fire-resistant flesh from their bones and char their skeletons to ash. They will not harm me, but you must assure me you'll keep your distance from the bait,*" Briar growled, disappearing in a shower of flames and fury down the street in pursuit of the pora.

"*If only I had a weapon-*" I challenged, but Briar's fury hit me like a truck, sufficing to shut me up.

"*You will stay where you are, especially considering what you lack. Her magic has been strengthened by a bond with Valencia, I can feel it. I fear it's enough to stymy the magic of others, possibly even stopper the magic of a shonte if such were to be turned against her. Exert some will power; do not rise to her bait. It would be a pity to lose your power before ever reining it in.*"

The bells of the keep chimed in warning to all, so loud I jumped in alarm, losing my footing as I ran to Brett and Kev. My knees hit the ground as I glanced over my shoulder toward the ongoing clamour. Seth had run out beyond the walls, directing his elite into the streets but not toward Brett, Kev and the bait magikier. Then this was a coordinated attack, and I could only assume others had fallen for it around the keep. What was it Seth had said? One stray pora was all it took…

Picking myself up, I burst back into a run only to stagger up to Kev, whose eyes were locked on Brett's back. Brett stood over the bait magikier, frozen in horror of what he had done. She sputtered, still clinging to life from the rebar on which she had been skewered.

The gurgling sound from the wet hole in her chest churned my stomach.

All the warmth left my fingertips, receding up my arms. My eyes transfixed on the slow collapse of the girl's chest, no longer heaving with the effort of breath. Then came the stench. Blood. Too much of it. Filling the air and stinging my nose.

My hands flew up to cover my mouth. It was all I could do to hold back my scream.

"Brett, what did you...?" I heard myself whisper under the tolling of the bells. I could only imagine the look of abject horror in my eyes, fixed on the girl's wilting body.

"This is war, Annie!" he snapped back at me, startling me into breaking my stare and looking at him. His eyes were wide, his hands shaking, and when our eyes met, his face crumpled. "She did something-" He choked on the words. "Something to Kev. She was burning him..." He collapsed before the girl, his knees hitting the ground hard. He sounded as if he'd entered a trance with his haggardly whispered, "She wouldn't stop-"

The click of Kev's lighter sounded beside me, and his subsequent shout in pain and alarm had Brett and I rounding on him, panic in our eyes. That same purple-tinged fire leapt around him, refusing to depart from a criss-cross trail around his torso before he extinguished it again. His clothes didn't burn, but his skin singed red. A phantom serpent of smoke encircled him in its wake, still following the criss-crossing path around his body.

Rasping for breath, he fell back with his eyes glued to his palms. "I don't get it," he snarled, "Why can't I control it?"

"Briar said the girl could plug up magic." The words escaped me automatically as my gaze trailed back to the body on the metal stake. "When you tried to turn it against her..."

"But she's dead now!" Kev shouted, louder than the raucous bells. He worked to collect himself, but he was quaking next to me. "Why can't I-? This shouldn't-!" He couldn't get a full thought out, shaking his head between his hands.

My eyes found Brett again, dragging across the corpse in front of him. "We should get back to the keep." My voice sounded hollow. "Before anyone else gets hurt." He flashed me a scalding glare, assuming it was a jab at him, but voiced no objections. Instead, he dragged himself to his feet and offered Kev a hand. When Kev didn't budge, still staring at the dead girl like she held all the answers, Brett grabbed Kev by the collar and hoisted him to a stand.

At the sight of a wet, red stain on Brett's hand, matching the growing red pool trickling to the ashy ground under the girl, vertigo hit the back of my throat and I sucked in a sharp breath. I fixed my stare on the ground as my legs moved mechanically with the brothers to the infirmary.

New patients screamed and sobbed in the infirmary, or else contained themselves in a catatonic hush like Kev. My eyes raked over them, searching for any sign of the pora disease. Would it show? How fast could I expect the infection to spread? Would I see the evil cultivating in them, an excruciating betrayal of the self? But they just looked like people to me. Terrified, in pain, and above all else, confused.

We set Kev down on Brett's empty cot as Faith hurried over to us, having seen us enter under the tarp. "Annie!" she called, snatching me up from my place next to Kev. "Are you hurt?"

"No, no. It's Kev-"

"What happened?" Faith demanded, turning her gaze down on the cot where he lay. Raking her eyes over him, she gritted her teeth, a hiss of breath carrying the words, "Another curse mark." She turned his chin to reveal the skin just behind his ear. I hadn't noticed before, but a violet X marked him there. Brett and I watched her for an explanation. "Kev," she said, turning his chin again to peer into his empty eyes, "Can you use your magic?"

"It won't listen to me," he muttered, finding his voice, "What's wrong with me?"

To my surprise, she had an answer. "A carmavi magikier cursed your magic. A couple others have been brought in with similar marks." She tapped a long, thin finger behind her ear. "They can't access their magic because it's been blocked."

"Carmavi?" I whispered, recognizing the word. Although I preferred to call my own magikier classification the more intelligible translation, divine, I had also heard it referred to as carmavi, in the same way Faith's mind magic also went by the gibberish title, phomara. All the carmavi magikiers I'd heard of – which were few and far between – were restricted from using their abilities because it messed with others' magic, like how mine twisted the will of centions. But I never thought a magikier would turn against their own, at least not to this effect...

Brett's pond-green eyes flicked to me, barely retaining any of the blue from his usual turquoise now that his eyes were cast under dark thoughts. "Can you undo it?"

"This isn't my magic." I shook my head, unable to meet any of their eyes. "I'm a carmavi, sure, but I can only trace my own connection back to the centions. Use their magic for myself – *on* myself – I don't think it affects others." Then again, I was hardly knowledgeable on the subject. It being a restricted magic, I'd only ever been advised against using it, and when I didn't listen, I'd incurred the wrath of the centions. "I'm sorry, Kev," I whispered, pressing my hand to his arm.

"It's not on you, Annie," he muttered, but his sullen eyes fell again to his open palms, as if trying to will this curse away.

"It's on Valencia," Faith growled, surprising me. Before I could ask, she was already explaining, "I've heard a few of the healers talking about it. Magic-blocking is one of the five known categories of carmavi magic, but it shouldn't be enough to indefinitely block another magikier's. That would take constant concentration, and even then, it's just not possible to hold it forever."

"But the bond Valencia makes..." Kev whispered, putting it together. He had been there the night I learned just how Valencia attained as much power as she had; by forging a bond with individual magikiers so they no longer relied on the centions as a power source, but on Valencia. This bond simultaneously heightened the bonded magikier's magic and opened a doorway for Valencia to use their augmented magic for her own. This was her best excuse not to flat out kill me; because she wanted my magic to manipulate that of the centions. But how could I make that bond with someone hellbent on destroying my life, on killing me to get her sister back, on slaughtering everyone I loved just to get her way-

I bolted upright with the realization our group was one short. "Where's Lin?" She could just as easily have been lured to the traps of Valencia's allies.

Before I could shoot into action in search of her, Faith stayed me with a hand on my shoulder. "She's underground with the stone-crafters. It's the safest place she could be." Of course Faith would know. It was the duty of a best friend.

Vhy'ry magikiers like Kev and Lin possessed unique magic involving the elements – Kev could control the size of a lit fire and Lin could shift slabs of stone – sort of like they honed specific facets of the shonte magic sheathed within me. They tended to do it better by a long shot, but they had more guidance and practice than what was ever made available to me.

"And she's smarter than that," Kev granted with a darkness in his tone turned inward on himself, "She'd know not to go beyond Dyval's barrier."

I fell out of my ready stance, no longer sure where to go. How to be of use. What to do in the face of the day's cataclysmic loss. Brett had taken a life, and now consumed himself with rubbing at the blood staining his skin, but what had I done? Nothing.

5

No Rest For The Wicked

WITH THE END OF FAITH'S SHIFT, SHE AND I WERE USHERED FROM THE Song brothers' despondent vicinity, leaving them to their respective cots in the infirmary. Briar still hadn't returned, but she popped into my head every now and then to calm my woes.

The healers said Kev would be released come morning if they couldn't do anything for him, and although I wouldn't say it aloud, I doubted the discovery of an antidote overnight. The moment Faith and I left their sight, Faith released a shaky breath. I turned to find her face drawn with exhaustion. The day's toils painted her pallid.

We took advantage of our allotted window – in alphabetical order – for the communal showers before bed, and descended into the basement feeling at least slightly fresher, even with a lack of shampoos and conditioners. News was already spreading regarding the coordinated ambushes' outcome. Groups huddled together around lanterns or on mattresses before sleep, whispering the day's gossip. Although I hung back with Faith, wary to let these images into my mind just before sleep, I couldn't help overhearing.

Seth had led his elite to fend off the ambushers and escort our lured people safely behind Dyval's barrier, healers rushing those cursed like Kev to the infirmary. But those infected by the pora, well, I heard a suspicious lack of news regarding them. Instead, I heard rumours and fearful whispers. The mere mention of pora left everyone on edge, instilling a sharp atmosphere in the keep like nails scraping on chalkboard in the back of everyone's mind. Though no one voiced it, we all knew anyone infected with the pora disease couldn't be allowed within the walls, if Dyval would even grant them entry, but people still made a wider berth around the infirmary, clogging up traffic in the main hall. It was too soon to know how many of us hadn't gotten away.

My face must have betrayed my thoughts, because Faith poked my side, shaking her head. "Get some rest. If today's any indication, we're gonna need as much as we can get going forward." Catching my eye, she added, "And you do deserve to rest."

"Ugh, what are you, my mental health triage nurse?" I mocked, settling down on the mattress assigned to me, pulled from the wreckage of the city. We'd been directed to mark our names on our new beds – partly to claim them as our own and partly as a means of collecting data on who made it this far.

Sighing in a long-suffering way reserved mainly for me, she grumbled, "You could do with one, considering," and flung herself on her bunk as I peeled off my leather jacket and tabard. "But this isn't forever, Annie. We'll get back…" My mind went to Mom. To our old lives.

I shook my head. "I can't put all my eggs in that basket. It's too much to hope, when so much has changed…" Clearing my throat of the thickness therein, tears so swift to gather in my eyes, I threw on a jokey tone of voice, seeming loud in my ears. "It's whatever, though! We're all rivers and whatnot, flowing endlessly downstream on the river of existence. Ten bucks says you can't find that most elusive cryptid, a permanent self."

Faith watched me with raised eyebrows, the quirk of a smile hiding in the corner of her mouth.

"But just because something doesn't last forever doesn't mean it never mattered!" I rambled to fill her silence. I raised an index finger to illustrate a point, but my voice was wobbly on the words, "Some would say the key to a happier life is being in a constant state of change and acceptance!"

"Okay, Annie," she chuckled, smiling fully now as she patted my hand. "You can be your own mental health triage nurse."

She was quick to fall asleep, but I lay restless, staring up at the dark-enshrouded ceiling as the military police called for lights out. At least this meant the gossip fizzled out, although small voices still chattered on the barest of breaths around me. There was too much to bear leaving unsaid.

It had to be midnight on this strange, alien planet where the sky never darkened – a side effect of the moon-bright ring painting rainbow radiance through the starless night – when I finally gave up on sleep. It wasn't by a lack of exhaustion, but rather, the flashes of images I didn't want to see playing out behind my eyes every time I endeavoured to close them. Lovejoy,

Dooley, Fisk, Allard, Shimura, Inspector Mayes... Names no longer belonging to the living, but to people I had watched pass the threshold. Even Kev, the expression of utmost agony on his face, eyes brimming with automatic tears, as a bullet ripped through him. I could hear the whoosh of breath leaving their lips, shouts of pain, guttural agony of life ripped from their bodies, like I was right back there watching it all unfold before me.

With shaky breath, I sat up, eyes open wide. I was glad for the silver beams of light filtering in from the high windows, a reminder that I'd escaped these horrors. But it wasn't enough to sit in this dim chamber, surrounded by the sounds of others' night terrors. I pushed off from my assigned mattress and crept out of the basement, making sure not to draw the attention of the military police quietly playing cards in a small side-room just beside the stairs.

At the top of the stairs, I stood hopelessly still with nowhere to go. My whole body dragged under me, weighed down by the need for sleep, but my mind was a livewire. The infirmary teemed with busy nurses even at this late hour, but they kept quiet for the sake of their sleeping patients. The ones who weren't kept up by their pain and discomfort, that was.

I imagined an equal hush on the upper levels where off-duty officers slept, the kitchens where night staff prepared tomorrow's meals, and the side rooms where office work took place, all in an effort to ignore the sobs, soft cries and barely-contained panic I could feel charging the air all throughout the keep.

There was a scuffle near the tall double doors of the keep, sending me instinctively into hiding under a veil of shadows. Military police shoved the doors open, ushering in a larger troop. At the head of the group, combat nurses carted in the wounded on stretchers, rushing them to the infirmary. They were met with a flurry of action and healers making space for these new patients. Behind this commotion strode Seth.

He teetered in the effort of keeping himself upright, only accepting as much help as he needed from the officers around him. The way he moved, or maybe it was simply the way he held himself, seemed off. I could hear his grunts from where I hid. The troop split, the majority leaving to carry out whatever orders he gave while only two helped Seth into the command room. After a moment, even they left him, closing the door softly behind them.

I quirked my head, furrowing my brows, because surely, if Seth was hurt, he shouldn't have been taken right back to work. But of course he wouldn't put himself out of commission. Not for anything.

Creeping silently across the marble floor, I chanced a furtive glance over my shoulder as I stepped up to the door of the command room. My hand found the doorknob – pull not push – and I slinked quietly into the room.

He sat at his desk, but his chair was pushed out, his eyes on the sabre laid across his lap with one hand trembling on the hilt and his other pressed firmly to his side. His hair fell over his face, casting a shadow over his unreadable expression.

"Seth?" My voice was small, but he startled as if I had shouted, head snapping up to meet my eyes. "What happened?"

He moved as if to get out of his seat, sheathing the blade, but with a wince, slumped back. "You should be sleeping."

"You're hurt," I whispered, my eyes transfixed to the blood blossoming across his white shirt. He shook his head unconvincingly.

"It was all a decoy. They were going for the water supply. I had to–" He grunted, pressing both hands now to his side. "Ow," he hissed through gritted teeth, attempting a smile through the pain for my sake.

"Are you going to be okay?" My feet carried me further into the room. "Someone should be here. I can go get a healer–"

"No, no. I'm not a priority," he assured me, but I shot him a look. The corner of his mouth turned up in a smirk. "Trust me. I'm something of a wuss when it comes to…" He gestured to his side, but this only revealed the sheer amount of blood slicking his hands. He bit his lip, pressing the wound again if only to hide it from me, but he should've known it was too late for that.

I rounded his desk before he could protest, unsure what I meant to do but certain I had to do something. After all, Briar had told me shonte magic could heal…

"May I?" I gulped, gesturing to his side.

I could feel the energy bundling up in me, eager to breach the surface of my being, like it had been in the bunker. This was a warm ball unfurling high in my chest, flowing freer with every beat of my pounding heart. It felt… radiant, like I sheathed a sun within my being. It had a goal, a path, and I pushed it along into my hands.

I knew what I wanted from it, and it wanted to be set loose, to sap my energy and blaze with a life of its own, just like in the bunker. I'd learned that day that the reins I had on this magic were fickle, more a cable plugged into my heart than any restraint on it. Even now, I could feel it thrashing against me, straining to escape my body, and run rampant in the world.

The drive to do something, to heal him, seemed enough in this moment to make up for the shortcomings that had blockaded my magic in training. My frantic energy – emulating that which I felt in the bunker – plateaued into a heady sense of peace; the magic itself soothed my nerves, or was it him? Whichever it was, in that moment, the world grew calm and so did I.

He could only stare down at me where I took a knee, level with his injury. His eyes were wide, their blue in stark contrast to the dark red spreading through his shirt upon his hands' removal. He set his jaw in discomfort, a flicker of pain in his expression over releasing all pressure, but I hastened to replace his hands with my own. The muscles of his abdomen clenched and rippled under my touch. I thought I heard his breath hitch, but my hyper focus pooled around his injury.

"You can do this?" There was no doubt in his voice, only avid curiosity which bubbled nervous laughter high in my chest.

"Guess we'll find out," I mused, closing my eyes. It seemed the right thing to do, allowing me to visualize my intention.

A peace of mind I seldom knew swathed my head as I imagined my connection to the shonte element, Nature, on a biological level. The kick of magic broke from its furled ball in my chest to course down my arms and into my palms. There, it stopped. Like a blockade at the final gate, it just wasn't passing through.

Pushing a little harder, I willed it to emerge. The power, the magic. To take shape upon reality how I imagined it in my head. I started with what little I recalled from high school biology, imagining my magic's connection to water and blood – drawing forth the blood vessels to enrich the wound with nutrients. To air and dryness – clotting the blood at the surface of the wound into a scab to stem the bleeding. To fire and body heat – burning away infection, dissolving what wasn't meant to get under the skin. To earth and flesh – stitching him back together with scar tissue. It was a lose framework of my intentions, but the magic so keen to escape me filled in the gaps.

The breath left my lungs in a gasp when that familiar slicing sensation reopened old wounds on the meat of my hands, the tap through which the magic escaped me. My eyes snapped open, gaze searching Seth for his reaction, but I could just as easily feel it.

The V-shaped cut of his abdomen tightened under my hands, a tangible tremble coursing up his back as he shut his eyes firmly against what I could only assume was pain. The spread of blood came to a complete and sudden halt.

"Seth?" I asked. He nodded, still with his eyes shut firmly, his mouth a tight line. "I'm sorry, I didn't know it would hurt-"

"It's fine," he rasped, his hand twitching up to his jacket's inner pocket, only to stop, remembering something, and drop back down. I recognized that motion – his drive to light up a cigarette. Since our arrival on Cellana, he'd been lacking that faint scent of cigarette smoke and sandalwood so familiar in his presence. Instead, he was leather and petrichor, blood and charcoal, and above all else, the freshness of this world's mixed fragrances. A heady aroma.

Cracking his eyelids open, he worked to put a smile on his face, matching the genuine gratitude in his eyes. But then I remembered my hands, still planted intimately on his person. Warmth boiled up my neck to the tips of my ears, and I pulled my hands back so quickly, my elbow banged against the edge of his desk. He sat up, reaching out to me with a look of concern, but the ease of his reaction distracted me well enough.

I winced through the flash of pain in my elbow, gripped tightly in my other hand, and shooed away his concern. "Did it work?"

He lifted the hem of his shirt, sufficing to heat my face as if he held a torch right up to my cheeks. His dark skin – taut over lean muscles – gleamed with blood both fresh and scabbed over, but no other evidence of injury remained. His gaze snapped back to me, slack-jawed and awe-struck. "That's – You're incredible..."

Was my face *actually* on fire? It sure felt like it. Oh god, what if my shonte magic caused me to spontaneously combust? Was that a possibility?

"*Not likely,*" came Briar's voice. I hadn't even noticed her presence in my head. "*You do make it terribly difficult to ignore you, Anelisha. Have you any idea the beacon of magical energy you just sent out?*"

"*Well, no, beacons are meant for* others *to notice,*" I snarkily responded, but my mind was elsewhere, because Seth just called me incredible. He was talking, too, but it was something about shontes and I just liked the way his mouth moved.

"*I have just witnessed the head of every pora in their camp turn abruptly in your direction. From several kilometers out, I might add,*" she noted, wearing a tone of disdain, "*You've made yourself a target. They'll know the distinct scent of your magic now. They'll crave it.*"

"*Oh...*"

"*Ah, so the threat of the ravenous plague-ridden guzzling your lifeblood to the last drop has no bearing on your romantic heart,*" Briar huffed.

She wasn't wrong. I never had my priorities straight. "*Yes, well, I suppose death is inevitable no matter how it happens.*"

I couldn't help my small chuckle at that, calling Seth to raise an eyebrow. "Briar?" he asked, to which I nodded, but her presence faded from my mind the moment I turned my attention away.

"Turns out using my magic is like sending up a flare for the pora." He flinched, transparently shocked, although I hardly thought it deserved such a strong reaction. With an intentionally lighter tone, I teased, "That bodes well for any diversion tactics you might have in mind." I couldn't help it, I was giddy with the success of my magic, or perhaps suffering from a dreadful lack of sleep. If I was exhausted before, I felt about ready to slip into a coma, now.

His eyes hardened, and my stomach fell. I'd reminded him of his work, and sure enough, he pushed up from his seat, stepping over to one of the bookcases lining the walls where he scoured the shelves.

Huffing my displeasure, I plopped down into his vacated seat and pulled my knees up to my chest. The nighttime chill – damp and pervasive within these marble walls – was already creeping into the keep. Now that I no longer burned with blush, it was hard to ignore.

I startled, catching sight of a dark mass flung toward me out of the corner of my eye, only to snatch a plush blanket out of the air. Seth met me with a smile when I glanced his way, but he was quick to resume his search. Wrapping myself up in the blanket, it was the resurging warmth in my chest that kept me comfortable.

"Okay, what do we know about pora?" I asked, partly for the recap. He glanced sidelong at me, smirking. Was I really so transparent?

"In comparison to the common magikier? They're stronger, faster. Durable. Drinking magical blood has been proven to have a regenerative effect on their sustained injuries. Some studies have even suggested a regular diet of magikier blood can halt the aging process for pora."

"They're immortal?" I burst, somehow managing to sound offended.

He blinked his eyes softly in that contented, cat-like way, edging on a smile. "It was a small study, and deeply controversial. Pora don't last long in captivity."

"Oh… Not all that immortal, then. Is that all we have on them?"

"Not hardly. When the pora disease infects a magikier, they lose their cention-given magic, but some develop a knack for suggestion, weaseling ideas, sometimes coherent thoughts, sometimes outright illusions, into another's mind with just a look."

"Gross."

He tilted his head, granting his agreement. "And they see clear as day in the dark-"

I shook my head, confusion knitting my brows together. "Hold up, they what? Then why would they ambush us in daylight? They gave up their advantage." I considered it. "Unless they wanted us to see them."

Seth nodded solemnly, running his fingers over the spines of books whose titles were illegible to me. Gold-embossed and written in some foreign language. "Fear of infection. Distrust in our ranks. Panic. That's what they want. But they'd already made their first attack without any of us realizing. I had our water-purifiers check the well once I heard pora had attacked. Like I thought, they'd used our distraction to taint the water, meaning to spread their disease without risking their numbers in a full-fledged attack. Luckily, we've had water-purifiers assigned to the distribution of water since coming here. When night fell, I had a taskforce attend the well, lying in wait for our enemies."

"Did you stop them?"

He gave a dry chuckle. "Our legionaries did. I can't say I was much help." I certainly doubted that but left him to his modesty.

"Legionaries, huh? Not soldiers?"

"They're called legionaries on Cellana. Part of the centions' Eternal Legion."

"Mm." I furrowed my brow. "Does the Eternal Legion not fight for eventual peace?"

"No, I suppose it doesn't," he murmured, and that seemed to be the end of it.

His search went on thanks to the sheer number of books he'd gathered from the ruined city. In the meantime, I spent a glance over my hands, testing the sting of stretching my palms. A fresh red stain soaked my bandages which desperately needed changing after this latest exertion of magic.

Absent-mindedly, I wondered if I could heal myself the same way I had healed Seth, or if the effort would merely cancel itself out. I spent a long time on this train of thought, too long in my sleep-hazy state, so much so that Seth startled me out of my internal soliloquy with a book slammed heavily atop his desk.

"Sorry," he murmured, catching my jump in alarm. The spine of the book creaked as he sifted through the large, vellum pages. By the look of it, this book had lived through age-old wars long resolved, if such a thing ever happened in the war-torn lands of the centions. He narrowed his eyes on a passage I couldn't decipher. It didn't look to be written in any recognizable script, at least to my untrained eyes.

"Whatcha lookin' at there, scholar?" I asked, and he glanced hastily in my direction as if he'd forgotten I was there. He closed the book with a dull snap, mushrooming dust and sending loose papers skittering off the desk.

"We can't hold out against pora forces. When it comes down to it, *we* aren't Dyval's priority, you are." And a poor one at that.

Dyval would happily ignore me in a truly dire situation, allowing me to perish, just to do away with the dilemma my very existence posed. Either keep me alive to fend off Valencia's victory or let me die, thereby taking away another unreliable powerhouse capable of threatening cention rule. But if she went out of her way to let me die only for me to survive on my own, I would have no reason to fight for her, or worse, I might choose to side *against* the centions. But, but, but, until that happened, I was trapped in my obedience. Sticking with the centions meant I could hold them to their responsibilities, and she would have to continue protecting everyone in the keep. So, we were stuck in a balance of feigned loyalties, a stalemate of conscious inertia, and I, for one, resented it.

We met each other's eyes, equally aware of these issues. I could see him teetering on the edge of talking about it, but I was faster, mocking, "An ancient book told you that?"

He shook his head and carried on, speaking more to himself than to me. "We won't last. Not with our numbers and no hope of reinforcements." He turned to face me without meeting my eyes, half-sitting, half-leaning against his desk. His hands were white knuckled on the desk's edge, his shoulders taut. "It's only a matter of time before the infection gets behind our walls and spreads like-"

"-the plague?" I put in. He nodded.

"We'll never have the chance to warn the Empress at this rate." Leaning back with his hips to the desk, he steepled his fingers, resting his chin on his thumbs. "We can't hide behind Dyval's barrier and we can't fend off their attacks forever. The people we lose in our skirmishes will inevitably end up on their side or..." *Dead.* His gaze flicked to me, the haggard lines of sleeplessness deepening with unease. He released a worn sigh. "I'm sorry, I don't mean to put this on you. Don't let me keep you from sleep."

I shook my head stubbornly, but any image of defiance or determination I might have mustered was surely smothered by the plush blanket cocooning me. "I could say the same to you. But we both know how effective that'd be." I looked up at him with an open expression, imploring, "Let me help. There are always more roads to take than what's immediately clear to us. We just have to look a little harder."

Sinking out of his tight posture, he nodded. A lock of hair fell out of place from behind his ear as a smile reached up to his eyes, glued to mine. "What's the off-road equivalent? To go on the offensive?"

"What, like, send an assassin to take out their leaders?" I chuckled, "Subterfuge and all that?"

Humouring me, Seth mused, "None of ours could make it on their own and hope to succeed. There's no balance to a taskforce of this calibre. Enough to pose a real threat would be a dead give-away and any less would be ineffective." A light went off above my head at his words.

"What about a shonte?" I shot back, if only to counter his point. It hardly even registered that I was speaking of myself until he stared down at me in horror.

"I wouldn't ask that of you," he automatically answered, "You said it yourself, your magic is a beacon. There's nothing subtle about you."

But I was already running with the idea. "Then I don't use it until I'm right where I need to be. When my magic goes off, it's like a bomb. If they have no headquarters, no leaders, then Valencia loses a faction. Seth…" A flame snaked up my spine, and I met his gaze with fire in my eyes. "What if I did it?"

"It's asking too much," he insisted, shaking his head. He never asked for anything, not from me. He merely watched and hoped with eyes I would be heartless to deny. Even now, he didn't ask me to drop it. Instead, he hurried to list the cons, "It's too much of a risk. You'd be vulnerable outside our protection, outside *Dyval's* protection. This is exactly what Valencia wants. And we're dangerously uninformed, ill-equipped, disadvantaged." He met my eyes directly. "You would run the risk of infection. The pora virus takes quicker to stronger magic. Or if one of Valencia's enhanced carmavi blocks your magic; then what?"

"But who else could?" I breathed and fixed him with an open look. "Give me an alternative, Seth."

His eyes begged me to reconsider, but he had nothing to counter it. Instead, he sighed, "We think the combined forces of pora and Valencia's loyalists must be in the heart of Arillia to sever the connection between this country and the other clans, to keep magikier reinforcements from spilling in. Considering the desolation of the City of Gates, we can't begin to estimate the sheer force of pora they must have gathered. Anelisha, this is too big, even for a shonte."

"But don't we *need* the heart of Arillia if that's where we'll embark from to warn the Empress?" I smirked to myself, taking some pride in my ability to keep up with this whole mess.

"You've barely begun your training. You haven't even mastered your connection to this magic," he tried again, voice dipping low in his plea for me to yield.

I started in surprise. "Did Briar tell you that?"

"I've asked her to keep me informed."

"The magic comes to me when I need it," I murmured, clasping my wrist against my chest. Like this, the blanket slid down my shoulders, a ripple of plush around my hips. "That's how I healed you. Seth, if I can help, I *have* to..." I didn't notice him move, but Seth's hands gingerly drew mine onto my lap, and suddenly he was there in front of me, kneeling where I had been.

"I know..." He held my hands with as much care as he had turning those old, fragile pages, revealing the fresh red stains in the fabric of my bandages. He wasn't surprised to see them, but a crease furrowed his brows and he closed his eyes against the sight of fresh blood. His nostrils flared and I expected a lecture, the likes of which I would have received from Faith or Brett or even Lin, but instead, Seth quietly breathed, "I wish they knew you like I did, before this power."

I tilted my head in surprise, asking, "Who?" if only to distract myself from the soothing press of his hands on mine.

He peered into my eyes. "Everyone who escaped Valencia because of you. They see the shonte you've become, and they cling to this image of you from the bunker. I can't say I haven't heard them talking about sending the *Champion of Blackano* to fight for us." He shook his head with the tilt of a smirk on his lips. "But you're so much more than that."

I wanted to slap a palm to my forehead for my obliviousness; I wasn't the only one thinking I'd been totally useless these past few days.

"You don't have to prove anything, Anelisha." The gentleness in his voice tugged at my heart. He released my hands, but the warmth of his touch remained, tingling in the tips of my fingers, and he pulled the blanket up on my shoulders. "You were already the sun to their distant stars, long before you took the power of a shonte."

Reeling, it was like my brain swooped suddenly out of my head, landing somewhere low near the base of my spine. My mouth opened and closed and opened again, searching for words, until a smile dimpled my cheeks. I could only breathe, "That was poetry..."

"Ah, I meant it to be cheesy." His lips tilted up in one corner, and when paired with his sleepy, half-closed eyes, made a valid play to stop my beating heart.

"Poetry is just fancy cheese."

He smirked, stifling a small chuckle, and stood up to rest once more against the desk. "I know all you want to do is protect the people you love but give me time to think of an alternative. This... this is a last resort. We can't rush into a plan that could cost us everything."

"Wouldn't everyone here be safer?" Because Dyval would choose them over me, and she would rest assured in my full support of that action. "We would only be risking me."

"Like I said," he mused, but allowed me no time to put his meaning together before he continued, "But until we come to a decision, you'll have time to work on your magic with Briar. You'll need to be prepared..." To use it. To *kill* with it. Oh god...

A mechanical nod had me lowering my eyes to the floor, but my mouth had a mind of its own, as usual. "Yep, yep, yep. Okay, sounds good. I like to have a plan, especially one I can procrastinate." Somehow, I was only now feeling the weight of the responsibility I'd taken on. No, the responsibility I'd volunteered. Sheesh, I really was such an idiot. I couldn't be trusted to make my own decisions, let alone plan a half-baked coup on bare minimum sleep. Sleep...

At the thought of it, my eyelids grew heavy. There was no running from it any longer.

"Can I..." I hesitated, ducking my head under the hood the blanket made, "Can I stay here awhile?" My eyes flicked to the couch along the far wall beside an old-timey radio transponder. Maybe it was the look in my eyes as I struggled to push down the reasons I'd rather not sleep in the basement, or maybe it was in my tone of voice, but Seth caught my meaning.

"Of course," he noted, although his tone pitched in surprise, "Make yourself comfortable. I'll work quietly."

"No, no, don't trouble yourself." I was tired enough as it was, he could've knocked down a wall and I doubted it would wake me once I was out.

Giving up his desk chair still with his blanket wrapped around me, I hobbled over to the couch and with all the grace of a tossed peanut, flopped onto the cushions. My wild curls flew out around me, a snarl of red locks cutting off my view. Although my back was turned, I thought I caught the sound of a chuckle escaping him.

"Where do you sleep?" I mumbled into the couch, hoping the exhaustion in my voice didn't blend my words.

"Here, mostly," he answered, the creak of his chair telling me he seated himself once again at his desk.

I clicked my tongue in reprimand. "No good. You're gonna screw up your back."

"Get some rest, Annie." I was too tired to register his use of my nickname, which was saying something considering how rarely he used it. My eyelids fluttered closed and my breathing slowed, but I still treated myself to the soft sounds of Seth pushing up from his seat to cross the room. I imagined him studying the war table where his scouts had marked enemy forces lying in wait, my mind likely doing no justice to the serious look that was surely on his face.

"You too, buckaroo," I slurred into the couch. With that, I was out.

6

Thanks, Brain

Day 4

IT WASN'T THE NIGHTMARE I WOULD HAVE EXPECTED, MAINLY BECAUSE it wasn't one of the recurring ones drawn from my lived experience. Somehow, that made it worse.

It felt dangerously real. I knew the creature to be a pora only by the nature of fear that raced in my chest, but this conjured monstrosity hardly fit the bill. As a matter of fact, I couldn't see much of anything. There were only two blood-red eyes – which, I felt pretty sure, wasn't even biologically correct for porakind – unblinking and hovering over me, and a mouthful of dog-like fangs spilling hot breath on the palms of my hands as a vise-like grip clamped my wrists together in front of me.

It was too dark to make anything out of the murky depths of the dream, as if I had found myself leagues deep underwater, a heavy weight crushing me, pinning me to the ocean floor and slowing my movements, but somehow in the logic of the dream, I could breathe. Frantically raking in breaths too short to be of any help.

Even so, all the breath left me in a guttural rasp when a pair of lips met the skin of my hands – skin, not bandages – spiking pain in the pull of blood from cuts already there and chasing white hot fire through my veins. I whimpered, unable to struggle under the weight of the void, darkness keeping me down. Rough hands, calloused and cold, drew my hands out further, to the mouth sucking at my palms. Hungry for more, for all of it, he trailed ravenously after the hot streaks of liquid dripping down my wrists. A weight planted itself atop my stomach, the knees of the pora digging in under my shoulders as his tongue dragged down my arm. I felt the brush of the pora's fangs teasing between his lips before their points dug into the soft skin at the hollow of my elbow.

Incoherent pleas for mercy ripped from my throat, lost before reaching my ears as my words absorbed into the darkness pressing down on me. The draw of blood, pooling in the mouth of the pora and spilling out around his bite, became the center of my being in this nightmare, a focal point of shooting pain. I thought I heard his involuntary moan, muffled against my flesh. Under the flooring weight, my back arched in the effort to buck the pora, but he was a rock, unmovable, his rigid hands clamping my arm to his mouth.

"This is the future you face, as you are now," a wicked voice boomed through the darkness. Although I knew I hadn't spoken these words, I recognized the voice as my own, and only then understood to whom it truly belonged. The voice of the girl whose body I'd grown up in, the body I had reincarnated into. Evelyn Lupei. "Does it petrify you, knowing this?"

With the startling sensation of being drenched by a bucket of cold water, I was suddenly aware of the dream, of the cobweb of phantasms thick as cotton candy and just as sticky crowding in on me, entangling me for Evelyn's picking. But Evelyn's voice wasn't a mere figment of my unconscious mind. It was hers, and it was real.

A shiver fingered up my spine as the pora's fangs pulled out of my skin, allowing the blood to puddle in the crook of my arm and trickle off my elbow. I hardly noticed for the new terror burgeoning high in my chest. Evelyn shouldn't have been able to speak directly to me. Even in a dream, I knew this.

By the thunder in my chest, heart hammering against the cage of my ribs, I escaped the dream. It all came crashing down around me, and I shot up from sleep, sitting bolt upright in the low lantern light as my eyes flicked furiously this way and that. For a moment, I had no idea where I was, panting and quivering, thrashing out of the plush blanket wrapped like a straitjacket around me. Clammy with sweat and nevertheless chilled to the bone, I couldn't help my shivering.

"Anelisha?" Seth's voice, husky with sleep, broke my panicked headspace envisioning shadowy figures in the corners of the room. Before I could figure where his voice had come from, he planted himself on the arm of the couch. He rested his hands on my shoulders, delicately but firmly, to meet my eyes.

Those mesmerizingly blue irises, flecked with ocean waves around the black pit of a maelstrom, guided me to the present moment, reminding me where I was, what had happened, who I was with. His eyes were my safe place, and outward from them, the world bloomed back into existence. By the eerie silence of the keep beyond this hushed room, I knew we had entered the small, dark hours of the night.

"It was a dream. You're safe." I couldn't be sure how many times he repeated this sentiment before I finally heard him.

"I'm not, I'm not-!" I gasped, pulling away with involuntary tears brimming in my eyes. "Evelyn-" I choked on her name. "I heard her voice. She's still in my head!"

He looked as if I'd struck him, fixing his stare on the floor with mouth slightly parted. "It shouldn't be possible…"

He swallowed, giving the impression of staving off vertigo. He knew as well as I the danger Evelyn posed. He'd defended me when she had an opportunity to kill me – no, to replace me. She'd tortured him in the same way a sociopath would cut the tail off a cat.

He ran his tongue over his bottom lip, fists clenching on his knees. It was a moment before his voice shook over the question, "Are you hurt?"

My hand automatically went to the inside of my elbow, but I was quick to reassure him, "She wasn't exactly *there* in the dream. It was just her voice." But Seth noticed my hand's movement, his face drawn with worry.

Gesturing to the elbow I clutched, he spoke with a strained voice, "If you've been injured…"

The fact of the matter was, it didn't hurt anymore than it had yesterday or the day before since the expulsion of shonte magic from my body had ripped through the flesh of my arms, but hesitation found me with the fear that my dream had left a mark. A mark of pierced skin and bruising. A mark taken directly from the dreamscape, like the first time Evelyn tried to kill me – and would have killed me if not for the healers. But here, we lacked the high-level healing facilities available to us in Blackano.

Lightning shot through my veins and buzzed in my brain. What if, when I pulled up my sleeve, unbound my bandages, and revealed the crook of my elbow, we would discover that my unconscious mind was more dangerous than anything these perilous lands could throw at me? There would be no avoiding my hastened ruin, no escaping my fate – the destiny carved out for me by the Lupei sisters.

"May I take a look?" Seth prompted, calling me back from the depths of my mind. The expression he wore spelled thoughts as despairingly urgent as mine.

Biting back the protest in my heart to see the truth, whatever it may be, I folded my sleeve over itself high on my bicep and peeled away the spiral of bandaging from there. The half-healed lacerations from mere days ago drew angry red ribbons where the bandages fell away, but I expected as much. A sickly smell of blood – metallic and old – filled the room, stinging my nose. I really should have changed these bandages sooner.

A moment from pulling away the pink and yellow-stained cloth around my elbow, I made the mistake of glancing up at Seth, only to find his stare disturbed on the mangled gore etched into my arm. My breath caught, my hand stopped, a flash of heat climbing my neck to burn my cheeks. He hadn't seen the full extent of my injuries before now, and what a mess I was.

"I'm sorry-" I croaked, but my words seemed to wake him from his horror, and he met my gaze with confusion in his eyes.

"Why are you apologizing?"

Blushing deeper, I ducked my head in a shrug. "Seemed appropriate?"

Seth's lips parted as his fingers reached out toward me, only to stop himself on a wavering thought. I moved to pull my sleeve down again, happy to pretend the dream had never happened, but he pushed through his tentative pause, taking my hand in his and with his other, picked up the thread of loose bandaging I had released.

"I'm the one who should be apologizing," he softly noted, undoing the rest of the bandaging with careful grace. Before I could protest his words, the crook of my elbow lay bare before our eyes and-

Nothing. No mark from the dream to further mar my already scarred-up skin.

A breath I hadn't realized I was holding rushed out as the cloud of fear that still clung to me from the dream finally dissipated. I fell back against the couch, still squeezing Seth's hand in mine, but his eyes were fixed on my elbow.

"And there we have it," I pleasantly sighed, "She doesn't have the tangibility to hurt me or there would've been a mark. All she can do is taunt me, and hell, what's one more voice of doubt in the back of my mind."

"What do you remember about the dream?" he asked, loosening his grasp of my hand, but I didn't let go just yet.

"It was dark," I murmured, shutting down the fear threatening to rush back, "A pora had me pinned..." The words trailed away from me when he

set his jaw, a hard look in his unreadable eyes, but I forced myself to continue, "It bit me, and that's when she spoke. Evelyn said this was my fate, or something along those lines, but even I can recognize a scare tactic when it's slapping me in the face."

"She's using *reality* as a scare tactic," he noted, a pained expression in the furrow of his brows.

I blew a nervous breath. "Hah ha, helpful..." Working to calm the resuming tremors in my fingers, I squeezed his hand.

He still hadn't torn his eyes from the spot on my elbow where the bitemark didn't show, but I could see a cascade of thoughts behind those sapphire blues, unable to breach his mouth. Whether the scar was there didn't seem to matter to him.

Lacing my fingers with his, I pressed his hand. "Sure, there are pora out there who'd be glad to sink their teeth in me, but Evelyn told me to be petrified, so I'm not gonna. I feel terror on my own terms," I declared, as if this was something to take pride in, "Which is to say, primarily in social situations."

He huffed a wry chuckle, finally meeting my eyes as his own hid worry behind the barest pretense of a smile. "I shouldn't have expected any less of you."

My face burned under his gaze, but he seemed to be hovering over his next words, wary to speak them. Instead, the rattle of talons on marble and the subsequent boom of the door thrown open introduced Briar into the room on sweeping wings.

Her voice appeared in my head with her arrival and rose in volume the closer she bounded, until she clung to my shoulders, filling my brain with, "*What disaster bars me from your head this time?*" Seth leapt back in surprise as she scoured me for answers, slithering in folds around my torso and licking the air suspiciously. With ruffled tail swinging indignantly, she hissed, "*I was unable to sense your mind until I had come within mere feet of you. By closing the distance, I found you, but this shouldn't have happened at all.*"

"Probably thanks to Evelyn," I hastened to say, a wave of exhaustion pulling the carpet out from under any competent explanation I could give. This only earned me Briar's dramatic head turn and dragonesque glare.

"*Your lax attitude toward the very being whose entire existence is dependent on a lack of your own astounds me. Probably, indeed.*" The little barbs on the tip of her nose nudged into my cheek, a warning headbutt. "*If she has not left you, then I've failed to notice an enduring aspect of her in you – the perfect copy that you are. I suspect whatever aspect of her consciousness that exists in you must be residual from the night she nearly ended your life.*"

"Yeah, but now she can't touch me, so..." I yawned, Briar's fiery warmth around my shoulders acting as a final balm to soothe the nerves my dream had frayed. A resurgent push for sleep weighed down my eyelids, but I worked to keep them open.

"*And yet her mere presence succeeds to supplant me from your mind. I can no longer hazard parting from you...*" Even Seth started in surprise at her words, bringing me to realize she'd included him in this mind link.

I started in alarm. "*But what about defending the keep?*" The thought projected from my mind before the words could reach my lips.

"*I've been assigned to you, shonte. Defending the keep was a means of defending you; if doing so gambles your safety, then the risk is too high,*" she decided, flicking her tongue. She didn't need to remind anyone of my disposition for getting myself into trouble which merited her caution. Even Seth wore an expression in his eyes conveying his similar line of thinking.

"And what about your search? You're sure we're on top of it?" Seth interjected.

Briar held silent for a moment, flicking her tongue in distaste. "*I know where* it *was hidden in ages long past, and though I swore to help the centions' children unearth them... I still hesitate to draw attention to them.*"

"There's no going back on your promises, Briar," he said, and I glanced between them, brows furrowing in my confusion.

"Is this about your sacrifice? To the centions?"

She swung her head back around to meet my eyes. "*I've mentioned something of this to you, once before, though not in detail. And, with your help, Knox, I might convince Dyval of one who may wield what your stonecrafters dig up.*"

I found myself losing the thread of their cryptic conversation, looking back and forth between them as I quelled the curiosity burning within me. I wanted to believe they would tell me if it was important, but more likely, they would only tell me what I needed to know. This was, after all, more of the centions' business.

Before now, I hadn't even considered Seth would put Briar to uses unbeknownst to me – and now, because of the latest barrier between our minds, he was losing perhaps his most powerful asset just so she could keep an eye on me.

A distant memory returned to me, involuntary and entirely unwanted. An echo of Clayton's voice weaseled into my mind with the words, *I guess the centions have their round-the-clock guard dog on you, after all.*

7

What Does Progress Even Look Like?

Day 12

THE STONE-CRAFTERS DISAPPEARED UNDERGROUND, A PURPORTED foray into the old mines under the City of Gates, but Briar didn't let me believe the tripe. Whatever it was they were so intent on digging up, it had everything to do with whatever she'd given up to centions.

Up top, the infirmary still buzzed with an overwhelming wounded-to-healer ratio, but a good few were released over the course of the week, including Brett.

With his release, Seth's elite assigned him to scouting missions beyond the keep where Kev had already been drafted since he lost his value to the metalworkers. I rarely saw the Song brothers after that.

Instead, I tested my hand in the healing department, meaning to work my magic like I had with Seth, but a finnicky inconsistency came with this new usage. For one, it barely worked, and when it did, it was on the most minor of injuries. Even then, the gashes on my palms reopened no matter the sutures knitting my skin back together. Honestly, I was just trading in wounds and never to my benefit.

Faith and Briar were the first to look for the blood on my hands. They took it as a signal to end my practice for the day.

"*If it causes you equal harm, then it is no success,*" Briar would repeat each time.

Worse was when I couldn't summon the magic at all, this being the more likely turn of events. The infirmary dulled with the disillusionment of all watching, to the point I couldn't bring myself to meet anyone's eyes when I finally gave up my mentally exhausting efforts. Those nauseating walks of shame brought about a worse twinge in my chest than the slight sting of expelling the magic.

"*I thought shontes were supposed to be powerful,*" I grumbled from my mind to Briar's after a long day of failure.

I opened and closed my hands as I trudged through the keep after her, absent-mindedly testing how far I could stretch the uncomfortable grooves dashing all hopes of palmistry. My feet dragged under me, the let-downs of the day like a tangible weight on my back. But Briar had insisted I follow her to the lower levels, explaining scarce little of her plans for me. The secrecy, I was used to, but I could have gone for a nap.

"*Don't be disheartened, young one. There was only one other shonte, who was well-trained for decades as the centions' weapon before he died in their wars. For all anyone knows, his great power could have been a fluke.*"

"*That's encouraging.*"

"*You are not so wrapped around the centions' fingers. I believe you will be greater.*" She considered it for a moment. "*That is, if you do not first succumb to an untimely but easily preventable death.*"

Rolling my eyes, I huffed in her mind, "*Okay, are you feeling a teensy bit bitter toward me or am I reading too much into your usual salt and vitriol?*'

"*Do you believe me ignorant to your thoughts after all this time, that I wouldn't perceive the plan that has occupied your sleepless nights since last you spoke with Knox? That's what I would call the catalyst to your preventable death.*"

"*And it's what Seth would call a last resort, so no need to worry. I'm sure his big brain will figure something else out before I get the chance to go out in a blaze of glory. I'm just practicing preparedness.*"

"*Pardon me, I had not thought you capable of precaution,*" she teased, flicking her tongue. "*Perhaps I've been harsh. I don't mean to, how did you put it, add another layer of stress to a hundred-layer cake? But this world is dangerous, and your plans have a tendency to fall through. It would be a valued comfort to know you can handle what it is you spend your nights brooding over, but it has been some time since I was last on Cellana. And how different it was, then.*"

Without warning, she dropped the connection between our minds. Suspicion fingered into my mind with the idea she meant to keep me from accidentally eavesdropping on her most valued memories, from a time before the centions muzzled her. But how could I blame her? As things stood, I was the magikiers' fist, and magikiers, the centions' legs. Dyval had us both on a short leash.

Or maybe I was all off. Her voice returned, fierce and rushed. "*Quickly, something's wrong.*"

"Wha-?"

"*Turn around.*"

Spinning on my heel, I nearly lost my balance at the height of the stairs to the basement in my search for whatever she meant. A disgruntled passerby staggered around me, surprised at my sudden change of direction, and shot me a glare as she passed.

Before I could smile a quick apology in her direction, I saw what Briar had, and a flicker of fear caught in the back of my throat. At the far back of the long vestibule, boxed into the corner. No, edging toward a rarely used side room.

If not for her brightly coloured hair, I wouldn't have recognized her. And then she was out of sight, shoved into the room.

"*I asked her to meet you in the basement. They intercepted her,*" Briar was saying, but her thoughts slipped between the cracks of my mind, drowned out by adrenaline. "*She's scared.*"

I'd broken into a sprint before I could fully register what I saw. Four much taller people crowded around one. The keep wasn't so busy in that corner, no one would have noticed if they weren't looking for it, and it had happened so fast, even *I* might've missed it if not for that familiar pink hair, even cut short in a pixie cut. When did she do that?

My feet skidded out from under me as I crashed through the doors, chasing the small group into the room. Not a room, a hallway. Briar extended a wing, compensating my balance, and with her long, snaking body, kicked off from the floor to keep me accelerating forward. More doors lined the length of the corridor, none standing out to me. They'd vanished.

"*Where-?*"

"*Third door down. Quickly! They've seen her face.*"

"*Her face?*"

Heart thundering against my ribcage, I burst through the door Briar had pointed out to me, whacking a body behind it. A week ago, this might've shot stinging pain through my arm, but now it was just itchy. I'd recovered fast with help from the healers, leaving no more than a latticework of pink lines all up my arms to show for my trouble. Only my palms still bore fresh wounds, even if the day's efforts had ended in failure.

"What's going on in here?" I shouted as a man hit the ground, flung off his feet by the swinging door.

"Annie?" Lin's voice found me, small and incredulous. She was on the ground, a bruise already forming over her brow.

Red stained my vision. "Get out!" The command ripped from my throat, bouncing off the walls of the closet-sized room, but I didn't move from my place blocking the doorway. *Come near me*, my fists implored them.

The four assailants scrambled away from me, backs hitting the claustrophobic walls.

"You don't understand!" a woman's voice shouted back, "She's one of them! Look at her!"

My eyes flicked briefly to Lin, but she looked no different than I expected, forgetting the much shorter hairstyle. Except… the scarf she had taken to wearing was pulled down around her chin, revealing the markings on her skin. Twisting red lines, a spiderweb of unnatural veins, branching out from the red spot in the middle of her forehead. The path travelled by a kirranite parasite as it attempted to takeover her body.

"She's infected," the man on the floor spat at Lin, although he was speaking to me.

"No, she isn't!" I shouted back, incredulous with outraged disbelief and loud enough to make him jump back from me. "She's a survivor like you! Like me!"

"But-"

"I gave her that mark when I kept a kirranite from making a host of her body!"

Silence rang in my ears in the wake of my words, the four attempted assailants each sharing a look of disbelief.

"What were you going to do to her?" I growled, sending a powerful kick at the feet of the man on the floor. "You're disgusting, dragging her here. To do what? Tell me!"

He quaked under me, raising his arms up to block his face as if he thought I would unleash hell on him. I wanted to.

"*Anelisha,*" Briar whispered in my mind, "*Do not fault their ignorance unless it is wilful. Fear is what blinds them.*"

"*But they were going to do something awful to her! There's no excuse!*"

"*You stopped them. You've forced them to consider the consequences of their actions. Let them feel this consequence, but let it be just.*"

"*Then give Seth their names.*"

She did as I said, easily rifling through their perturbed minds, and I filed each name away in my own head, to remember what these four were capable of.

Clenching my fists at my sides, I committed their faces to memory, staring hard between each of them. "Figure out what pora look like, and don't ever take serious matters into your hands again. *Idiots.*" My voice shook, the words falling out of me like lead. It sounded too reminiscent of Val's fury with her own followers, men and women who had taken her cause and run with it, spreading terror and flames in their wake. Was there no escape from morons?

With that, I stepped aside, moving into the room toward Lin as the four of them scrambled to get out. Quaking fingers pulled her scarf up high on her face, to the iron rims of circular goggles befitting of the metalworkers, whose tinted lenses blocked her eyes from view. She even styled her pink-dyed hair – roots a dark brown – so the pixie cut covered her forehead. When matched with a stone-crafter's leather apron, gloves, utility belt and knee-high combat boots over Arillian shirt and pants, she hardly let a sliver of skin show. And now I knew why.

"Are you okay?" I crouched down in front of her, meeting her at eye-level no matter that I couldn't see past her lenses.

She nodded but didn't speak, sniffling under her scarf. Tentatively, I reached out to her, but she caught my hand, pinning it down next to her. "I'm fine. Please, Annie, I don't wanna talk about it."

"But they-"

"It's not their fault I look like a monster," she hissed, but must have seen the fire in my eyes, for she hastened to tack on, "We're not talking about this, remember?"

"Fine," I grumbled, but pulled her into a hug, squeezing her tight. The better to avoid staring at the bloodred pattern carved into her warm complexion, or more accurately, the efforts she took to hide these markings. "As long as you're okay…"

"Actually," she shakily huffed, coming to a stand, "I was on my way to you."

I hadn't seen much of her – or anyone, really, besides Faith and Briar – between helping in the infirmary and passing out on my mattress. Now, all I could think of were more instances like this one. A week of having to hide her face, of keeping away from others' paranoia, of isolation. I wanted to ask if this was why she'd cut her hair, but I refrained. I should've gone to see her every day.

More and more questions besieged my mind, battering the ramparts at the tip of my tongue, demanding to be asked, but I held off. It was only too bad that meant I couldn't think of anything else to say. My jaw clenched, mouth a thin, white line.

"Briar said I was chosen to finish the excavation," she continued, filling the silence, and tilted her head uncertainly toward the dragon sprawled across my shoulders. "It's been such a tight-lipped business; I should've realized the shonte was involved."

"Me?" I said, glancing toward Briar as my eyebrows climbed high on my forehead. "I wasn't told about any of this. Just that you've been digging toward… well, something."

Starting out of the room, Lin was happy to keep the casual conversation going. "You're off to bigger and better things, I'm sure. And speaking of, is it just me or is she getting bigger?" Peering sidelong at the little dragon, Lin planted both hands on her hips and quirked an eyebrow – one of the few bits of her I could see – before nodding to herself. Truly, she was sprawling; her tail wrapped thrice around my waist and the bat-like fingers on her wings knotted in the material of my sleeves, just to anchor her lanky size. "She is."

I hadn't noticed before, but Briar never could've used her length to propel me forward like she did in the hallway before. "But she didn't grow an inch in Blackano-" I was saying, only for Briar to shake her narrow head, invisible eyelids blinking sideways – too much like windshield-wipers to look normal.

In both my mind and Lin's, she explained, "*I told you, Anelisha. The centions have lifted only their most unfounded punishments from my being, including their restraints on my body. Did you think they kept me trapped in that metal figurine simply because they could not handle a creature of this meagre size? Not hardly. When they first released me from that insufferable prison to watch over you, they ensured I would remain… manageable. Now that you face greater peril, and now that you've spoken some sense into Dyval, they've allotted me another measure of freedom.*"

Behind the slight tint of the goggles, Lin's eyes sparkled with intrigue, pouring herself into this easy distraction. "Fantastic. How big will you get?"

I wished I could be as outwardly surprised and delighted as Lin.

"*I do doubt I'll return to my former magnitude, but suspicion tells me they'll allow a... significant growth spurt to take place.*"

"Kev'll get a kick out of this," Lin noted, "But I'm not here to fawn over your second puberty." She seemed so normal, bouncing back too easily, too quickly, after what just happened. I had to bite my tongue again to keep from asking just when this had become her normal.

"*Correct,*" Briar mused, "*I believe the time has come for our shonte to receive a worthy weapon, and through too many insufferable arguments with Dyval, Knox and I have pestered our keeper into approval.*"

We emerged back into the main hall of the keep, and with that, she leapt from my shoulders, unwinding her long tail making up half my height, and caught the stale air of the keep under her white and gold, stained-glass wings. From here, and with my eyes now trained on the little differences Lin had so easily noticed, Briar's slinky body didn't look quite so slinky. As a matter of fact, she looked sturdier. A little less serpentine, a little more feline. Once-stumpy legs now looked to have absorbed all the length her deep-chested torso forfeited, although the difference was only minor. Most glaring of all was her wingspan, looking greater even than her full length, tail included. It boggled my mind, not the difference, but my failure to notice it earlier.

"*Follow,*" Briar commanded, and dropped the connection between our minds.

"Hey, uh," Lin muttered, rubbing the back of her neck, "Don't tell the others about what happened, okay? No one needs to know."

"Sure, but can I ask one question?"

"Is that the question?"

"Lin, tell me this hasn't happened before..."

She fell quiet, and I couldn't even hope to read her expression for the measures she took to conceal it. "Come on, we don't want to lose sight of Briar," she finally said, nudging an elbow into my side like I hadn't spoken at all.

Heaving a sigh, I yielded to her subject change. If she didn't want to talk about it, I wouldn't push it, but leaving it open ended like this didn't alleviate any of the weight on my chest. If nothing else, I could at least lighten the atmosphere I supposed was doubled in intensity for her.

"Our little drama queen always needs to make an exit."

"Yeah, Kev's been calling her the dramagon."

A light chuckle escaped me. Of course Kev would. God, I missed him – I wondered if he knew what was going on with Lin.

The brothers would have had a good excuse to see Lin, as she worked part-time with the stone-crafters and metalworkers assigned to repair weapons and armour for the scouts and to supply processed materials for their outposts when not working on the excavation. Sure, her magic only let her break down the great chunks of ore our miners retrieved, but Brett and Kev would've gone out of their way to visit her whenever they could.

They would keep her safe if anything like this had happened while they were around.

Shaking off the rapid digression of my thoughts, I muttered, "I just hope she knows I'm capped at a brisk walking pace."

Flying circles overhead to measure her speed while Lin and I navigated the meagre crowd, Briar led us deeper into the keep.

We followed the glint of gold near the ceiling beyond the length of the main hall and through a number of labyrinthine doors at the other end. Lin already knew the way well enough, but I was just doing my best to keep up.

Finally, we came to a stone supply chamber. It hardly looked out of the ordinary, but Lin got to shoving aside a stack of crates hiding a stone slab of a door blended seamlessly into the wall, and I jumped to help her heave it aside.

The deeper we went, the more our shared curiosities caught up to us. Me, who had no idea what Briar was taking us to save some connection to her sacrifice to the centions and her dealings with Seth, and Lin, who had spent the better part of the last week excavating this pit with a unit of handpicked stone-crafters, each held to a confidentiality agreement and given little information save one key advisory: whatever they did, they were not to touch whatever it was they unearthed.

Behind the door, a spiral staircase drilled deep into the bowels of the keep where the stone-crafters had been digging down. I couldn't fathom how deep it went, but the pit was precise, and Briar was assured in whatever we would find at the bottom.

Plucking out a makeshift torch from one of the crates, I stuck the tip out in front of Briar. "Can you light this?"

"*I wouldn't encourage carrying an open flame where we're headed,*" she chuckled, as if tickled by some inside joke. Nodding her prickly chin toward the stairs, I peered down to find a warm red blush emanating brightly from the stone steps wherever shadow met them. A glow-in-the-dark staircase, then – be it magic or some kind of alien rock, I was none the wiser.

"So, we're descending into this claustrophobic hole in search of some *worthy weapon* when I literally make weapons for a living," Lin clarified over the echo of our footfalls on stone. The steel plates on the toes of her boots clicked every few steps. Soon enough, the red light awash over the tight space of the spiral staircase consumed us. "Is this an insult to my craftsmanship, or should I count myself blessed just to come along?"

"*The excavation is nearly complete, and Knox figured it best to restrict those who encounter what is buried here to a minimum, but the weapon awaiting you still requires a stone-crafter to wrench it from its casing. Whatever you do, Catalina, you must not-*"

"Touch it. Yeah, yeah, I know."

I shunned the thought that I should have been able to move rock and stone just fine, if only my magic was reliable. Instead, I chirped, "And here I thought you wanted to keep the temptation of the fight out of my hands?" Lin raised an eyebrow at the tone I failed to hide, glancing uncertainly between us.

"*Even so, it is imperative that you have a means of properly defending yourself. It isn't enough that you possess a power you cannot yet control, or worse, a power that could be stripped from you in the same way Kevin has been severed from his.*" Although I hadn't meant it as a rhetorical question, I wished she hadn't answered. "*If you can wield this weapon, then you are achaion.*"

"Gesundheit? Did you just sneeze in my brain?" I grumbled back.

"*A warrior befitting of the fight, Anelisha,*" Briar groaned in my mind, evidently rethinking her choices, "*To be achaion is to possess the heart of a dragon, quite literally. Do you recall my brief lesson on the dragons of Cellana?*"

"It… rings a bell?" For some reason, all that came to mind was the *Dark Side of the Moon*'s album cover, but I doubted that was what she meant.

"*Only six weapons of achaion have ever existed, wrought from the remains of my kin, made from the great ones' molten bones. It was the centions' tradition, long before magikiers and pora and the petty squabbles of littler things. You will face the trial of achaion the moment you make contact with the weapon-*"

"A trial?" I squeaked, cupping my chin in hand. "You watched me fail to use magic properly for two weeks and now you think I'm – ahem – befitting of the fight?"

"*I watched you try and try again these past two weeks, relentless in the face of failure, in fact impelled by failure to try ever harder, and so I have faith. It is your heart and potential that will be judged, for ability can be learned.*"

I made a face but withheld my skepticism.

"*The six weapons of achaion were lost in the wars between centions and aethuri, or so it was thought. Whisked away, stolen, traded, and buried, they have each come to their own hidden tombs one way or another, locations of which only I possessed knowledge for many ages, but it was this knowledge I gave up to the centions in the trade for your life, Anelisha. The weapon to which I take you now has been Dyval's secret for many centuries. Here in the depths of the City of Gates, buried by stone, story, and shadow, the dragon-bone glaive, once the crimson emberbreast, Fiamme, has long rested.*" She slipped up, a feeling of struggle arising between our minds, an echo from hers. "*For you see, Fiamme lives on in this weapon of achaion, and hasn't deemed any worthy even to look upon her since the fall of dragons.*"

"Oh..." Lin and I met eyes, a red gleam catching in the perfect discs of her goggles.

"*Oh, indeed. These were weapons wielded by the centions themselves. Why else did you think they hunted my kin to extinction?*"

"I didn't know..." I breathed, unsure what else to say.

"*There's much you don't know, but I would not bog you down with the infinite transgressions of tyrants. We should focus on the present.*"

"And this glaive, it's just buried in the rock bed under the City of Gates? For how long...?" Lin put in.

"*Long ago, the deep underground in which we now find ourselves was a vast lava lake. She sank into the molten flames, and over time, magma became rock. A coffin fit for a dragon. She is buried here, with the history centions buried beneath the trampling feet of their magikier armies.*"

I stopped myself on the cusp of apologizing. I only wished the words meant anything coming from me, but the past was the past. "Dyval's okay with this? With me having a weapon like this?"

"*She permitted your trial, yes, but it's my understanding she expects you'll fail.*"

"Great." I rolled my eyes, making an effort not to speak my mind. Instead, I deduced, "Hold on, so you asked for this?"

"*I did, and so, too, did Knox, though indeed, Dyval first reacted with reproach and scorn at the suggestion. While yes, I would rather Fiamme lie forgotten in the hovels of the world, to rest in peace for all eternity, I am no longer the keeper of the resting places of my kin. For that, I'm glad it's you who will face her trial first before any other.*"

We three fell into a morose silence, darker even than the hollow in which we found ourselves.

The stone walls of the spiral staircase changed around us the deeper we descended, until there were no more bas-reliefs carved along the sides or frescoes painted on the underside of the steps overhead, the likes of which could have told ancient tales of heroes and wars, of lost cities and plagues, of gods and demons, if only we stopped to study their craft. But we wasted no time. The walls became smooth, as if eroded into shape by eons of running water.

From chalky limestone, the walls met at a seam with a crystal-flecked stone I couldn't identify, then a dark, ridged stone – sulfuric in my nostrils – like volcanic rock, each seeming to be stacked one atop the other, an afterthought of ages building upward. The steps beneath our feet grew narrower within the limits of the acute triangular slabs they'd been cut into, always of the same, red-radiating stone. If not for the strange light illuminating the steps beneath our feet, we would have long ago been plunged into tar-thick darkness.

"We're gonna have to walk back up all these stairs," Lin groaned when Briar made no indication we were nearing our destination.

"*I fear we may walk them empty-handed. I have yet to sense the glaive.*"

"You don't even know where it is?" I grumbled.

"*I know where she should be. But it would seem, we can no longer bank on shoulds.*" She hummed a contemplative note in our minds. "*The two of you must continue to the very last step. Wait for me there while I fetch your ecological empath. If the weapon has been stolen from this place, it does not bode well for any of us.*" An undertone of profound uneasiness tinged her voice, but I was stuck on the surface level.

"No, no, wait. Don't bring Brett into this," I interjected, shaking my head. Memory struck, playing a movie reel of images behind my eyes. A girl sputtering for breath as her lungs collapsed, perforated by a metal rod; the look of panic and helplessness in Brett's eyes; her blood splashed on his hand. "Unless you're planning on carrying him back up all these stairs, I say we give him a break."

"Trust me, he's all breaked out," Lin put in with a wave of her hand. "The healers fixed him up enough to send him on scouting missions, and even if they hadn't, he'd still bend over backwards for you."

Ignoring my enduring complaints chasing circles in my head, Briar ended the discussion with a decisive, "*I've summoned your Brett to investigate this sacrilege.*"

Lin and I continued our descent and were happy to have a moment's rest when we eventually reached the final glowing slab. There were no sculptures or murals here, only sandpapery rock that was warm to the touch and a coating of dust on the floor, all looking as if they had been carved by nature, not by hand. The walls were surprisingly flat, boring even, for a place where the weapon of achaion had been kept. Sweat slicked the back of my neck as we sat waiting for Brett and Briar. The muggy heat was too stifling to speak, but I could only imagine how much worse it was for Lin in her head-to-toe garb. Still, she wouldn't shed her heavy layers.

When they finally joined us, Lin teased Brett's complaining which had come echoing down to us with his descent. Blowing a lock of brunet hair out of his face with a roll of his eyes, he moved his hand in a circular motion, gesturing for us to get on with it. I couldn't help smirking up at him, but he wasn't looking at me. As a matter of fact, he fastened his eyes anywhere but on me.

"So what am I doing down here?" he asked, looking to Briar who leapt from his shoulders back to mine. As soon as she settled herself around my neck, he was looking away again. Lin quirked her head to one side, looking between us unsurely. Then I wasn't just imagining it.

I thought I noticed a speck of blood on his hands, flashing an image of the girl on the stake behind my eyes once again, but when I peered closer, getting a proper look, there was nothing to see. Stupid, I scolded myself, why would there be blood on his hands?

Ousting such thoughts from my mind, I couldn't help thinking that day – the day Kev lost his magic, for I couldn't find it within myself to address the *other* affair – was the last time I'd really spoken to Brett, and now, with all that time to stew, he couldn't look me in the eye. Maybe that was why he hadn't come to visit me like he had with Lin. Maybe… he didn't want to see me.

Dark stains among the navy blue and black hues of his typical Arillian scouting uniform – leather gloves and bomber-style jacket over a t-shirt tucked loosely into high waisted cargo pants, and silver-clasped combat boots up to his knees, perfectly outfitted for utility, mobility and stealth – kindled dark imaginings in my mind of the skirmishes beyond the walls. His missions. It was a moment before I caught myself staring and finally wiped the perplexed expression off my face.

Briar either didn't notice or didn't care, getting straight to the point. "*Focus your magic. Return to the fall of the city. Who came through here to burgle the weapon sheathed in stone?*" she demanded, "*For whoever it was had some inkling of a truth lost to time. This goes beyond the work of pora or kirranites or magikiers and is likely the hand of Valencia who led the attack. Who now wields a weapon of achaion, and who champions her forces where she is not.*"

"Those are some strong assumptions," I put in, but Briar's gaze held pointedly on me. It was one of those rare few times I grasped her unspoken meaning. If the Valencia's Cellana Corps had one leader, one champion, decapitating it would be an easier feat. But after all the talking up Briar had been doing over the weapon of achaion, the seedlings of this plan didn't exactly earn my vote of confidence.

Brett tucked away his look of confusion and nodded obediently, sitting at the base of the spiral staircase and closing his eyes to reach his magic. A bead of sweat from the heat dripped down the length of his sharp jawline. It didn't help that we crowded each other here in this claustrophobic sauna, no more spacious than a closet. Lin climbed a couple steps higher to give him some room, and I followed suit, sitting with her to await Brett's verdict.

My thoughts echoed away from my mind to Briar's eavesdropping, "*You know, an hour ago I had only a fleeting idea this weapon existed. Now it's just another problem.*" Maybe, if it hadn't been important enough to talk about before, the whole subject would just as inconsequentially shimmy around the pitfalls of relevance.

"*An ill-considered hope,*" Briar commented.

I crossed my arms. "*First the great, big Lupei secret, and now this whole achaion business. Don't you just love it when these things come out of left field?*"

"*Valencia has age and memory on her side. She's always made a habit of using the centions' secrets against them, having been one of the few outsiders tasked with burying them. That the centions keep their secrets to this day only lends further advantage to their truth-bearing enemies. Valencia knew to release the Kaipracan's wrath on this world to escape that pit of legend, Vincladimhús, all those ages past. Now, it seems, she has knowledge of at least one of the weapons of achaion and has imparted this knowledge to her trusted disciples.*"

"*Go figure. For someone who never did her homework, she's really levelling the playing field with extra credit, huh?*"

"*I don't think you understand the gravity of what we've discovered. If Valencia was ever to wield a weapon of achaion, it would spell the end for us. We would be wise to retrieve the glaive before our absolute defeat comes to pass.*"

"*That's great, Briar. What a cheery thought.*"

"*We are fortunate, at least, to expose Valencia's champion through this setback. We'll know who to target from the host that felled this city.*" By the pensive weight to her tone, I couldn't help the feeling she was using an encoded double-speak I wasn't privy to.

"*Who to target, huh? So... I take it you're warming up to me and Seth's little brainstorm the other night?*"

"*Not hardly.*"

Wary to ask her opinion, I glanced sidelong at her as if I could read her reptilian expression, only to cave, prodding, "*Well...?*"

"*My take on the subject? As things stand, I doubt you're enough to guillotine Valencia's force in Arillia. Had you been accepted as achaion, wielder of Fiamme, it might have been a different story-*"

I could do without the hypothetical. "*So that's what this was all about?*" My heart sunk low in my chest. "*It's because I'm going nowhere as a shonte?*"

"*You mistake slow progress for outright failure when you allow yourself to be blinded by the end goal. You're learning at a reasonable pace in a time of rash action. That is no fault or error you can control.*" She must have sensed the doubt in my mind, continuing, "*I never expected you to grasp the minutiae of this wholly misunderstood magic with only two weeks' practice.*"

"*But I don't have time to take things slow,*" I grumbled, and had to refrain from imagining what it meant to be out of time; the hardships Seth's elite faced in protecting the keep. Did Briar know something I didn't? A stupid question, really. When didn't she?

"*Unfortunately for your training as a shonte, we cannot afford to fall behind our enemies. The danger we face staying here any longer calls for a revision of plans. With four months of combat instruction under your belt, I would suspect you're better equipped to handle a weapon than magic, and I happened to know of one that would put you above all the rest, even with your limited experience.*"

"*Emphasis on limited. I only took extra training with swords, shields and bows. And, if I'm being honest with myself, we barely scratched the surface. If I'd known-*"

"*You're many things, but you're not clairvoyant. Your training with a sword will surely come in handy. That your classes covered the basics of polearm training should have been enough for Fiamme to pick up where you faltered. If the glaive was still here. Paired with your explosive outbursts of shonte magic in the worst of circumstances, and with myself by your side, I would have had smaller doubts as to your likelihood of triumph. But as things stand...*"

"All fair points..." I granted aloud, forgetting the privacy of our words.

To my right, Lin nodded as if her suspicions had been confirmed. "So it *is* a secret conversation. I figured either that or you seriously zoned out on me there." At her words, the mental connection fizzled out.

Wincing, I admitted, "A little bit of both. Hey, sorry for dragging you into this little unsolved case by the way. All to work up a sweat and sit around doing nothing."

She shrugged, leaning forward to rest her elbows on her knees. "I'm technically on the job, but it's nice just to get to see you." She fiddled with the edge of her knee-high boots. "I think about it a lot, you know. What would've happened if you hadn't..." She gestured up toward the mark on her forehead.

"Nuh-uh, don't do that to yourself-" I was saying, but lost my train of thought when she shook her head, pink tufts of hair parting to reveal the bloodred circle in the middle of her forehead. Just as quickly as I noticed it, her hair fell back over the mark.

"I thought losing Raina was the worst thing that would ever happen to me. I know, childish. But I did."

I ducked my head, remembering my part in their break-up, even if I didn't have as much to do with it as I once believed.

She must have been thinking the same thing, because she admitted in a small voice, "I blamed you, and I let that get between us. Even after I realized the truth, I was still angry with you. There was no real reason, I just couldn't let it go. If you hadn't saved me like you did, I... well, I would probably still be that person."

"I wouldn't blame you, after everything," I murmured, staring down at my hands. And yet, I couldn't help disputing myself. How quickly, how sharply, had Lin turned against me – rightfully so from her point of view, but still at the drop of a hat. The spiting words and bitter pain between us couldn't be so easily undone after all those months left to stew, and Lin knew it.

Before her, I had no idea the people I held so dear to me could become something resentful and heart-wrenching. My childhood bullies hadn't even been so unpredictable, but we were hardly close, not like it was with Lin. I had believed her my closest friend, the person whom I confided in and in turn confided in me... But even Brett broke my heart in the end. Roxy became fed up with me. Dahlia hardly bothered with me. And Faith, my own sister, had seemed a rival to me – albeit only by Val's poisonous whisperings in my ear.

People terrified me, conduits of change who often failed to communicate just that. They were sailing on such different streams from mine, always faster, always obscured from me, and how could I possibly keep up?

"Then let me just say," Lin spoke up, snapping me out of my inner digression, "I was only angry, even after I knew you weren't to blame, because I wasn't – I'm *still* not over Raina. It's hard to stop loving someone, and it made me bitter, but I'm sorting out my feelings. Or, you know, trying my best."

"But you shouldn't have ended up in the delinquent center, and to deal with that on your own? I feel like that's on me. I mean, it's on Valencia, obviously, but she only went after you because we were so close..." Even now, I was always going to be the bullseye Valencia threw for, but what did she care if a missed throw meant hitting the people closest to me. As long as I had them, she had leverage.

She waved her hand. "I wasn't totally alone. Faith came to visit as often as she could-" Leaving me to Val. "-but I never talked about it with her. It took me realizing how hard break-ups are, and messy, and confusing, to finally realize how I was acting."

As she spoke, her eyes flicked to Brett, the slight tilt of her head in his direction and the raise of her eyebrows illustrating her point. I was too caught up in my own contemplations to grasp her meaning at first, but her eyes spelled the message out for me behind her tinted lenses. My heart leapt to my throat, putting the pieces together and dropping my former destructive notions.

She continued, "And I only really looked at myself and my actions after realizing I could've been erased by the kirranite parasite. I was taking it out on the people I'd attached all these strong feelings to. Namely, you."

She met my eyes with a meaningful look. There was another apology in her gaze, but this time, not on her behalf. This was no longer about us.

"It made sense to me, putting up a wall to fend off any more pain. It only ever hurt so bad because I thought the world of you. I just didn't want you to hurt me again."

"Oh..." Her words peeled my heart twice over as I decoded her meaning.

"Don't get me wrong. Now, more than ever, you're more than just the world to me. But what can I say, I was fourteen espresso shots of pure bitter teen energy. And sad. Still sad, though." She shrugged, as if to move quickly on from this confession, but I spoke up before she could pile on more words.

"But you're not going through that alone, not while I'm around."

For those last few months in Blackano, I had found myself wedged in a rut of depression. There was so much going on that the stress had turned into despair and isolation, but in that quiet space of sadness, everything in my life had come to a standstill. If not for that, I was sure I wouldn't have made time to process my own feelings.

Gulping back the emotion in my throat, I somberly spoke, "When the sadness slows you down, take time to heal and feel the emotions that come with recovery. You might find a new perspective in all the darkness. One that leads you to a glimmer of light."

She patted my knee and met me with smiling eyes, shining and warm. "I think, in a way, I already have. But I'm not the only one you should be consoling." Leaning in close, she whispered in case Brett could hear beyond the concentration his magic necessitated, "I'll be the first to say he's got his faults. Maybe just because of that, well... don't let his feelings do *all* the talking. Now more than ever, you need the people who care about you around."

I attempted a nod and a smile, but it felt a farce. She thought this was all about our break-up. That he wasn't meeting my gaze because of lingering sentiments. Although the notion left me blushing despite the circumstances, I doubted that was the case.

I wasn't surprised Brett hadn't casually brought up the girl whose blood stained his hands, or the look on my face when I saw what he had done. He could probably guess the slimy, sticky feeling under my skin even thinking back to it, now, and for *that* reason, he wouldn't look me in the eyes.

I knew this was true by the distant echo of his panicked shout, "This is war, Annie!" reverberating between my ears. How many more would he kill under that justification? How *many of us* would become killers as those words heated the ice in our veins? Would I? After failing to take the lives of those who massacred my protectors in Blackano and would have executed my friends. They were still trying to kill the people I loved, which begged the question: Would I become a killer too late?

If Valencia's champion truly did steal the weapon of achaion and had been judged worthy to wield Fiamme like Briar said, would I even stand a chance?

"I'm sorry if that felt a bit pushy," Lin added, quirking an eyebrow, "I'm not trying to pressure you into confronting him."

"No, no, you're just trying to help-"

Brett jolted out of his trance, glancing around the warmly lit space in momentary confusion. My mouth snapped shut, quite suddenly remembering the subject of our conversation was seated two steps down from us. In chorus, Briar shook herself out on my shoulders, seeming to wake from a daydream. I took that to mean she'd been inside his head as he relived the memory of this place.

"So?" Lin asked, keeping her cool much better than I.

"You're not gonna believe this," he chuckled dryly under his breath, glancing up at me from under long eyelashes. "A whole team was down here, led by a man I only caught a glimpse of in my vision for Knox. *He* was the bombshell on the battlefield, the one that levelled the city center, and he turned these walls to dust to get the glaive. That guy, he *radiates* power. And standing there by his side, his right-hand man? They called him Simon Beckett."

No way. That name had haunted me for months, and now, it seemed, I'd stumbled across his apparition. Shaking my head in pure incredulity, I huffed, "Unbelievable."

8

New Plan

Day 15

EVERYTHING FELT LIKE IT HAD COME TO A STALEMATE, BUT I WAS ON THE sidelines. Briar was putting out fires with Dyval what seemed like every day now that the weapon of achaion had officially gone missing. Meanwhile, Seth and his military police – I had heard them nicknamed his dogs for their obedience – had become engrossed with the outer defense, far beyond the perimeter of the keep. I hadn't seen hide nor hair of him since the night I healed him, lending a louder voice to the persistent buzz of anxiety in the back of my mind.

Briar had spoken to Seth of the missing weapon when she first revealed this latest misfortune to Dyval, but there was little he could do about it, either. Not while we remained pinned down in the City of Gates.

His elite kept the rest of us on a need-to-know basis, and in turn, we kept our noses clean behind the pulsating mirage that was Dyval's protective barrier. At the end of each week, small groups returned for their allotted rest and recuperation as guards on the walls of the keep. If less returned to swap shifts, no one was the wiser. Somehow, it was the stable numbers in the infirmary which told of a grislier war.

I didn't see Faith around the infirmary these days – or at all, since the dividers went up between mattresses in the basement – only because Briar pulled me out of my shoddy practice. Instead, the little tyrant had me working on meditation, sitting still for hours on end in the effort of communing with alien nature. Put simply, that meant three days of zero progress, but at least this allowed my hands some time to heal.

I'd gotten better at abstaining from itching the scabs off my palms. I'd also gotten better at stowing my complaints when I proved time and again to be a failure of a shonte, as Briar was having none of that mentality.

So there I was after another day of fruitless and admittedly self-deprecating introspection, sitting cross-legged next to Briar catnapping in coils just as the sky darkened with a spattering of raindrops, when I noticed the voice of Seth Knox beyond the wall. By his no-nonsense tone, I figured he was speaking to officers changing shifts before nightfall. His gruelling plight to stave off our collective doom left him with a deep huskiness to his voice, but that hardly seemed out of the ordinary these days.

"... shepherding a herd just south of us. With the pora tainting crops outside the city, we only have one option. We fence off a section of the grounds for the herd, cut our outdoor space in half and pull the general magic-users out to care for the animals. A stuffier keep for fresh milk and meat... What we really need to do is expand these walls." He caught himself on the verge of digression. "Report this to Ramona in the command room. Thank you."

I stepped up to the gate to find Seth turning away again with the new shift of legionaries who'd taken their week's rest as sentinels around the keep. Oh no he didn't.

"Hey! Seth!" I called out to him, jogging to catch up before the guards at the gate could stop me. He stood a little straighter, peering over his shoulder in surprise. By the lack of Briar's prattling in my mind, I assumed she was still asleep under the tree where she wanted me to pretend to be a shonte.

"Anelisha? It's dangerous outside the keep-"

I stopped myself a moment from spouting, "Well, same goes for you, our commander, our leader, the man in charge whose head is his defining characteristic, not his guns, no matter how much he wants to do everything, and who *should* be holed up in the safety of his war room for that exact reason." No, I couldn't say any of that in front of his subordinates. Instead, I came up with the wildly improvised excuse, "I need inspiration." Spontaneity was my middle name, after all.

Seth came to a full stop, turning to meet me with a questioning expression. The other officers paused a few steps ahead, waiting for him.

He was somehow more dishevelled, with dark circles around bloodshot eyes, a short beard growing in, and strands of onyx hair falling into his handsome face while a worn-out elastic band held the rest back. He looked like the walking dead, and although he wore even this shockingly well, I wanted to tuck him into bed, any bed, and keep the whole world from bothering him until he got some goddamned rest.

"Not that it would be inspiring to see our people get hurt. I mean, of course their bravery and sacrifice *is* inspiring-!" I cut myself off, gathering my thoughts. "I just think I should see the state of things. To really grasp my magic like I did in the bunker, but this time, try to understand it." The last time I felt that connection to my magic was in the process of healing him, and I'd been too caught up worrying about him to care that I'd finally managed to access it.

Shaking his head so his tied hair bounced back and forth, he pointed out, "If you use it, the presence of your magic will gather pora for miles." Even with that adorable hair action going on, a pained look creased his eyes. "Contrary to what we would have our enemies believe, we don't actually have enough manpower to hold off a concentrated attack of that magnitude."

"I'm not here with a death wish, and you know the last thing I want is to put anyone else in danger. I promise I won't use it, I'll stay behind our defense, but I *need* to feel it." Just like Briar wanted. But as I spoke, I felt my stomach drop at the lie. If I was being honest with myself, I really just wanted an excuse to talk to Seth – but how petty was that. He'd been so busy these past couple weeks. I just wanted to make sure he was doing okay.

The rain came down harder now, darkening the leather over his shoulders and tickling my scalp. Now more than ever, he was petrichor and leather. "I'm not sure this is the best idea, but if you think it's necessary…" He seemed to be waiting for me to interrupt, to think back on it and decide against this crazy plan, but the words got stuck in my throat. Finally, he nodded solemnly. "We make our shift changes at the east bastion, hardly a hot spot for enemy raids. You should be safe enough there," he granted, doubt still colouring his voice, "But will you stay close to me?"

A grin ranged up to my eyes. "I may be prone to finding trouble, but you can rest assured, there's nowhere I'd rather be."

The tired creases under his eyes smoothed into smile lines. "Don't get too comfortable. These days, it's like trouble shadows me." Tilting his head toward the fresh batch of officers – a gesture to resume marching – he offered me his hand.

The updraft of hot fire in my chest brought a moment's hesitation, just long enough for him to realize he'd offered to hold my hand. Before he could retract the offer – a flash of something like dejection in his eyes – my hand snaked out to press his palm. Fastening my eyes to the wet spots in the carpeting ash where raindrops fell, I hid my face and the blush thereupon behind the curtain of my wild, red curls. The warmth of his fingers intertwining with mine crackled fire all up my arm, hottest where I felt his touch.

"Your sister and friends have been a huge help." We walked behind the troops, just far enough to entertain some sense of privacy. "Ever since we took Faith on as a combat nurse-"

"You what?"

He glanced over at me, a slight expression of surprise in his eyes. "I thought you knew. She volunteered her help on the front. The best use of her magic is in cases of sedation. She's proved a valuable asset in the two days since her transfer."

No wonder I hadn't seen much of Faith. "But... Is she sleeping at the first defense?"

He seemed to realize his mistake. "She insisted. But you can rest assured she isn't throwing herself into needless peril. She's a combat medic, not a legionary. The Song brothers are especially protective of her when they return from scouting ops."

"Right..." Maybe I could see them too, now that I was headed to the first defense. I'd be sure to knock some sense into Faith or at least demand why she hadn't told me about any of this. It wasn't like I'd ever done anything like that... I tugged on my collar, frowning. She probably thought I'd overthink her decision. Pff, I could prove her wrong.

A moment's hush returned my attention to the warmth of his hand. Part of me nagged that he'd pull away if I left room for him to realize we didn't *need* to be holding hands.

"So, have you slept at all or am I witnessing a new world record?" I blithely asked, as if we weren't headed out to the first defense of a siege I'd heard scarcely little about.

"I'm sure *someone* has a worse case of insomnia than me," he dryly chuckled, hardly a real answer. "Have you made any progress with your magic?" By the closeness of his voice, I knew he'd turned his head to look at me. To meet my eyes, but I couldn't chance looking back. He'd be able to read everything in my face. If he didn't already know.

"I, well, I'm out here for a reason." Quieting my voice and leaning in closer to him, still without turning to look at him, I asked, "So... have you come up with any alternatives?"

He paused, but I knew he understood my meaning. Finally, he breathed, "I'm worried if we don't act soon, there won't be a time to do so." His words were almost inaudible even to me.

"Then I have to-"

"Anelisha," he cut in, and his other hand tucked my hair behind my ear to reveal my face. Holding my eyes, he simply stated, "You're not expendable." But all I heard was, *You're not effectual.* There was no value to my magic while I was the one in possession of it. Flashes of the littered dead – in the bunker, the streets, the delinquent center – leaked through the wall around my heart. The injured and the desolate hobbling from the fields to the keep. Survivors were a minority, but the fight was far from over.

If Briar was in my head, she would've shot down this train of thought. I couldn't police my mind like she could. All I could do was turn it off. Turn everything off.

I focused on the blue of Seth's eyes and the warmth of his hand pressed to mine, swinging between us as we marched along a well-worn path. Where yellow ripples and flecks of green made a turquoise pond of Brett's irises, Seth had starbursts of white around his pupils like white caps on ocean waves.

He looked away to the distant battlements, to our first defense holding against nightmares in the killing field where ground was hard-won. "We'll figure something out." By his blind insistence, I assumed he'd noticed the distance behind my eyes. An attempt at reassurance. "I'm sure of it." He didn't look sure.

"You don't have to lie to me…" My voice was flat, dull in my own ears, and I worked to shake the emotionless haze so quick to settle over me. "Are you scared?"

"No." His answer came automatically, his gaze still intent on the manned battlements.

"Why not?" I demanded, but my own line of questioning turned inward. Was *I* scared? If yes, then my inaction was cowardly. If no, then what the hell was wrong with me? But I couldn't even tell which it was.

Was I empty?

"I can't afford to be scared for the sake of everyone following my lead," he said in answer to the question I forgot I'd asked.

"That doesn't mean you can't still be scared," I pointed out.

He shook his head. "The last thing I have left to be scared of is losing you." Because my death was the key to Valencia's ultimate victory. That was what I had become. Maybe, that was what I'd always been.

"What was the first thing?" I thoughtlessly asked to fill the space of silence.

The pain of betrayal in the set of his jaw, the furrow of his brows, the tight line of his lips, showed me all the answer he couldn't bring himself to say. Levi Videl.

I should have known, and I probably should have left it there. But he was still holding my hand – I held on tighter – and I couldn't think what else to say. "So… have you figured out why he did it?" Such an idiot. "The whole *LeVal* team-up?" Shut up! "Who could've seen that coming?"

"Actually-" His voice was strained, his gaze turning down to his feet. "-those are the questions that keep me up at night. More than the death, the pain. More than all the terror this world has to offer. I try to understand why he would side with Valencia. And I come up empty-handed." Confusion made a tempest of his eyes, dark, intense, and crushingly deep. He pulled his hand out of mine to reach once again for the pack of cigarettes that just wasn't there. Whatever warmth had surged in me now chased after his retreating touch, withdrawing through my fingertips until there was only the chill of the soaking rain.

"Maybe… I can attempt to distract you with the wit of banter?" I offered.

He shook his head, smirking. "Oh, that's not necessary."

"That's probably for the best, considering I'm not all that witty," I murmured around the barest smile, but my heart weighed too heavily in my chest for the real thing.

If there was anyone who brought out Seth Knox's lighter side – a side I only ever caught in glimpses – it was Levi Videl. In a bizarre turn of events, something similar could be said of me and Val, before she was Valencia.

She had come to know me in those four months better than anyone ever had, and she used that to destroy me. I could do nothing but watch in the aftermath of her efforts as my life came crashing down around me. She made me realize… in a world full of others, control was an illusion. No, worse than that. A *delusion* fabricated to ease the hard truths of this chaotic reality we all shared. But I had Briar to remind me that only I oversaw myself.

When that fanciful pipedream of control flew out of Seth's hands with Levi's betrayal, who did he have?

"I'm sorry." I tucked my hands in my pockets with thumbs polishing my knuckles. "It's not fair. The power other people have over our lives without even realizing. It's worse when they realize but just don't care. It shouldn't be that way, but it is…" I looked deep into his eyes, searching for something – I didn't know what. "But maybe you can't understand why he did what he did because you're nothing like him, and isn't that enough to know he's not worth agonizing over?"

We were coming up on the battlements as he opened his mouth to speak. I could see the leaden agreement on the tip of his tongue as a dead look filled his eyes, but I refused to leave it at that. As the officers filed into an easternmost stronghold built into the angular bastion jutting out from the wall, I stopped Seth under the overhang by the heavy iron door with a hand on his arm.

Shaking my head, I met his gaze with softness in my own. "Sometimes, we just have to accept that some things are out of our hands. That the best we can do is let go, no matter how hard it is to do that. Not out of surrender or weakness, but because in most cases, there are others you're better off sharing the unpredictability with. People who make decisions that fit with you instead of actively working against you. They're the ones worth your while." Gulping back hesitation, I announced, "I hope I'm one of those people. I'm here for you, Seth. And you can count on that."

The rain dripped into his eyes from one long, dark lock of hair hanging down and curling onto his forehead. There was too much to read in his face as the pounding rain filled the pretense of space between us. The twitch of a smile in the corner of his mouth, the empathy in the set of his brows, the sadness in his gaze. His pupils were blown, dark voids swallowing up the ocean tides as rumination detained him behind his eyes. The onslaught of too many thoughts was visible even to me as his regard tracked down to my lips, my neck. He looked like he was going to kiss me or say some desperate thing or fall apart altogether.

Before he could act on any of the signals he was giving off, the wall exploded.

9

Wuh-Oh

DISCLAIMER: THIS WAS NOT THE INSPIRATION I WAS LOOKING FOR – HELL I wasn't even sure what I expected to find out here, but I should've known it would involve some form of trauma. Currently, that meant blunt-force head trauma.

The stone wall splintered and burst apart before I could even register what was happening. The deep, grating *karoom!* of the explosion left my ears ringing, followed by pain when a golf ball-sized rock struck my brow over my left eye. For a moment, I couldn't feel my legs, and the next thing I knew, I was flat on my back and Seth had thrown himself on top of me, crouched defensively over me with one arm covering the back of his head and his other propping him up over me. A decent-sized stone thumped off his back, bringing a grunt to his lips muffled by the pitter-patter of dust and rocks showering down around us, rebounding off the shield he made above my body.

"Told you," he huffed as the last of the pebbles plinked off his back, "Trouble everywhere I go, even at the east bastion." A shadow fell over his face. "And by some massive stretch of the imagination, I'm the one leading this whole operation–"

"You just saved my life!" I gulped, choking on my heart fluttering high in my throat, "So yeah, you dummy, you've definitely got a high approval rating out of me. That being one for one on my hell yes!"

Rolling his eyes in mixed amusement and incredulity, he blinked, noticing something on my forehead. It was a moment before I felt the warm pool of blood gathering in the hollow of my eye socket and the stinging cut on my brow from whence it leaked.

His eyes went wide, his voice a hushed breath, "You're bleeding-"

Pressing the injury under my palm, I tried to stem the flow. "What can I say, I'm no lucky charm either. Although now I'm wishing I'd said goodbye to my loved ones before I came here."

The ground shook again, the distant crack of splitting rock alerting us to a secondary assault at another location along the wall. A pair of officers rushed to help us inside, the bastion's interior our only viable refuge in the wake of the massive hole blown into the wall nearest us.

The more I moved, the hazier the corners of my vision became, until I found myself seated on a bench at the back of a bustling room, watching Seth's shoulders as he received a situation report at the war table just in front of me. Faith had volunteered herself into *this*? I peered around the room – the war table consuming a sizable portion of the available space – in search of her face or the red medic's belt among those present. There was no sign of her, but she could've been anywhere along the circumference of the battlements making up our first defense.

My head spun in the hubbub of responding magikiers – those capable of patching up the walls and those assigned to defend them. Losing track of the flow of events, I pushed myself to focus on something smaller, more manageable, in case of a concussion. I'd been banged up enough at this point to recognize a problem when it clocked me across the noggin.

Peeling my palm from the sticky wetness congealing over my brow, I stared at the sheer volume of blood coating my hand. I doubted my face even needed that much blood; save for all the blushing I'd been doing around Seth. Sheesh.

Someone was bandaging my head before I'd even noticed their approach. As the legionary girdled my head with gauze, I watched Seth speak with the officers around the war table overseeing the defense of this bastion. This wasn't the first time he'd protected me. As a matter of fact, this was disturbingly like when Evelyn pulled out all the stops to try to kill me; he'd shielded me with his body and been impaled before my eyes. While it wasn't his physical body – he had been dream-walking in my subconscious – I knew by the agony on his face that he felt it as if it was. This time, it was real for him. He could've been hurt. He was lucky he hadn't been killed!

A snap of familiar energy fizzled through me, tingling against my insides like bubbly champagne. It was the same energy I'd felt when I found Seth bleeding in the command room. This was what I was here for, or so I told him – better not waste my opportunity.

Closing my fist in a tight ball, I unleashed my mental feelers to the rock and stone of the wall before I could lose the thread of magic again, touching this power churning in my core without allowing it to escape me. I felt the soles of shoes pounding through passages within the walls like insects crawling on my skin. My wandering energy clashed against others' magic pulling stone up from the ground to patch the missing battlements. Still, I stretched myself thin through the vast connections of earth and rain – stone and soil, grass and trees, their roots as deep as lakes. The further I extended these fingers of magic, the more I could feel.

Pora.

Their feet hit the ground hard, sprinting with such power and speed to their stride. From the-

"They're underground!" I shouted, startling even myself. "Magikiers – tunnelling through stone to get under the walls!"

"It was a distraction," Seth growled under his breath, his back still turned to me. He barked out commands, but I tuned him out, honing into my connection with the earth. If I could just count the footsteps, count the feet. There were too many, certainly more than the number of feet I could feel scrambling like ants within the wall.

Unlike the scuttling of responding legionaries, a dignified stride ascended a staircase I hadn't noticed behind an iron door. Seth met the man when he emerged – he had a smooth-edged face built for smiling – and gave him a run-down of the situation. We were outnumbered, and our enemies would soon flank us from behind.

"Yes, I see," the man said in a heavy Slavic accent, seating himself at the head of the war table and shrugging off his overcoat.

I sensed the shift in the earth just before I felt it collapse. Our enemies weren't the only stone-crafters in the area. Our own had toppled the enemy tunnel down upon its moles, and for a split second, I almost believed that was the end of it.

Raking in breath, I reported what I felt. "The tunnellers held off the cave-in over their own heads and continue to move forward." I held my eyes shut firmly in concentration. "But the pora. The collapse only pinned down a handful. The rest, they're digging their way out of the rubble." As for the other magikiers who'd marched behind the tunnellers, I tasted their blood soaking the earth, metallic in the back of my mouth.

"Where will they surface?" asked the thick-accented man, taking off his glasses to fix his regard on me. With a start, I realized this cherub-looking gent was the company commander, the leading officer at this estimated one hundred-troop-strong bastion. Dog tags dangling from his neck read Brigadier General Lyovin Alexeyich and the decorated Arillian overcoat draped over the back of his chair confirmed his rank. A man of his stature would have overseen the entire eastern regiment.

"A few paces past the wall, to the left of the bastion." Opposite the explosion. "But the tunnellers-"

"How many pora?" he asked.

"They're moving too fast-"

"Night is almost upon us," he noted to Seth, who held his chin between forefinger and thumb in contemplation. "It would be too easy to lose them in darkness..."

The Brigadier General tipped his chin toward the awaiting officers, and with that tiny gesture, a centuria of legionaries departed the stronghold to ambush those clawing up from the tunnel. The handful who remained pointed their rifles through embrasures in the walls, guarding the bastion from a frontal assault. I wondered whether the Brigadier General was a telepath, or if they simply had protocols in place.

"What does the shonte have to wait for?" burst a legionary with the loud and stiff conduct of one addressing a higher-ranking officer, but she watched me over her shoulder. It was a moment before I recognized her as the officer who'd given me my new clothes the other morning.

Scrambling for the right words amid the buzzing in my brain, I could only spout, "I can't. My magic-"

"Shonte magic. *Powerful* magic." Brigadier General Lyovin's hooded eyes lit up with an idea as he spoke, circling a finger as if to illustrate the cogs turning in his head. "And pora, they're like moths to flame."

"More like sharks to chum-" I was muttering but cut myself off before I overstepped my bounds.

In the wake of my muttering, the other troops whispered between themselves. Brigadier General Lyovin allowed them this moment as he turned to Seth with a plan. Too many voices. All of them saying the same thing. Bait. A flash of the girl skewered on a metal stake stung behind my eyes. No. No! That wouldn't be me! My connection to the earth snapped back with all the momentum of an elastic band pulled taut, hitting me hard in the chest and winding me where I sat.

"Enough!" the Brigadier General's voice silenced the room, and he opened a palm in gesture to Seth.

Nodding to the Brigadier General, Seth spoke in a measured tone, "Our only hope won't be reduced to bait on a hook." He stood tall, glare scalding any who dared oppose him. Brigadier General Lyovin leaned back in his chair and clasped his hands over his abdomen, holding his gaze on Seth. Among everyone present, only he appeared unmoved by Seth's declaration, so Seth doubled down. "We defend the shonte at any cost. Without her, we're lost."

The shonte. That was all I was to them. He had said so himself. They had no idea the danger they would face if I were to truly use my magic, calling a storm of pora down on my position. No idea at all... I shouldn't have come here, and not for any reason I'd expected. I averted my gaze from the desperation in the legionaries' eyes, trained on me like they'd stumbled upon an oasis in a barren desert. The shonte they'd built up in their minds was a mirage.

Leaning in toward Seth, Brigadier General Lyovin coolly probed, "Why did you pull her from the keep?" He kept his voice low enough to avoid rousing the troops, but I heard him.

"That's, uh, my bad..." I murmured across the war table, but Seth was saying something about my training and Brigadier General Lyovin did nothing more than catch my eye with an intrigued glint in his.

The officer who'd spoken – an athletic woman with a beauty mark like Marilyn Monroe and a haircut that reminded me of Mom's old pictures from the nineties – wore a perturbed expression as she watched me. Her voice was low, her tone puzzled, when she finally breached the threshold of proper conduct.

"What's the hold up? Did our champion expect something different from this world?" she fumed, unnoticed by Seth and the Brigadier General still taken with their discussion. "This is the war you trained for. The whole reason we were each hand-picked to be magikiers. Not born but *made*. I may have chosen my position as a legionary, but you're only here among us because the centions, glory to them, saw the warrior in you. They saw that you can – that you *will* – do what you must."

"It's not that simple-"

She shut me up with a hard glare. "But it is. When you've finally got your enemies right where you want them, you take pride in the kill. Because you understand that it's them or you." I shrank from her words, but she only leaned in closer with fire in her eyes. "Here, only the strong survive. But remember, we're only here because the centions chose us, aware of our strength." Gritting her teeth, she hissed, "Now act like it."

Boy would I love to, but the centions didn't choose me. Knowing what magic would run through me as a magikier, they had no reason to power me up like this, except that I was reckless. I nearly lost my life in a car crash and in turn, they nearly lost their leverage – Evelyn's reincarnation, killed at seventeen by her own bad driving. What a joke. They only transformed me because I'd endangered the reincarnated body of their prisoner, their hostage. Not because I was strong of mind and will, the way magikiers were meant to be, but because my mortal fate was inconvenient to them at the time. A stupid reason to be uprooted from an adequate life, and a downright cruel reason to leave Mom all by herself. But that was it.

Second guessing her earlier tone, she gritted her teeth through the cordial introduction, "Corporal Mika Trist," and offered her hand. Hesitantly, I shook it. "Will you fight?" she demanded, measuring her tone. Before I could answer, her eyes flicked to the Brigadier General, and she stood bolt upright.

Brigadier General Lyovin had stood from his seat, calling the entire room to attention. He gave a salute, dismissing their ready stances, and rounded the war table to speak privately with the officer in charge of the remaining troops. The rest of the room quieted, observing him, but Seth strode over to me.

"How are you feeling?" he asked in a soft voice, watching Mika leave my side. She busied herself with putting the roll of gauze away, and only then did I realize she must have been the one to patch me up. "You're looking a little… overwhelmed."

"Pff, sure." I shook off my inky thoughts, breaking from the tar pit of my mind. "Overwhelmed-overschmelmed. I gotta say, I'm feeling surprisingly coherent for a potential concussion victim."

He fixed me with an amused expression. "I can take you somewhere safer until the raiders fall or withdraw-"

"And what if they don't?" He trusted me to make good judgements, but what sound reasoning had brought me here? It was selfish and rash of me to jeopardize myself like this, no matter that I'd done what I set out to.

"Then this bastion will be compromised. We'll fall back on contingency plans to maintain the security of the keep." Blanching, I sank in my seat. I really had to stop asking the hard questions; I was never ready for their answers. Noting my expression, he attempted a reassuring smile. "But we've faced worse raids and learned from our victories. The tunnellers are our main concern."

"I could try to cut them off-" He stopped me with a look. "Yeah, yeah, yeah. My magic's a beacon, I know." Sending him a sly side glance, I noted, "I was the one who told you that."

"I've made the Brigadier General aware, as well." He made an obvious effort to keep from glancing at the gauze wrapped around my head, heavy with blood and partially obscuring my left eye, as he offered me his hand for the second time today. That's right, I had yet to get up from my seat, but that was partly due to the pulse beneath my bandaging threatening to undermine any pretence of balance.

Taking his hand, I broke a sweat simply in the effort of retaining some measure of dignity. Go figure, as it turned out a little chunk of rock to the skull made finding footing on a flat surface feel like ninety-degree rock-climbing. It didn't get any easier when Seth led me to the stairs from whence Brigadier General Lyovin had emerged.

"What's down there? And why's it so deep?" I motioned to the endlessly dark tunnel forking off alongside the height of the stairs. It looked how I imagined the digestive tract of some great stone giant would appear from the inside.

"That's the Chute. There's nothing for us that way," Seth answered, closing the iron door behind us before helping me descend the magic-carved steps.

"What kinda chute goes straight to hell?" I thoughtlessly kidded, only to realize afterwards what would go down a chute as large as this, here beneath the front lines. A shadow fell over his eyes, insinuating the truth in my jest. Gritting my teeth against the discomfort churning in my stomach, I averted my eyes and began faster down the stairs. "Well alrighty then, time to distract woe with comedy," I muttered under my breath, but before Seth could notice I'd spoken, I loudly burst, "You know what's ironic?"

"Hm?" he hummed in distraction.

"You remember when I launched myself under a hundred-fifty or so pound body falling at top speed from a few stories up? And I had nothing to show for it, medically? Not even a scratch. Well, it's looking like a single, stray pebble is the battering ram to my skull's ramparts." Catching Seth's eyes, I drove my point home with a raised index finger and an uttered, "Ironic, unfair, and I'll be the first to say, it would *behoove* you to require hard-hats out here."

"You think you have a concussion?"

"Maybe not. My name's Anelisha Knight and I'm still cracking jokes at inopportune times, so it can't be *that* bad-"

"And those two things imply the other?" he chuckled absent-mindedly.

"Don't they?" I smirked, only for my feet to stumble under me, wiping the amused expression off my face as I missed my footing down a few steps.

Seth practically lifted me off my feet in his one hand, snatching me in close before I could fall down the stairs, surprising me with his strength. Adrenaline shot through my veins, and I was laughing against his chest.

"Ugh, it feels like all the juice in my brain's been turned to sludge! I'm chugging at half-speed, Seth, and this train's about to crash."

"Do you want me to carry you?" An unspoken resignation glinted behind his eyes.

I gaped up at him. "Has that been an option this whole time?"

A hush fell over us, the silence of the deep Chute behind us seeming right at our backs. Then he did something I'd never known Seth Knox to do. He laughed.

It was a full laugh, a real laugh, as he scrutinized the look on my face. Maybe this raid was the last straw to break the camel's back or his insomnia had finally gotten the better of him, but in that moment, I learned that when Seth Knox laughed, he wheezed. And when he wheezed, he squeaked cute little intakes of breath. God, if Levi was ever treated to this side of Seth, I couldn't fathom what impossible thing Valencia had promised to lure him away.

Seth covered his mouth with both hands to try to stymy his laughter, obscuring the light that had come into his face and drawing space between us with his back hitting the stairwell wall. Irony shone in his eyes.

"What?" My attempt at an offended tone came out meeker and more curious, but I crossed my arms over my chest nevertheless to hide the delight fluttering there. What a wonderful sound, his laughter, so immediately addictive. "Am I that laughable?"

"Not at all. It's just... it *is* ironic. All of it. And how deep the irony goes-" he breathed but there was no more mirth in his voice as he shook his head against whatever ideas had so tickled him. Composing himself, he failed to speak with a level tone, "That I'm the head of this operation. Commander of these people. Fighting pora on the side opposite Levi. That you'd be here with me. Of everyone, I should be the last person taking you to safety, but the people you salvaged from our dying country would sooner hide behind you than ensure your wellbeing. And what am I supposed to do? You don't know what you are to me-"

"Seth," I interrupted, catching his shoulders and meeting his eyes, "After everything you just said, it's pretty obvious to me that's *why* you're the first person I'd go to. You make me feel safe. I trust you."

Peering openly into his face, I tried an encouraging smile, seeking to soothe the stormy seas brewing in his eyes, but his gaze caught on the bandaging around my head and he pressed his mouth into a thin line with fists clenched at his sides.

"My apologies. I shouldn't be speaking this way." The storm in his eyes settled as swiftly as it had arisen, leaving hollow formality.

"No, that's not what I-"

Taking my hands from his shoulders, he closed his palms over mine. His gaze softened on me, watching me full in the face with a pitying expression. Any hint of his previous laughter had vanished from this gentle regard, leaving only that former courtesy, always keeping himself on a short leash.

"I'm glad Valencia couldn't break your trust." He smiled that polite smile. "But there was a lesson in it all; you said it yourself. Nothing's fair – not in this world or the next, from Earth to Cellana. Remember that."

"Sort of hard to forget," I huffed. "You do realize you're all over the map with these emotional ranges, right?"

"Yes…" He frowned. "I apologize if I'm scaring you."

Scoffing, I waved a flippant hand. "You could never."

We resumed our descent. Seth maintained a light grip on my hand in case of another trip up, but the tact of his touch implied even this overstepped his comforts. I couldn't let this silence persist.

"Well, uh, on the subject of trust, did the Key-Keeper know? From the very beginning, he said not much would be normal around me. Is that because he knew about me, about Evelyn, about all of it?"

There was a slight tilt to his eyebrows in poorly concealed surprise, but he answered, "He was aware who you are."

"And he passed that knowledge on to you and Levi?"

"For the most part, yes," he nodded, a crease forming between his eyebrows.

"So I was never just another magikier to you?" This certainly explained his lack of surprise – besides the surprise of having his heart immediately ripped out, I supposed – to see Evelyn in my dream. But nothing would change the fact he had kept this terrible secret with the ease of breathing… "Why keep me in the dark?"

"We had special orders to accommodate you, and special orders to keep it quiet."

"And these special orders. They came from the centions?" I guessed, earning his wooden nod. "Have I ever mentioned how much I *despise* secrets? Theirs in particular?"

"I can't say I feel any different. We weren't aware of your importance, not really. They had us under the impression the reincarnation of Evelyn's mortal body would never step foot in Blackano, so of course, when they brought you to us asking that we say nothing, and then everything that followed... there was no preparing for Valencia's return considering our limited knowledge."

"Even at the top, they kept a lid on what you knew. Well, I've certainly had enough of the centions' secrets. Do you know what a weapon of achaion is? Or why they killed the dragons? Do any of us know why we fight for them, really?" I huffed, but Seth's hand had gone stiff with unease around mine, a feeling of separation in the air between us as he removed himself from my heretical rambling. Heaving a sigh, my voice came out quiet with hesitancy as I asked, "Can we make a pact, just you and me? I expect it from them, so it only hurts in a literal sense when their secrecy stabs me in the back, but from you, that would be too many kinds of hurt... So, what d'ya say, partner. No secrets?"

He slid his eyes sidelong toward me, wide and vulnerable. "No secrets..." he echoed, toeing the line between doubt and want. I stuck out my pinky, drawing a smile across his face.

"Let me start, and you might not like this, but..." I bumped his shoulder, catching his pinky finger around mine. "I didn't actually have a good reason to come out here except to talk to you, because I'm dumb like that."

"But you tapped into your magic?"

"Yeah, things turned out for once-" I shrugged. "-but that's no excuse. Briar makes up a hundred percent of my impulse control and she just happened to be taking a nap." I ducked my head in a shrug, fighting the warmth of a creeping blush.

"If you just wanted to talk to me, why didn't you say something? I could have set aside a time." A hint of humour tinged his soft tone.

"I don't know where everyone gets the idea I'm some sort of good conversational partner, or articulate in the least. And organized? Not even close. I hardly ever say anything useful or informative." I shrugged again, small and meek. "But that's my big secret."

He hesitated, letting the silence draw out as his struggle to find words showed plainly on his face. I decided to help him along.

Flashing my teeth, I asked, "Back in Blackano, I heard Levi's hair was insured for big bucks. Rumour or *absolute legend*?"

I did it! Seth laughed his husky laugh, smiling fully up to eyes.

We had approached the base of the stairs where lantern light spilled out over the final steps where shadows of officers flitted back and forth. Although the heavy stone walls of the bunker muffled their voices, I thought I heard a familiar intonation murmur, "Hey, I recognize that voice." After a moment, he spoke again, louder and directed at the stairs. "*Annie*-body there?"

Yep, that was definitely Kev, and I didn't need Lin's subsequent, "Oh my god, Kev," to realize it.

Halting only a few steps from the opening into the bunker, my eyes went wide in alarm and turned on Seth. "What are they doing here?" I hissed.

"The scouts must have returned from their–"

I rounded on him, emotion buzzing in my head like the gonging of a bell, my skull being the bell. "Brett's nineteen, he can make these decisions, and Kev's toeing the line at seventeen, but Lin's a *kid*, Seth. Where's the age gate? She has no business being here!"

"I didn't realize, when we requested stone-crafters to maintain the bunker… I didn't think someone her age would enlist," he explained, but there was no excuse I could accept. Optimism had him continuing, "But we might've stumbled onto a bit of luck, here. The best close protection comes in trusted friends."

"I'm not a fan of body guards," I protested, giving myself over to anything else – Seth's eyes, my anger at Lin's placement here, the general distress of this whole situation – to avoid a mental highlight reel of my last close protection team.

Leaping the last steps, I burst into the room with eyes raking over the surprising number of industrial workers and military police sleepily pulling on their gear. The attack must have woken them, but I didn't linger on the drowsy atmosphere, instead rushing to Lin in her head-to-toe gear, and the brothers in their scouting uniforms, all seated together at an out-of-the-way booth stacked with weapons by the base of the stairs. They waved me over, but my heart still hammered in my chest, taken aback by their nonchalance.

One by one, they flinched at the sight of my bandaged head, the brothers' faces dropping, but I didn't give them a chance to question it. Striding up to the small trio they made, tucked away in a corner of the room, I lowered my voice to a growl. "You do know this bastion is under attack *as we speak*?"

"Yeah, why else would they wake us up," Lin noted around a yawn. I could see she made an effort to avert her eyes from my blood-soaked bandage, even behind her tinted goggles. "And before you blow up at me, they needed stone-crafters to secure these bunkers. You know, hero work."

"You can be just as much of a hero from the keep."

She smirked. "And let these two goofs rake in all the glory?" She draped her arms across the brothers' shoulders, leaning back in the booth. They met glances over her head, each wearing a look of exasperation.

"Your safety's important to me, Lin-"

"And *your* safety's important to the whole wide world but here we all are. What are you doing here, anyway?" At her words, Brett's posture stiffened, and Kev watched me closely, each of them anxious to hear whatever terrible news had pulled me out of the keep.

I blushed under their stares. "Hey, don't go turning this around on me just yet, I'm not done with you. This bastion wouldn't miss one stone-crafter."

She rolled her eyes. "Sure, but I can't be associated with you and *not* pull twice my weight. Just ask Faith."

"Is she here, too?" My eyes combed the room one last time, catching a number of red belts the likes of which Faith would be wearing, but none were fitted around the waist of a no-nonsense ginger. The one time I had the mental ammo to sit her down for a lecture, she was nowhere to be found. Honestly, that girl only operated under one energy, and it was hubris.

When Lin hesitated in the effort of recollection, Kev answered, "Nope, they got her up at the Fortress of the Damned."

I rounded on him. "I'm sorry, the *what*?"

"You don't have to worry about her, only the legionaries are damned up north," Lin casually explained, calling my look of shock down on her, but I was speechless.

Seth stepped up beside me, clapping a hand on Brett's shoulder. Brett eyed the hand out of the corner of his eye. Seth hardly noticed. "Good to have you back, and perfect timing, too. Would you mind keeping Miss Knight's company until the danger passes?"

Brett raised an eyebrow at me, apparently forgetting he'd refused to make eye contact the last time we were together now that Seth was involved. The set of Brett's mouth spelled an ostensible distaste for the other man, although he seemed to expend a great effort trying to hide it, enough to trump his surprise at finding me here. If I had to guess, the greatest issue he took with Seth as of the present moment was his escorting me into this mess at all. And that was all mere conjecture.

"I'd still like to know *why* you're here," Brett grumbled in an exasperated tone, edging out from under Seth's grip.

Kev chipped in, "Can you blame us for wanting to know what brings our champion to the front line?" Although his tone was playful, my spirit wilted at the moniker, like lead on my heart from the mouth of my friend.

There was no getting around it. "Oh, just more bad choices," I chuckled, hiding behind a smile. I could feel Seth's eyes on me, could practically hear the question sheathed in his regard, but I acted my answer by ignoring that which I told myself shouldn't have upset me as much as it did.

"Bad choices *and* a touch of drama? Sounds like a sleepover," Lin teased, "You've singlehandedly made my night."

"Ugh, I guess I am spending the night here, huh?" My eyes flicked to Seth, taking in his evident distraction which stole him away from the conversation. I wondered how long he would stick around, here with me where it was safest, or if he'd already decided to leave me in the capable hands of Brett, Kev, and Lin in favour of whatever duties awaited him on the surface. Whichever it was, he was hesitant to leave.

"Briar's not joining us?" Brett asked, nodding to my unusually exposed shoulders.

With a shrug, I considered, "She must've had a hard day of bossing me around. I left her cat-napping."

I knew her to be lazy, hell, that was the most she lay bare for me to know about her, but this was verging on peculiar. I figured she would've caught up by now, or at the very least barged unceremoniously into my mind to demand my whereabouts. Clenching up, I recalled her worries regarding the latest development with Evelyn. There was a very real possibility she'd been barred from my mind and simply couldn't find me. God, I hoped she wasn't worried.

Sucking back a breath, I played up a casual tone in my admitted, "Which was something of an oopsie, in hindsight. Those rascally bad choices, always lurking where I least expect."

Brett sighed, palming his forehead in a gesture I'd come to recognize as his backwards way of showing amusement. I couldn't help my smirk, over which Lin and Kev met each others' eyes only to roll them in synchronized mockery.

"Will you be alright here, if I...?" Seth asked me and gestured back to the stairs, although he seemed to have taken the unspoken interaction between Brett, Kev, Lin and I as answer enough to his question.

"No secrets?" I huffed, "Yeah, I'll be fine. But if you stayed, I'd be even better." Catching his soft smile, I felt my face heat up as I hastened to add, "I wouldn't have to worry about you."

I could feel the eyes of my friends on me and Seth, but nothing compared to Brett's wave of rolling dichotomies crashing sidelong into me, threatening to knock me off my feet. As outwardly civil as he could be with someone of Seth's high rank, the friction in the air was unmistakeable.

Ultimately, Valencia had taken advantage of my crush on Seth to drive a wedge between Brett and me when we were dating; I certainly couldn't blame him for his reservations. But I couldn't bring myself to read his expression with a glance out of the corner of my eye, least of all to meet his gaze straight on. Not after the months I'd spent feeling like a snake every time I fell for Seth a little more, at Brett's expense.

Oh dear lord, was this a love triangle?

No, only a distraction. At that moment, a violent commotion rang in my ears, calling all attentions down on a scuffle near the far corner of the subterranean barracks. For a second, I could make out nothing from the bustling confusion, only to catch a blinding glare of light right in the eye, reflected off a metal edge.

I fell back a step at the sight of a blade protruding from the chest of a wailing officer, thrashing terribly on the end of the sword as blood dribbled down his chin, and with searching eyes, I found the culprit there behind him: unmistakably pora in the way its jaws locked around the man's throat. Some of the industrial workers screamed, flinging themselves back from the sudden appearance of enemies in our midst, other officers ran for the pora with weapons drawn, but I stood frozen with the vivid memory of my nightmare breathing ice down my neck.

All I could think was how? How had it gotten there?

Then I saw it. A blonde woman had her hand on the pora's back as he defended the corner, only to disappear in the blink of an eye and reappear again with her hand on two more pora to join in the ensuing skirmish. Each time she reappeared, flickering in and out of focus like an object caught in a mirage, there were more pora under her hands. Until a loose arrow plunked deep in her chest just under her collarbone, the whistle of air loud in my right ear.

Startling out of my momentary lapse in cognitive processing, I whipped my head to the right to find Brett with a scouting bow from their table, his arms dropping from the release position. A hard look, detached and terrifyingly calm, shone in his eyes.

"Get out of here, Annie," he said in a lethally quiet voice, his unbroken stare fixed on the skirmish. "Knox?" For this, he chanced a fleeting glance out of the side of his eye, demanding Seth react.

Leave him? A pang of anxiety struck at my heart like a coiled viper, piercing pain in my chest. Adrenaline flooded my veins, rooting me to the spot as tendrils of that familiar, unwieldly magic lashed out from my toes to the stone beneath my feet. It took great restraint just to keep from unleashing the magic clawing at my seams, desperate to engulf the bloodbath ahead of us in the earth and forever forget that Brett had just taken another life before my eyes, and now expected me to leave him here to a similar fate.

Instead, I focused on the sensation of weight on the other side of the back wall, feet lined up in droves but holding still, perfect for counting. "There are forty-two on the other side of that wall. Pora or magikier, I can't tell," I announced with a finger pointed in gesture, "But they're just waiting..." Waiting for the magikier tugging at the stone wall to finally break the wills of the stone-crafters on this side. Along the stone threshold barricading our enemies from overwhelming the barracks, the conflict of energies contained a hint of something recognizable – but not in the sense that I'd encountered it before – reminding me of pink hair dye and a flat voice.

"You can sense them?" Kev gaped and met Brett's wary look before returning his gaze to me, "Is it the best idea to be using your magic around pora?"

"I'm not really using it, just seeing through it." I glanced over to Lin, who sat forward in the booth, fingers steepled in front of her scarf with a look of utmost concentration behind her tinted lenses. I was certain it was her energy among several others holding up the walls against the magikier's augmented ability.

Kev stood just ahead of her. Unable to rely on his blocked magic, he had a mace at the ready. I did a double take; maces didn't exactly spell stealthy scouting ops, but even Brett was reaching for one of his own from the small pile of armaments on the table.

It was a moment before I understood why we'd apparently resorted to Neanderthal melee. While blades would only glance off a pora's practically unbreakable flesh, negating any use of piercing or slashing weapons, their insides – particularly the cranial cavity – weren't quite so enduring. Tougher than rhino hide, enough to shrug off bullets like a bullet-proof vest, but not cushioned enough to absorb the impact. But all I had were the weights sown into the knuckles of my gloves, and I highly doubted that would be enough to do any real damage.

"We should be going." Seth's voice called me out of my mind, his offered hand the focal point of my unfocused eyes.

"Now that's asking too much…" I breathed, a knot of embarrassment tightening in my gut.

What was it Briar had said about selfless selfishness? Turning tail hardly felt selfless. But even if I stayed, my support would be a hollow farce, unarmed with nothing but the bomb of my magic to defend myself. The kind of powerful magic pora would have delighted to taste on their greedy tongues. Briar said they'd recognize its aura after they caught that first whiff of my power almost two weeks ago. It wasn't unthinkable that the pora had followed my magic here.

As if on cue, a pair of yellowed eyes – pupils blown and sockets sunken – met mine. The world slowed around me; the walking disease broke the skirmish line with a seemingly effortless horizontal slash through the waist of an officer just under his breastplate. The officer collapsed in halves, raising bile at the back of my throat, and the creature of the night lunged straight for me.

10

Last Resort

I FELT THE SWORD'S GRIP BEFORE I NOTICED SETH PUSH THE INEFFECTUAL weapon into my hand, drawing me behind him and toward the stairs in the same action. Acting the barricade between us, he caught the pora's blade on the back of a chair he'd drawn up like a shield in his other hand. Like this, the blade's sharp edge slashed into the wood and wedged there.

Ducking under Seth's arm, I stepped in close while the pora struggled to free his weapon. With a precise manoeuvre lending all my weight to the attack, I butted the pommel of Seth's status-symbol up into the pora's chin. His teeth jarred together with a loud crack, sending him lurching backwards as he lost his grip on his weapon.

Seth stepped quickly in around me, swinging the chair like a baseball bat into the side of the pora's head. He barely ducked in time, launching himself at me with a crazed look in his discoloured eyes.

Without thinking, I braced into a sturdier stance and angled the blade at the pora's diaphragm where I'd learned to navigate around the ribcage, instinctively meeting his charge. Rather than pierce his dermal armour, the sword merely acted a thin, metal barrier between us as my arms absorbed the shock, maintaining four feet of reach space.

A mace swung in from the right, but the pora was faster, wrapping a hand around my blade and leaping cat-like to the side before this new assailant could bash his skull. The sword flew out of my grip, only to be turned on Brett chasing after the pora. As he passed, he growled back at me, "What are you still doing here? Go!"

"Oh, as *if* you really thought I'd leave," I grumbled under my breath, but Seth stepped in close to me again, nudging me toward the stairs with a gentle hand on the small of my back. He'd wrenched the pora's sword from the chair, keeping the weapon for himself this time. Probably to keep me from launching back into the fight.

"You think you'll ever quit being an idiot?" Brett dryly huffed, planting himself defensively in front of Seth and me.

"Man, I sure hope so," I smirked, although I could feel the wild look in my eyes, wide on Brett and the pora posturing for a true brawl. I knew it was a long shot even as I implored, "Come with me?"

Kev answered for him, "I don't think that's up to us." He flanked the pora, swinging his mace. He didn't have his brother's strength, but he was quicker and with a decent opening, he could get a couple licks in, all the while keeping an eye on Lin where she was safely tucked into the corner of the room. Her fists were clenched on her thighs, posture stiff in the effort of maintaining concentration to hold up the wall.

A quick glance around the teeming barracks lent the impression our invaders were targeting stone-crafters, only held off by the remaining officers. Bodies littered the ground, not one of them pora. Even so, the initial shock of the attack had begun to fade, and our side had finally organized themselves in fighting formation.

Just not organized enough to notice the woman with the arrow protruding from her chest as she dragged a red stain across the floor. She looked like all the other bodies scattered around, except for her bright, honey-blonde hair framing her face from a bun that had come half undone with the battle, easy to miss when I meant to avert my gaze from the dizzying bloodshed. I only noticed her when she was right at my feet, having skirted the pora and the fighting to reach me, but Seth reacted first.

It all happened so fast.

One second, I was reeling away from the woman's extended fingers, prepared to backstep out of her reach, and the next, Seth had taken matters into his own hands. I pirouetted back several steps before I'd even registered his guiding hand on my arm, spinning me out and away from him as if we were two dancers on a stage all our own. I might've steadied my own footing if not for the sudden vertigo sending me entirely off balance. The stupefying pulse of the cut on my brow launched nausea in the pit of my stomach. The bottom step caught my ankle, toppling me over the stairs where the stone edges struck my back, winding me.

Before she could stop herself, the woman's hand met Seth's ankle, directly where I once stood – but she must have realized who he was. In the blink of an eye, they were sucked into a void of nothing, swallowed whole by thin air, and transported together out of the room. Just like that, Seth was gone. Abducted by the enemy in my place.

Shock coursed through me like a bolt of lightning traversing my nervous system. I struggled to rake in breath as horror froze me where I'd fallen at the base of the stairs.

I struck the ground with a balled fist, releasing an animal cry. "I had it, you idiot!" My heart hammered in my chest to the drumming in my ears. I would have eluded her grasp on my own! He had no reason, no *right* to step in my place…

Although I knew he was gone, my eyes raked the room for any sign of him, only to land on the far wall. Movement battered the earth just beyond, implying a scuffle. She'd spirited him away to the other side! And he was dreadfully outnumbered. But I could get him back!

"Annie!" Brett's voice snapped me out of my link to the magic. Cognizant again of my own being, I thought my heart might beat out of my chest. "Your magic's too strong. If you use it, they'll all come after you!"

"But they took him!" I growled. Red tinged my vision as I honed back into the earth, only to find the scuffle had passed just as suddenly as it occurred. I tasted the woman's blood, hitting the back of my throat so powerfully, I choked on it, but something else had happened. The bleeding had stopped – maybe she'd run out – or she'd been healed. As for Seth, there was no accounting for him in the stillness of the small legion beyond the wall. If she had been healed, she would have been able to steal away with her catch, and what a prize to carry home: the Key-Keeper of the City of Gates.

Before I could react, three bodies came at me at once, hauling me up the stairs and out of the barracks. I thrashed against them, blind to their faces and deaf to their words as only one thought coursed adrenaline through my body. He thought I couldn't take care of myself, only to face abduction in his defense of me.

The stairs quaked under our small troop, rupturing in spider webs of fissures that spread to the walls, spitting rocks out at us. Tremors strong enough to vibrate in my bones threatened the fortitude of the entire underground base, causing the ground beneath our feet to crack unevenly and drawing up jagged peaks and near-vertical slopes of sharp stone all around us.

One of the hands lost their grip on me, and only then did I notice Kev roll his ankle on a shattered step. Brett caught his brother before he could tumble down the stairs.

I heard Lin curse under her breath. "You need to stop before you make everything worse."

A jolt shook me out of my catatonia at the realization she was speaking to me, and only then did I understand the seismic shocks were my doing. And yet, the skin of my hands didn't sting, nor did any warm wetness stain the palms of my gloves. I couldn't feel the telltale signs of having used the magic save a slight, ringing headache, but there was no question, I'd caused this earthquake.

It was worth stating, I hadn't meant to. A quick search through the tendrils of my magic sent my stomach plummeting, for the earthquake hadn't been contained to the stairs.

There were no more feet behind the far wall of the barracks, only bodies. Rock and stone had been brought down on the heads of all those who would have slaughtered us – by me, I had done this. But this… this was a massacre.

I sank in my friends' hands, entirely too aware of what I'd done by the wave of metallic tang hitting the back of my throat, seeming to drip all down my interior, colouring my insides red with the blood of unseen enemies. I gagged on a foreign sensation like my heart just upchucked every emotion I'd ever felt, dried and spent of any positivity.

Pouring myself into my wandering magic, I frantically searched for the feel of heaving chests, breath stirring up the settling dust, any sign that I hadn't…

There! And again! Movement stirred beyond the far wall, of rocks being shoved off bodies and strong arms picking themselves up. There was only one explanation for so many survivors: they were all pora.

With a little more searching, I found the blood I sensed by the touch of my magic came only in small patches leftover from the teleporting magikier. Her arrow wound, I assumed. But what brought true relief to my being, was the fact that it was her blood, and her blood alone, that I sensed soaking into the earth. She must have zapped out of there with her hands truly full, having plucked out the other magikiers there with her, including Seth, and as such, had left these durable pora to the fight.

"The magikiers retreated…?" I murmured, drawn too far by the reach of my magic to meet the eyes of my friends.

"Whatever just happened, they stopped trying to bring down the wall," Lin noted, "But no normal magikier should be capable of teleporting more than one or two others at a time."

We four shared an uneasy glance. "It's gotta be Valencia's bond," I noted.

"Has to be," Kev muttered, dissatisfied. "How many does she have under her belt?"

"This is Valencia we're talking about," Brett put in, rolling his eyes. Old grudges really did die hard.

"But the teleporter still needed to make physical contact first, or she would've gotten you," Lin considered, nodding in my direction. A small glint of hope had entered her eyes, shining bright behind her goggles, and I understood why. The enhanced capability of a domenth-bonded magikier still had its limits…

But there was no time to dwell on it. Pora still clawed at the stone. "Our stone-crafters can barricade against pora, right?" Because I'd given them something to crave, so desperately I could feel the crack and snap of fingerbones breaking upon hooking into the magically hardened stone.

I didn't understand. Had the company stolen what they came for? But the woman had failed to capture me… Unless, I was never her target to begin with. Seth had said, after all, trouble seemed to be following him. I could see no other reason for the sudden retreat of the magikiers. In reaching for me, she'd caused Seth to forget himself.

Brett, Kev and Lin dropped me in a familiar seat, back where I started. For a moment, my mind was thrown for a loop, believing I might have imagined everything as I found myself right back where Corporal Mika Trist had bandaged me. And yet, even this optimistic delusion abandoned me with Seth's grave absence hanging on my heart like a weight, wrenching on the beating organ with a vise-like grip as if to split it in half.

"What are we gonna do?" Kev rasped close to my ear. Whether he was talking to me or someone else, I couldn't tell, but I gave him my answer anyway.

"Wallow?" The sardonic joke felt wrong on my lips as I wiped at the fresh tears in my eyes. Now wasn't the time for emotion. Louder, I announced, "We just lost our commander. We have to go after him-"

"Commander Knox was taken?" came the syrup-thick accent of Brigadier General Lyovin from the head of the war table. He motioned to Kev to close the door from whence we came. "How could this be? He took you below where it was safe."

"Not anymore," Brett mused. Seeming to notice who he was speaking to, he snapped suddenly to attention to report, "A troop of forty or so pora are lying in wait behind the far wall, but they seem to have lost their way in, sir."

"Then we bolster stone-crafter numbers to fix the problem." He glanced to me, a twinkle in his eyes. "And you, shonte. You caused the earthquake?"

"It wasn't my intention-"

"Are you fast?" he interrupted, waving off my apology.

"I can run, if that's what you mean."

"You said you wanted to give chase, no? To go after Knox." He gave a half-shrug, circling a hand in a casual gesture which made it hard to believe he registered the gravitas of our situation. "If you're fast, you may catch up." He caught my eye with a clever smile. "And when you do this, I suggest you use your shonte magic. You, over anyone here, *could* save him, *could* lure the pora from city walls, and in doing so, *could* save everyone of whom we speak. The pora will give chase to you alone, if they sense your magic is headed in another direction. We here will be free of them, or at least, a good number of them." Another half-shrug. "But, of course, you're limited by your ability. So I ask, are you fast? Because we here are pressed for time."

Dipping my chin in a nod, I balled my fists on my thighs. I could be fast… but it was this kind of reckless decision-making, ill-conceived and dangerously impulsive, that brought me here to begin with. Could I really throw myself into even greater danger, knowing Seth would have done everything in his power to keep me safe?

A grave look came over the Brigadier General, seeming hardly to fit on a face as warm and as frank as his. "I am aware, as I'm sure you are, that there is no fleeing the City of Gates until something changes. Our enemies make a ring around us. Our allies are driven out of Arillia. We are backed into a corner, or so it would appear." He leaned forward, cupping his chin with his elbows propped up on the war table's edge. "Our situation will not change without sacrifice, but this was too steep a price for our commander. Now that he's at stake, the question is directed at us. What are *we* willing to sacrifice?"

I held his level gaze, my heart beating high in my throat.

He gestured casually with a flick of his hand in my direction. "You are an instrument of change, shonte. And while you may be our champion, we, the whole, need a commander who is dutiful, humane, and insightful."

"I understand," I choked around the lump in my throat, "We spoke of a plan to infiltrate the heart of Arillia. For me to cut off the head of the faction, to scatter their forces and weaken their resolve..." My friends started in surprise at that, but I kept my eyes on Brigadier General Lyovin. "If they brought Seth back to whoever's in charge of Valencia's Cellana Corps..." I trailed off, doubt creeping into my mind.

How did I know they hadn't set up facilities for prisoners of war elsewhere in Arillia? I blanched to think the very notion of prisoners of war was lost on our fiendish enemies. But if that was the case... No, the heart of Arillia had to be their most fortified position, and if this siege had been all to capture one man, then surely, they would have made arrangements to keep him captive.

"Let me be clear," the Brigadier General spoke softly, "I do not ask this to abuse your abilities. I defer this decision to you, and to what you believe Knox would have wanted. If you choose to act, you will be assigned a vanguard to escort you behind enemy lines. As well, if you choose to stay, you will be assigned close protection to escort you back to the keep. Whatever your decision, you may tell anyone who asks that I commanded it. Understand, there will be repercussions one way or the other."

I started in surprise at his words; I couldn't just throw him under the bus to save my own skin.

"There is a price for every choice we make," spoke the Brigadier General, "At least this once, I will pay it for you."

Before I could give my answer, Brett burst, "I request my assignment to this mission, sir. Whichever she chooses." Although Kev blanched, his dread transparent, and Lin flinched in surprise, they steeled themselves and followed his lead with nodding heads, standing at attention on either side of me.

"Lin-" I chastised, but she elbowed me in the side, her seething glare sufficing to shut me up. In her eyes was a warning; there was no convincing her to stay behind, not as long as I was in danger, and least of all if Brett and Kev were coming with me.

Brigadier General Lyovin's face glowed with a smile, granting them their request with a nod of his head. "You have noble friends. Good."

I opened my mouth, floundering for the right words to undo their pledge, but the look in the Brigadier General's eyes told me there was no way he would send me out there alone. It wasn't just my life on the line when it came to my decisions. It had taken me this long to fully realize – finally clear to me in Seth's glaring absence.

A high-ranking officer burst in as words failed me. He had blood spattered across his heaving chest. In three strides, he crossed the room from the front door and saluted the Brigadier General before bending low to his ear. In a quiet voice, he reported, "A second wave of pora have been spotted charging in from their camps to the north and south. No formation. No recognizable leaders. Enough to overwhelm and overrun us."

I glanced at my friends. It was either leave them here or bring them with me – as much as I hated to admit, the latter seemed the less anxiety-inducing.

"I see. They come for you, I assume," Brigadier General Lyovin mused in my direction, sitting back in his seat and rubbing his knuckles in deliberation, "We could do with that distraction now. So what do you say? Time runs ever shorter for us."

The officer looked between us, putting the Brigadier General's meaning together. Confusion furrowed his brows, disapproval set his jaw, but he held his tongue in the presence of a senior rank. I wasn't the only one facing consequences by choosing to leave the City of Gates. I could see it in the shadow that fell over his eyes, his hands steepled in front of his chin; if Brigadier General Lyovin let me go like he intended, he'd be breaking the very rules set down by our lost commander. There would be legionaries who agreed with him, like Corporal Mika, and others who understood the massive risk, not just to everyone still sheltered in the City of Gates but to all magikierkind if I was lost beyond the walls.

But surrendering Seth wasn't an option.

"I'll do it," I breathed, "Whatever it takes."

11

If the First Ingredient Is Failure, Improvise

My words seemed to set the world to fast motion. Surely, Brigadier General Lyovin had to be some sort of telepath. With just one look from him, the handful of officers in the room knew exactly what to do. Even Brett, Kev and Lin leapt suddenly into action, debriefing with the Brigadier General as they grabbed gear for the road and packed self-cleaning water bottles which would filter any water we came across.

Meanwhile, I felt as though I'd been captured in the eye of a storm. I could only stand still as hands hooked a sabre and scabbard on one hip and a mace on my other, and on my back, a scout backpack containing equipment, rations and updated maps among other things. They said the leather I was already wearing – boots, tabard, jacket, and gloves – should be enough to keep a pora's wolf-like canines from ripping into me without overheating me in a fight, but even so, they handed me a roll of leather wrappings as extra padding to stow on my person wherever I saw fit. The last thing anyone wanted was for me to lose what made me their champion to the bite of a pora. Once we were all geared up, the Brigadier General went over the plan one last time with Brett, Kev, Lin and I while four other officers readied themselves to escort us across the battlegrounds.

It was a strange dichotomy, this simultaneous feeling of readiness under these officers' practiced care and of dread as I led my friends to likely doom. I couldn't meet their eyes. I had never wanted to turn tail so badly as in this moment, to run back to the keep and curl up in a ball in the basement. I had come here expecting censored horror to churn my stomach but ultimately unlock some fantasy of righteous anger, only to find genuine terror hidden just around the corner of my daily life. I was an idiot. And now here I was, hours later, preparing to toe the edge of darkness on the measly hope I wouldn't be consumed by it. Hours later, still an idiot, but a necessary idiot if this was what it meant to get Seth back and give our forces on the walls a shot against the horde.

I wished Briar could have been here with us. Her silence seemed to confirm the dissonance in my psyche going by the name of Evelyn. What I wouldn't have given to have Briar's input on that whole situation, let alone everything else. What was it she had said – about the likelihood of my success if I had Fiamme's glaive, my magic, and Briar all at my disposal? I was one for three on that scoreboard. But it would take far too long to retrieve her, and we were pressed for time with great legions of pora descending upon the east bastion. Instead, Brigadier General Lyovin sent a runner back to the keep with a message of the route I'd been instructed to take.

Brett assured me that would be enough for her to find us, but I had my doubts. Things rarely tended to work out for the better around me.

It wasn't half an hour before we were on our way out of the City of Gates. A pair of stone-crafters carved out a tunnel beneath trench lines and battlefields, walking ahead of us. Four armed legionaries strode in formation around me carrying lanterns and maces, their footfalls heavy, their weapons at the ready, and among them, Brett and Kev strode silent as ghosts, a cat-like grace to their movement.

Just watching them, the difference between legionary and scout became glaringly apparent to me, even with only a couple weeks in the position. Strong leaders among phomara magikiers had a tendency to saturate certain traits among their subordinates, or so I'd heard in the basement chatter. But even the best magikiers couldn't permanently enhance others' skills. Not like a domenth could.

I didn't ask any names. For some reason, I believed that would keep these legionaries safe, unlike Lovejoy, Dooley, Fisk, Allard, and Shimura, names I would never forget. But it did feel impolite to walk among them as strangers, knowing I could be the reason they lost their lives today. A heavy thought, and one I promptly suppressed.

We came to a strange, unshapely wall beneath the earth, some kind of rock-hard wood which stumped the stone-crafters but didn't surprise them. Enemy fortifications. This was the hard part – our enemies would be watching the length of this wall for escaping tunnellers.

"We haven't been able to cross this wall. No woodworkers, you know. But there's gotta be a gate where they come through," explained Lin in a small voice, motioning to the wall of alien lumber. "We never see them cross this barrier from the surface. They just kind of-" She gestured with her hands. "-appear in front of us."

"You've been out here before?"

"I meant it more as a general we." Huh, so only I was heartless enough to drag a kid out into the field.

Shaking off this notion, I lit up with an idea. Just as the group was beginning to tunnel upward, I interrupted, "Wait, wait, I have something for this!"

Like I had at the bastion, I could try to feel around for any tunnels on the other side. I could help! But of course, the one time *I* could carry the team, the kernel of magic inside me was nowhere to be found. It probably didn't help that I had so many eyes on me while I searched within myself for the power I knew to be there. Power I just couldn't tap. And without it, I certainly couldn't enforce my will on the natural world, nor could I spread my senses through the earth.

"Why not?" I growled under my breath and shut my eyes tightly. Where was it? It was there just half an hour ago! Now, there was nothing.

Brett leaned in close, keeping his voice low so only I would hear his leading question, "Didn't Briar say you shouldn't rely on emotion?"

Sure she had, but when had that ever worked for me?

A rational voice uncannily close to Faith's popped into my head, reminding me that my disbelief and anger when Seth was taken had just about doomed the east bastion and was what called for this course of action in the first place.

"Fine," I muttered, shoulders slumping. Only then did I feel the expression that had tipped off Brett, having furrowed my brows and set my mouth in a tight line – I couldn't be more obvious. I glanced up under my eyelashes to the restless group, muttering, "You can just ignore me. Sorry for the hold-up."

"It was worth a try," Kev said as Brett motioned the stone-crafters to mine to the surface. They probably would've gone ahead even without his gesture, but he wore a satisfied expression to be heeded.

"Yeah..." I muttered, trudging along behind the stone-crafters. By Kev's standard, the last two weeks had also been *worth a try.* I just hoped this negligent magic wouldn't give out on me before I could do my part for the Brigadier General's diversion tactic. Mine was a pivotal role, after all.

The channels our stone-crafters made to circumvent the lumber walls must have been common scouting routes, letting out in a forested area Brett and Kev seemed to know well. We surfaced under the roof of a shelter disguised as a bush, but the interior was nice enough. Embrasures in the walls revealed our forested surroundings illuminated only by wandering constellations and the moon-bright ring across the night sky. Even that pale lustre wasn't enough, raining through the high canopy in patches and limit visibility to a bare minimum beyond the confines of our wardrobe-sized shelter.

From the moment we were to step outside, the nocturnal pora would be able to ambush us with ease, here just behind their camps. But that was why I hadn't come out alone. As soon as we surfaced under the cover of the camouflaged scout post, Brett was hard at work with his magic, checking around for recent enemy movement in the area. It was a slow-going process but gravely necessary.

Kev and one of the legionaries went with him, while the rest hung back with Lin and I in the shelter, cramped in together as our superiors pointed out the direction to the next and final scout post beyond which I would set up the diversion. From there, they re-explained we would have to find the disused train tracks which would lead to the heart of Arillia, a great city they called Cerenthior, making abundantly clear we weren't to get too close to the tracks for the ambush spots all along their length. Seemed simple enough.

I was never one for backpacking. More of a cottage girl, myself, although I hadn't been to one since Dad left – it belonged to his side of the family. Even so, I convinced myself the coils of anxiety writhing in my gut and the jitters in my fingertips were poorly denoted excitement. Yeah, I could get behind an expedition through nature – alien nature that positively wanted us dead. And what luck that I would be with my best friends – those I least wanted to endanger.

Yeah... Now seemed like a great time to start second-guessing myself – not that I had ever stopped. I was in desperate need of a confidence boost – and out here, I wasn't likely to find one. Yeesh, what I really needed was some way to get rid of that cynical voice in my head, turning every thought sour. As long as I could just do what I was told and not be totally useless.

"You good?" Lin probed, nudging an elbow into my side, "That's quite the hundred-yard stare you've got goin' on."

"Sorry." I shook off the mood that fallen so suddenly over me. "Distracted."

"Save the distractions for our welcome home party. The scouty boys are back and we're about to head out."

"Right," I muttered, glancing up to Brett, Kev and the officer near the door. I hadn't even heard them come in. My voice pitched as low as my spirit on the words, "Any chance I can convince you to head back?"

"Hmm?" Lin hummed, having missed my words. But she would be pissed if she knew I had it in my head to go alone. If it was the other way around…

"Nothing."

Glancing over at me, she looked me up and down with concern behind her tinted lenses. Assuming the reason for my diffidence, she stumbled over herself in assuring me, "We'll find him, Annie." She seemed to combat the naturally flat tone of her voice, bringing a rare softness to her words.

"I know we will." I nodded sharply. "There's no going back without him."

She winced. "Well, we'll find him one way or another, won't we?" She ducked her head, wary to speak her mind, but I knew what she meant. These were pora we were up against and Seth was a born magikier, last descendent of the original magikier. Magic was woven into his very DNA, which meant the pora virus would have a stronger effect on him, could even corrode him completely. But this was *Seth Knox* we were talking about. He carried more authority over a thousands-strong faction of magikiers than any non-cention or non-Emperor before him, and he had close ties to me. He was valuable to Valencia, and certainly to Levi Videl. They couldn't afford to waste him to a magic-rotting disease.

I assured myself in this, refusing to imagine any alternatives as I hissed through gritted teeth, "He's alive out there, and we're going to bring him back. We just have to act fast." The severe determination in my voice echoed memories of Val, her speeches and her promises, but I shook all thought of her from my mind.

"Annie?" Brett spoke up from the other side of the room, "We have our route. You ready?"

"Ready as I'll ever be," I huffed, stretching my arms over my head and listening to the leather crinkle over my shoulders. I wanted to shove my friends back down the mouth of the tunnel and seal it behind them – Kev didn't even have his magic while that cursed mark was still branded behind his ear. Instead I said, "Let's go."

Brett was the first out the door, leading our little expedition of four. He and Kev knew the scouting routes well enough to direct us. Lighting our lanterns would've only drawn unwanted attention, which left us to our limited night vision. I kept Lin by my side, and Kev made up the rear. Though

I knew the chafing of our clothes and the crunch of the nature-ridden forest floor underfoot were but miniscule sounds in the vast, open night where strange howls filled the air and high branches rustled with the weight of nocturnal predators, the noise we made funneled into my ears at maximum volume, raising my heartrate and shortening my breath.

Only minutes into our departure, Lin took my hand, pressing my palm in comfort. Unbelievable. Even in the kind of darkness that obscured everything beyond a five-foot radius, she could read me like a book.

We shimmied around tree trunks the width of vending machines, grazed past itchy underbrush up to our waists, slogged through indistinguishable, ankle-deep mud puddles from the day's light downpour, and swatted at bugs we could only hear, never see. I couldn't be sure just how long we walked before Brett raised a fist in the light of the ring and pointed out a boulder with a second skin of moss sprouting barely grown saplings. We'd reached the next outpost, and even more surprising, we had done so without a hitch.

But here was where it got dangerous.

The outpost itself was no larger than a shed with a small underground bunker, but from the moment I stepped inside, I felt as though I'd just unwittingly walked into the opening scene of a horror film, evidently the result of its situation so close to enemy lines. Eerily vacant, with food and weapons stores ripped to shreds and shrouded in dust, an abundance of signs pointed to the failure of its operation, but I wasn't sure I wanted to know any more about it than what I could see. Ransacked, raided, and razed to the ground, now it was nothing more than a landmark for us. A checkpoint.

"Are you hyperventilating?" Kev asked in a whisper upon closing the outpost door behind us.

"Who, me? *No*," I choked around my rapid breathing, waving a flippant hand. Sure, I felt like I was stuck in a bubble and my air was running out, but I wouldn't admit to it. Then came the rambling. "I assure you; this ventilation isn't hyper. If anything, *I'm* the hyper one. 'Cause this mission is... hype..." I winced.

"Ooh boy," Lin huffed under her breath.

"Are you sure you're up for this?" Brett asked.

"Psh, of course I am." I waved a hand again, the same hand. It was especially unfair that this, my go-to casual gesture, came across with the same emotive charge as a nervous laugh and a green complexion. "And even if I wasn't, I have to be, right?"

Brett met me with a look of disbelief. Kev and Lin met eyes across him, each raising an eyebrow with cartoonish theatricality.

"Well, would you look at the time-!" I announced louder than intended, earning a chorus of shushes. In a whisper, I bade, "*Right,* so just stick to the plan. Don't die, be safe, and please survive-"

"Annie," Brett muttered.

"Uh-huh, uh-huh. Good talk, team," I said, voice pitching almost at a high squeak. Before my blush could steal away what little remained of my dignity, I made a pair of finger guns toward the door and headed out with a palm to my forehead, leaving Lin and Kev to find their positions while Brett tailed close behind me, a silent phantom in the darkness.

Not far from the outpost, the forest became denser with walls of rampant shrubbery and undergrowth reaching up to my waist at its lowest, such that Brett and I were forced to swing our sabres just to carve out our path in the thickest parts.

A whirlwind of doubts orbited my mind as we followed the constellation centered upon Cellana's north celestial pole which the legionaries had indicated for us: five radiant points making up Cerae's Crown, the middle of which stood eternally motionless in the night sky. A ceiling of foliage shrouded my view, leaving me or Brett to climb high into the boughs every now and then to be sure we hadn't lost our way. Even then, I couldn't help wondering just how far they wanted me to go, if I was cutting our venture too close to the train tracks, or if I was taking entirely too long. Most of all, I plagued myself with thoughts of failure. The nearer we approached, the steeper the hill I felt myself rolling down, out of control and racking up speed. What if I couldn't reach the magic?

"We should be far enough behind enemy lines," came Brett's voice. He'd welded himself into the greenery, his silhouette indistinguishable from those of the trees and shrubbery under what few strands of the ring's light lanced through the high canopies.

Stopping for a moment, I listened – I still couldn't sense anything the way I had back at the bastion. To my surprise, I did hear the faint gurgling of unseen water. "Yep. We're here."

An underground stream rushed beneath the earth, or so the legionaries said. I had everything but fire at my disposal – it should have been ideal – but I just stood there staring down at my feet as worry after worry rushed faster through my head.

Brett cleared his throat, calling me back to attention. "So that means you should be doing something, doesn't it?"

"I'm working on it." Escaping the barbed wire mesh of my mind, I tacked on, "You should stay behind me in case I..." *Can't control it.*

"Don't worry about me. Just do what you have to." I couldn't tell his location from where his voice emanated, bouncing off the trees and muffled among the rustling leaves. He really was a ghost.

Shutting my eyes tightly, I fought the rapid flutter in my ribcage, imagining Briar's voice guiding me toward my supposed connection to the world around me.

When nothing continued to *not* happen, Brett's voice returned, advising, "Now might be a good time to get passionate."

I winced, stuck on Briar's teachings, but that nagging voice of doubt reared its ugly head in the back of my mind, recalling all my disappointing flops under her guidance. Right now, I didn't need to be in tune with the magic – I couldn't wait for it to be symbiotic – I just had to control it.

Giving a nervous chuckle, I conceded, "You know what? That's not a bad idea. Scratch that, it *is* a bad idea, but also maybe our only option. So definitely stand on that rock right there." I flapped a hand toward a shoulder-height, stump-shaped object amid the sea of leaves where a strand of light hit just right, a good distance away from me.

"Standing on this rock," he obediently announced, and appeared out of the darkness with a lithe little vault onto the natural stone platform.

Shaking out my nerves, I hopped from foot to foot, exhaling through gritted teeth. "Okay, I got this, I got this-"

"Annie."

"Yup, hurrying up."

Closing my eyes again, I let the setbacks of the past two weeks wash over me, augmented by the sheer disaster of today. The issue was, I was already grossly aware these problems stemmed from my poor decision-making. The initial burst of adrenaline at Seth's disappearance had vacated my bloodstream, leaving only frayed nerves and overthinking to trap me in my head. At the heart of it: I was running circles in an endless loop. Valencia only managed to ruin my life in Blackano when I succumbed to my lowest emotions and the behaviour that followed; how was this any different? Now, I stood between the scales balancing life and death for everyone at the walls, all because I lost control and my magic blew up, calling down hell on that position. And what was my solution except to lather, rinse, and repeat, but apparently, I'd run out of hot water! This was an entirely too literal example of fighting fire with fire!

Electricity fizzled around me, sparking like fireflies in the air with a dry crackling sound. Beyond the charged haze, I caught Brett's reminder, "The water, Annie." A note of worry was plain in his voice.

"How am I supposed to redirect this?" I hissed through my teeth, finding a foothold in the magic through the buzz in my bones, a dry echo of the energy in the air.

"*I* don't know!"

"Of course you don't. I don't either! What am I even doing out here?" I groaned under my breath, sinking low on my haunches and pressing both hands to the ground, closer to the coursing water beneath the earth. "How many bad ideas can one person have in a single day?"

"You can't be limited to a number," Brett casually noted in a parody of his flirting voice – the only difference was a playful lilt which once had the power to leave me rambling for words. I shot him a look.

"Not helping."

The rush of running water growled loud in my ears as I knotted my hands in the fine stalks of alien grass threaded with twigs and pine needles. The snap of electricity jolted out of my fingertips, sparking small bolts of light into the grass from which plumed puffs of smoke. My mind followed the trail of energy into the earth, a path which sent small critters burrowing in the dirt, and which bloomed low in the earth upon making contact with an underground stream not fifteen feet below me. Perfect. Now if I could just redirect the output of my energy to the water... But it was like trying to hold onto sleep after waking; the harder I focused on the magic, the more I felt it slipping between my fingers.

"You know how I never know what I'm doing?" I chirped, still with eyes closed and hands on the forest floor. Innumerable tree roots drank from the underground system of flowing water, my electricity branching up through the contact to several trees surrounding us. Leaves showered down over Brett and I, probably to do with my magic, but I had no idea what I was doing to make that happen. "Oh my god, I'm a danger," I groaned in frustration.

"Actually..." Brett pondered and seemed to light up with an idea by his sudden movement. I felt his footsteps on the earth more than I could see or hear him moving in this darkness.

"Where are you going?"

"To be in danger."

I jolted in surprise, the instinctive thought to stop him zapping from mind to magic in an instant. Before either of us could react, a tree root jumped out of place to trip him up. He went sprawling to the ground. "Sorry!" I burst, leaping to help him. "I didn't know I could-"

He moaned, holding his foot. "Did you just taser me with a tree root?"

"Well damn if I did because that's not what I was going for." Embers glowed with life along the length of the tree root, a damp smoke billowing off the well-watered limb. "What were you thinking? That kind of impulsivity's gonna turn you into another me, and nobody needs another me!"

He scoffed, rolling his eyes. "I figured you always manage to get the magic working when someone's in danger. And it worked… kinda."

"Yeah, but that's not exactly ideal," I growled, "Now stay on your rock and let me figure this out or I will *intentionally* taser you."

"Didn't you just use it, though?" he pointed out, nodding down to my hands. I blanched with the realization he was right. But when I stripped back a glove, what I had taken for stress sweat was proven just that, making my palms clammy, but not too warm, not too wet, not blood from the paper-thin cuts that came with expelling this magic.

"It worked like it was supposed to…?" Shaking my head, I balled my hands into fists as if to force the blood to the surface of my skin. "This won't call them to us – Is that really what we're trying to do? Oh my god, and I tasered you! Can you stand? Can you run?"

He tried, pushing himself up to a stand, but upon testing his foot, he raked in breath between his teeth and shook his head. "Just give me a minute. You didn't do any real damage."

"You don't have to be all macho about it-"

He waved me off. "Well, now that there's a genuine danger, maybe you'll find it easier to raise the water."

"Oh yeah, because it's just that easy," I snapped, matching his tone. Before he could put in his rejoinder, I gestured northward under the compass that was Cerae's Crown. "Walk it off in that general direction. I'll catch up."

"Splitting up is a bad idea."

"Just think of it like you're clearing my path," I shot back, fending off the urge to roll my eyes.

"No." He crossed his arms, sitting in the dirt with me. "I'll be the damsel in distress you so desperately need. Save me, oh strong and powerful shonte. Raise the water."

"You're unbelievable!"

"I am," he mused contritely, as if it couldn't be helped.

"You know what *is* believable? You, downplaying the pain you're in because you don't like to have feelings, and using this as an excuse to stay off your feet." Pointing a finger in front of his face, I sang, "Ah, ah, don't even bother denying it. I know I'm right, because *I'm* a bad shonte."

He quirked his head to one side, wearing a look of exasperation. "Weird brag."

Flapping my hand, I huffed a lock of hair out of my face. "Yeah, wrong tone. Whatever."

"You're wasting time," he pointed out, "And I'm not going anywhere without you, so..."

"Fine!" Whether he'd meant to or not, this sour mood he'd incited, when combined with the very real panic of knowing pora were soon to be upon us, made a great headspace to find my footing in the mental minefield of shonte magic.

The electric spark that had filled the air around me was snuffed out the moment I hurt Brett, but the magic's sensation remained, so I counted that as a minor win – my first win of the night. In place of the electricity, I homed in on the water I'd detected below. Droplets clung to tree roots, soaking into the wood, but I demanded more. Capitalizing on the roots' absorbency, I drew the water through and over them, acting a perfect highway up which I pulled the rampant streams to the surface en masse.

For a moment, I feared my supposed progress was mere imagination, but I hardly had time to worry. A low gurgling introduced a flood of puddles bubbling up at the base of the trees, rising swiftly as the underground streams siphoned increasingly faster to the surface. The ground under my knees softened, soaking into my clothes as the soil turned swiftly to a suctioning mud.

"Ah! Get up!" I cried, hopping to my feet only to entrench myself up to my ankles in mud.

"I'm trying!" He struggled to copy my movement, but the dirt had become something closer to quicksand when mixed with the rising water, hungry for something to refill the space where streams once flowed deep beneath.

"This is exactly why I told you to leave!" I pointed out, grabbing hold of him with both hands and yanking him back toward the stone – on which I had also told him to stay. My feet wouldn't budge under me, sinking deeper into the soil the more I tried to move.

"I'll get myself out of this, you just keep focusing on raising the water!" he directed me, but I couldn't see how he would free himself on his own.

Already, the water had risen to my knees, rushing around me with enough force to knock me off my feet if they weren't anchored in mud. Still I had to pull the waters higher if we wanted to begin this quest properly.

Brigadier General Lyovin had said our best bet to elude pursuing pora would be to draw up the subterranean rivers and block them off – apparently pora durability meant equal sinkability – but at this rate, the river would best me before any pora had the chance to show up. I was the least in-control master of my own fate who ever lived.

"Oh my god," I groaned at the onset of a poorly timed idea, one hand reaching for the nearest tree branch a good two feet out from arm's length, "I could've just gotten rid of the earth covering the underground streams. That would've done it."

"Where was this masterful thinking two minutes ago?" he snapped, forfeiting his futile efforts to escape the suctioning mud. At this point, his legs – which had been crossed, the dummy – were just about sunk.

"Oh, I don't know, maybe it was buried under my panic at having tasered you? Oh, that's right, after you tried to *spook* me into the magic."

He scoffed. "Are you blaming me?"

"Why yes, Brett, I think I am! But that doesn't matter now because we're both going to die here." A hysterical pitch had entered my tone.

"Not if you do something about it." He had the audacity to massage his temples while the rising waters darkened his shirt low on his chest. I hardly heard him over the static in my brain.

"This was a terrible idea! But where's the surprise, all my ideas are at least a little bad-"

"You're hung up on all the wrong things," he groaned, hands splashing in the water.

I gesticulated wildly, spouting, "I am the death of you! How are you only mildly offended by this-?"

"Annie!" he burst, whacking my thigh nearest him to snap me out of my frenzy.

"What?" I snapped, "What could be more important than our impending doom?"

"Stop panicking, just fix it," he stated in an even voice, "Use the same magic that got us into this to get us out, you idiot." Narrowing my eyes at him, I scrunched my face in an overexaggerated glare.

"Leave it to you to keep your head in a situation like this," I grumbled under my breath and shut my eyes tightly, pouring my focus into the mud surrounding our feet. I could work with mud.

I didn't bother rewiring my mind from my connection to the water, a connection I had to maintain to keep it rising. Instead, I balled my fists around the familiar pain in my palms and envisioned the water making a bubble of space around Brett and I.

Immediately, the mud dried around my ankles, pulling back to release Brett's crossed legs as all moisture fled our vicinity. He shoved up to a stand and leapt onto the rock I'd assigned him with but the slightest wince at putting weight on his foot.

"I saw that," I noted over my shoulder, catching his gaze.

"And I see pora," he retorted, nodding in gesture past me. "Across the water."

"They're fast," I gulped.

"They're pora."

I shot him a glare. "How close?"

"Close enough to see. You're gonna want to speed things up."

"And would you say you're a *strong* swimmer?"

"Please don't," he sighed, recognizing the futility of his entreaty.

I shrugged, raising my palms innocently. That was his only warning before I shut my eyes and, maintaining my little bubble of air, pulled everything up from beneath the earth. The sting of escaping magic trailed fresh wounds up my arms as I let the crashing waves disturb the soil, shoving the forest floor down where the streams once flowed so as to create banks on either side.

There was more water than I knew what to do with, flooding the forest in branching paths and shoving the earth out of the way to accommodate this new river, but I focused on keeping it just large enough to force our pursuers into a detour upon chasing us. For this diversion to work, I had to give our enemies the impression they could catch up to us, otherwise, there was nothing stopping them turning right back around to rejoin the siege on the city.

I flowed away from myself on the rush of the tide, escaping my minuscule body to explore every curve, every nook and cranny, every hidden den in this vast forest with all the jubilant discovery of the water I rode. It had to admit, it was difficult to rein myself in, let alone the water.

A hand caught the handle on my backpack, dragging me up from the water. I hadn't noticed it encase me, crashing through the barrier of my little bubble, but I hadn't felt like I was drowning. Without even realizing I'd been fully submerged, I resurfaced to white-water rapids. Sputtering for breath, I fought the weight of my gear with every attempt to swim, keeping my head above the water only by the hand on my backpack and the flotation device tailored into it.

A rough point raked across my thigh – the shape of the water flowing around it suggested to my mind a tree branch, steadfast to the tree trunk. My left ankle wedged between branch and trunk, becoming snagged and jerking my entire body. In an instant, the water consumed me, flowing up my nose as it dragged against me.

My mouth filled with muck, shoving scratchily down my throat. Automatically, I coughed and sputtered, trying to rake in breath, but there was only rushing water, burning against my lungs. My own screams warbled eerily in my ears, the phantom wail of the drowned.

I strained to reach my captured ankle, fighting not only the powerful current but the drag of the backpack, seeking urgently to float. There was no way I could win out against both. My fingers scrambled to unbuckle the belt across my chest, desperate to rid myself of this wrenching weight, only to fumble uselessly with the prong.

Still, I couldn't help gulping in mouthfuls of this filth water, tearing fiery trails down my windpipe. I couldn't tell if the edges of my vision were fading or the water was getting deeper, pitching me into utter blackness. I'd released it all from the ground and simply carved out a path for the parade – it was its own beast now, and it was trampling me.

Finally, I unclasped the belt, losing the backpack to the current. Angling myself behind the girth of the tree which had so ensnared me, I found small relief in the obstacle it made for the rushing waves as I pulled myself in close. Upon clasping my ankle in hand, I probably could have exerted a little more care dislodging myself. Instead, I yanked up, scraping through boot and skin alike to free myself in my panic.

Free. I clung to the tree, shimmying up as my lungs screamed at me to gulp in air, even if it meant swallowing this whole river first. I couldn't help myself. I gasped for breath, pulling in another mouthful as my body spasmed. If not for my legs wrapped around the tree, I would've been lost to the current right then, but I forced myself to keep moving, climbing the tree as fast as I could manage while my body shut down. I needed air. It was all I could think. All I could feel. The crushing pain in my chest, heaving against the water already consumed.

I couldn't see anything, focused only on climbing, but the sound of the rushing water roared louder in my ears. Or was that the roar of blood behind my ears.

My hand reached up – air! I wrenched myself higher, surfacing in the open breeze once again as I gulped in breath, only to choke on the water already sloshing around inside me. Hacking up mouthfuls, I clung shaking to the tree simply struggling to breathe.

"Annie! I thought-!" Brett choked on his words, his disembodied voice reaching me on the wind – precious air.

"I'm here!" I called back, voice grating, broken and wobbly with unstifled tears. "Are you okay?"

"I made it to the other side! Swim over!"

Oh, to hell with that idea. "But I lost my bag!"

"Then forget the bag! The riverbank isn't too far! Just swim to my voice and I'll throw you a rope!"

"Uh-huh," I muttered under my breath, weighing my options, "It's his idea, not mine… That's gotta count for something." Except I couldn't imagine a worse alternative. At this point, I was ready to build a tree house atop this fine, broadleaved plant and retire a disparaged hoax of a shonte.

"Come on, Annie! Our back's wide open!" All the more reason to spend the rest of my days right here, but I conceded.

Trembling, I pried my fingers from their involuntary grip on the tree, leaving pockmarks in the waterlogged bark where my nails dug in. I couldn't see the riverbank in this darkness, only reflections of the ring's light on the waves, but Brett's voice didn't sound dreadfully far. "Keep talking!" I called out to him and, gulping back a breath, tossed myself once again into the churning water.

It was a little easier to swim this time now I had Brett's voice to follow. Especially when the end of his rope plopped into the water next to me and he dragged me in the rest of the way. Soaked like this, his hair was as dark as his brother's and clung to his face. I'd rather focus on that than the agonized look in his eyes, desperate and unnerved.

"I'm never going to another water park," I sputtered as he hauled me up from the crashing waves. Clutching his hand, I crawled tremulously onto land looking and feeling like a drowned rat. Once I got my legs under me, he had me in his arms, his chest heaving rapidly under my hands.

He shook his head in exasperation, raining droplets from his hair, only to pull abruptly back from me with his hands on my shoulders. I swear I saw him roll his eyes through this veil of darkness, and he removed even that welcome touch. "Mhm, because you have that kind of self-restraint." Though his voice was strained, the sarcasm came through just fine.

"You doubt me," I huffed, lying flat on my back now my overburdened body had a moment to rest. I could've kissed the dirt, rejoicing in my return to land.

Hunkering down, his eyes shifted left and right as he caught his breath, his dark eyelashes gathering beads of glimmering water. We weren't out of the woods yet, literally or figuratively. "Kev and Lin won't be too far from here. Can you walk on your own?"

"I should be asking you-" I was berating, drawing myself up to a stand, but red-hot pain flared up my leg the moment I put an ounce of weight on my left foot. "Ooh! No, ignore me. It's just a scrape-"

"There's blood everywhere," he growled under his breath, catching my calf to give it a look.

Glaring up at me, he lifted a large flap of leather draping uselessly from my not-so-intact boot, sopping wet and trickling red. Beneath, he revealed a nasty scrape, pebbled and dribbling blood in thick streaks. A heartbeat of heat pulsed in the wound, radiating warmth in my ankle.

"How am I supposed to protect you, Annie? I should be taking you back. You did what the Brigadier General said, you lured those pora away *and* bought us time with this obstacle while we put some distance between us and them. Great. But we should circle back to the City of Gates-"

"If we circle back, there'd be no point in forcing a horde of pora to detour around all *this.*" I gestured back to the impromptu river. "We'd meet them at the halfway point, and then what? Even if we made it past them, we'd be returning empty handed."

"Annie-"

"Talk to me about turning back when we have Seth." The sting of fresh air on my open wound faded to a background hum as I met Brett's eyes, determined to prove my grit. Water fell down his face in shining rivulets, catching light like constellations on his skin, but I did my best to ignore just how pretty he looked in this moment. Wringing out the water in my hair, I stared him down until he raised his palms in surrender.

"Whatever you say," he sighed, and began pulling off his backpack.

"What are you-?"

"You wear this so I can carry you on my back." Standing up, he held the drenched backpack out to me. I eyed the thing, then him.

"Fine, but I'm not buckling it," I grumbled, taking the bag.

12

And That Was Just Step One

"WHAT TOOK YOU SO LONG?" KEV'S VOICE INTRODUCED HIM FROM THE surrounding obscurity where he blended with these small, bleak hours of darkness hedging on morning.

Brett merely grunted as he hobbled up the forested hill – not quite so dense on the incline – in his weariness with his weighted trek. I did my best not to revel in his warmth now the night's chill bit into my dripping wet clothes, gnawing ravenously on my back.

Kev gave a feeble chuckle, appearing between the trees alongside us. "I'm only kidding. We caught the tail end of that mess."

"Great," I rasped. My rattling lungs hadn't forgiven me just yet for all the murky water swallowed. I could still taste the river like my tongue had sponged it up.

He poked my side. "So, uh, you okay?"

"I did what I was supposed to. Used my magic, lured the pora, built a *river*? *And* no one died. I'm better than okay."

"I'm covered in your blood," Brett gruffly pointed out, then to Kev, "Med-kit?"

"On it," he nodded, zipping off again into the darkness.

"Spoilsport," I huffed next to Brett's ear, resting my chin on his shoulder.

"You really have no idea when to be serious, huh."

"The fruit of optimism is bountiful, Brett. And I can be *seriously* optimistic when I least want to," I mused between chattering teeth, gesticulating with arms draped over his shoulders and hands in front of his face, making a wet, squelching noise with the soaked leather. Red droplets leaked down from the hems of my gloves.

He boosted me up on his back, getting a better hold on my legs wrapped around his middle. "You're shivering."

"I noticed," I smirked, although admitting to it didn't exactly solve my problem. The leaves rustled overhead with a cold draft, and I trembled just the same. "But I'd be more worried about my arms."

"Trust me, I'm worried," he sighed, a curtness to his tone.

"Of course you are." A sad smile crossed my face as I tilted my head to study him. His hair was dry, stuck up in odd places and interwoven with leaves and twigs from the river, but wavy like I had sometimes seen it just after a shower, before he had a chance to brush it. A lock of brunet fluff had fallen into his eyes. In them, he wore a hard look, focused and composed as he scoured the ground for adequate footing among gnarled roots and uneven terrain. "For what it's worth, I'm sorry."

"It's not your fault you got hurt-" He cut himself off, biting back words he didn't have to speak for me to hear: But you could have been more careful.

"I don't know about that," I smirked, shrugging as I watched his baby blues rove over the forest floor, "I *did* directly cause my own injury. My river and all that. Hey, you think they'll name it after me?"

"How big did you make it?" he scoffed, somewhere between amusement and exasperation.

Biting my lip against a smile, I mused, "That's a good question. I guess we'll find out when we strip off these gloves, huh? It honestly feels like I'm wearing wet socks on my hands, Brett. Not ideal. The longer my fingers stew in this lukewarm me-broth, the less I want to have fingers."

"Just keep your you-broth-" He winced, having stooped to my level. "-contained for a little longer. We don't want your blood diverting any stray pora from the lure you set."

"Yeah, yeah," I huffed, opening and closing my hands so the liquid rushed around my fingers, an inadvertent expression of disgust scrunching up my nose as I did.

"If it bothers you so much, stop focusing on it."

"Impossible, you'll have to distract me."

"Kev'll be back soon with the med-kit."

"Is that the best you've got?"

"It's the most I'm willing to give," he wheezed upon reaching the top of the incline where he stopped, taking a moment's breather. "Somehow, I convinced myself you'd be less... *you* about all this."

"A false hope," I teased, grinning against his shoulder. "On the contrary, your being here is making it much easier to take any of this lightly."

I meant it as a compliment, but he groaned, "Please tell me that's the blood loss talking."

"Why, am I annoying you?" This hardly came out the light-hearted snub I'd intended, but considering he'd called me annoying before, I probably should've seen the sinking feeling in my chest coming. Before he could speak, I interjected with overcompensated flippancy in my tone, "Don't answer that."

He shook his head with a sigh and resumed his slow trudge through the ever-thicker woods, ducking under low-hanging branches and elbowing through nets of enmeshed saplings hiding tripwire roots and, likely, several diseases' worth of alien ticks. My face fell, his absentee answer hanging over my head no matter that I demanded his silence. That was, only until he grumbled under his breath, "You're not annoying, you're..." He searched for the word. "Irrepressible."

Grinning, I glanced off toward the trees, hiding my face behind my wild, red hair as my heart skipped a beat, too similar to older days. Shunning that uninvited feeling, I let the comfortable silence grow between us.

We weren't too far from the campsite Lin had handcrafted with her magic when Kev found us again. While Brett still held me, the younger of the two brothers pulled off my tattered boot and bound my ankle in cloth bandaging. The scratch all down my thigh didn't need immediate care, more of a nick than a deep cut, which I considered for the best since there was no getting to it without first taking off my pants. And as for my arms, well, we held out for the security of Lin's haphazard, underground sanctuary before going anywhere near that mess.

Kev led us the rest of the way to a rock den Lin had carved out of a steep crag hidden among the hills and camouflaged behind a matching tarp. We'd left the sounds of the rushing river behind, a good distance to ensure the pora would have more than enough trouble catching our scent, let alone finding us. It was a welcome comfort in the backs of our minds, especially as the dim glow of lantern light hemming the edges of the tarp, acting as a door to our small abode, made up all the evidence of our presence to be found from outside the den.

Brett lowered me to my feet just outside the nook, and if our hands stayed in contact a little longer than was strictly necessary, neither of us remarked upon it. Immediately upon entering the cramped space, hopping on one foot under the tarp, I was slapped in the nostrils by a metallic odour of salt and meat that somehow managed to smell both wet and cold. Hardly appetizing, but when Brett and Kev shimmied in behind me, Kev rubbed his hands together, licking his lips, and Brett's stomach growled.

The low ceiling forced us to sit after we dropped our bags and weapons by the opening, our knees pulled up to our chests to make room for the lantern in the middle with our elbows clashed at our sides.

Lin sat at the far back of the den, having prepared our meagre feast of rations, and with a wave of her gloved hand, met us with reflections in her lenses, the lantern light glaring back where I might've seen any expression in her eyes.

"I was almost concerned," she teased, voice flat as ever, and handed me a tin of gelatinous substance. This, scouts called food, but it looked more like a dog's meal to me.

"Not yet, gotta get these off," I muttered, waggling my fingers in front of her face and sending a splash of blood to the stone floor from the leather hems. "Whoops." Careful to keep the contents of my gloves from spilling out entirely, I dragged my arms out from the repulsively slick insides, revealing blood-drenched hands up to my elbows.

Gagging on her meal, Lin lurched back, nearly hitting her head on the stone wall. "That's more disgusting than anything that could come out of a tin can. What happened?"

"It's not as bad as it looks! I promise, I've just been stewing-" I stopped myself as Brett shook his head in his hand.

Kev and Lin shared a horrified look – or so I assumed, with her goggles negating any effort to emote – but I tied off the ends of my gloves and stashed them in an empty tin case.

Opening my mouth to speak, I couldn't get a word out before Lin shoved my allotted tin toward me. "Eat first before I decide we need to force feed you." She eyed me up and down. "You look like a drowned rat."

"Are we positive this is even edible?" I muttered, studying the label on the tin – illegible with water damage.

"We've had it on every scouting op," Kev put in, motioning between himself and Brett. The corner of his mouth quirked up into a lopsided smile. "And that's how you dodge a question."

"You poor souls," I breathed.

"It's everything you need out here," Brett assured me, rolling his eyes.

Swallowing my doubts, I took my tin of definitely-not-dogfood and wolfed the gelatinous meat sludge down like one of its target demographic. After that first bite – how could anything be so salty – the rest went down quickly. I hadn't realized how hungry I was, depleted and starved after the long day I'd had. Brett, Kev and Lin ogled me like an animal at a zoo, but I hardly noticed as I licked the tin clean.

All the while, I held off the urge to wince as every move I made wrenched apart the cuts carved out of my fingers and palms, irritating the lacerations up halfway to my elbows where the blood had clotted and the scabs dried over. Instead, I plastered on a smile, set the empty tin aside, and raised my hands, palms facing out.

"See? No big deal. Good enough to eat with and not nearly as bad as it was after the bunker."

"I don't know, seems like a big deal when you lose that much blood," Lin noted, gesturing to the semi-inflated gloves sitting in the tin case. Thinking on it, she shrugged. "But I have to give you credit, you got the job done. Just keep your blood-encrusted everything away from me."

"You're seriously encouraging her?" Brett bickered, sounding an awful lot like Faith now that he had an audience to back him up. He turned to me with an utterly unhelpful, "You shouldn't have pushed yourself," and I shot him a scowl.

Folding my arms over my chest only to immediately jerk them back for the sting of contact, I huffed for what felt like the hundredth time in the span of our walk, "I didn't push myself. I did what I was told."

Brett opened his mouth to speak, frustration in the set of his jaw, but Kev leapt in first to say, "And there's no undoing it, now. You'll just have to arm yourself with actual weapons from now on."

"Which falls in line with the Brigadier General's plan!" I cheered, nudging his side to convey my thanks, "I can't use it again without sending up a beacon. This was a one-and-done deal, and now that the deal's done, I wash my hands of this magic." I mimed dusting off my hands, wary to touch my palms where the worst of the cuts gouged deep.

"Until we reach Cerenthior," Brett added, a note of ire darkening his voice, "Where Valencia's forces – including *pora* – are all gathered up. Where you'll have to use it again if you want to beat her top general."

"Is that what we're calling him?" I mused, but he cut my tease short with a sharp look.

"I've seen him in my visions twice now, Annie. He was dangerous even before he had the dragon-bone weapon-"

"Fiamme. She's a glaive-" I interrupted, much to Kev's surprise and confusion, but Brett ignored me.

"-and with it, he's entirely too dangerous to take on in – what – hand-to-hand combat? Was that your plan?" Hah! A plan? He really thought I had one of *those*?

"Obviously, I'll be going into that fight as the shonte," I muttered, heart beating loudly in my ears, "But until then, I'm just me. No, until then, this is about finding Seth-"

"Sure it is," Brett snapped, the room dropping to glacial temperatures, "Except you and him were brainstorming this botched assassination plot long before he was taken. Isn't that what you told the Brigadier General?"

"Like, five hours ago." I flapped my hand as if it was nothing but gulped back the stress rising in my throat, tight as a hand's grip. Was the nook shrinking? There was hardly enough room as it was for the walls to be closing in on me.

Lin nudged my right foot, my good foot, with hers, noting, "You should've told us about your plan."

"Even if any of you were around to hear it, it wasn't concrete yet. I could hardly even call it a plan-"

"I'd say," Brett muttered.

Pointing a finger at him, I shot back, "You know preparation has never been my strong suit, so you can go right ahead and take that up with Seth. But don't, he was very sleep-deprived and had a lot on his plate. And, frankly, I can't imagine he's any better off now-"

Kev cleared his throat indiscreetly, tilting his head toward Brett's jaded expression, and I furrowed my brows in a frown.

"I'm being serious!"

"Doubtful," muttered Brett, but he rummaged around in the med-kit, resurfacing with an antiseptic wash. Gesturing for me to open my hands, he doused my cuts, clearing away the coat of mostly dry blood as I gritted my teeth, raking in breath. "The least you can do is take care of yourself."

"Hey, be sparing. We already lost one bag's worth of supplies," I remarked, rejecting the bottle in favour of rubbing the stinging fluid up my arms to wash the blood from my skin.

"We did?" Lin gaped, pulling a wince out of me which I could just as easily blame on the flaring pain of the antiseptic rinse.

"Yeah." I showed off my ankle, a bloom of red already staining my fresh bandages, as if to illustrate a connection between this and the missing backpack. "That's my bad." The number of facepalms in the nook outnumbered me three to one.

"Maybe we should just get some sleep," Kev suggested, sliding down with his back on the wall, knees still bent so he looked like a wet noddle, and folded his hands over his stomach. I hadn't noticed them all finish their meagre meals, but the tins lay empty in the case with my gloves, now a trash bin.

"I second that," Lin huffed, grabbing her bag and wrenching her bedroll free.

Kev offered me his, noting I'd lost mine, with a not-so convincing, "I run hot anyway," after which he licked his finger and poked his knee, making a sizzling sound between his teeth.

Rolling her eyes so dramatically I could discern the action even with her goggles, Lin whacked him with her pillow, walloping his defensively raised elbows. Brett had already zipped himself into his own sleeping bag, having rolled over in our limited space, feigning sleep.

Even with Kev's warmth, that glacial air had yet to clear..

13

Off The Rails

Day 16

BRETT WAS THE FIRST TO FALL ASLEEP, HIS DEEP BREATHING AN OLD COMFORT I had nearly forgotten.

Strange, how quickly I fell back into that old addiction of falling asleep with him – in his arms, waking up to his embrace, to his breath fanning over my neck. I remembered the first time I pressed my face to my mattress the morning after he slept in my bed – I'd passed out on him while we were studying together, late into the night. We both knew it was just an excuse to hang out. And I had woken up, shocked and delighted to find the trace perfume of his lavender-scented soap still clinging to my mattress, summoning images of his cute, fluffy bedhead in my mind. Of course, Lin had then walked in on me lying face-down on my bed with a goofy smile plastered on my face.

He didn't have that lavender-scented shampoo anymore, but while he dozed next to me, it was all I could smell.

Shoving the soft memory out of my head, I turned over, away from Brett but toward Kev and Lin. At my movement, Kev whispered in a soft voice, "Still awake?"

Lin grumbled, "I am now."

It took some heavy focus on my part to finally tune them out, but I closed my eyes and centered myself on Brett's rhythmic breathing, matching his even breaths with my own like I used to in Blackano. Hours passed in the effort of sleep, restless and so quiet, I could hear the whispers of grass stalks in the frigid wind of the night, along with the cracking and whipping of clashing branches in the treetops.

I couldn't sleep, not in this alien forest walked by powerful, unseen creatures of the night, legions of whom had been lured to an area not too far from where we lay hidden. Fact of the matter was, once we laid our minds to rest and turned off for the night, we became vulnerable to those very beings. Images of fangs and blood lurked behind my closed eyelids.

It couldn't have been far from morning before I finally managed to doze off, only to wake shortly after at the sound of an animal scuttling around outside the tarp. I startled out of a half-sleep with my head on Kev's bony chest, feeling like I'd blinked the night away only to open my eyes again to a medley of aches and pains.

My heart jumped to my throat but the shuffling and rattling that had stolen me from the doorstep of sleep sounded too small for pora. Judging by the clamour it made, I could only assume the animal was making off with our tins, taking the entire case that had acted as our trash bin even though we'd fastened the supposedly airtight lid atop it. From then on, the bone-deep cold kept me up. If not for that, it would have been the tossing and turning of my friends.

With the early morning light slicing in along the edge of the tarp where our little thief in the night must have weaseled in, the last dregs of sleep lifted from my mind. No one else, though. Just me. And I was at the bottom of the pile.

There was no getting out of this without waking everyone up, but for the first time all night, they slept peacefully. No tossing – Brett had apparently removed his elbow from Lin's side. No turning – Lin didn't even have her foot in Brett's face. And most amazingly, no snoring – looking at you, Kev.

Now, what kind of friend would I be to wilfully disturb their well-deserved rest, especially after the stacks upon stacks of racked up calamities that plagued us yesterday? Well, I would be the same person from yesterday, wouldn't I? If I was really going to take things seriously like Brett wanted, the first step was to let go of the gentleness currently anchoring me to the bottom of the dogpile. The longer I basked in this small luxury, the more daylight we wasted and the slower we would be to find Seth.

With a pre-emptive wince, I gulped back a big breath, and with it, blared, "Wakey, wakey!"

The little nook droned with lethargic groans and spiteful grumbling. Lin rolled away from me, folding her pillow over her head to cover both ears. Brett bolted upright in his bedroll only to then slump forward, rubbing the sleep from his eyes with hands that could very well have weighed tons for his sluggish movements.

This left all of Kev's weight on me, his head smacking the ground and his legs sliding off his brother. Kev moaned and threw a hand to his forehead, attempting to sit up in the same action by jabbing an elbow in my side. My hands flew out automatically, shoving him the rest of the way off me so he flopped onto the cushion of backpacks lining the wall with an undignified squawk.

"M'awake," he slurred, standing up on all our things and teetering back into the wall like a drunk. "What time's it?"

Brett peered out through the tarp he was already in the process of taking down. "Sunrise."

Lin managed a few more snoozing minutes as Brett, Kev and I groggily packed up our campsite – I was careful with my aches, most significantly my injured ankle, but the bandages beneath my boot did a fine job of compressing and dulling the pain. She might have stolen a couple more winks, but she sat suddenly straight in her sleeping bag, scrambling to readjust the round-rimmed goggles she'd slept in and making the rest of us jump as she whipped her head left and right.

"What?" Brett demanded, glancing furtively through the opening in the stone as if expecting to find someone lying in wait outside.

"Briar just-" she was saying, but before she could get the full thought out, a whistling of wings cutting through wind sounded from the sky, and someone *did* appear in the opening, albeit only for an instant. Brett leapt out of her way just in time as Briar twisted, pulling in her wings, and bulleted into the tight space, striking me with all the force of a speeding truck.

"Agh-!" The sound was punched from my chest as Briar – not quite the little critter she once was – knocked me right off my feet. I was only lucky to have Kev there to cushion my landing, but even so, the both of us went sailing into the back wall, only for him to trip over Lin, and for all of us to go tumbling atop her. Brett merely watched from the entrance, hiding his amusement with the barest hint of a smirk tugging at the corner of his mouth.

"*I searched through the night once I was made aware of your wildly irresponsible plan! It must be unadulterated madness that you acted such. Or had it slipped your mind, the dense curtain that it is, who hides behind? And dense, indeed! What folly has you ambling unconcerned to your demise?*'

"Nice to see you, too," I wheezed, yet to recover as Kev and Lin writhed beneath me, moaning and groaning their complaints.

"Who hides behind-?" Brett was asking, bringing me to duck my head between my shoulders with a wince, but Briar wasn't done chewing me out just yet. Honestly, I was glad to avoid the question.

"*The range at which I can contact your mind grows shorter. You're only fortunate I can trace the minds of your companions unobstructed. But asleep? That was the challenge.*"

"Well, great! So you can find Seth, too!" I cheered, but she waved her head left and right on her spindly neck.

"*If I could, I would have said as much. I've been long in the effort to no use. Either he's been unconscious this whole time or-*"

"There is no or. You'll just have to keep trying," I cut in harshly, and cleared my throat of the sudden seriousness to have overtaken my tone. "I would've gone back for you if there was time-"

"*Had you done so, you would not be here at all. But I've seen the river you manifested and the camps of pora all along its length, eager to cross. Word spread fast of your escape from the City of Gates, not just among your own. A league of those who once lay siege on your comrades' walls now bear down upon you. Once their magikiers catch up, they'll cross the river with ease.*" She bit back her anger, licking her scaly lips in dissatisfaction. "*It's unsafe to linger here, and yet more so to go back.*"

"So...?" I murmured, staring up at her where she had planted herself on my chest, less the manageable size of a cat but rather like a medium-sized dog. I'd been more observant of her swift growth since Lin first pointed it out to me and boy had she grown. At this rate, she'd be the size of a small house by the end of the month.

Caving, reluctance entered her tone as she announced, "*So I will be joining this ill-advised expedition.*"

"That's great!" I beamed, lifting her under her arms and placing her in coils on the floor. The more she grew, the shorter her torso appeared, increasingly lithe, athletic, subtle, in comparison to her legs, seeming like stilts now unlike the stubby little appendages they once were.

"*Is it? There are some foes beyond even me, and many I have not yet been tested against. When you strut so haphazardly into danger, remember those you drag along behind you. And on that topic, there is one other who accompanied me to find you, whom I saw fit to properly chastise your insolence.*"

Blanching, I gasped, "You didn't-"

"Anelisha!" the enraged voice of my sister called my attention to the open entrance, through which I found Faith marching to meet me.

"Oh! Fantastic timing, Faith! We were just talking about you!" I squeaked, while in my mind, I asked Briar, "*How'd you get her across the river?*"

"*By air and much toil.*"

Leaping to my feet to a chorus of grievances from Kev and Lin, I met Faith's furious approach with an overly cheerful, "Looks like the gang's all here, huh?"

"Do you even realize the uproar you caused?" she raved as she squeezed in through the opening in the rock, looking like she hadn't slept a wink with dark bags under her eyes and her ginger locks protruding from a tousled bun. Nodding her acknowledgement to Brett as she passed him, she strode right up to me, prodding my shoulder with an accusatory finger. "Losing not only Seth Knox, but the shonte? All in one night?"

"The alternative was to lose the wall, so..." I mused, weighing the options on my hands and giving a shrug. "And for what it's worth, Brigadier General Lyovin gave me permission to throw him under the bus. You know, he was the one who sent me out here."

"And you just took that at face value, did you?" Faith groaned, throwing her hands to her temples and pacing the narrow space of the nook. "Lyovin Alexeyich is facing severe punishment for his actions last night. General Griffith stepped up in Knox's absence and temporarily stripped the Brigadier General of his title. He's on trial before Knox's advisors for treason!"

Aiming my thoughts at Briar, I asked, "*And Dyval?*"

"*Feigns blissful ignorance. She's doing exactly as we anticipated; protecting your people to the detriment of your prospective lifespan.*"

"*Finally, some good news.*"

"*Is that what you'd call it?*"

Faith was still ranting. "How are you so sure Lyovin isn't one of Valencia's Liberation Front spies? Did you even stop to consider who to trust? *Anyone* from Blackano could be working for her. For all you know, this could be some elaborate scheme to get you killed!"

A heavy silence filled the overcrowded nook, her words hanging stale in the air. Kev and Lin met glances, still sprawled on the floor and hesitant to make any sudden movements while Faith fumed over them. Brett's expression had fallen into one of suspicion; I could practically see the gears turning behind his eyes as he racked his brain for any hint toward the Brigadier General's true character – or, I supposed, the *ex*-Brigadier General.

"I didn't think-" I was saying, voice meek in the shadow of her words, but Faith cut me off.

"I know, Annie. That's my point," she lamented, rubbing her temples with a jaded sigh. "You can't just go around trusting that everyone has your best interest at heart. Keep that up and you'll wind up dead." Just past her shoulder, I saw Brett give a slight nod, while to my rear, I heard Kev's sharp intake of breath between his teeth.

"You're not pulling any punches, huh?" I muttered, squeezing my fists tight at my sides. The air felt thin in this cramped space, like I was inhaling nothing and exhaling everything.

"My bark isn't as bad as a pora's bite," she noted, sounding somehow too loud for the nook. At her words, a flash of my old nightmare struck new terror in me, as fresh as if I was back in the grasp of that shadow-cloaked pora from the darkest corner of my subconscious.

"So much for sugar-coating it," Lin huffed, earning a snappish rejoinder from Faith which devolved quickly into a nook-wide bickering, but my attention escaped me as pain shot up my arms, originating from the inside of my elbow where I knew no injury to be.

"*Step outside,*" Briar advised in my jumbled mind.

Almost automatically, I vacated the nook, silencing all within as I stepped over Kev and Lin and brushed past Faith and Brett to escape the shrinking stone walls, entirely too small a space for five people and a dragon.

"Where are you going?" Faith demanded, but I stopped just outside where the air was clean and the tight knot in my chest could relax.

Rounding back on her, I met her gaze through the opening in the stone with a fire in mine. "I'm going forward. Look, Faith, I'm pretty sure we've passed a point of no return, and nothing you've said changes the fact we're out here to get Seth back. Whether the Brigadier General is on our side or not has no bearing on what I set out to do. And if it comes down to it, I'll do everything in my power to beat Valencia's champion." My eyes flicked to Brett. "Even if it means facing pora to get to him."

"But *how*, Annie?" Faith insisted.

I didn't quite have an answer to that question, but I stuck to my guns. "Contrary to popular belief, I'm not intent on getting myself killed! Disrupting Valencia's plans, and whatever that entails, is second *only* to rescuing Seth."

"And we'd be remiss to hold you back," Lin spoke up from the back of the nook, raising a thumbs-up for me to see, answered by Kev's, "Hear, hear!" Faith shot them a look, but sighed, dropping her hands at her sides.

"From where I'm standing, it looks like you're in just as much need of rescuing as Knox, but by all means, lead the way," she finally grouched, defeated and bitter about it. "It's not like we have any other options with that river at our backs."

"Like I said, point of no return," I grinned, transparently overcompensating, and earned a roll of her eyes.

Within a couple hours of travel – slowed to accommodate my injuries – we had already split into pairs at intervals of several feet. The two grumps, Brett and Faith, led the way and our very own definitely-not-morning-people, Kev and Lin, made up the rear, leaving me to trudge along between them. Briar had taken to the skies, scouting out our route and reporting back to the only minds she could reach, which was to say, everyone's but mine.

In the absence of my friends' company, I'd taken to humming a little ditty under my breath with rambling lyrics on loop in my mind. It went something like, "Everything hurts, everything hu-urts, but just a teensy-tinsy bit, so I don't mind-"

Our separation didn't stop the bugs of all shapes and sizes swarming us in these dense woods, biting through the bandages on my arms and buzzing in my ears – Lin would laugh every now and then behind me as Kev attracted all the bugs near them, flailing and thrashing loudly in the underbrush to thwart them off. From the front, Brett shushed Lin's laughter, only for her to continue in sarcastic mockery, duller in her staccato, "Ha ha ha..."

It wasn't exactly ideal – as a matter of fact, I could have gone without watching from the sidelines as my ex had a grand ol' time filling my much more socially competent sister in on all that she'd missed – but it was better than being stuck in the middle of non-stop arguments. After just one wakeful night, we'd been at each other's throats all morning. I hated to think what would become of us after a few more, and with Faith and Briar now sharing our limited food, water, and shelter supplies to boot.

It was encroaching on a red-sky evening before Brett slowed our pace just a hundred yards from the disused train tracks. There, we maintained our distance in the enshrouding treeline where we lay low, hidden among thorns and prickly underbrush as we limited our complaints to the occasional audible gasp and grumbled, "Ow!"

In our distraction with the threat of lurking pora and pesky pinpricks finding chinks in our armour, it was Faith up ahead who noticed a hunk of animal remains upon treading directly through it.

"Ugh, watch where you step," she groaned over her shoulder for the rest of us, plugging her nose against the stench of the shaggy lump now wafting up to meet her. Upon kicking off the sludge now caking her foot, the toe of her boot clanged off a hollow tin, making a small, metallic sound.

"Hold on a minute..." I murmured, and bounded ahead to halt the group, where I parted the grass for a better look. Kev and Lin ran up behind me, quiet with unease.

The animal was strange to me – reminding me of a large rodent even ripped apart and left an unspeakable mess, but looking to have had not four, but eight long, furry legs, each ending in wolf-like paws – but that wasn't what I was looking for. There beside it lay the tin case from last night, albeit now terribly beat up and emptied of our trash.

I froze. "Brett, I need you to tell me what happened here."

He quirked his head to the side wearing a dubious expression, but crouched down next to the poor, butchered animal and closed his eyes with the words, "Just give me a minute."

"What is that thing?" Kev asked, peering over my shoulder with a grimace on his face. "Some kind of... doggish spider? A scuttlepup!"

"We're not naming it that," Lin mused, seating herself on a raised tree root with her elbows propped up on her knees and a mace in her lap. The power and exhaustion in her eyes spelled a battle-ready mentality.

"Exactly. If you'd been paying attention in class, you'd know this is an Arillian greyback burrower," Faith noted, pointing out a tuft of sleek, grey fur on what must once have been the abdomen of this dubiously mammalian-arachnid hybrid.

"You're both clowns. It's obviously a wolf spider," I noted as I circled the area in search of footprints from whatever or whoever had ripped the animal apart, only to discover we'd flattened the vegetation with our own tracks, covering up anything that might have been there before. Heaving a sigh, I gave up my meagre tracking attempt. "Leave it to an alien planet governed by gene-splicing, near-omnipotent fascists to make wolves into eight-eyed arachnids complete with paw mandibles and too many leg joints. Wolf spider, I'm telling you."

"But those already exist," Kev ruminated, a hand on his chin, "And I hate them. Now scuttlepup-"

"Arillian greyback burrower-"

"We don't need the biology lesson," I teased, peering into the mangled tin case hidden in the brush. "Unless that can explain how it ended up dead after raiding our camp last night." A drop of red had dried onto the outside of the tin.

She blinked, a hint of alarm in the set of her brows. "Seems to me like you could do with one. These animals are highly venomous and can be territorial during their mating season-"

"Nice to have our walking encyclopedia back," Lin chuckled.

Clearing his throat, Kev announced, "If they're so dangerous, then for communication's sake, I just want everyone to know I'll be sticking with the indisputably superior terminology of scuttlepup. If I see one, that's what I'll be yelling."

"But that's not-" Faith cut herself off, folding her arms across her chest. "Sure. Call it whatever you like."

"Wolf spider," I declared, grinning mischievously as both Kev and Faith groaned their disapproval.

Before our bickering could go any further, Brett twitched out of his vision and opened his eyes. He shot to his feet, gaze sharp on the field just beyond the trees where distant train tracks cut through distant hills. The rest of us fell quiet, watching him for an explanation.

"Good instincts, Annie," he rasped, out of breath, "They must've sniffed out your blood when this thing opened the tin and ripped into your gloves. A gang of pora came from the tracks and guzzled what they could of your blood from the animal's guts." He stopped himself upon noticing my look of disgust at his description.

"No need to wax horrific about it," Lin mused, drawing herself up to a stand with a back stretch and a groan as she raised the hefty mace over her head. "So, what's our plan of action? Where'd they scamper off to?"

"We're not going after them," Faith stated as if it hardly needed mentioning.

Kev had an uneasy quality to his voice with his hesitant suggestion, "Better to deal with our problems than let them deal with us, though, isn't it?"

"See? Kev gets it," Lin mused.

"No, no, no. Don't lump me in with your bad ideas," he cautioned, waving his hands out in front of him, only to clap his hands together and glance toward Faith, granting, "But she has a point and I'm in complete agreement."

"How is going after them any different than hand-delivering them their favourite food? And anyway, I thought you scouts were supposed to be masters of *stealth*?"

"I, uh, I wasn't the best scout. Just an ace with an arrow, really," he smirked, earning Brett's chagrined nod from behind the hand covering his face.

"You still haven't told us which way they went," Lin added, poking Brett's side with an extended index finger. "They obviously know she's here if they were lapping up her blood. As long as we can't find them, they could find us, or worse, ambush us."

"Brett?" Faith tried, as if expecting him to side with her.

"Well," he reluctantly noted, "Some good news for once. We aren't alone out here."

"I think that's what we'd conventionally call *bad* news-" Kev was saying, but Brett continued.

"The pora weren't alone, either. There had to be ten, maybe twenty others with them. Not pora. Not kirranite. Whatever their association with these pora, they were in rough shape."

"Captives of the pora? Of the Liberation Front?" I leapt in. Faith made a dissenting noise, paired with a likewise expression on her face. "What were they doing out here?"

"They passed through carrying empty baskets and crates, but I'd say it's a safe bet whatever was originally in them was dropped off at the tracks."

"Could've been transporting resources quarried from the forest," Lin contemplated. "The kind the Liberation Front would need to hold Cerenthior since seizing it."

"From the snippets of conversation I could pick up, these prisoners were displaced from the City of Gates or some other town razed by pora. They headed off in that direction." He pointed due east, a perfect ninety-degree angle from the route we were meant to follow.

Ignoring the twinge in my ankle, I ducked my head between my shoulders and decided, "If these are prisoners of the Liberation Front, they're exactly what we're looking for."

"We're looking for Knox," Brett corrected me, "He wasn't there, Annie. Not with that group."

"But that teleporter couldn't have taken him directly to Cerenthior in one trip," I insisted, "They had to have stopped somewhere along the way, right?" And if we didn't have to go to Cerenthior, I wouldn't have to face Valencia's champion – at least, not yet. I could wait until I had a better grasp on my magic. Until I was ready…

"How far off-course would this prisoner camp be?" Faith considered, tapping a finger to her chin. "With our limited information, it's an even gamble chasing this thread could either benefit us or throw us off completely."

Brett shook his head. "The most I can do is track them step by step."

"Well what gear were they carrying?" Lin deliberated.

"Mm! Good point," Kev praised before asking of Brett, "A day's worth? More?"

"Not even a bedroll," Brett recalled, "All the prisoners had were the baskets in their arms."

"Which would imply they're less than a day's walk away. That's barely even a detour!" I beamed. Dragging myself up to a stand, I hesitated a moment from packing up and met the eyes of my friends, asking, "Objections?"

"Not a one," Kev colloquially mused, hopping down from the boulder. And so, we set out again, cutting our break short in favour of catching a head start on our detour.

"Think you can pick up their trail?" I decided, and Brett huffed his assenting sigh.

The trek was touch and go, requiring us to pause and wait for Brett's verdict every so often before we could continue. In our ample downtime, Faith kept herself busy refilling our water bottles and taking inventory of our remaining supplies now our numbers were so skewed – really just pulling all the provisional and logistical weight around here. Meanwhile, Briar flew circles overhead, hidden among the clouds as she kept watch for encroaching enemies. That made a grand total of three out of six active contributors, two of whom were late drop-ins. Not the best track record.

We stopped as the sky darkened to night and the brilliant ring drawn across the cosmos radiated a colourful hue. Another night, another makeshift den comprised of jaggedly cut rock and not a lot of living space. Briar kept watch from the trees as we slept.

Day 17

I EDGED OVER TO LIN DURING OUR FIFTH OR SIXTH STOP OF THE MORNing – I'd already lost count – facilitating Brett's time-consuming tracking technique. We had set up here as the sun approached the ring in the sky, soon to cast a vast shadow ushering in dew and frost across the land.

We'd claimed this fine clearing for our quick lunch break where we sat upon a bed of moss, speckled with the heads of flowers which poked through and blossomed, and where vines enshrined the boughs of encircling trees reaching high to the last few minutes of sunshine. Surprise, surprise, there was only more of that meaty goop to restore our strength, but at least this encouraged us to eat fast and rest longer while Brett took a reading of the area.

Lin had situated herself perfectly to catch the most rays before the sun disappeared behind the ring, finding the best spot this particular coppice had to offer, which had sunlight glaring off her lenses and completely obscuring her eyes.

With her scarf pulled up over her nose and her goggles blocking the rest of her face from view, I couldn't be sure if she'd already nodded off, but when I came close, she made a small noise like a chuckle.

"Is this how you creep up on people?" she teased, "You could do better. You do have size on your side."

Scowling, I huffed, "I'm not creeping up on you. I'm just..."

"Bored?" she supplied, the sound of a smile in her tone. "Or have you come to seek my counsel because you've started second guessing yourself?"

Rolling my eyes, I dropped down to the forest floor next to her. "You know me too well. And it's for that exact reason, you should know I'm not the one to be the one making these decisions. Of everyone here, I'm not-" Sitting up straight so the light no longer obscured her eyes, Lin turned a look on me and I bit my tongue. I plucked the grass at my feet, muttering, "Brett and Kev are the scouts, not me."

"Which is why they're off doing scout things," she said, throwing a hand outward to where Brett meditated, trance-like, and waving her other arm in gesture to wherever Kev had ended up. "Look, I've come to terms with the fact we're all probably going to die out here, but that doesn't mean we can't take a few bad guys with us-"

"That's not encouraging," I muttered.

"But backed by a heroic attitude," Kev chipped in, appearing on the other side of the rock so suddenly, Lin nearly fell off in her surprise. "I can commend that-"

She shoved at him, begrudging him for having scared her.

Briar shot through the hole in the forest's vast ceiling, bolting into the clearing where she caught the wind under her wings and landed next to me. So near, her words seeped into my mind for the first time today. "*I'm curious, will you repeat your mistakes and fail once again to properly dispose of your trash?*" By the reactions of my friends, either jumping in surprise or wincing their guilt, I assumed she'd included everyone in her *pleasant* conversation.

"It's not like I've got another set of blood-soaked gloves to lose track of," I chuckled weakly, smacking my lips to try to cleanse the salty aftertaste in my mouth.

She flicked her tail like a peeved cat and made a sound like a sigh. "*Unfortunately, I've been unable to trace the scents of those who drank of your waste, nor any who hide in this, the Khuloces Forest. Life is rampant here, and so too, magic. So old, so powerful, I cannot discern the grains of sand from the beach.*"

"The Khuloces Forest?" Faith hummed in contemplation.

"*One of the last Great Forests of Cellana where magic was born. What a shame that even this place has been tainted by your wars. Now, even the trees grow angry.*"

"Sounds ominous," Lin blithely chipped in as she rounded the circle we made, collecting our empty tins in a bag. Tying off the end, she held the bag out to Briar, such that Briar arched her back and edged away, eyeing it suspiciously. "Would you mind tossing this somewhere far enough away to throw any pora off our trail?"

"*Ah yes, because one trash planet is not enough,*" she grumbled, but took the bag in her claws and swept off into the darkening sky, soaring amid the scintillating, multicoloured shine off the edge of the ring where the sun had begun its eclipse.

"Hey, don't pollution-shame me. This is a valid strategy!" Lin called after her and plopped back down in the moss, leaning back with her hands behind her head and her ankles crossed. "Damnit, now she's got me thinking about eco-footprints on an alien planet…" she grumbled.

When Brett roused from his trance, he pointed out a hidden trap set by the pora. Lin recognized the kind of trap once he pointed it out, and she was able to deactivate it. His body trembled with overexertion as his magic ran thin, but he made sure to check every new area diligently. Upon finding more traps – four more, to be specific – he set his jaw, nodded, and steeled his nerves to continue this mental workout.

There was no more resting her eyes for Lin as she worked closely with Brett to dismantle the traps in our way. They squabbled all the same, doubling the time it took them to get anything done. It wasn't until the sun hovered low in the sky, just above the horizon, that we found our destination – and only because Brett knew where to find the secret entrance.

The forest wasn't quite so dense in these parts, instead deepening such that it reminded me of the ocean floor, pitched into darkness beneath leagues of waves – in our case, leagues of rattling branches and leaves, filtering green-hued remnants of the day's withering light to the moss and fungus at our feet. The trees must have reached a couple hundred feet high and were at least ten arms' lengths around, stretching their boughs horizontal to the forest floor in a perfect ceiling.

Unlike the ones back by the City of Gates, these trees had bark like elephant skin; grey, wrinkly, dry, and surprisingly spongy, with a feel like an eraser to the touch. Their roots spiralled out from the trees' base, moss-coated or sunken in the forest floor, as thick streaks of yellowish-grey.

Brett stopped us not far from a sheer cliff face buried among the trees, pointing out one particular tree growing out of the rock. The tree itself was wider than most and covered the forest floor with colossal roots thicker than any of us were tall in a half-circle out from the high natural wall. Blending among these gnarled serpents of wood and moss – the largest of which could have been carved into great ships – was the wooden entrance to a hidden tunnel, or so Brett's visions had shown him.

"This entrance is watched by a couple of Liberation Front vhy'ries, a tree-shaper and a stone-crafter, on the other side," he remarked, "I know the knock pattern but-"

"We can't just waltz in through the front door!" Kev squeaked, half-hidden behind his brother no matter that we'd stopped a safe distance away.

"Yeah, that," Brett blandly noted, "Any ideas?"

"Briar, could you scout around and map an overhead layout for us? The Khuloces Base can't be entirely underground," Faith called upwards, toward the boughs overhead. Somehow, I understood she only spoke aloud for my sake.

As expected, I didn't hear a peep from Briar, but I caught a glimpse of her golden scales as she soared skyward in a high spiral around the trunk of the colossal tree. I could only assume the others received some form of response from her by the subtle signs of their body language.

After a moment, Faith continued for the rest of us, "In the meantime, we should set up camp somewhere we won't be noticed."

"Finally," Lin groaned, "I'm starved."

I was content to comply without voicing my feelings – that they sent Briar away, that they could hear her when I couldn't – as I simply trailed along after our de facto leader, Faith. By nightfall, Brett located a deep crevice one of the prisoners had mined out of the cliff face, seldom traveled by their captors, and from deep within it, Lin carved a den branching off from one side.

I sat beside Kev as they did, careful to remain hidden from view as the moon-washed night dipped the world in shades of grey. These neutral tints illuminated their work with dancing rays of pale light passing between the wide, fanning foliage high up above, rustling uproariously in the nighttime gales.

Every now and then, a fresh gust of bitter winds would funnel at high speeds between the trees, blasting us so emphatically it had our jackets snapping and my hair flapping every which way. The cold sliced through each layer of my outfit like I had nothing on at all, and the force of the winds themselves seemed enough to knock me right off my tired feet.

A day and a half of walking with these injuries had drained me more than I'd realized.

14

Fireside Talks Hit Hardest

Day 18

When I finally slipped into the realm of dreams, it seemed my mind had resorted to a different kind of torture. The torture of nostalgia, of memory, of softness and security. There was no death, no pora in this dream. Only the pain of a past made untouchable by the present.

The bed was plush, the duvet warm and wrapped around me, only up to my waist. I knew I was back in my room in Blackano even before my eyes fluttered open. A soft haze crowned the edges of my sleepy vision, fraying the edges of this sleep-induced memory.

A mix of signals merged and blended in the room, depicting the time Lin had spent here as my roommate in her vast assortment of clothes and the neatness of the closet, interspersed with little details, like red cups forgotten and tipped over in the corner of the room, bottles lining the top shelves of our desks, and an unmade bed, marking Valencia's time as my roommate. In the realm of the dream, it made sense.

Neither of my temporary roommates were there, but my bed was full.

Dream-Brett snoozed on his side, curled around me with his legs hooked around mine and his head on my shoulder so his fluffy bedhead tickled my neck. Like this, he avoided the light of the morning sun which would glare into his eyes from the window. It was his favourite thing to complain about, but he always volunteered himself to take that side of the bed. The dummy.

It was then I noticed he was wearing his blue and white plaid shirt. I'd only ever seen him wear it once. He bought it the day before at my suggestion and I'd promptly spilled coffee down its front the next morning, ruining it.

I supposed, in the context of the dream, that meant this was the morning I would lean down to meet his lips as he sat eating cereal on the couch in the common room, eager for a kiss, and dump my boiling hot mug over him in my distraction.

Smiling into his hair, I hiked up the duvet to my chin, surrounding myself with warmth, and inadvertently covering him up to his nose.

"Too warm," he moaned, his voice muffled against my shoulder. I patted the side of his face, running my thumb over his cheek. Groaning, he turned his head toward my touch and pressed a kiss to my palm, sending a tingle up my arm. "Too warm," he repeated.

"You can always take off your shirt." My directness surprised him; I was never one to ask for strip shows. Maybe it was because some distant, half-awake part of me knew I would soon be the end of this cute, plaid shirt of his.

He quirked an eyebrow at me, inviting me to watch as he drew himself up in bed. The duvet pooled around his waist as he donned a roguish expression and began slowly undoing the buttons, teasing each one open with a new, more ridiculous model pout, all the way down to his navel. With a hint of dramatic flair, of which he seldom indulged, he ripped open his shirt and slid it off his body before rejoining me under the duvet, wrapping his arms around me as he did.

"Better?" I asked around my laughter, catching the side of his face in my palm as I stroked my thumb over his mouth. "Or did that just make you hotter?"

"You tell me," he grinned, and I kissed him in reply. In these soft, private moments, he had a tendency to smile more than my heart was ever prepared for, each one kinder, gentler, fonder than the last.

If our cocoon was warm before, it was now a furnace. Dream-Brett's torso blazed with heat, burning against me through my clothes. Wriggling in his embrace, I got a good grip of my sweatshirt – okay, *his* sweatshirt which I'd been using as a nightgown the past few nights – and pulled it up over my head.

He gave me room to shrug it off, propping himself up on his elbows with his arms caged around me. I didn't put on a show the way he had, simply trying my best not to hit him in the face with all my struggles to undress.

The oversized sweatshirt hit the floor with a soft thud, the only sound in the room, maybe even the whole world. I was hesitant to look up at him, aware that he was taking me in but thinking only of the opinions sheathed behind his eyes. He didn't let me dwell in my apprehension, brushing his finger under my jaw to urge our eyes to meet. Finally, I peered up under my eyelashes, feeling my face burn with blush.

Dream-Brett gazed back at me, lust making his eyes blaze green.

That same half-awake part of me knew what was supposed to happen next, for it had already happened. He had kissed every inch of me, murmuring into my skin that he loved me. All of me. And I had operated on instinct as wave after wave of blinding hot desire crashed over me, spinning me in a maelstrom of heat and love. The world beyond his touch faded to nothing, unimportant, and I didn't care if I ever resurfaced. The only thing that truly mattered to me was with me.

The maelstrom eventually calmed into a heady peace, and when it did, his eyes were the colour of a beautiful sea, clear and bright.

But not this time.

Instead, as I gazed up at him, the pinprick pupils in his eyes began to bleed. His irises filled with it. Red. Absolute red, swimming at the edges. The room darkened around us, morphing away from the comfort of my old Blackano dorm room. The bed disappeared under me, instantly stripping away to white tile floors, belonging to the delinquent center where my world first ended. The rest of the dorm room expanded outward into the keep's basement with a too-high ceiling and seemingly limitless space, all of it shrouded in deepest shadow. The heat cut suddenly out, and I noticed the duvet had disappeared, having slipped off his back when his arms made a cage around me. Snow blew in from the open window – what open window? – and lightly dusted the top of his hair.

A globule of the impossible blood gathered at the edge of his right iris, accumulating mass as it escaped the surface of his eye. It splashed onto my cheek, burning so hot, I heard my skin sizzle at its touch. But I was frozen – no, I was stuck. Stuck on something, wedged up under my ribcage. A downward glance showed me the sharp edge of a broken rebar jutting out from my naked torso, my flesh frayed and stretched by its protrusion. I wanted dearly to scream, but all that came out were the gurgles of blood sloshing in my lungs.

My wide eyes searched the empty space around us and finally landed once more on the red pools of his eyes hovering over me, pleading mercy to equal silence. All he did was smile, the uncannily wicked expression curling high in the corners of his mouth. The man above me was unrecognizable, but he was at once unmistakeably Brett.

And he had his hands closed around my throat.

Murderer...

The unnervingly familiar voice whispered through my mind, resonating off the claustrophobic darkness until there was nothing but that word. Meeting this all-encompassing voice, a clear laugh rang out from above me, breeching the pounding of blood in my ears – unlike the whisper, this laughter felt grounded in the reality of the dream. It chimed prettily just outside the darkness still sneering that accursed word.

You love a murderer and yet condemn me, though I am powerless.

The darkness shifted as the piercing laughter grew louder, until it wasn't mere shadow that surrounded us, but pitch-black hair. *Her* hair. A simple turn of her head revealed her pale face from the void of raven-black locks which had blended so seamlessly with the abyssal nothing all around. She pulled away from where she had been leaning into Brett's ear, camouflaged amid the darkness, to reveal the ghostly vision of Val Darling – not the crimson-haired archangel, Valencia Lupei, who had never been anything but evil in my eyes. This ghost of an old friend looked just as I remembered; that confident smirk quirking up the corner of her mouth as her lips dripped poison into his ear.

As she turned to face me, the first voice cut suddenly short, its surround-sound echo of hissing whispers finally running out, but in the same instant, Brett's grip tightened, vise-like around my neck until all I could retch from my windpipe was blood. There was no air. Not in my lungs. Not in this room. Not anywhere. Only thick, bushy darkness and viscous red.

"Good," Val Darling whispered into his ear, but I could hear her clear as day, "Just like that-"

I jerked awake, my eyes flashing open to the real world as my heart raced in my chest. For all the discomfort in my joints and the exhaustion in my muscles, I might as well have forgone sleep entirely.

It was like a crust of sand had grown under my eyelids while I slept, and no amount of rubbing them cured this dry sensation. Shivers wracked my benumbed body, slick with a layer of cold sweat. And all the same, the last dregs of my nightmares stayed with me, like a lurking presence hidden among the shadows all surrounding me.

For a moment, I couldn't remember where I was or how I'd gotten to the bottom of this pitch-black pit, finding only a disturbing similarity between this darkness and the darkness of my dream. My own shaky breaths were the only tangible sensation in my vicinity, heaving with the effort of escaping the tendrils of dread still enshrouding my mind. A nightmare, I told myself. It was just a nightmare.

Oh, how I wished Briar had easy access to my mind again, if only to ask her what the hell was going on with my subconscious to dream up something like that.

I shoved the memory of it from my mind, focusing on what was real and around me. The blanket – yes, there was a blanket – had abandoned me in sleep, probably stolen away by Faith as she was prone to do.

The cloud of sleep eventually cleared from behind my eyes. Even so, I had to work to calm my breathing and to stifle the shivering that had taken root in me as the sweat cooled on my skin, inviting the night's deep chill. Cold, too cold.

A fire would have been nice.

With nothing but a passing thought, a fleeting whim, I beckoned warmth to my numbed hands. A bright flicker of light sprouted between my palms, warm not just in colour, which leapt to the dry leaves and twigs at the back of the rock den. The wisp of flame burgeoned with brightness cutting through my otherwise pitch-black surroundings, illuminating the sleeping faces of my friends around me.

I could only stare at it.

This fire, so small and yet so powerful, had sprung from me without any hassle at all. No pain in my palms, no blood on my hands – no fresh blood, anyway. It was like the times I'd managed to sense the earth and feel it as if it were part of me, but this had come to me naturally, without prompting.

If Brett or Faith or even Lin woke up to see it, they wouldn't believe it. At least, they wouldn't believe I'd conjured it without attracting the attention of all those pora hidden away in the Khuloces Base.

Carefully, I cupped my hands around the small, dancing flame and with it, slipped out of the small den. I tiptoed deeper into the tunnel beyond our little nook, the firelight glowing dimly in my palms, barely illuminating more than a foot ahead of me, but its warmth enfolded me.

Under the splash of soft, rippling oranges and yellows, the deep crack in the cliff face seemed rather a mosaic of warm colours. I plopped down on the ground, away from everything in the depths of the crevice, and lay the little fire on the soil in front of me. This little fire I had made with pure thought. But how?

Tiny embers crawled up in front of my eyes as the twigs burned into ash and charcoal. Gathering more fuel for the fire so it would grow, I wracked my brain for an explanation as to how I'd managed to make it in the first place – to use my magic so effortlessly. For the life of me, I had no answers. Instead, all I could do was let it warm my hands and feet and allow its light to chase away my nightmares.

I shook my head, rubbing my hands together over the glowing hot coals, and sat by the edge of the fire now brimming with glowing hot embers. Fond reminiscences of better days, sloshing drinks, and friend-filled nights washed over me, taking me back to a distant bonfire in my memory where I had lounged merrily between Val and Brett as we passed a bottle between ourselves. How strange a thought, following the terrors of my dream.

I shook out the memory, tainted now as all things were, and had to remind myself those were oblivious days, with drinks pushed into my hands, and enemies sporting masks in the likeness of friendship.

Letting the warmth and smells of my surroundings erode away the memory, I purged my mind of this undue fondness – which had come with the thought I could go really for a drink right about now. Here, hidden in the walls outside the Khuloces Base where the Liberation Front hid their prisoners of war, tears stung my eyes.

How did it come to this?

The earthy scent of this crevice in the cliff face mixed pleasantly with the smoky musk of the fire, clearing the last vestiges of sleep from my mind, only to be replaced with the weight of melancholy.

If only I had the choice, I would fold from this game of tricks and deceit. A sigh escaped my lips. If only. But Valencia had already set the rules for her cruel game, and there seemed no way of escaping it now.

She had sowed treachery among us magikiers and managed to break our kinship, to turn us against each other no matter that her real targets were the centions, and her pieces had moved expertly into position. Pieces whisked away from her opposition, so easily coerced in the face of the centions' negligence and ignorance – their utmost failure to see magikiers as sentient agents. And here we all were, caught in the middle of an ancient dispute.

After all, it was that very conduct which had stoked the domenths' initial rebellion.

The lives lost in Blackano would never be recovered, and Valencia's provocation of this conflict was the cause, the corruption… but I couldn't help thinking, here in the warmth and solitude of this crevice, that the

Liberation Front's demand for liberty and dignity even over life and security had a place on the centions' battlefield. The Liberation Front had only gained traction because of the rot in the centions' fascistic government. Most notably in the case that our unquestioned sovereigns refused to treat us, their pawns, their playthings, as anything but.

What did I know, really, of the centions' countless transgressions? Nothing. They had no reason to inform us, and everything taught to us was composed by centions. Briar had helped me to see that, but other new magikiers would never know the lies and omissions in their learning.

While I had Briar to keep my eyes open, the Liberation Front had Valencia, who not only opened her followers' eyes, but closed their fists, and bared their teeth.

At its core, the Liberation Front was a push for change.

The murder of my most timid roommate and the disappearance of my most outspoken, the slaughter of the Inspector's entire team, the razing of Blackano... I wondered, would Valencia's bloody uprising be celebrated over the bones of the terrified and naïve in years to come?

If she had meant to do it right, she wouldn't have done it like this. I had to believe as much... and yet, she'd spoken of opportunists and anarchists meddling in her plans. Had they done so to such a degree that she'd lost complete control by the end? I shuddered to think, if not for them, her rebellion might have been peaceful. She'd certainly tried to make it so, or else she wouldn't have taken her time trying to sway *all* of Blackano to her side. She had almost succeeded, too, until the arsonists got their hands on a matchbox or twenty.

If they hadn't started rioting and setting fires and using dirty scare tactics, magikiers might not have been fighting magikiers that day. Not unless the centions pulled in loyal reinforcements from Cellana to stifle the rebellion – and if that had happened, I couldn't even begin to imagine just how many lives would have been lost. It would have been an all-out war.

Instead, Dyval relinquished Blackano to the Liberation Front that day, and those of us who sided with the centions had been driven out. That the secluded little country fell into Valencia's open hands, cut off from the world of magic under the centions' rule. I wondered if it would become a forgotten landmark of the past, ephemeral in the minds and memories of those of us who escaped. In saving us from Valencia's rebellion, Dyval had once again turned her back without confronting the problems in the society she was meant to govern.

Fact of the matter was, when Valencia had the chance to speak with Dyval, she chose to fight her instead.

Now, Dyval safeguarded the City of Gates as a means of appeasing me, but I couldn't say how long that would last – or if she would only do so as long as I held my new power, a constant, unspoken threat on the conditions that I support the centions and oppose the Lupei sisters.

I hazarded a glance over my shoulder, half-expecting to find a cention eavesdropping on my mind, but the only judgement I found came from within.

You don't want the dead to have lost their lives in vain... or the centions' civility to be fleeting... How can you not see that you and your enemies are one and the same?

The accusatory words felt foreign in my head, an intrusion wrought by something just out of sight, although the voice certainly sounded like mine. A hint of memory took me back to just over two weeks ago when the word "shonte" had entered my head upon activation of my untrained magic, as a result manipulating the powers of the centions to imbue me with such power. At the time, I thought little of it. It had sounded like my own inner voice, but thinking back to it now...

Before I had a chance to truly register the writhing, shadowy tendrils slithering through my mind, nor the wicked chuckle echoing in their wake, drawing up images of Evelyn just as I had seen her in my dream, a monster on whose wings our body would ride into the apocalypse, something soft and warm fell over my shoulders.

I jumped in surprise, grabbing for whatever it was, only to find a blanket had been draped over me. In my perplexed hesitation, I nearly leapt out of my skin when Brett plopped down next to me. He glanced sideways at me, raising his eyebrows, and grabbed a stray stick to stoke the fire.

"What are you doing up?" His voice was sleepy, his eyes dark and heavy. In this lighting, I almost couldn't make out the colour in them.

"I couldn't sleep." The idea crossed my mind that Evelyn might have illustrated the very nightmares that kept me from a good night's rest, but I shoved it aside, afraid of what might happen if I gave it too much thought. Snuggling into the blanket, I held my hands over the fiery embers, but it was no longer the cold that had me shivering.

"You shouldn't go off on your own. We *are* camped out right next to an enemy base."

"Yeah," I murmured around a yawn, letting him distract me from the turmoil in my head. "I'm sorry if I woke you."

"You didn't," he interrupted without looking my way, his eyes fixed on the small burst of flames he'd managed to coax out of the coals. I wondered if he knew how I made the fire. "But you should've woken me up, anyway. Not just me, any of us. We're here to protect you, but you make it so difficult."

"You need your sleep-"

"And you don't?" He heaved a heavy sigh. "The rest of us aren't here to dismantle a guerrilla faction or even to rescue Knox. We're here to protect you so *you* can do those very unlikely things. It'd just make our job a hell of a lot easier if you weren't always stumbling over your own feet with exhaustion."

"Mhm, because that's my biggest problem," I teased.

"It sure is one of 'em." Drained of energy, he heaved a sigh, rubbed the meat of his palms over his tired eyes, and ran his fingers up through his hair. "You know, you're doing that thing again."

I quirked my head to one side, raising an eyebrow. "What thing?"

"Oh, you know." He wore a flippant tone of voice, but I could tell he was mocking me. "When you pretend nothing's wrong, even though nothing's right?"

Another flash of memory, illustrating Evelyn in all her terrible glory, struck my mind's eye. My curious expression fell into a scowling pout, obstinate. "I have no idea what you're talking about." Shooting him a smile he promptly missed in his refusal to look at me, I teased, "Besides, one thing is going right. You came to check up on me."

"That's not right *or* wrong. Just natural." He said it so offhandedly, like correcting a math mistake, I almost didn't register the significance behind it. But the next moment, he lost his Brett-smile, which was to say, not a smile at all, but a general sense of contentment sheathed behind his eyes. Even from this angle, catching only a sliver of his profile, I read this barest shift in his expression like I was fluent in him. "Annie, I want you to be honest with me." He hesitated, letting a long pause stretch between us. "Are you afraid of me? Because of what I've done?" He had emptied his voice of all emotion, almost too soft to make out over the dying crackles of the fire, but there was a different kind of power behind it, such that took my breath away.

Memory of my dream rushed back to me, and that voice, that word. Murderer. I fumbled to ask, "Why would I-?"

"I heard you mumbling in your sleep," he said, like I should have expected it. "But I should've known. You saw what I did to that woman outside the keep, the one who took Kev's magic away, and to the teleporting magikier at the bastion. You know what I do with the scouts."

I jolted in surprise. At least on the topic of the scouts, I'd assumed they merely scouted as per the name, but I supposed I had seen blood on their uniforms. I held my tongue, unsure what might come out if I opened my mouth.

"I've ended lives," he stated, ice cold in the heavy silence, "What do you think of that?"

I tripped over my words. "It was self-defense. Or… or you had to, to defend others. Like when you saved Kev." But a buzzing fog had rolled in, clouding my mind. I never thought I would hear him say it so candidly. To speak of the blood which dripped from his hands, invisible to the eye but nevertheless there, having gushed from the throats of nameless enemies. Ever present.

He held deathly quiet. Out of the corner of my eye, I noticed the tremble in his hands, clasped tightly around each other. "What about duty?" he finally said.

"What *about* duty?" I asked, echoes of Valencia's spiels racing through my mind and mixing with all I'd been taught of the centions' wars. Duty to whom? Was it Levi's duty to betray Seth, or Valencia's to torment me? Was it the centions' duty to slaughter dragonkind and bind Briar to the form of an inanimate hunk of metal for centuries, conscious and helpless? Was it the duty of the centions, of the domenths, of the powerful, to subjugate the weak? Was it everyone's duty to destroy and injure and kill under empty promises of obligation and order? The justification couldn't possibly outweigh the cost. More than that, I couldn't find the reason behind any of it, nor did I want to. And maybe that was why…

"War isn't as simple as self-defense, is it?" He shut his eyes, heaving a breath, and pressed his white-knuckled hands as if he held his entire moral code in his unyielding grip. "And that's what this is. You've been given a mission. Because of your strategic value, you now have a duty to stop Valencia's champion before he leads her Cellana Corps to destroy everything the centions built for us, and you'll have a dilemma to face when others get in your way. Kill or let live. But *can* you kill?"

"Hey now, that's-" He shook his head against my irreverent tone, tripping me up, but I continued in a hiss, "That's a bit reductive for the weight of the situation, isn't it?"

"You can't win a war by asking nicely. There are people out there who'll never listen. Who've already accepted that they might have to die for their cause and see killing you as their best bet to survive. They're relentless, they'll refuse to stop until you're forced to stop them. And if you don't, your mercy becomes their cruelty."

My heart dropped to the deepest pits of my stomach as I floundered for the words to dispute his stance, for there were none. There was only the surge of emotions awash over the beaches of my mind.

"Valencia has her champion, but everyone's a threat. You'll see what I mean when you face them tomorrow." He met my gaze, maintaining a hard fortitude in the shadow of his eyes, so much so, it was like staring directly into the sun. I glanced down at my hands over my chest, clutching the hem of the blanket to keep it wrapped tight around me. "So, can you?"

My mouth hung open, at a loss for words.

"That's what I thought. The way you looked at me that day, I knew you hated me. I couldn't stand to look you in the eyes."

"I could never hate you," I corrected him, the words escaping me with the ease and automation of breathing. Still, I fixed my stare on the dying embers.

"The way you looked at me… I knew you'd never taken a life, not even the day Blackano fell, not even when Valencia had everyone at her disposal hunting you like an animal. A lot of people got blood on their hands that day, not just the Liberation Front."

"You…?" I glanced up again, but he'd turned his face away from me, hiding his expression.

"The woman outside the keep wasn't my first. What they did to Dahlia… I was *so angry*." His voice wobbled. "I'd never felt so helpless, so alone. I don't even remember how it happened, like I blacked out, but I went after them. I knew what I was doing, what I'd done. I'd do it again."

"Brett," I pleaded, although I wasn't sure what I was pleading of him. Reaching out to his hands, I let the blanket he'd draped over me fall from my shoulders. The fluttering movement drew his glance, and my hands froze far from his. Tears glinted in his eyes, burning with the light of the fire.

"I felt nothing," he whispered, shaking his head. "Every time, I feel nothing."

"That's not true," I hissed, fury glinting behind my eyes as if his words were an assault against me. "I saw your face outside the keep. You were in anguish."

He made a strange sound, like laughter, but it was too dry, too cynical, full of something bitter. "I was afraid of what you'd think of me. Nothing else."

"I don't know why you're lying." Although my voice shook with emotion, it was anger that coiled in my chest. I reached more fervently for his hands, but he pulled away. That didn't stop me frowning intensely into his face.

He met my expression with a pained half-smirk, a forced expression to stifle the dark chuckle I could practically hear in the air between us. "So, you only take *everything* at face value when it's what you'd rather hear?"

"I was there! I know what I saw, and I know that you're lying – or, or at least *exaggerating.*"

"Yeah, you were there. The woman was no longer a threat, but you saw what I did to her. You, Anelisha Knight, who only ever tries to save people, never to hurt them." Although his voice was mocking, there was a twinge of remorse, of sadness in his tone. I was certain of it. "*I* knew what you thought of me."

"Well sure, I thought you panicked. That you reacted on instinct. That you were protecting Kev!"

"And I killed her." I flinched at his words, recoiling back from him. Goosebumps raised on my arms. "Would you have done the same? Would it even enter your mind?"

"I would have saved Kev," I whispered, but a different memory arose from the dark waters of my mind, reawakened only weeks ago when Evelyn attacked my subconscious. A distant memory of a knife in my hand and the neighbourhood kids sprinting wildly to get away from me. I'd failed to protect the family dog from them, but what had followed was truly monstrous. *I* was monstrous.

"That much is a given," Brett softly mused, unaware of the darkness behind my eyes, "You would have gotten him out of there. You would have defended him, maybe even incapacitated her, but you wouldn't have done what I did. Maybe, if I hadn't been there, she would've been captured. Maybe, once we had her, we could've forced her to undo what she did to Kev. Or maybe she would've worked her carmavi magic on you. Whatever would've happened didn't, because I ended the situation in a way I don't think you could have." He leaned back on his hands, rolling his eyes, but it seemed a ploy to rid himself of his tears. "So what are you doing out here? Our enemies won't stop until we're dead or they are, but you can't take a life. Are you going to make the rest of us do it for you?"

Aghast, I shook my head vehemently. "I would never do that to you-"

He shot me a scathing look, and I bit my tongue. Each of them had come along as my close protection; my safety was their top priority, their *only* priority. If I ran headlong into danger while limiting how far I would go to defend myself – if my enemies saw weakness in me, reluctance to act, and took advantage of that – then wasn't I asking exactly that of my friends? To kill for me…

"I didn't sign up for this mission because I thought you could do it," he muttered.

"Ouch." I attempted a lighter tone to stifle the heavy atmosphere weighing down upon us, but my voice wobbled, and it came out more pathetic than anything else. "Then why?" I kicked myself for asking.

He raised his shoulders in a shrug, distancing himself behind his eyes. "I'm here to pick up where you falter."

"Here I thought I had your vote of confidence," I huffed, only half-sarcastic. His silence blew the rest of my sarcasm out like a candle. "From the moment you heard the plan, you thought I was the wrong choice…"

"Of course I did. Annie, this mission, this life, it isn't you."

"But you never wanted any of this either! Why am *I* the failure for keeping my conscience?" I burst, earning his withering glare.

"That was the first thing I had to kill."

"Okay there, Edgelord, saying the first morbid thing to come to mind doesn't make you cool."

He groaned, slumping back and raising his face to the stars. "And here *I* thought we were having a serious conversation."

"We are!" I snapped, my voice cracking like a whip. Silence bloomed in the shadow of my outburst. A smooth, low feeling crept up in me, polishing out the rough edges of mischief and teasing until there was only sombre memory. The silence between us grew, until finally, I couldn't keep the images coursing through my mind contained any longer. I began slow, reluctant, but honest. "You know, when I was little, the neighbourhood kids thought it would be fun to ride my dog like a horse." He glanced sidelong at me, unsure where this had come from, but I continued, "They were the same kids who'd bullied me and stepped on me for years, and I let them do that. To me. But when they hurt her… when I saw her collapse under one of the bigger boys through the kitchen window, and it looked like she just… broke, it was like something in me snapped, too. Before I knew it, I had a knife in my hand…"

He furrowed his brows, drawing a crease over the bridge of his nose, and although I could see the questions piling up behind his eyes, he let me continue at my own pace.

"By the time I got outside, they were already running away. They knew what they'd done, but they were scared. It took me a long time afterwards to realize they never meant to hurt her. But in the moment, all I knew was they'd broken her back. She wasn't even whimpering; she was so still… so I threw the knife at the biggest kid. It… it hit with such a horrible sound. Wedged deep in his shoulder. His parents took him for stitches and his family moved away later that year, but when the kid hit the grass, I felt every organ in my body drop to my feet. He was crying, snot running down his chin and he was *terrified* of me, paralyzed by fear – I thought I really had paralyzed him – and screaming bloody murder. In an instant, I was next to him, pulling the knife out of his shoulder to try to fix what I'd done, and I could hear myself apologizing. Again and again. His blood was everywhere, I'd never felt so disgusting…"

Brett's mouth was a thin line, his eyes turned downward. I doubted he knew what to say, but I couldn't stop myself going on.

"He shoved me away and ran off into the woods after the others, and all I could do was sit there, for so long, staring at his blood on the knife. At the pain I'd caused, but Pepper was still dead. Hurting that boy hadn't changed anything; I'd only made things worse and I knew it. I *felt* it, like I'd been doused in grease and oil that couldn't be washed out. All the kids in the neighbourhood hated me, or maybe they were just afraid of me. I started living life out of the corner of my eye. Keeping my head low, because if I didn't, I'd hear what they all said about me. I didn't need their words to *feel* like a monster. Eventually, even their parents turned against my mom…"

Brett opened his mouth as if to speak but stopped himself. I could see that he wanted to turn this around, to reassure me somehow, but he didn't have the words.

"When I finally went back inside that night, there she was. Mom. She looked at me like I'd become the thing I felt like I was. I couldn't let go of the knife even when she told me to." Holding out my hand, I gestured to the faint, white line of the scar under my thumb. "She had to wrestle it out of my hand… I don't want to do that again, Brett. No one can make me that angry little monster."

He was quiet for a long moment, turning the words over on his tongue, until finally, he said in a flat voice, "These aren't kids we're dealing with, and this isn't some suburban neighbourhood where the only things you have to worry about are judgement and gossip."

I shook my head. "I never cared that the other kids wanted nothing to do with me. I was fine on my own. The thing that stuck with me, that I can still feel to this day, was that disgust. Disgust at myself. Hurting others is the lowest thing a person can do. Nothing's gained from it – it just makes everything worse, for everyone. But if I can help people… help them change for the better–"

"These are pora we're talking about, Annie. They won't change."

Tearfully meeting his eyes, I breathed, "How do you know that? The only way to bring more good into the world is to give them that chance. To learn and grow and choose a peaceful life."

"That's dangerously naïve." His voice swept a chill through my bones, but the tears poured hotly down my chin, hotter than the hum of warmth dancing across my face from the simmering coals of roasted underbrush. Brett startled at the sight of wetness streaking my cheeks, cutting through the grime of our travels, but he balled his hands so his knuckles pressed the cold stone of the ground and held his glacial gaze. "If you can't do what you set out to, then there's no point trying. Call it off."

He let these words hang in the air between us, weighing down upon me like sandbags over my shoulders.

"How can you say that?" I whispered, fighting the pathetic wobble in my voice. My head shook left and right, seemingly of its own volition. "I can't just– I'm not going back without Seth. It's *my* fault the City of Gates lost its commander. If I can't even save *one* person…" Something changed in his eyes, bringing me to trail off.

"You'd fight the whole world for him."

"What?" I sniffled, wet and nasally with emotion.

"I think, for the first time since I met you, I'm starting to understand you."

Clearing some of the thickness from my throat, I demanded, "What's there to understand?"

"Why you throw yourself in the middle of an unfair fight like your body's a shield. Why you get into shouting matches with anyone who talks down to your friends. You give and give and give, and don't care that it's self-destructive, but the rest of us don't work that way. You think it's all you can do to be a good person–"

My eyes narrowed on his. "You're wrong, and possibly projecting. I don't have to throw myself into a fight to feel good about myself."

"Could've fooled me."

"It's not about fighting! If *helping* each other was everyone's baseline, we wouldn't be in this mess!"

He rolled his eyes. "That's a nice sentiment, but we *are* in this mess. Personal philosophies won't change the reality. If you're killed trying to rescue Knox, everything he did to protect you will be in vain. The one person who's even half as destructively selfless as you are will have suffered for nothing. He let that Liberation Front snake capture him so she wouldn't get to you-"

"You think I don't know it's my fault-?"

"That's not what I'm saying." He barred any hint of emotion from his tone, keeping his voice low. "Do you not see the situation we're in? We're camped out on the doorstep of some Liberation Front Base on a *hunch* that Knox might be here. The moment we get in, *if* we get in-" He snapped his fingers, startling me. "-they'll be on us like that, and any one of us could be killed. Devoured, even. *Turned.* We're *all* gambling our lives on this."

"Your realism is starting to sound a lot like pessimism," I grumbled, wiping savagely at my tears. "As long as I don't use my magic, I'm indistinguishable from any other magikier. And if they're taking magikier prisoners anyway, who's to say they wouldn't let us live?"

The turquoise of his eyes glittered with equal parts frustration and displeasure.

I bit my lip, brows furrowing, but steeled myself for the promise I knew he was afraid to ask of me. "Look, Brett, if things aren't looking good tomorrow... If it starts to look like we won't make it, I'll give the signal to retreat. Okay? If it's hopeless, it's hopeless. But we can't know until we've tried."

"And you think *you* can judge a hopeless situation?"

"Better than you can, apparently! I just... I don't want to be the sword. I don't want you to be one, either! Or Lin or Kev or Faith! Just promise me you won't kill for me!" I burst, only to watch the expression fall from his face and his eyes go blank with disillusionment. I could see the realization depressing into him that there was nothing he could say to change my mind. Ironic, I supposed, considering the capacity for change was the foundation of my argument.

A stark silence pushed in on me, the lack of a buffer between my last words to him and his cold taciturnity thrumming loudly in my ears.

After a moment, he stood. "Fine. If you're so determined to invade a Liberation Front war camp tomorrow, you might as well get some sleep."

He dowsed the last dregs of the dying fire underfoot and offered a hand to help me stand. Tentatively, I took it and followed him back with his blanket wrapped around my shoulders.

The bitter chill pierced into me twofold in the absence of my fire and the presence of Brett's frustration. Locking my jaw against the chattering in my teeth, I found myself spiralling into the same strain of thoughts as those which had plagued me before Brett's arrival, albeit this time without the safety net of emotional stability.

The thing was, I was faced with a seemingly unsolvable problem. To flaunt my power, hold it to others' throats, threaten lives with this massive privilege I'd stolen out from under the centions; I'd be no different from the evil I kept at bay. Hell, I'd be a poor rendition of Evelyn, her might and her malice reincarnated along with everything else I was because of her.

Killing had to be more than a last resort for me, but Brett was right. These were pora we were going up against. They were once magikiers – like me, my friends, and just about everyone I had met since first entering Blackano – but were now quite literally bloodthirsty monsters. And yet, they had the presence of mind to put aside their more monstrous qualities and team up with Valencia's force of magikiers, ignoring their allegedly insatiable bloodlust.

As far as I was concerned, that alone proved their capacity to not only rein themselves in, but to choose peace with magikiers. And could I blame them choosing the side that was fighting for their rights, to pardon them of the age-old grudges the centions held against pora, kirranites, and domenths alike?

And yet, because of their choice, I was easily any pora's number one target, and a delicious meal at that. They had no qualms about killing me. There would be no hesitation on their part.

So where was I meant to draw the line?

We reached Lin's hidden den in the stone, but I couldn't wedge myself inside, not yet.

There was no helping the broken croak of my voice as I whispered, "I'm sorry, Brett. I'm so sorry." The tears welled up in me again, burning hot in the back of my throat. "I don't know what to do…"

His arms were around me before I'd registered his movement. He engulfed me in a hug, squeezing me so tightly, I could barely breathe – or maybe that was a result of the tears burning at the back of my throat.

He held me against him for a moment more, my face nuzzled into his chest, his hand on the back of my head and fingers running through my hair.

I couldn't hug him back with the blanket enfolded around me like a strait-jacket, but I relaxed into his welcome embrace, even while conscious of the tear stains I was undoubtedly making on his shirt.

His breath was warm against my neck, flashing soft, intimate memories through my head. "You don't have to know what to do," he whispered, sending a shudder down my spine, "Let me take care of you."

"With everything that's going on-"

"I won't let anything happen to you. I'll do what you won't, conscience aside."

What little warmth had returned to me vanished like the fire put out under his foot, chased away by a shockwave of ice threatening to stop my heart and squeeze my lungs into useless raisins.

I wanted to scream at him that the last thing I wanted was to make a murderer of him, but the words lodged in my throat. In that moment, a murderer was all I could envision behind my eyelids.

He had killed out of anger, out of fear, out of duty. He drove that woman outside the keep onto a stake; he impaled her with his bare hands. He lodged an arrow in the teleporter at the bastion with no reservations. He was a hunter, not a scout. Ruthless. Instinctive. Cold. And he didn't let himself show remorse, if he had any at all.

My mind chugged to a halt, glazing swiftly over with frost and snow until every ounce of me lay muffled under a thick layer of white. I felt nothing.

He let go of me, but I couldn't remove my empty stare from the ground. I couldn't bring myself to look at him. If I did, I would only see a man coated in blood. I could almost hear it dripping from his fingertips…

"Here," I automatically said, removing the blanket from my shoulders, but he stopped my hands.

"Faith took yours, didn't she?" His voice had changed again, drawing up a great distance. "Keep it."

15

To Vindicate a Detour

"SLEEPING BEAUTY AWAKES," LIN TEASED AS I SAT UP, BLEARY-EYED AND wrapped up in Brett's blanket.

I was too tired to do more than acknowledge her words with a nod, shaking out the red cloud that was my bedhead. For all the candyfloss muddling my brain, nausea unsettling my stomach, and aches and pains stiffening my muscles, I might as well have gone the whole night without a wink.

Faith and Brett sat together near the entrance to our hidden den, discussing whatever plan they'd spent the morning hatching, informed by Briar's nighttime scouting operation. Lin busied herself packing up our meagre campsite, and I was soon enough informed that Kev was up ahead, keeping lookout from the mouth of the crevice that sheltered us.

My tired eyes kept flicking back to Brett.

Part of me wanted to pull him aside, to talk about everything he said last night, but I'd rather he felt comfortable enough to speak openly with me again, and for all I knew, bombarding him with a follow-up would close those walls right back up around his heart. The other part of me couldn't get that godawful dream out of my head.

"Here," Lin said, and tossed a can of scout rations into my lap. My stomach turned over – it was too soon to eat, and certainly too early for the intense saltiness of this particular meal. She patted my shoulder and returned to packing, allowing me a moment to shrug off my deep sleep.

The word must have gotten out that I'd finally roused from sleep, for Briar chose then to bullet in through the small entryway. She swept her graceful wings in close around her long, ribbon-like body and caught my shoulder with her two front paws, coiling herself around my torso like a garland on a Christmas tree, except she weighed about as much as an anaconda.

My inner voice echoed with my reactive thought, "*Ugh! If she keeps up this growth spurt, she'll break me in half!*" and I startled with the slow realization Briar was in my head.

"*This growth spurt is out of my claws, just as whatever you may find within the Khuloces Base is out of yours.*"

"*So I take it you still can't tell me if Seth's in there?*"

"*You make it sound as if it's my choice. All I can say with any certainty is he's locked in a slumber I cannot breach, nor can I find him unless this changes. If this changes.*" She flicked her tongue in dissatisfaction. "*And on that topic, it ails me to think I'll never find you if you're separated from your friends. I would almost suggest you don some leash between you so as not to get lost.*"

I heaved a hefty sigh, earning an eye roll from Lin. "If anyone's wondering, Briar's sage word of the day is paranoia," I grumbled for the group at large, but only Lin paid me any mind.

"Let me guess, she's telling you to be careful?" she teased over her shoulder and sat back on her heels, finishing up packing our meagre campsite. With that, she dusted her hands together over another job well-done. "Have you considered taking her advice?"

"*Now, will you at least heed her advice to follow mine?*" Briar mused, and I could hardly contain my amused frustrations.

"*Seems like a roundabout way to do it, but sure. I live by the buddy system, anyway,*" I conceded, hoping rather to stymy the headache burgeoning in my mind with Briar's presence. She must not have noticed, for her lengthy explanation of the overhead layout of the Khuloces Base which she proceeded to push into my brain. At the very least, it was something to think about while I forced down my underwhelming breakfast.

By her reports, the cliff face we'd burrowed into turned out, rather, a thick wall encircling a box canyon, or more accurately, courtyard of cut stone, at the back of which overlooked the Khuloces Base. Her view from above had shown a series of tunnel openings along the inner circle of the cliff wall, one of which we could safely assume led back to the hidden entrance in the hollowed root. Whether this meant multiple exits or a series of underground tunnels, she couldn't say, but her interest rested with the Khuloces Base.

We had come into a stroke of luck with our positioning. Exactly opposite our location within the cliff wall, nestled against the wall of the box canyon providing a measure of natural fortification for the Khulous Base, was a raised, stone butte upon which sat the fortified base itself, heavily patrolled and teeming with Liberation Front radicals of all creeds.

"*Exactly opposite? Like, their base of operations is just on the other side of this massive crack in their defenses?*" I mused between our minds, "*Huh. Well how 'bout that.*"

" *Your luck must finally be changing to have discovered this unfinished breach of which they do not seem aware.*"

I paused in contemplation, cupping my chin in one hand. "*Brett said it was one of their own prisoners who mined this part of the cliff, right? They must not have realized they were digging* toward *their captors.*"

"*You think this a failed escape route? From... the outside.*" With a flick of her forked tongue, she extended her wings in gesture to the deep crevice in the cliff wall all around us. " *Why would they not just hide as we're doing?*"

"*Good question. It's just too convenient, isn't it? For us, that is.*"

Her wing swept toward Faith and Brett near the back of the nook where they had their heads together, drawing maps and plans on the rock. "*Not convenient enough. Your stone-crafter alone cannot breach the rest of the way through this open tunnel unnoticed. Not unless-*"

She cut herself off just a moment before Kev appeared through the opening of our nook, a frazzled look in his eyes. "We've got company."

All eyes landed on him as he pulled himself inside. "The good kind or the bad kind?" Lin asked as Faith and Brett quickly gathered their packs on their backs, prepared to make a break for it.

"What good kind?" Kev asked, momentarily confused, but shook himself out of it and continued on a rush of breath, "The door hidden in the root opened up. There were pora – maybe ten or more – and a handful of magikiers wearing the soaring heron of the Liberation Front on their coats. They led a line of prisoners out, with ropes linking them by their ankles, all holding pickaxes or pushing mining carts. We gotta go–"

"Linked at the ankles?" Brett interjected, a note of surprise colouring his voice. "They didn't have those kinds of restraints in my visions."

A beat of silence passed between us; voices replaced with the almost audible whirring of gears in our heads as we puzzled out this latest development.

"Worst case, they caught whoever's been digging out this trench," Lin considered, "Group punishment?"

"If that *is* the case, this isn't a hiding place, it's a funnel," Faith said, pushing the last pack toward Kev and flapping her hands to usher us out. Briar bolted from my lap before we could crowd her in our departure, catching a current of wind under her wings upon which to climb high into the green-tinted rays raining down from the foliage.

One by one, we leapt out of our nook and into the half-finished tunnel, this scrapped attempt at freedom carved out of the cliff face. My curiosity got the better of me. I couldn't help but peer out from the narrow mouth, only to discover the forest crawling with labourers, ropes slithering through the underbrush to connect each of them at a distance of twenty or so feet. They all wore dark and heavy bags under their eyes, their steel-blue coveralls hanging off wiry bodies and their belts wound tight around too-thin waists.

Nearest to us toiled a man in his late twenties or early thirties – hard to tell with the layer of grime deepening the shadows on his pale face – with bicoloured white and dark brown hair styled in such a way, the dark brown half mostly covered the white half. He was armed with a weathered pickaxe like all the rest, but it seemed rather a prop in his hands as he feigned the labour he'd been tasked with, grumbling cantankerously to himself with each half-assed swing.

"Ah, Annie! Get away from there!" Kev squeaked in a tiny voice, pulling me back into hiding. My back hit his chest as his hit the wall and he continued unbroken for the others, "They're all out there, where are we supposed to go?"

I shook my head, stepping out of Kev's hold. "Shouldn't we get a sense of how many prisoners there are? They need our help just as much as Seth does, and, well, the enemy of my enemy is my friend, right? They could help us."

"Annie," Brett groaned, disillusionment in his eyes, and to his left, Faith shook her head. Before either of them could state their evident disagreement, however, Lin was speaking with a hand to her chin, pondering the legitimacy of my idea, and the whole lot of them descended into hushed bickering.

Reluctance entered Briar's tone. "*If you are to ask their help, just remember to hold your blathering tongue should anyone speak of shontes and champions. I'll make myself scarce and keep an eye from the canopies, lest I draw unwanted attention where secrecy reigns.*" As far as I could tell, her words were reserved for me alone, and were almost inaudible beneath the headache pounding more incessantly now than before between my ears.

"*And please, for the sake of my sanity, make no mention of Valencia, and none whatsoever of Evelyn. Understood?*"

"*Geez, I'm not that much of a chatterbox.*"

"*So you would say. It pains me to realize, although I'm certainly not surprised, that any degree of skepticism would be foreign to you. All I ask is that you maintain a principle of vigilance. Not just here, but everywhere. You should realize by now; danger lurks around every corner. For you, and for those who follow you.*"

Her echoey presence in my mind fizzled and popped with the effort of keeping the line between our minds open at this distance, but at her words, memory of last night's conversation with Brett battered me over the head. With it came a flash of something else. Suddenly, I was back in the City of Gates where our own people had attacked Lin simply because they made assumptions about the marks on her skin. These prisoners wouldn't show her any kinder treatment if they made those same assumptions.

I peered sidelong at Lin, wondering if she was thinking along the same lines as Briar, as me, but her expression remained expertly hidden behind her scarf and goggles, along with the markings on her skin.

I had no words for her, neither to protect nor comfort her. I couldn't force her to face what she had so emphatically refused to acknowledge that day.

Instead, I gave a sullen nod. "*I can't afford to be naïve anymore, huh?*"

"*You never could. Now, in facing Lupei's Liberation Front here on Cellana, you repay the debts of your naivety.*"

Her presence faded entirely, the connection between our minds breaking, and the headache began to recede.

"Hi there," drawled a voice from nearby, catching us all by surprise.

The man with half-white hair stood adjacent to the mouth of the tunnel, his neighbours on the rope tether hard at work a good twenty or so feet from us and deep in the effort of ignoring him entirely, but his eyes were on us.

Flicking a finger out from the fist pressing his jaw in pensive contemplation, he blandly remarked, "I expected rats might eventually move into my secret tunnel, but it's hardly been a week. Who are you?"

He leaned all his weight on his pickaxe clutched in his other hand like it was a cane, peering around Kev so his jaded regard could affix to me. A glint of something like intrigue entered his eyes.

Following the path of his gaze, I found my sleeve had ridden up, revealing fresh scabs and inflamed skin adorning the latticework of cuts climbing up my hands. Inhaling sharply, I balled my hands into fists and hid them in my pockets.

"What happened? Lost a battle with a butter knife?" he droned, suspicion intermingling with mockery in his tone.

Brett bluntly interjected, "It wasn't pora, if that's what you're asking." His defensive tone came across accusatory, as if egging on a fight. Kev jabbed him in the side, shooting him a warning look.

"Even if it wasn't pora who did it, pora can still use it," the man with half-white hair said matter-of-factly, turning his nose up at us.

With this slight tilt of his head, his glossy dark brown locks fell over the tips of his ears, drawing my gaze to the dry, dead locks of white better suited to someone twice his age. I couldn't help thinking this strange pigmentation testament to his time here.

A crooked smile framed his words, "You should know better than to keep open wounds out like this. Especially so close to..." He tilted his head, gesturing back toward the Khuloces Base.

"I *do* know better, but I lost my gloves, and I didn't pack another pair-"

"Did you forget to pack your healer, too, or are you just teasing fate for the fun of it?" He sounded incredulous, and Brett's glare deepened.

"Are there healers here?" Kev tested, a pinch of hope glinting in his eyes.

The half-brunet man seemed to weigh his options. Finally, he said, "What luck. You've stumbled across the one and only."

"And you'll heal me?" I let a hopeful intonation imply my urgency.

He tapped a finger to his chin in contemplation. "Did I say that?"

Faith made a noise of disgruntlement, a half-stifled, "Tch."

"Why were you digging this trench?" Lin spoke up, and with a backwards gesture, continued, "You must've realized you were burrowing deeper into this place?"

He blinked, what I could only assume was surprise at our knowledge. "Yes. That was my intention."

"Why?" Faith demanded.

"Am I under inspection?" He caught himself, seeming to recall his earlier curiosity. "Answer's no, *you* are. And for that matter, who are you people? I'm in enough trouble already; give me one good reason I shouldn't-" He raised his hands with pickaxe clasped between them in gesture toward his captors, but I didn't let him finish the thought.

"We can help you-"

"Annie," Brett hissed under his breath, but the man made a small sound, halfway between a scoff and a chuckle. Sinking the butt of his pickaxe down to the ground, he propped both arms over the head and leaned in over it with a devilish smile turned on me.

"Help me? How suspicious of a group of absolute strangers. Did you come all this way *just* for me?" He arched an eyebrow at us. "Altruism like that, it's enough to make a man paranoid."

"And why's that?" Brett asked, but I flapped a hand in his direction, wary to scare this remarkably dodgy man off.

I jabbed a thumb toward the back of the tunnel, deep into shadow and cliff rock. "We want what's on the other side of that tunnel, just like you. We have a stone-crafter-"

"Curious," he mused, running the word over his tongue as a glint of intrigue shone in his eyes. "You wouldn't happen to know what's hidden inside that base?"

"Hidden?" Kev prompted.

"Stored, buried, stashed. Choose your pick," he mused disinterestedly, "Or have you come to rescue those damsels in distress, their highest-priority prisoners?"

I twitched at the words, thinking immediately to Seth, and ducked my head between my shoulders upon noticing his clever eyes, glinting with curiosity, on me.

"Well, which are *you* after?" Lin demanded, blunt as ever.

He turned his nose up at her. "None of your business. But you said you could help me-"

"You'd better change that attitude, old man. I'm your stone-crafter."

"Perfect," he grinned, but not an ounce of enthusiasm leaked into his laconic voice. "And wouldn't you know it, I'm feeling charitable. You scratch my back, I'll scratch yours." His sly eyes slid toward me. "Show me your hands."

"My...?" I glanced down to my hands, catching Brett's subtle head shake through my peripherals.

"In the event we *are* caught, you'll be marginally tougher to infect with the pora disease and significantly less of a threat to me. How's that sound?"

Hesitation gripped me, Briar's warning about trusting these desperate people resounding in my head, but what choice did I have in these circumstances.

He heaved an impatient sigh. "Take it or leave it, but you can't stick around me with open wounds-"

"Fine," I snapped, stepping forward, but Faith stopped me with a hand on my shoulder.

"I don't know-" she cut in, but I shushed her with an insistent look.

"He's a healer, Faith." And a stuck-up snob with a silver tongue, but I could ignore that for now. With reluctance in her eyes, she released my shoulder, and I pulled my hands back out of my pockets, opening them to reveal the worst of my slices.

He winced at the sight of my injuries, making an obvious effort not to gag as I gingerly rolled my sleeves up over my elbows. Even Kev sucked back breath between gritted teeth at the grisly sight.

Wearing an expression of clear disgust to be touching my open injuries, the man with half-white hair brushed his palms over mine and got to work.

What energy I possessed in myself sapped from me the moment his magic hit, slamming into me like a truck. So he was one of *those* healers – the type that used up the injured party's energy to hasten the healing process, rather than simply undo the damage itself.

I had to stifle my complaints in my throat – healing was healing, and I certainly needed it.

He worked just enough of his draining magic on me to stitch my skin back together, closing the scars into pink, raised lines, but it was enough to leave me woozy with lethargy. At the very least, my ankle was comfortably walkable again.

"So we have an agreement," he said, catching my healed palm in hand and giving a firm shake as if that cemented it. "You owe me, now. Really, they would have sniffed you out within the hour if I hadn't done this for you, so let that reflect in our collaborations going forward."

"Sounds oddly like entrapment," Lin sarcastically noted.

A pout turned down the corners of his mouth, but he disregarded her words with a wave of his hand and moved on to the next order of business in complete ignorance of her tone. "Unless you want to paint a target on our backs, you'll quiet down. The ravine echoes something fierce."

Brett's face contorted into a frown. "Is that a warning or just your fancy way of telling us to shut up?"

"Couldn't it be both?" answered the man with half-white hair, clasping his hands in front of him and swinging on his feet. He swayed like a tree caught in a powerful breeze, tall and slender on long legs. "If we're caught down this way, you'll be no better off than me. No use to me, either."

Shaking his head in his hand, Kev groaned, "And that's all we are to you, huh?"

As he spoke, Faith made a gesture I understood to mean we should ditch this guy and figure a way to do this on our own. I shot her a look demanding how we were supposed to know the intricacies of this place without a seasoned prisoner – and one who'd evidently been gathering intel, at that – in our crew?

"Do we have a better plan, or any plan at all?" I whispered out of the side of my mouth, much to Faith's shy, over-the-shoulder glance toward her and Brett's incomprehensible scribblings on the backwall. By her lack of response, I could only assume the answer was a no. "So…?"

"Okay, buddy," Brett sighed, "What's your plan?"

16

Long Road to the Khuloces Base

My weapons felt heavy in their holsters as we packed up the last of our campsite. All the while, the man kept watch at the mouth of the trench from an otherwise sleepy expression as he feigned manual labour. Maybe that was just his natural resting face, pale with dark circles under his eyes entirely unrelated to the caking of dust and silt trapped in his pores. He certainly didn't look like he'd be of much use in a fight, but whatever insider knowledge he possessed could keep us from confrontation entirely – or at least, that was the hope.

"Don't expect much from the rest of them," he noted over his shoulder for us and lifted his chin in gesture to the other prisoners, all the while not making eye contact so as to maintain the illusion we weren't there. "When the punishment's magic suppression and the enforcement's a slew of pora salivating down your neck, you tend to gravitate toward complacency."

"Not you, though," Faith aptly noted, "Why's that?"

He lifted one shoulder in a casual shrug. "Everyone needs a healer, and unlike you lot, those without a death wish maintain a baseline of the most essential magikiers, for prosperity's sake. They wouldn't waste me so haphazardly."

"Most essential?" Lin scoffed. "You sure think highly of yourself."

He slid his gaze sidelong at her and winked, somehow more jaded and patronizing than kittenish. "Well, there's no accounting for taste, is there?"

Kev winced. "What if they prefer a healer who doesn't sap his patients' energy on their deathbeds?"

The man huffed, seeming to take offense at Kev's line of thinking, but granted, "You're right on the money. They've been trying to coerce me into some cult-y pact to *enrich my magic*, but I know a thing or two about the cost of power."

"Great responsibility?" I guessed.

He met my small jest with an unimpressed expression. "Not quite. But they won't risk destroying my magic if they think I might still give into them, so I've been mulling it over. As things stand, I'm untouchable."

"And how long's that gonna last?" Brett huffed under his breath.

"I assure you, I'm a compelling actor. It's how I sleep so soundly at night, curled up with a cozy sense of security in this maximum-security prison." His tone dripped with sarcasm, enough to make me wonder just how much of this declaration was ironic.

"But here you are, one of the miners working the quarry. Not exactly high-profile," Lin remarked.

"Take that up with them. *I* know I deserve better."

It was enough to make me wonder what constituted a high-profile prisoner, and enough to make me hopeful. Seth was a Knox after all, maybe the last descendant of the first magikier. Surely, that had to count for something. At least in the way of politics.

With a "Psst!" Faith beckoned me over, away from everyone else.

When it was just the two of us at the back of the little nook while the others busied themselves with packing up, I lowered my voice and asked, "Uh... What's up?"

"Are you sure about this guy?"

"Well, I do sort of owe him now, don't I?" I flexed my healed hands, evidence to the recompense owed.

She sighed, shaking her head, but there was a fondness in her eyes. "You set the bar too high when you do everything out of the goodness of your heart and expect everyone else to do the same. We're stuck with this headache in human form, and sure, he's a healer and he knows how to navigate the base, but-"

"We shouldn't look a gift horse in the mouth. Without his tunnel, we'd struggle on our own to get into the Khuloces Base." I deliberated over my next words, grumbling, "Sure, I don't trust the guy, but he wants to get in there just as badly as we do. Isn't that enough?"

"He's a man with an agenda, and we have no idea how we'll fit into it once the truth comes out about who and *what* you are."

"How's he gonna know?"

Pointedly, she raised her eyebrows and tilted her chin downwards, a careful and perfected expression which forced me to hear my own words and, by them, talk myself out of whatever it was she didn't agree with. I'd seen it all before, so often she deflated my flimsy excuses, but not this time.

"Oh, come on," I sighed, "Ran-Out-Of-Hair-Dye over there talks about us like we're bumbling toddlers, we're as far from a cause for scrutiny as we can be."

"Until he sees what you can do, which he will, because you told him we'd help him. You made his problem our problem. Hell, Annie, we don't even know what he started this tunnel for–"

"But we're using it." I shrugged, raising both hands with palms facing the ceiling. "I feel pretty safe letting him think we're just tools for his disposal. It's a bit of a give and take if you think about it."

"Hold on a moment, let me just count the scores for a sec." She paused for dramatic effect with finger tapping her chin, an illustration of concentration. "He doesn't rat us out immediately, *heals* you, and lets us use his tunnel to the fortified base. That's three favours. And us? We have Lin finish the tunnel. That's a big one. And we lend a hand in his escape. That's two."

Catching my face between my palms, I groaned into my hands, "Your kindergarten level math is truly mind-blowing. So what if the scales aren't totally balanced by the end? Him not ratting us out shouldn't even count!"

"Yeah, and if we're caught, he *definitely* doesn't face a greater risk because he made that choice for us. There's no *way* he could hold that over our heads." Sarcasm dripped from her words, so gratingly triumphant in her reasoning. "He's bound to find out the truth about you, and what do you think he'll do with that one favour still owed, then? Abuse it, maybe?"

A bitter *tch* escaped me as I scrunched up my face into a baulking expression, disgruntled and notably complaintive in the set of my mouth.

"Annie," she warned, "You know I'm right."

I waved my hand in a circle as if rifling through an imaginary rolodex of counterarguments. "I'm still unconvinced. He just doesn't come across as the type to care about the things that make others' lives difficult. Namely, every single thing currently fueling my anxiety."

"Ugh," she groaned with a miserable inflection, and dropped her shoulders with her face raised skyward.

"It's just, I'd sooner expect him to hate the drama of it all and try his very best to ignore us. Which could be a good thing, under the right circumstances."

Eyes as tired as the moot point she continued to argue, Faith cupped her chin in hand and gave me that annoying, patronizing look that meant I'd dug my own grave. I heaved a theatrical sigh, but she was the first to continue in a tone I knew to mean she thought she'd already won the argument and now had no idea why it was still happening, "If we can't trust him now, how can we trust him then?"

"Hard to argue with a hypothetical, you know," I grumbled, shaking my head, "We just have to take a chance on him, and if he becomes a problem, we'll deal with him. We have numbers on our side, and he *is* just a healer. Not all that threatening if you ask me."

She paused, thinking it over. "Ah, fine. I guess." A jaded grin made wicked with the spark of mischief in her eyes leeched away her tired expression. "And who knows, maybe his paranoid hypervigilance will counterbalance your… you-ness."

"Uncalled-for." I thought it over. "But fair enough."

The sound of shuffling toward the front of the cave caught our attention as the subject of our discourse wiggled out of the rope tethering him to his mining group. Taking the end in hand, he snaked the long rope rather down a narrow crevice so as to feign his hard work and wound it around a stray root jutting out of the walls to fix it in place.

"And they fall for that?" Brett's tone was derisive as he watched the fugitive at work, but the man waved off his reservations with a grunt.

"Hasn't failed me yet," he sighed, wearing a listless tone I could hardly consider present, one certainly unconcerned with sanctioning our collective judgement toward him.

Absent-mindedly, Kev nudged the rope aside with the toe of his boot. "If it's so easy to get out of your restraints, what's keeping anyone here?"

"You forget how many prisoners here have had their magic stripped upon arrival. And even those lucky enough to keep it wouldn't risk a solo trip through the Khuloces Forest."

"Isn't freedom worth the risk?" Lin put in, earning the man's jaded glare.

"It astounds me how unaware you are of the peril you blundered through to get here." Striding back toward the depth of the tunnel, he beckoned each of us after him with a hand over his shoulder and the words, "Come parade your ridiculous rabbit's feet this way."

We set out through the long, winding tunnel in near silence, our guide walking alone at the head of the group with a makeshift map open under his freckle-spattered nose for all the natural cracks, twists, and forks muddying my sense of direction, for one. I couldn't tell if he was trying to memorize his own map in the dim lighting of the tunnel or if he was realizing he needed glasses.

Faith, Brett, Kev, Lin, and I trailed along after him like his little ducklings. Not long into our hushed hike, I'd realized he didn't have dog tags like the rest of us – he hadn't asked our names, but he must have taken note of our helpful accessories, foregoing introductions.

Instead, his steel-blue coveralls, weathered with outdoor labour, flaunted a white patch no larger than a nametag on the back with black thread lettering detailing name, magic, blood type, and other finer points I didn't stare long enough to decipher through the tunnel's poor lighting. And wouldn't you know it, after all my gawping to catch his name, I found myself stumped on the pronunciation.

The name on the patch spelled out Cillian, and for the life of me, I couldn't figure whether to pronounce it with soft or hard C sound. From what little I knew of him, he certainly seemed the type to have a mocking jab prepared for any situation, needing only the slightest offense to trigger a verbal assault. Suffice to say, I walked in silence behind him.

"*God*, how long did this take to shovel out?" I groaned, an idle complaint with no intended audience, but my eyes flicked to Cillian's back and an idea gleamed behind my eyes. I raised my voice slightly to ensure he heard my next words. "What's so worthwhile on the other end of this tunnel, if not people?"

As if sensing my gaze, he dropped his shoulders and lowered the map, peering back at us. "Was that supposed to be directed at me?"

"You'd know best," Brett answered, wearing a tone of ill-disguised suspicion.

He conceded agreement with a half-nod, half-shrug and passed an offhand glance over the dog-tags dangling around Brett's neck. "What can I say, Brent? I'm inquisitive by nature, and there's a secret up there I plan to uncover. Not to mention I get to stretch my legs without the weight of a tether. That's an added benefit."

Snorting in disbelief, Lin gestured around to our general vicinity, including our little gang, with wide open arms. "How does any of *this* benefit you?"

"Have you ever been cooped up in a musty hole in the ground for a number of months you forgot to start counting, no hope of escape, and escorted to the doorstep of freedom everyday just to throw your back out mining resources for your captors' armory? No? Then I'll leave you to your assumptions."

"I think I'm starting to get why no one misses you when you're away digging this trench," Kev mused in a tone laced with sarcasm. I elbowed him in the side, shooting him a look, but Cillian made a sound somewhere between a chuckle and a snort.

He raised an index finger toward the packed dirt caking the ceiling, a glint of dry amusement in his eyes. "Here's a handy piece of advice, kiddo. Keep the talking to a minimum. You've been blessed with a vapid smile, so use it; people find simplicity endearing." He turned back toward the front, returning his nose to the map. "Just whatever you do, don't disturb the trees." Kev, Lin, and I shared an incredulous look but kept quiet.

"Will talking disturb the trees?" Kev extrapolated.

"Do the trees have ears where you come from?"

Kev grumbled under his breath, huffing and puffing in annoyance. Changing the subject, he strained against his frustration to ask, "So what's with the hair?"

"Only a result of morbid curiosity," Cillian simply answered, a conclusiveness in his tone implying we shouldn't hold our breath for elaboration.

Blowing a lock of hair out of his eyes, Kev gave up any manner of small talk, and the tunnel was filled once more with the sounds of our shoes scuffing dirt and stone.

Eventually, the tunnel opened skyward into a roofless space, cast under shadow by a spider web of tree roots knitting between the silt-coated walls of the ravine, and the boughs and branches even higher above that. Underfoot, the faint blue glow of bioluminescent waters trickled between shattered chips and jagged plates of the weathered rock floor. These rivulets of light pooled in pits eroded from the uneven ground with wisps of steam rolling over the surface, catching these colours in low swirls. I could only assume these babbling brooks came from a system of natural hot springs deeper into the ravine.

This theory proved correct some ways down as we arrived at the back of the tunnel, a larger space wedged open by natural erosion and dotted with deep, steaming pools of the bioluminescent water so common in this area. A natural bathhouse hidden in the ravine, and the stopping point of the man's hard work. Here, he'd been faced with the slower process of mining sedimentary rock, rather than simply shovelling out the soil which had blocked the ravine's passage, and so here, he required Lin's stone-breaking magic.

"This is you," Cillian announced, tossing his pickaxe to Kev so he had no other choice but to catch it, and with a hand on Kev's back and the other on Lin's, shoved them down the mined passage together. It was only big enough for two at a time and even that was a tight fit, leaving the rest of us with the idle job of keeping lookout.

Dusting his hands off on his pant legs, Cillian ambled back to the hot springs with a yawn and a hand running through his hair.

"All in a hard day's work?" Faith mocked, to which he merely rolled his eyes and plopped down along the edge of the nearest pool, pulling forth his haphazard map once more.

It was easy enough to ignore them while Cillian paid us little to no mind, and I busied myself rather with skipping from rock to rock around the circumference of the deep valley, an outstretched hand brushing along the dirt-caked walls which came loose at the slightest touch.

Brett sat cross-legged near the entrance, settling into his usual trance to observe all that Cillian had been up to in the long process of this ill-advised break-in.

"I wouldn't if I were you, empath," Cillian lazily called without taking his eyes off the map laid out across the stone in front of him.

"He can't hear you," Faith put in when Brett didn't respond.

"That's unfortunate," Cillian smirked, and not a moment later, Brett jumped out of his trance, a deep blush reddening his neck and face. "Can't get this kind of privacy in the communal showers."

Still beet red with blush up to the burning tips of his ears, Brett shot the smirking man a glare he didn't look up to see, only to quickly avert his gaze again and push up from his seated position. After a moment's hesitation, he ambled over to Faith, following along beside me where I stood on a tall boulder at the other end of the open space.

"This'll take all day," Brett grumbled when he came near, and I had to contain my amusement for the last traces of fluster still lingering on his voice.

"Oh?" Faith half-chuckled, earning Brett's withering regard. "Did you get a sense of how long it's taken him?"

"No."

Clamping down on the traitorous smile tugging at the corners of my mouth, I measured my expression and hopped to the next rock, but Cillian's wry chuckle echoed off the walls of the ravine to us, succeeding to draw the blood to Brett's face once more.

To our collective surprise, it was Brett's begrudging suggestion, once Kev and Lin took a break during the dark hour as the sun passed behind the ring across the sky, to make use of these natural facilities while we were here and the world cast under shadow.

Steam softened the air collected in the depths of this geologically eroded ravine, wafting off the still waters of the hot springs into which we waded, each of us blind for the thick darkness captured here. In this moment, I could believe myself in a pleasant solitude. My head was too spacey to pay the rest of them much mind as I instead focused on cutting through the grime staining my skin with a strawberry-scented lather Cillian had pointed out to us which he'd stockpiled from the prison camp and kept in buckets along the stone ridges.

He'd sloshed one of the buckets in a wide display of its contents with the words, "Found this in the officer's showers. Heard they use this stuff to keep the stink of magic off them so pora don't-" and circled a finger beside his ear with a low whistle. "I like to think it's kept me under their radar."

Waves of steam rolled off the water's surface, just thick enough to catch the cave's shadows and offer another measure of privacy. Nevertheless, I averted my gaze respectfully from the others washing nearby.

Once the initial glee of soaking in a hot bath passed, I got to work washing my travel-worn clothes in the hottest basin near the back, where the shadows were so deep, I could barely see my hand in front of my face. The creeping exhaustion of Cillian's healing magic hemmed the edges of my mind as I fell into the mindless automation of scrubbing out the dirt, grime, and blood that had become one with the weathered material.

As the sun peeked out from behind the ring, I hung my clothes on the rocks to dry, myself wearing only my romper undergarments, wrung out by hand and damp against my freshly washed skin. I had found a shaded section of the baths near the edge of the hot springs and plopped down on the ridge with my legs in the soothingly hot water, lost in my own world.

So it came as a surprise when a bather surfaced from the water right next to me, hair slicked back and scattering droplets over my legs as the water split around him. He faced forward from the edge, not looking at me, but spread his arms along the rim of the pool in the aspect of utmost relaxation.

Betraying myself, I squeaked in alarm, falling back from the man with half-white hair. My legs kicked up a spray of water as I went, dousing him yet further and fraying his aspect of relaxation as he adopted the look of a disgruntled cat.

"Enjoying the amenities?" he flatly greeted in a dulcet tone as if he wasn't casually lounging in his birthday suit. Sure, there was a thin veil of steam skimming the opaque waters, but I was still acutely aware of the fact he had nothing on.

I glanced around for the others, but Brett had grabbed the pickaxe, joining Lin in her laborious reprisal as Kev took up a hidden lookout position back down the tunnel we'd come from, keeping a watchful eye, and Faith sat herself down with Cillian's near illegible map. For all her big talk, Faith was doing a shoddy job of keeping an eye on this man – but could I blame her, considering his apparent penchant for nudity.

With broad shoulders and an otherwise slim frame, his malnourishment showed in the lithe, agile muscles defined under shrink-wrapped skin. Svelte and anorexic. That said, I made a point to fix my stare on anything but this apparent exhibitionist.

"Not as much as you are, apparently," I grumbled, admiring the wall, "I'd appreciate a little privacy."

"So would I, but it would seem this became a public bathhouse the moment you and your friends arrived." He was so close, I could see the perpetual exhaustion in the downward curves of his dark-lined eyes, but one would never guess it from his venomous voice. Who knew a tone could carry so much condescension in so few words?

"Ugh." I shuffled my legs and began to move away, but he held up a hand, like an aristocrat signalling his servant.

"I just want a word. You *are* the ringleader of your little circus, aren't you?"

My expression fell into a muted glare. "If that's what you want to call it, sure."

I thought I saw a smirk curl the corner of his mouth, but the expression was so small, and the ravine so dimly lit, it was too easy to mistake. "So, I take it you know your way around the Khuloces Forest?"

"Well, no…"

Now I was sure he wore a lopsided grin. "Can I ask *why* you're so interested in delving deeper into this place? And no lies this time."

"Why would I lie? And why so curious?"

He shrugged, his eyes on the cat's cradle of roots and branches overhead as if searching for something, anything, to resolve his ennui. "Consider me an interested party."

I edged another few inches away. "That doesn't answer my questions."

"Doesn't have to. You're here to answer *my* questions–"

"Actually, I'm here to wash up–"

"Priorities change. I'll let you get back to that soon enough, but for now, indulge me." He glanced back at me over his shoulder, a glint of light catching in his sly, downturned eyes. "What do you expect to find in the Khuloces Base?"

"You really can't wrap your head around the idea of people helping people, huh?" I huffed, shuffling further away. He hardly seemed to notice or care.

"I'll believe it when I see it."

"You *are* seeing it."

"Sweetheart, there's no saving *anyone* from the Liberation Front. Prisoners here resign themselves to whatever life this is for them. There's no value in broken things, and no reason to risk something as precious as your own lives for anything so worthless," he mused with the inflection of an adult talking down to a child, only to momentarily lose himself behind his eyes in contemplation, but he shook off whatever train of thought he'd been following and continued, "So no, that can't be the reason you braved the Khuloces Forest and hand-delivered yourselves to the Liberation Front. As the proprietor of all your I.O.U.s, I'd like to know what really brought you here."

Heaving a sigh, I brought my hands to my face, smoothing out the exhaustion behind my eyes, which he piled onto me twofold. "You could win an Olympic medal for the mental gymnastics you're pulling off right now."

"It wouldn't, by chance, be a weapon?"

I quirked my head to one side, catching the side of my face in one palm. "What weapon?"

"You and your merry band of idiots are from the City of Gates. That much I've gathered. And stories travel, even in times like these. Something was taken from beneath the city when it fell. Something powerful. Is that what you're after?"

A light flicked on above my head, and I had to fight off my look of understanding. He could only mean the weapon of achaion, Fiamme's glaive.

Shoot, that was a factor I hadn't considered.

Noticing his impatient expression, I hastened to answer, "No. At least, I don't think we'll find it in some random, backwoods base. Why, is that what *you're* after?"

"The odds that it's here are too slim to go to all this effort," he mused, and my face must have given something away, for his expression changed and he faced away from me once more, "You wouldn't happen to know what's so special about it? Besides the obvious?"

"The base-?"

"The weapon."

Narrowing my eyes, I did my very best to make my tone sound oblivious – an easy feat for the likes of me. "It's just some fancy, historical weapon, isn't it?"

He harrumphed unhappily and conceded with another shrug. "Shouldn't you know *something* about your enemies before running off to meet them?"

"Conventionally, yes, but-" Before I could get the thought out, he dipped back under the surface of the water, leaving me just as suddenly as he'd appeared. What a strange, strange man, but his line of questioning had stirred up new concerns, clouding my head with worry as I plucked the rest of my outfit off the sun-warmed rocks – still damp but wearable.

17

What's A Break Without a Breakdown

I EMERGED FROM THE HOT SPRINGS ENVELOPED BY THE PLEASANT earthy scents of the ravine and the strawberry of our lather as warmth steamed off my squeaky-clean skin.

Figuring I could do with a break from Cillian and his enervating line of questioning, I plopped down on the stone slab next to Kev at the lookout point, situated perfectly for a wide view of the tunnel entrance from behind rocky cover. I must have surprised him, considering the sudden, purple burst of light in his palm which he hastened to hide from view.

I furrowed my brow in concern as I gently but quickly took his wrist, turning his palm up to reveal a latticework of burn marks seared across his flesh. A purple spark leapt between the pads of his fingers, biting deep wherever it touched.

"What are you doing?" I hissed under my breath, just low enough to avoid catching anyone's attention. Kev slipped easily out of my grasp, shooting me a look, but I persisted. "How did you get fire down here?"

"I got a spark off the pickaxe before giving it to Brett. It's fine, it's just practice." A wince creased his eyebrows, not in pain but in concentration to keep the lick of fire alive in his grasp. No matter his efforts, it snuffed itself out with a puff of smoke and he clenched his fist, swearing under his breath.

"But the carmavi mark-" I objected, only for him to shake his head, locks of deepest black falling into his eyes. Like this, I caught a glimpse of the mark behind his ear, burning neon bright while he struggled against its enduring hold on his magic. Softening my tone, I pleaded, "Kev, you don't have to do this to yourself."

"I can't afford to be useless anymore-" He cut himself off, anticipating the protest on the tip of my tongue, and quirked a self-deprecating smile my way, full of shame and apology. "Don't pretend I haven't been."

It was still a struggle to wrap my head around this carmavi magic which he'd been living with for so long now. I simply shook my head, watching him re-wrap his hands with a long strip of cloth from his pack, hiding his long, guitarist's fingers now raw and red with his efforts, a vibrant clash with the last chips of black, grey, white, and purple nail polish on his nails.

"Everyone else has something. You're, well, you, but Brett's the scout, Faith's the field medic, and Lin's the miner... which is only fitting for our resident minor. Couldn't resist the pun."

A traitorous smirk lifted the corner of my mouth at his lighthearted quip, reflected in Kev's own smile, but even this was quick to slip away in a return to his former gravity.

"Everyone's earned their place on this team. But this, for me, it's all I'm good for. I'm dead weight without it, you know that." He said it so matter-of-factly, I almost missed the small twitch in the corner of his mouth, fighting off a bitter frown.

Glancing sideways toward Faith at the map, and to the crevice down which Brett and Lin could be heard sheering away the stone, last night's argument echoed between my ears once more. I kept my voice low in my assurance, "You have nothing to prove to me, Kev. It's my fault you're here."

He scoffed and sent me a sidelong smile. "Fault? Nah. I chose to stick with you, I just want to earn my place by your side." He tapped a finger to his chin in a mock pensive gesture. "Which is saying something, considering our current predicament, or the fact you volunteered yourself to single-handedly take down an insurgent regime. And now, here we are."

"I didn't say I'd... Not an insurgent *regime*..."

He met me with a knowing look and all I could do was groan into my hands, having somehow never thought of it that way.

"Got a little perspective on that one, huh?" he teased, "But keep in mind, if you have a panic attack, I'm gonna have a panic attack-"

"No, no, that's not gonna happen. Just let me, I don't know, apologize? You didn't have to– you shouldn't have had to– I'm sorry."

"Uh-uh, no more apologies, and put the puppy dog eyes on hold."

I smirked into my hands, dragged down my face. "Just on hold?"

"You heard me right. I recall one Brett Song-" Brett was striding out of the opening to the crevice with the collar of his shirt in hand, wiping the material over his glistening face, and his head snapped up at his name. "-once claimed your masterclass puppy dog eyes to be, and correct me if I'm wrong, weapons of mass suggestion?"

"What are we talking about?" Brett called over to us as he clapped Cillian's shoulder and passed the pickaxe off to him. This in turn caught Faith's attention, leaning back on her palms to glance between us as if watching a tennis match. Some lookouts we were.

Grumbling under his breath about sexist labour distribution, Cillian shimmied sideways down the narrow crevice and disappeared to work as Brett crouched down by the pools where he splashed the hot water onto his face and resurfaced with a worried expression in the crease between his brows.

Now that we had all eyes on us, Kev closed his wrapped hand on his knee, expertly concealing his fresh burns, not even a hint of pain in his mild expression. "Oh, just how Annie's gonna win the day with empathy and eye contact. I, personally, think it's a foolproof plan. Or, you know, a fool-necessary plan, but that's my favourite kind."

Faith rolled her eyes, but Brett gave a dismissive shrug. "For what it's worth, it's the best plan in our arsenal. And we've run out of time to re-evaluate." Judging by the cynicism in his tone, he didn't sound exceedingly confident in it, either.

His cynicism must have been contagious, for it sprouted something in me. Who was I to throw them into danger in my defense without even knowing if we would face something as formidable as the glaive of Fiamme, or the champion who wielded it?

"So, we're really doing this, huh?" I worked to steady my breathing. "Weird how these things sneak up on a person."

"I don't think it did much sneaking," Brett mused without looking my way. Though his tone was scathing, the affection was there, always shining through.

"Mm," Kev granted, "If anything, this whole mining business might've given me tinnitus."

"Ah, well, you got me there," I chuckled tightly, and worked to get a grip on my pitch. "Mhm, okay!" Clapping my hands, I nodded my head and pursed my lips in a determined expression – my game face. "Is it pep talk time or what? As team leader, I feel like that's on me."

Brett stifled a derisive chuckle, a sound I recognized to mean he was checking himself out of the conversation, but Kev waved an encouraging hand, urging me onward. "Infect us with your uncanny optimism."

"Coming right up, my good sir," I teased in a poor imitation of a maître d' but hesitated, raising an index finger to illustrate my pause. "Just gimme a sec to unearth said optimism."

"Annie," Brett began, the corner of his mouth quirking up into the bare minimum of a smile as he pulled himself back up to a stand. It was easy to miss, but my eyes were trained to notice. "You might be the only one here in need of a pep talk," said the man who had only last night implied we were rushing to our deaths.

I gasped in offense. "Nuh-uh, you couldn't give a pep talk to save your life. And I don't need one, anyway! We only have one option, and it's to keep moving forward."

"And if he isn't here?" Brett tiredly noted with an almost mindless automation, habitually the devil's advocate, but I wasn't about to have the same argument twice. Nor, it seemed, was he.

As if only just hearing himself, he huffed a weary sigh, running his wetted fingers through his hair, but his shoulders dropped, and he leaned back against a jagged stone ridge. He didn't have to say anything else; I knew what he would say without needing to hear it, that he would ask me to see things the way he did, tell me to call it off before we found ourselves unable to turn back. I could see it in his weary eyes, he had made his judgements and deemed our efforts futile, our operation doomed.

Faith and Kev shared a wary glance, noticing the sudden drop in the atmosphere.

My eyes flicked to the crack in the wall through which Cillian had disappeared, listening for the clinking and clattering sounds of his labour. Satisfied he wouldn't hear me over all the noise, I continued, "This is the mid-point between the City of Gates and Cerenthior. This is our last window of opportunity to rescue Seth before they have the home advantage."

"This doesn't look like a home advantage to you?" Brett dryly remarked.

"Anyway, we can't just pack up and take our business to Cerenthior after we've *seen* what's happening here."

"And what do you expect us to do about it?" he groaned, sliding his hands up his face and sighing into his palms. "You can't shoulder every problem in the world."

"Good news for you, it's not the *whole* world. I just happen to care about the parts of it I'm entrenched in." Making my point, I gestured to the trench in which we'd found ourselves. "Literally."

"Fine. You've already made up your mind." His voice was muffled by his hands, directed more to himself than to me. "Why do I even bother?"

"Why do you?" I shot back, a vitriolic note in my voice I hadn't intended.

He fell quiet, and the space around us became a vacuum, silence pounding in my ears. Damnit, why did I say that.

My hands began to shake, but I clenched them into fists and ignored the incessant vibration. "There's no other option here. So, no. No pep talks for me, thank you very much. I do what I set out to with *all* my heart, a bullet train on pristine tracks, if you will. And fear's just the fuel."

"I doubt aggressively lampshading it makes it any less of a personal pep talk," Faith reviewed, wary to intrude on the awkward atmosphere Brett and I had created.

"Joke's on you, I don't even know what lampshading means," I grumbled in a small voice, crossing my arms over my chest with a pout. A sound of whistling winds caught my ear and a glint of golden movement caught my eye. I perked up when my thoughts echoed in my head, "*Aha, a welcome distraction!*"

"*I grow weary of hiding out of sight, too far to reach into your mind. Why is this outsider still among you?*" Briar's voice spoke softly through my head, somewhat muffled with a skin-prickling sort of radio static, two steps from normal, like the warning buzz you feel just before a migraine. "*Pardon the discomfort my company brings. It seems your mind grows further from my reach with every passing day. But for what reason do you keep this stray whose mind is so closely guarded?*"

"*He's the one who made this tunnel. You might be interested to know; he was asking me about the weapon of achaion not ten minutes ago-*"

"*This piddling magikier knows something of them?*"

"*Well, not really. Just that there's a weapon out and about in Arillia that our worst enemies got their hands on— Hey, on the topic of all the dangers awaiting us at the other end of this tunnel, how much of a liability am I, really, when it comes to pora sniffing out my magic? Without using it, I mean.*"

"*They will likely gravitate toward you, but I doubt they'll realize. They're not honed sensors as some magikiers are. They can't pinpoint your exact location lest you send up a flare. The same way you're unaware of the dead center of a continent when you stand somewhere upon it, the breadth of your aura is far too vast to denote your proximity.*"

"*Oh.*"

"*Now I have a question for you. What madness drives you to the fangs of monsters in the company of this discourteous individual? Do you trust this new guide of yours, after everything I've said to you?*"

"*That's two questions. And, well... I don't really have an answer for you.*"

"*If you care to know, what little I can gather from the mind of this man travelling with you is only that he thinks quite little of you. Indeed, he hardly likes and only barely tolerates any one of you. Although I could say the same of your friends' feelings toward him.*"

"*Yeah, he has a bit of a, uh, disagreeable disposition.*"

"*So I gather, but I find his knowledge of the weapons of Achaion intriguing.*"

"*Why's that-?*"

"*I simply cannot fathom what purpose you see in dragging another into this, making a mess where one already exists. Yes, I have noted how the fields of his mind burgeon with knowledge you and your friends have yet cultivated, but I sense also a danger in this wanton inclusion of one already bound up in complicated webs of his own.*"

"*For all your scorn, I think I just caught the barest hint of a compliment tucked away in that little tirade.*"

She ruffled at my teasing tone, like a red tinge in my mind. "*For as long as you keep this tomcat around, I'm made to stalk after you as a wild creature in the foliage, feigning that I am not even here.*"

"*You could come down-*"

"*Tell me you do not intend to show your hand simply because he's playing the same game.*"

"*Yeah. Or, uh, no. Definitely,*" I mused, unsure how she wanted me to respond. Before she could snap at me, I continued, "*Look, he's done nothing but help us – and annoy us, here and there. I don't get what's so suspicious about that.*"

"*What have I said, time and again, of your haste in trust,*" she groaned in my head, "*Have you even bothered with a plan?*"

"*It's kinda hard to get a plan going without staking out the place first, isn't it?*"

"*Yes, because your tendency to procrastinate pondering what causes you any manner of stress has little to do with it.*"

"*Okay, okay, I'll think about it. You can go back to the treetops now.*"

She answered, perhaps unintentionally, with a wave of frustration which crashed over my mind and further frayed some of the white noise muffling our connection. Without another word, it fizzled out completely, and I was left alone with my thoughts.

I couldn't help my small grimace at this failure of communication as a delighted shout caught in my ears and Lin stepped out of the crevice in the wall with a gesture for us all to come along. I fell behind the group, my eyes on the canopy high overhead, combing the banana-yellow foliage and coal-black branches for a hint of gold to suggest Briar's hidden and aptly camouflaged presence.

The tunnel through the stone wall of the deep ravine wound upwards, slate stone steps taking us up and up and up towards the surface of gnarled roots and protruding rock formations. Our route rose out of the ravine to a towering stone forest overgrown with vegetation and monolithic trees built like umbrellas. The spattering of rocks towered like skyscrapers in some places, jagged tips peeking out over the treetops, and in other places only stuck several feet out of the rich soil suctioning the soles of our shoes underfoot.

Cillian's knowledge of the land made zero sense to me now that we'd departed the ravine, as he didn't seem to be following any visible landmarks, least of all in relation to the incomprehensible map even Faith had failed to decipher.

The sun had almost set, and I could feel the tension rising as it became increasingly apparent the base still hadn't come into view. Not only that, but Brett's mouth had become a thin, white line in his effort to keep it shut, an enduring struggle to compose himself every time Cillian opened his mouth.

We were shuffling single file through a narrow ravine between monolithic stone formations, the walls of which pulled apart into dirt under my hands, when Lin had had enough. With stomach grumbling and voice lowered on idle complaints, she aired a string of grievances from the back of our little line-up between Faith and Kev.

"You're preaching to the choir," I heard Kev whisper from the rear, quietly enough that I had to strain to catch his words. "I thought the base would be closer than this."

"He keeps saying we're almost there, but we don't even know if he's taking us in the right direction," Lin agreed in an undertone, stumbling slightly over a knotted root which poked up through a crack in the harder dirt under our feet.

"We wouldn't be able to tell either way," Faith noted just as quietly.

Kev made a sound of doubt. "You said the dramagon did her whole scan for hidden intentions, though, right-?"

Cillian cleared his throat from his position at the front of our single-file line, an obvious interruption. "I hear you prattling on back there. You'd tell me if the plan is to get captured, wouldn't you? Do let me know, I hate being left out of these things."

"Prick," Lin hissed between her teeth.

"But I *am* curious what kind of person gives themselves such an awful codename as *dramagon*? A telepath, I have to assume." He blew a lock of hair out of his eyes with a world-weary sigh. "Of all the magikiers to have tailed us, it just had to be one of those, huh."

Before I could register his question, I snapped, "Why is everything out of your mouth an insult?"

"And why are there other people if not for mocking? See, I can ask pointless questions, too. But let's not get side-tracked. You haven't answered me," he noted, squeezing himself out of the gap into a valley below a towering cliff face. He held out a hand in front of Brett's face to block his way, jamming up the gap. "Well? Where's your telepath?"

I could practically see the steam lifting off the top of Brett's head as he seethed in silence, a challenge in his unwavering glare held on Cillian, but we were stuck, our arms pinned close to our bodies by the narrowness of the space.

"Your whole gang does a fine job playing the fool, by the way. You had me convinced you lack the combined braincells to scheme."

My skin prickled at the thought Cillian had led us here on purpose. No, I reasoned with myself, he couldn't have, not with Briar listening in on his thoughts. Unless...

Turning my head back to Faith, Lin, and Kev, I demanded in a whisper, "When was the last time you heard from Briar?"

Kev quirked his head to the side, unsure why it mattered, but Lin exhaled in realization and answered, "It would've been about an hour now. Kev?"

"All I know is the sun was still up at the time. Why-?"

"Faith?" I asked.

She furrowed her brows, wracking her brain for answers.

"Briar, huh?" Cillian interrupted, impatience in his tone. "Great, that brings the score to two weird names and still no face to pair them with. Care to give a little more before I feel compelled to threaten?"

"Is that not a threat in itself?" I shot back at him, finding myself more annoyed at his personality than the state of affairs.

"Good catch," he mocked, and conspicuously rested his other hand on the butt of his pickaxe. With the hand that barred Brett's way, he made a circular motion to urge our explanation. "See, the problem is, I don't much like telepaths, so go ahead and call yours out of hiding. Not too loud, mind you. We *are* just outside the Khuloces Base."

"We are?" Kev squeaked, and worked to calm his tone. "Why are you doing this *here*?"

"It's not like I had much control over *where* you would betray my trust. I will say, it's a shame I won't have all the clownfish in one barrel for my distraction, but I digress."

"You were going to ditch us?" Faith guessed on a low growl, earning Cillian's sigh.

"Intentions, intentions. Why does everyone look for intentions? Is it so unsatisfying that I do my best work on impulse?"

"Then *impulsively* change your mind. We don't have to split up here!" I snapped, failing to stifle the surge of anger in my chest.

"In the category of intentions not had, it was never my intention to die for whatever failing cause you've all followed here. I'll give you a moment to make your peace with that-" He paused. "Satisfied?"

Biting back the venom in my tone, I spoke in a deadly calm voice, "I get it, you don't want us knowing what you're after, but news flash, buddy, we don't care."

Smiling, he met each of our eyes and pointedly said, "Anna, Bart, various other stragglers, you were only ever going to be my diversion, but that mental crowbar of yours has officially compromised me. Your *dramagon* makes each and every one of you a hindrance to everything I've been doing. Know what that means?"

"Nothing good?" Brett fumed, a challenge.

Shooting him a lopsided smirk, Cillian ran his fingers through his hair and raked his gaze over our surroundings. "Too bad your telepath's a coward. I thought they were supposed to be the empathetic ones? Oh well." He clicked his tongue with a shrug of his shoulders, as if the situation was unfortunate but unavoidable.

"Wait-" My eyes flicked to his pickaxe, then to Brett, the buffer between me and Cillian. If Brett tried anything, he would have an automatic disadvantage. Surely, he wouldn't be so rash. And yet, his words from last night resurfaced in my head, running circles around any coherent thoughts I might've had. *I'll do what you won't.* "She would've come by now if she knew what was going on!"

"Unconvincing," Cillian critiqued, boredom in his tone. "Just because you got stuck with a cowardly telepath doesn't mean they're any less of a snake in the grass. Although, you should really be in the market for a replacement."

"She's not a danger to you!" I made an effort to withhold my glare. "Just let us go, Sillian."

"I-" He paused, staring at me with a strange sort of expression. "What did you call me?"

"Um… Sillian? Am I… Oh goddamnit, I'm pronouncing it wrong, aren't I?" Giving a weedy smile, I attempted to ease the situation with a weak, "Well of course it's not a soft c, that would just be *silly*. Heh?"

He made a noise of dissatisfaction deep in his throat, his brows high on his forehead. With a jaded look in his eye, he glanced sidelong at Brett, muttering, "Must've been a bad day for democracy when this one was made team leader. You *do* realize every instance of your journey is evidence to the fact you're in over your heads, hm?"

"Careful, we might get the idea you actually care," Lin groaned from the back.

"And what a speaker I would be to turn lights on above empty heads," he commented around a scathing smile. I opened my mouth, then hesitated, unsure how to respond to this back-handed… compliment?

"Does that mean you do or don't care?" Kev chirped from the back, but Cillian paid him no mind. Instead, in one fluid motion, he pulled the pickaxe up into his hands, gave it a one-handed flip, and with a fluid motion, caught the grip in his palm with the dull point pressing Brett's cheek.

Brett flinched at the contact, a slight exaggeration as he shifted into a better position. The stance was almost indiscernible, but I knew his fighting style well enough to see the plan in his posture. He could knock the pickaxe out of Cillian's hands from this stance, easily disarming him if he slacked his grip, except Cillian's white-knuckled hold was anything but slack. So Brett merely fumed, unmoving, awaiting the perfect moment to strike.

Giving a theatrical yawn, Cillian twisted his wrist just enough to tap the pickaxe to Brett's nose with a request of, "Telepath, please. We don't have all day."

"*Briar? Can you hear me?*" I attempted, to no response. Panic clamped tight around my throat. An hour since she was last heard from, and now radio silence… "Our telepath might be in a rougher spot than us."

"Sure, sure. That's a better excuse, I'll give you that, but does it *change* anything? Sooner or later, those pora up there will sniff us out, and I'd prefer to be well on my way by then."

He gestured up toward the top of the cliff with the pickaxe only to freeze up as his aim fell directly on two distant figures. Exactly where he pointed the pickaxe stood two tall forms at the stone ledge of the cliff face at his back. From here, they looked like nothing more than silhouettes cast against the light of the ring bisecting the sky – surely, we who were still trapped in the gap between stone formations were masked by shadow and shapes. Not Cillian, who stood out in the open, waving a pickaxe around and making a scene in the deep valley.

Swearing under his breath, Cillian caught Brett's chin between thumb and forefinger, looking between Brett's eyes and mine as he hissed, "If anything you've said to me is true, you'll save me."

Brett pulled away with a look of disgust for the other man, seething with detestation, but Cillian raised his palms in a shrug as if to say it was on our conscience either way, and with that, gave a hefty swing of his pickaxe.

Except, the swing didn't make contact with Brett. Rather, he swung the pickaxe into the fragile wall of soil to the right of Brett, hooking a solid chunk and yanking out a sizeable dent in the soft slope which immediately came toppling down as the rich mound of silt burst forth.

An avalanche of dark, moist soil came tumbling down, filling the narrow gap where Brett and I stood, but not quite reaching Faith, Lin, and Kev behind me. The thick silt encased our feet, our legs, rushing swiftly up to my waist and swirling high around Brett's shoulders in a surge of dense, inescapable mass, trapping us.

In my struggle against the flow of heavy soil, I strained to maintain a view of Cillian. He tried to make a break for it, cresting a hill in the valley just visible over the slope of dirt encasing Brett.

A mirage shimmered in Cillian's path and out stepped one of the shadowed figures directly in front of him, clotheslining him and knocking him off his feet with her sudden appearance.

His back hit the ground, hard, and he let out a loud, whining wheeze. She must have been a magikier and a teleporter at that, but at this distance, what really struck me was that I recognized her. The familiar honey-blonde hair was raked back into a meticulous bun, pulled so tight, it hugged her scalp.

Sucking back a breath, my heart stuttered on a beat with the realization, this was the teleporter who'd taken Seth. With that same breath, I choked on a lump of soil and wheezed against the dirt banging on the front door to my lungs. If she heard anything from us, our whole group was done for, and there was little chance of saving Seth, Cillian, or ourselves.

"So, are you brave or stupid?" the woman demanded, pointing a blade to Cillian's throat.

"Ugh, neither," he groaned, lying back down with arms and legs spread-eagled across the ground. "This is pure, unlucky happenstance."

"Oh?" She stuck the tip of the blade under his chin, testing the elasticity of his skin. "Who were you talking to?"

"My very large retinue of bodyguards. Give it a moment, they'll be on you like dogs on a bone." He glanced up at her under his eyelashes. "Better start running."

She scoffed, focusing her gaze now entirely on him. Well I'll be damned, he'd given a lie so near to the truth, he'd covered it up entirely.

"And why would *you* have a retinue of bodyguards?"

"Couldn't you tell?" Cillian doubled down on his naturally presumptuous tone and gave a grand flourish of his arms from his sprawled position. "I'm a very important person."

"Mhm," she mused, a note of distaste flavouring the hum. "You're certainly *special.* The kind of special that would have a man make his great escape deeper into prison just to get himself caught throwing a temper tantrum at rocks."

He made a noise deep in his throat, somewhere between a scoff and a chuckle. "What an offensive assumption."

She stepped on his wrist, pinning it down. "Don't think I haven't heard of the man with half-white hair. You picked a bad time to come to Arillia, Bojack."

At the unfamiliar name, Brett and I shared a quizzical look, momentarily forgetting our situation in the Chinese finger trap of the soil.

"That *is* your name, isn't it?" the woman carried on, wearing a triumphant tone like she'd won some unspoken game of wits.

"Well, now hold on a minute," Cillian – or was it Bojack? – choked out, "I get this all the time, but you see, *I've* heard this Bojack's white hair is on the left side. His left, not yours. An easy mistake to make, I'll give you that." He gestured with his free arm up toward his own head of bicoloured hair, the white half on his right. "I'm flattered, truly, but you've got the wrong man."

"*Mhm.*" My head spun with the effort to keep up.

"Ah… friend of a friend?" he muttered, giving up the ghost. "Let me guess… Lana?" Judging by the way he said it, he was only guessing the first woman's name to cross his mind, but it just so happened to be Mom's name.

"Svatka." Her voice was flat with disillusionment.

"Gesundheit?"

I heard the thud before I realized she'd hit him. "You're a special case, Bojack. If all the stories are true, hardly a pawn of the centions, but a piss-poor ally in general."

"Fair enough. So where does that leave us?"

"I'll give you a choice. Join the fight for freedom – from the centions, from oppression, from injustice, all of it. And I do mean *fight.* Or be made an example of their systemic brainwashing before a high-profile crowd."

"And how would I do that?"

"We'd take a little off the top. Have I made myself clear?"

"Clear as a bell, darling," he sighed, sarcasm dripping from his tone. "I'm assuming neither is still a valid option?"

With a cruel laugh, she leaned down, pressing into the wrist under her foot, and caught his other arm as he threw it up to block her in case of another sucker punch. The moonlight bent around them, shimmering in an abrupt mirage. Just as suddenly as she had appeared, the woman disappeared once again, taking Bojack with her.

A pair of arms encircled my waist, wrenching me sideways out of the soil, as a third hand with cracked nail polish clamped down over my mouth. "Shh," Faith hissed in my ear, the restraining force around my middle. Kev released my mouth and reached past me to retrieve Brett, knotting his fist in his shirt and yanking, albeit with some manner of finesse so as not to disturb any more of the soil.

Kev whispered, "I don't think they realized we're here."

"Yeah, well, he'll throw us under the bus if we don't get moving, fast," Brett noted just as quietly, shaking the dirt off his boot as he stumbled back onto level ground.

"I doubt it." I glanced back toward the growing mound of dirt blocking our path to the Khuloces Base, to which that Liberation Front teleporter had surely taken him. "We're his only hope, now. And we're not giving up on this place just yet."

"But he did this to himself," Kev matter-of-factly stated like that could excuse the circumstances.

"Doesn't matter," I said in a deadly quiet voice, head ringing.

Lin's jaw dropped, a glint of moonlight reflecting off the lenses of her goggles. "You're kidding. They'll be on high alert now."

Faith nodded gravely. "Not just pora, but Liberation Front magikiers, too. If we weren't in over our heads before…"

"Yeah, yeah. We're down a guide and a dragon. But that doesn't change the mission." My heart cinched at the thought, but I shoved it down. Briar could handle herself, I had to believe as much. "Let's just stick to the plan," I decided, laying the overconfidence on thick. Faith, Lin, Brett, and Kev passed looks between themselves, partway confused but mostly just shocked at the notion of having a plan. Catching this, I sighed, "It's a figure of speech."

"It really isn't," Faith groaned.

18

Time Won't Be the Only Thing Getting Crunched

THE KHULOCES BASE CROUCHED ATOP AN EQUALLY STOUT PLATEAU shrouded beneath towering tree branches. The way up or in was hidden – hardly unexpected, especially if they had teleporters to act as transit – and the very same pull-apart loam that we found in the narrow ravine coated the plateau's sides. It would have been a hell of a lot easier if we had Briar to airdrop us in, but I'd rather not think about what was holding her up. Instead, I set my mind to just one task at a time. First: ascending the fifteen-foot height of unclimbable dirt. Hmm…

"We could really do with a teleporter of our own, huh?" Kev noted from his seated position atop a snaking root several times his width.

"I'm light enough. You could probably boost me up and over, right?" I considered, tilting my head toward Brett and Kev as I appraised the distance, resting my chin in hand.

"Not on your own," Brett said flatly, crossing his arms.

"Ooh-kay," I huffed under my breath, cutting a crease between my brows with a frown, "Shut down my brilliance, that's fine."

Before he had a chance to register my words, Faith bumped Lin with an elbow. "There's got to be a solid foundation hidden in all this sludge. What are the odds it'd be stone?"

"In our favour, that's what. And you might just be onto something." I could hear the grin in her voice, and she yanked her gloves up to her elbows.

"Hold on a second-" Brett cut in, but Lin waved him off with a flippant hand.

"A little magikier flair won't turn any pora heads." With that, she shoved her hand into the soil, rummaging around in the cliffside.

She pressed deeper, until she was up to her shoulder in cold, wet dirt and complaining about these very attributes. The temperature had already dropped considerably since the sun went down, calling forth a heavy fog around the mammoth trees.

"And the verdict is...?" Kev prompted.

Sputtering dirt as if it had somehow seeped through her mask, she wrenched her arm back out with a completely soaked-through sleeve. A small cascade of soil tumbled out after her arm, sprinkling to the mud-ridden ground in an awful likeness to tapped sewage. "It's all dirt as far as I can tell. I've got nothing to aim at."

"Damn," Faith muttered, pursing her lips. "You think we'd be used to the fantasy of convenience by now."

Lin tapped a finger to her chin. "Well wait just a minute. If you boys chuck *me* up there, I'd be closer to the foundation."

"Wha-?" I was about to object, but Brett and Kev nodded to each other and positioned themselves around her. "Oh, so when I suggest going up there alone, it's too dangerous, but sending in the fourteen-year-old, that's totally fine. No moral qualms there-"

Lin patted my shoulder in consolation. "*Someone* has to put your good ideas to use. They're rare enough as is."

"I- Hey! Your misplaced confidence doesn't change the risk factor-"

"You're one to talk," she wryly chuckled, and with that, tapped Brett and Kev's shoulders, which was apparently the universal signal for lift-off, for with that, they sent her sailing high overhead with one synchronized and powerful launch. She pirouetted in the air, giving me a small salute as she went, and landed unceremoniously atop the plateau where she fell out of view over the edge.

I heard her gasp against the chill of the mud as she waded against her own weight dragging her deeper down into the consuming sludge. The wall bucked and protruded around her as she disturbed the soil clinging to whatever geological components made up the plateau, such that the dirt looked to be alive, heaving with breath. By the small sounds she made, I imagined Lin struggling to keep her head above the soil as she floundered for anything to hold onto.

"We'll pull her out if she goes under," Faith assured me, having most certainly caught the abject horror I could feel mangling my expression.

"That won't be necessary," Lin's voice came back to us from over the ledge, huffing and puffing with the effort of pulling herself free, but unperturbed as she ever was. "The soil gets clumpier and more reliable away from the edge. But, uh, we didn't consider that the foundation might be, like, pure quartz or something… 'cause I'm pretty sure this mucky stuff's clay."

"Can you do anything with quartz?" Brett called back in a hushed voice – barely discreet as he battled the wind's whistling and howling.

"Quartz is a crystal." Not an ounce of patience could be found in her tone.

"Crystal's like rock."

A disembodied, "Yeah, well, not enough like rock," met his remark.

"I didn't realize you had such picky magic," Brett droned in frustration, crossing his arms over his chest. "Do you have a *preferred* rock?"

Her head popped up over the edge, her neck craned at an awkward angle, just to glare daggers down at him. "I'm not a shonte, I don't have control over every naturally occurring solid, just like Kev doesn't have control over any moderately warm temperature. *He* needs a flame. *I* need a clump of minerals, to make a fissure that reduces part of it to its smallest mineral components."

"Nobody asked for a science lesson-" Brett was saying, but Faith jabbed him in the side and gave a shake of her head, putting her foot down on their childish bickering.

Out of the corner of my eye, I noticed Kev glance down at the burns on his hands. There was a contrite expression in the tired lines under his eyes, just barely visible in a thread of light from the star-speckled sky.

Bumping his shoulder, I shot him an encouraging smile and cupped my hands around my mouth, reminding Lin in a loud whisper, "Cillian sorta put his life in our hands and his death on our collective consciences, so maybe save the magic tutorial for later?"

Pursing her lips, she muttered an unenthusiastic, "Oh, right," and disappeared once again over the ridge.

A soft rumbling emanated from the plateau. With it came an avalanche of soil pulling apart at the seams. A jagged crack opened like a slice taken out of a pie, drawn through the mud with larger slumps spilling to the ground in easily climbable mounds. And there at the very back of the parted soil was a stone ridge cleft in two, and Lin swinging her legs over the side from an out-of-sight nook.

"You coming?" Though she manufactured a bored inflection, I could hear the triumph in her tone. A victory of worth. Maybe it was because of what Kev had said, but I found myself noticing these little indications of pride in usefulness – and my own lack thereof.

Upon ascending the plateau, we were met with stone walls which rose up from the foundation without a seam or a cut. This, at least, didn't pose as much of a challenge as I initially anticipated – a distant commotion emanating from within the base appeared to have drawn any potential lookouts away from their duties on the wall walk.

Kev went first to scout the section of the wall we'd decided upon, and when he gave us the signal, the rest of us crossed the distance in a crouching sprint. Crouched over the dip of an embrasure, Kev reached a helping hand down to the rest of us as Brett hoisted from below. First went Lin, then Faith, then me, and finally, Kev and Faith each grabbed hold of Brett's arms, pulling him up after us as Lin and I kept watch on the other side.

We five lay flat on our stomachs across the wall walk, peering out over the edge into the courtyard below. From the height of the wall, I could see everything. A gap in the canopy overhead ushered in the pale luminance of the night sky, shimmering over puddles which dotted the flat stone. This dim lighting managed to illuminate most of the cluttered courtyard where discreet silhouettes blended into shadow, humanoid forms loitering by walls and seated on the indistinct shapes of barrels and crates.

Livestock pens contoured the courtyard where they reached up half the height of the walls with downward-slanted stone roofs. The ground around them was littered with straw, feathers, and other materials Brett noted would be perfect for silencing our footsteps. Not only that, but there was some sort of construction underway, using a pulley and winch system on a rotating treadwheel crane with several large slats of lumber on its elevated platform.

The courtyard itself was half-moon shaped and framed by the wall built directly into the stone structure toward the back. One gated entrance – a portcullis, I think it was called – with a dark overhang seemed the only way in or out of the dark building. Behind it, a dark tunnel sank into hard stone to hem the walls of shale and grit. It must have burrowed deep into the cold, dark depths beneath the Khuloces Forest.

There. That had to be it – what we were after. We had come to the place where this sect of the Liberation Front kept their high-priority prisoners. And there neighbouring it stood a small stage, raised from the ground and adorned with a dark-stained chopping block.

"I just want everyone to know, if it comes down to a contest of magic between me and a handful of stone-crafters, I don't stand a chance," Lin noted in a hushed voice. "To make a structure like this, and I have no doubts that building goes deep into the ground, it would've taken months for any less than five normal magikiers, and that's not even taking into account Valencia's whole domenth-bond hoopla."

"So stealth's the game, is what you're saying," Kev whispered.

"I'm saying we're screwed if we're caught, but sure, that's a nicer way of putting it-"

Leaping into motion, Brett grabbed Lin and Kev by their collars, pulling them down, and held his index finger to his lips. Before he could answer the demand for an explanation in each of our eyes, an unfamiliar voice reached us from below. Harsh and wet, like someone with a nasty head cold, the very sound of it had me recoiling on instinct.

I didn't need to see the speaker to know what he was. Pora.

"... damn pests, using magic like it's nothing to us," the disembodied voice berated in a mocking tone. "Did you see the one they just brought in? Honestly. It's like they can't be bothered to give us a break. Not even the damn hostage gives a rat's ass!"

"We better get a taste if they're gonna go wasting him anyway," grumbled a second, but the first still had more to his tangent.

"It's like, did they forget we're here? I thought they were supposed to be afraid of us? Our *uncontrollable bloodthirst* and all that bull?"

"They're magikiers, Finn. You think they care even a little what it feels like? Did you care at all when you were one of 'em?"

"I'll decide whether or not to be pissed about it, thank you very much. I swear, if that hoity-toity teleporter keeps jumpin' around like that, her muscles'll atrophy. You'd think it'd kill her to walk a few steps."

"There ain't much that couldn't kill a magikier," chuckled the other, "Unless we're talking about whatever bombed our brains the other night."

"Whatever the hell that was, it couldn't have been a magikier."

My hands clenched into fists, thumbs absent-mindedly worrying my knuckles. How many days out from the east bastion were we? And these pora had felt my magic – no not just felt it, been *bombed* by it.

"Think it's one of Lupei's?"

"The Liberation Front's been talking about a shonte." My breath caught high in my throat. "Felt more like Tenebret to me. Couldn't think straight till I got my hands on a bloodbag, and even then, anything I drank tasted rotten by comparison. Is that normal?"

"Hell if I know. You've been pora longer than me."

He snorted and spat on the ground at his feet. "Can't seem to get it out of my nostrils."

"Least you didn't pull an O'Malley. Damn fool grabbed a couple new recruits and bolted."

"He didn't!" the pora gasped, clearly making an effort to keep his voice low.

"I'm tellin' you! Broke rank to chase the insufferable scent like a goddamn animal. Even got Garett thinkin' about deserting – don't tell anyone I told you that. It's pora like them who give us a bad rap..." Their voices passed out of earshot, growing quieter as they moved off. Still, I dragged the meat of my thumb over the skin of my knuckles, pulling at the wounds Cillian – Bojack, I supposed – hadn't fully mended. A slight ache tingled beneath my skin.

O'Malley and a couple new recruits... My traitorous mind brought up an image of the dead scuttlepup – wolf spider, I obstinately reminded myself – that had been ripped into by pora hunting my blood. Hunting me. A shudder coursed up my spine.

No, this wasn't the time or place to get caught up in distant dangers. Clenching my fists around my thumbs, I shook off the sticky feeling of tar coating my insides. This was a time for heroism and victory.

"They've moved off," Faith whispered as Kev and Lin pulled away from Brett's hold on their collars.

I released a breath I hadn't realized I was holding, shooting a look out the side of my eye toward Lin. "They felt you use your magic, but I don't think they realized they were on a straight path to the source."

Faith nodded, contemplation shining in her eyes as she cupped her chin in hand. "And by the sound of it, they can't differentiate one magikier working their magic from another. They thought it was the teleporter."

"But they sensed it, anyway," Brett put in, "If stealth's the game, we'll all need to refrain from magic."

"Easy for you to say. Not like I'm the *only* one-" Lin was saying, but Kev held out an arm.

"Now's not the time. You hear that?"

We all fell silent, straining to catch whatever he had. All I heard were the mighty creaks of age-old branches filling the space of silence leftover in the wake of his words, and the chirping and croaking of strange creatures intermingling with whispers of soft winds brushing over the forest floor behind us, and... and something unspeakable. Low, so low I could barely make it out, but booming. Distant, as if leagues of land stretched between its source and my ears, but vast. The puddles speckling the courtyard rippled, catching pale beams from the light of the ring in the sky, with each far-off tremor. Rhythmic and barely discernible. Like…

The blood rushed to my toes, leaving me cold and choking on breath. Like far-off footsteps of some great and lumbering thing. Impossibly huge.

19

Go Big or Don't Go Home

"WHAT THE HELL IS THAT?" I SQUEAKED, BARELY AUDIBLE THROUGH MY choked-up windpipe.

"An inhabitant of the Khuloces Forest, maybe?" Faith's voice trembled.

Brett shook his head. "Whatever it is, it's far enough away, and no one down there seems to be bothered by it. Ignore it for now. We have smaller fish to fry."

"*Much* smaller," I breathed for fear of speaking any louder within range of whatever could make such a far-travelling ruckus. A silly precaution, I was aware, and yet so naturally capable of overpowering common sense.

In my distraction with the distant clamour, I jumped at the much closer sound of a familiarly haughty voice from behind the portcullis. Much like the faint booms of gargantuan footfalls far off from us, Bojack's inimitable voice sounded like it was getting closer. Indeed, the ground-shaking footfalls had grown somewhat in volume, like thunder clapping louder and more frequently the closer the storm clouds drifted overhead.

Shaking off my distraction, I re-centered myself and abandoned my over-the-shoulder glance. No thanks, uncanny sense of foreboding, I'd pay no more mind to the thunderous clamour bouncing through the impenetrable darkness, thank you very much. Instead, I honed my attention on the goings-on within the courtyard.

The portcullis gates groaned and began their slow, dragging ascent. From within, two adjacent lines of shadowy figures emerged. Bojack's bi-coloured hair gleamed under the moonlight, denoting his presence heading the line of prisoners, each hobbling with heavy-looking weights around their ankles. They didn't rattle or clang off the filth-covered stone like metal would, but rather scuffed and scraped like stone grating over stone. More indication to the work of stone-crafters.

The heavy clamour of weighted feet dragging across the courtyard nearly obscured the slithering hiss and jangle of metal chains linking each prisoner together by their ankle cuffs.

They couldn't have been more than fifteen feet from us, but Bojack made enough of a spectacle of himself to keep all eyes on him. Leaning in toward the pora stationed by the gate, or perhaps away from the magikiers restraining him, he loudly complained, "If this is meant to be my welcome party, you should consider replacing your party planner. On that topic, if the spot's open, I've been told my parties are to die for-"

"For the love of god, could we hurry this up?" groaned one of the silhouettes behind him, "If it weren't for these cuffs, I'd have beaten your head in already."

"Now, now, the only one beating anyone to death around here is me. As you can see, *I'm* first up to the chopping block." Blithe in the face of public execution, he chuckled at his own play on words.

"Yes, that *is* your general situation," sighed another among the throng with a faint Irish accent.

An orange glow emerged from beyond the gate, growing warmer and brighter until a pair of magikiers stepped out, making up the rear of the two lines and holding large, controlled flames in the palms of their cupped hands. Even from this meagre distance, I noticed the nearby prisoners shy away from the heat.

"More vhy'ry?" Faith guessed in a barely audible whisper.

"Fire-keepers," Kev granted with a nod, "To keep the pora in check, I bet."

Brett dipped his chin in an absent-minded nod, too focused on whatever he was counting on his fingers. "So, from what we've seen and estimated, we're dealing with three pora, one teleporter, two fire-keepers, and possibly a handful of stone-crafters. Either those five unverified magikiers down there are all stone-crafters, or any number of stone-crafters are hidden away inside that building. That's an unsettling number of ifs."

"That's *one* if," Lin flatly pointed out.

"One if and eleven enemies," Faith noted, "That we can see."

"Not the best odds-" My voice cracked. "-but I'm sure we've faced worse. And hey, we'll have thirteen prisoners on our side."

"Cillian included," Kev chipped in.

"Twelve on our side and one on Cillian's, then. We have the advantage of numbers."

Brett shook his head. "You heard what that teleporter said. He's to be made an example of. They'll be expecting him to start trouble."

"Which should give us an edge," Lin argued.

"How are we supposed to rescue him if he's the center of attention?"

"You have to admit, he's a phenomenal diversion. Getting Seth out of there will be a piece of cake," I reminded them, only for ice to shoot through my veins at the realization…

"Yeah, speaking of, I don't see him down there," Kev noted without even a hint of the panic I could feel coiling around my heart. "That teleporter said this is an example for *all* the top-notch prisoners, right?"

Whipping my head back around, my eyes raked over the courtyard, scanning the prisoners' poorly lit faces for the only one that mattered. On some distant level, it felt rude admitting this even just to myself, but Cillian, or Bojack, or whoever he was, had only ever been a means to an end. Seth was the whole reason we ventured all this way. Seth was *my* priority. Seth was… hah, that's strange, he wasn't anywhere to be seen, but that couldn't be – he *had* to be here.

"I doubt they're doing this in shifts," Lin noted, whapping the back of Kev's head for the dumb question.

"Not helping-" I choked out, but my voice was so small, I doubted any of them heard.

"So if Knox is here, we should be able to see him," Faith tacked on over my failing voice, the final nail in the coffin containing my trampled hopes.

"He wasn't brought here." My voice shook, but never rose louder than a whisper. Damnit. *Damnit!* "They must've sent him to Cerenthior!" And to a seemingly inescapable fight.

Chasing Seth to that occupied city meant confronting the subject of Brett's most disheartening visions. The nameless man who felled an entire nation with an army of magikiers and pora alike, who took the dragon-bone glaive for himself, and who I was supposed to put out of Arillia's misery as the shonte. Seth had gone to the formidable company of Valencia's champion, her top general, while we allowed ourselves to become distracted. Misguided.

"What was the point of any of this!" I hissed, wiping furiously at the indignant tears so swift to spring to my eyes.

"I'll give it you straight, Annie, it's starting to look like there wasn't one-" Kev was saying, but Lin whacked him again, knocking him away. In the same motion, she grabbed my shoulder and directed my gaze to the courtyard.

"What was the point? Look at all those people down there. Thirteen captured. One of them, admittedly, a dirtbag who deliberately glued himself to your conscience. You're gonna tell me *you* of all people don't see the opportunity to do some good here?"

I flinched back from her words, my heart sinking somehow lower in my gut.

"Stop making it sound like a cakewalk," Brett shot back, vitriol in his tone, "Annie's right to run from an avoidable confrontation. There are thirteen prisoners, sure, but they're being watched by more captors than we currently have eyes on."

Faith dipped her chin in a pensive nod. "If we retreat now, we can live to find Knox later."

Lin shook her head, her pink fringe parting over the red mark in the center of her forehead. "I'm with you whatever you choose, Annie, but you need to be true to yourself. Leaving now, it'll eat away at you. I know it will."

"Stop it," Brett growled and sidled up on his elbows closer to me, "I know it's a foreign concept to you, but you need to think about yourself. How can you help anyone if you're dead?" His eyes implored me to call it off like we'd spoken about last night, a silent plea to follow through on my promises, but all I could do was lower my gaze and bite my lip against the surge of emotion hitting the back of my throat.

In a small voice, I spoke my truest mind. "We can't just leave them."

"Annie." His voice carried a warning, an unspoken ultimatum.

"I know what I said to you, but it's not hopeless."

A tetchy noise grated in his throat. "Just senseless, then."

Brett and Lin fell into a quarrel of harsh whispers, mediated poorly – in fact, failingly – by Kev, but the emotion had drained me, and I mentally checked out of their argument. I felt Faith's hand on my back, a gentle pressure supporting my decision, but she held silent. She must have come to the same realization as Lin.

Down below, Bojack was waltzing up to the chopping block, his hands bound and a burly bear of a man clasping his shoulder so tight, I could see the dimples his oversized fingers made from where I was. Bojack wobbled slightly along the way as the earth shook again, but no one seemed to pay these tremors any mind, so I wouldn't either.

Twelve prisoners stood huddled together at the front of the platform, boxed in against the elevated stone by seven magikiers, two of whom bore flames in their cupped hands. A clear distinction drew an invisible line between these magikiers and their pora cohorts. Like grotesque statues, the two pora we had overheard earlier held their posts closer to the building, and the third stationed herself just adjacent to the platform, facing the crowd with her back to us.

While my friends bickered in hushed voices between themselves, the Liberation Front magikier at the far end of the line of prisoners read off a sentence I didn't care to tune into. It was more for the audience's sake than Bojack's, I presumed. But for all the effort gone into this, only one in the line of detainees seemed to be paying any attention at all, the rest too beaten up and bloodied to escape their own evident suffering.

In the very middle of the line-up, one prisoner stared up at Bojack with a look of dumbfounded disbelief.

Something about this young man caught a wire in the back of my mind, twanging with a sense of… of what? I couldn't fathom what had my heart stuttering on a beat, just for a moment. Nor what caught my breath high in the back of my throat.

Ren…

I started in surprise at the disjointed thought, barely even a word.

Sure, for a prisoner, his dishevelled brown hair had a certain sheen, pulled back into a messy bun with a single strand of dark hair tumbling down before his eyes, but I wasn't this much of a hopeless disaster, was I? Enough to lose my cool at the sight of a dirt-caked boy? No, this feeling, whatever it was, held a peculiar familiarity devoid of memory. A second-hand response–

Bojack tutted disdainfully, purposefully interruptive, and the sentence-reader's grip on the page tightened. He was leaned in close over the speaker's shoulder, eyes flicking side-to-side as he peer-reviewed his own death sentence. "I see you've made three spelling mistakes."

One thing I was sure of: we didn't have *time* to bicker. Only to act. And when I was most unsure of a situation, I had a tendency to act with the utmost, oft misplaced confidence.

"Okay, listen up. Kev and Lin, go left. Brett and Faith, you go right. Take the wall walk to flank from ten and two and knock out those pora on either side of the building if you can. Lin, your top priority is breaking the prisoners' stone shoes. Got it? Good. Let's go."

"Wait-!" Brett hissed, but I was already on the move.

Giving my friends no chance to argue any further, I dropped down from the wall and swung from the roof of the sheep – or maybe boar? – pen below, landing lightly on the balls of my feet with bent knees among the pig-eared yet woolly, tusked animals – the small half-bleating, half-snorting sounds they made covered any noise from me.

I was lucky these six large beasts with coats of dapple-grey fleece only snuffled at my feet and bumped me around without much of a reaction to my presence. They could have blown my cover easily. Instead, I clambered over the gate of their pen and lowered into a slinking crouch.

Yeah, I was really doing this.

My heart pounded high in my throat. My palms, slick with sweat, slipped on the wood fencing of the adjacent pen to which I clung. Three words circled my head in an endless loop. *Get to Bojack.* It was all I had to do, tackle one task at a time.

I scanned the crowd in the middle of the busy courtyard, all of whom had been gathered on the other side of the platform. As expected, all eyes on–

I froze. Among the prisoners and their captors, one pair of eyes met mine across the courtyard, the same pair that had been rapt on Bojack with exasperated incredulity. This emerald-hued gaze belonged to the only attentive prisoner, the one who wore his tousled hair up in a poor excuse for a bun. Tall, broad-shouldered, narrow hips; he had the toned look of an athlete.

He could be of use.

Sporting an expression like his brain had stalled in the effort of processing what he was seeing, he managed a semblance of covertness as he stared at me. Finally, he bobbled his head, as if shaking off his momentary surprise, and gave a subtle tip of his chin toward one of his captors at the edge of the group – now that I got a better look, I recognized the teleporter's honey-blonde hair, raked back into a tight, military-style bun.

When I glanced back to him, he made a similar gesture to the magikier reading Bojack's long-winded death sentence – at this length, it was nothing short of a manifesto – followed by a final tilt of his head toward the pora next to the stage on which Bojack impatiently tapped his foot.

The dishevelled prisoner surely possessed some great affinity for body language, for I immediately understood; these were the head honchos of the

Khuloces Base. With that, he sent me a conspiratorial wink and returned his gaze to Bojack as if he hadn't just partaken in this impromptu heist with me.

Looking around, no one else seemed to have noticed me – just the perceptive young man. With heart pounding against my ribcage, a smile tugged at the corner of my mouth. Good. We now had *two* men on the inside, even if one was a complete stranger, and the other, a raving egomaniac.

No matter this shred of progress, our time was running out, made all the more evident when the man restraining Bojack grabbed the back of his neck in a fist as large as Bojack's entire head. The mammoth-sized man shoved him down to the chopping block, the loud *thump!* of what was likely blunt force head trauma echoing off the surrounding walls.

"*Ow*, stop it," Bojack whined on reflex. Seeming to realize the absurdity of his plea, he let out a bubble of demented laughter – surely the Stockholm syndrome couldn't have set in so fast – and hushed up with an audible gulp. It was like he didn't know how to react, and could I blame him?

Kicking myself into gear, I crept forward under deep shadows cast by the pens and the wooden crane. No guards had bothered to cover the rear of the platform but getting close enough to take cover was risky.

Risk or not, I had few precious seconds to reach Bojack before he was done for–

"Can we pause a moment? I'm a little unclear on something," came a jaunty voice, deep and confident. An Irish lilt in his voice implied the ghost of an accent he'd grown mostly out of. This guy again.

With a hasty glance across the platform, I found the speaker to be the perceptive prisoner, disturbingly casual in his interruption of the execution's next and final step. His neighbours in the line-up gestured nervously for him to let it go, whatever it was, their faces drawn into frowns and grimaces as they passed shifty-eyed glances between each other, but he waved off their concern.

"Does this bleak outing now mean death penalties are on the table, or is there a prerequisite to it? You'll have realized the man you've got up there is a convicted felon across Cellana, wanted dead or alive in most countries and pursued by bounty hunters of all creeds. I'm only curious, as this one's a bit of a special case. The rest of us, well, we just don't fit the bill, do we?"

"What are you getting at?" groaned a jaded voice.

"It's just, you're framing this as capital punishment, but I'm hardly concerned for *my* well-being. I don't quite *feel* expendable enough, I suppose."

I was certain, if his captors weren't so stunned by his audacity, they wouldn't have let him get a single word out. Instead, the courtyard held its collective breath. Bojack turned his head under his captor's hand to get a better view of the crowd, this slight movement sending ripples through the heavy tension in the air, and he huffed a lock of dead, white hair out of his eyes.

I almost couldn't believe my eyes. The stranger had seamlessly pivoted the crowd's attention away from Bojack, taken entirely upon himself.

Grabbing the figurative bull by the horns, I snuck across the span of courtyard to the platform, and nearly leapt out of my skin in alarm at the sudden, wild tremble in the ground, bucking under me from a far-off source. The tremors were getting worse, but they covered any sounds of movement I might have made as I took full cover behind the platform, my back to the raised stone. Less a platform, more an altar, I supposed. And Bojack, the sacrifice.

"Are you volunteering yourself for the next available slot?" the teleporter's recognizable tones of contempt chimed in. "For all the trouble you've been, you've more than earned it."

"Trouble? That doesn't sound like me," reflected the prisoner with a dollop of honey sweetening his tone.

I peeked up over the edge of the platform. Bojack's left foot lay within arm's reach as he knelt over the chopping block, but I couldn't just yank him out from under his hulking subjugator's vise-like grip.

Peering up the monumental back of the executioner who had Bojack pinned under him, I mentally flipped through my options. No magic. No real back-up, either. Not until Kev, Brett, Faith, and Lin started breaking prisoners' chains. Just my sabre sheathed on one hip and my mace hanging from the other, paired with the element of surprise facilitated by the stranger's ongoing distraction, but that wouldn't last long once I revealed my position.

As I wracked my brain for a plan, moonlight glared into my eyes off something just beyond the towering executioner. Following the gleaming reflection, my eyes adjusted to the metal-framed platform of heavy lumber dangling from the wooden crane. A thick rope – hooked to two durable cables with all four ends looped around pegs protruding from each corner of the platform – held these materials aloft over the head of the pora standing next to the platform.

Now there's an idea. I just had to time it right.

The distance from my place of cover to the crane couldn't have been more than a hop and a skip away, but I'd be passing close to the pora. At the very least, she was just as distracted as everyone else with the stranger's discussion about– I listened in–

"... and they cut the line. Sent me out to sea on a shoddy raft with nothing but a trowel to defend myself, and they didn't even know I'd taken it! Current would've strung me along a straight path to the overrun Isles, but I paddled like my life depended on it, mainly because it did, with that damned gardening tool and by the time I made it back to port, they were already holding my funeral. I swear, thespians that they were, they even had tears in their eyes. Lovely folks, just not the most hospitable captors. Not compared to you lot, anyway..."

Okay, I had no idea what he was talking about nor how he had gotten to this topic, but whatever he was on about, he held his audience captive.

Peeking out in the direction I meant to go, I observed the pora lady for a moment, watching the way her jaundiced and bloodshot eyes shifted between the stranger and Bojack, and the way her hand twitched eagerly toward the single-edged sword sheathed over her back with the long handle poking up just past her strong-hand shoulder. Judging by her restless tics and ready posture, she would win the contest of haste if she caught sight of me.

I slinked around behind her, moving quickly and close to the ground to reach the heavy body of the crane mounted atop a rotary device. A set of wooden planks made up a short staircase to the treadwheel operating the crane's pulley system. With light feet and slow movements, I climbed the steps, taking care not to make a sound.

The view from this meagre height showed the entirety of the courtyard, including a direct route to Bojack, obstructed only by the pora loitering under the platform held aloft by the very rope spooled next to me.

My window was fast closing. The stranger's affinity for meandering speech wasn't running out – he had a limitless supply, by the sounds of him – but his audience retention had begun to slip. Quickening my pace, I unsheathed my sabre with a hiss from its leather scabbard and tested the blade against the rope. I'd have fared better with a toothy saw blade, but I made do with what I had and began cutting along the length of rope held taught against the arm of the crane.

Glancing out of the corner of my eye, I saw the teleporter grab the stranger by his collar and yank him in close, growling some form of insult or perhaps a threat directly into his face. My heart skipped a beat, but this staggering concern was only fleeting.

Whether it was his carefree posture – with shoulders thrown back and his core engaged as he leaned all his weight on one leg – or his closed-eyes smile making light of the situation, I wasn't worried for him. Not only that, but *he* hardly appeared bothered. Every ounce of his being waved off all concern, an aura of casual confidence shucking off whatever the world threw at him.

No such luxury extended to the pora positioned under my improvised assault.

The rope snapped – at the sound, the stranger grabbed hold of the teleporter's shoulders, keeping her from using her magic lest she bring all the chained prisoners along with her. There was no escaping what came next.

The rushing sound of rope-burn whipped through each metal loop along the crane's arm, chasing the heavy platform, and was joined by a commotion toward the back of the crowd derived from the two other pora. Standing over their haphazardly slung forms were Brett and Kev, bodies contorted in the act of swinging their maces. They were still following through their swings when the platform dropped onto the third pora's head, flattening her like the Wicked Witch of the East beneath it.

Just like that, all three pora lay immobilized on the ground.

Having announced ourselves with the kind of gusto that opened rock concerts, Lin and Faith threw themselves at the crowd before the remaining Liberation Front could gather their wits. Lin pressed her hands to the two nearest prisoners' stone cuffs while Faith provided her cover, and with two loud cracks, the cuffs split in half under her palms, freeing both prisoners whom Faith promptly outfitted with our extraneous weapons. Lin had no use for hers, instead focused on freeing the prisoners.

Before the Liberation Front magikiers could adjust to the situation, I vaulted the railing in front of me, propelling myself from the height of the stairs.

Time felt as if slowed as I soared through the air from this meagre height. In that sensation of timelessness, my gaze combed the ground below, showing me exactly where I needed to land, and who I needed to hit first.

I let my body roll from my feet to my thigh to my upper arm when I landed on the stack of lumber on the crane's load-bearing platform, scaling the meagre slope onto the stage where Bojack lay prone. In the same fluid motion, I rolled back onto my feet and bounded from the lumber, engaging my core muscles to thrust the heels of both my feet into the chest of the bear-like executioner.

The wind rushed out of him under the heels of my boots, and he sailed back several feet, flying right off the platform. Not a moment later, I landed on my side and swung around into a lunge.

From beyond the stage came a loud popping sound following the man, and a cloud of energy like a shimmering bubble shoved him back toward me from palms thrown out behind him. Energy expulsion magic – precise enough to have sliced clean through Bojack's neck, if my deductions were correct.

Fast, fast, I had to react faster than he could get me. I had to do *something.*

Giving myself no time to second-guess my actions, I stepped on Bojack's back and grabbed tight hold of the sentence reader cowering ahead of him. In the same motion, I thrust my sabre to the sentence reader's throat, so automatic, so mindless, the very act of it oozed a sticky cruelty from my heart. This, a bluff I desperately hoped no one would call.

With my heartbeat pounding in my ears and adrenaline rushing through my veins, I shouted the first thing that came to mind, "Drop your weapons and lie face-down in the dirt! *Now!*"

By the wide-eyed terror and slack-jawed fear I saw in the faces all around me, I doubted anyone realized I was only parroting bank robbers I'd seen in movies. The world trembled again, seeming to punctuate my words, and the courtyard fell still and silent.

The echo of my harsh voice reverberated in the air around me, the sharpness of my tone feeling somehow unfamiliar. My lips had shaped each word but some other power had coloured my voice the red of malice.

Before I could dwell on this peculiarity, the magikier in my grip shifted – my shock at his nerve considering I had a blade to his throat did nothing for my reaction time.

It was a split-second before I noticed the discolouration of his skin, and only then did I realize he'd turned the flesh of his throat to stone. A stone-skin magikier.

A rock-hard elbow jabbed up toward my face, but instinct alone had me ducking out of the way just in time, watching out of the side of my eye as this one-hit knock-out grazed past my ear.

With slipping grip, I threw my sabre – aiming for the ground at the feet of the chatterbox who'd given us the distraction we needed, but one of his peers swooped down to claim it before he could – and in the same action, extended my arm holding onto the stone-skin's collar.

The stone-skin wobbled in a failed effort to find his balance after throwing that jab, automatically latching onto my arm, and gripped the edge of the platform by the toes of his shoes. With that, I readjusted my hold on his collar and with my free hand, drew the mace from the leather strap on my hip.

An idea shoved to the spotlight in my scattered and panicking mind and I overexaggerated its heft to make a performance of raising my weapon over his head. A silent threat.

An image of pure, shining confidence appeared in my mind's eye, taking the form of the only person I had ever known to wear it well: Val Darling. "Neat trick. I wonder how hard I'd have to hit you to break you to pebbles?" The words poured out of me on a hiss of breath, sending a chill up my spine at the unfamiliar hint of sadism in my voice.

He gulped, loud and obvious, seeming to see right past me to the image in my head. He trembled under my grip much as the ground shook beneath my feet, and rescinded the stone from his throat, peeling back the layers of bravado to reveal his hidden dread.

"Cillian – Bojack – his weapons," I commanded and removed my foot from Bojack's back.

Watching me quietly, he pulled himself up to his knees, his hands still bound, and patted down the stone-skin magikier. Any weapons he found, he tossed to the prisoners Lin was still in the effort of freeing. One by one, the freed prisoners took up arms and turned them on their former captors.

It happened so fast. Blood splashed over the ground, shouts and cries filled the air, and I bellowed automatic commands at the rest to surrender, voice breaking over my barely masked plea.

Most who remained did as I commanded, dropping their weapons and falling to their knees in the hay and the dirt, where they pressed their foreheads to the filth in fear. A shrill ringing peeled between my ears. Four dead littered the ground around them.

"Do as she says, or it'll be your heads!" Brett barked at them, the sharp clap of his shout startling the rest into obedience, and they dropped their weapons on mere reflex. Kev and Faith swooped in, confiscating what they threw down.

A deafening silence filled the courtyard as everyone within wavered over what to do next – the Liberation Front's teleporter had fallen unconscious in my nameless ally's chokehold, their stone-skin magikier had been duped by my bluff and quailed under the threat of my mace, and their pora lay motionless on the ground among those slaughtered by the freed prisoners.

This base had been compromised within a span of mere seconds – too fast for anyone to react – and the six blood-spattered prisoners Lin had already freed were armed with the weapons of their captors.

"What next? Huh?" hissed the stone-skin under my mace, "You think you can get away with this, just the four a'you?"

"You think there are only four of us? That's cute." My voice hardly sounded my own, giving everything over to my performance of Val Darling's confidence in the wake of this bloodshed.

Some part of me felt this wasn't a lie – how could there only be four of us. I felt such a powerful presence within, so powerful, it seemed to be talking through me. Maybe that was why he so readily believed me, snapping his mouth shut with a quivering chin.

I tipped my head in Brett and Kev's direction, automatic in my movement and unable to speak for the weight in my lungs. They understood this unspoken command meant they were to lead the rescued off the premises, and they set immediately to action. Two of the armed prisoners kept the Liberation Front down on their knees while Brett and Kev boosted the others over the wall. Lin, meanwhile, kept up her efforts while Faith watched her back.

"To lower casualties," I added in a strange voice, an offhand remark to shake up the stone-skin. Our whole operation would surely take a turn for the worse if he or any of our foes gained even a shred of composure.

A small sound of muttered cursing caught my attention and I glanced out of the corner of my eye to Bojack only to find that while looking down at him, I couldn't see any of the dead, as if what I couldn't see bore no weight upon my conscience.

As I watched, he shuffled on his fettered hands and knees in a failure of subtlety as if to go with the other rescues, but I hooked the toe of my boot on the rope binding his hands and yanked him back.

"Where do you think you're going?"

"To safety? I'm sorry, does that not constitute a rescue mission?" His twitchy eyes flashed to the crowd, intent on something I didn't care to discern through all the commotion.

Somehow, in my own incredulity with this absurdity in human form, a cup of relief had been added to the sea of anxiety churning in my chest. If nothing else, this clown of a man was a harmless problem, but one I could emotionally handle – which made it something I could prioritize in this moment of panic burgeoning high in my throat.

"Don't go getting smart with me-"

"If that's your main concern, I suddenly understand why you've never bothered raising the bar for cognitive thinking among your crowd. You would appear to be the bat among rats as far as thinkers go-"

"You ungrateful-!" I fumed, steaming out the ears, "No, I don't trust you as far as I can throw you, so you're gonna stay right where I can see you. And you know what, while you're at it, why don't you go over some ideas on how to approximate someone who isn't *excruciatingly obnoxious*! Just sit still and don't make a fuss!"

"Mm, I don't know. You're asking a lot of me."

"Wha-? How!"

"I've never not made a fuss, not a single day in my life."

I was sure I felt a vein throbbing on my forehead as I shut him up with a withering look. "We came after you – *saved* your *life*, actually – so if you could just pretend to be worth saving, I'd really appreciate it."

"You drive a hard bargain," he remarked, tone dripping with sarcasm, and earned my red-tinged glare. A strained, coward's smile picked up the corner of his mouth and he surrendered with a pair of open palms, sitting quietly beside me with legs crossed, his chin in his hand, and a gaping yawn stretching his mouth. "Wake me when I'm no longer in life-threatening peril, then, would you?"

"Are you so unbothered?" grunted the stone-skin.

"On the contrary, I am simply bothered." His eyes went wide on something or someone in the crowd, and he ducked his head between his shoulders, averting his gaze. Although I knew better than to let myself get distracted, I couldn't help my own glance in Brett and Kev's direction, silently wishing they'd hurry up and boost all the freed prisoners over the wall, but Lin could only break the chains so quickly. I was stuck here holding a hostage and maintaining a bluff with nothing else to do but feel myself getting antsier by the second.

Just then, and directly in front of me, the sound of an elbow plopping down on the platform's edge caught my ear, and I spun back around to address this new interruption. "What now?"

At the end of the platform, the stranger who'd proven himself quite helpful had his elbow propped up on the stone with his head resting on his filth-caked knuckles and the unconscious teleporter gripped tightly under his other arm.

So close, I could see through the muck, grime, and unkempt stubble of his unkind imprisonment, insinuating an elegant jawline, dark eyelashes, sharp nose, and charismatic smile to pair with the emerald hue of his eyes, the bronze of his skin, and the dark, sun-streaked locks of his hair wound up in a bun. He was, unfortunately, handsome. But he was also close enough that I could *smell* his unkind imprisonment, and I might as well have been back in the boar pen for the stink of him.

I doubted he noticed his own stench, for he batted his eyelashes and exaggerated his leaning pose against the side of the stage. Even now, with all that was going on, he was wreathed in smiles and gazed up at me from contented cat eyes. For no reason I could discern, he looked like he was about to strike up a casual conversation with me.

In that somewhat diminished Irish lilt, he optimistically began, "Heya Red, masterful execution of the breakout. Really, I'm just happy to be a part of it."

"Yeah, thanks for the distraction," I said uncertainly, glancing out of the side of my eye toward Bojack, who merely shrugged his shoulders before returning to his attempted nap.

"Ah, don't mention it. I only came over to say, whatever you've got goin' on here, I'm in."

"E-excuse me?" How many surprises was I going to endure in this trying endeavour, and from the very persons in need of rescuing, no less. "You don't even know what you're signing up for."

"Frankly, I've got nothing else going on, so I might as well..." His words trailed off, an easily read allusion to some impending request.

Looking him up and down, I measured the indignance in my tone and groaned, "Why does it sound like you're about to ask me for something?" Honestly, it was like herding cats with these Arillians.

"Funny you say that." He flicked a finger out in Bojack's direction, tipping his head toward him so the stray locks of hair framing his face fell prettily askew. He obviously knew what he was doing. "I'll just come out and say it, will I? As luck would have it, you have the bounty I've been hunting there under your foot. Don't know if you heard, but there's a high price on his head. Now, I'm personally not in it for the money- *aaand* I see I'm losing my audience."

I passed a wary glance between Bojack, the stone-skin, and the handsome stranger. "This really isn't the time."

"Unfortunate, that," he mused as if his terrible timing was as regrettable as it was unavoidable, "Can I ask that you forgive my impatience a moment longer? After a few months in a dark pit with nothing but angst-ridden revolutionists for company, it's a bit of an adrenaline rush seeing my objective wrapped up like a present two feet in front of me."

"I think that speaks to something else entirely."

He smiled – not like he'd ever stopped smiling – and his entire face brightened with this slight shift in his expression. "Anywho, I'd be happy to take the wily little rake off your hands. Or scrape him off the sole of your boot? Whichever you'd prefer." He waved his hand placidly as he spoke and beamed up at me so expectantly, I almost pitied him.

"I… What? No." Aiming for a covert glance, I flicked my gaze hastily to the stone-skin. This stranger's absurd level of comfort with me was doing neither of us any favours.

"No?"

"Sorry to disappoint, but I just risked my life for this guy. I'm not about to give him up to the first person who comes asking."

"Ah, you could never disappoint, sweetheart."

"Don't call me sweetheart."

"What would you prefer?" he asked nicely. He made it all seem so inconsequential with a closed-eyes grin, but I could tell he wasn't done.

"Anything other than sweetheart, *sweetheart.*" Though my tone was thick with sarcasm, dripping vitriol, he seemed entirely unperturbed.

"No problem, love."

"Ugh," Bojack grunted, shifting under my heel, and motioned in my general direction for the other man's sake. "I wouldn't if I were you, this one'll get you killed."

"How charming," smiled the stranger, "But let's stay on topic, yeah? What d'you say, Red? Would you have a change of heart if we called this little trade-off recompense for my help here?" He waggled the limp body of the teleporter enfolded in the crook of his arm.

Any former sympathy I had for him – whom I'd assumed had abetted our little heist without any ulterior motives besides his own freedom – vanished in the blink of an eye, and I narrowed my gaze. "So you only helped us to get your hands on Cillia- damnit, Bojack?"

"Well, Mad Jack, but-"

"How many names-?" I shook off my exasperation. "No, better question: Do magikiers on Cellana do *nothing* outside their own self-interest?"

A spark of fascination shone in his captive regard. "I'd like to think not, but I'm curious; what does that make you?"

Damnit.

"Whatever. I said it to him, I'll say it to you; he's not leaving my sight." The blithe stranger opened his mouth again, the slight smirk on his lips implying he already had a counterpoint prepared, but I cut in with, "It's non-negotiable, so just drop it!"

"Non-negotiable?" he echoed with furrowed brows and pouting lips as if genuinely disheartened by my rejection. I supposed this was as far from a smile as he'd come since I first laid eyes on him. "Not to talk your ear off in the middle of a prison break, but I've been on this bounty for near a year now with just a picture for reference. I tracked stories of the man with half-white hair, all the way from Schevon."

"I don't know where that is." Even the stone-skin looked surprised at that, a derisive expression breaking through the slowly fading fear painted in broad strokes upon his face.

"If I may break down the main points of my journey for you, then?" the stranger carried on, pulling a groan out of Bojack which I might've echoed if not for the façade I was struggling to maintain. "I tracked him 'cross land and sea, never knowing a soft bed or an ample meal, and *always* running out of funds. Jesus, Mary and Joseph how it got away from me. It was fierce desperate altogether until I finally cornered the slippery layabout in Cerenthior. Got him locked up by accident, I'll admit. Wasn't my intention, but I'd gotten used to rolling with the punches by then. Ah but the punches, they just kept punching. You can imagine my surprise when this fresh war cropped up out of nowhere, and me caught up square in the middle of it. Didn't even see them comin'. Knocked me clean off me feet and I woke up here. Not many can say they were the very first bludgeoned unconscious at the outset of a war, but I'm pleased to hold a record for something."

"Riveting," I drily noted.

"Yes, I know. So here I find myself in this fine establishment after said series of unsolicited adventures-"

"A fine establishment for swine-" Bojack grumbled out the side of his mouth.

"Uh-huh..." The stranger did his best to ignore him, much like Bojack made it apparent in his aloof pose that he was trying his darnedest to feign our nonexistence. "All that to say, wouldn't it be more satisfying, for both myself as the bounty hunter, and you as my fortuitous friend, if I could walk out with the bounty that got me into this mess? The driving purpose of my life this past year? Subtract from that my detainment here, of course, which was notably devoid of purpose or an appreciation of *life* in the standard sense." He drew air quotes around the word with his free hand. "But I digress."

I pursed my lips and tilted my head as if in contemplation. "No. Frankly, I have zero attachments to your bounty hunting gig *and* a conscience I'd prefer to keep clear. You'll just have to be satisfied with your freedom."

The stone-skin's eyes cut back and forth between us as if following a tennis match, the fear that had once widened them to copper pennies subsiding. But my attention was in the wrong place.

Movement caught my eye, my only warning.

A lock of the teleporter's glossy blonde hair had twitched, falling over her face to reveal steely grey eyes fluttering open. The stone-skin shifted in my grip at the same moment, an unconsciously coordinated attack as he reached for my mace and wrested it out of my grasp. With split focus, I lost sight of the teleporter in all the stone-skin's writhing about and misplaced my footing from Bojack's bindings.

It all seemed to be happening in slow motion as I felt more than saw the turn of the tide in the Liberation Front's favour.

I couldn't react fast enough when the teleporter burst into action, blinking through space to move faster than should have been possible – and directly through the chest of the stone-skin. His body had blocked her from view, and her hand had snaked out so fast, I couldn't hope to track her movement with my eyes even if she were within my line of sight.

Her arm burst through the stone-skin's unarmoured chest, blinking in and out of space as he bellowed in agony, and she closed her grip around my wrist. Just like before when she stole Seth away from me, she took me by surprise.

In a flash, she'd taken hold of me, and not a moment later, the world pulsed and bloomed around us. Not only the teleporter and I, but the stone-skin's body and the chatty stranger, too, who still held onto her.

As she worked her magic, the world pulled away as if the stage curtain on which all things were illustrated had been drawn back, revealing instead an entirely different setting.

A headache emerged in my effort to figure out where we'd ended up, head spinning dizzily with motion sickness. Though I hadn't moved an inch, I found myself in a deep, dark chamber, boxed in with only one exit where shadows blocked the way. Immediately, my senses were struck by an odour of pungent veggies mingling with the ranker scents of sawdust and clay heavy on the air, only then muted by the must of mildew in the corners.

Directly above, albeit muffled and distant, an uproar of voices and violence drew my attention to the ceiling of this dimly lit room, illuminated by a line of hanging lightbulbs on ceiling hooks. That could only mean…

The stranger yelped, dropping the teleporter on instinct, who doffed the wheezing and struggling stone-skin from her arm with another flicker of movement. The stone-skin hit the floor hard and went still.

A dark pool bloomed all around him as my insides became a wintry tundra. I found myself falling away from the sight, retching in the back of my throat as I stumbled back against a body. Shallow breaths and a fluttering heartbeat met the back of my head at the stranger's chest-level.

Dazed, I tipped up my chin, face turning upward to find his face more than a foot over mine, his eyes wide with alarm and seeming to pose a question as they met mine. He patted my shoulders with either hand, stepping back from me as he breathed more to himself than to me, "Well… I was feeling too privileged today anyway."

As if my bad luck were contagious, when he stepped backwards, he was enfolded into a looming shadow and yelped again for the spines protruding from this towering darkness. They jabbed into him and caught up the material of his prison garb, and from the shadowy mass, one shell-encrusted arm snaked out, encircling him to knot its overly long fingers in his unruly hair.

He was screaming an unmanly cry, flailing his arms out wildly in a futile attempt to escape his unmistakably kirranite captor's vise-like grip, but he dared not wrench away while the kirranite tangled its prickly hand in his hair.

In turn, the kirranite made a strange choking noise, somewhere between a hiss and a gurgle, and bashed him over the head with its thorny elbow. The stranger's body slumped down to the floor, a streak of blood running swiftly from a gash carved out by one of the innumerable barbs deforming its glossy black carapace.

My trembling hands balled into fists at my sides, and my eyes skirted around the body of the stone-skin, unable to look at the death laid out before me.

"How could you do that-?" My lifeless whimper carried an echo of the deranged confusion buzzing madly in my head, and I turned my empty stare upon the huffing and puffing teleporter. "He was on your side… He trusted you and you *plunged your fist through his chest.*"

A hissing sound came from the exit, but I couldn't tear my eyes from the teleporter. The air around me whipped like a storm, chasing my hair up toward the ceiling as the floor quaked beneath my feet, but this wasn't like the other times my magic had poured irrepressibly out of me. This time, it wasn't an expulsion of my will, but an extension of the emotion unfurling in my chest. The blank anger, the vacuous rage. A new kind of despair.

"What's wrong with you!" A violent rumble shook the room, jostling dust from the walls and ceiling, but in the wake of my words, the room calmed swiftly to a deafening silence, just like any other earthquake among the sporadic tremors.

"He was in the way," the teleporter wheezed, still catching her breath, "Maybe now the others will remember; we don't compromise, and we *don't* hesitate."

I shrank back from her callous words, only to find my upper arm pricked with needles, so thin and razor sharp, they poked straight through the fabric of my sleeve. At the slight sting, I spun, coming face to chest with a second kirranite.

This was the looming shadow which blocked the only exit – a narrow, stone staircase leading up. Horror greeted my racing heart at the sight perched atop these stairs, the source of the hissing.

On the bottom steps were four swollen and bruise-coloured pora who ogled the stone-skin's body, leaking excessive red. Their reflective pupils dilated to such an extreme, they consumed all the colour of their irises, with the added horror of their bluish-green veins protruding in a latticework over the discolouration of their oily skin, shiny in the light of the flickering bulbs. Disturbing shadows were cast from these pulsing veins in unnatural patterns, making hellish designs across their faces.

The rage in me diminished, replaced by a meek, ugly creature of fear and disgust at the sight of them. Something in me screamed to run. My feet wouldn't budge.

The teleporter stumbled several paces back from me and tripped over her own feet, tumbling unceremoniously to the floor by the far wall.

Cracked, flickering and grime-encrusted lightbulbs illuminated the room, just enough that I could see her lips were drained of colour and she struggled to rake in breath. Magic use so soon after rousing from her oxygen-deprived sleep had left her overwrought and in need of recovery time.

In other words, she was weak.

"What's this?" one of the pora in the stairwell hissed in that grating, choking voice I had come to associate with their disease. "Bit off more than you could chew?"

"Can't you hear what's going on up there? Why aren't you helping?" she snapped back at him and flapped a hand toward the kirranite blocking the stairs. It dipped its prickly head and shoved past the pora at the foot of the stairs without a word. I could only guess it was off to level the playing field up above.

Stopping momentarily, it turned and grabbed hold of two pora at the back of their little gang, an unbreakable grip dragging them along much to their grumbling complaints. Even though their numbers had been halved, I still couldn't bring myself to look the two remaining pora in the eyes.

How fast the tables turned, and bloodshed. It was too late for the stone-skin, lying pale and motionless on the floor just behind the crates. All I could do now was count my own odds.

The room we'd been zapped to was small and cramped, a storeroom off the stairwell on the verge of running out of supplies. At a glance, the same fall-away soil from around the plateau had been caked thickly onto the walls, a last defense to keep out or at least bog down stone-crafters like Lin. Several knee-high boxes and crates crowded the room. They'd get in the way in a fight…

With my only supposed ally knocked out at the remaining kirranite's feet, I was on my own in this enclosed, underground chamber, but not alone. I felt it worth reiterating, it was just me against the teleporter, a kirranite, and two pora, on which front I was not only outnumbered but *heavily* out-matched.

A new commotion reverberated overhead even unto the sound of stone raking against stone, as if wrenched apart with earth shaking tremors still coursing through the land. Battle was surely making a bloodbath of the courtyard – but I couldn't let that horrifying notion distract me now.

"You almost had us, I'll admit," rasped the teleporter, sitting up with her arm propped on one of the crates, "Don't you know better than to start monologuing when you're winning?"

"I wasn't monologuing!" I gritted out, edging away from the pair of pora blocking the stairs, and threw out a hand in gesture to the unconscious stranger, "This idiot just wouldn't stop talking to me."

The teleporter nodded as if she suspected as much and pitied me, none-theless. "Try having him as a prisoner."

"No thanks. If you couldn't tell, I'm somewhat opposed to that sort of thing." Pivoting my sights toward the teleporter, least threatening of every-one in the room, I narrowed my eyes to a glare and took another step in her direction and away from the stairs. "You know, for a self-proclaimed

Liberation Front, you have a bad habit of taking away others' freedoms. And lives."

She shrugged, readjusting her position on the floor so she could lean her head on her knuckles. Slowly but surely, the colour was returning to her face. I didn't have long to make my move. "Says the one defending centions. You can get down off your high horse, I'm not in the mood to argue with a brainwashed brat-"

"I'm not arguing with you, and I don't intend to." And yet, there was no escaping with action. Words would have to do. "Think you can level the playing field just long enough to communicate, or does the idea that I might say something you agree with scare you that much?"

She quirked an eyebrow at me. "I could ask the same of you. I'd bet no one has ever told you the thing that makes magikiers so special."

"I'm guessing it's the magic?"

"We have the rare gift of self-improvement. The ability to *hone* our magic. Sure, we only have the one trick up our sleeve, but with time, effort, and a little creativity, we can shape it into something unique and powerful."

"Yeah. That's the whole point of Blackano."

"Not quite. We were unintentionally designed this way, and when the centions realized what they'd created, they capped our potential. As long as we're bound to them, we'll always have cement shoes holding us down."

"So is that what making the bond with Lupei does? It tethers magikiers to *her* rather than the centions, and gets rid of the cement shoes?"

She quirked her head at me as if surprised I knew of it. "It frees us from our banal existence under the centions' constraints and lets us work on ourselves – refine *our* magic – as we please."

"Forgive me if I sound dismissive, murderer, but it sounds an awful lot like you're doing this for power."

She chuckled darkly, shaking her head. "Of course you'd think that."

"It's hard to think any differently when you use agency as an excuse to hold power over others. Not even over centions, but other magikiers!"

"You think we didn't try the peaceful alternatives first? They weren't listening, and never would unless we made a real, tangible statement."

"You're *killing* people! You're tearing down the ones you say you're trying to help, and *nothing* is being fixed. It's magikiers feeling the brunt of your rebellion, *not* centions."

"Until we've freed them from their blind obedience, the centions' pawns aren't exactly giving us much choice-!"

I laughed, a dry and unhinged note. "Nothing but a practiced statement, an excuse to make yourself feel better. Tell me, are these Lupei's words ad verbatim, or do you paraphrase for fear of plagiarism?"

She actually had the audacity to look offended. "The centions would have us all die for nothing–"

"It stopped being about that the moment you started burning down countries built *by* magikiers *for* magikiers and destroying *our* communities. You killed your own ally for nothing!"

She sneered in my face, but it only spurred me on.

"You've dedicated yourself to a cause that tries to justify murderers under the guise of taking down murderers. There's a touch of hypocrisy somewhere in there, don't you think?"

"You're comparing apples to oranges," she hissed.

"Am I? Blackano was supposed to be safe, but because of your cause, countless people have been killed and displaced. In a country built specifically for the safety and training of magikiers, safety *ensured* by the centions–"

"You have no idea what they've done to us! Blackano was the epitome of privilege, built to fabricate blind trust between magikier and cention, but here? On Cellana? We're like pigs to the slaughter."

"So you're telling me the City of Gates looked like that before you got there? And what about him?" I dipped my chin in the stone-skin's direction. "*Stop* putting yourselves on a pedestal. No one deserves to tower over others."

Her glare deepened, casting stark shadows over her face as her lip curled into a sneer. "You say this, but the dirt on my hands doesn't distinguish me from any one of your friends up there. Jericho knew the cost. He died for the cause he gave his life to, and he'll be remembered, his name celebrated. He would be proud!"

Nausea roiled low in my gut. "Who would take pride in dying at the hands of a friend? You've solved nothing, and people are still killing each other."

A glint of dry amusement darkened her eyes. "So what you're telling me is you're harmless."

"*How* is that your takeaway?" I burst and shook my head, refocusing myself, but she flashed me a wicked smile, her attitude shifting toward condescension, and fury boiled in my chest.

"It would seem we've come to a moral stalemate. You and I are two brick walls jabbering at each other. But one of us is more of a hypocrite than the other. Shonte."

"What?" My voice faltered, giving me away. There went any chance of talking my way out.

The sound of a foot sliding off stone had me snapping my head in the pora's direction, only to watch as one of the two slipped off the last step. "Shonte?" the other echoed, intrigued, and raised her nose in my direction as if to sniff out my magic.

The teleporter snapped her fingers, drawing everyone's attention, but her shrewd eyes were on the pora, and she slid her gaze toward the kirranite. "You, keep those two in check. He wants her alive."

Without a word, the kirranite marched toward the stairs, where it situated itself firmly between me and the two salivating pora.

"Who's this *he*?"

She ignored me like I hadn't spoken at all, and I hardly thought she meant to. In her excitement at discovering my identity, I doubted she even heard me. "We've been told to keep an eye out for any redheads by the name Anelisha coming from the City of Gates, and I'll say it. I had to read those dog-tags five whole times to believe it. I never thought *the shonte* would have such a weak mindset."

I opened my mouth to retort, but the look on her face caught me off-guard. One of focus and deep concentration.

With a static-y fizzle and a *pop!*, the dog-tags around my neck materialized in her hand. She caught her breath, the focused look in her eyes replaced by a self-congratulatory smirk. So, she could do more than just teleport around – she could pull little items like dog-tags off people without even touching them! By the look on her face, I could only assume she was still honing this application of her magic.

"Anelisha. It isn't the most common name around." She gave a breathy chuckle and jangled the metal plates in her hand. "*You're* the shonte I've heard so much about. And you're so... You're so..."

"What?" I demanded, cross, as she looked me up and down.

"Small." I twitched, on the brink of launching myself at her, but the look in her narrowed eyes stopped me, a spark of recognition lighting them up. "And you're the one I reached for at the City of Gates."

Instead of a full-on frontal assault like my fists so called for, a sour expression pursed my lips and I glowered down at nothing, internally cursing my poor foresight. Why had I kept my dog-tags on? To cater to *Bojack* of all people. Ugh. "You got me."

She shook her head in bewilderment. "I have to ask. What's the most wanted person on Cellana doing wandering around the Khuloces Forest?

You do realize the bounty on your head is in a league of its own? For the capture of your commander, I got a pretty promotion and authority over this base, but for you – hell, I can't even imagine…" She trailed off in her glee, thoughts racing too fast for her mouth to keep up. I could see the gears turning behind her eyes. "If I'd known back in the City of Gates…"

"Yeah, about that-"

Her eyes lit up in sudden understanding. "You won't find your commander at this base. That must be why you're here – it can't actually be for that swine, Bojack. But you're way off course. Your commander will have reached Cerenthior already. By now, Tenebret probably has him in his personal custody, safe and sound behind all the defenses of that impregnable city. Who knows, you might've caught up with him by now."

It was like she knew exactly what to say to pinch my heart, but I rolled my eyes, crossed my arms, and masked a sidestep toward her with an exaggerated lean on one leg. "That's the second time I've heard that name today." My voice shook, betraying my true feelings. Still, I continued, "Who the hell is this Tenebret?"

The teleporter quirked a grin at me, her gaze sliding down to my feet, noticing my approach. "Now who's the idiot talking too much?"

Before I could react, the air phased around her, consuming her in a haze of refracted light. I couldn't move fast enough. In the blink of an eye, she was gone, leaving me stuck in this claustrophobic room with the kirranite blocking the pora at the stairs, and the stranger's still unconscious body on the ground behind the crates.

Well, that didn't go at all like I wanted.

20

Not Literally!

I OBSERVED MY CAPTORS, MY BACK TO THE WALL. NO EMOTION LEAKED through the kirranite's prickly mask – hiding this hivemind parasite's poor, overshadowed host – but the pair of pora watched me with ravenous wonder and curiosity shining in their watery eyes.

Like those other pora had spoken of outside, these two knew enough about *the shonte* to want a taste. Whatever aura I had given off the last time I used my magic, it was enough to start them salivating as they ogled me, now.

I blew out a lungful of air, making noises with my mouth. Awkwardness blanketed the room as I wracked my brain for something to say. "So… *super* sorry if I sound ignorant asking this, but are pora actually as ravenous as everyone always says you are?"

The pora to the right of the kirranite cocked his head to one side, apparently dumbfounded by my line of questioning.

The other gruffly answered, "Depends what you've heard, and who it's in reference to. I can only speak for myself when I say, well, no?" He was somewhere between mocking me and speaking civilly.

"Why?" the one on the right teased, not an ounce of civility in his tone, "You finally starting to understand the gravity of your situation?"

"Garett," warned the first, shooting him a look behind the kirranite's back.

I quirked my head to the side. That name sounded vaguely familiar. It was a moment before I recognized where I'd heard it before. This was the one those other pora had briefly mentioned, the one who'd considered breaking rank to hunt me down.

At the thought, a light bulb flashed on above my head.

A fresh plan took shape in my mind, half-baked and if I was being honest with myself, way too reckless to merit the slightest consideration, but it was all I had at present, and the situation wasn't looking to get any better the longer I waited around, certainly not for the people – Brett, Faith, Lin, and Kev included – up top fighting for their lives.

Fact of the matter was, I could think of no other way to escape with the zonked-out stranger, and I couldn't just abandon him here.

"You've all heard of the shonte, I take it?" I began.

Both pora's eyes shone at the word. There was no doubting I would regret this.

"I heard pora have a pretty intense reaction to, uh, well..." I retreated from the word, watching their eyebrows rise on wrinkled faces. "If you've got any burning questions, now's the time to ask 'em."

They stared at me, faces painted with bewilderment at my frankness, and equal wariness. In turn, the kirranite crooked its spike-lined skull subtly toward them, angling a wary eye on the two loose cannons behind its back.

Good.

I took this to mean I'd read their shaky dynamic correctly. For as stupid as this plan of mine was, at least there was some merit to it.

I slid my gaze from one to the other. "What, you mean to tell me you're not even the slightest bit curious where I came from? How I got this magic?"

On a low hiss of air escaping the tight shell that encompassed it, the kirranite reminded its overeager cohorts, "Keep your filth from her veins."

"Filth-?" chided one of the pora, Garett, but the other whacked him across the back of his head, shutting him up.

"She is to be brought before him. Unspoiled and alive."

The pair shared a wary glance behind the kirranite's back. They knew as well as I, this kirranite was connected to the swarming, shadowy mass of its colony hivemind, all possessing the bodies of stolen hosts like this one. Whatever this kirranite came to know, the rest in its colony would know as if they themselves had experienced it.

It went without saying, if these pora pulled any stunts on this lone kirranite, they'd have an entire hive to deal with.

But, as things stood, there was only one kirranite there in front of them. Only one to hinder them should they act fast. And speed was one of the prime benefits pora had to their name.

I watched the cogs turn behind their discoloured eyes, these pools of insatiable curiosity catching in the dim light. It was the clandestine sheen in their furtive glances that confirmed it for me.

All they needed was a push in the right direction.

"Well," I mused, skirting closer to the trio at the stairs.

My eyes flitted to the stranger on the floor as I approached, making sure to park myself behind the crate nearest him. I propped my elbows up on the crate and cupped my chin in both hands with an expression of pure innocence plastered on my face.

"If you're not overeager to ask your questions, I guess it's up to me. So what's so appealing about our blood? Does it taste like something else to pora? Oh! Do different kinds of magic have different flavours? And on that topic, do pora eat, like, real food or do you get by on blood alone, 'cause then I could sort of see where the stereotyping comes from – not that that, uh, excuses it..."

At this bizarre line of questioning, even the kirranite shifted its dubious glance from the pora to me, a hint of confusion breaking through its emotionless mask.

No wonder Bojack thought I had a death wish; I certainly wasn't making a great case for myself. Nevertheless, I'd stumbled upon a genuine curiosity I hadn't realized was on my mind and blithely pursued the train of thought in the absence of a response.

Quirking my head to the side so my hair fell over one shoulder, the ends pooling in wild, red tresses on the crate, I ruminated, "Okay, bear with me on this one, but if there's such thing as unique tasting blood per magikier, and if pora do actually eat food, then has anyone opened a gastropub for fine dining combinations, or am I the only one thinking about these things? There's gotta be restaurants for pora-heavy demographics-"

"Please stop," sighed the pora on the left, second-hand embarrassment in the wince on his face. I tended to have that effect on people. "I know what you're trying to do – or, I thought I did until you kept talking."

The other, Garett, leaned in closer behind the kirranite's shoulder, gaining ground in my direction. "I can't tell, is this nervous rambling or what?" An ounce of malicious intent leaked into his preposterously innocent tone, but the kirranite made no indication it had picked up on it.

Shrugging my shoulders, I made a face of uncertainty with my tongue stuck out between pursed lips. "Can't say I have an answer for you."

Another considerable tremor in the earth sent the hanging lights dancing, their dim luminosity shivering over the room, and shook dust from the ceiling, loosening a sliver of soil from its packing against the wall. Whatever was causing these earthquakes could only be getting closer, but I focused myself on the pora and on escaping this room. I couldn't afford to become distracted, not with my friends' lives on the line up top, nor the annoying stranger knocked out on the ground down here with me. There was too much at stake.

The dancing lights rippled over the kirranite's glossy, beetle black eyes devoid of sclera, turned up toward the ceiling. In that instant, I realized there were no eyes on me as all three investigated the worsening integrity of the room. I had this one chance to surprise them – the only question was how.

Without thinking, I threw myself forward. Because *that* was the logical conclusion when one's life was on the line, right? Leave everything to a hunch and hope for the best? Yep, that was *definitely* the right thing to do when stuck at an absurdly one-sided impasse!

I vaulted the crate in front of me and threw my weight behind a palm strike, only to slam my bare palm on the kirranite's barbed forearm, raised as a shield to fend me off. I heard my skin tear as my palm grazed its prickly hide and felt the warmth of my blood rushing to the surface. It pooled in my clenched fist.

Perfect.

The kirranite shoved me back, and I disguised a few extra steps among my stumbling so I could plant myself beside the stranger's unconscious body. He twitched in his sleep when my heel nudged his side, but otherwise didn't stir. Damnit, don't tell me I'd have to carry him.

Raising his nose, Garett huffed the air and actually shuddered. "Incredible," he whined in a breathy voice, brushing up against the kirranite's blockading shoulder. He bared dagger-like fangs and licked his swollen, off-coloured chops, eyes intent on my clenched fist. "Like a hot-blooded chihuahua, this one. What did you think you'd accomplish, there?"

With this slavering pora pressed against its back, the kirranite met the end of its patience. It rounded with a terrible, guttural noise and swiped a clawed hand at the pora, forcing him to spring away and crash backwards up the stairs. He was faster than the kirranite, but when it came to a kirranite's sheer strength, one good hit could have downed him permanently.

Snuffling and snorting like a posturing bull, the kirranite went after the other pora as well with a kick aimed for his shins, driving him off. "You slop-brained fleas would waste a shonte so carelessly? Disgusting, selfish creatures."

"Cool it, beasty. We didn't do anything." An insolent tone coloured Garett the pora's words as he picked himself up from the steps, dusting his hands off on his clothes. Looking up, his eyes found me around the kirranite's girth, nostrils flaring and a nightmarish grin curling the corners of his too-wide mouth. "But you could at least bag some of that on her hand for us, couldn't you?

The other chipped in, "It'd be a waste to let it dry and flake."

Garett nodded, heaving breath. "It's only a scrape. Wouldn't do her any real harm if you bleed her a little extra." It was a moment before I realized he only heaved breath in the effort of scenting the stale air for my blood.

"Enough for a mouthful," chirped the other, excitement raising the volume of his voice and ushering in a frenzied tone.

Blood filled the sclera of both pora's eyes, their irises shining redder than before – each a reflection of the fresh blood upon which their intense stares were fixed.

"Get back, lecherous scum!" roared the kirranite, but it was like a switch had clicked on in both pora, and they launched themselves forward in unison, even shoving at each other to get by.

In an instant, the atmosphere in the room shifted, becoming sharp and volatile as all three in front of me leapt into action. Not just the pair of pora scrabbling for me, but the kirranite who grappled one by the windpipe and bashed him down against the stairs, causing his neck to jut out at a strange angle. The pora named Garett managed to slip the kirranite's grasp, dodging zealously around it too fast for my eyes to follow. Before I could move out of the way, he was upon me, wild-eyed and ravenous.

Now, there was never a point in my life at which I couldn't confidently call myself an abysmal decision-maker, but in this moment, with my scraped-up hand tucked between my back and the floor, and my other arm barring the pora from my throat as he gnashed his slavering fangs over me, my knack for choosing the path of *most* resistance became abundantly clear.

Sucks to suck, I guess.

I managed to wedge just enough space between Garett and myself to get my feet under his hips. Before he could grab for my ankles, I flicked a glance in the direction I meant for him to go and kicked with all my strength.

In a last-ditch effort to firmly plant himself on top of me, he grappled for a hold on the arm I was using to bar him but failed to wrap his discoloured fingers around my wrist. Without anything to hold onto, he went sailing backwards.

I was lucky in my aim, propelling him directly at the suctioning loam coating the walls, into which he promptly sunk.

Racing to my feet, I wasted no time grabbing the unconscious stranger under the arms and hauling him over both my shoulders, where I held onto him by an arm and a leg. Although he was slender, maybe even underweight after his time in these awful conditions, he towered over me in height even more than the average man and probably doubled my body weight even malnourished. I groaned against his weight crushing down on me but set off toward the stairs nonetheless, adrenaline spurring me on.

I only had this one chance, while my captors were either too busy with each other or thrashing their way out of the clinging soil to notice my egress. I bolted between them, mounting the stairs two at a time with the stranger bobbing uselessly against my back.

Fingers clamped my ankle – the same ankle that had been wedged in the tree, the same ankle Bojack had already worked his magic on, the same ankle that now clicked when I walked – and nails raked against the leather of my boot, wrenching my foot out from under me.

I hit the steps hard under the stranger's weight, bashing my shins and elbows against the stone ridges. The stranger thudded against the stone next to me, heaving a pained gasp as he did.

Sucking breath through my teeth, I kicked backwards, but the hand was wrapped around my ankle so tightly, my very bones seemed to creak under his biting grip.

My world zeroed in on the sight of my hands in front of my face, scratching desperately at the stone, the sound of nails shredding and of pounding blood. Panic surged, cold and dizzying, through my veins.

A loud tear found my ears, followed succinctly by a chill on my bare skin. I knew without looking back. The flap of torn leather on the ankle of my boot had been ripped open.

I could practically feel his teeth teasing against the skin he'd revealed, imagined his breath lapping at the place he would bite. Distantly, I heard myself screaming.

Before I could register what was going on, a new pair of hands grabbed my arms, heaving me up the stairs as a long leg swung over my head. The kick collided loudly against bone behind me and the hand on my ankle disappeared, sending me flying up the stairs in all my haste to escape.

I had a split second to realize it was the stranger who'd saved me. He'd finally woken up and leapt immediately back into the swing of things.

He wrapped an arm around me, hoisting me to my feet, and helped me up the stairs. Letting him guide me, I passed a wary glance over my shoulder toward our assailants. The pora who'd grabbed me lay sprawled at the base of the stairs, a sizable dent in the side of his face and a dazed look in his crossed eyes as he spluttered and wheezed incoherently. Good riddance, Garett.

Movement drew my eye, and I caught a brief glimpse of the kirranite, still struggling against the better-mannered pora. Considering the hivemind to which it belonged, I could only assume this kirranite had already signalled for reinforcements to cut us off, the only reason I could figure it would let us escape while it dealt with these defectors. Even so, a wave of relief crashed over me to be rushing off in the opposite direction.

"Sorry for the wait, I could swear I usually rouse faster from a bludgeoning. I like to tell myself it's one of those things the body develops an immunity toward," the stranger was saying, but I could hardly focus on his words, instead absorbed with matching his long-legged pace. He half-carried me up the stairs with an arm around my middle, which was probably for the best considering the flash of pain which coursed up my left leg whenever I put weight on my ankle.

I rested a moment at the height of the stairs as he contemplated the first fork in our path here in this labyrinthine anthill of a fort. Finally, he pointed an index finger down the leftmost corridor illuminated by a string of grimy lightbulbs and offered me an arm to help maintain my pace.

Taking it gratefully, I asked in a quieted voice, "You don't have a concussion, do you? Can you remember your way out of here?"

"Oh, certainly." He considered his words. "The remembering part, I mean. Although I'll apologize in advance for only knowing the long and winding way. I'm sure there's a shortcut we'd rather take, if only I knew it. As for the other matter, I'm still hesitant to diagnose the drumming in my head."

"I doubt most concussion victims would be this articulate."

"You'd be surprised. My last one, I had to read a declaration of peace before a sizable crowd. I'm told it went well. The peace didn't last, of course, but I was already hunched over the public toilets losing the finger foods by then."

"From… from the concussion?"

"Poisoning, actually. But that's beside the point. I'm sure I'm fine."

I could only stare up at this baffling man as we hobbled hastily along, mouth parted in incredulity. Even now, there was an air of charm about him that dressed his actions and his words in a casual enthusiasm, brandishing a relaxed ease and subtle consideration in the way he comported himself.

"You're uncannily chipper about all this." I couldn't keep the wince off my face as another shot of pain speared through my ankle. I'd put the faintest pressure on my leg, catching an uneven cut of the floor underfoot, but even so, it shouldn't have hurt this much.

"Better that than dead, and honestly, I thought I'd be the latter by now. I have you to thank for that, don't I? Matter of fact, besides a few regrettable intervals, this gloomy evening has turned downright sunny since you came along."

Narrowing my eyes on him, I tried to gauge his sincerity, but there wasn't a single hitch in his campy demeanor. "What, still buttering me up to get your hands on Bojack?"

He smirked. "Can't hurt to try, love."

I groaned. "Let me stop you there. I *cannot* handle the pet names, dude."

"Ah, you hate to see it. Could I get your real name, then?"

Eyeing him, I blew an exasperated breath and grumbled, "Throwing my name around all willy-nilly just signed my near-death warrant, so maybe not."

"Well mine's Dorian," he carried on, unphased, and turned down another branch in the winding tunnel system. Immediately upon stepping foot in this new corridor, he broke into a coughing fit and covered his mouth with his free hand, rasping against his palm, "Ugh, hold your breath for this part. We're passing through solitary."

The stone walls to either side of us ended abruptly, instead replaced by metal grates revealing dark pits thirty feet deep. Filth littered the floor, closer resembling the boar pens up top than accommodations for people. Lamplight at the other end purchased a strong, golden glow through a narrow opening, cast across the walls and floor and cut with dancing shadows on the smooth stonework.

Then came the stench.

My nose crinkled and I couldn't help but sputter for breath. Like rotten food, mold, feces, and infection all packed into one reeking mouthful, the eye-stinging fumes could've combusted at the slightest spark. This cesspool of noxious odours hung heavily in the stale air, pushing against my nostrils to pervade my poor, unassuming lungs, but I clamped both hands over nose and mouth alike.

"Funny thing, calling it solitary as if *that's* the major punishment here. As if I'd be worried by a little loneliness and not this sensory torment."

"You lived in this?" I wheezed, muffled against my palm, and struggling against the instinct to breathe.

"Not voluntarily. But it did teach me to pick my battles, that's for sure, and this one, I don't intend to lose." He hurried down the corridor, lifting me against his side to cross the distance as quickly as possible. Sliding to a stop just before the end of the hallway, he set me down and hazarded a gasping breath. He made good use of it, speaking all in one go, "I think I can safely say no one with a nose would lie in wait for us here, but the gate to freedom's coming up, and you can call me paranoid, but I suspect an ambush."

"Kirranites and all that," I puffed, feeling the blood rush to my face in my continued refusal to breathe. He nodded, seeming satisfied that we were on the same page in this tome of uncertainty.

He motioned to the frayed edge of my already weather-worn sleeve and mimed ripping it off, then gestured to my bloody palm. Happy with any excuse not to open my mouth, I tore off a long strip which I wound several times around my palm before he helped me tie it into a knot, tight against the wound.

"And how's your foot?"

"Unbitten." One-word answers were all I could manage.

"No-" He cut himself off with a small, involuntary laugh. "Can you put weight on it? Can you run?"

By the alarmed look in my eyes, he got his answer, and he conceded with a shrug.

"Eh, we'll make it work." He clapped his hands together, making a soft noise as new determination shone crisp in the emerald of his eyes. "Good huddle."

Hah, he really thought he did something. Nope. Not for my general state of distress, anyway. But the stench was too rancid to put my true feelings into words, so I nodded along and followed his lead.

We made it two steps down this reeking corridor before a disembodied shout halted us in our tracks. A raspy voice, guttural with disuse, clapped startlingly loud off the damp, stony walls. An incoherent garble of sound. It was a moment before my brain registered the words buried therein.

"That you again, Dorian? What's going on up there?"

"Helena!" Dorian burst, surprise in his eyes, only to clap a hand over his nose and mouth to block out the smell. From behind his hand, he continued in a nasally voice, "They gave you my spot, did they?"

A sliver of light across half her face was all that illuminated her. Otherwise, she was shadow and shape buried in the dark depths of the nearest cell. From what I could see of her, she was a stony-faced woman wearing an expression in the slack of her jaw and furrow of her brows which illustrated the impression that we'd lost our wits.

She raised a bony hand to the dash of light cast across half her face, shading her eyes against the dim lighting behind us, and with the knobbly fingers of that same hand, beckoned us toward the bars.

I was hesitant to approach, instead combing our surroundings for a key by which to free her, but Dorian strode happily forward to lean against the hard stone rods walling her off.

This broad-shouldered woman with biceps the size of my thighs and in serious need of a visit to the dentist for a couple cracked teeth and one missing altogether sat with her back against the far wall of her cell and her elbows propped up on her knees.

"Who's this with you?" she demanded in a gruff voice, tired and yet casual in a way I wouldn't expect from someone trapped at the bottom of a hopeless pit.

"I'm not so much focused on the who, but the what," said Dorian. "And *what* she is is our ticket out of here. You're welcome to tag along if you'd like."

Her mask of filth, worn like a second skin over her face, cracked with the lines of a cold smile, empty-eyed and serpentine. "You know you're not getting out of here, Dorian. Doing the same thing over and over, always expecting a different result; it's a sign of insanity."

He made a disapproving sound, half-way facetious and entirely unphased by this eerie visage swathed in darkness and filth so far below. "You made that up."

"They'd probably release me from solitary if I turned you in."

"Oh?" A hint of genuine curiosity lightened his unserious tone. "And how do you intend to do that from down there?"

Veins bulged on her neck and forehead, a visible strain to keep herself from belligerence, and she steepled her fingers at her chin.

Before she could lash out at him, I interjected, "I take it you must be an important person if the Liberation Front's trying so hard to break you–"

"Not anymore."

"So humble," Dorian tsked, and turned to me. "You're speaking to the Captain of the Arillian Spire."

"Meaning-?" I was saying but shook my head against distraction and continued for the woman down below, "We can help you escape. Is there a key-?"

Leaning forward against her knees, she looped her arms around her legs and clasped her hands in front of her as she caught my wavering gaze in the steel of her eyes. "Who are you to make such promises? Some reckless kid who's convinced yourself all it takes to save the day is a pinch of pretended heroism. It would be a waste to gamble my life on those lining themselves up for death."

"No key," Dorian answered in her stead, in fact ignoring her cynicism entirely, "Stone-crafters raise or lower the bars as needed."

"Goddamn. Don't they get tired of carrying magikierkind on their shoulders?"

I could tell he was smiling by the shape of his eyes, no matter the hand still covering half his face. "There's a reason the centions make so many of them."

"No kidding." With a small kick, I dislodged a sizable rock from the floor. "Now watch me break all their hard work the way the cavemen intended it."

With a grand, flourishing gesture, he took a wide step out of my way. "By all means."

I probably should have let him do this part considering the state of my ankle, but I balanced my weight on my other leg and reared my arm back with the rock clenched in hand. The first swing chipped at several of the stone bars, the second bashed clean through a few of them, and the third left a crumbling hole in the stone defense.

My fingers trembled as I dropped the rock at my feet and the muscles of my arm and shoulder complained, but I wiped my palm off on the skirts of my tabard and stuck my head through the hole. It was large enough that the woman down below would have no trouble climbing through.

Problem was, she made no move to get up.

"Come on, take my hand!" I called down to her, reaching through.

She watched me, as still as the dead.

"We don't have all day-!" I was shouting, nose wrinkling against the smell even stronger in proximity to her cell, when my foot began to slip. I felt myself toppling forward before I could register the gunk underfoot, sliding me down the slight decline into the pit. Just as suddenly as I felt myself moving, I wasn't.

To my right, Dorian had his hands stuffed in his pockets, standing like a flamingo on one leg as the other barred my momentum, blocking me from falling in. His leg, extended at a ninety-degree angle, was level with my sternum.

"Careful there."

"Whatever," I grumbled, pushing off from the bars to escape that near disaster and the suddenly horrendously obvious height difference between he and I.

"Pains me to say it, Red, but she's a stubborn one. We shouldn't waste any more time here."

"But…" I was ready to argue, but there was a hint of contrition in his eyes, nearly hidden away by his manufactured smile. The protests died on my tongue.

"Don't get me wrong," he continued in his jaunty tone, "You've done your due diligence. You gave her a way out. That's more than most would've done."

A final glance in the Captain of the Arillian Spire's dismal direction was all it took. She wasn't even watching us anymore.

"Fine."

I couldn't get my mind off her as we hobbled around the corner. Dorian had his arm slung around me again, helping to carry my weight as we entered a long corridor with several side chambers. Each open archway along its length revealed unlit side rooms and potential hiding places for our enemies. Or, added an acerbic voice in the back of my mind, other oubliettes hiding more broken prisoners like the Captain. That slithery voice teased notions of Seth, projecting him in place of the Captain in my mind's eye, but I shook off such thoughts. The teleporter had confirmed it already. He wasn't here. I couldn't risk my friends' lives searching for him in this cursed place any longer.

At the corridor's end, another fork in this absolute maze of an underground fortress made me think we were never going to get out of here. The harsh smell had begun to clear up – or maybe I was getting used to it the longer we waded through it – as we moved down the hallway on the tips of our toes, as quiet as we could be.

Our shadows circled around us as we moved through the dim lighting, cast across the floor and leaping from wall to wall. It was enough to have my hair standing on end no matter that I knew they were our own. Inaudible shouting and harsh thuds traveled through the thick, sound-muffling ceiling of the corridor, illustrating a nightmare in my mind of what was happening up top. In contrast, the musty air around Dorian and me brimmed with a skin-crawling silence, pushing against my eardrums until the pounding of my blood intermingled with the thumping of feet and bodies above.

Movement drew my eye, and I nearly jumped out of my skin upon registering a dark form looming against the wall to our left, only to find Dorian had peered into the leftmost archway, leaning away from me just enough to cast an unnaturally long-necked shadow.

"See anything?" I whispered, barely catching my own voice over the thunderous shocks of my heart hammering my ribcage.

"These rooms were all lit up before…" he mused.

I spent a glance toward each of the eight pitch-black rooms. "So, we should assume they're all traps?"

"I'm not so sure. I never counted more than five kirranites at a time while locked up. Their colony doesn't keep their slurry here, either, or I'm sure I would've been subjected to it by now. Hard to charm your way out of captivity when all you have to work with are emotionless husks and repressed idealists, *so* I leaned a bit too heavily into my fallback plan, which is to annoy my way to freedom."

"And how'd that work out for you?"

"Well, I *am* still kicking, so I'd say better than expected."

He tilted his head toward the end of the hallway, signalling us to keep moving. We did, hugging the wall and slinking along faster than before with our eyes on the darkness sheathed behind each looming archway. Staring so deeply into them, my eyes played tricks on me, showing me movement where there was only shadow and warping the borders between light and dark until it looked like some amorphous *thing* approached from each doorway. But the corridor was as still as it was silent, enough to hear a pin drop, save our hasty shuffling from one end to the other.

"Huh," Dorian happily mused upon rounding left at the fork while still clinging to the wall. He still had his arm under mine, my hand clasped around his wrist, providing a welcome support to give my ankle a break, and I practically hopped on my other foot, careful not to scuff my boot or knock any pebbles for fear of giving away our location.

With only one way forward and no side rooms, the stairs to the portcullis gates directly ahead marked the end of our little maze adventure, a sliver of moonlight cascading down the steps to find us. "Maybe they figured we'd know better than to try walking out the front door?"

"There was an alternative?"

He shrugged his shoulders, bringing his thumb and forefinger to his chin in the aspect of contemplation. "Not sure, but it's always nice to be overestimated-"

Mid-speech, he cut himself off and whirled around, pulling me behind him by the arm I still held onto. A set of prickly talons swung past me, and the kirranite to whom they belonged sailed after them, having apparently thrown itself at me. It launched itself again, but I managed to dodge it myself, or rather, to dodge behind Dorian, only to find it had rejoined its peers.

Dorian made a strangled noise in his throat like a yelp, raising both arms defensively in front of him. Positioned squarely between me and our assailants, he faced not one, not two, but three kirranites blocking the way we had come. I, meanwhile, accepted the uselessness of my damned ankle and leapt onto his back. He squawked and floundered for balance as I wrapped my legs around his middle, half-strangling him with my arms around his neck and certainly deafening him with my cry, "Run!"

With that, I steered him back around with an arm thrown forward and a finger pointing to the stairs. To my relief, he listened to me, all the while yelling in fear and panic as he held onto my legs. He launched us up the stairs as if I weighed nothing, and slipped to a stop, stumbling up a few steps in his haste, upon finding the portcullis gate had been dropped. The teleporter awaited us at the height of the stairs, guarding the thick metal chains which controlled whether the gate went up or down.

"Ah, feck," Dorian swore under his breath.

To our rear, the three kirranites blocked the way we had come, and ahead, the teleporter held her ground. They had us bookended on the stairs, and Dorian hesitated on the middle step with his body turned halfway to keep an eye on both sides.

He huffed a lock of hair out of his eyes, unable to brush it away while he had his hands clasped under my knees. "Well, they didn't overestimate me, they just outsmarted me. Figures."

"Figures?!" I cried in disbelief.

"Happens more often than not-"

He cut himself off as the floor shook tremendously under his feet, jostling him down a couple steps. The teleporter at the height of the stairs stumbled back against the wall, crying out in surprise.

Beyond her, through the metal grilles of the portcullis gate, I saw the silhouetted treetops shake violently in the light of the ring – our only warning before they parted like the red sea, jagged and jutting fingers as thick as tree trunks clasping them in great bunches. From the darkness between these monolithic trees wrenched apart like stage curtains, there emerged an impossible, towering creature swathed in pale moonlight.

A shimmering object flashed out in front of the giant, catching white and gold scutes across the long, serpentine neck of a familiar figure. She shot out from the dark mass of the forest's looming shadows and into the air above the courtyard. Chasing this golden streak, a second pair of arms with hands the size of suburban houses snaked out from the shadows, claws like vine-smothered boughs raking across the courtyard of the fort and sweeping through the stone as easily as if it were melted butter.

It took me a moment to register what exactly I was looking at between the bars of the portcullis gate. Then it clicked. This thing – the cause of the earth tremors – was a multi-armed giant encased in tree bark, softened only by moss. And it had its sights set on Briar, clapping rounded hands in attempt to catch her like a child trying to catch fireflies in their bare hands.

Briar, meanwhile, dipped and flitted easily out of the tree giant's grasp, teasing it like this was a mere game, but with every new clap and strike, the giant tore more out of the fortress, sending rubble flying and people scattering.

She had brought the cavalry.

But Dorian and I were still trapped between the portcullis gate and the kirranites, and the tree giant was making quick work of dismantling this entire base.

The teleporter shouted something toward the courtyard, lost to the clamour of the giant's destruction, and with that, disappeared in a haze, absconding this increasingly foul situation. Simultaneously with her desertion, the kirranites made a play to seize us, but Dorian had already rushed the steps – not one to neglect an opportunity, I supposed, even if it meant sprinting full speed toward a handsy giant.

"Ack-!" Dorian cried, finding his legs swept out from under him. He twisted at the waist, dragged backwards down the stairs, and in that same action, propelled me some of the distance to the top. I clambered up the rest of steps on my hands and knees. We'd both be buried down here with the apparently heedless kirranites if I couldn't wedge open the portcullis.

I reached out to the chain, so close to pulling open the portcullis as I heard Dorian struggling to bottleneck the kirranites at the base of the stairs, when a splitting headache ripped through my skull. As if it would do anything, I threw my hands to my ears, crying out in shock and pain. "*Anelisha!*" Briar's voice called in my mind.

My thoughts tumbled out of me. "*It hurts! It hurts! Get out of my head!*"

The headache passed, and with it, the connection to Briar's mind. Something was seriously wrong with me – and I couldn't help thinking it had everything to do with Evelyn – but that wasn't the most pressing matter at the moment, and I focused myself once more, grasping for the chain.

"Stranger!" Dorian's voice reached me not a moment before I felt the string of thorns jabbing the flesh of my ankle and a shell-encased hand clenching securely around it. The injured ankle, wouldn't you know it – it just *had* to be that one, huh.

This was the only thought I had time to register before I found my poor, bruised body once again banging off each stone step in a downward haul, elbows clunking off each edge and my one free leg flailing wildly in spastic attempt to connect a kick with any part of my captor.

I had a fleeting moment to register the flash of gold divebombing the portcullis gate – shimmering wings tucked in tight to the narrow body – before Briar bulleted into the stairwell through the grilles of the gate. Her slinky body wedged just momentarily in the small space – before her growth spurt, she would easily have fit – and she caught her talons on the metal as her back half whirled spasmodically behind her, like a ribbon in a tornado.

Giving a feral push, she bolted the rest of the way through and collided powerfully with the kirranite grappling me, meeting it with a scrabbling of sharp talons on shell and a sound like nails on chalkboard.

The kirranite fell back from me, releasing its hold on my ankle, and I scurried backwards on my hands until I hit the wall, gulping down uneven breaths.

Dorian's loud yelp broke through the static muffling my headspace. "We can rest on the other side of the gate, no?"

"Right," I huffed under my breath and crawled up the steps once more, grimacing against the dull pain in my elbows.

A brush of air disturbed my hair directly adjacent to me, and a voice I hadn't expected to hear again filled my ear. "Oh no you don't," cooed the teleporter, lacking the grace not to gloat, "You really thought I'd leave without you?"

"Well what took you so long?" I snapped back at her and went to throw a punch, but she flashed out of sight and appeared on my other side.

While my head was still turned in the other direction, she grabbed a fistful of my hair and pulled me up by the skin of my scalp. I spun on my heel to face her as she opened her mouth for a witty retort.

All she spewed was blood.

I hardly had time to register Briar's lightning-fast reflexes, having bounded from the kirranite behind me to the teleporter's shoulders, where she promptly slashed her throat – talons painted red.

With a deafening buzz in my head, I barely registered the flash of pain across my back as I hit the steps, too stunned to catch myself. I couldn't do anything but stare up at the teleporter's desperate look of fear and shock as her lifeblood poured in a rush of red across a sharp line drawn from earlobe to earlobe.

The flood of gore cascaded from her gaping throat, raining hotly over me, and bile scratched at my esophagus, pushing at the lump of emotion caught in the back of my throat.

A flash of the girl on the metal stake battered me over the head, superimposed over the sight lurching in front of me. Then the stone-skin, his life stolen by this dying woman.

"Good…" The shrivelled word ripped out of me on a broken breath.

She pawed at her throat, crashing backwards against the steps as weak fingers groped for her exposed airway, as if to apply pressure to the overflowing ravine of red.

Another headache burgeoned between my temples, carrying the sharp command, "*Go!*" With that, the stab of pain in my head passed, but in its place, a hot ball of pressure pushed behind my eyes, threatening to spill tears onto my cheeks. I scrambled automatically toward the gate – opening now as Dorian yanked on the chain and Briar held off the kirranites.

I stumbled through, unaware of the throbbing in my ankle, and Dorian leapt out after me, allowing the heavy gate to come crashing down behind him. But there was no escaping the tumult – not yet.

The courtyard into which we emerged shrouded us in its frenzied air, pushing in on me from all sides.

Briar swooped through the holes in the grated metal behind us, smacking into my back with enough force to knock me off balance, but my hand was anchored to Dorian's – I hadn't even realized I was holding onto him – and I caught myself on my good foot as she wrapped herself around my shoulders.

She steered my aimless flee with her weight, leaning heavily to one side or the other so as to drag me to meagre safety from the giant's attempts to catch her. With each near miss, long, tree-like talons scraped through the ground in the wake of my adrenaline-fueled sprint.

"*Why did you bring this thing here?*" My unnerved thoughts echoed back to me, alerting me to the open link of my mind.

"*I was ambushed this afternoon, or perhaps I surprised the great, lumbering creature, but I haven't been able to shake it since. I attempted reasoning with it, but its mind is too young, and fascinations too distracting.*"

"*It's been after you all day?*"

"*To ask is to rub salt in the wound. Never let me call you frustrating again after the nuisance this lumbering thing has been. I had hoped to keep it from harassing you as well and so made a wide berth of you. Too wide, it would seem, as I eventually lost contact with your mind. I took too long to realize you were in trouble, but once I did, I figured I could make some use of its fascination with me-*" The connection fizzled out as she spoke, her words blending into the background noise swiftly filling my head.

I could hear Dorian shouting in bewilderment beside me and could feel his hand clasped around mine to keep from losing me. People screamed and yelled all around us. My brain buzzed in the effort to sort through the chaos.

The last of the firelight snuffed out with the sudden onslaught of rock and stone flying out from the giant's attacks, pitching me into a new blindness as my eyes strained to adjust. Without sight, I found myself surrounded on all sides by the sound of the giant's limbs plowing through stone, of shrieking, of crying, of crackling flames; the smell of blood sharp and sweet in my nostrils, of smoke and charred wood, of the sewage smell released from the rifts taken out of the ground, revealing the prison areas underground – everything blurred together, feeding the state of utmost confusion coiled taut around my brain. I could make sense of nothing, not even my own body, stuck on autopilot with Briar co-piloting from her perch across my shoulders. Inescapable disorder.

Until I heard them. Four distinctly familiar voices over the clamour of unfettered mayhem. Brett, Faith, Kev, and Lin – Bojack, too, but his voice brought no great relief to me like theirs did.

Following the sound of their voices, my gaze was drawn to the dark silhouette of a half-toppled wall. I managed to right my mind just enough to race in this direction. It was all I could do, crawling over upturned boulders and mounds of debris, dodging aside at the whistle of the giant's swinging limbs, ignoring everything else.

Pain shot up my leg with each step, muted by my determination. It was just enough to ignore while this final stretch extended before me. Dorian clasped my hand tighter, dashing to keep up.

"You know the ol' boost and hoist?" he wheezed as we approached the wall, and I made a sound like agreement. Briar shot off from my shoulders, zipping past the giant to divert its attention while we took this moment to ascend the wall.

I fumbled to find Dorian through the darkness as he took a knee, clasping both hands over his thigh. He caught my good foot and hoisted me up the way we'd been trained in Blackano. I soared up the meagre height of the wall, hooking my hands over the ledge by instinct alone without any way to see what I was doing, and pulled myself the rest of the way up. Like this, I spun, lay down flat on my stomach, and reached an arm down for Dorian.

I heard him skip back a few steps, then launch himself forward, running up the wall to grab hold of my arm. The scrabbling of his feet on the stone alerted me to his position, and I caught him. Gritting my teeth, I hauled him over, dragging him up the wall onto the catwalk beside me. The moment he had his feet under him, he was helping me back up to my feet as well. He crossed the narrow catwalk with an encouraging pat on my shoulder and lowered himself down the other side of the wall where the muffled sound of his feet hitting the soil met my ears.

"Jump down, I'll catch you!" he called up to me, and maybe he could see me, but I sure as hell couldn't see him – or damn near anything, for that matter.

Dangling off the edge of the wall, I released my grip, shutting my eyes tight, and fell – right into his arms. Good, I doubted my ankle would've been too happy with me if he'd missed.

The clouds thinned, casting a thin veil of pale radiance from the ring in the sky over the plateau, helping my eyes to adjust to this pitch-black night. Finally, I could see again.

Brett, Faith, Kev, and Lin were no more than dark spots half-hidden in the shadow of a massive tree, gathered together around what I could only assume was Bojack by the glint of white caught on the lighter half of his hair. An increasingly loud and argumentative tug-of-war had unraveled between them.

"We're going back!" Brett snarled, earning Bojack's lacklustre huff.

"Oh, no need to ask my permission. You can die at your own discretion. Just leave me out of it."

"And let you run away again? Yeah right, man! You're more slippery than a leech!" Kev shot back.

"Let the record show, I resent that comparison."

"You're right, it hardly fits. I've never known a leech to be so enamoured with the sound of his own voice," Lin deadpanned.

"Just leave him, he's the one who ratted us out in the first place," Faith growled.

"Blatantly untrue, but she makes a good point. I'll be on my way-?"

There was a sound of a scuffle, followed by Brett's grunted, "Oh no you don't."

Dorian chuckled beside me, taking a moment to appreciate the chaos. "We should intervene before they start throwing more than just words at each other, yeah?"

"He'd deserve it."

My voice must have carried, for when I spoke, my friends' voices died down, their heads snapping in my direction.

"Annie!" Faith cried, relief swelling her tone.

Dorian nudged my side, failing to hide his clever smirk. "I'll pretend I didn't hear that."

With a roll of my eyes, I grumbled, "You can call me Annie. It's a nickname anyway."

"But I much prefer my nickname for you, Red." God, this unremittingly positive energy of his was like a warm aura against my back.

Refusing to humour him with a response, I instead crossed the short distance of the plateau and waded through the deep mire along the ridge – soaking my clothes in the process and, hopefully, washing out the teleporter's blood – to join my friends. Faith raced over to meet us halfway, where she swept me up in her arms and squeezed me in a hug that could've broken bones.

"You look awful, what happened?"

"I'm fine, just tired," I huffed, and she must have noticed the odd note in my voice or the darker stains on my clothes, giving me a fretful look.

A flicker of gold caught in the corner of my eye, and in came Briar once more, divebombing into my jacket and coiling around me, hidden under the soaked-through material. Her rapid growth became ever more apparent to me as I felt the seams of my jacket strain to contain her. In such a short amount of time, another couple feet had been added to her length, not to mention the bulk of her increasingly feline build.

"*You forget the situation. Go! Quickly!*"

I wasn't the only one to break into a sprint at her command. Brett hoisted Bojack over his shoulder like a sack of potatoes and raced off, falling into step alongside me with Kev and Lin close on our heels. Dorian hastened to catch up, his eyes fixed on Bojack.

Finally – *finally* – we left this foul place, escaping into the woods from whence the tree giant had come, having freed the detained and destroyed the base, even though Seth was never here.

For everything we did here, I couldn't help the feeling that it was all for nothing – we would never catch up with him now, not without going straight to the heart of Arillia where horrors stained the lands red, where masses of kirranites and pora assembled with the Liberation Front, and where I would undoubtedly have to face Valencia's champion, wielder of the dragon-bone glaive.

So much for short cuts.

21

Suffice to Say That Could Have Gone Better

WE RAN UNTIL THE WORLD-SHAKING TREMORS HAD FADED TO A BACKground noise, rumbling vaguely under our feet. My left ankle had swollen to twice its normal size by then, thick against the leather of my boot, but I focused on avoiding the roots threatening to trip me with each step and kept my wincing to a minimum. Dorian was the first to stop and help me clamber up the larger roots whenever we came to one, soon joined by Lin and Faith while Brett struggled to keep his grip on the ever-complaintive Bojack slumped over his shoulder and Kev kept an eye on our surroundings.

Only once we deemed it safe to stop and rest – as birds began to chirp and the dark of the night began to clear, ushering a soft tinge of blue into the black veil overhead – did Bojack take that as his cue to start… clapping? With bound wrists, his toil to maintain an aspect of snark was truly a sight to behold.

"You really are something. I've never seen anyone turn such a bad situation infinitely worse, and in record time!" His eyes were locked on me, but I stuck out my tongue and averted my gaze, plopping down in a small, mossy valley between monstrous tree roots to give my ankle a break. Having witnessed a tree giant with my own two eyes, I couldn't help my new suspicions toward any tree in our vicinity. "Don't get me wrong, I'd never expect any less having known you for *one* day, but you sure kept me on my toes. Figuratively of course-"

"Oh, enough," Brett groaned, dropping him carelessly off his shoulder. Bojack thumped to the moss bed beside me with an undignified wheeze.

Struggling to wiggle into a better position with his hands and feet still bound, he slugged across the ground – a failure to disguise his attempt to inchworm his way to freedom.

"Stop that," Faith warned, seating herself on the high ridge of a ginormous root from which to keep watch of our surroundings.

Although she tilted her head in Bojack's direction, I noticed her eyes slant toward Dorian, her unspoken suspicions evident in the subtle glance. He hadn't said much as we fled to this hidden hollow in the wood, and I could read the curiosity in each of my friends' eyes, wondering why he was with us at all.

"So what happened?" I finally asked, letting the burning question roll off my tongue. "With the other prisoners, I mean. I didn't see them…"

"Most of them got out. The rest scattered as soon as that *thing* showed up," Brett explained without looking in my direction. Ah, so we were back to that, were we? I supposed nothing had changed between us, not even in the face of this slight, almost catastrophic victory.

"Then the teleporter blipped the rest of the Liberation Front out of there in seconds flat, and this little coward made a break for it with his tail between his legs," Lin tacked on in her flat tone, "Shuffled his way right to some pora slobbering over his blood. So we stepped in."

"And not a thank you to be heard," Kev melodramatically griped.

They carried on, but the clamour of adrenaline in me had quieted to a melancholic monotone at the mention of the teleporter.

So that was where she disappeared to, even though she'd killed the stone-skin without hesitation. One to squander our victory, one to ensure a retreat. The same woman who brutalized her own ally had prioritized saving the remainder of her people over abducting me when she had the opportunity. *Ample* opportunity.

She could have gotten away, but she came back for me and now lay dead in the ruins of her promotion.

A shiver coursed up my spine.

"But," I went on in a shaky voice, "You freed all the prisoners, right? Before the tree giant showed up?"

"Yep," Kev chipped in, "Mission success."

Mission success, but still no Seth. All we truly got out of this detour was confirmation he'd been taken to Liberation Front-occupied Cerenthior.

"Freed but not safe," Bojack chimed in from the forest floor, "And as we all know, those of us kept in the quarry could have made a break for it at any time. We *chose* not to, and why's that, do you wonder?"

"There's nowhere for them to go," Kev guessed.

"Nowhere that wouldn't need defending, and defending necessitates numbers," Bojack mused, quirking a clever smirk in the corner of his mouth, "But you did away with that little problem, didn't you? And after that commotion? Everyone who wanted out will have flocked there like moths to a flame."

Faith caught her chin between thumb and forefinger, deep contemplation in the furrow of her brow. "And the Liberation Front doesn't know about it?"

Raising his shoulders in a lazy shrug, Bojack spoke his next words around a yawn. "That's the gamble. And the flame." With that, he extended his bound wrists out ahead of him and cleared his throat. "A little help?"

With an indignant grunt, Brett leaned forward to undo Bojack's bonds, but only until Dorian stepped forward, finger raised with an interruption fast on his tongue.

"Actually," he began in that care-free and jaunty tone of his, "I'll ask that you leave those knots be. It'd be a great help to me."

Brett quirked an eyebrow, evidently unclear on the why of it all, but he raised his palms in surrender and backed off. Bojack hadn't exactly made a good case for our protection in all the time we'd known him.

Aiming a beaming grin at Brett in thanks, Dorian plopped down on the moss bed across Bojack from me with a soft thud and sprawled out comfortably with his hands behind his head and his ankles crossed.

"Heya, bounty," he greeted for Bojack, completely oblivious to his confounded audience, or just plain ignorant of our snooping. He smiled out the side of his mouth toward Bojack, who squirmed uncomfortably between us.

Groaning loudly, Bojack threw his head back with the sort of melodrama I'd sooner expect of a toddler. Catching Brett's eyes, then Lin's, Kev's, Faith's, and finally mine in an attempt to provoke our pity, he whined, "They made us eat gruel off the floor and now you won't even untie me! What did I ever do to any of you?" He paused, thinking on his words. "Don't answer that."

Making his annoyance painfully obvious, Brett turned his head away with his arms crossed over his chest. In our reluctance to humour his bellyaching, it was Dorian who did all the speaking. "You'll be happy to learn they had us mopping the floors until our hands were bloody just yesterday, so at the very least, there was *some* measure of good hygiene attempted."

My jaw dropped, aghast. "That's what the place smelled like *clean*?"

He nodded but the corner of his mouth lifted in a half-smile, half-wince, conceding the deplorable situation he'd escaped. "And now I think about it, they probably just wanted any excuse to soak up our blood for later. I probably should've guessed, considering the preference for absorbent wash-cloths over, I don't know, bandages? Why didn't that strike me as odd at the time…?"

Bojack blew a lock of white hair out of his eyes, a glint of relief in the first inklings of dawn they reflected. "Sounds like a hazard for pora infection. Or even the normal infection-infection. Let's hope for the latter."

"How about neither," I chipped in, "He did help us, and therefore you, you know."

Bojack scoffed. "I'm not exactly benefitting from his survival, now, am I?"

"You are, though," Dorian pointed out, saccharine sweet. "You might even thank me for covering your hide back there."

"I was nearly beheaded, and in record time."

"Keyword: *nearly*," he chimed, and proudly tacked on, "A distinction owed to yours truly."

"I don't do life debts."

"Eh, what'd I expect. He said you'd be difficult."

Bojack shot him a glare and turned over on his other side to find himself face-to-face with me. Without missing a beat, he demanded of me, "Do you want directions to the soon-to-be ambush site or not, Little Miss Altruistic? Just think how many people are running straight into a trap at this very second."

A worried wince drew a crease between my brows, but I raised my head, propped up on my knuckles, to peer past Bojack and find Dorian's eyes. "He who? Not-" I searched for the name. "-Tenebret?" This line of questioning only earned me perplexed looks from both Dorian and Bojack, and the tally for confusion hit maximum capacity among our little group. Okay, so decidedly *not* this mysterious Tenebret.

As if to magnify the general state of confusion colouring the atmosphere around us, Briar chose that exact moment to poke her head out through the collar of my jacket. This must have been the first he caught a good look at her, because Bojack gave a high-pitched shriek, startling away from Briar's lizardly head and shuffling backwards on his hands until he collided with Dorian. Steadying him, Dorian caught his shoulders.

"What the hell is that thing!" Bojack wailed, making a failed effort to throw his hands out in self-defense while they were bound behind his back.

"*That name, where did you hear it?*" Briar's voice echoed in my head, sending a bolt of pain from one temple to the other.

"It's in my head-?!" Bojack shouted, volume rising, and Brett, Lin, Faith, and Kev barraged him with equally loud shushing. He blinked up at them, astonished at their lacklustre response to what was evidently blowing his mind. Dorian, meanwhile, peered around him in abject fascination, mouth agape and eyes shining.

"She's a dragon," I briefly introduced, "And the telepath you stirred up all that trouble over. Do you see why we weren't parading her around?"

"Oh yes, how dare I do the exact thing you would've done in my situation. Irredeemable scoundrel that I am."

"You were already planning on ditching us! In the *Khuloces Base*, Cillian, we would've died!"

At my use of the name he'd originally given us, he huffed a breath out the side of his mouth and waved a flippant hand. "The jig's up, you can stop calling me that."

I nearly asked why he'd seen fit to use an alias in the first place, but Briar leapt in before I could speak, growling in my head, "*You'll answer my question first.*"

I answered out loud to keep Briar away from my deeper thoughts, "Right, sorry. The Liberation Front was tossing that name around. But judging by the way they spoke about him, and the way you're reacting, he sounds important." Not just the Liberation Front, but the teleporter whose convictions had rivalled Val Darling's, whose lifeblood now reddened the moist silt scabbing over my outfit.

"*That is... strange.*"

"Why? Who's Tenebret?"

"*Don't speak his name aloud.*" She constricted my waist with her serpentine body. "*Don't even think it.*"

"Ow! Hey! What, is he some sort of clairvoyant?"

"*Yes. And so much more. To speak his name, on your tongue or in your mind, is to invite him into your headspace. You, especially, should venture to wipe the very subject of him from your memory.*"

"Well, that's just not fair," I grumbled.

"A magikier wouldn't be-" Faith was saying, but Briar interrupted, swinging her head around to face her.

"*A magikier, he is not. I would urge you to remind yourselves this is Cellana, not Blackano. Here, the magic is ancient, powerful, and diverse. I'm amazed you can forget, having only just fled the wrath of a tree giant, young though this one was-*"

"*No one's forgotten the tree giant,*" I sighed in my head, only then realizing she was broadcasting my thoughts. "Are you gonna tell us who he is, or would that only set off his magic security alarms?"

"*He's known by another name in casual conversation, more of a title, the meaning of which has long been lost to time,*" she mused, "*The Kaipracan.*"

"The-?" I raked in a sharp breath and felt my skin prickle under Brett's startled eyes. "Well, that's not fair at all! What's he doing on their side?"

"*I do doubt one such as he would be involved in all these theatrics. An evenly matched contender against the centions themselves has no place in the low boil of the Liberation Front's petty tumult. He wouldn't lower himself to such tripe.*"

"That's some high talk for the ultimate enemy," Kev noted.

"*An enemy ever supreme, unmatched by all creatures of magic who've yet faced him, save one.*"

"Who?" I demanded, leaning forward.

"*The cention who first imprisoned him in Vincladimhús and perished not long thereafter at the hands of her brethren who feared her power. If you wish to rouse a force to defeat him, you will not find it in battles past. No, I daresay you will not find it at all.*"

"Great," Lin dryly commented, the sound of a zipper alerting me to the fact she'd pulled open her bag. "You know, bad news doesn't go so well with a snack break."

"Ooh! Snack break," Kev echoed, followed by another *zip!* as he ripped into his own pack.

Speaking exclusively to me, Briar's voice echoed off the walls of my skull. "*Your friends have the right idea. Let the Liberation Front throw his name around. Let them incite his wrath while you steer clear of it.*"

"*You're so convinced the Kaipracan can't be working with the Liberation Front, but what about Valencia? They knew each other personally-*"

"*Enough.*" A flame of indignation coloured her tone, surprising me. "*There's no more to say on the matter.*"

"*Isn't there?*"

"*I will not speak of him any longer.*" Her long body shifted around my middle, squeezing me as she readjusted herself, and like this, she coiled her neck back around to nestle in my jacket. The connection between our minds dropped with a pop and fizzle of the headache she'd inflamed between my temples, leaving only my own frustration with her.

Releasing an indignant huff, I scooted over the moss to lean my head back against one of the larger tree roots. How Briar couldn't see the correlation here was astounding to me. The Kaipracan, tyrant of Cellana, commander of pora and kirranites alike, enemy of the centions, and released by Valencia herself… these breadcrumbs added up all too well.

22

Chance Encounter with a Tree Hugger

Day 19

I BLINKED AND WHEN I OPENED MY EYES AGAIN, BRETT WAS CROUCHED down in front of me. I nearly jumped out of my skin at the sight of him, whacking my head off the root behind me.

Dawn had stretched unto daylight and with it came a gradient of colours from the pink and gold kaleidoscope of the high canopies to the lush greens of the vibrant and aromatic underbrush crawling over the spectacularly uneven forest floor to the soft bluish glow of oversized fungi hidden in deep, soil-rich crevices. In this way, a rainbow of colours portrayed this lively environment across Brett's face hovering so close over mine, splashes of colour catching in the brunet tones of his hair and gathering in the pools of his eyes.

"You're pale," he began, making his voice impassive no matter the concern evident in the set of his jaw.

"And?" It came out more snappish than I intended.

He matched my tone almost instinctively. "And you couldn't judge a hopeless situation, but that's no surprise." He worked the muscles in his jaw, a visible effort to keep his voice calm. "I was worried. You ran off without telling us anything-"

"That's not true. We had a plan-"

"That wasn't a plan!" A shaky breath escaped him, and he lowered his voice again. "Why did you run in alone?"

"It worked, didn't it?"

"Barely," he growled, "And now look at you. You're pale. You can't even stand. What happened?"

I startled again at the feel of Briar slithering around my middle in the plush of my jacket, enough to poke her head out and flick her tongue at me. "*Like a child, she would rather start an argument than admit to being hurt.*"

I gasped aloud, offended at her blatant betrayal, but before I could speak in my own defense, Brett had already plopped down beside me, legs crossed and eyes combing me for injuries.

"Let me get this straight. You didn't call it off when you should have, ran in blindly, disappeared on us, *and* got hurt? I think that's bingo." His voice was flat, but I felt his disdain like a slap to the face.

I pushed away his hands going straight for mine and easily read his assumption. He thought I'd used my magic. Somehow, that only stoked the fire of irritation building so swiftly within me. "Can you just leave me alone? Please?"

"You really want that?"

"Yes!"

"*Liar,*" Briar snarked, before severing the connection between us once more. The low hum of the headache her very presence incited cut suddenly short, like loud TV static flicking off. It was starting to look like these headaches were becoming a regular thing.

No one else was hurt – I was the only one limping, the only one with a headache from Briar's mind link, the only one still reeling from the events at the base, and apparently the only one worried about this whole Tenebret dilemma – at least, that was how it seemed. And Kev was worried *he* was the weakest link? Yeah right. "I can take care of myself."

"All evidence to the contrary!" Bojack unhelpfully crowed, and Dorian bopped him on the head, waving a finger in front of his face like a chastising mother.

"Yeah, well-" I began, rounding on him, but Brett stopped me with a hand on my mouth.

He pressed his other palm to his face, massaging the exhaustion from his eyes, and turned to Dorian. "Where's she hurt?" Obligingly, Dorian stuck an index finger out in the direction of my left ankle.

I shook my head and folded my arms as Brett removed his hand from my mouth to gingerly investigate my swollen ankle. Faith kneeled down on my other side, pressing cool fingertips to my skin. With her touch came that recognizable sensation of numbness – this overpowering magic she had finally learned to use in small doses. Her concentration consumed her, working to siphon only enough of her magic into me to keep the pain away without knocking me out, and Brett got to work figuring out the problem and how to fix it. Just like he always did.

Shooting a heated glare past Brett, I caught Dorian's gaze, but he made a flourishing hand gesture as if to say *you're welcome.* I could only groan. "I guess I found my new nickname for *you.* Traitor."

He masked a soft laugh. "I can live with that." Returning his attention to Bojack, he added, "As for you-"

Bojack tilted his head back toward the rest of us. "Take it up with them. I have no social stamina for pointless arguments, and they've apparently got dibs on this." He gestured to himself, bringing the rest of us to roll our eyes in unison – maybe the only thing we had done in unison since setting out from the City of Gates.

Dorian perked up in surprise, meeting my gaze once more with curiosity in his. "And why's that? What's he to you if you're not bounty hunters?"

"A guilt trip," Lin tossed over her shoulder, "And a disastrous guide."

"Ooh," Dorian hummed the sound around a triumphant smile, "Lucky for us, that uncomplicates matters some."

"Oh?" Kev prompted.

"I mean him no harm," Dorian beamed as if this statement alone merited a trophy.

I folded an elbow over my eyes with my head leaned back on the root, tuning out the discomfort in my ankle as Brett tested the injury between his hands, deadly silent. "You just want to... what, abduct him? Is that even legal?"

Like his smile, even Dorian's small, amused chuckle was contagiously cheery. "I have orders to bring him back to the Clan Leader of the Schevonian Isles-"

"A man devoid of power since the plague," Bojack cut in, "Why bother."

Dorian laughed him off with a wave of his hand. "The Orange Sages might be gone, but he's still the Second Clan Leader-"

"Remind me again, leader of what? You said it yourself, they're *gone.*"

Without removing my arm from my face, I grimaced against a twinge in my ankle beyond the numbing agent of Faith's magic and in a tetchy tone

I hadn't intended, reminded them both, "But what for-?" I gritted my teeth, reining myself in so I wouldn't reflexively kick Brett in the face.

"Well, the arms of achaion," Dorian simply said, and all of our heads snapped up in tandem, all eyes on Bojack.

"So you do know what it is!" I gasped before I could think to play dumb, and a chorus of sighs and various other noises of disapproval passed around the circle of my friends. Even Briar shuffled her wings in distaste, and so with fingers steepled in front of my chin and pursed lips, I continued more carefully, "How much do you know?"

Bojack's brows had raised nearly to his hairline, watching us all. "Just enough not to go manhandling another one myself."

"Another one?" Faith echoed, ears pricking at the insinuation.

"Well aren't you perceptive."

Brett sat up, peering over his shoulder at Bojack. With his movement, a faint blue glow from the bioluminescent fungi spattering the lower cliff faces of the nearby ravines sieved past him, illuminating part of Bojack's face and catching in the white of his hair. "You've held a weapon of achaion before?"

"I didn't take the weapon from the City of Gates, if that's what you're insinuating."

"I know that," Brett snapped, taken aback by his tone and yet matching it with equal accusation in his own. "I saw what happened that day."

A spark of intrigue entered Bojack's eyes. "Oh?"

"But how did-? Where did you-?" Kev gasped with sudden understanding, as if the pieces were clicking together in his mind. "Is that why you smell like magic, like those pora were saying?"

"Sure," he jadedly huffed, "If that's what you want to talk about right now, why not. If it weren't for the melatonin dispensary of my magic, I'd have a much bigger problem than early-onset greying."

"So you're just constantly using it?" Lin demanded, "Like, right now?"

"Mhm."

I already assumed the answer, but I couldn't help asking, "Do you have to?"

"Unless I want to die in my sleep."

Voice flat and gears turning, Faith breathed, "A weapon of achaion did that to you?"

"My price for curiosity. I knew I wasn't worthy of a weapon of achaion, but I wanted to know what would happen. Maybe I thought it would accept me and banked on the idea I could heal away whatever happened if I failed. If you couldn't tell, I was young and full of hubris."

"*And what did you do with it, the weapon of achaion you came into contact with?*" Briar asked throughout each of our minds, startling me. Not just for the suddenness of her intrusion, but for her needing to ask at all. Bojack must have had his mind under lock and key if even Briar couldn't pick it for the truth.

Was this why she found Bojack so intriguing? Because he'd already found a weapon of achaion, a weapon he couldn't wield himself? Did she suspect it from the first moment she tried to rifle through his mind?

"That's valuable information, isn't it?" he grinned, taking obvious pride in our utterly flabbergasted expressions, "And I'm the only magikier alive who knows the answer." He bubbled with mocking laughter. "Why do you think the Empress wants my head? Because I'm a scoundrel? Because I don't play nice?"

"It probably contributes," I muttered.

Narrowing his eyes into a glare, he crinkled his nose in distaste. "She didn't like me digging up old bones. None of the Clan Leaders did."

"And for that reason," Dorian beamed, "I'm taking you back to the Second Clan Leader of Schevon. Sounds reasonable, no? So if you wouldn't mind, I'll just be taking him-"

"Now wait just a minute," I interjected, looking for any excuse to get more time and therefore more information out of this man. "None of us know the way to the- what was it?"

"The soon-to-be ambush site," Bojack helpfully supplied, an infuriating smugness nestled in the corners of his mouth.

"Right. Not without you and Bojack," I continued, meeting Dorian's eyes with resolution behind my own. "We're the only ones who can help them."

Losing some of the wind from his sails, Dorian deflated some, but still not enough to lose his happy-go-lucky smile. "It's a bit of a detour. I could give you directions."

"*If only it were so easy*," Briar spoke up, my partner in crime, "*I am not so well-versed in the ocean-like currents and mutability of this ancient forest. Sky-scraping trees which move and come alive, monolithic stones that appear and disappear. I know not the ever-changing landscapes, nor are any of us fluent in this foreign language of mental mapping. The Khuloces Forest is a troublesome labyrinth to those like us.*" Her thoughts in our heads came with a sludge of distaste, vexed by her inadequacy and loath to admit her imperfections – few and far between though they were.

I plastered on a smile for Dorian, gritting my teeth against a wave of pain from my ankle, and settled back again. "There you have it. We'd be lost without him, but he's all yours once we get there."

Bojack dropped his jaw, shocked and appalled. "You would hand me over, just like that? I thought we had something."

Brett sat back on his haunches, releasing a sigh. "Either way, we need a healer. This looks sprained."

Faith pushed more of her magic into me, shrouding the pain and numbing my leg up to my hip. Beyond the sedated buzz taking root in my mind, I could barely think straight, rendered practically to a daze.

Brett must have seen the light dim behind my eyes, for he slid his glance toward Bojack, weighing our options. His healing magic would leave me drained, but Faith's sedation magic left me loopy and did nothing to actually fix the issue.

Problem was, we'd already missed a night's rest. Dawn stretched her bluish fingers over the horizon, and the militants from the base we'd destroyed had scattered somewhere in our vicinity, or so we could assume – by the looks of things, we were on a straight path to pulling an all-nighter and had only one place to go: the site of an impending ambush.

Finally, Brett caved, "Alright, Bojack…"

He fixed his posture at his name, remembering to look down his nose at us as he fiendishly noted, "*Most* essential."

After a quick rations break, and after Bojack worked his literal magic on my ankle, I held onto consciousness with the same gusto I would have used to latch onto Kev's back had I forgone Bojack's help – like a koala cub clinging to its mother. As it turned out, fixing the problem in my ankle was either on par with the last bout of healing magic Bojack had worked on me or required even more of his pyrrhic ability, and as such, sapped my energy in an equivalent exchange.

Considering the exhaustion already weighing down on me from the too-many-hours I'd spent not only awake but supercharged with adrenaline, it hardly mattered that I could walk painlessly on two feet – scratch that, *mostly* painlessly. Instead, I now tripped over any root in my path and teetered with every step, bleary-eyed and constantly fending off an endless slog of yawns.

Amid the haze of my exhaustion, I was drawn into conversation, stumbling over my words as much as my feet. My brain chugged at half the speed of my mouth.

"Did you find who you were looking for?" Bojack asked, and it was a moment before I realized he was speaking to me. "Couldn't have been this unremarkable tart." He gestured vaguely to Dorian.

"Well… no," I murmured.

"Great. So what I'm hearing is it was as much of a waste of time for you as it was for me. And now you're throwing me to the dogs after I was nearly *killed*. Have you no heart?" Bojack griped and descended into petty grumbling.

"*I* wouldn't call it a waste of time," Dorian chipped in, but Brett spoke over him.

"No, Bojack's right. We haven't gained anything."

Dorian fumed quietly beside Bojack's grumbling, but I was simply focused on avoiding eye contact with Brett. I felt his gaze on me and imagined the malcontent and frustration I would find in those sea green pools. He had every right to be angry with me. I did exactly what I said I wouldn't, only to turn up empty handed.

"Well, I wouldn't go *that* far." To everyone's surprise, Bojack had leapt back into the discourse, albeit deadpan and dripping with sarcasm.

Massaging his temples between his index fingers, Brett noted, "I was agreeing with you."

"No, no. You did gain *something*, just not the thing you were after." He held up both index fingers to illustrate his point, and elucidated, "Bragging rights. Honestly, that's the undisputed silver to whatever gold you thought you'd unearth there."

Somehow, his enthusiasm toward the bit only made our alleged reward infinitely less desirable, and he relished in our melancholy.

It wasn't long before Brett sat us all down again to work his magic, if only to enforce a temporary silence on the group. I hesitated between my desires to smooth things over with him and to avoid him at all costs. Turns out, I didn't have to. He kept his distance from me and delved straight into his magic before anyone could interrupt.

The early morning dragged on. Birds had begun to chirp even though the sun had yet to rise, and I was feeling sick with exhaustion.

Bojack, Dorian, and Brett led us in an utterly dysfunctional show of collaboration, for which Brett showed no patience toward either man – Bojack, I could understand, but I couldn't figure what Dorian had done to deserve his shortness. Kev kept lookout at a meagre distance with Briar's help, reminding me almost of a falconer and his falcon. Meanwhile, I stumbled along in the middle of the group, elbows linked up with Faith and Lin's ever since I nodded off mid-stride and walked into a tree. A nauseous feeling had been roiling low in my gut since Bojack healed my ankle, a constant reminder of my body's begrudging surrender of hope for sleep.

Stuck in this half-awake state of mind, dream-like imaginings replayed our entire fiasco at the fort behind my eyelids. I swore I could feel the spatter of warm liquid hitting my skin again and again each time the image of the teleporter's death rang shrill and insistent in this looping memory reel, and my automatic reaction, a slimy, sticky feeling in the whirlpool of my memory. *Good.* I had spoken that word aloud in the face of her brutal death.

I caught myself glancing toward Kev and Briar up ahead, eyes fixed to the golden glimmer shining over her scutes. How could she slash someone's throat so automatically, so trivially? She must have thought nonlethal force wouldn't have stopped the teleporter from making off with me, but she'd killed her, and in that fleeting moment, I had celebrated her death.

We stopped at what we collectively agreed was the halfway point, even though only Bojack really had a grasp of where we were going. For all the rest of us knew, he could very well have been taking us in the complete opposite direction, and assuming as much, Brett had made crystal clear what would happen to Bojack if he did.

Faith and Lin sat me down next to a modest-sized pond at the base of the crater-like trench, sinking down on either side of me with their arms still chain-linked with mine. Bojack flung himself across a boulder shaped much like a lounge chair near the high bank behind us formed by a shelter of roots and erosion while Dorian kept an eye on him, but Brett, it seemed, had had enough of them. He marched up to Lin, Kev, and I, squatting down next to the water and refilling his waterskin as he grumbled heatedly under his breath.

"How's it going with the dream team? Get anything out of Bojack yet?" Faith teased.

He shot her a glare. "Of course not. He talks in circles. Sure, it's all about him, but it's never what I'm asking. And Dorian's no better."

"Briar?" Lin asked.

"*The bounty hunter knows as much as has been given freely to us, but the bounty... His familiarity with deflecting the magic of telepaths is not only impressive but unsettling for a magikier, and a healing magikier at that. To have a mind so trained against intrusion...*" she answered, but there was distraction in her tone, resounding and distant. Rampant suspicions and theories blipped from her mind to mine, too fast and too sporadic to unpack with any coherence.

Shaking his head between his hands, Brett blew an exhausted huff of breath and continued in a firm tone, "We're ditching them the moment it becomes an option. I can feel myself unhinging."

"Well, hold on," Kev spoke up, "If they know the way to Cerenthior-"

Brett desperately shook his head, a pained look in his eyes. "No. No, no. I know where you're going with this, and I'm putting my foot down. We're not asking those two for directions. I'd rather die."

"Cool, 'cause that's always a valid option these days," Lin sarcastically noted, "You did see the literal tree giant, didn't you? We have *no idea* what's in store for us on our own. So maybe put your ego down instead of your foot and we can get somewhere."

"It would be an advantage to us, if we had more time with him," I noted, but my heart wasn't in it, and all the gusto I might have mustered disappeared when Brett made a face at me. I winced in apology but gave a feeble shrug. "He has knowledge not even the centions had until Briar was forced to give it up. That's big."

"And whatever he did with that knowledge, it made him an enemy of just about every magikier on Cellana. Even the Liberation Front wants him dead. Let's just hand him over to Dorian and be done with him before he figures out something he shouldn't," Brett insisted with a pointed look insinuating *I* was the something.

With that, the bickering started anew. Scratch that, I wasn't sure it had ever really stopped.

I closed my eyes and leaned my head back, raising the waterskin Faith, Lin, and I had been sharing to my lips. Before they could raise their voices, I cut in, "Why are we arguing this. Dorian's a bounty hunter with his own responsibilities, he's not going to put them all on hold to join us to the certain doom capital of Cellana."

Begrudgingly, Faith was the one to explain, "Schevon's a straight shot north with Cerenthior at the halfway point. He'd have to go out of his way to *avoid* it."

I could practically feel Lin's triumph radiating off her. "I'm sorry, weren't you siding with Brett on this one?"

"Dissing her just as she's coming over to your side? I thought you were better than that, Mullet," came Dorian's voice, and Lin's hand shot up to the nape of her neck where the pixie cut had already begun to grow out. There Dorian sat, cross-legged on the bank just behind us, smiling that dopey, harmless smile with his chin cupped in one hand and Bojack's tether clasped in the other.

"Can't imagine why," Lin grumbled as Bojack muttered, "I didn't."

Ignoring the both of them, Faith shot back, "I haven't changed my mind."

"Well, at least you're exploring all the angles, even if you're lacking some objectivity. Naturally, I've been mulling it over since I heard where you're headed. The more the merrier, as they say."

Brett swore under his breath, turning back to the water and splashing a handful over his face. Streaks cut through the grime of travel caked onto his skin.

I quirked an eyebrow at Dorian, perplexed. "So, think on it. We'll leave it up to you whether you come along or not."

Lin nodded. "Until then, you should start putting together a case to convince the people out of a healer. Desperate times and all that."

An offended scoff called our attention to Bojack, who wore an expression of sheer distaste. "I can't help but feel I've been reduced to a bargaining chip." Disbelief and resentment coloured his tone.

"Best bargaining chip in the business, as things stand," Dorian dotingly patronized him.

"Is that the word on the street among bounty hunters? And I wasn't informed? How inconsiderate to leave one out of their own repute."

"And knowing that would have changed things?" Brett scoffed.

"I could have used it to my advantage back there. Maybe I wouldn't have ended up on a chopping block."

"Yeah, wouldn't put it past you," Kev groaned.

"I guess I still could. Out with the idiot, I'll turn myself in for a pretty price."

"And who's the idiot in this case?" Lin jabbed, then turned to Dorian. "How'd it take you this long to catch this guy?"

"I blame the war," he noted, but shrugged and found my eyes once again. "Until I'm done with this bounty, there'll be no me without he or he without me. We'll be attached at the hip, in a very literal sense. I'm only hoping that won't be too inconvenient for you."

"This is Bojack we're talking about," Faith reminded him, and Dorian gave a humble dip of his chin, owning up to the reality. Bojack huffed another disgruntled complaint.

"I shouldn't have brought this up," Brett quietly muttered under his breath, more to himself than to any of us, but his words breeched the sleepy haze swathing my head.

Speaking around a yawn, I put an end to this discussion. "It's not like we're dependent on each other. If it works out, it works out."

Giving a nod, Dorian delicately granted, "Right. We'll leave it at that, then."

I snuck a peek in Brett's direction, finding a soft glimmer in his eyes. Relief. But even that slight expression soon snuffed itself out. For once, I could practically read his thoughts on his face – an echo of the shy-to-hope look he had worn when I first promised I would call off our detour to the Khuloces Base if things weren't looking good, and the disillusionment that followed when I didn't, now pitched against the context of this latest promise.

My heart sank in my chest, and I averted my gaze.

Dorian conceded with his usual docile smile, and nudged Brett's side with an elbow. "So, teasing me with the prospect of good company was just something you felt like doing?" he mused, and grinned with a glimmer of mischief in his eyes as Brett grumbled something and moved off, making a wide berth around his tormentors.

I found myself half-smiling as I watched the two of them. Everything seemed to come in halves when sleep pushed against the frayed hems of consciousness.

In the lull of the conversation, a small sound caught my ear. "Mmph!" came a muffled voice from somewhere nearby. For a second, I wondered if I'd come to the stage of sleep deprivation where I'd started to hear things, but it would seem, I wasn't the only one to notice the little sound.

All at once, everyone around me bolted into action, all except Bojack who had taken up his temper again.

"Who's there?" Brett shouted in a warning voice, raising his mace from its holster. Kev backed him up with one arrow notched on his bow and two more held in the same hand for rapid fire, aiming between the trees without releasing.

"Mm-mm!" the muffled voice returned from somewhere closer than I initially realized.

Dorian stood up, staring down at his feet, and kicked the root on which the bank sloped. Ancient and dense, I didn't expect the root to budge when the toe of his boot met the wood, and yet...

"Mmph!" The voice sounded like it was right under us.

Kev's jaw dropped and he sheathed his arrows again. "Someone's buried under the roots." He glanced back toward the water, calling my attention to the small, almost imperceptible signs that this trench was freshly cut out of the forest floor.

"What are the odds?" Bojack mused, deadpan and unimpressed. "In present company, I would've expected a kirranite slurry. This group is its own bad omen."

Dorian turned his pensive regard up the length of the mammoth tree, and visibly gulped. In a quieted voice, he mused, "Hmm, so it looks like we've made our camp on the roots of a sleeping tree giant. Hard to differentiate from the local flora, these beasties."

"Another one?" Lin hissed, and rounded the root in search of something.

She bent down on the other side and an ear-splitting *crack!* told me she'd unearthed a rock to shatter. In response, the root curled back on itself and recoiled away, slithering back into the forest floor. The bank shuddered at its movement, creating a small avalanche of dirt, and in its wake, revealed a hollow. There, huddled inside, was a frazzled-looking man.

Bojack took one look at the excavated man and groaned his own rendition of Lin's statement, "Ugh, *another* one. No, nuh-uh. We're at maximum capacity, bud. No more tagalongs."

"Are you alright?" Faith fretted, ignoring Bojack and instead hurrying to help the poor man out of the pit that had just moments prior been covered by roots as wide as he was tall.

Kev strode along after her, offering a hand to the man as well. "What happened? Did you come from the Khuloces Base?"

"Course I did!" huffed and puffed the man, refusing Kev's helping hand in favour of Faith's and scrambling out of the pit.

"And... are you...?" Kev attempted.

The man shot him a dirty scowl. "What, you think I'm some flea-bitten pora? I got out when I could. Cluster of earthquakes sent the place into complete anarchy." He peered around Faith toward Bojack, surprise raising his eyebrows nearly to his hairline. "Cillian?"

"What happened?" Brett demanded, stepping up between Faith and the dirt-encrusted man. With this slight shift, Brett slid into a stance I recognized from our training sessions. He held his mace low, but his grip was tight. He was subtle, appearing casual, but his feet were shoulder-width apart and properly angled, knees slightly bent to spring into action at a moment's notice. He was ready for a fight, or to knock the others out of the way of an attack, but I was only glad he'd hesitated to raise his mace outright.

I shifted to get a clearer view around him, finding even this slight movement difficult while my body yearned for sleep.

"Bunch of us made a break for it when that first earthquake hit. Didn't expect the pora to go nuts. Some new squad came in, raided the place lookin' for a Shawn?" He didn't sound certain about what he was saying, but when Brett squeezed his temples and dropped his weapon to his side, heaving a sigh, the man figured we understood what he didn't. "You know this Shawn?"

"You wouldn't happen to have, uh, misheard them?" I asked, feeling my heart pinch in anticipation of the worst. I'd heard it straight from the horse's mouth, after all. Pora from this very base had gone rogue chasing after *the shonte*. Now, it seemed, they'd even turned against their allies.

"Obviously, they didn't find who they were lookin' for, or they wouldn't'a lost their tempers." He brushed off Kev's helping hand, turning a cold shoulder toward him. "So, this Shawn. That one a' you?" He looked Dorian up and down, but Dorian merely smiled back, and his gaze landed square on Brett.

"Well, no. None of us go by Shawn," Kev interjected, and gave it a second thought, flicking his eyes to Bojack. "Unless that's another one of your aliases."

"Do I look like a Shawn to you?" Bojack shot back, and everyone went back to disregarding him. Even Dorian, calm and quiet in the face of this confrontation, placed a warning hand on his shoulder to shut him up, but minded the rest of us inquisitively. Judging by the eager sheen of his regard, it took everything in him just to hold his tongue.

Lin reminded the man, "We just pulled you out of the ground and you're already accusing us of, what?" She chuckled humourlessly. "Having a common first name?"

"Obviously that's not the end of it," he growled, taking a wide step back from Faith, Brett, and Kev. "What do them pora want?"

"It's complicated," I started, and the man rounded on me with a heavy glare.

"I was close to the gulch when they fanned the quarry followin' a scent on the air. Ran long as I could and when I finally stopped to rest, the damn trees must've figured I needed a cuddle. I been stuck in that pit for hours; thought that was it for me, that I'd end up mulch for the damn roots. So yeah, you better believe you're gonna tell me what I wanna know."

"*Say less and you may find yourselves better off,*" Briar reported in each of our minds, although it appeared by the lack of a reaction from the man himself, she'd blacklisted him from her broadcast. "*If his memory has any merit to it, his prerogative once bedlam reigned was to debase himself, feigning injury so the able-bodied would carry him away to safety. And when they were cornered, he watched those who helped him struggle to fend off their detestable foes and fled while all their backs were turned to him.*"

"*Great. We don't need another Bojack,*" came Brett's internal grievance in the conference call of Briar's telepathic mind link, echoing with the telltale signs of an unintentional response. Bojack whipped a glare in his direction, but by the look of shock on Brett's face, I doubted he'd expected Briar to share his thought with the group at large.

A slight sting caressed my skull, pushing against my brain and pounding with my blood. Another headache, so instantaneous now whenever Briar reached into my mind.

"*I recognize some of the pora in his memory from your visions, empath. Those who devoured the animal by the tracks, do you recall? It would seem they've grown in number.*"

The tracks…

There was no doubt in my mind, this was the same group of pora who'd been tracking us since we left the City of Gates, who'd devoured the scuttlepup – wolf spider! – to get at my blood. I could only assume they'd lost the trail at the quarry, where Bojack had closed my wounds and where I'd washed the apparent homing signal off my back. That, at least, offered a reason for their violent lash-out, although it did nothing to excuse it.

"*Careful,*" Briar's voice returned, "*He's got his eye on your packs and a propensity for petty theft.*"

"Yeesh, you really know how to hold a silence. Enough to make a man paranoid." He eyed each of us, letting his gaze linger on Faith. "Like you're talkin' to someone I can't hear."

Lin leaned forward, contempt in her tone. "Is that a problem?"

He hardly paid her any mind as Brett stepped up closer to the man, blocking his view of Faith entirely. The cocky expression on his face wavered, but he squared up, nonetheless. "What, are you so gutless, you let the preteen do all the talkin'?"

"I'm fourteen, so–"

"Shut it, kiddo. This discussion's above your pay-grade. Or should I say school grade?" He seemed to find himself hilarious, a roguish curl stretching the corner of his mouth.

Brett shook his head, frowning. "Don't be disrespectful."

Nodding, Kev thumped the wooden length of his bow over the man's head and punctuated his brother's words with an avid, "Yeah!"

"Ah, hey-!" the man complained, pawing away the bow. The heel of his boot caught on the uneven ground and he stumbled back until he was up against the base of the nearest tree. Whether this trunk belonged to a tree giant, I couldn't tell, but whatever it was had no reaction to the soft collision.

"Just so we're clear," I began, glancing out of the corner of my eye toward Bojack who'd first introduced me to the problem I now sought to circumvent, "We do have a telepath among us, and we know you're a self-serving coward and a thief. That said, you can still come with us to the meet-up point."

"Excuse me?"

"That's where you're headed, isn't it?"

The man stood there for a long moment with his back to the bark, mouth agape and a flabbergasted expression on his face. His wide eyes flitted to Brett, then to Kev, then back to me. I could practically see the gears turning in his head, and he finally sputtered, "Who the hell are you people?"

Bojack chuckled out the side of his mouth, more akin to blowing air than a real laugh. "Trust me, pal, you don't want to know."

"*He feels cornered, and though he is a snivelling rat, he's of the desperate sort,*" came Briar's voice, this time exclusive to my mind alone, "*You may want to talk him down from reckless action before the window closes. As the leading expert in such activity, I'm sure you can manage.*"

"*Is he dangerous?*" I asked through the sensation of having my brain cleaved in half, keeping my response to a minimum no matter the ache her words invoked across my skull.

"*He can make himself and whatever he touches invisible to the naked eye, but he's acutely aware of the fact he is without a weapon. Whether visible or invisible, he cannot block the presence of his mind from me. So, no. I would not call him particularly dangerous.*"

"*Mhm, that's great, but your invisi-snitching won't do me much good if it comes with a headache.*"

"*The pain persists? That shouldn't be...*" Her words trailed off as her presence disappeared from my mind, and with it, the sting of the headache.

Turning my attention once again to the man now approximating belligerence, I had to raise my voice over the apparent spat with Bojack that had cropped up in my distraction. "We've done nothing but offer you help. Did that get lost in translation, somehow?"

Bojack smirked as if my intervention had won him the argument, and the man glared daggers at me. "And how's that, hm? The way I'm understandin' it, you and this Shawn fella are the reason for all this!" He threw his arms out in gesture to his surroundings.

With a wide, theatrical yawn, Lin leaned back against the high bank with her elbows on the ridge and crossed her ankles. "And the way I'm hearing it, you want to try your luck out here by yourself. Look, if you're dead set on mulching yourself for another tree giant, more power to you, but you're not seeing the bigger picture. This is my *saintly* friend's way of offering you a measure of protection while you walk where we can see you."

I couldn't help thinking she'd laid it on a little thick, but I was too stunned at her tenacity to say so – or say anything, for that matter. We stood like statues, shocked into silence, save Bojack who had the audacity to cackle like a witch – a fitting laugh for him.

And that was that.

When it came down to it, the man stuck to his guns, and bolted the moment Bojack started whooping and hollering, falling over himself to get away. I was too concerned with the assumption Bojack had lost his mind to notice the man make a run for it, and by the time I did, it was too late.

I couldn't help thinking, perhaps the man was right to run from us, so as not to be wrapped up in whatever game of the damned followed at my heels. I had only to consider the path of destruction we'd left in our wake since leaving the City of Gates, and the pora who continued to tear it up behind us.

We'd extended a hand and invited him to put his trust in us, and for all we knew, he was better off putting as much distance between us as he possibly could. Maybe that was what Bojack found so laughable.

23

Not Exactly Masters of Stealth

Unlike last time, Bojack let us know when we were getting close, and Briar took off into the trees, enmeshing with the golden rays of daylight filtering through the high canopy.

The foliage was denser in these parts, carrying deep shadows below the heavenly gold glow trapped in the leaves so infinitely high above, those colossal limbs entangled like a ceiling of bramble. But it wasn't totally dark here in the forest's depths. Glowing blue mushrooms the size of horses grew in patches along the bases of only the thickest tree trunks. Like neon umbrellas over our heads.

We had to hack and slash our way through the colourful fungal undergrowth thriving beneath the glow of the mushrooms, dulling our blades on their rubbery stems, and breaking a sweat in our effort.

By *our*, I of course meant Brett, Lin, Faith, and Kev. Not me. Nobody seemed to trust me with a blade at this late stage of sleep deprivation. So instead, I watched them work alongside Dorian's expert babysitting of Bojack, and the thought crossed my mind that any one of these hewn fungi could be some heretofore unheard-of magical creature like the tree giants. With nothing else to do, I simply counted us lucky the toadstools and verdure weren't fighting back.

"We're here," Bojack mused in a dull, sing-song voice. At his words, Faith held out both arms to halt our slow crawl through the thick underbrush. A sheet of vines and creepers speckled with yellow, pink, and blue flowerheads stood just ahead of us, blocking our path.

She gestured up the curtain of growth to a woody knot of low boughs on a colossal tree where a small, almost imperceptible marking in the bark denoted the presence of people. Relief swelled in my chest, although it felt a lot like sinking into sleep. Catching myself stumbling with a near tumbling sway, I worked to find my balance and reminded myself how close we were to rest. That this place was safe, and this latest detour wouldn't be for nothing, not like the last.

"Finally," Kev wheezed and sheathed his sabre, making for the natural drapery. Before he could take another step, Lin clasped his arm.

"They're expecting an attack, remember? They might have set traps."

Faith lifted her chin in gesture to the high canopies, indicating Briar's intel as she relayed, "Not to mention there's a lookout just up ahead."

Briar couldn't reach my mind from the height of the trees, but Faith had assured me she and Briar were maintaining a mind link for safe measure. Even though I was more zombie than person at this point, even that smidgen of exclusion – unintentional as it was – squeezed a lonely sensation in my chest.

With a hand cupping his chin, Dorian leaned in closer to me, an aspect of Sherlockian analysis in his countenance. "So we're going off the assumption they don't like us?"

I shrugged, but Lin snickered, "I don't see why. We gave them a fleeting reprieve from their *most essential* magikier."

Bojack shot her a glare, but Dorian was still contemplating our situation and spoke up with an index finger raised to the sky, as if this were a lightning rod for a stroke of genius. "Why not just announce ourselves?"

Brett scoffed, stepping up next to us. "We have it on good authority to be cautious in new places."

"Good authority here meaning past experience," Bojack chimed in, modelling a dubious expression in my direction. Under the slight glow of a nearby mushroom, his white hair took on a prettier, azure hue.

"So what now? We just wait and hope they don't shoot first when they find us skulking on their doorstep?" Faith asked, and Brett heaved a sigh, rubbing a jaded hand over his face.

"Yeah, that's a good point," he huffed, and with a beckoning gesture to Kev, urged his brother's scouting help. "We'll just have to find them first."

"You do realise I was once a valued member of the mining community?" Bojack spoke up, "If you send *me* in first–"

"No," everyone spoke in unison.

Dorian gave him no time to sulk about it as he stepped up toward a chest-high toadstool upon which to sit. In place of coherent complaints, the utterly indisposed man made a strangled sound while being towed along by the tether connecting them.

"Do I need to reiterate the potential for traps?" Lin hissed after them in as loud of a voice as she dared.

"I'm not going anywhere far-" As he spoke, his foot dropped to meet the ground, except there was no ground to meet, and he cut himself off in his surprise.

The thick moss that had grown over the forest floor under his foot flew up in a burst of bluish greens around his leg, revealing a small hole in the ground, more likely a snake's den than a planned trap, but bearing the same result.

With a short and haggard shout, his one leg plummeted into the small pit, bringing the rest of him down as well, and Bojack couldn't help his burst of laughter, short as it was before his bindings dragged him down after Dorian.

Brett rounded on them with a glare as their fleeting cacophony bounced off the monolithic trees, a vast and resounding echo. Lin had her arms up around her head, ducking under this fresh feeling of scrutiny from unseen eyes.

"You okay?" Kev groaned out of courtesy. Dorian lay on his back on the ground, hands clasped neatly over his stomach, with one leg absolutely missing in the moss bed. He wore a rare, disgruntled expression, partially hiding the perpetual smile in the curve of his lips.

"This hurts my ego more than anything else," he mused in his Irish lilt, "But who's to say I did fall. A tree giant might have shifted its roots right when I stepped down."

"How terrible," Bojack snapped, "Oh, how dreadful a thing to happen to you of all people. Me? Oh, I'm just *fine*."

I couldn't help but let loose a soft chuckle, offering each of them a hand with the chastising words, "Get up."

A noise beyond the curtain of vines froze each of us in place, distant and hard to make out, but undoubtedly a voice. I perked up at the sound, making a move to introduce ourselves to whoever approached, but in that same instant, Brett's hand was on the small of my back, and we hit the ground – or rather, I landed on Dorian's chest hard enough to leave him wheezing.

"Get down!" Faith whispered, pulling Lin and Kev low as well.

"One step ahead of you, love," Dorian roguishly remarked through his efforts to catch his breath, and I covered his mouth, flattening myself to get as close to the ground as possible. We lay together in this dog pile, hidden behind a knee-high wall of fungi-covered root and moss, and fell into a hush.

My heart pounded in my ears. All it took was a moment of shock. Tensions were already high enough as it was, adding to it could be a fatal mistake.

"Are they Liberation Front?" Kev whispered, only vaguely audible through the weight suspended in the air.

I felt more than saw Brett shrug his silent response.

Whether they were Liberation Front or not, so deep in the Khuloces Forest, even friends looked like foes under the wrong light.

There was a second shout, the words somewhat more audible this time, but muffled as though by a piece of clothing over their mouth.

Moisture retained in the moss soaked slowly into my pant legs, cold against my skin, but I ignored this mild discomfort. Dorian shifted under me, likely facing a worse discomfort with his entire leg sheathed in the earth, but he soon gave up his futile attempt to free his leg of the hole.

"I swear I heard something," a female voice called, closer than the first. My hand covering Dorian's mouth clenched in surprise at her proximity – just on the other side of the root. My heart leapt to my throat, beating rapidly in my ears.

None of us moved, entirely too aware of the danger we faced if we alarmed her. No matter what side she was on, she would have no reason to hesitate.

"Could've been anything," the first answered, approaching. By the adolescent crack in his voice, I placed him at no older than his mid-teens and in drawing that conclusion, my mind raced with overanalysing conjecture. Was it more or less likely that someone as young as he would be among the Liberation Front, or was this proof of his being a freed prisoner from their base?

I had no answers.

"And *anything* could be dangerous," the girl shot back, "We're in the heart of the Khuloces Forest, Henri. It's a wonder this place hasn't gobbled us whole."

"That's what we keep *you* around for."

"It doesn't work like that. And- Hey! Get back here. I told you splitting up negates my magic!"

"Then don't go running off without me?"

"But I could swear I heard something." At her words, he made a sound like a scoff. She continued in a sassy tone, "You wanna go off on your own? Fine. Not like I was taking *your* health and safety into account-"

"You're worried about me? That's cute."

"It's not cute! And I'm not worried about you-"

"You're right, not cute at all. Adorable is the word I was thinking of." There was triumph in the boy's voice, and both pairs of footsteps moved off, although their argument persisted.

A glare of blue light reflected off Lin's lenses into my eyes, calling my attention, and for a moment, I thought I saw her shoulders droop, her eyes lower, sadness drawing her face, but the expression disappeared the moment she caught me looking.

"What's wrong?" I silently mouthed.

"Nothing," she muttered in a muted voice, earning Brett's expressive body language reminding us to be quiet.

Too late.

"Okay this time, I *know* I heard a voice! Who's there!" the girl shouted, followed by the light tap of footsteps jumping atop the root hiding us.

We all looked up just in time to catch the glint of gold overhead, and then Briar was on top of the teenage girl. Not attacking, but restraining within the coils of her long, boa constrictor-like body.

The girl couldn't help but release a muffled scream into Briar's rough hide, struggling helplessly against the unbreakable hold restraining her arms at her sides, but the boy we had heard leapt up to her defense.

"No, no, wait!" I cried, fumbling to get my feet under me, but the tangle of my friends kept me down.

"Who the hell are you?!" he yelped, utterly unintimidating, but his round eyes found my face and then lowered to the dogpile consuming me. His jaw dropped and his voice cracked on the exclamation, "Cillian?"

Dorian answered with utmost authenticity from the lowest position in our pile, "I apologize for the scare, but you can call us friends. If I'm understanding things correctly, you escaped the Khuloces Base, too?"

A momentary silence met his entirely-too-casual introduction, during which I met each of my friends' bewildered expressions with equal astonishment. In the wake of his words, Briar slowly, gently, released her hold on the girl so her long body lowered to the forest floor. The last of her weight flopped heavily to the ground and she slithered over the fungal undergrowth and moss bed to me, forked tongue flicking at the pair standing over us in an obvious warning.

An awkward sound escaped me as I scooped Briar in close, away from these hostile strangers. Her head didn't budge from its spot, golden eyes transfixed to her potential targets, and neck lengthening to account for my wrenching her long body away. "Sorry about her."

Finally, the girl recouped herself with panic in her eyes and fury on her tongue. "What the hell is that thing?"

"A dragon. Briar. She's nicer than she seems... well, when she wants to be-"

Shaking out the confusion knitting her brows, the girl stopped me with waving hands. "Who are you people?"

"Well-" Dorian began, but she pulled forth a short spear which looked to have been carved from the very trees surrounding us, a warning in her eyes. As far as I could tell, she was armed to the teeth with an assortment of less obvious weapons. The hilts of hidden daggers poked out from under a short fringe lining the sleeves of her oversized jacket and she had a bright red fanny pack on her hip which could have concealed any number of small weapons. Even her bouncing, blonde hair was tied back with what looked like a wire garrotte, commonly used to strangle people. In light of that, I'd even go so far as to mark her wire-rimmed glasses as a weapon, cracked across the left lens and badly bent so the right side made a wide berth from her ear.

Over the sound of Briar's hiss, the girl growled, "Careful how you answer, or you'll be a dead man."

"A dead *friend*," Dorian corrected in a surprisingly charming voice like this was a totally normal situation to be in. "Believe it or not, our little troupe is here to lend a hand."

Before he could dig himself a deeper hole than the one he'd quite literally fallen into, I burst, "He's telling the truth!" unsure how else to back him up. My decree seemed adequate for him as he nodded with shining eyes and gestured to me as though I'd provided irrefutable proof of his character.

"The truth about what, that I don't believe it?" the girl retorted in increasing frustration.

"No, about the hand," I happily informed her, and extended my own in offering. Both teens stared at me like I had the plague, and from beside me, Lin let loose a wry laugh, apparently finding absurd amusement in all this.

The girl's gaze found Lin, and the shadows practically melted away in the burning radiance of her glee before she blanched, averting her regard.

She was swift to readjust herself, but everyone and their mother had seen that telling reaction, and she must have realized it, for suddenly she was grinning down at us, all former airs dropped. "Cat!"

With that, she lowered her spear and waved off the fairly obvious concerns of the boy beside her. After a moment's hesitation, he settled back into a more casual stance.

"Oh, it's you." There was a playful lilt to Lin's otherwise deadpan voice, immediately falling into some pre-established dynamic she had with this stranger.

The girl beamed somehow brighter. "What's with the get-up*?* I didn't even recognize you." She passed a fond regard over Lin, resting on her vibrant pink hair with a few inches of dark brown roots. Lin fidgeted with the hem of her scarf, pulling it up higher on her nose so it met the bottom of her iron goggles. "Except for that pink mop on your head."

It was in that moment, after fully processing what the other girl had said, the realization struck me: we could have been calling Catalina *Cat* this whole time but stupid me, *I'd* been too drunk to put that 2-piece jigsaw puzzle together and ended up with Lin. Like *linoleum!* And the rest of them just went along with it, as if that were somehow more acceptable than *Cat!*

"Pink mop? You said you liked it," Lin snapped, voice muffled against her scarf, as she sat up straight. By this point, the rest of us were all dropped jaws and bugged out eyes, astounded at this genuine chance reunion.

"Not with those roots," the girl teased, but a drop in temperature filled the space between them as Lin was no doubt reminded of her time in the delinquent center – the reason for the roots. Scoffing, Lin shrugged, closing her arms over her chest and leaning back against the wall of soil at her back with one leg propped up on her other knee. Not a sliver of skin showed, and for all the aloof bravado in her pose, she looked smaller than I'd ever seen her, drawn into herself.

"Wait, you two know each other?" I burst in time with Faith's more polite inquiry along the same lines, but my voice was louder.

"Oh, right." Haphazardly gesturing to each of us, Lin introduced, "Annie, Faith, Kev, Brett, this is Taylor. My old roommate." As Taylor gave a two-finger salute for the group at large, paired with an exaggerated, grinning wink, Lin tilted her head in my direction. "You're her 2.0."

I must have been more exhausted than I realize, for I was at an utter loss for words. "What are the odds of that!"

"Apparently higher than either of us thought."

"What can I say, it's just my luck," Taylor chuckled like it was an inside joke.

Lin was quiet, so much so, I could just about see the gears turning in her head. Finally, she turned to face Taylor head-on, muttering, "Is this what you call luck? You nearly javelined my friends here."

"C'mon, Cat. I told you I'd find you in Arillia."

"But *I* told *you* there was no way I'd choose Cellana," Lin reminded her, a suspicious look entering her eyes. "How strong is that power of yours, anyway?"

Taylor smirked. "Look, all I had to go off was a feeling. You know, *the* feeling." I furrowed my brows in contemplation. Based on what they were saying, I could only assume her magic had something to do with sensing future events... powerful stuff. "You can't blame me for that."

"No, guess I can't."

Pursing my lips, I wriggled out of the disassembling dogpile and came to a conclusion. No, I would not start calling her Cat just because this girl was better at nicknaming than me – Lin was our thing and so Lin she would remain. What she had with Taylor – or was rediscovering with Taylor – was something else entirely.

Offering a hand to Lin, Taylor asked, "So how'd you find us? I didn't think anyone told Cillian about this place."

"Valued member, huh?" Brett noted under his breath, a hint of amusement colouring his tone.

Cross, Bojack blew air out of the side of his mouth and turned his head away. If he could fold his arms, I was sure he would have. "We write our own stories, ass."

The boy, Henri she'd called him, jumped down after Taylor to helping the rest of us to our feet. Then there was the problem of Dorian; stuck in his little hole. Brett and I dug out the earth around him with no help from Bojack, and pulled Dorian from the earth, lifting his leg free. In the same action, we practically dragged Bojack along like an unhappy cat in a harness.

"Thanks," Dorian huffed, "Any longer and my pantleg would've soaked right through."

Bojack spent a glance over him. "It's completely drenched."

"Oh... oh my, my leg's gone numb," Dorian murmured worriedly, "You don't think the nights here have quite reached frostbite temperatures yet, do you?"

"Now's not the time," Brett groaned, kicking Dorian's shin.

"Ow! Wrong leg!"

"Good! You're as bad as him!" Brett shot back, sticking a finger out in Bojack's direction. "You could have gotten us killed!"

Bojack raised his bound hands in the air with an index finger stuck up, blithely remarking, "Not only do I resent that, but it's also untrue. *I'm* at least helpful."

At that, we all turned a disbelieving look on Bojack with varying degrees of exasperation in our expressions. Even the two newbies in our group joined in. He hardly noticed, wholly unbothered by our unanimous disagreement.

With the quirk of a smirk crinkling her eyes, Lin patted her old roommate's shoulder. "So, you gonna lead us back to your secret hideout or what?"

"Do I have a choice?" Taylor teased, and motioned toward her peer.

He sighed and signalled for the rest of us to follow, but not first without turning a wary eye on Briar with the words, "Send that thing away. You're not bringing it in with us."

24

Wrench In The Plan

THE RUNAWAY PRISONERS MUST HAVE HAD A TREE-SHAPER AMONG them, for after a complex series of knocks, the bark at the base of the colossal, vine-dangling tree twisted and weaved into a brand-new knot in the wood, creating an entryway just large enough to step through.

I felt the change in the atmosphere the moment we crouched through the hole in the deceptive tree trunk. The refuge into which we stepped was only as large as the enormous tree was wide, overpopulated with thirty or so people in a single, wooden hollow.

As my feet hit the ground on the other side, I noticed a woman with her hand on the interior bark, pale and smooth as if sanded down by magic. She must have been the tree-shaper who made this safe haven. Dark shadows contoured her eyes, sunken and empty with a lack of sleep to match our own. This had been a long night for everyone.

As Taylor and Henri strode in at the back of our group, the tree-shaper snaked out both hands and nabbed the two of them by their collars, one in each hand. "One of you better start talking!" she warned, voice strained, and refused to let either go until they did.

I staggered on my feet, swaying slightly too far this time, but a hand caught my shoulder. Glancing to the side, I found Dorian's gentle smile, and the world seemed to pass us by. He guided me down to sit by the entrance, speaking in that irreverent way he did, but his words merely slipped through one ear and out the other. Someone deeper in the room caught his eye as he stood back up, bellowing their name as he moved off with Bojack in tow.

The world raced past me, as if in fast motion.

In the mild security of this makeshift tree fort, all the tension my body held in the effort of getting here dissipated, replaced instead by heavy weights making stones of my limbs. Even my eyelids strained to fight off gravity's hastily intensifying mass. I couldn't fight it any longer.

Sleep overtook me like waves crashing over a beach, but the dream that awaited me offered no rest.

It hardly felt like a dream at all, and I soon understood why. I wasn't alone.

"Finally, Anelisha..." Seth breathed on a haggard breath from his place slumped against a familiar desk chair, tucked in behind the cluttered desk I'd seen once before in his office back in Blackano.

The minutiae of the dream finessed even the smallest details, filling in gaps my memory would have omitted. Even Levi Videl's desk was there – definitely something I would have left out – and all his things. But I didn't have time to think about that, not when Seth sat just in front of me, looking notably worse for wear.

I rounded his desk in a frenzy, only to hesitate, unsure what my hands wanted to do. Finally, I leaned back against the edge of the desk and folded them in front of me to keep from touching him. "You're here- Are you okay? This is your magic, right?" Dream-walker that he was.

He nodded, a strained expression on his face although he tried to hide it. "I'm sorry I couldn't reach you sooner-"

"I pulled an all-nighter!" I gasped in horror, "If I hadn't- It's my fault-"

"No, it's not that," he softly assured me. A slight smile burrowed through the exhaustion sculpting his fine features. There were bags just under his sapphire eyes, new creases illustrating unimaginable horrors in the lines of his face, and his lips were ashy with dry, chapped skin. "I'm sure it has more to do with what's been happening on my side. Just, please, you're safe, aren't you?"

"Uh..." How best to tell him I'd run headlong into danger the very moment he was taken, created a river to attract pora away from the City of Gates and right to me like moths to a flame, then infiltrated said pora's Khuloces Base, where Briar – not me! – brought a tree giant through like a wrecking ball? "Like, right now? Yeah, I'm safe."

He raised an eyebrow, skeptical, but didn't press the matter for the sudden dizziness behind his eyes. He caught his head in the palm of his hand, falling forward with his elbows propped up on his knees. He'd only been gone three days, but by the look of him, it could have been three months.

My hand rushed out to catch him, but my fingertips slid through him like he was no more solid than water.

"I couldn't make myself material." And I couldn't figure a reason why he would lie about something so trivial, but a small, almost imperceptible note in his tone implied dishonesty. He huffed, recollecting himself, and continued, "As soon as the carmavi magic wore off-"

"It wears off?" Thoughts of Kev darkened my ever-shadowy mind.

"These days, it's hard to say. It stopped affecting me, though, and I contacted each of my generals in the City of Gates as soon as I realized."

Of course. Business as usual.

"I even tried Levi..." Now that, I wasn't expecting, but he chuckled dismally to himself and let the remark die on his lips. "I'm running thin on magic, but I wanted to see you anyway."

I tried not to let that little compliment shoot fireworks off in my chest. Emphasis on tried. So instead, I asked, "Are you okay?" With that first question, the floodgates broke. "Where are you? Where are they taking you, I guess, is what I should be asking. And who has you?"

He chuckled mirthlessly, shaking his head. "I only have half-answers for you. I've had an... *eventful* last few days."

"What did they do to you?"

"It's what I did to myself. I figured they must have been after me because they knew I had the key, that it was only a matter of time before they took it off me-"

My eyes must have gone round in my alarm, for he cut himself off and averted his gaze, rubbing the nape of his neck.

"What, like the gate key? The key that bridges the gap between worlds? *That* key? Do you still have it on you?"

"I was stupid. I thought I could use it to escape them after the teleporter handed me over to her superiors. That, or they would take it from me..."

My brow furrowed, grasping for understanding, and then it clicked. "You went back." It wasn't a question. Back to Blackano. To Valencia's conquered domain.

He nodded, giving a dry gulp. "It was like she was waiting for me. She was there the moment I stepped through. I didn't have time to react."

"That's why Briar couldn't reach your mind..." I whispered, my dizzying confusion plain in my voice. "You weren't even on this *planet.* But you're able to reach my dreams?"

"Lupei threw me back after she was done with me. Whatever she wanted; she must have gotten it, but it's all a haze..." He shuddered. "She left the gate open when she first took me so she could send me back when she was done with me."

"But you closed the gate first," I whispered, hoping beyond reason. "You had to."

He met my eyes with a tired sadness in his. "She closed the gate on her side. Anelisha, she has the key-" His voice hitched with emotion, but he cut himself off with a quaky breath. "I gave it right to her."

"You couldn't have known..." My voice was meek in the face of his emotion. To see that glossy shimmer well up in his eyes, to see the light catch in it as it spilled down to his chin – I felt something in me shatter. "You did what you thought was best."

His voice still shook. "It wasn't enough."

"The Liberation Front had you – they *still* have you! It was only a matter of time before they found it themselves."

He drew the back of his hand across his face, a twisted smile in the corner of his mouth. "All I did was cut out the middleman."

Silence blanketed the room, so uncannily real in the realm of our shared dream. So, Valencia had the Key-Keeper's key, capable of opening a gateway between Blackano and Cellana at the discretion of its possessor... She could arrive on Cellana whenever she so desired. Wherever.

And yet, it wasn't thought of this bleak future that hounded my mind. "What was it like?" I whispered, an image of Val Darling flashing behind my eyes. "To be back there?"

He paused, a hint of contrition entering the knot of his brows. "It was unrecognizable. As if to rub salt in the wound, she had Levi give me a tour..." He trailed off, his eyes becoming distant with a thousand-yard stare.

"Typical Val," I groaned, but caught myself a moment from missing her – no, not missing her, but remembering her. What she used to be. What she was to me. It was a tainted feeling, dark and painful.

He shook his head, as if snapping himself out of the memory. "Since I've been back, the Liberation Front hasn't stopped moving me around. They only took the hood off to splash water in my face, but I have an idea of the journey north. We reached Cerenthior by train only last night."

I wanted to ask more about Blackano, about Valencia, even about him and Levi, but I quelled the storm rampaging inside me and let him change the subject, asking instead, "The trains are still running?"

He nodded, wincing at the movement. "They've turned each station into kirranite slurry sites. I've never heard of so many clusters so close together like this – they're usually more territorial creatures, at least from colony to colony. But they've even got pora patrolling the tracks."

"Talk about interspecies cooperation. Who'd of thunk the Liberation Front would introduce corporate team-building strategies to the bogeyman."

He actually laughed, ragged, pained, and distinctly thick with emotion carried over from our previous subject, but a laugh, nonetheless. For all that had happened the past few days, and even in the wake of learning Valencia now had a free pass to Cellana in her pocket, my heart still fluttered in my chest at the sound of it.

"Where in Cerenthior? Give me something to work with."

He glanced up into my eyes, narrowing his own. "You shouldn't leave the City of Gates. Especially not now that Lupei can appear whenever she feels like it."

"Too late for that," I half-laughed, but all the humour had left him, replaced instead by new horror.

"I knew they were avoiding my questions," he muttered under his breath, and shook off the thought. "Stay away from Cerenthior. These magikiers, even the kirranites, know exactly who I am, and exactly who *you* are. They have orders from Lupei herself to use that to every advantage they can muster. Don't make me the bait on their hook."

"Psh, I'm a little smarter than a fish-"

"Why do you think she sent me back?"

"But-" Dropping my gaze to my hands, I bit my lip to keep it from trembling. "You can't ask me to leave you to *this*."

"I'm asking."

"Well, I can't oblige! We need our commander back."

"You don't. I spoke with my advisors. The City of Gates stands strong, I assume because of whatever you did. The attacks have dropped remarkably in number and frequency. They're doing better than they ever were before-"

"That's great news, but it changes nothing. You're still stuck in occupied Cerenthior with Valencia's champion. Who is he, anyway?" I stopped myself a moment from spouting Tenebret's name, instead sputtering, "The Kaipracan?"

He verged on a startled laugh, surprised at the conclusion I'd drawn. "The champion who met me here is a man."

"What, like the Kaipracan isn't?"

Wearing a stunned expression, likely at the realization of just how terrible a student I was, he mused, "He's a monster. Not even his second form could be so… No. It can't be him."

Furrowing my brow, I couldn't help but frown my stubborn disbelief. I'd sooner believe Seth was off his causation-correlation game. Brett's visions had shown him a man in the City of Gates, and I had simply assumed he was a man when the Liberation Front at the Khuloces Base spoke of this *Tenebret.* If Briar said Tenebret was the Kaipracan's name, I had to trust it.

Still, I hesitated to speak it out loud, even in a dream. Briar's warning had circled back to the forefront of my mind, and so instead, I asked, "Well, does this champion's name start with a T?"

Seth watched me like I was from another world. "Anelisha, this was meant to be a goodbye."

I stared at him, not understanding. "Well, surprise! I'm probably already halfway there so you can save your goodbyes for the T man."

He sighed, bringing a hand to his tired eyes as if to rub out the confusion behind them. "What are you talking about?"

"Briar said he has some sixth sense when his name's mentioned, so I've taken up nicknaming," I explained, but Seth was shaking his head, and honestly, I was losing the thread of the conversation, myself.

"Cerenthior's in bad shape. Teeming with more pora than magikiers, and fresh kirranite slurries in every patch of shade. The only way in or out is through the railway tunnel, but they keep that guarded around the clock. There's no getting in unnoticed." Not like the Khuloces Base, where luck had favoured us for once – and even then, we would've been goners had it not been for the absolute wild card on Briar's tail. "Don't throw your life away for a lost cause-"

"You're not a lost cause. You're here, right in front of me, and soon enough, it won't just be in a dream."

He started shaking his head again, but I leaned forward, reaching to steady him even though I knew I couldn't truly touch him. If not for his ghostly intangibility, my thumb would have brushed his sharp cheekbone, my fingers would have been tangled in his hair. He peered up into my eyes, one of the few times I felt taller than him, and almost seemed to lean his head toward my palm.

"Trust me, Seth. I'll figure something out."

"I'm not asking you to." His voice was surprisingly gentle, a sympathetic coax, like he was talking me down from a ledge. "I know what we spoke about before, but everything's different now. I've seen the ruin of Cerenthior, and there's nothing left to save. Not in Arillia."

"But-"

"If you've already left the City of Gates, then carry on north. Circle east around Cerenthior and cross into Schevon. The Liberation Front hasn't gotten through yet, I've heard them talking about the skirmishes at the winter border-"

"I'm not abandoning anyone!"

"You wouldn't be abandoning the City of Gates if you inform the Schevon clan of what's happened. Of what's *really* going on. The fact that Lupei has the key... They need to know what's coming. This message has to reach the Empress before Lupei's return, or it's over for us all."

My head shook of its own accord, wild red curls flinging from side to side. "If I know Valencia, and I do, she'll only strike when the moment's right. She'll have a plan, and she'll wait, and she'll wait, and she'll keep waiting until all the pieces fall into place, or she's forced to act. It's sort of like her thing."

"Be that as it may, this is so much bigger than just you or me-"

"You're right, but it's not so big that Arillians no longer matter." It came out on a hiss of breath, my fury escaping me like steam. "Stop only looking at the bigger picture. There are survivors out here, prisoners who fled their camps, and they're *suffering*. I'm with a group of them..." And because of me, pora went ballistic. Because of me, they had no other choice but to run into even greater peril. Wherever I went, whether it was Arillia or Schevon or Loruna, pora would follow. "I *have* to help them and I'm *going* to help you. As a shonte, it's my responsibility to do what I can, isn't it?"

"You can't help everyone." He stopped himself and sighed. "But there's no dissuading you from trying, is there?"

"You know me." Better than Brett did, apparently. "So you're not allowed to give up just yet. Got it?"

He didn't answer, rather turning his eyes down to the floor under heavy eyelids and long, dark eyelashes. I pulled back from him, hesitant to speak for the despondence sheathed there in his empty gaze.

"I won't be long," I promised. "No more detours."

His back jumped, and it was a moment before I realized he'd given a dry laugh. "You've been detouring?"

"Oh, just seeing the sights. You know how it is," I teased, and he laughed again, that noiseless exhale. Pursing my mouth, I resolved to get him to laugh for real, at least once more before the dream was spent. "This is an *alien* planet, and I'm somehow the only one aware of that fact. It's *cool*!"

"Does it really look so alien?" He let himself be distracted, apparently just as aware as I was there was nothing more for words to solve. Not right now, anyway. "I'd heard the centions, glory to them, took inspiration from Earth's ecosystems."

"If that's the case, they failed big time. Wolf-spider-hybrids don't exist on Earth and thank goodness for that."

"You sure they aren't just hidden away somewhere in Australia?" he teased, bringing a wide smile out of me.

"Even their spiders aren't as big as the ones here. And I haven't seen a single familiar plant since we got here, by looks *or* smell. Hell, even the trees here pick up their roots and wander around!"

I nearly thought I'd gotten somewhere with him, pulling him back into a lighter conversation, when a third speaker entered the chat. Sure, she used my voice; it just wasn't quite *mine*.

I felt the weight of her voice approaching before I heard it, and then it was everywhere, all-consuming noise. "You smile and you laugh now, but when you come face to face, will you admit to your sins?" Evelyn cackled, as if broadcasting her voice over an unseen intercom in this memory of Seth's old office. "Will you still believe me the only monster present?"

Seth's head snapped up, raking his eyes over the room in search of her, but it all came down around us. In the blink of an eye, the walls were stripped bare, the floor pulled out from under us, and only darkness welcomed me, just like the last dream she'd invaded. Seth flickered before my eyes once, twice, and disappeared entirely, ejected from my head.

"Hey!" I shouted into the emptiness, balling my fists at my sides, "We were having a conversation! Can't you mind your own goddamn business!"

"This is my head, too," her voice answered me from nowhere and everywhere at once, "In fact, more so mine than yours."

"Oh, shut up! This is *my* life!"

"What life you steal from me. You're nothing. A delusion. A figment of my rotted mind scrabbling to replace its lack with some poor impersonation of me. Not for long. I wake, and have been waking, since first we were reunited, me and my body. And just like the dream-walker, you, too, will disappear."

With these last words echoing incessantly in my head, I bolted upright, waking from this restless sleep, heaving and shuddering. The cold had seeped through my clothes while I slept.

A quick glance around my environment – the tree's interior, one large room bustling with people – settled the racing of my heart as I spotted Lin and Kev seated with the pair from before. Kev leaned back with a makeshift ukulele – he must have pestered the tree-shaper to make him one and strung it himself while I slept, although I was surprised he hadn't gone the extra distance and asked for a guitar. Several others had gathered around him as he played, but it seemed everyone in the tree fort positioned themselves close enough to hear his music.

I wasn't sure where Brett and Faith had gone off to, nor Dorian and Bojack, but I staggered up to my feet and made my way over to Lin and Kev.

"Hey," I began in a scratchy voice, hoping it wouldn't give away the thrumming of my heart against my ribcage after that rollercoaster dream. It hardly felt like I'd slept at all.

Lin waved, but she was intent on whatever Taylor was saying. Kev must have noticed the look in my eye, because he offered his ukulele to one of the older teens who'd been watching him and patted Lin's knee before coming to a stand, excusing himself from their small group to link arms with me and walk me away.

In an undertone, he asked, "What's up?"

"Geez, did someone slap a Something's Wrong sticker on me or is it just that obvious?" I could hear the teen strumming the strings behind us.

"You look worse than you did before you passed out."

"Oh, that's much better, thank you." Idly, I wondered if I'd looked a downright mess in the dream, too. Would Seth have conjured anything to change my appearance? To doll me up? I doubted it, which only reaffirmed that it had in fact been a nightmare, not a dream. Embarrassment rushed up to heat my face, undoubtedly burning red.

"You good?"

"Actually, I, uh… I spoke with Seth." And Evelyn. Again. But Kev didn't need to know that part. What was it she said? That she'd wind up replacing my consciousness eventually, no matter what lengths I went to avoid it? Yeah, I'd rather not talk about that any more than I'd care to discuss the inevitability of death during an outright war, thanks.

He cocked his head to one side, reminding me in that way the Song brothers often did how puppyish he looked when confused. "Isn't that a good thing? What'd he say?"

"Just that Valencia has the key, and he wants us to abandon all hope and run to Schevon. But I told him no."

"Valencia has the key? What key?" He gasped in horror. "The *gate* key?"

"Keep your voice down!" I hissed, "She hasn't done anything with it yet."

"But how'd she get it?"

I flapped a hand as if to fan away the mental image of tears rolling down Seth's face. "Doesn't matter. She's not here yet, so we'll deal with that when it becomes a problem. Preferably years down the line, like the chronic procrastinator she is." Moreover, I just didn't want to accept the reality that I would be seeing her again, sooner than I would have ever imagined.

"So… what did you say no to? That she has the key?"

"No! That we're running to Schevon."

"We're not?" He shook his head between his hands, pressed to his temples as if this was the only thing keeping it screwed on. "Why not!"

Snapping my eyes back up to meet his, I hissed, "Seth's alive and they have him in Cerenthior. There's a tunnel… A well-guarded tunnel… And about a billion pora and kirranites by the sound of it. But that doesn't change anything!"

"It doesn't?" He sat me down by the far wall, pacing in front of me. "Okay, so disregarding the fact Valencia could appear at any moment while we're completely disadvantaged out here on our own… Mister Knox is usually the plans guy and he's saying go to Schevon…"

"Mhm."

"And the plan we're going with directly disobeys the will of our appointed commander?"

"Yeah…" What confidence I'd mustered in my voice before had already run dry.

He made a sound with his lips. "Doesn't sound favourable, I gotta say. Actually, it sounds the opposite of favourable. Like going to Cerenthior's a *really* bad idea."

"I *know*," I groaned and dropped my head in my hands, letting my hair fall in long, wild curls around my face. In a small voice, I muttered, "But what other choice do I have? I'm supposed to be this *Champion of Blackano*, the *shonte*. So why do people keep telling me to run away?"

Dropping down next to me, he made an equally confused sound in his throat, but he gathered me up against him and I leaned into his embrace, pouting against his shoulder.

"Could be because we don't wanna see you get hurt," he considered with a hint of playful mockery dancing on his tone, and I squeezed his arm affectionately, but we both knew his words weren't enough. Only action, having Seth back in front of me, freeing Arillia from the wicked tyranny of the Liberation Front, keeping the people I loved safe from Valencia's far-reaching influence, only *action* could fix the persistent ache nestled deep in my chest.

But what action could I take? Brett had said it himself; I couldn't do what needed to be done. When I came face to face with the Liberation Front's champion, what was I to do? Even the teleporter, who knew me a grand total of ten minutes, had called me harmless.

And yet, when her lifeblood spilled over me, showering me with fat, red droplets, my mouth had shaped the word, "*Good.*"

Shaking off these ever-darkening thoughts, I grounded myself back in the present moment, reminded myself of what was real, what was tangible, that I was seated here beside Kev, and focused myself on the one thing I was sure of. "I can't leave him there. You didn't see him. He looked..." *Like he was dying.* "Just... don't tell Brett about this, okay? Or Faith. I'll tell them myself. Once I figure out how to make them understand..."

Kev held silent, simply patting my arm with his free hand. This small gesture, a comfort in itself. "That's probably for the best," he finally yawned, "Considering we have a meeting to get to."

Shooting him a sidelong look with one eyebrow raised, I couldn't mask the confusion in my voice as I asked, "With who?"

25

One Tough Cookie to Crack

NOT FIVE MINUTES LATER, I SAT IN ONE OF ONLY TWO WOODEN CHAIRS on either side of a table filling the otherwise drab, barely furnished side-room carved out of a school bus-sized tree branch, opening and closing my hands. Faith, Brett, Kev, and Lin stood behind me, from whence I noticed a sound of nervous shuffling. The soles of their boots on – you guessed it – wood floor. Everything was made of wood, carved directly from the hollowed-out tree.

I was tired sure, but the static energy in the air had my hair standing on edge, nerves wracked to bits. A sound of wood rapping on wood called my attention to the doorway, and in strode a giant of a woman, the barest hint of a limp from her wooden peg evident in the sway of her shoulders. With the pant legs of her coveralls rolled up over her shins, I noticed the discolouration and odd shape of her left leg and realized after a moment that it was made of wood. A makeshift prosthetic.

She dropped down into the seat across from me and I could swear the whole branch shook, or maybe that was just my heart pounding against the cage of my ribs. Something about this woman, whether it was the raised, white lines of scarring like lightning bolts traversing her chin, lips, up to her right eye, or the chips and cracks in her jagged teeth, or even just the barrel-chested athleticism of her silhouette – whatever it was, the mere sight of her sparked my fight or flight reaction.

"So, uh," I began, wary to say the wrong thing, but having failed to mentally prepare myself for this, I spouted the first thing that came to mind. "We come in peace," I announced like this was a normal way to greet another human being. I was pretty sure I heard a chorus of palms slapping against foreheads from behind me, but I didn't dare break eye contact with the glowering lady.

As if unable to help herself, Lin sarcastically critiqued, "Are we aliens visiting from another world?"

"Well, in a way-" I was saying, but the scary woman interrupted me, voice as cold as an arctic gale, and loud as a thunderclap.

"Who led you here?" she barked in a croaky voice that could've made a wolf spider's back crawl. She had two whole feet over my meagre five-foot height, but it was the deadly look in her eyes that had my heart tripping on a beat. I instinctively recoiled, hairs standing on end.

"Uh, well," I uneasily began, shifty-eyed and rubbing my knuckles uncomfortably.

Faith placed a hand on my shoulder, leaning forward with uncrackable confidence in her smile. "The short story is Cillian, or as we've come to know him, Bojack led us here. But if you want to know why we're in the Khuloces Forest at all, the long story goes a little ways back. Like you, we're survivors of the combined force of pora and magikiers who laid siege on Arillia. The difference is you have knowledge and experience that we don't. We came through the gateway just nineteen days ago to find the City of Gates in ruins, and we've been struggling to hold it ever since. When our commander was taken, we took it upon ourselves to get him back. Our ecological empath found one of the Liberation Front's routes crossing our path and his observation led us to the Khuloces Base, where we had hoped to find and rescue our superior. And so here we are."

The woman eyed Faith, a scowl carved into her face. That Medusa gaze flicked to the rest of us, her brows settling into a dissatisfied expression.

When her cold regard fell upon me, an animated nod shook the wild mane of my hair, and I stuck a thumb back towards Faith. "What she said. I may be in the talking chair, but don't let me be the mouthpiece." At my words, the woman had to keep herself from massaging her temples, clenching her fists a moment from doing so. "And on the topic of our commander, he reached out to me-"

Both Faith and Brett startled at that, jostling in my peripherals. "Just now, when you were sleeping?" Faith asked.

"Mhm. But we didn't have long to talk." I clamped down on my tongue. No way was I about to admit to the interruption which shortened our already fleeting reunion.

"Clearly. You were passed out for, what, half an hour? Less?" Lin recounted.

"Well, he gave me the gist of the situation. He said the Liberation Front called their forces away from the City of Gates."

"And toward us..." Brett presumed, bringing a hand to his chin, a contemplative look entering his eyes.

"Exactly. Right now, it's safer there than anywhere in the Khuloces Forest. And there are people there who could use the help of some locals." My resolute gaze landed square on the woman in front of me. "See where I'm going with this? I take it you're the leader around here-"

"Captain of the Arillian Spire," she corrected me.

A light flashed on above my head and the pieces clicked together. "You again?" I gasped, connecting the dots of recognition in my mind. I knew her voice sounded familiar! "So you got out!"

"If I hadn't, you would have brought the whole place down on me." There was no emotion in her voice, no passion. Only a statement of fact.

Rubbing a hand over the back of my neck, I raked in breath between gritted teeth in an apologetic wince. "That was actually the work of a, uh, tree giant-" I was saying, but a foot bumped the back of my chair and I shut my mouth in favour of a tactical silence.

She hardly cared for my petty excuses. "Give up, move on, and live another day. These are the words I lived by for I don't know how long. Somehow, I get the feeling you've never had a passing thought in the same vein."

"Giving up isn't exactly an option-"

"And we can't risk staying in Arillia any longer, not even for your people. We leave tonight for the tunnels on the outskirts of the Ceren Mines. We need all the stone-crafters we can get to carve passage through the mines north to Schevon." Her stony gaze landed on Lin. "It may take months, but we don't have much choice-"

"Months!" I burst and balled my hands into fists on my thighs, an image of Valencia's looming return casting deep shadows over my mind. "We don't have months-"

"We have neither the numbers nor the strength to attempt a crossing over land. This way, and only this way, do the people here have a chance of making it across Liberation Front-occupied Arillia without confrontation. And you have a stone-crafter."

A flash of heat boiled low in my gut, sending a fog of steam to cloud over my mind, white-hot with fury. "Is that a threat?"

"As I said. We need every stone-crafter we can get."

"You're not taking Lin." My voice shook dangerously, but there was no longer any meekness to it. "We're not abandoning the people still boxed in at the City of Gates, and we're not leaving our commander in the hands of the Liberation Front. I won't burrow underground like a mole when I can do something!"

"Drop this blind hope-!" She cut herself off with a cruel scoff, a suffocating silence following in the wake of it, like the tide going out after a crashing wave. "You better wish they greet your commander with death, and soon, or you'll be the one crushing the thing that follows' skull when it tries to take a bite out of you."

I shuddered at the image, mouth gaping like a fish as I searched in futility for words.

"You know these pora are different," Faith spoke up, careful not to impose but potent in the severity of her tone. "They're in league with a rogue faction of magikiers which began in Blackano. A faction we witnessed the birth of. Who've now taken Arillia by storm and intend to do the same across Cellana. They have use for captives beyond keeping livestock, and our commander, the youngest Knox and apprentice to the Key-Keeper of Blackano, is undoubtedly a high priority hostage to ransom with the centions."

Really, she should've been the one doing all the talking. Why my friends saw fit to sit *me* down in the speaking chair, I couldn't fathom.

The Captain's cold stare from eyes as black as beetle shells settled on Faith behind me, seething icy tendrils to every corner of the room until no warmth remained. When next she spoke, her voice seemed the bitter winds of winter whispering over unscathed snow.

"You watched the birth of this bloody revolution, did you? Then tell me. Why weren't we warned? Our pieces held still on the chess board, and pora razed our country to ash and dust, unchecked. Magikiers turned against magikiers, and the centions were nowhere to be seen. Did they turn a blind eye to us just to watch their precious Blackano burn, too?"

"You can't blame us for the centions' silence. Dyval made her grand appearance, but too little, too late. We still lost Blackano," Lin growled, but she may as well have said nothing at all. The Captain's level regard held firm on Faith.

Faith refused to buckle beneath this bone-chilling stare, voice as strong as ever when next she spoke. "You aren't the only ones who felt abandoned by the centions as the Liberation Front proved how real their threats had always been."

Staring between Lin and Faith in mixed disbelief and disapproval, Brett dutifully remarked, "If not for Dyval, glory to her, we'd still be stuck there." His voice was stiff with obligatory respect for the centions.

"And you, an ecological empath from the toppled City of Gates," the Captain dismissively continued, sliding her eyes to Brett, "That's your magic, isn't it? Did you witness it, the fall? Did no one there think of Cerenthior, our *stronghold*? The impregnable city of Arillia? Confirm my suspicions for me. Is it that our riders, rather than warn our clansmen, sent for reinforcements from the north? That the Schevonian Clan Leaders knew and did nothing, forsaking us to rot and disease, just like the Empress, while locked behind her iron walls, abandoned the East in our time of need? Like the centions, who've gone dark in recent years. Tell me how hopeless it was, empath, that our own allies wrote us off long before the end."

Brett hesitated, before speaking in a tight voice, "I assumed the trains were ambushed outside the City of Gates, no matter which direction they sent their messengers. Metalworkers and stone-crafters, they could have cut off all exits before the attack."

"A forgiving assumption," she sneered, "Riders sent with intent to warn the First Clan Leader of Arillia would have reached Cerenthior by train with enough time to prepare before the siege on our capital. If they had, Arillia and her people would still stand. But riders seeking aid from Schevon would have taken an express route and bypassed our cities. This... this is the only explanation for the devastation that followed." The futility in her tone came through twofold in her collapse back into her seat, an elbow propped up on the arm, and her head propped up on leather-bound knuckles. "And still, you would rather stick around in Arillia and wait to die with all the rest," she remarked, wry and withering.

"If we ran off to save our own skins, we'd be doing the exact same thing that doomed Cerenthior," I insisted, but the corners of her mouth only curled into a vitriolic grin, mirthless and cruel.

Measuring her voice, she ignored my input and relayed as if giving a report, "An unstoppable force of pora streamed into Cerenthior, something we thought unfeasible, in the dead of night. They were silent as the plague they brought with them. The Arhillin, our greatest strength, had no warning, reacting only as well as they could within their divisions, but communications were down, and chaos spread like wildfire. There was no time to secure our people in the fortified chambers at the heart of the Ceren Mines. They flocked to the Spire instead, unaware pora had already infiltrated the First Clan Leader's keep. She and my superiors had locked themselves inside to withhold the fast-proliferating infection. By the time I reached my station, a vast majority of my colleagues had already fallen in battle, and all those who sought refuge in the Spire were piled high against the doors, fingertips sanded down to the bone and claw marks carved out of the stone. To this day, I still couldn't tell you how they infiltrated the city so flawlessly, but I know how they won.

"Daylight brought a short relief. I was among the Arhillin who salvaged the main city and pulled the people back to the Ceren Mines, only to find it overcrowded and rank with those hiding infection. The very people we protected became our enemies as they succumbed to the disease, roused into ravenous bloodlust come dusk of the second night and driven to madness by the infection boiling the magic from their blood. We few Arhillin who remained in the aftermath of that blood-washed night retreated deeper into the Ceren Mines, but we'd reached a dead end. There was nowhere left to run. We had no choice. We worked our stone-crafters to death, pushed them to the limits of their magic until they could no longer move. Some were so weak, they simply stopped breathing. But by daylight the next day, the rest of us had a way out.

"Four hundred were with me. No more than fifty made it to the Khuloces Forest behind me. I knew the dangers, but somehow, I didn't think death would hound our every step, a shadow we couldn't shake. We were dropping like flies as more and more succumbed to the forest or to their injuries. Retreating here, hiding in the Khuloces Forest, all we did was prolong the inevitable. We discovered too late that the Liberation Front had already taken the Khuloces Base… That magikiers, our own people, would betray us so profoundly, as to destroy their own kind… I wish I fought and died by my Clan Leader's side rather than endure this relentless torment. I've had enough of sacrifice. If it means saving these people, those who've endured what I have and who are here with me now, then I can stand to be a little selfish. Let those who abandoned us know the feeling."

She released a shaky breath, and there was only silence.

The simple act of breathing felt as if to pull the walls in around me like a vacuum, tight and claustrophobic in the wake of her words. After a beat, I sat forward in my seat with a hand reaching out across the table, palm up imploringly. "Did you do what you thought was right? Every time, in the moment, was it the most right option?"

"I-" She cut herself off, swallowing dryly. "I didn't ask for consolation."

"It's not consolation. I just want to understand," I said, surprising even myself with the graveness in my tone. "The Arhillin with you were tasked with protecting those people, and you worked your stone-crafters to death-" I tripped over my words, choking on the thickness in my throat. "But you knew your people needed an escape route. Their deaths weren't meaningless, even if it shouldn't have happened in the first place. The infected, and the three-hundred and fifty who couldn't make it to the Khuloces Forest, and those who succumbed even after making it here; *none* of this should have happened and wouldn't have if the Liberation Front hadn't razed Cerenthior. Captain, they will *keep* razing magikier cities if we don't do something about it."

"And what can you do?" she spat.

"*We*, Captain. You have to admit, your people here would give ours in the City of Gates just the edge they need to survive Arillia. To *escape* Arillia with you. You're not out of the woods yet – literally."

"Is this a joke to you-"

"The Liberation Front didn't give us a choice when they attacked; not in Blackano and not in Cerenthior! It doesn't matter that the centions chose not to react, there's no changing that. It matters what *we* do. It matters that we do our *best*. That we do what feels *right*, the most right thing that we *can* do," I snapped, "All we can choose is what we do next with these screwed up lives of ours. *You* fought on, made difficult decisions, protected those you could, and now you lead these people in this refuge. *You're* still here, *you're* still alive, so choose *your* next move."

Clenching her fists so tightly that I could see the white of her knuckles, she snapped, "I have, or do you see some better option I've failed to grasp?"

"I see a lack of hope in you, Captain. And because of it, you would condemn Arillia and all its remaining people to the will of the Liberation Front."

"Hope?" she scoffed, "Hope implies a future. There's nothing ahead if our own have turned against us."

"The Liberation Front on Cellana are a rogue faction lacking solid leadership. If we just band together-"

"Band together?" she laughed, losing herself to incredulity, and lifted her chin in gesture back to the main chamber, "In case you hadn't noticed, most everyone here is either too weak or too injured to move on their own. If you're looking for a fight-"

"They're already fighting! They're fighting for their freedom, and honestly, who isn't?" Grinding my teeth, I banged a fist down on the table. "For every loss along the way, there's only fury to fill their place! So, why are you taking the coward's way out when there are people in the City of Gates who need to get out of Arillia, too! There's something bigger coming-!"

"Annie!" Brett cut in, the strength of his voice rattling my skull.

Closing a hand on my shoulder and pulling me back against my seat, Faith quickly noted, "I'm so sorry, we're not trying to offend you. We've had a long day."

The Captain's top lip curled in distaste, a crease forming between her brows, and she leaned forward in her seat, unsettlingly close to me. "You can't shame me for keeping these people alive."

"Alive but six feet under. What are you surviving for if you won't help others out of the same situation?" At my biting words, Faith's fingers dug into my shoulder, her hand clenched tight. Even so, I held my glare level with the Captain's.

"And what are you dying for?" she snapped, standing up sharply to dwarf me in her shadow.

I burst onto my feet as well, hardly putting a dent in our height difference – not to mention how this clouded my eyesight over with a sudden headrush. It didn't matter. I was livid. "When I first met you in that cell, you were like a wounded animal in the wild, lying down and waiting to die by whatever got to you first. Never once expecting someone to help you. But that's the difference between animals and people. People *care* about each other. We take risks so others don't have to struggle and suffer. When we can't see beyond our own self-interest – when we stop offering our help to those who need it most – *that's* true death for all. The death of civilization."

She stared at me, taken aback, and silence filled the room. Stuffy and suffocating. There was no triumph behind my words, and no crack in her composure.

"Get out." For the hostility in her eyes, her voice was surprisingly calm, measured, cold. Faith squeezed my arm reassuringly as I began to turn, disillusionment settling into my bones like the first snow of a long winter, but the fierce-eyed woman raised a hand, halting our egress. Her eyes were locked on me. "No, no. You stay."

The room went still. My friends hesitated to move, but amid their reluctance, I fell back in my seat, the winds taken out of my sails in the wake of my words. And yet, she wanted me to stay; there was still something left to be said between us, and she was willing to hear it, to say it.

That had to count for something.

"It's fine," I assured them without removing my eyes from the Captain's. Then, with venom in my tone, I added, "Stay with Lin."

"Annie-" Brett began, but Kev tapped his side with a pointed look, and slowly, eventually, they each filed out of the room.

The very air seemed to suck out behind them, leaving behind a vacuous chill which sunk deep into my bones. Quite suddenly, it was just the two of us, caught in a silent staring contest, an unspoken challenge to make the other flinch first.

The Captain's glacial eyes stared straight through me, reading the pages of my open book so effortlessly. And she was a stone-cold wall, daunting and infinite so as to cast an impenetrable shadow over everything, consuming me in her darkness.

"It would seem I can't talk you out of your suicide mission, and I doubt you'll survive your own hubris," she jeered, "but if you're so determined to fill their gullets, let them choke on your bravado." All the ridicule leached from her expression, becoming solemn and serious. "If it comes to it, if a pora has you between its teeth, you have one choice. You choose death. Understand?"

"I don't think that's-" I was saying, but she raised a hand for silence.

"You either understand, or you go back to Blackano, to learn properly that this is the only way. They're nasty little things who like to play with their food. To lick the blood off their blades and form a link with your magic, until they have more control over you than you do. Once they've tasted your blood, they can make you see things, *do* things. They'll mess with you until you no longer know what's real and what's not. But if one of them gets its teeth in you, you take that sabre you keep on your hip, and you run it through your heart while your skin's still soft. Do you understand me?"

"Yeah... Yeah, I guess-" I muttered, although anyone who knew me would have recognized the lie, an empty promise.

"If you don't, one of them will have to." She raised her chin toward the door, through which my friends had disappeared.

The hair raised on my arms, a shiver running up my spine. "I understand." But the crack in my armour felt rather like the opening of a floodgate.

I averted my gaze, catching my breath, and found how it hitched on a note of despair. Not quite a sob but verging on one. All at once, the weight of my conversation with Seth, his despair, his hopelessness, his attempted goodbye, hit me over the head like a match of worry striking the flint of this argument, and it set me aflame, melting the ice around me as I sank forward, my head in my hands.

"So *please* try to understand what I've been telling you," I gritted, feeling the wetness of unsolicited tears fill the lines of my palms. Fresh frustrations coiled around my heart at this, and I wiped furiously at my eyes, refusing to cry. "I don't know what else to do. I can't turn back, but I've learned of a new threat to the City of Gates. And hearing you talk of duty and responsibility to your people- Well, *they* need to go with you! Not just for their sake, but for the sake of all magikiers on Cellana!"

She clearly wasn't expecting this display of unchecked emotion, as she was rendered briefly speechless, but her surprise was as fleeting as my silence. When she spoke, it was with a deadly calm. "You're like a child begging for a toy that isn't theirs. Not once have you shown me an ounce of respect. Some would call it passion, and those are the kinds of saps who might value that in you or even admire it, but I find it a particularly repulsive trait."

"Call it whatever you want, just consider what I'm saying to you-"

She disregarded me with the wave of a flippant hand. "You must realize you're leading your little flock to their dooms. And what a waste of a stonecrafter that would be."

"And what about all the magikiers at the City of Gates? Hm? Leave them where they are, and they'll be the first to face what's coming-" She cut me off again, this time with a loud bang as the side of her fist bashed the wooden table between us. I nearly winded myself, startled backwards against my seat by the suddenness of it.

"Do it yourself if you're so gung-ho about it."

"I was assigned a mission; I'm *going* to see it through. Saving Seth, rescuing our commander, well, that's shaping up to be a personal goal at best, but my real purpose in Cerenthior is unavoidable."

"Oh? And what would that be? Besides finding yourself a nice grave to jump into."

I levelled my gaze with hers, but there was no fury in it this time. No tears, no self-righteousness. Only sincerity. "Here's the CliffsNotes: I have to face the Liberation Front's champion before their messiah arrives by way of the gate key she took from our commander. The clock is ticking, and I can't waste any more time."

She quirked her head to the side, inquisitive eyes fixed upon me. "And you have some knowledge of this alleged *messiah*? Or is this just another assumption to add to the long list you've catalogued for me-"

"I knew her personally in Blackano and learned to fear her. When she comes through, there will be no hiding from her. No outrunning her. Not as long as she's welcomed to Cellana with Arillia already tucked under her thumb and the Liberation Front's champion at her beck and call. *Nowhere* will be safe if I don't accomplish what I set out to." I released a quaky breath, an unpleasant heat spreading across my chest and face for the intensity buzzing within me. "But if I can send the other refugees from Blackano out of her line of fire, then even if I fail my mission, at least they'll be on track to spread the story of everything they endured in Blackano and everything they've seen here to Schevon and to Loruna. The message will reach the Empress and magikiers will prepare for war. It's the only way to give them a fighting chance."

With furrowed brows, she folded her arms over her chest, leaning back from me. "You didn't mention this when your friends were in the room."

"They wouldn't like me telling you the truth."

Keeping an appraising eye on me, she paced behind her chair, and finally clenched the back of the seat with white-knuckled hands. "Those at the City of Gates would see us coming and assume we're spies of the Liberation Front. What proof can we offer that we're not? They wouldn't go with us; they would shoot on sight."

I shook my head, leaning forward. "You don't have to go alone." For once, I had a plan. Not a good one, mind you, but one I would see through.

26

Fork in the Road

"HEY, CAN WE TALK?"

I poked Faith's side, nudging her toward a less crowded area within the tight-spaced tree fort. Dorian and Bojack had rejoined Kev, and Lin had her old roommate by her side, but I could feel their eyes on me, most notably Brett's as he stood off to the side. I supposed I couldn't blame them wanting a better explanation of what had happened after they left than the one I gave.

Something in my voice must have tipped Faith off. She was immediately suspicious with a dimple forming and an eyebrow raising, but went along with me, anyway. "About what?"

"We came to an agreement, the Captain and I. She's going to take the people at the City of Gates to Schevon."

"That's not our concern-"

"It is. We owe them our help-"

"We do?" Faith scoffed, wearing a tone of mock surprise, "I thought you bargained away Briar's freedom to enlist Dyval for that particular task?"

"Hey now, Briar did all the bargaining, I just made myself enough of a nuisance for the centions to want me dead. Come on, Faith, we're not leaving them there. I gave a whole rousing speech about, like, moral obligation to each other or whatever."

"What do you think taking them to Schevon will solve? We haven't even found Knox."

"It's not that simple," I exhaled sharply, striving to gather my wits about me.

She narrowed her eyes. "Then what aren't you telling me? Because it seems pretty simple from where I'm standing." I could practically hear her insinuation as if spoken aloud. She wanted to know why Dyval's protection was no longer enough.

Steeling my nerves, I had to avert my eyes with a hand rubbing the nape of my neck to explain, "Well, I was only concerned since… since Arillia needs to be evacuated before Valencia arrives."

Ever the perceptive one, she pursed her lips and leaned her weight on one hip, tapping a finger to her chin in the aspect of consideration. "Spoken like someone who knows more than they're letting on. Like someone on a time crunch."

"Funny you say that…"

She leaned in close, the fire of urgency burning in her eyes, searing me even as I tried to look away. "What did Knox say?"

"That she has the gate key." I met her eyes in time to see her trying to build an argument off this new information, but she floundered for the right words in her stunned silence. So I continued, "And the Captain and I realized while talking back there, the City of Gates won't let just anyone lead them away, even to safety. They'll need a couple familiar faces-"

Outrage contorted my sister's face, and she cut me off with a look, knowing and sharp. "I won't leave you alone out here."

"I'm not asking, and I won't be alone," I said, willing myself not to crumble under her stare. "And… not just you. With Brett's magic, the leadership you've already shown, and the Captain's understanding of the Khuloces Forest, you'll all get back to the City of Gates without issue-"

"Not happening-"

"Brett's a phenomenal scout, and you're the equivalent of a full shot of morphine, but more than that, you're a diplomat and a strategist. Your mind is wasted here with me, here where you would be easy pickings for Valencia. Once you get back to the City of Gates, you'll not only have a purpose, but also the protection of Dyval. You have to know what Valencia would do if she got her hands on you-"

"So you want us to hide while you risk your life for Knox." Her voice came out flat with distaste.

"No! I want you to have an army at your back and Dyval as your shield. You can help the people I can't. You have to get everyone moving to Schevon." Seth's pleas came back to me. "I need you to spread the message that Valencia's coming. Magikiers everywhere need to be prepared, or she'll just keep doing the same thing she did in Arillia and Blackano." Whether anyone would listen was a source of anxiety I would leave for another day.

Just as I had intended, Brett was near enough to hear the whole thing, and he chose now to butt in. What I hadn't anticipated was the dejected look on his face when he did, stepping up behind Faith with his head lowered and his expression expertly neutral. A sea of unspoken thoughts and feelings stirred within the blue of his eyes, but all he said was, "So this is what you came up with?"

"I dunno, I think it's one of my better ideas, maybe the best I've had so far."

"Is that saying much?" he muttered.

"Hey," I shot back, but memory of our conversation by the fire struck again. "Well… probably not, but I believe in it. This is what I want for you. Both of you. To save lives, not… you know…"

My words sparked a seeming confirmation in his eyes, and he hung his head in a slight nod, hiding the tightness of his mouth. This was the same face that had broken up with me that day in the library. Fighting to be cold, to be unattached, but mostly just at a loss.

"I won't argue with you," he murmured, almost too softly to hear, "If you really believe in this plan, then I'll go with it. I've spent too long holding you back."

"Brett," I murmured, but I didn't know what to say.

He shook his head, insisting I listen. "I know I've been holding you back, Annie. Because it's all I can do when it comes to you."

"That's not-"

"I argued and I fought with you at the Khuloces Base, and what did you do? You ran off. You got hurt. You could've been killed, and in the end, it didn't matter that I was there. Because all I did was try to hold you back." He shook his head, dark hair falling into his eyes. "Every interaction with you feels like a push and pull against me. But if I can do this for you… if you want me out of your way…" He trailed off, for a moment leaving the impression he was waiting for me to correct him.

I wanted to reassure him. To say I needed him here by my side. But I couldn't lie to him. "It's for the best."

He gave another small, stoic dip of his chin in concession. "Fine, just tell me you'll be smart out there."

"I'll try to think like you."

"We've already seen how that goes. Try again."

"Okay, well, I'll have Briar, Lin, and Kev with me, and we'll have Dorian's guidance. Does that count for anything?"

Faith leapt in, "We don't even know if we can trust him, and we certainly know we can't trust Bojack. We're not leaving you." She shot Brett a glare.

"Yes, you are. We owe everyone at the City of Gates that much."

"But-"

"If not for them, then do this for me. Seth made it very clear, Valencia's instructed her Liberation Front to use whatever advantages they can find over me. They now know he's one. And I doubt they're ignorant to what you are to me."

"We knew the risk," Faith hissed, stepping closer.

"But I can't risk you!" I shot back.

"Annie, I can't-" Faith pleaded, gulping back emotion. Her voice softened. "I can't risk you, either."

"Well that's not up to you, is it? Valencia and her Liberation Front are out to get me. That's the way it is. But if I can keep you safe, and if you can help all these people, then maybe it's worth it to be the target of an insurgent militia. At least I can feel like this wild goose chase and the casualties attached to it aren't all for nothing." Because in the end, Evelyn would always win. She would be there when mortality inevitably got the better of me. Hell, she was already here, buried somewhere in the depths of my mind, lingering just outside the bounds of consciousness.

Facing Brett, I continued in a curt tone, "Valencia likely won't arrive so soon after getting her hands on the key. She'll want to scheme up something grand, so you'll have to work fast. I'll keep the Liberation Front's eyes on me, give you a chance to double back with the Captain and her people-"

"Another diversion?" he derided, "You realize you couldn't have done that alone last time?"

"Call it a learning experience."

"It was a near-death experience, and you know it."

"Now's no time for semantics," I countered.

"Please don't tell me this is your well-thought-out plan?" Brett sighed, apparently convinced I didn't have one at all.

I was eager to answer, for once prepared for this pop-quiz of a conversation. "As a matter of fact, it is. I'll create another diversion like I did for the Brigadier General, but this time, I'll clear a path to the northern end of the forest and follow that toward Cerenthior. The Captain said it's not too far from here, and I figure it'll cut down our walking time without any trees or roots or slopes in our way. Then I'll have Bojack there to patch me up afterwards."

"You'll be exhausted," he matter-of-factly noted.

"Kev can carry me." I sure hoped he wouldn't mind. "And if our enemies somehow catch up to us, we'll have Lin and Briar right there to help deal with them. Dorian, too, I guess." But he had Bojack tethered to his hip, a package deal, so I hardly counted him a reliable support.

"You're going to trust them knowing what you are?" Brett remarked, pensively poking holes in my plan.

Faith shot him another scathing glare. "You're really considering this?"

"Well she's not wrong. What can you or I do against Valencia when she comes? We need strength of numbers if we're going to pose any kind of challenge to her, and the rest of Cellana needs to be warned."

But he'd found the pitfall in my plans. I would need Bojack's healing once I used the magic, at the risk of letting both him and Dorian in on the secret of my unique abilities. And how could I trust one such as Dorian – the smooth-talking bounty hunter that he was – or worse, Bojack – did he even need a qualifier – with that kind of secret.

"I'll have a chat with Dorian, see where he stands in all this, and if he doesn't stand on our side, we'll just have to convince him."

"And how are you going to do that?" Brett scoffed, all too aware of our new acquaintances' respective stubbornness.

"Puppy dog eyes, remember? I'm telling you; I've thought this through."

Faith shook her head, stubborn as she ever was. "It really doesn't sound like it."

"That's just because it's coming from me."

She was still shaking her head. "It's too reckless." Brett nudged her side, and she huffed her displeasure before rounding on me again. "Keep Briar with you at all times."

"I will."

"And if anything happens, I want her to tell me right away. Hell, I want daily check-ins! I know she can reach me from whatever distance."

"Sure, I'll pass on the message."

"No, you know what, I'm gonna have a talk with her right now."

She began toward the tree-shaper, but I caught her arm and she let me stop her, leaning into my hand. "I'm not sidelining you, Faith. I swear." Shooting a glance toward Brett, I continued, "Not either of you. But I need you to do this for me. For *them.* The people at the City of Gates are scared and slow to trust. They won't let strangers in on their own, out of fear they might be spies, but if they're with you..."

Her mouth turned down in the corners, a crease forming between her brows, but she sighed and rolled her eyes. "Fine, fine." She clasped my hand on her arm, and with that, shot me an encouraging smile no matter the deep melancholy sheathed within her eyes. "Guess I didn't need to come running after you after all, huh?"

"Can't blame you wanting to make a dramatic entrance."

She chuckled softly. "I'm still gonna talk to Briar. And if there's any way to help you from where I am-"

"I know you'll find a way. But your top priority is getting everyone to Schevon. Okay?"

A reluctant smile tugged at her lips. "As you command, Miss Champion."

It wasn't long before we were packed up and ready to go. Faith had spoken with Briar, then Faith and Brett had spoken with the Captain a little more. They got everything sorted in record time – much sooner than I would've in their shoes. By the time Lin, Kev, and I were packed and ready to head out, Faith and Brett had everything squared away.

The send-off was small, a gathering next to the obligatory tree-shaper there only to open the door for us one final time.

Dorian was still saying his goodbyes to a number of individuals, ranging from his fellow former prisoners of war to those he'd only just met, whom he'd hit it off with right away. All the while, Bojack slouched and sulked behind him, apparently forgotten by his former community. I did my best to ignore that whole spectacle.

Nudging into Lin's side as Kev clapped Brett's shoulder and Faith traded words with Taylor, I muttered, just soft enough for Lin to catch, "You know I'd suggest you go with her if not for the Captain's tendency to, uh... use up stone-crafters."

Her head snapped to face me. She probably thought I couldn't see her watching Taylor past the tint of her goggles. "And what would you do without your trusted stone-crafter, huh? Even if the Captain wasn't an awful human being, you couldn't get rid of me that easily."

I gave a soft chuckle, but I couldn't help my sullen glance in Taylor's direction, nor the sour feeling that I was taking Lin from an approximation of a normal life.

27

To Trust or Not to Trust

WE HAD BEEN ON THE ROAD FOR A COUPLE HOURS, DRAWING UP distance between us and the tree fort, but the time seemed to fly. Without Brett, we didn't stop every hundred or so paces to check the area for activity. Hell, without Brett, I couldn't be sure we weren't walking straight into enemy territory. His ecological empathy seemed a luxury we'd taken for granted now that he was no longer with us, but it couldn't be questioned, our pace had just about doubled.

It wasn't difficult getting Dorian to talk, it was just a matter of getting him to talk about the right thing. Both he and Bojack had already made it obvious enough, they were masters of directing conversations in their favour and away from topics they would rather avoid. Case in point, we hadn't gotten another peep out of Bojack on the subject of the weapons of achaion, though we tried, tried, tried again.

We trekked in a single file line with Dorian and Bojack at the back, Kev ahead of them, me ahead of him, and Lin at the helm, finding paths through the thick underbrush as we crawled over colossal roots and kept our footing down vast knolls in the woodland. One would think to conserve their breath for the full-body exercise of this off-road trudge, but not Dorian. Especially not once he noticed what Kev was up to.

Like he did in the ravine, Kev must have stolen another spark of fire from the torches in the tree fort, for he bounced a tiny flame between his hands like a hot potato as we hiked. But nothing had changed. The small plume was still tainted purple and biting back at his palms for the curse mark on his neck, and his eyes still carried that sour, fixed expression.

I watched as Dorian's eyes flicked to the X behind Kev's ear. "Had a run in with a carmavi magic-queller?" he asked, "Any idea who it was?"

Kev met my eyes with uncertainty, and I raised my shoulders in a half-shrug, as if to say, whatever it took to get those two talking. So he made a face and through his concentration on the flame still hopping between his hands, answered, "Whoever she was, she's dead now. Why? You know anything about curse marks?"

"Some. They had a carmavi magic-queller at the prison, to keep our magic tempered."

"So you lost yours, too?"

"That was the case, until Drew took his life. Problem is, my magic's not exactly of the sort to be used, so it wasn't much of a loss, or a gain once I got it back."

I quirked my head to one side, pondering his words. So this carmavi hadn't made the bond with Lupei? That hardly seemed likely, considering most everyone from the Liberation Front was souped-up on the bond, certainly all those she'd posted to Cellana for their cause. What was it the teleporter had said about the bond? That it merely removed the lid on magikier magic? So this carmavi, whoever he was, hadn't trained himself to the same level as the one who'd marked Kev – to a level capable of making the magic permanent. Or he'd only trained himself to have this effect on a larger number of magikiers at once, rather than pooling everything into one. And now, while both lay dead and rotting, only Kev still had the lock on his magic.

Dorian read our expressions with apparent ease, confusion sketching a line between his brows as he asked, "So what is it about these magikiers that makes them so much stronger? Can't say I haven't noticed the power imbalance there and I, for one, find it terribly unfair."

A sting of pain invaded my mind and with it came Briar's voice. "*I wouldn't advise advertising the bond Lupei makes, for the likeliness it holds to convince more to her side.*" She'd curled herself around my middle again, hidden in the bulk of my jacket to keep any more tree giants from finding a fascination with the golden shine of her scales.

"*Funny, I was just thinking the same thing.*" Even if I *could* trust Dorian with this information, I couldn't just give it away freely, not with Bojack listening attentively behind him. The headache passed – she had been keeping our chats short like this to save me from the pain – and I answered out loud for Dorian, "We're not sure what it is, but the magikier who cursed Kev is dead, and *he* still has the mark. Do you know any way to get rid of it?"

I heard Kev rake in a sharp breath, whether holding it in anticipation of Dorian's response, or in response to yet another burning lash from the untamed flame bouncing between his hands.

"I wish I did." He hesitated a moment before blithely noting, "You'd think someone with the power of a shonte could do something about it. Although I admit, I don't know much about shonte magic, either."

"What?" The word snapped out of me on a hiss of breath, and my feet halted under me. Kev jumped back in alarm so as not to catch my hair on fire, only to bump into Dorian who caught his shoulders to steady him.

Dorian continued, unfazed and exuding a mild-mannered confidence, "I only figured, since you're that shonte everyone's been talking about. Aren't you?"

I rounded on him. "How'd you know-?"

"Annie!" Lin groaned, and slapped a palm to her face, making a muffled sound against the scarf pulled up to her nose. "If he didn't know before, now he's certain."

"I-" I cut myself off, at a loss for words.

"*How very smooth, Anelisha,*" Briar quipped in my mind, and took her leave once more before I could ask her to gauge Dorian's thoughts on the matter.

"Well, the question stands!" I burst, "How long have you known?"

"Since our friend from the roots went on about a Shawn. I just hadn't had the chance to bring it up 'til now, seeing you wanted to keep it secret and all. I'll admit, I was in the effort of fitting the pieces together since I met you. For one, not many magikiers would take a team of three to storm an enemy base swarming with pora, kirranites, *and* rogue magikiers. For two, all those stationed at that base sure had a lot to say about this shonte person. And three, you seemed a high priority target to them, Svatka especially."

"Who?"

"The teleporter. She was a bounty hunter like me, went by the name Svatka though I never had the pleasure of meeting her before she fell in with the wrong crowd. And then, well..."

Bojack's eyes glinted with intrigue from over Dorian's shoulder, intent on me.

"And what do you plan to do with this information?" Lin demanded.

"Do?" Dorian pondered, "Well, it'd be a fine thing to see a shonte in action, if that counts as doing."

"I can't just use it whenever I want. It's not a magic trick," I muttered.

"Just a magic?" he teased.

I rolled my eyes, smiling, but turned back around and resumed our previous pace. A slight sting across my forehead was my only warning before Briar's voice sounded off in my mind. "*Pardon the headache. Your friends wish to speak with you in private.*"

Before I could register what she meant, Kev's voice echoed in my head across the line she had opened between our minds. "*I dunno, Annie. Maybe Brett was right. Maybe we should cut them loose.*" He paused, considering it as he kept pace with me. "*He's known about you since the Khuloces Base and said nothing.*"

Lin gave a small, almost indiscernible nod to my right, mulling it over. "*We can't trust him; we don't know a single thing about him, except that he and the teleporter were apparently colleagues.*"

"*And then there's Bojack,*" Kev put in.

Lin and I both made noises of disgruntled agreement across the connection, but I granted, "*We can't deny, I'll need healing afterwards. This is bound to be a big one, maybe my biggest use of shonte magic to date.*"

"*So it really does rest with Bojack, huh?*" Lin considered.

Kev hiked one side of his mouth up into a skeptical expression, nudging into me from my left. "*But you've healed people before, haven't you?*"

"*A few times in the infirmary, yeah, but I doubt I'll be able to heal myself. Every time I managed to get it working, I opened the same cuts on my hands that I always do.*" Always, except when I healed Seth. Or those times I shook the earth and launched my senses through the ground. Or the time I shocked Brett. But I still couldn't untangle the common denominator between those occurrences. Besides panic, but I was always at least somewhat panicked, and I still managed to hurt myself most of the time anyway, so that was hardly a sound hypothesis.

Sensing my scattered train of thought, Briar mused, "*A safety net is not usually laden with spikes, Anelisha. Allow another's help, just this once. And if he betrays your trust a second time, I'll char him to the bone.*"

"*Hey, now, none of that,*" I warned, "*We don't talk about charring our allies to the bone. Hell, we don't even talk about charring our enemies to the bone, got it?*"

"*Our allies, huh?*" Kev remarked.

Lin made a small, dissatisfied sound low in her throat, forgetting this conversation was happening in our heads, and covered it with a terribly fake-sounding cough. The mind connection fizzled out on the strangled sound.

"Bless you?" Dorian offered, and she gave a nervous chuckle.

I stifled a laugh of my own, and said aloud for Dorian's sake, "I should tell you, this magic is hard to control, harder to summon, and dangerous for those around me when I use it."

Bojack leapt in then, reasoning, "Because pora will be on you like flies on honey?" as if this solidified whatever point he'd been making with Dorian.

"Apt of you to put that together," Kev grumbled.

"Obviously, magic as strong as that could only be a lure," Bojack shot back, apparently offended Kev would doubt his deductive reasoning.

"Those pora at the base spoke about a bomb of magic down near the City of Gates. Said it set into them like radiation after a nuclear explosion," Dorian considered, "You really dug under their skin, from wherever you were." A note of darkness haunted his voice with memory. I could only imagine what he had experienced, locked up in a place with pora so riled.

"I'm sorry-"

"Only the worst of them let it consume them and that's hardly your fault." He returned to his normal, nonchalant tone, and I could practically hear that perpetually affable smile in his voice, "You're not responsible for their actions."

"Still, I'm sorry for what happened. In the end, it's a direct result of my using it." And here I was, about to use it again, now on an even larger scale than before. I let out a shaky breath, and with that, began my long, winding, and terribly inarticulate explanation of the plan.

Bojack wore a dull, practically asleep expression as I tried to lay out my thoughts in an organized manner, my eyes flicking to him every now and then. He was, in a way, the true target of my proposal. It was difficult enough gauging how much he absorbed – he was like a high school student who'd rather be anywhere but in class. That was, only up until he realized what I wanted from him.

"Oh, so now you'll admit I'm essential. When you want me to paint a target on my chest in your blood. That's quite the turn of events, considering I don't feel much like helping."

"A turn of events implies you were ever helpful to begin with," Lin noted, but Bojack inconsequentially waved her off.

"Too little too late, oh tagalong snatchers of mine." But he was in no position to argue, and though petulant, nettled, and more than a little deflated in the ego department, he did the one I never expected from him: he went quiet.

"So..." I muttered, hesitant to look him straight in the eyes and instead focusing on Dorian. "Having said all that, do you still want to help us?"

Dorian slid a sidelong glance toward Bojack, but without waiting for his response, warmly shrugged, "Bugger it, why not. I suspected you were special since before I decided to tag along, didn't I?"

"Well, don't get too excited, but you're about to see first-hand what happens when I use it. Fair warning, it's not pretty."

"I find that hard to believe." There was a small thud from behind, and I glanced back to find Dorian had caught Bojack's wrist as he'd apparently made a grab for his belt. More disappointed than anything else, Dorian remarked, "Hey, now. I thought you agreed to play nice."

"Under old conditions, sure. But I won't empty my veins to pora. They have a particular liking for my brand of magic-"

"You say that about everyone," Kev noted.

"This time I mean it!" Bojack snapped.

How he managed to appear entirely unaffected by Bojack's frustrating demeanor, I'd never understand. Instead, Dorian simply reminded him, "I wouldn't wilfully endanger you; you're my charge."

"Great, so we're leaving?"

Smiling wider, more like the Cheshire Cat than his usual pleasant aspect, Dorian shook his head. "Nah-ah, we both agreed to help these fascinating people at one point or another, and since you failed your go at it, you'll just have to make it up this time around. Have a heart, Mad Jack, being a good Samaritan every now and then never hurt anyone."

"You and I have heard vastly different stories."

"Oh? Well I'm not all that moved. Yours are usually *only* stories."

Folding his arms, Bojack huffed his half-white hair out of his eyes and turned his face away, apparently dissatisfied to be outsassed, outclassed, and all around outmatched by his warden. "You shut your pretty mouth," he grumbled.

Dorian bumped his side with an elbow, noting, "Have you never heard the saying, leave the world a better place than you found it?"

"Doesn't apply."

"Out of a refusal to face your own mortality?"

"I was taken from the only world I cared about."

Dorian's face fell, and before I could stop myself, I was speaking. "What does it matter which planet you're on? You're still surrounded by good people."

"Not to toot your own horn?" he cynically noted. He met each of us now with a wolfish grin and empty eyes, a haunting combination. "This world will take my life no matter what I do, so it might as well rot for all I care."

"And everyone in it?" Kev demanded as Lin scoffed her disagreement.

"Sure, why not."

At that, Dorian vehemently shook his head, folding one arm over his chest, holding his elbow as he raised his other hand, index finger out, to illustrate his point. "*You* haven't been to the Fishery District in early spring, and it shows. When Mister Grey fishes carnispisces from the rivers running down from the mountains and sweet Idina, who put me up for three weeks, cooks them into a stew to end all stews."

"Your point?" Bojack droned.

"They were the first people I met on my hunt for you, and they set a bar that's only gotten higher wherever I go. And you're saying to do away with *everyone*? That's absurd."

I caught myself smirking and quickly hid the expression, but my eyes still shone with resolve for what lay ahead. Nodding in determination, I linked elbows with Kev and Lin like we were in *The Wizard of Oz*. "Who knows, maybe the real terraforming will be the friends we make along the way."

"That doesn't even make sense," Kev chuckled, his teasing tone bringing a welcome lightness back into the conversation.

"She's doing her best," Lin jabbed back at him, and some of the pressure on my shoulders lifted.

Yeah… Maybe, just this once, I could do this.

Briar coiled just barely tighter around my middle, reminding me she was there and listening just before she popped into my head to note, "*Your determination is admirable, but do not forget the reality of what you face. You could barely cling to consciousness the last few times you attempted such an immense expulsion of magical energy. And now you expect to have it further sapped through this magikier's healing. Prepare yourself, Anelisha.*"

Before I could address her in my mind, her presence disappeared again. I had to admit, I wasn't a fan of these little pop-ins. And though I knew she hadn't meant to, in the wake of her words, that tiny hint of confidence I'd felt had crawled back into its shell.

28

Easier Said Than Done

NOW IT WAS JUST A MATTER OF USING THE MAGIC, PARTING THE FOREST to the northern edge where occupied Cerenthior awaited us, and sending up this massive flare. Only then would Briar signal Faith and all the rest to begin their departure for the City of Gates while all pora in an incalculable radius bore down on me, just over three hours out from the tree fort. Faith, Brett, and the others would be good to go, but us? Well...

I shuddered to think of all the ways this could go wrong, but Kev, Lin, and even Dorian filled my ears with all the ways this would go right. Briar, thankfully, muzzled herself through their encouragement. And before I knew it, I was sitting cross-legged in a small grove beside a peaceful-looking pond – Lin, genius that she was, suggested it to wash off the blood afterwards – with my palms flat on the moss beneath me. My friends stood in readied stances behind me, and Briar lay coiled like a snake on my knee watching me.

Sunlight streamed hot and bright through the high foliage, tinted greenish yellow on its way down to us, and glaring off the sheen of Briar's scales back into my eyes. I reminded myself there was no rush, not like last time, but the magic felt no nearer.

Surely, I'd learned *something*.

Shutting my eyes tight, I breathed slowly and steadily as I let myself envision the air from my lungs intermingling with the air of the forest. Air that rustled the leaves – their surrounding whispers sounded louder in my ears – and caused the high branches and treetops to creak and whine. Within the cage of boughs and trunks, the forest air seemed a living creature all its own, breathing the free air from beyond, and oxygenating the lifeblood of the forest.

My heartbeat stuttered in my chest as I felt the crawling of small critters under my palms. It was a moment before I realized they weren't crawling on my hands, but that I could feel them, deep within the earth beneath the moss, busy in their tiny halls. A scrabbling of small talons high in the treetops, higher than I should have been able to hear, seemed to itch at the inside of my skull until I felt the flutter of wings disturbing my air – no, not my air, the forest air.

I felt myself swaying at the height of the trees, and travelled down their trunks to their roots – the breadth of this system carried me out in all directions, linking me between hundreds, no, thousands of trees whose roots had knotted in a marriage of the Khuloces Forest. And I felt it. The edge of the forest. By the heat of the sun on the leaves, like heat warming my own face, I judged the northern edge we sought, and with that, found a straight path between it and my body's position. For a brief moment, I felt myself not as me, but one of the multitude of creatures contained within the forest I had become. I could feel my friends' feet on my mossy floor, like bright spots, pinpricks, amid the vast green.

When I pulled the water from the ground to create that river, it hadn't felt like my own creation. The water wanted to rush and run, to cut through the earth making way for its exploration, and I had merely allowed it that freedom. Now, I had become an observer of the forest, a vast, interconnected entity, and I could feel every little lifeform roaming its inimitable contents. And among them, countless wandering souls, feet ambling in all directions – human and otherwise, I could feel them all like the insects under the moss, each footstep a small vibration in the vast system alive around them.

I drew myself back to the straight path north I had found, reminding myself somewhere in the back of my dispersed consciousness of what I was meant to do. But there was a big difference between feeling as one with the forest and moving entire sections of the forest. The magic snapped back like an elastic pulled taut on my first attempt to dig my feelers into the dirt and shove it aside.

The breath rushed out of me as I whipped back to my body, but I gritted my teeth and forced the magic out again, back to where it had been. It dragged against my will this time, raking across the moss and earth. I dug in my claws and tore. It was easy to push aside once I got started, a thick layer of it similar to the waterlogged mire like at the Khuloces Base. Earth flew up to either side of the path along a line drawn by my magic, banking high to encase the trunks of trees shoved to either side. Heat swathed my arms, tugging insistently on my focus to force me back toward my body. No, I was making progress.

I tore the magic further out from my body, racing down the path now as I bulldozed the forest floor out of my way. All the way to the edge. Yes, I could see it. The northern edge of the Khuloces Forest. Earth sprayed out to either side of me as I bulleted through the forest floor, carving a deep ditch out of the world straight to the edge.

That's when I felt them. The stampede of feet crashing through the bramble, bounding over rock and stone, advancing on my position. Feet heavily and unmistakably pora bolted at impossible speeds toward my defenseless body. They were fanned out across the south and southeast parts of the forest closest to the City of Gates, but one group struck me in particular.

A pack of pora emerged from a familiar hollowed out tree, the refuge governed by the Captain of the Arillian Spire. This large group had unearthed their former prisoners' refuge just as predicted, but not those who had taken refuge there. And now, their attention was called to me.

I snapped back to myself, only to entrench my consciousness in the pain roving hot fire up my arms. A scream broke from my throat, and ended on a choking, wet gasp as I folded at the waist, wanting to clutch my arms for the strange chill over my flayed skin, but merely holding them out in front of me, fingers spread over the red soaked moss.

"Annie!" someone was shouting, but I could hardly breathe for the tightness in my chest, let alone focus on anything outside the rampant agony spearing up my arms.

A cloud of colour sank down in front of me, blurred by the overflowing tears obscuring my vision, and something took hold of my shoulders. Rather than the shooting pain I expected from this contact, a new warmth flowed from this touch, caressing over the wounds lacerating my shoulders, my upper arms, my forearms, my wrists, my hands, a path that darted straight for my heart. Slowly, the pain receded and eventually faded to a background buzz. My broken sobs became snagging breath and occasional hiccups.

"You're okay. You did it." Lin's voice sounded off just behind me. It was a moment before I felt her hand on my back, almost too gentle to note. Afraid to touch me.

I could only watch as the deep slices over my arms knitted back together into sore, pink lines. Darkness hemmed the edges of my vision, tugging me into the welcome abyss of oblivion.

Through the static abuzz in my brain, I noticed Dorian had one hand on Bojack's neck, forcing him down in front of me, and his other hand on my shoulder, steadying me. There was horror in his eyes.

"See?" I croaked, "Told you it isn't pretty…" I couldn't be sure I'd even spoken these last words as unconsciousness swooped over me like an eclipse, throwing all into black nothingness.

Hardly a second seemed to pass, and I bolted upright. The world spun around me, and I raised a hand to my head. It was a moment before I realized there was no pain coating my arm or squeezed out by the press of my palm to my forehead.

Drawing back, I noticed my hand was whole, with only a choppy spider-web of pink lines to show for my use of shonte magic – not a single cut left gaping. With a heavy head, I peered around in search of Briar, and was surprised to find I was moving. Or rather, *I* wasn't moving, but the person carrying me was.

I fell back against Kev's chest, woozy with vertigo, and mumbled an apology for squirming. He held me in a princess carry, moving surprisingly fast for the burden he carried – namely, me.

"I'd rather you wiggle around a little than keep looking like death incarnate," he chuckled, although the playful note in his voice sounded forced, strained. A front for fear.

Letting my eyes roam, I found the world a gradient of browns beneath a radiant sky of yellows, oranges, and reds – sunset, and Briar's fiery gold scales hanging against it in a steady glide overhead. When had it become so late? It was morning what felt like mere seconds ago…

After a moment of empty-eyed staring, I realized this was the ditch I'd dug out with my magic, no more than ten feet across with high walls banking on either side, at least twenty feet high and crawling up the trunks of tipped or leaning trees. Already, colourful underbrush crawled over the height of these walls and dangled down on either side of us. The forest had already set to reclaiming my path. By some foreign knowledge, I knew the other sides of these long, book-ending walls would show a barrier of overgrowth and dirt ten feet high but found some solace in the notion. With any luck, the forest's rapid growth would prevent attacks from either side.

Turning my gaze forward, I found Lin maintaining a moderate jogging pace as she led the way. To Kev's rear, Dorian met my glance with a full-faced smile and a greeting wave, matching our pace as Bojack wheezed complaintively by his side. He knew as well as the rest of us, pora were undoubtedly funnelling down this ditch, close on our heels.

"Ugh, how long was I asleep?" I groaned, earning Kev's laugh over his laboured breathing. I had to wonder how long he'd kept up this pace with me in his arms. Could I have done the same? Certainly not in this state…

"All day. How's your nose?"

"My nose?"

"You faceplanted pretty much the second Bojack healed you. And *somehow-*" He emphasized loudly, speaking more over his shoulder than to me. "-he didn't think to catch you."

I tested it, scrunching up my face. "Feels fine."

He returned his attention forward, but his eyes darkened, withholding words unspoken. Before I could ask, he continued, "We managed to wash most of the blood off your arms, but your clothes got pretty badly stained. There was… a lot."

"I'm sorry-"

"Nah-ah, I knew you'd try to apologize. You built this whole road, Annie. We've been on it for hours, with just a short lunch break around noon, and I still can't see the end. Talk about underselling yourself, this is beyond incredible."

I held my tongue before I could spout this supposed *road's* eerie resemblance to little more than a fast-overgrowing ditch, and the fact I could've died building it. If not for Bojack's healing, I probably would have, from blood loss alone. But somehow, I had only slept for *one* day. When I first used shonte magic in Blackano, I'd been wiped for days without anyone using my energy to heal me, and I hadn't even used it to such an extent.

"*Is it not obvious you've improved? Every time you flex this muscle, it becomes stronger, and you become ever more capable,*" Briar's voice returned to my mind, bringing me to realize the headache hadn't dispersed.

"*That might be the most reassuring thing you've said to me.*"

"*I'm proud of you, Anelisha, but I can't ignore the sheer amount of magic you spent today. The wounds ranged high on your shoulders. You know what would have happened had they reached your heart. Having a healing magikier on hand wouldn't have mattered.*"

I fell quiet, pensive in my silence. Until finally, "*I couldn't feel my body until I snapped back into it… I wouldn't have even known until it was too late.*"

"*That's what I feared.*" She sighed in my head.

"Does something hurt?" Kev asked, noticing the unease in the knot of my brows and the set of my jaw.

"No. I'm just… thinking."

With another hour of moderate-paced travel, and a momentary lapse in speed when we came to a section of the path lost to new growth and what was perhaps the van-sized footprint of a tree giant, we finally reached the edge of the Khuloces Forest.

The path opened like a river spilling into the ocean onto a far-reaching valley. Set against the horizon was a tantalizing city skyline shaped around a colossal tower – the Arillian Spire. Another burst of tears sprang to my eyes at the sight of it, or perhaps by the sting of ash on the winds. Thick plumes of smoke and shadow-casting clouds of ash hung over the great city like a mourner's veil.

Here at the edge of peril, flanked on either side by dooms of a different sort, we stopped for a quick meal. I wolfed mine down in seconds flat no matter the questionable content of these scout supplies, starved and still hungry even once finished. But we only had so much to go around. It wasn't long – in the wake of rations which seemed only to invite my hunger rather than quench it – before we set out from the mouth of the ditch to cross the valley.

Dorian and Bojack led the way as the only ones of us who knew the whereabouts of the train tunnel into the city. I had mentioned it in my explanations, making sure to note the Liberation Front had taken Seth through this tunnel. I had no doubts it would be heavily guarded, but from what Dorian could report, it seemed the only viable hole in the impregnable walls of Cerenthior, designed to withstand the monstrosities of the Khuloces Forest on its doorstep and all the forces of the Kaipracan. We were in desperate need of a real plan, but it was hard to look ahead while paranoia had me shooting glances over my shoulder.

Our meal break came to an end and I was back on my feet, insisting I carry my own weight much to Kev and Lin's dismay. We moved at a snail's pace, slow enough to make my skin crawl. I knew they were just trying to accommodate me, but it did nothing to help the dark recesses of my mind.

I'd had enough nightmares to know what it felt like to be chased by unseen monsters, to feel them behind me like my own shadow no matter all the hasty glances over my shoulder revealing empty air.

This persistent unease crept into my chest, coiling about my heart like barbed wire on a spool. Pora would never give up this hunt, and the best I could do was hobble at a slightly faster pace toward the city their terrible force had seized.

Even so, my affinity for mental gymnastics of the simultaneously anxious and optimistic variety had Cerenthior's looming shadow looking like the ribbon at the end of a long race, the only thing pushing me forward. There, where the Liberation Front had Seth. There, where Simon Beckett, one of the many instruments of my dismantlement in Blackano, stood at the beck and call of Valencia's champion. There, where Valencia's champion wielded the fabled dragon-bone glaive, the legendary weapon of achaion made from the bones of the crimson emberbreast, Fiamme.

I had to get *there.*

All had grown quiet in this bone-deep sense of foreboding. Even the world. Dusk fell into night and the ring across the sky shone its ever-present radiance overhead, drowning out the stars in its light. But the darkness felt thicker here in this field of tall grass and clothes-catching nettles.

My left ankle panged uncomfortably, yanked back when the sole of my boot suctioned to some sludge-like substance underfoot. I stumbled slightly, only to find I'd stepped in some sort of tar-like substance caked between the tall stalks of barley grass.

"Ugh," I muttered and wrenched my foot free, scraping my boot over the grass. The tar didn't rub off no matter what I did, instead staining into the leather like a shadow.

"Something wrong?" Lin asked, already drawing her mace as she came to a stop.

"Nothing, I just stepped in goop." Yeesh, I hoped it wasn't the other thing that rhymed with goop. Well whatever it was wouldn't budge.

"Goop's a happy stretch," came Dorian's voice from up ahead, keeping that same measure of distance he'd maintained since taking Bojack on – just far enough to keep Bojack's personal space from overlapping with the rest of ours should he try anything. "We must've run them out of the forest."

"Run who out of the forest?" Kev demanded, pulling his bow off his shoulder and glancing around the seemingly empty field. A fierce glint in his eye reminded me of Brett, the same way a caricature immediately brings to mind the original. It must have been the downturned curve of his mouth, closed just too tight, lips just too white, which betrayed his fear.

"Not a who, a what," Bojack grumbled.

Nodding matter-of-factly, Dorian pushed the thick tar around with a plucked stalk. "This is what's left behind when you force an eviction notion on a kirranite slurry."

Seeming to recall a passage from our studies, Lin's lenses gleamed in the fading daylight as she recited, "With no host body to contain them, the shadows fall apart, leaving a snail trail of darkness that thickens into slop and dies off." She caught her fist in her palm. "Like black licorice left too long in the hot summer sun."

"Gross," I muttered on a low breath, feeling every sound I made like a clap of thunder in the vast hush of the field. There was only the melancholy rustle of bitter winds combing through the barley, and something else, something quieter. I couldn't place it.

Dorian's gaze followed the puddles of tar deeper into the barley field, and he furrowed his brow. "This trail looks fresh."

"Of course it is," Bojack groaned, "Not like we weren't already on a leisurely stroll to our collective demise."

Dorian wagged a finger in front of his face, still smiling. "Keep in mind my stance on your wilful endangerment, yeah? I won't let you be reduced to a mindless host."

"It'll sure be hard to hold you to that when I'm a mindless host."

"Somehow, you make it the favourable outcome," Kev noted with the barest quaver in his voice.

"Speaking from experience? Yeah, couldn't agree more," Lin tacked on, the both of them earning Bojack's sidelong leer. I had to say, the expression had lost some of its intended effect, the same way saying a word too many times will make you forget its meaning. But neither Kev nor Lin noticed the look he shot them, intent rather on combing our dusk-darkened surroundings.

I heaved a weary sigh and on the same breath, whispered, "This just became a life-or-death situation. Lay off the guy, both of you."

"Yes, listen to your leader," Bojack snubbed with a faux-aristocratic sneer, and Kev made a face like he couldn't fathom why that insult was so effective.

Dorian shook his head. "Applies to you, too, bud."

"Oh, I'm bitterly aware, but you must be projecting if you think I care-" He cut himself off as his face changed, wry sarcasm morphing suddenly into an expression I'd sooner find on a cornered and terrified rabbit.

It was a moment before I registered the haggard rasp of breath emanating from the tall grass just behind him, sending a visible shiver down Bojack's spine. Lin and Kev seemed to realize it wasn't just the wind at the same time I did.

Bojack reacted first, the closest of our meagre group to the small, almost imperceptible noise. All the colour drained from his face as he leapt behind Dorian, both hands clutching Dorian's waist to face him toward the sound. His living shield hardly seemed to mind, throwing one arm out to protect

Bojack. In the same action, Dorian entangled the chain linking them around his wrist.

"Hands off the belt," he quietly warned out the side of his mouth, and Bojack grumblingly obliged, gliding his hands up to the unarmed bounty hunter's shoulders instead.

The silence of the night carried impossibly small sounds to us, deafening now as I held my breath high in my throat. A wet schlep of flesh falling over itself through the barley, somehow never resting its significant weight in any single step. The rush of grass parting for this unseen, inhuman entity making a beeline for us. Damp bones chafing amid the sodden sounds, grating and scraping and clacking together in a quiet disharmony of movement.

For a silent moment, we all peered into the impenetrable darkness sheathed between swaying threads of barley grass. Kev notched an arrow with two more in hand, aiming toward the sound of shuffling, and Lin flexed her grip on her mace, reaching for her sabre with her hand, as both stepped closer to either side of me. Against kirranites, none of these weapons could do any real harm.

But most kirranites I'd seen had human hosts, taking on their height. The thing that approached hid seamlessly amongst the waist-high barley. Whatever constituted a kirranite slurry, I was soon to find out.

The barley stalks parted… and disappeared.

My mind scrambled to keep up as a section of the field blipped out of view before my eyes. It was a moment before I realized the stalks had been consumed by shadow, and the pieces clicked together in my mind.

I'd already seen a kirranite slurry twice before, but I had never smelled one. An acerbic odour of burning rubber stung my nostrils, pulling a jerk reaction out of me to cover my nose and mouth.

A flash of the first kirranite slurry I'd ever seen crossed my mind: the tar-like pit Valencia had crawled out of. Then the second: attached like a swarming mass of shadowy leeches to her wings, writhing and wriggling among the threads of her feathers. But this, what slopped out from the barley and devoured it in shadow, was a heaving and convulsing form all its own, moving of its own accord. A myriad of hostless kirranites.

This particular slurry dripped and oozed off bones licked clean, dragging a disassembled corpse around with them the same way a snail drags its shell. The slimy tendrils of darkness clung to the hollow chest cavity, taking turns in the cage of its ribs, but constantly shifting like waves on a beach.

My eyes darted to find the face, an instinctive reaction, but the skin had slopped from the muscle, eyeballs turned to sludge in their sockets, and what flesh remained fastened too tightly, stiff as dried jerky, to the chalk-white bone.

A dry heave scratched up my throat, and I clenched the hand already on my mouth, forcing my meagre meal back down. It wouldn't do me any favours to lose it now.

Even so, my feet were frozen under me. I couldn't bring myself to move, but Briar shot into action.

She swooped down from the heavens, a flicker of gold amid the stars before she lit up the field with her fires. The slurry of ever-contorting shadows wrapped around the emaciated corpse was engulfed in her flames, a terrible shriek escaping the shell of its roasting chest cavity as what flesh had clung to its face melted down to blackened bone.

Kev and Lin shielded me from the heat of the flames, all of us turning in towards each other, but a flash of movement caught in the corner of my eye. The slurry sloshed outward, distorting into an elongated and completely unnatural arm, and bolted through the air like black lightning around the wildfire of Briar's breath. In the blink of an eye, the impossible, shadowy arm wrapped around Briar and whipped her to the ground.

A noise ripped out of me, somewhere between Briar's name and an incoherent cry, and I broke from Lin and Kev, stumbling over numb feet. The fires had caught on the barley, forming a wall between us. My heart drummed in my ears, off-beat and erratic as the fires towered higher, roared louder, spread faster.

"Annie, stop!" Kev shouted over the deafening noise in my head.

"Let go of the fire," Dorian's calm voice was like a balm to the panic banging pots and pans in my chest, "He can't control it in a contest against your magic."

"Wha-?" I snapped back to myself, and all at once, the pyre dimmed, losing the accelerant of my magic and half its height. With the barley feeding its ravenous hunger, it still spread, just not as wildly.

Kev swore loudly from beside me, and I turned just in time to catch the purple flames criss-crossing over his chest, biting into his clothes and singing his skin. The curse mark held true, barring him access to his own magic except to turn it against him.

Panic rose up in me again. It had been too long – Briar hadn't resurfaced – that *thing* had her! A flash of memory wrenched me out of the present, back to some of my final moments in Blackano, when Valencia shot a mere fraction of these kirranite shadows into Lin. I had almost lost her in an instant...

How many seconds had it been since this slurry took Briar down? Time seemed almost to stand still. Too long, it had been far too long!

"Annie? Annie, come on, we need to get out of here!" Lin's voice echoed strangely between my ears, but I could only stare straight past her. It was a moment before I registered what I was seeing.

Dorian had one hand on Kev's shoulder, the other extended out toward the fires. Following this path with my eyes, I started in alarm to find the flames reaching toward something just beyond them, too exact, too calculated, to be natural. With a snap of his fingers, the flames fell into line not with Kev's will, but Dorian's.

Briar burst through the golden wall, scales shimmering as the last shadows which clung to her seared off in the fire. She latched onto my statue-still body, hot against my skin. The blistering sensation seemed distant in the background of my consciousness, a footnote to the tidal wave of relief washing over me. I enfolded her in my arms, clutching her to me like she was my last lifeline.

Briar's wings wrapped around me, sheathing me from the heat as the flames rose in a spinning inferno and crashed down on the field where we had last seen the slurry, scorching belligerently until all that was left was black, charred earth.

The flames devoured themselves into smoke, and the world grew dark and still in their wake, pitch-black in the endless gulf of a cloudy night.

Nothing, not even the bony remains, was left of the slurry.

Then, there was shouting.

"What the hell was that?" Kev snarled, wrenching away from Dorian's touch. An animal look in his eyes spelled his loathing. To be used, to be useless on his own.

Dorian raised both palms, stepping back from him and nearly bumping Bojack in the process. Of all of us, only Bojack wore a dull expression, a clever glint in his eyes implying his hidden suspicions had been confirmed.

"Well?" Kev burst, demanding an explanation.

"I'm a magic-stealer." The words fell out of him. "Surprise?" He attempted a charming smile – which wasn't to say the smile wasn't charming, simply not charming enough to detract from the situation – and quickly continued, "I'm not exactly meant to use it, being an Untouchable and whatnot. Magikiers like me aren't permitted to so much as think about it, except in special circumstances, and I, for one, would consider this fairly special–"

"Dorian Cyrus," I whispered, and he started in surprise, glancing my way.

"Why does that name sound familiar?" Lin muttered, furrowing her brows.

I quirked my head at her, surprised. She wasn't with me when I first came across this name. "I don't know why you'd know it, but I read about a Dorian Cyrus back in Blackano."

"Oh?" Dorian pleasantly chimed in.

"You're a carmavi magikier." Like me. Shaking off my confusion, I worked to recall, "You remove, collect, and replace magic..." And if memory served, he was restricted from using it by law. Just like I had been and, I supposed, still was. They never taught me how to use my magic, but Dorian seemed not only capable but adept with his.

"That's a stellar memory, but those archives overexaggerate my ability. I can only remove the magic of a magikier I'm touching and use it as my own. A magic-stealer through and through, but only as long as I'm making physical contact."

"Like Rogue!" Lin leapt in but ducked her head shyly when all eyes turned to her. "From... from X-Men..." I could hear the blush in her voice as she grumbled, "Give me a break, she was my first TV crush..."

Dorian tilted his head with his smile, an expression entirely too sunny for the late hour. Not to mention the peril we'd just faced. "Sure, but I have a little more agency in whether or not I use my magic. Emphasis on *not.* The authorities would've put me down a long time ago if I couldn't keep it under wraps."

"Good for bounty hunting, though," Bojack snidely remarked.

Dorian covered his mouth facetiously in the aspect of complete and utter shock. "And disobey the oaths I took? Whatever are you implying?"

Kev folded his arms and turned his head away, muttering just loud enough for us to hear, "We should keep moving. Every second we waste here, pora catch up."

"Right," Lin granted with a curt nod, but her eyes were on Kev, carrying a fresh concern.

We started up again, and the distance drawn between Dorian and the rest of us seemed a gaping chasm. At least he had Bojack to keep him company – or maybe that was more of a punishment.

I held onto Briar as I walked, refusing to let her go, and she eventually settled in my arms, but she didn't open a connection between our minds. Whether she wanted to save me the headache, or simply didn't want to talk about it, I felt her absence like a tangible thing no matter that she was there in my arms.

"How are your hands?" Lin's voice sliced through the thick darkness in my mind, calling me back from its depths.

"My hands?" Oh, right, the magic had poured out of me again.

Gathering Briar up in one arm so her long, draping body hung over my shoulder and coiled in the crook of my elbow, I raised my other hand and opened my palm under my face, focusing through the thick darkness to find any sign of injury.

Nothing.

Not a single scratch, just the pale pink lines leftover from Bojack's healing.

Lin quirked her head to one side. "Maybe you didn't use it?"

"Oh, she used it," Kev put in, "It was all I could feel when I tried reaching out to the flames."

"It's happened before. A few times now," I muttered, resetting my hold on Briar's anaconda-like body – in recent weeks, she had become more deep-chested, more muscular around her shoulders and hips like a prowling predator rather than a snake, but she would always remind me of a serpent in the heavy length of her neck and tail. "It doesn't flow out of me, it just… is me? I don't know how to explain it…"

"Let's just hope it didn't send up another flare, not so close to Cerenthior. They'd pincer us," Lin contemplated.

I searched for the words, to explain that it didn't light me up in the same way sending my feelers through the earth hadn't alerted the pora to me before. It was a different flavour of the same magic. A flavour that flew under their radar, that didn't scar me up, that *worked.* But the only word I found was *inadequate.* This was the flavour of magic I should have been using, but I could never summon it when I needed it, nor could I control it when I had it.

So I stayed quiet with an assenting huff and hoped they would drop the subject.

My lack of control had nearly cost Briar her life, or worse, made her into a mindless host for that slurry. I tightened my hold on her, and in response, she slithered around my waist, squeezing just slightly more than usual. A silent reassurance.

Reassurance? Do you think yourself capable of using this magic as I have?

The words weaseled into my mind like an intrusive thought, spoken in a voice just like my own. For a moment, I accepted it as my own, startled by the notion.

Enough dancing around the truth. This flavour you speak of is mine and mine alone. But imposter that you are, you take credit for all that I am.

My breath caught, recognizing not the disparity of voice, but of tone.

Evelyn.

The moment I could name her, the looming presence in the back of my mind disappeared. My body shuddered, fingers quaking, bottom lip trembling. She was getting closer.

"Annie?" Kev coaxed, ever the observant one.

"Hmm?" Even my voice shook, and it was the final nail in my coffin.

"Whoa, hey. What's wrong?" Lin's usually flat tone carried a softer note than I was prepared for, and to my greatest horror, tears sprung to the corners of my eyes at her question.

It was a stupid reason to start crying, but now that I'd started, I couldn't stop myself. I shook my head, hair flying out to either side of me. A flicker of red, my own red locks, returned me to the dream in which Evelyn had revealed herself. All fiery red hair and blazing wings, like a vision of apocalypse. My body, turned against me. And now, too, my mind, my magic.

"I'm fine," I assured them no matter that I sounded the complete opposite of fine. But how could I tell them Evelyn's presence only seemed to be growing in my head? How could I tell them she was *talking* to me while I was awake? Was that why Briar wasn't speaking to me? Had Evelyn barred her from my mind again?

The intrusive words came back to me, and I registered what she said.

She'd been using my magic, and without opening the cuts on my palms, at that. Was that why she pushed the idea into my mind that day? Spoke the word that would forever change my life? Was that why she wanted me to have this power? The tiny sliver of her that had entered my body was doing a better job of being a shonte than I was!

This was the power of a domenth, only a fraction of the power I would be going up against when Valencia came to collect, an inevitable future now that she had the gate key.

"Hey!" Kev interrupted, placing a hand on my shoulder to stop me walking. He had to bend slightly to meet my eyes. "What's going on? Is it the kirranite slurry-?"

"Oh, no, no. Nothing like that-" Damnit, why was I tossing aside a perfectly usable excuse? "-heh, you know me, just another meltdown. Nothing out of the ordinary!"

"It's at least somewhat out of the ordinary," Lin noted, voice still too soft, too worried, to unclench the fist of emotion from around my heart. She glanced toward Cerenthior. Yes! An easier explanation than the truth.

"Valencia's champion..." What, existed? Awaited me right around the corner? Had done something horrible enough to Seth to make him want to...? I shook my head, as if that could rid me of these paralyzing notions. Good one, me, in feigning dread, I'd just uncorked another source of anxiety. "Uh... well, he's sure out there."

I couldn't think what more to say, but I didn't have to. Kev and Lin immediately understood.

"For now, we just need to worry about making it there," Lin assured me, "Then we can rest and save our worries for tomorrow. Okay?"

I screwed up my face in a wary grimace. "Okay..." Easier said than done.

Kev patted my shoulder and we picked up our former pace. "It would help if we knew what he looked like. Hey Briar, any chance you can get an APB from Brett?" His eyes flicked to where Dorian and Bojack bickered a good distance ahead.

Wiping at my eyes, a note of confusion entered my voice. "What, you don't think Brett would've put two and two together if the man he saw in his vision was tall, pretty, and irrepressibly giddy?"

Furrowing his brow into a frown, he shrugged and glanced away again. "It's just, he was hiding the fact he's a carmavi. He can take anyone's magic. That's shady as hell."

Lin considered it, granting, "For as rare as they are, the Liberation Front does seem to have a lot of carmavi magikiers."

"You're kidding," I scoffed, "*I'm* a carmavi magikier, what does that say about me?"

She met me with an exasperated look. "You're also a shonte. Scratch that, *the* shonte. You're a special case, Annie. Doesn't count."

"They had him imprisoned! You should've seen the conditions they kept him in."

"Imprisonment for the sole purpose of some twisted belief-system conversion therapy. And he was there for months, certainly long enough to be effective." Her voice shook, and I remembered her time in the delinquent center back in Blackano.

Although society in Blackano had passed that whole institution off as lawful, even necessary, the delinquent center was no more innocent than the Khuloces Base. I'd never asked her much about it, but Faith had more than once insinuated the indoctrinating treatment she'd endured in that place, and for the simple crime of contacting a loved one on the outside.

Kev and I fell quiet, but Lin tapped a finger to her chin, leather glove to cotton scarf. "I seriously doubt he's the champion, but a little doubt isn't enough to make me trust him. We've known enough Liberation Front nuts to recognize their pattern, and they have a habit of playing the long con."

She didn't have to say her name for me to know exactly who she meant. From Val Darling to Valencia Lupei, Lin had a point.

29

Glimmer in the Dark

WE CARRIED ON IN A SOLEMN SILENCE, LISTENING FOR ANY OTHER SIGNS of danger lurking in the tall grass. Distant crackles of thunder met our straining ears, and the pleasant scent of rain swathed my buzzing brain.

A storm brewed off the horizon – just our luck. But something else had the little hairs on the back of my neck standing on end, goosebumps chasing up my arms.

I was sure of it. Something out in the cloak of darkness had its eyes on us.

The tall grass rustled, rippling in the breeze, and a glare of light shone off Lin's goggles directly into my eyes. A sidelong glance in her direction revealed a flicker of movement caught in the reflection. A shadow peeking out over the tall grass, human-shaped and moving against the wind.

I snaked a hand to hers, grasping her wrist insistently. "Something's out there."

"You noticed it, too? I figured it was just the nightly paranoia setting in." Dorian's voice was soft, muted so as to let the rustling of the grass hide his words. He spun on his heel, walking backwards to face the rest of us alongside Bojack's forward march.

"You think it's another slurry?" Kev guessed and raised his nose to the air for that telltale scent of burning rubber. He dropped his pace, so he fell behind, making up the rear with his hand on his bow.

A backwards glance told me almost as much as the clipped tone of his voice. He kept an eye on Dorian, distrusting and intent on the man who'd manipulated his already cursed magic.

Bojack scoffed, stopping dead in his tracks with arms crossed huffily over his chest and his head turned haphazardly over his shoulder. Like this, he peered out of the corner of one downturned eye at the rest of us. "And if it *is* a slurry, what do you expect to accomplish with a bow and arrow?"

Dorian snagged at the waist, caught so suddenly on the end of the chain tethering them, he nearly lost his footing. Sporting a contrite expression in apology for Bojack's behaviour, he resigned himself to halt alongside his ward and hear him out, whatever he had to say.

Not me. "Okay, first of all," I interjected, stopping as well, "Whatever's out there, it's human-shaped. And secondly, if you don't have anything nice to say, shut up."

"What she said," Kev immaturely tacked on, bringing me to drop my head in my hand. "And whatever it is, the fire was probably what attracted it, so you can doubly shut up. There's nothing subtle about a towering inferno in the middle of an open field."

Rubbing the back of his neck, Dorian clicked his tongue and offered up an apologetic smile. "Yeah, that's my bad."

"Of all the illustrious deaths I could have had, it had to come to me in a boring, old field, surrounded by idiots..." Bojack groaned into his hands and dragged them down the sides of his face. "Would anyone care to come up with a plan or are you banking on another mercy capture?"

Now that he mentioned it, that didn't sound like such a bad idea, but Lin was already snapping out a retort. "I don't hear you coming up with anything."

"It hasn't even been an hour since the last time your impaired sense of self-preservation nearly cost me my life, and you're still inviting death like it's a distant relative during the holidays. Excuse me if I figured I'd play task delegator for the waking nightmare of executive dysfunction that is this miserable band of travellers– mmph!"

I was fairly sure Lin and Kev had already tuned him out, but his bitter words came out muffled nonsense as Dorian stepped in behind him, clasping a hand over his mouth. "Talk about inviting death. Keep your dramatics to a low simmer, will you? You're making a scene."

Muffled against Dorian's palm, Bojack grumbled, "You're out of your goddamn mind blaming me."

"Hush now, darling," Dorian cajoled, refusing to let up his grip. I swore I saw the stalks of Bojack's eyes in his exaggerated eyeroll. Facing the rest of us, Dorian continued, "So Red says it's human, and if that's the case, it's best to assume there's more than one. Question is, magikier or pora?"

Kev notched an arrow. "Let's hope magikier."

"Let's not. Nasty little buggers when they're not on your side, I'll tell you that much."

Lin scoffed. "And you expect me to believe pora are somehow better?"

"Good point." His measured gaze slid toward the rustling of the grass. "But I've a preference for seeing my enemies coming, and pora aren't exactly known to attack with the upper hand of invisibility. Or any number of other magikier tricks."

Kev swore under his breath and lifted his bow, tracking the rustling in the grass with an arrow notched on the drawstring. Grabbing his arm, Lin furrowed her brows with a shake of her head.

"Don't waste your arrows."

Stepping up to Dorian, I met his eyes with a steely regard and rested a hand on the hilt of my sabre, a weapon I had yet to draw in self-defense. "So, Liberation Front magikiers?" If not for the squeak in my voice, I might've come across like I had some mettle.

He softened his regard. "If I had to make a guess."

With a sharp nod, I pursed my lips and tightened my grip. "Well, if they already know we're here, and I think it's safe to say they do, we don't have much choice but to stand our ground."

"Right you are."

"Thing is-" I gestured between Lin, Kev, and myself. "-the three of us have to enter Cerenthior. By whatever means."

Wincing, Dorian tried for an encouraging smile even with furrowed brows, but where sympathy crinkled his eyes, an expression of contempt mixed in with the shock rounding Bojack's. Even Lin and Kev raked in startled breaths behind me, and Briar tightened her coils around my middle in the folds of my jacket. We must have woken her.

"So-" Dorian paused as if collecting his thoughts. "-you're going to *let* them capture you." An unreadable note lowered his voice.

"They haven't attacked and I, like a degenerate, am in desperate need of a B and E scheme. Having an escort in sounds like a manageable first step."

"You don't want to put a *little* more brainstorming into it?"

"With what time? Anyway, if they wanted us dead, we wouldn't still be talking."

"Astute observation, Sherlock," Bojack mumbled into Dorian's palm as a deep resolve came over his captor's expression, hardening his gaze.

"Then we're coming with you-"

"No you're not," I protested as Bojack growled into his hand, "Is now really the time to bandwagon on stupid ideas?"

"Now, now. The pickier we are about doing the right thing, the more we're just part of the problem."

"Part of? You're my *entire* problem."

"Why don't you ever listen to my opinion?"

"Because mine's better. And you're an idiot."

"Okay, but consider this-"

"I'm the only one doing that!" Bojack burst into his hand, muffled and muted. Heaving a sigh, Dorian unclasped his bounty's mouth to wipe his palm off on the leg of his pants. Like a kid forced to eat his least favourite vegetable, Bojack stuck out his tongue with an exaggerated grimace. "Are you finally ready to hear reason?"

I never understood Brett quite so well as I did in that moment as an overwhelming need to squeeze out the frustration between my temples nearly got the better of me. Hell, even I wanted to ditch Tweedledee and Tweedledum, here.

"Uh, Red?" Dorian noted as my fingers itched to massage away the space they'd rented out in my brain.

Flicking a glance toward him, I expected to find his happy-go-lucky smile awaiting me, only to start in alarm at the polar opposite expression he wore. His gaze was fixed just past my shoulder, eyes darting back and forth, round as pennies, and mouth slightly agape. A breath escaped me, high in my throat as I spun on my heel to find whatever had caught his attention.

I nearly leapt out of my skin at Bojack's world-weary sigh. "Looks like that's it for talking." Only then did I register Kev and Lin's silence.

They'd vanished entirely, nowhere to be seen beneath the pitch-black shroud of this starless night.

"By your own reasoning, does this mean they're dead?" Bojack musingly continued, tapping a finger to his chin in the aspect of philosophical consideration. I jabbed an elbow back, ramming his solar plexus. His wheezing and sputtering brought a touch of relief to the spinning terror alive in my mind, calming my nerves just enough to clear the white noise abuzz in my senses.

Movement caught my eye, drawn to a patch of thrashing grass stalks, and there at their base, a dark mass writhing on the ground. Blinded by my shock as much as the dark, I strained to pick apart this bizarre sight of incomprehensible shadow. A bulbous orb raised off the blob from which long limbs extended with fingers scrabbling at the dirt. It felt a short eternity of blankness before a glare of light caught on a pair of lenses. Lin's iron goggles.

The sight before me suddenly clicked in my head. Half her body had disappeared, dangling down in some deep pit. She dragged herself across the ground, swallowed waist-deep in the hole – I could only assume this was a stone-crafter's doing – and pinned under some invisible force, gagged by whatever pressure had her scarf clinging to her face like a second skin.

My feet were moving before I'd fully registered what I was seeing. Kev must have been swallowed whole, Lin only managing to save herself at the last second because of her magic, and even then, something had her pinned and mute. Instinct propelled me forward, only to collide with a force I couldn't see. In that brief moment of collision, a dark apparition of a man hunched over Lin and clad in a strange uniform met my eyes. The next moment, my feet flew out from under me, too much momentum for the sudden impact in my path, and he was gone.

"Get away from her!" I shouted, haggard, and kicked wildly in search of an ankle to wrench out from under the invisible magikier. Like a scythe, my leg sheared through the grass stalks, but nothing of substance stayed my destructive path. Rather, a hand clamped around my throat, almost large enough for the thumb and index finger to meet at the nape of my neck. Again, he appeared, hovering over me like a vision of death as the stars stolen from the spotless dark of the sky popped before my eyes.

"Protecting one of them? You're disgusting," a deep voice snarled above my face.

Gold filled my vision as Briar snaked up the man's arm from her nest in the bulk of my jacket. He launched himself back from me in alarm, crying out even as he disappeared into thin air, denoted only by Briar's whirlwind of attacks on his imperceptible person. My hands went straight for my bruised throat, a fit of gagging, wheezing coughs tearing up my deprived lungs.

What followed was chaos. We were surrounded – they came from all directions. A quick glance over my shoulder offered a discouraging sight, grainy with darkness whether from the lack of oxygen reaching my brain or my godawful night vision. Dorian had been forced down from behind, pinned atop a flailing Bojack and restrained under a pair of these uniformed magikiers. Ahead of me, two more made a beeline for Lin. And Kev… I couldn't see him anywhere.

But the invisible man's words, so acidic with disgust and contempt, returned to me.

"Wait!" I croaked, extending a hand toward Lin with outstretched fingers, but she was too far to reach. "She's a magikier! We're magikiers! Please, we won't fight you!"

A woman's voice emanated from the heavy shadows. "Then where do your loyalties lie?"

Bojack gave a dry laugh, curt and sharp, into the dirt – once again muffled. "With whoever's holding the most effective weapon, and right now, that's you, honey."

"Ignore this gobshite; he was born without a moral backbone," Dorian mumbled into Bojack's back where his face was burrowed, pinned down under a gloved hand belonging to one of the two uniformed assailants on top of him.

"We, well..." I weighed my words, but I had to face the facts, the truth was my only option here. And so, I told it all, from who we sought in occupied Cerenthior to the journey we'd taken to get this far. They didn't need to know the background details of all that had happened in Blackano or the specifics of my magic, just that we had come from the City of Gates and opposed the Liberation Front, and boy oh boy did they let me go on at length about that particular subject. As I spoke, Briar returned to me, landing on my legs with her wings extended out to either side in defense of me, but no one made a move. Until finally, with everything laid bare, I hesitantly asked, "Can I, maybe, get a sense of *your* loyalties? After everything I've shared?"

"You're in luck." A hand extended out to me, helping me up to my feet as Briar scaled my legs and torso to drape herself heavily over my shoulders, far too overgrown to truly belong there anymore. "We share a common enemy."

"Great! Really, that's awesome, so let's maybe backtrack a step and sort out the little mishap where you *buried my friends*? There was another guy here with us, you know!"

At my words, the field opened up, and Kev clawed his way out of an underground pocket. He scrambled back to the surface of the world, where he toppled onto his back, heaving for breath, and simply shouted into the night. Lin clamped a hand over his mouth, having pulled herself out of her own pit, and shushed him with an index finger in front of her scarf. This only succeeded to morph his incoherent shouting into a gibbering rant muffled by the material of her glove, hands flailing in gesticulation. But there was only relief in my chest, swelling powerfully at the sight of him, alive and well if riotously indignant.

A breath I hadn't realized I was holding flew out of me. "Oh, thank whatever's out there, you didn't kill him." An odd note had entered my voice, punctuated with a breathy chuckle. I planted a hand on my hip and with my other, brushed a stray tear from my eye. "Hah. You know, there's a good chance I might've snapped if you had. Can't say what I would've done! So maybe next time, you can use your words before attacking random strangers minding their own goddamn business, hm!"

A sigh emanated from the darkness nearby and I took a wide step, crossing the distance to Kev and Lin in a single stride. As I helped them to their feet, that same female voice dully noted, "Had you been discovered by any other faction besides Arhillin scouts, you wouldn't have been shown any mercy at all. You would've been killed outright."

"Untrue. We *just* destroyed a kirranite slurry-"

Lin elbowed me in the ribs, cutting me off, but I'd already said too much.

"With fire and smoke. You realize you set off a beacon with that little stunt, don't you? And on that subject, now's no time to loiter. Muzzle that beast of yours and pick up the pace."

Briar hissed, spitting embers, but she begrudgingly lowered herself back into the folds of my jacket where she remained.

"Where are you taking us?" Lin demanded.

"Exactly where you wish to go."

30

The Legion on Their Doorstep

IT HAD BEGUN TO RAIN BY THE TIME WE FINALLY CROSSED THE VALLEY with these six Arhillin scouts, and Kev had his jacket over his bag to protect the ukulele packed inside. Dorian and Bojack strode just up ahead with one of the scouts, having apparently already forgiven them, with a young man whose voice Dorian had recognized once the initial chaos subsided.

Just six magikiers – I'd wrongly assumed their numbers had swarmed us in the tens or twenties, maybe even thirties – and they'd picked us apart in mere seconds. I tried not to linger on that disheartening notion, our utter defeat a slap in the face of our ambitions. What was I expecting to happen once we reached Cerenthior? It wasn't like we'd see massive, unwarranted improvement overnight, and here we were, a day out from our destination, having only just pathetically succumbed to a group of *six*!

It was all I could focus on as silence ruled the rear of our travel group within the white noise of the rain – even Dorian's voice up ahead was but a warbling dissonance just outside the self-contained bubble of my mental presence. Briar still wouldn't speak to me, but her absence only felt like Evelyn's presence. And sure, I had done my best to shut out all thought of Evelyn, too, but that had only numbed me.

Within minutes, the downpour came down so hard, we could hardly see the city walls ahead of us. My hair clung to my neck and back, raindrops tickled my scalp, and heavy winds sprayed yet heavier droplets into my face every now and then, but the worst was the ground's refusal to absorb any of the rain, making a massive puddle of the flats.

These drylands stretched vast and exposed from the outer walls of the city to the frayed edges of the barley valley. Blackened remains of vegetation implied this land was once part of the lush valley, but now it simply looked dead. Just like the obscured silhouette of the looming city. Just like everything in this downpour.

Except for a faint, fiery glow which flew through the sky from the city and crashed down closer to the middle of the drylands. There, where distant light broke through several deep cracks dug out of this no man's land. We realized what they were immediately. Trenches.

The Arhillin scouts were escorting us back to their warzone.

Kev, Lin, and I slowed our pace, speaking in quieted voices no matter how far we were from the trenches. Kev suggested we skirt around the attacking force. Lin pointed out we could use the help. I simply stared as another steaming fireball launched at the trenches. How could these Arhillin stand it? To watch their brothers and sisters in arms reduced to ash on the Liberation Front's doorstep?

Even through the deluge and the night, I made out a surprising number of legionaries scrambling to put up tarps to catch and disperse the fast accumulating water. Far behind the trenches, out of range of the city's defensive siege weapons, the white top of a medic tent beckoned the wounded, and beyond that stood an array of countless canvas tents. So many, they faded into the pale obscurity of the downpour.

In our mucky approach, we observed the Arhillin legion, Arillia's finest warriors, gathered here to retake their capital and bustling like ants in their tunnels. The rain would fill their trenches at this rate, drowning their progress and pushing them back to whatever trenches they might have left behind in the more water-absorbent valley.

I could feel Lin and Kev's excitement to either side of me as we approached, but there was none to be had in myself. Rather, my stomach dropped, disheartened, to think how long they had been here, fighting this war of attrition, without gaining much ground at all. How impossible this task began to seem, pitched under the gloom of their futile efforts.

Not five kilometres out from the camps, our Arhillin escorts stopped us approaching any further without announcing ourselves and advised we stay here so they could go ahead. While we waited, Lin fashioned a white flag from the bandages in her backpack, working against the rain to make it visible, and Dorian edged closer to us with Bojack at his hip.

"I don't have to ask you not to make this difficult for us, yeah?" he implored, nudging Bojack's arm with an elbow. "Considering you're on the Empress' most wanted?"

"No promises."

"I suppose I wouldn't trust your word, anyway." He punctuated his teasing tone with a wink, and Bojack attempted to blow a pesky lock of hair out of his eyes, but it was slicked down by the rain and caught in his eyelashes.

It wasn't long, with Lin waving her makeshift flag, before a small company of uniformed magikiers in unmistakably Arillian garb splashed across the swiftly inundating flats on horseback – except, the closer they came, the less their mounts looked like horses, their bodies too wide, and sporting oxen horns which stuck out to either side. Even their lumbering gallop wasn't right for a horse, but they were fast, agile. Shrinking away from them, I could only think how easily even one of these great and imposing beasts could trample me flat into the ground.

They crossed the distance before Lin, Kev, or I could figure out how best to greet them and slowed on their bizarre mounts several feet in front of us – more like bison than horses now I got a better look at them. The conclusion Dorian seemed to have drawn was to shuffle in front of Bojack, blocking him partially from view, which Bojack gladly accepted.

Horns stuck out to either side of these beasts' large, low heads with fleecy manes covering the head, chest, and shoulders, and even thicker blue roan hide like that of a bear coating the rest of their wide bodies. Clouds of steaming hot breath escaped large, wet, and snuffling nostrils. Large hooves kicked up the scorched earth.

The legionaries atop these beasts drew their long, curved sabres, ready to attack at the slightest misstep on our part, and wouldn't you know it, our lovely escorts hadn't returned with them, leaving us to fend for ourselves. This company's armoured black and blue uniforms covered them head to toe, with silver masks covering their faces – well, all but one of them. Their indisputable commander, wearing a decorated coat like Seth's over a glossy black cuirass, dismounted and approached with an intimidating stride.

Briar snaked out from where she hid in the bulk of my jacket, crawling up to my shoulders and extending her wings to shield our much smaller group from the rain. She wreathed my shoulders, the two pairs of thumb talons on her front feet digging into my jacket, and the raptor-like claws on her back feet clasping my upper arm, but her elongated body seemed to float around me like a ribbon in the wind. When paired with the majesty of her wings, I had to admit, she was a sight to behold. And she had her sights set upon the company captain.

"Briar..." I whispered in warning, watching the rest of his company stiffen and urge their mounts forward but she squeezed my shoulder reassuringly.

The captain raised a hand, signalling his company to back down. She hadn't opened a connection between our minds, but I assumed she had done so with him.

In the silence of my seeming exclusion, I couldn't help comparing him to the only other Arillian captain I'd met, the Captain of the Arillian Spire. For one, he seemed to notice Lin and Kev's existence, so that was already a plus. And he wasn't missing any limbs, nor did he look terribly starved. The end of his beard was tied off in two short braids and he wore his salt-and-pepper hair in a ponytail of dreads, his thick eyebrows dark in contrast to the lighter brown of his eyes set into a kind visage, with a smiling mouth under a broad, pierced nose. He couldn't have been *less* like the Captain of the Arillian Spire, with his unguarded expressions and broad, robust physique. The only trait they shared was their above average height. And, it seemed, their authority.

Recognizing this, I tried not to wilt under Briar's weight, but it was like my body was on strike, demanding bedtime. I could feel myself sinking, but only until the captain's eyes flitted to me, and my back straightened automatically, a weary smile plucking up the corners of my mouth.

"Hi!" I sang before I could figure out something better to say. My saying anything at all almost felt like an intrusion on whatever conversation Briar had taken him into. I could only hope the scouts had passed along a decent reference, but I doubted we'd made a good impression on them.

He tilted his head as if listening to the rain and glanced back to Briar, then again to me. It was worth noting, he had to look down maybe two whole feet to find my eyes. "Pleased to meet you, Anelisha. If you don't mind me asking, *how* are you going to break the enemy's defenses?"

"Oh..." I internally cursed Briar. That was quite the misplaced confidence she had in me. Was I the only one concerned we'd just been taken down in three easy steps by a team of, I repeat, *six*? "I will! Definitely will, uh, do that. But right now, we desperately need rest." I gestured to my small group.

When the captain's gaze roved over the others, nodding to each of them in turn, Dorian gasped, "Jacob Cole?"

I glanced sidelong at him, about to shush him, but his eyes were lit up, and the captain met him with an exuberant smile. I felt myself relax, albeit only by a smidge. Subtle though he was, I saw him pull the tethering chain taught, drawing Bojack in behind him to better conceal his high priority bounty.

"By gum, you're alive!" the captain, this Jacob Cole, guffawed, throwing his arms out wide.

Lin and I shared an odd look at his turn of phrase, but in a single stride, he crossed the distance to Dorian and clapped a hand on his shoulder, pulling him into an embrace. Only then did I realize how strange a thing it was to see Dorian dwarfed in comparison to another, and boy oh boy did Jacob Cole tower over him in height as well as pure muscle mass – I had to wonder how his mount hadn't broken its back beneath him, even with the build of a draft animal.

He boomed a laugh, pulled back from the hug and jostled Dorian's shoulder. Even now, I noticed Dorian's white-knuckled grip on the chain, guiding Bojack outside Jacob Cole's direct line of sight. "It's great to see you! I'll admit, I thought you were done for."

Rubbing the back of his neck, Dorian grinned up at him. "Yeah, so did I. 'Til this one came along." He gestured to me, and Jacob Cole turned his blindingly bright smile on me, somehow outshining even Dorian's.

"Well come on, then, let's find you all a tent." He gestured to his entourage, then motioned to Briar on my shoulder, advising, "You'll want to hide the dragon if you plan on sleeping tonight. The Arhillin will swarm you with questions if they catch sight of her."

And that was that. Jacob Cole walked us back to the camp with his mounted warriors making up the rear. His own strange mount trailed loyally after him, snuffling and nudging his back as his voice boomed over the pounding rain, recounting stories of the long war and weaving tales of the Arhillin's impressive feats.

I perked up at his allusions to the champion, leader of the force occupying Cerenthior who rarely made appearances in battle. Few had laid eyes on him and lived to tell their story, but those who did came back speaking of insurmountable power and a terrible weapon. Bojack's eyes glittered at his mention of it.

Tidbits about Jacob Cole leaked through his accounts. A man of County Chthial, he was the Third Clan Leader of Arillia – more than a captain, it would seem – and after a force of pora bolstered by the fall of Cerenthior ran through his cities, razing and devouring how they pleased, he had gathered his greatest warriors and the Second and Fourth Arillian Clan Leaders from County Eloth and County Yitela, respectively. With all their remaining forces combined into one Arhillin legion, they laid siege on Cerenthior in attempt to take it back and had been creeping up this no man's land outside the walls ever since.

"Do you make a habit of personally greeting everyone who approaches with a white flag?" Bojack interrupted.

Dorian dropped his head in his palm for all his wasted effort, chuckling tiredly. "Sorry about him."

"The bounty you've been after?" asked Jacob Cole, a tinge of something hidden in his tone, but he didn't need Dorian's nod to confirm as much considering the very obvious chain between them. He extended a hand to Bojack, who eyed it suspiciously before taking it, only for Jacob Cole to shake so vigorously, he could have dislocated Bojack's entire arm.

"You can call me Cedric Laurent," Bojack bitterly remarked, pulling out of the handshake prematurely, "Charmed, I'm sure."

"I know that moniker," Jacob Cole noted, although his recognition didn't seem a surprise. He leaned down to Dorian's ear, sliding his eyes sidelong to catch the withering regard Dorian held for the man of many names. "You realize this one's on more most wanted lists than there are organizations handing them out? Same goes for Bojack Hart, Sacha Rose, Cillian Gray, Basil Devereux, Jasper Matheson, I could go on..."

"Funny you say that. I once stumbled across a list comprised entirely of my alter egos."

Jacob Cole raised a scolding eyebrow for Dorian, driving home his point. "The Empress is offering to pay his head's weight in gold."

"Now that is auspicious! Know any good illusionists?" Bojack tittered, shaking out his battered hand, as Dorian gave an inward groan and dropped his shoulders.

"Yeah, I know."

With a pensive nod of his head, Jacob Cole eyed Bojack. "Grimshaw wants the credit for his capture?"

Dorian shrugged his shoulders, still smiling. "I would assume so, but I've no place to talk. I'm just the deliveryman."

Narrowing his eyes, Jacob Cole continued, "As Clan Leader, his duty is to the Empress, as is mine. Keeping this one from justice would be high treason."

"That it would."

"And here you are getting your hands dirty. You sure Mad Jack's worth the trouble?"

"I don't question Master Hamish's orders."

Under his breath, Bojack remarked, "Master?" with a funny look in his eyes, but quickly hid the expression with a curled grin. "I won't pry into your personal business. So, let's get back to the point."

"Which was?" I groaned, massaging my temples. At the very least, I was happy to let them have the spotlight I'd rather avoid. I was still in the effort of decoding what Briar evidently and misguidedly thought I was capable of.

"A Clan Leader's life shouldn't be risked so recklessly. Certainly not an Arillian Clan Leader. I hear you lot are hard to come by these days."

Ignoring the spit of venom in his snide tone, Jacob Cole grinned, wide and roguish. "I appreciate the concern, but I saw the smoke on the horizon like anyone else. We were prepared for a fight. That said, if I'd known the first wanderers I pick up waving a white flag would be accompanied by a dragon, an old friend, and a shonte, I would have greeted every wayward soul to pass this way with a five-star meal and a smile."

I blanched, staring down at my feet. So, Briar told him the truth. That was a surprise, considering her whole trust-no-one stance on most interactions, but I supposed he was a person of merit, considering his rank. Kev and Lin must have picked up on this too, squeezing closer to either side of me with an eye fixed on our jolly escort.

He waved off his company as we entered the camp, striding through deep puddles and kicking up mud between large tents bustling with legionaries. In the distance, another fireball crashed over the trenches, but now that we were closer, I watched it break against an invisible force hovering above ground level. Magic and defenses, but no countermeasures I could see.

No matter the late hour nor the winds and rain, magikiers defended their keep and held their ground at the trenches, and yet were still leagues out from the only opening in the wall. I wilted under the heavy weight of expectation thrust upon me, to do what no one before me had yet achieved.

Jacob Cole was true to his word, inviting us to a hearty meal of barley grain cereals in his command tent as his assistants sorted out our residence for the night. Not exactly a five-star meal… unless you'd been stuck exclusively eating scout rations the past few days, like us.

One of his assistants served us at a sturdy wooden table, stained with coffee rings and chipped along the edges. Even so, the furniture had a certain class about it, blues and silvers adorning the fabric walls of the tent and breathing life into the torchlit space. The table stood low to the floor surrounded by eight, silver-threaded cushions embroidered with cerulean floral designs on which we sat in a circle.

As I ate in relative silence, Briar stole bites from my spoon, still tucked away in my jacket no matter her ample coils and large, folded wings. Even with my dour mood, the tent was hardly quiet. Dorian and Jacob Cole caught up properly over a couple malt beers, the atmosphere electric with happy chatter even as Dorian kept a close eye on Bojack. Just as close an eye as he kept on the attendants in the tent, a hand always resting on the chain.

You'd hardly think this was one of three commander's tents in an ongoing, months-long siege on the city. Certainly not once Kev pulled out his ukulele to much clapping and singing from our host. The warmth in the tent seemed to rise, and I found myself forgetting the world outside, if only for a moment.

Dorian drew Lin and I into the conversation as the meal came to an end, each of our bowls licked clean. One of the assistants returned with more mugs to accommodate the rest of us, but I turned mine down, eyeing the barrels of beer stacked near the back of the tent. Had Val been here, she wouldn't have taken no for an answer. Maybe, if tomorrow wasn't too important to risk a hangover, I might've said yes.

"So how do you two know each other?" I asked to distract myself, leaning around Bojack who downed his entire mug in one go as soon as it was filled.

He lounged across two cushions next to Dorian, feigning his own absence as he signalled the assistant, who must have been a decade older than him, for a refill. He seemed to take some pleasure in this mild exercise of authority.

Jacob Cole tapped a finger to his chin in contemplation. "It's been, what, four years now?"

Dorian leaned across the table to meet my gaze, smiley as he ever was. "I was fifteen when I arrived in the City of Gates, a bit young to head out to war, so they assigned me to the Schevonian Isles as an assistant to the Second Clan Leader there."

"That explains the Master bit," Bojack grumbled as he motioned for an exceedingly sarcastic toast, and continued, "I thought you were a bounty hunter?"

Dorian conformed, downing the last of his beverage if only to appease him. "That's what Master Hamish had me become. Good pay, good work.

Cellana always has need for bounty hunters." For Kev, Lin, and I, he tacked on, "Grimshaw Hamish, he's the Second Clan Leader of Schevon."

"Most know him for his forty hertz voice. I know him as a pain in the ass," Bojack sighed, swirling his drink in hand.

"He saved your life," Dorian pointedly sighed, but seemed to realize his mistake in trying to chastise an incorrigible grumbler, instead turning back to the rest of us. "*Anyway*, I met Jacob Cole through Master Hamish. The Clan Leaders of Arillia, Schevon, and Loruna gather a few times each year, so I got to know just about everyone."

Jacob Cole hooted another boisterous laugh and nudged Kev beside him with an elbow. "Now that's an understatement. The lad might as well be Grimshaw's own flesh and blood-"

"Always one to take in strays," Bojack tutted.

"-but you've grown on each of us like a fungus, kiddo. I ever told you you're like a nephew to me?" A devilish grin took up Jacob Cole's face. "Twice removed."

"Is that why you spoil me?" Dorian laughed as Bojack motioned to the assistant again, this time insisting he refill Dorian's mug as well as his. "Thank you," Dorian smiled as the assistant complied.

"You build families wherever you go, huh?" Lin noted, and Dorian waved a flustered hand.

"Has the Empress ever been to any of these meetings?" I chimed in, doing my utmost to come across casual. Here we were, on the edge of occupied Cerenthior, and I was only just now learning we'd been travelling with our best bet at contacting the Empress all along.

"Mhm, her Imperial Majesty makes yearly visits to each Clan Leader. I've only met her once or twice, and I've had stress dreams ever since." He brought his freshly refilled mug to his lips, a quiet consideration behind his eyes.

As if reminded by our mention of the Empress, Jacob Cole leapt into yet another of his epic anecdotes, excitedly recounting stories too grand, chivalrous, and fanciful to be totally true, but all I could focus on were the fresh ideas taking shape in my head.

The more Jacob Cole spoke, the more Bojack weaseled more drinks into his and Dorian's hands, posing questions every now and then to poke at the topic of the weapon. Jacob Cole didn't seem to realize what it was or what it signified, or perhaps it was his intention to say little on the subject, but Bojack soon gave up his subtle interrogation.

More and more beers went around to all but me and Lin – she was old enough to go to war, but still too young to drink – before one of Jacob Cole's assistants returned, having finally sorted out our temporary residence. With that, Lin, Kev, and I excused ourselves from the command tent in favour of sleep, led by the equally tired-looking assistant. As we walked the mucky path between rows upon rows of large tents, Briar bundled herself in the bulk of my jacket, a failed attempt at discretion. At least no one called me out on my lumpy looking midsection.

Our tent was just like any other, with an empty weapons-rack out front and eight empty cots rolled out on the tarp floor inside. It was obvious enough to me; this tent was once occupied by legionaries no longer with us, evident in the dark brown stains only half washed-out of the cots' cloth material. Even so, Kev and Lin discarded their heavy travel gear and flopped onto their makeshift beds. Kev passed out the moment his body hit the somewhat cushioned fabric, and Lin was soon to follow.

I let them sleep, organizing their packs in the corner, and doffed the heaviest of my own travel gear, including Briar. Here in the tent, she ran little risk of being seen, but the plan that had taken shape in my mind saw a different purpose for her.

"So, you might not like where I'm going with this, but how long would it take you to lure some tree giants across the valley?" I began, and reflectively added, "They'd have to be big to do any real damage to a wall like the one around Cerenthior, bigger than the tree giant at the Khuloces Base." Catching myself on the verge of digression, I turned my regard down toward Briar and implored, "Thoughts?"

She leapt onto one of the cots, wrapping about herself in coils, but her large, reptilian eyes were fixed on me. After a long moment, she flicked her forked tongue and whipped her tail in frustration.

What confidence I had mustered toward the product of all my brainstorming at dinner deflated. "You still can't talk to me?"

She shook her head. It wasn't like I hadn't already figured as much, but I frowned, nonetheless. It would've been nice to hear her thoughts on this haphazard plan of mine, if it could even be called a plan. Even with all the brainstorming in the world, it would always be my bouncing ideas off her cynical realism that paved the road to my best course of action. Or so I had learned since first meeting Briar.

More than that, I needed someone to talk to. To open up about everything, spill all the secrets I'd kept bottled up inside this past month. Briar was one of only two people who knew about Evelyn – that she was still in my head, albeit not to the dire extent I had only recently come to realize – and the other was currently being held captive somewhere in Cerenthior.

I glanced sidelong toward Kev, who breathed deeply with his face smushed unflatteringly against his cot. Then to Lin, already snoring as she lay curled on her side.

Heaving a sigh, I pulled the blankets from their packs and flapped out the dirt accumulated from travel before spreading them gingerly over my friends. Even so near to the front lines of this war, this was the first time since leaving the City of Gates we would be able to rest safely and soundly. I wasn't about to wake them.

Briar made a noise behind me, a cat-like chirp, and I glanced back at her over my shoulder.

"I know you don't want to leave my side. You promised Faith you wouldn't. But you have tonight. I'm not going anywhere."

She glowered back at me.

"The wall needs to come down somehow, and the only other way I can think to bring it down is with my magic."

A low growl rumbled deep in her chest.

"Yeah, yeah, Cerenthior's teeming with pora, and that's exactly my point. If you fly out to the Khuloces Forest right now, you'd have all night to find as many tree giants as you can. Just the sight of you was enough to mesmerize that first one. Imagine how many you could lure out to the walls of Cerenthior if you were really trying. Imagine our advantage."

She flicked her tail again, the ruffles along the edges of her jaw quivering irritably, but she must have figured there was no arguing without a voice of her own. She bared brilliant white fangs at me, snout rippling with her snarl, but she unwound herself in quiet compliance. Unfolding her wings, she dug her talons in and pushed powerfully off the floor, sending unused cots skittering across the tarp. In a blast of stirred up air, she bolted from the tent and was gone.

My breath hitched as a flash of memory burned behind my eyelids. That claw-like arm from the kirranite slurry had caught her up in it even as she attacked, had slammed her to the ground. "Be safe out there!" I called out through the tent flaps, but I doubted she heard me over the rain.

The sudden loneliness in the tent seeped into me like a bone-deep chill. With that, I set myself to the last of the tasks I meant to wrap up before bed. Sure, I was beyond exhausted, but it wasn't yet midnight and my clothes needed cleaning – the blood stains from earlier today would do me no favours come tomorrow. Lucky me, I had noticed a laundry basin on our way to the tent. Unlucky me, it looked like the blood from my arms had soaked through all my layers.

Huffing my discomfort at getting undressed as fast as humanly possible in the corner of the tent – and pleading fate to let me off the hook just this once by keeping Dorian and Bojack from walking in on me – I tied my hair up into a bun and threw on the patterned chiton we had taken with permission from the underground refuge. And so, feeling the chilly night air in places I would have preferred not to, I gathered up all my clothes, along with Lin and Kev's from the unkempt piles they'd left on the floor, and retraced my steps to the basin. Firelit lanterns hanging off metal pikes in the ground lit my way, casting shadows of the resting legionaries loitering around their tents.

I felt some of their stares as I passed and readjusted the pins holding up my chiton each time the hair on the back of my neck stood up, but no one approached me. The rain was still coming down, although not as hard as before, but a large tarp held up on stilts kept the basin from overfilling. That wasn't to say my chiton and laundry load weren't already soaked through by the time I got there.

Barrels to the right of the basin contained more of that strawberry-scented lather like from the underground refuge, which I scrubbed into our clothes until the basin water turned an almost opaque ruddy brown.

Only with fierce lathering and rubbing did the blood stains lift from the material of my clothes, enough to have the water sloshing up over the sides. All the while, my mind churned as busily as the choppy ripples in the basin. Water I should have been able to control as easily as Evelyn allegedly could – through *my* magic.

How many times had she used my magic through me without my knowing it?

The few times I'd managed to use it the way she took credit for – sure, she was mad at me for claiming those little victories as my own, but I was just as angry with her for doing the same – had been in the midst of deep and overwhelming emotion. Feeling the City of Gates' enemies burrowing in the earth, sensing the life in the forest to find the Captain… Evelyn certainly had nothing to gain from any of *those* times the magic responded to my will, seemingly of its own accord.

Hardening my stare down at the water, I pulled the bloodstained cotton of my jacket sleeve taut between my hands. These stains were deeper than the ones on my other clothes, almost black with blood.

"If you can control it yourself, why would you use it exactly how *I* wanted to?" The words whispered out of me, a direct address to the free-loader in my head.

No response. Of course there was no response, what was I expecting from *Evelyn.* The living – or half-living – nightmare which plagued my waking mind.

Narrowing my eyes, I focused on the water as it stilled around my hands. I imagined it sieving through the cotton of my sleeves, pulling with it all remnants of the blood that had soaked them. This vision encapsulated my mind, but I didn't force it, rather giving into the idea of it. Like a river eroding the riverbank, carrying away the dirt and grit as aquatic vegetation filtered out this contamination.

I thought I saw the water stir all on its own, just for a moment, but a nearby ruckus of feet splashing through rainwater and a loud, hollering voice barged in on this breakthrough, calling me back out of my head. It was a moment before I registered Dorian's Irish lilt amid all the unintelligible shouting, just in time before he cut himself off and the sound of feet splashing through the muck grew near.

"Isn't it a little late to be doing laundry? And torrential?"

Recognizing Bojack's voice, I glanced over my shoulder to find him stumbling toward the tarp's meagre shelter through the rain, weighed down by Dorian hanging off him. Water dripped from the ends of their drenched hair, falling onto bright red cheeks, aglow with too much drink.

They must have been pointed in this direction by one of Jacob Cole's assistants, or told the number of our shared tent, but I was simply amazed they'd gotten this far at all, considering how obviously drunk they were.

"Heya, Stranger, fancy threads," Dorian beamed, nodding to the folds of my chiton clinging to my skin as he hopped up on the lid of a detergent-filled barrel with swinging legs. Bojack jerked forward by the pull of the chain, crashing against the side of the barrel and nearly losing his balance entirely. He caught himself at the last second with windmilling arms and shot Dorian an overexaggerated glare. Heedless of Bojack's withering regard, Dorian blithely continued, "Care to yell with me? S'fun pastime in a storm like this. Does wonders for the stress."

I nearly took up the strange offer but shook my head and stifled the urge to laugh. "Stress, huh? I didn't think you were capable."

He shot me a curled grin. "In this society? If I'm being totally honest, fealty to the Empress is on a backburner for me at present. And it's *your* fault." He straightened a finger at Bojack.

"Me?" Bojack gasped, "What did I do?"

"What *didn't* you do?" Dorian slurred, mussing Bojack's white locks. "Ugh, I'm in no state to list your transgressions. You'll just have to live with my frustration."

I couldn't help but chuckle lightly. "Sounds like you two had a fun night?"

Groaning his displeasure to be caught up in casual conversation, Bojack rested an elbow on Dorian's thigh, causing Dorian to jump with a charley horse. Ignoring his perch's evident discomfort, Bojack leaned his head against his knuckles and drooped under his own weight, eyelids fluttering tiredly.

"If by fun you mean exhausting," he huffed, ever the sourpuss. Red-stained lips stood out against his pale, albeit rosy, complexion, suggesting Jacob Cole had brought out the wine after Lin, Kev and I left. His head lolled, elbow sinking sideways until he was practically draped across Dorian's lap as he whined, "Is it just me or have I lost my tolerance?"

"It's not just you," I mused, still chuckling.

"You, too? Drunk on life, I take it?" Disillusioned sarcasm dripped from his tone, but Dorian clasped his hands together and leaned forward over Bojack, eager to weigh in.

"Lemme tell ya, captivity did a real number on my tolerance."

"Is that so?" Bojack tiredly moaned in the effort to stave off a yawn, hardly seeming to care that he was still part of this conversation as he struggled to keep his eyes open. He had one arm wrapped around Dorian's waist and the other folded under his head across Dorian's lap.

"Or, hmm, maybe it was the last time that did it."

I winced. "You have a *last time*?"

Dorian waved a hand conversationally. "If I had a nickel for every time I've been taken hostage, I could get a bubble gum off a gumball machine."

"Not to poke a hole in your metaphor, but I think those only take quarters," I pointed out.

"I wouldn't say you poked a hole so much as *popped my bubble*. Heh?" He patted a beat on Bojack's back with a snickering, "Ba dum tsh," and stifled a self-satisfied chuckle.

"How aren't you and Kev the best of friends?" I groaned, massaging my eyes in amused exasperation.

"But you know what I mean? Twenty-five cents in nickels, sure, it isn't much. But when it's the number of times pora and kirranites and all the Kaipracan's folk have flat out refused to do me in like they do with everyone else?" Closing the pads of his index fingers to his thumbs, he drew his hands out to either side of him and slurred, "The nickels are stacking."

I quirked my head to one side, meeting his unfocused eyes. "What, like, even before the Liberation Front?"

He nodded emphatically, shaking droplets from his hair. "Not to sound like I'm descending into madness, which I very well might be, but as far as I'm concerned, it goes all the way back to the Kaipracan."

"Madness, indeed," Bojack mumbled into his arm, unimpressed, "Surely, this counts as a delusion of grandeur and I'll be released on the premise I've been captured by a lunatic. No sane person puts himself at the heart of conspiracy only to convince himself he's a wanted man. And not the good kind of wanted, either."

"But everything goes back to the Kaipracan, doesn't it?" Dorian tried again, his tone pleading at least for me to understand where he was coming from, but I could only shrug.

"I don't know, does it?" I recalled what Briar had said about this Tenebret person, and the Liberation Front's repeated mention of him. But Dorian didn't seem to hear me, dragged out to sea on the tides of conspiracy.

"Like he doesn't want me dead. I've seen what happens when he wants magikiers dead, and I mean *really* wants them dead. He always gets the job done, whether he sends pora or kirranites. But every time, I've been the sole survivor, the lone hostage, gathered up with only a handful of others plucked off the battlefield here and there..."

He rambled on, lost behind his eyes and seeming almost to have forgotten he was speaking at all, but I'd heard enough to reinforce my old theory. He was a carmavi, after all, and Valencia only let *me* survive her assault on Blackano because she wanted my carmavi magic, saying she'd rather make the bond with me than flat out kill me.

No matter what anyone else said, it was obvious enough to me the Kaipracan had a potential stake in Valencia's war, bearing in mind his infamous abhorrence for the centions. The cooperation of pora and kirranites with the Liberation Front was undeniable. Not to mention, Valencia was the one who freed him from their shared prison all those eons ago, at least according to the history books centions wrote for our teachings – and I already knew just how omissive those could be.

"Were you the only carmavi imprisoned by the Liberation Front?" The words poured out of me, cutting him off mid-thought.

Quirking his head to the side ever so slightly with the ends of his water-darkened hair falling into his eyes, he murmured, "How did you...?"

There it was. But a blockade stopped me at the edge of confirmation, posing the unanswered question: what would the Kaipracan want with carmavi magikiers? Lin had astutely noted the surprising number of carmavi magikiers in the Liberation Front considering their rarity among magikierkind. Carmavi magikiers, who had stifled Kev's magic and kept Seth from reaching out to anyone. There was no doubt about it, they were a hot commodity when fighting other magikiers. But in the end, they were no more advantageous to have than any other magikier. If the Kaipracan really was rounding up carmavi, I doubted it was purely a matter of correctional thinking. If that were the case, he'd do better to round up every magikier he could get his greedy hands on.

Pursing my lips, I averted my gaze from him. "And Bojack, a rossicar healer, was the first and only one taken to the chopping block. A scare tactic."

"Yes, thank you for reminding me as you diminish my worth," Bojack sleepily interrupted, his voice husky and grim. Dorian slouched over him, wearing a contrite expression in recollection of the execution his charge had very nearly succumbed to.

"I'm sorry, I don't mean to brush off what happened to you," I murmured, lowering my head and turning back to the basin where my jacket hung suspended just under the surface of the water, only to discover the stains on the sleeves had vanished. I jerked in surprise, breath catching.

For a moment, I stood completely still, simply staring down at this evidence my magic worked. The last threads of our conversation snipped clean from my mind as I pulled a hand from the water, checking my palm.

Nothing. No cuts. Not even a scrape.

The corner of my mouth curled into a grin. Evelyn certainly had nothing to gain from doing my laundry.

31

It's the Little Victories

THERE HAD BEEN NO HINT OF A LIE IN EVELYN'S VOICE WHEN SHE TOOK credit for these harmless splurges of magic. Then, it seemed little more than an exertion of my will through her magical affinity, as if I were channeling it through *her* rather than my fragile body…

Evelyn couldn't have had the level of control she'd implied.

"That was certainly a switch," Dorian noted, drawing a smile on his cheeks with both index fingers in gesture to my own.

"Ah, sorry, I'm a bit of an emotional mess."

"Aren't we all?"

"Speak for yourself," Bojack mumbled as if in his sleep.

Ignoring him, Dorian flapped a hand unworriedly. "All vibes are welcome here. So what's on your mind?"

"Well, I was just thinking…" My mind consumed me with notions of what this could mean. Of how I could put this to use.

"Happy thoughts?" Happier than the muddy waters of our last conversation.

"Sprinkle some fairy dust on me and I might just fly."

"Now that right there…" He waved a finger around lazily, closing his eyes. "That's a kind of magic I can get behind."

I smirked, nudging his knee with my elbow. "Don't go passing out on me just yet. I can't carry the two of you on my back." Even this had my mind racing with ideas of how to use the magic I had finally exercised without hurting myself. Could I shift the ground under them like a conveyor belt?

"And miss out on the last few conscious hours I'll have with you? Unthinkable," he slurred, even as he lowered his chin to his forearms folded over Bojack and smiled so contentedly, his eyes looked more like crescent moons. Under him, Bojack breathed heavily, his mouth slightly parted in sleep.

That was fast – suspiciously so.

"The last few hours, huh?" I remarked, losing some of my steam. "You don't want to chance sticking around a bit longer?"

"Jacob Cole isn't as partial to Master Hamish as I am. If he knew…" He pursed his lips, seeming to make an effort to catch himself before he said the wrong thing. "And anyway, Mad Jack's a wily one. Spend too long with him, and he's bound to find some means of escape. Least, that's what I've been told." His eyes flitted downward, half-hidden from me beneath long, dark eyelashes as he checked to see if Bojack was still awake. Seeming satisfied with whatever conclusion he'd drawn, Dorian met my eyes again with a roguish glint in the emerald of his own, whispering, "I think he's been trying to seduce me, but I *doooon't* think he realizes this belt comes with a key."

Throwing a palm to my forehead, I couldn't help my bubbling laughter. "Well now he does!"

Dorian ducked his head, eyes going round with another downward glance, only to find no change in Bojack's sleepy aspect. Flapping a hand, he gave his final verdict, "Pshh, *no*. He's a write-off."

"You realize he's still technically on his feet." I gestured to the very obvious leaning stance Bojack had taken up, bent across Dorian's lap, sure, but standing, nevertheless.

Without opening his eyes, Bojack mused, "Enough with the slander. As conventionally attractive as you are, I'm not trying to seduce you, Chuckles." He paused, a slight smirk picking up the corner of his mouth, still with his eyes closed. "Although the fact you would think so suggests you're seduced, effortlessly on my part. But at my age, there's nothing less attractive than a-" He scrunched up his nose in distaste. "-teenager."

"I'm nineteen," Dorian noted.

"Exactly, you're a nauseating train wreck. A toddler with more emotional range."

"Oh my god," I groaned, turning back to the basin. "You were pushing drinks on him all night."

Dorian gasped in a shock so genuine, it looped right back around to melodrama.

"That's not seduction," Bojack dryly noted. Alright, he had me there. "Now if you'd please lower your voice, I *am* trying to sleep."

"We'll go to the tent in a moment," Dorian assured him.

"You've been saying that all night," Bojack moaned, "So much for being true to your word."

"Drunk Dorian is a horrible, terrible liar, and you're just going to have to live with him a little longer-"

"Ugh!" Pushing up from Dorian's lap, Bojack flopped down to the rain-washed tarp on the ground instead, lying on his back with his hands drawn up just slightly by the chains around his wrists. "Enjoy a tarnished conscience once the hypothermia sets in."

Peering over the edge of the barrel with wide, apologetic eyes, Dorian asked, "Are you cold?"

"Oh? Was it obvious?"

He frowned down at Bojack.

I caught myself smirking and quickly hid the expression. For all their buffoonery, the realization struck me that I might actually miss these two once they were gone. Well, I might miss Dorian at least.

As I hung the now soaking wet but squeaky-clean clothes on a line under the tarp, I mused over my shoulder, "You know, I might have a way to warm you up."

"That doesn't sound ominous in the least," Bojack cynically remarked from the floor, but his shivering gave him away.

"I'll test it out on the clothes, then, how 'bout that?" I grinned, a renewed enthusiasm light in my chest.

"Mhm, so we're talking magic?" Bojack deduced, "And you think that's a good idea? Here? On the edge of the newly instated pora capital of the world?"

"But that's the thing. I might've figured it out."

"Might've?"

"I can't know for sure until I try, right?"

"Are you asking me to enable you or are you just an aficionado of stalling for time-?" Bojack was grumbling, but Dorian shushed him, flapping a hand in front of his face.

With a roll of my eyes, I centered myself. Under my breath, a whisper escaped me, too low for either of them to pick up over the rain. "Okay, Evelyn, work with me here. I know to send it through you now, so maybe it'll be easier..."

I was still talking to myself as I reached out and touched the wet fabric of the clothes stretched across on the line. Releasing a breath, I crossed my fingers, and with that, situated myself mentally in a cozy room lit only by the fireplace against the wall, in front of which I sat with my feet practically pressed to the iron screen. With rain pattering on the window, damp socks drying rapidly in proximity to the heat, the warmth of freshly baked cookies sitting warmly in my stomach, it was more than mere imagination. This was a memory, vivid and welcoming.

With it, I summoned thoughts of steam and saunas, water evaporating under a hot summer sun, and tied it back to this moment as I imagined it lifting from the clothes under my hands until they were dry. It was hardly an instant before I felt the clothes drying under my hands, even before I realized the magic was in effect faster than it had ever taken effect before.

Jubilation warmed even me, out here in this rain-wet chiton, only for it to dry against my skin, warm as my socks had been that evening after an hour by the fire.

Grinning euphorically, I turned to Bojack to find both he and Dorian staring back at me in shock and awe – Bojack didn't even try to hide it, to my surprise. Their hair had dried. Their clothes, too. But more than that, even the water at our feet steamed up and evaporated like an impromptu sauna.

Closing my eyes, I let the memory go, focusing instead on the pounding rain here and now, plunking off the tarp overhead. The warmth stayed with me, but I no longer radiated it. And when I checked my hands, joy sang in my chest to find not a scratch upon my skin.

"I did it!" I cried, beaming up at Dorian, and launched myself at him in a full-body tackle. It was meant to be a hug, but in his current state, he hardly had the balance to catch my weight when suddenly flung at him. Still, his arms wrapped around me as we went down together, hitting the tarp on the other side of the barrel from Bojack. Dorian coughed out his lungs with a rasping wheeze, and a loud thump from Bojack's side made me think his chains were probably too short. His pained groan confirmed it.

But none of that mattered right now.

I sat up, the folds of my chiton rippling out around us, and showed my unblemished palms off to Dorian. "Look! I'm not even hurt! The magic didn't rip out of me, it just… It *was* me!" Me and Evelyn.

Crawling out from behind the other side of the barrel, Bojack tapped his noggin and contorted his expression back into that characteristic withering smirk. "Impressive. And how long did that take you to figure out?"

"What's really impressive is how quickly you can find something to nitpick," I shot back, but laughter bubbled high in my chest.

Even as Dorian shone a smile back at me with a gleaming brilliance in his eyes, glimmering with a delight almost on par with my own, it seemed a hollow victory to celebrate with someone who hardly knew me. For a split second, I wished Brett were here. Or Briar. Or Faith or Lin or Kev. To see me just this once when I hadn't failed. To watch me slowly master this power I had been struggling with for so long.

"What changed?" Dorian wheezed against the pain of having the wind knocked out of him. Getting his elbows under him, he sat up slightly to meet my eyes. Only then did I realize how close our faces were, mere inches apart. I had him pinned down, one hand splayed over his chest, my knees bookending either side of his waist and the ends of my chiton, the sole article of clothing I had on, pooling around his hips.

He must have come to the same realization by the intermingling of our breaths – clouds of condensation in the cold night air. Suddenly, he was blushing fiercely, leaning back on an elbow with a hand in front of his mouth as he tucked his head between his shoulders. I scrambled to get off him, heart thundering in my chest as I went tomato red, myself.

"Now who's seducing the drunk?" Bojack dryly noted from just past the barrel. He lay flat on his stomach with his chin resting on his knuckles, peering at the two of us.

"Am not!" I squeaked, frantically rearranging my dress.

We must have looked like fools to anyone watching, and even though that was nowhere near out of the ordinary for me, the very thought of it only made the blush sear hotly down my neck, pooling like molten lava in my chest. Maybe because I looked less like a fool and more like a floozy...

Flustered and waving my hands around with no real goal in mind for them, I cried, "I'm sorry, Dorian, I didn't mean to-"

"No need to apologize," he laughed, sitting up properly with a knee bent to prop up his elbow, resting his head against his knuckles. Though the blush still blazed red to the very tips of his ears, he beamed that wide, authentic smile, and the racing of my heart calmed some. "I definitely didn't land square on the iron ring or anything-" He cut himself off upon catching sight of something over my shoulder, the smile dropping from his face.

I spun, eager for a distraction, only to blanch at the sight of a struggling pora, dragged along between a pair of legionaries. They had her by her wrists, lugging her backwards toward an imposing tent bigger than the rest.

Behind a cage of metal bars locked over her face and belted with leather straps around her cranium, she howled for freedom, but the legionaries were deaf to her complaints.

She quieted as they dragged her past us, in perfect view of our little refuge from the rain.

Jaundiced eyes snapped to our trio, passing from Dorian to me to Bojack, and her bloodred lips shaped a yellow smile.

A tremble shivered down my back. Had she noticed us because I used my magic? But there were no cuts!

"Continuously using your magic like this, you must be delectable!" her distant voice crooned over the rain, and she snapped her jagged teeth at us in a threat made empty behind that mask. The legionaries towed her along, adjusting their grips under her arms, in a rush to reach the blood-spattered tent whose flaps slopped in the wind and the rain.

Bojack scrambled away, pressing back into Dorian and I with a shout of, "Flattery will get you nowhere, honey!"

"A little presumptuous to think she means you, no?" Dorian pointed out, but when I glanced between the gnashing, thrashing pora and Bojack, I could hardly contain my surprise to find her eyes intent on him – not me.

I remembered what he'd said before, what felt like so long ago now. He was always using his magic, he had to lest the trial of achaion ravish his magic, his body, and leave him for dead.

He crawled higher on Dorian in his scaling panic, pointing a fervent finger ahead of him and raving into Dorian's chest, "You promised to keep me safe, bounty hunter!" I wondered if Bojack had even bothered to learn Dorian's name in all this time.

Tilting his head to me, Dorian wore a jaded expression as if to say, "See?" with a gesture to Bojack in his lap. His squirming only came to an end once the legionaries hauled their catch into the tent.

Huffing a mild laugh, I pulled myself to a stand and dusted off my chiton. "Okay, I think it's about time for bed."

"Couldn't agree more," Bojack pointedly remarked as Dorian opened and closed a hand like a ventriloquist dummy mimicking his speech.

We made it back with only semi-damp clothes because of the persistent rainfall. Dorian helped me carry the laundry load and dropped it on one of the unused cots before pointedly tossing the key Bojack needed across the room and faceplanting down on a cot of his own.

This manner of plopping facedown to bed had Bojack dragging along after him, only to miss the cot as he hit the ground. Complaining at length, he shoved Dorian over to make room for himself, but even as bitter as he was, he begrudgingly snuggled up against his shoulder to fend off the cold.

Dorian was out like a light within minutes, but I wasn't so lucky. Whether it was the giddy euphoria of puzzling out how to use my magic or the thunderous and rhythmic rumbles of the war at the trenches hounding me at the border of oblivion, I couldn't lay my racing mind to rest. Nor, it seemed, could Bojack.

Several minutes of stuffy silence had passed, broken only by the distant clamour at the trenches, before he spoke, as if waiting for Dorian's breath to deepen with sleep. I wouldn't put it past him.

Through the darkness, his dulcet voice found me. "You'll face the champion tomorrow."

I paused a moment, contemplating feigning sleep, but a quiet curiosity encouraged by the giddiness in my chest pushed me to answer. "Is that a question?"

"No. I'm sure your unparalleled recklessness can overcome a two-hundred-foot wall." Sarcasm was his native tongue, but I got the feeling this time, his words were genuine. "So will you do something for me?"

I propped myself up on one side, leaning my cheek against my knuckles, and peered over at him through the dark. "I've already signed myself up to do the impossible. My agenda's booked."

"That, you have," he yawned. A faint glow from the torches outside our tent caught in the white of his hair. "So what's one more thing?"

"Such sound logic," I groaned, a tinge of amusement colouring my voice, but dropped the playful tone as I muttered, "Let's hear it, then."

"Allow me to preface with a fact. This champion, who you seem to think has some connection to the Kaipracan-"

"-is the Kaipracan-"

"-has a weapon of achaion. Obviously, that's a problem. As far as the centions are concerned, a weapon of achaion in any hands but their own is a death sentence with their signature on it. But you're the shonte, they'd make an exception for you."

With a roll of my eyes, I dropped back onto my cot. "Not hardly."

"That so? Not the most agreeable lot, are they?"

"You're one to talk. You don't exactly give off a benevolent vibe." I considered it, furrowing my brow. "Yeah, actually, remind me again why I should do anything for you?"

"Because it's not for me." He paused, the tent filling once more with the low hush of slow breathing and flaming torches. Finally, his silvery voice returned through the stillness, a whisper dripping into my ear. "If you bring it to me, I'll reunite it with its five brothers and sisters."

"Five!" I burst, but he was quick to shush to me. Forcing my volume to a harsh whisper, I tried again. "You have the other five? How? Where did you-?" I fumbled for words, tripping over boundless curiosities, and all the while wishing Briar were here to offer me counsel. If she were here, she'd know exactly what to say, but just like with Faith and Brett, I had already sent her off, leaving me stuck with my own incompetence.

"If you want answers, bring me the last weapon of achaion," Bojack hissed across the tent, "It was the only one I couldn't get to in time."

Dorian fidgeted in his sleep, latching onto Bojack by his side with a groggy roll, and that was that. The offer stood in the silence between us, hovering over me in the wake of our conversation, and sleep seemed yet further from my reach.

32

A Dream Come True

Day 20

IT HAD TO BE EARLY DAWN BY THE TIME I FELT MYSELF SLIP INTO A FAMILiar lucidity, aware of the dream I had entered. A dream already awaiting me. I should have realized I would find no peace of mind even in sleep. When, truly, was the last time I was afforded the luxury of peace?

Rather, I was back in the war room from the City of Gates, and just as I remembered it, Seth sat in the chair behind his desk, only now, he looked even worse for wear than he had back then. More than that, he seemed different. A deep, unrelenting sadness clung to him, a shadow cast even when his face lit up at the sight of me.

"Anelisha," he said, carrying the weight of a thousand questions in my name. The last he'd seen of me, Evelyn had grown stronger in my mind, enough to interrupt our dream. But I'd rather he didn't pay that little calamity any mind. Not right now.

Forgetting my exhaustion, I rushed across the fabricated room to meet him and reached out to embrace him only to hesitate a moment from touch when he flinched from my hand. I wasn't even sure if I *could* touch him, or if he'd made himself intangible again, like the last dream. Maybe he didn't want to risk what had happened in the first dream, when Evelyn had slaughtered him in every way imaginable. The very thought of it was like a punch to the gut.

Derailing this train of thought, I hopped up onto his desk, swinging my legs over the edge with my hands clasped on either side of my thighs, and broke the ice with the first thing to come to mind. "Guess they haven't caught onto your magical shenanigans yet, huh?" I considered it, smirking half-heartedly. "The Liberation Front must be full of slackers."

"If only," he mused.

"And?"

"The City of Gates is doing well, if that's what you're asking." His eyes glinted, a spark of something like amusement lighting up in them. "Actually, I received some strange news regarding a rag-tag group of survivors led by our own Miss Knight and Mister Song. You wouldn't happen to know anything about that, would you?"

I grinned, leaning forward on my hands propped up on the edge of the desk. "They already made it back?" I supposed it was a shorter trip without all the detours and hapless wandering. "And? Are they going to Schevon?"

Returning my smile, he granted me a nod. "I had to give my advisors a small push in that direction, but they're going." He faltered, lacking the strength to maintain his smile. The soft expression fell instead to dereliction. "Can I ask you to go with them, or are you still determined to rescue me?"

"More than that, I'm just outside Cerenthior."

His gaze lowered to his hands in his lap, disheartened. "Even down by two?"

"And up by thousands." I leaned forward, unable to help myself from reaching a hand to his face, as if my touch might bring back his smile. "This is the last night they'll have you, Seth. I swear."

I nearly jumped at the feel of his silken hair running through my fingers, although I did pull back in surprise. His eyelids fluttered softly closed, for some reason wearing an ashamed expression, and parted his lips softly to speak.

I spoke first. "Don't feel responsible for whatever happens tomorrow." As if saying that would mend the deep misery behind his eyes.

Softening my regard, I leaned in toward him again, this time cupping my hand over his cheek, the meat of my palm resting along his sharp jawline. I'd never touched him like this before, but he leaned into it.

"I've learned so much more in these past few days of travel than I did in all the time I spent cooped up in the City of Gates. I feel like I've seen so much of Cellana, learned so much about Arillia and the people who live here. I've even learned to use shonte magic without hurting myself and, sure, I've only tried it in small doses, but that's still something. So no matter what happens tomorrow, don't be sorry that I chose you."

He brought a hand up against mine, gliding up my palm so our fingers intertwined against his cheek. "That's..." He gazed up into my eyes – I'd never been taller than him before but sitting on the desk allowed me a good measure of height. "How?" he breathed, wonderment in his tone.

"Oh, uh..." Somehow it seemed unwise to tell him I'd only managed the magic through Evelyn. Through the realization she had a hand in it, but her hand responded almost involuntarily to *my* thoughts and memories. Would he want to hear that? Probably not. So instead, I bit my lower lip, tilted my head to the side so my hair fell over my face and rippled down my chest, and roguishly teased, "Trade secret?"

With an amused roll of his eyes, his gaze followed the wild tresses of my hair, and his eyebrows raised. "Why are you dressed like a Greek goddess?"

I glanced down to find myself wearing the very same outfit I had worn to bed, which was to say, the chiton dress... and nothing else. Now I really was blushing.

"Oh! Hah ha," I squeaked, bubbly with awkward laughter, and recoiled into myself as I readjusted the folds of my dress at my knees, memory of that awkward moment with Dorian bouncing off the insides of my skull. "Just laundry day in the apocalypse."

From woeful eyes heavy with unfathomable torments, he watched my hands play with the ends of my dress, stretching the hems. The corner of his mouth twitched up into the barest hint of a smile, and he pushed up from his seat, only to stumble on his feet, eyes glossing over for a moment.

"Whoa, hey!" I caught his arm, reeling him in against the edge of the desk. Shaky breaths escaped him, small and shallow. He leaned his whole weight against the antique wood, supported by my knees to either side of him and propping a hand flat on the surface. Closing his eyes, he rested his forehead against mine.

"I have to try one last time," he breathed.

"Wha-?"

"Please, Anelisha, I'm asking you to leave Arillia with your friends. I'm glad to hear your travels have been enlightening, so keep travelling. Don't stop for me-"

"What did I just say!" Taking his shoulders, I pushed him back just enough to meet his eyes. "You used to believe in me."

"I do believe in you." He shook his head, the tips of his hair sweeping his brow. "I'm just... I'm not-"

"What, worth it?" I growled, frowning up at him. "There's a war happening here. It's *been* happening. For months, Seth! People in trenches, people *dying* left and right!" I couldn't even bring myself to listen to Jacob Cole's stories tonight, either a pyrrhic victory or a loss and never anything in between. "But even if I was just doing this for you, nothing you say can stop me."

"I figured I couldn't convince you," he sighed on a haggard breath, wilting under my hands. All the strength seemed to leave his body, and he leaned his hips against the edge of the desk to prop himself up.

A warm sensation sent tingles up my spine at the realization of just how close we were. Not a breath between us, the warmth of his body amplifying mine, my hands gingerly resting atop his shoulders and his planted on the desk to either side of my thighs. So close, I could see the exhaustion his weak smiles failed to conceal.

Looking between his eyes, I furrowed my brow and pursed my lips. "I think you've been awake too long." I seriously doubted he could use his magic in his sleep.

"I could say the same to you. Except now I'm the one keeping you from sleep. Proper sleep." He brought a hand to his face, running his fingers through the soft puff of black hair falling over his forehead. "And the night before you attack, too. I should let you go-"

"Don't!" I slipped my hands from his shoulders up his neck, cupping his jaw so he was forced to meet my eyes. "You have no idea what it means to me. To see you here, alive. To be here with you..." My breath hitched. "Don't leave me just yet."

My gut swirled to be caught under his gaze like this. Before I knew what I was doing, I was leaning into him, chasing the feeling.

His mouth parted under mine, igniting a fire in my chest at his taste, but he pulled away before I could relish in it, his mouth still open with shallow breaths. The tip of his tongue slipped into view to trace the curve of his bottom lip. Like he, too, wanted to savour the lingering taste of me.

At first, I didn't know what to do.

My entire body buzzed like I'd been struck by lightning, heart threatening to beat out of my chest, but everything in me centered on the point where my lips had met his, pushing and insistent. I had kissed him. I'd really done it.

The question was, should I have done it?

A beat, and then his mouth crashed against mine with almost bruising urgency. I could feel him losing himself in the fast-escalating kiss.

Calloused hands gathered me against him, flush against his chest, deepening the kiss in our intimacy, and I wound my arms around his neck. He escaped the dark cell of his mind in his exploration of me, his fingers finding the hem of my dress, riding it up in folds as his palm streaked hot fire up my thigh. His other hand braced the small of my back, pressing just enough to set off fireworks in my gut.

This was really happening. Well, it was *really happening* in a dream, but that had to count for something with a dream-walker.

I hooked a leg around him, aiding my hasty scoot to the very edge of the desk. This seemed to snap him out of it with a moan ripping up his throat, and he broke the kiss with his forehead on mine, breathing hard.

Roving his hands up to my waist, he squared my hips, drawing up a meagre distance as his thumbs pressed the cut of my abdomen. This simple touch bolted another shiver up my spine, and I had to wonder if he knew what he was doing to me.

Obviously not, when he breathed, "This isn't what you want." His eyes widened, as if startled by the timbre of his own voice.

All I had for him was a note of belligerent disbelief at his words, but I worked to quiet the agitation he'd stirred up in me. "I don't know what gave you that impression." How long had I been wanting this without ever thinking it would happen? Shoving aside the pining animal in me, I demanded, "Just… tell me what's wrong and we can talk it through."

He met my eyes, a hint of something like surprise in the storming oceans staring back at me. Surely, he couldn't have thought the turmoil spilling out of him was in any way discreet.

"It's selfish of me," he finally admitted in an awful, terrible, *loathsome* return to formality, audible in his very tone of voice. How he'd managed to pull a complete one-eighty, I couldn't fathom. Or, I supposed, it was more of a three-sixty return to the former heaviness of conversation. "To indulge myself, to do this with you when I'm…" His quiet sigh brushed warmth over my lips. "It's not fair of me to get your feelings involved if it's just going to end-"

"Stop talking like that!" I snapped, knotting my fists in his collar. Fire burned in my eyes, molten hot tears brimming at the edges of my vision. "The only selfish thing you're doing is resigning yourself to death! Can't we have something nice? For once?"

Melancholy was etched into the lines of his face, sharp with anguish. "I'm being realistic."

"Well it's not doing anyone any favours," I grumbled, loosening my hold on his collar but not yet letting go. These were dream clothes anyway, it wasn't like the shirt would wrinkle. "You said they know what you mean to me. They won't kill you."

"I never thought they would."

My eyes snapped up to his, a hiss of breath escaping me. "Then what end-?" Sudden understanding struck, cutting me off. Red filled my vision, but my heart tore in half, spearing pain deep in my chest. "You…? You wouldn't do that-"

"You don't understand my position. You can't." His eyes gleamed with moisture. "It's better if I-"

I clapped a hand over his mouth, shaking my head furiously. My voice wobbled over the words, "Do *you* know what you mean to me? Has it somehow slipped your radar that I've been falling for you this whole time?"

The audacity in this man, to look at me with such wide, startled doe eyes! He pulled my hand down from his mouth, but that shocked look of his didn't budge. "I…"

"I'm sorry, are you *blind*!"

"I didn't-" He cut himself off, confusion in the crease between his eyebrows.

Dragging him in by his collar, I met his lips again, as if to kiss away the tainted notion he'd insinuated. He startled for just a moment but welcomed me with an almost instinctive response. Petite as I was, his large hands nearly encircled my waist as he drew me flush against him, his thumbs pressing the sensitive dips of my abdomen. He must have known what he was doing, causing my breath to hitch high in my throat.

He broke from me again. "Wait, wait," he gasped, "Since when?"

"I said this whole time, you incorrigible dingus!" Tears brimmed in my eyes, my breath coming out ragged. "From the moment we met!"

"You're angry with me?" he whispered, brushing a wild, red tress of hair behind my ear.

"Of course I am! After what you said?" I cried, a lump in the back of my throat, a fierce blush burning hot against my face, so hot he had to have felt it. "I'm furious! I'm confused– I don't know what to– Ugh, you can't just…" The words tumbled out of me and trailed off into wild hand motions, illustrating the chaos of mismatched emotions thrashing about my insides.

"I'm sorry," he murmured, so soft, so gentle it hurt. "I won't."

"You better not!" I growled, knotting my legs around him possessively. "Ever!"

He leaned into me, regarding me with heavy-lidded, vulnerable eyes, and placed a soft kiss on my forehead. "Okay."

"Good," I grumbled, wiping at my tears, and quickly changed the subject for the debilitating ache low in my chest. "I can't believe you didn't know. I guess I never acted any other way around you. But *you're* the one who almost kissed me that night on the stairs."

Cocking an eyebrow at me, he turned his gaze upwards as if rifling through the archives of his memory, beckoning a lost file to come out of hiding.

"You don't remember? Back in Blackano, you came down from a work party for a smoke. You'd been drinking."

"I'm sorry, that was… inappropriate of me."

"Really, Seth? You're saying that right now?" I pressed another kiss, resolute and fierce, to his lips and pulled away to find a small, reluctant smile nestled in the corners.

He chased my mouth, slower this time, steadier, and with a gentle fervour. Tiptoeing around me, like he was unsure if I still wanted this. I wracked my brain for a way to show him I did, to let him know just how much I wanted this, but I was walking on eggshells, too.

I released my hold on his collar, ghosting my hands down his chest and feeling his muscles ripple under my light touch. Roving back up under his shirt, my fingers found the pebbled skin of a scar, and my hand lingered over this mark of memory. The wound I'd healed. Small, shaped like one of the many ring stains on his work desks.

I had always run the risk of losing him, from the very moment I met him. Even in Blackano, he had been a target for the Liberation Front, taken captive and assaulted during the attempted assassination of the Key-Keeper. He was Levi Videl's counterpart, the good to his partner's evil, and that had drawn a clear target on his back.

There was never a moment I hadn't been so close to losing him forever, but now, I feared he would lose himself first. He was always so distant from me, even now…

Making a small sound against my mouth, he tightened his hands around my waist, and in one fluid motion, lifted me right off the desk, braced against his body, as he spun until he was sitting where I had been with me in his lap.

The breath rushed out of me as his mouth trailed kisses down my neck, nuzzling in the crook of my collarbone. His hands clawed and crawled up my thighs, then ran up my sides, restless and needy. But his mouth on my skin, just where neck met shoulder, was a magic all its own.

A small noise escaped me, choked at the end. "Is Seth Knox giving me a hickey?" I gasped, feeling his teeth graze my skin and maybe draw a bead of blood, but I wasn't about to tell him that for fear he'd stop. His tongue sent another pleasurable shiver down my spine. "You know it won't be there when I wake up."

His chest rumbled, vibrating under mine as I leaned into the wonderful sensation of his mouth on my skin. Was this really happening? My heart-strings plucked and twanged like a chaotic song taking shape in my chest, at once elated and terrified. To be this close, it would only hurt so much more to lose him. He had to know this… didn't he?

Finding the hem of my dress again, he skimmed his hand up my leg, caressing the sensitive region along my inner thigh. Flames licked up from the pit of my stomach, steaming hot up to my face. The thought suddenly struck me. How far would we go, here in this dream created by his magic? There was nothing stopping us. Hell, there was nothing *but* us.

Was this happening too fast?

Another part of me derided the very notion. Not fast enough, it said. But then came that anxious voice again, wondering if we should stop and talk about… No, I couldn't even name it in my mind, that wicked word I was dancing around even now, let alone say it out loud.

Instead, I figured I should just let him have this. Have me.

I didn't have time to unpack that mildly concerning thought before another shudder of pleasure disrupted the train wreck of my mind, his lips leaving a trail of red marks down my neck and over my collarbone. I bit my lip to stop myself making a sound, tasting the salt of my tears. I couldn't escape my head, not even now that I had him under me. This, all of this, was so different from what I thought it would be.

That it was different from Brett didn't even begin to cover it. It had never been a delirium when I was with Brett. Was it supposed to be? Like it was right now. Like a flash bomb had gone off in my brain. Like I was living in the fallout, my exploration of Seth the only thing grounding me through the blinding white desire, wanting desperately for him to feel as good as he made me feel, to feel as alive as I felt, to *want* to be alive.

Like a circlet of confusion crowning my head, small, satellite reminders of Dorian orbited my messy mind, of finding myself atop him in much the same position. That tiny moment with him which had meant nothing but still felt like something.

Maybe… maybe it felt so different because I never placed Brett on a pedestal like I had with Seth. Since the very moment I met him, I had to shield my eyes from the sun against which I pitched him, gazing up the length of his ivory tower of my own making. And now here I was with my knees bookending his hips, sitting on his lap as his teeth teased my sensitive skin – I never would've guessed he was a biter – and relishing the feel of his hands on my bare skin. Here I was, terrified my words had meant nothing.

Though I had long wished for it, I never really thought I would get to have this with him. Now, those thoughts had morphed into something new, something worse. A fear of losing him.

The time and place had never been appropriate, least of all now. I couldn't get it out of my mind. The suicide – there it was, the elusive and terrifying word – he likely hadn't stopped contemplating simply because I asked him to. And here I was, the night before an impossible siege, the kind that had, until now, taken months just to inch across the scorched plains, let alone reach the enemy's true defenses.

There would never be a time for us. So why was this happening now?

"Seth." My voice broke over his name. "This isn't a goodbye."

He rumbled against my throat, "Hm?"

"You're... you're not doing this as a goodbye..." I couldn't stand to make it a question, to beckon his answer.

"If it was, I wouldn't just be kissing your neck," he chuckled, and went momentarily rigid in surprise at his own boldness. Good to know I wasn't alone in shock and, admittedly, titillation.

"Ah, now I understand," a third voice interrupted, wicked in tone but soft in volume. "Getting what you want was all it took for you to reconsider your *tastes*, was it?"

I started in surprise, recognizing my own voice in my ears.

Seth leaned back from me, a hint of alarm in his eyes, but I shook my head.

"That wasn't me." I dropped my head in my hand, my blood still thrumming with all he'd made me feel, as Seth's body froze beneath me. "Damnit, Evelyn, just leave us alone!"

Glancing around, Seth breathed incredulously, "Since when did you start talking to her like this?"

"Like she's a nuisance? Because she is!" Combing the room for her, as if I would find her simply standing there, watching us like the absolute creep she was, I shouted, "This is a private moment!"

"Yes," she answered, her voice ringing off the very walls of the dream in a rush of sound like waves crashing on a beach, closing in on us from all sides. "An isolated corner. A stolen kiss. And something more. You tested it once before..."

"What the hell are you talking about?" I shouted into the void from whence she spoke. A void beyond the stage of Seth's old war room. The anger came so easily to me with emotion already piled so high in my heart.

"Selfish indeed," she sneered, ignoring me with the same ease she displayed in existing just outside my consciousness. I hated her. More than I had ever hated anyone or anything. "You'll never be alone with her. There's only me."

"Talk about selfish," I snarled, but Seth's grip tightened around my hips again and he set me on my feet beside the desk, unable to meet my eyes. My knees buckled under me, still weak with all that had just happened, but he steadied me.

A shadow fell over his face, dark and deep.

"No, Seth-"

"I shouldn't have kept you from sleep." The dream began to unravel, walls crumbling, floor consumed by shadow.

"Wait-!"

I bolted upright in my cot, cold and alone in the tent as rain pounded the fabric and a horn sounded off in the distance. The waking world glared back at me, oversaturated and grating on my consciousness.

Bashing my fist on the ground beside me, I growled between gritted teeth, "Damnit!"

33

Another Goodbye

"WHAT'S YOUR PROBLEM?" I GRUMBLED OVER THE POURING RAIN AS I left the tent, finding Bojack holding a prolonged groan beside Dorian who packed up the saddlebags of one of those bison-rhino animals. Armoured bison, I'd heard Jacob Cole uncreatively call them. I was sure Faith could have confirmed or denied the nomenclature if she were here.

Bojack hardly acknowledged my presence, fixing his glare on the mug of water – collecting rainwater just as quickly as he was drinking it – clasped between his hands. But he interrupted his own groaning to answer, "All my problems are derived from either too much or too little coffee. Currently, I've had none for a grand total of six months."

"Cellana has coffee?" I absent-mindedly muttered.

"I wouldn't live in a world that doesn't."

"Hey, finally something we can bond over," Dorian mused without looking up from the drenched saddlebags. Making another disgruntled noise, Bojack flipped a lock of hair out of his eyes and sipped his rainwater with all the delicacy of a man who'd been poisoned. In a way, I supposed he *had* poisoned himself last night.

I snuck a peak at him under my eyelashes, wondering if he even remembered the offer he made me. To bring the dragon-bone glaive to him, to reunite the weapons of Achaion. By the sounds of it, he knew where the rest were, hell, he might have even stolen them into his own personal collection, a private museum. If that were the case, he had an ultra-powered arsenal at his impotent disposal. No wonder there was such a high bounty on his head.

"What?" Bojack grumbled, noticing my stare.

"Lin and Kev?" I asked, the first excuse to pop into my head.

In answer, Dorian turned his head, blocked the glare of the luminous cloudburst overhead from his bloodshot eyes with one hand, and gestured off with the other toward the mess tent in the same vicinity as the laundry basin. "They're getting you breakfast from the mess. You should hope they fill your bowl to the brim; it was delicious."

"You couldn't even keep the broth down," Bojack dryly noted.

"At no fault of the chef."

My stomach rumbled at the mention of food, only to turn over with nausea, again at the thought of food. On so little sleep, my very organs felt out of place. Or maybe that was a symptom of the overwhelming anxiety I kept on a backburner in my mind, shouting all sorts of things at me from a distance. At the top of the roster, it shouted that *today was the day*!

"Speaking of stews and chefs, we're stopping in at the Fishery District on our way back. If you love Idina's cooking even half as much as I do-"

"I'll what? Forgive you for kidnapping me?"

Dorian groaned, like he'd heard it before. "This isn't a kidnapping. You're wanted dead or alive by more Clan Leaders than I can count on my fingers across Schevon, Loruna, and *Trime*, my guy. Cellana's biggest hotspot for magikiers trying to *escape* the bounds of law and order."

He gave a small *tch!* noise, making a point of averting his gaze. "And? You can still call it what it is whether I'm the world's most wanted bachelor or not."

Sighing, Dorian noted, "You're lucky I found you first."

"Mm yes, then this growing sense of foreboding I feel must just be a rush of overwhelming gratitude! I'd drop to my knees and thank you if not for the chains." He rattled them as he spoke with an animated full-body wiggle, driving home the heavy sarcasm in his voice. Dorian could only rake a hand through his hair, already dead tired of Bojack's antics no matter the early hour.

"You could always stick a gag in his mouth, you know," I noted with mild humour, simply content to observe their bickering now that I knew I wouldn't have to put up with Bojack for much longer. Together like this, they emitted an atmosphere all their own like a neon bright bubble radiating out from them. To enter it was like standing just a little too close to a firework show. A pleasant distraction, a showy affair, but nonetheless socially exhausting to be around. At the very least, they kept my mind off the genuine explosions in the distance.

"It feels too cruel to take away his favourite aspect of himself," Dorian mused. Leaning back against his armoured bison, he tilted his head to one side and smiled his pleasant smile at me. "So, any idea how you'll do it?"

Nodding to the armoured bison, I deadpanned, "Is that thing a secret mind-reader and are you stealing it's magic?"

"Funny you say that, mind-reading's my cover if the wrong person ever asks about my magic," he commented, expertly casual save for the softness in his regard which spelled his reluctance to head out just yet. We'd known each other less than three days, and yet his departure felt like the breaking of a fellowship. Again, I was struck by that odd sensation I'd felt upon first laying eyes on him. Like I knew him from something, somewhere, just beyond the bounds of memory.

"I… I have an idea what I might do," I muttered, glancing back toward the towering walls of Cerenthior and the train tunnel through which the Arhillin hoped to make their entrance. The heavy rainfall made the city appear more like a shapeless grey blob looming more than two hundred feet high over the camp, but sunlight filtered through the clouds, offering a better view than we had last night. Shimmering silver and an abundance of blues. The city's high walls couldn't contain the soaring heights of the buildings sheathed within, radiant with gleaming, white windows in the few places where they hadn't been shattered or knocked out, leaving only darkness within the frames. Even from here, the Arillian Spire seemed to cast its colossal shadow over everything.

"Idea, singular?" Bojack mocked.

"I'm leaving room for improvisation," I snapped back at him.

"Goodness me, how could I forget. The power of improv is crippled by-" A scandalized gasp. "-*forethought.*" He cupped a hand under his chin, batting his eyelashes with diamond dewdrops jumping to his high cheekbones. The sarcasm practically oozed off him. "You must be firing on all cylinders today."

"Be nice," Dorian tiredly chided, and gestured between Bojack and the armoured bison with an insistent pat on the saddle, splashing in the puddle gathered there.

Although grumbling, Bojack complied, swinging a leg over the saddle with a boost from Dorian. "Call it constructive criticism, then."

Ignoring him, I landed my gaze square on Dorian. "Actually, I had an idea how you could help me." He beamed premature agreement back at me.

"You're headed back to Schevon, right? To Grimshaw Hamish, the Second Clan Leader there. Could you tell him the survivors of Blackano and Arillia are on their way? They're seeking refuge in Schevon from the Liberation Front."

He nodded with that closed-eyes smile I'd already grown so accustomed to. "Nice, short, easy to remember."

"Well, that's not all. I know this is probably asking too much, but you said the Empress makes visits to the Clan Leaders."

He sucked a breath between his teeth, guessing where I was going with this, but I plowed on before he could object.

"Send her a message. Ask her to Schevon. Faith and Brett can explain everything to her, better than either of us could with a long-term game of telephone."

"Someone's after telling her what's happened here, surely." A wary look had entered his eyes, the smile slipping from his face. Even Bojack watched me with slack jawed disbelief, stunned by my request.

"Unless she knows the full extent, whatever she's heard is irrelevant. This is all just a precursor to the war that's coming. A war for the survival of all magikiers, with two championing pieces. A shonte-" I turned two thumbs in toward my chest but paused uncertainly before saying the rest. "-and a domenth."

As I spoke, a dramatic streak of lightning coursed across the sky, followed shortly by the low growl of an earth-shaking thunderclap. I hoped Briar wasn't flying too high in this electrical storm. Though I steeled my nerves and refused to look away, a shudder I couldn't stymy rushed up my spine.

"Domenth?" Dorian echoed, mystified.

"Ever heard of Valencia Lupei?"

"The failed rebel?" Bojack scoffed and waved off all his former concern. "For an immortal, her legacy spends more time on the pages of dry, old textbooks than the realm of relevancy."

The ghost of a smirk plucked at the corner of my mouth as I imagined the tangent Val would go off on if anyone ever said as much to her face, but even that slipped away when I considered how she would react as Valencia. That side of her, the side she'd embraced at the outset of this war, gave little value to words. Only retribution.

"They'll have to write whole new textbooks to cover everything she's done."

Although Dorian raised an eyebrow, there was a hidden cleverness ablaze behind the light-hearted front he put up. Even with the bare minimum information, I could see the cogs turning in his head, trying to find where the pieces fit together. His curiosity about the powered up magikiers, the reason for the Liberation Front's sudden and overwhelming assault on Arillia, why magikiers would ever choose to fight alongside pora and kirranites. I could see him dissecting all of it. But he didn't push me for answers, instead giving a humble nod with a compliant smile.

"I'll pass on the message, but I can't promise Master Hamish will allow me..." Heaving a sigh, he glanced furtively over his shoulder and in a clandestine voice continued, "I can't say much, but Master Hamish is onto something, and it'd be wise not to bring the Empress into it."

"It'd be wiser to ready the magikiers of Cellana for a war they're drastically unprepared for."

Knitting his brows together with an expression like he was being torn in half, he shook his head. "I... I'll speak to Master Hamish, but even then, to think she'd make the trip at a time like this... Unless, well, I'm sure even the Empress would leap at the chance to meet the hero of Arillia. Once the dust settles, of course." For a moment, I didn't know who he meant. Not until he met my confusion with esteem in his regard.

"Me?" Somehow, I hadn't given much consideration to what I would do after the battle. The realization struck me, disturbingly cruel in the back of my mind. Even after all my big talk, I hadn't planned for victory. "Yeah... I guess I'll see you in Schevon."

"That part, I look forward to." He threw an arm around me for a parting hug, practically lifting me off the ground against his side, but I hesitated on a goodbye. I was all too aware how permanent one might be on a day like today.

He was still smiling as he hopped up on the armoured bison behind Bojack, who waggled his fingers at me in a parting wave, oozing with scathing pomposity. Such a taxing standard of irreverence to hold oneself to. No wonder he always looked so exhausted, never helped by his half-dead hair. I waved back with a genuine smile and stuck out my tongue at him for good measure.

Bunching the reins in one hand, Dorian clicked his tongue, signalling the large animal to begin the final leg of their long journey. It snuffled loudly, kicking up mud under it's even-toed hooves, and they were off. Dorian's large backpack blocked the pair of riders from my view as they plodded down the line of tents. Soon enough, the storm's misty grey spray swallowed them up.

The whim of a smile tugged at the despondence written into my face, too meek to lighten my heavy expression. "I hope I won't keep you waiting." The words escaped me on a whisper, whisked away among the winds and the rain, and drowned out by another thunderous clamour raging across the sky.

34

And Away We Go

SUFFICE TO SAY, THIS HAD BEEN ONE OF THE LONGEST WEEKS OF MY LIFE.

Jacob Cole and the other Clan Leaders of Arillia called an assembly of almost sixty people, each accompanied by two or three of their own exalted warriors. The presence of such immense power all contained within the command tent was almost enough to clog up my airways, pressing in on me from all sides. These were magikiers unlike any I'd met before, the greatest warriors of Arillia, and they had all come to discuss how I would champion their legion.

Lin, Kev, and I sat next to Jacob Cole and his troop, feeling entirely out of place the whole time. We held our tongues as they spoke of me like I wasn't right there, but under the long table at which we all sat, Lin and Kev held either of my hands, squeezing their support every time the tone of the long and gruelling discussion shifted into darker territory. These mighty strangers spoke of me, sure, but at each mention of *the shonte*, the distance between this elevated entity and my own identity grew ever vaster.

Briar must have informed Jacob Cole of her mission, for the assembly built their entire plan around the presence of a tree giant wrecking crew. It wasn't until he numbered three that I realized she likely had a mind link open with him at that very moment from wherever she was, keeping him in the loop of her success.

I receded back into my mind, jealousy rearing its ugly head no matter how ridiculous I knew it to be. Briar couldn't speak to me, but I would've felt a hell of a lot better about everything if I was in her loop, too. If she was in *my* head. But even my own mind had fallen to Evelyn's jurisdiction in her mastery of whatever trick barred Briar entry. Evelyn, the channel through which my magic finally worked like it was meant to. Evelyn, who wanted my very consciousness snuffed out like a candle on a windy night.

And so, I sat and seethed beside Jacob Cole throughout the long assembly, only half-listening as a slurry of absurd predictions for the day yet to unfold terrorized my wearied mind. As antsy as I was to get on with it, the dichotomy within me wrestled my equally loud spirit of procrastination, willing the assembly to carry on forever that I might never have to face what lay ahead.

"Once the walls are breached, the city will fall in no less than a day."

"Your words would inspire confidence, if the walls had ever been breached."

I tuned out completely about halfway through, catching myself on the verge of a panic attack and panicking evermore at the thought of it. Champions weren't supposed to have panic attacks. No one else was having one. Not here in this overcrowded tent, teeming with people and voices and an unspoken madness the rest of them didn't even seem to notice.

Stars popped across my vision. A barbed wire wrung out my heart, threatening to tear it straight through my ribcage. I couldn't tell whether time had slowed to a standstill or if everyone was simply staring at me, silent and judging as they ran down the clock to my inevitable failure. I caught myself on that last thought, reason pushing through the jumbled mess of my mind to remind me such fatalistic wording would only get me down. Thanks, brain. As if fatalistic wording was my biggest issue right now.

I couldn't figure how long it had been since the assembly ended, or even what conclusion they came to. I couldn't even piece it together when I asked Lin and Kev for the way my brain shut down, muffling their words between my ears and shredding whatever information managed to break through the mind haze. Finally, Lin took my arm and wrote it out in ink.

Before I knew it, Jacob Cole's assistants were fitting me with the armaments of dead legionaries in preparation for the battle. My errant and unruly red curls spilled out under a glossy black helmet with a Y shaped opening for my eyes and mouth. In it, I felt like a horse wearing blinders, but it almost made it easier to ground myself in what was happening in front of me. Almost.

They proceeded to wrap my arms and legs under my normal clothes with thick layers of cloth and leather, preventative measures in case I was swarmed by gnashing, clawing pora. Great. I might have started hyperventilating then if not for the bizarre dissociation distancing me from this mind-boggling reality I had entered. Atop it all, I wore a glossy black breastplate like those of the Clan Leaders.

The blues of my woolen jacket sleeves and knee-length tabard accentuated the look, surprising even me with how much I resembled a genuine warrior. Lin couldn't help but roll her eyes when I pointed that out, and Kev almost laughed.

Once dressed and ready, Jacob Cole ushered Kev, Lin and I into an army truck, rain drilling the canvas overhead. The camp was alive with busy legionaries, pounding rainfall, and splashing puddles. Everything seemed to be in motion, everything except us.

I sat quietly between Kev and Lin, awaiting the time when we would set off for the trenches, and feeling like an out-of-place turtle with a large leather and steel shield buckled to my back. With my sabre and mace sheathed on either hip and a long-handled hammer leaning against my knees, I was more like a snapping turtle.

The message inked onto the skin of my arm played repeatedly in my head, as if Lin had inscribed the words into the very tissues of my brain.

Briar brings the wrecking crew.

Wall comes down.

Stay with Jacob Cole.

"That's not very helpful," I grumbled without realizing I'd spoken aloud. Jot notes were meant to be mnemonics, but Lin probably didn't realize I was anything but mentally present for the debriefing.

"Hm?" Kev murmured. His knee bounced rapidly beside me, almost as fast as the pounding of my heart. Seventeen years old.

"We'll be okay," Lin insisted, squeezing my hand. I hadn't realized she was still holding it. "Just don't fall out of the truck and do as you're told. Okay?" Fourteen years old.

My head spun, a sickened feeling creeping into my gut. She shouldn't be here. Of everyone, *she* should have stayed back at the City of Gates, where Dyval's protections would have kept her safe.

"I'm not sure I could fall out of this truck if I tried." My feet felt shackled to the floor, along with all my internal organs and maybe even my sense of self-worth. They didn't need to know that part, though.

The earth shook, rattling the metal frame of the truck, and for what felt like the millionth time, my mind scrambled to dissect whether it felt more like a siege attack colliding against the barriers over the trenches or a distant rumble of thunder, refusing to acknowledge the truth of what it was. Another shockwave from the slow encroaching footfalls of tree giants.

Briar had been instructed to lure the tree giants around the outskirts of the camp, ensuring they didn't just storm through.

"You good?" Lin asked, to which I sent her an incredulous look.

"No, I can't say that I am," I said in too high of a pitch and let my head fall into my hands. "Sorry. I'm not helping."

"At least you're communicating," Kev chipped in, and caught his chin between thumb and forefinger in thoughtful contemplation. "Me, well, I have no idea what to say. Our resident optimist is all anxiety-ridden–"

Thumping Kev on the head so he cried out and clasped both hands over the spot of pain, Lin prodded my forehead with the index finger of her other hand and pushed until my face was no longer buried in my hands, forcing eye contact. "Annie. Seth's behind those walls."

"That's what I'm worried about," I stammered uncertainly, flicking my eyes every which way to avoid her iron goggles. "He visited my dreams last night. I… He…" How could I even begin to say it? That he would kiss me, only to announce it a goodbye. That he would even consider giving up, after everything I'd done to get him back… Was it a lack of faith in me, or–

I shook my head against such a horrid thought, reminding myself just how exterior I was to Seth's situation.

"We can't even begin to imagine what they put him through," Lin whispered contritely, as if reading my mind, "Even in so short a time. But whatever they've done to him, it all ends today."

My stomach turned over at the thought, vertigo hitting the back of my throat. "Sorry, but I don't think a pep talk's gonna fix anything right now–"

"Who's looking to fix anything? We're just havin' a chat," Kev pitifully mumbled as he rubbed the top of his head, a scowl carved into the shape of his mouth.

"But you have to admit, this whole thing would feel incomplete without one of your trademark speeches," Lin interjected.

"Me? I thought you were giving the pep talk?"

"I don't do pep talks."

Kev pursed his lips thoughtfully, "And mine just don't compare."

My gaze turned downward, fixed on my hands in my lap as I waded through the murky waters of my mind for the right words. They wanted a pep talk, but I couldn't even find the pep, let alone turn it into talk.

"Hey," Lin murmured, an uncharacteristically soft note in her voice, and hooked a finger on her scarf to pull it down below her chin, showing red welts on her lips.

She raised the heavy, tinted goggles off her face, resituating them like a headband at her hairline, and met my gaze with a fierceness in her own, but I started in surprise at the sight of her eyes. Once merely bloodshot, there was now no white left in the sclera, instead a glossy bloodred encasing the brown of her irises which, too, were different.

Like amber tiger eyes, the iris made up most of her visible eye, perfectly round with a pinpoint pupil in the center. The tint of her goggles had hidden them for so long, I hadn't even noticed this drastic change as it occurred. Now, the band of her goggles bunched her bangs high up on her forehead, revealing the red spot in the dead center and all its branching arms, like too many veins spiderwebbing her face. These, the marks of surviving a kirranite parasite.

"I don't think I have to remind you, you're two for two saving my life and Brett's with your magic, both on your first day having it."

Nodding, Kev chimed in, "I'm pretty sure you're a qualified rescuer extraordinaire, and that's all we're here to do. Rescue extraordinarily-"

Shaking my head, I averted my eyes from Lin's before she could catch me staring. "Is it? Am I really here for *one* person? I've been telling Seth over and over, it's not just about him, and it isn't! These people are fighting, they're *dying*, for Cerenthior. They're willing to lose everything to run the Liberation Front out of Arillia. I have to help them."

"Then we'll help them," Kev simply said.

"I'm the shonte. I'm Valencia's number one target, second only to the centions. No one else should be as intent on putting an end to the Liberation Front as me."

"We're agreeing with you, Annie. So why does it sound like you're having an argument with yourself?" Lin remarked, picking up on the telltale signs of a trailing thought in my voice.

The words poured out of me. "No matter what I do, I stand the chance of making everything worse. Hell, I'm the walking, talking embodiment of 'it could be worse'. Pora will come running if I push my magic like I've been doing, but if I don't try to use it, then I'm no better than an untrained legionary. And if I'm *that* useless, then who's to say we'll ever get past the walls? No one prepared me for this, I didn't even prepare myself. I refused to face the facts, and now Seth-" I choked back last night's tears. "What if he already-"

"Sounds like you're ignoring the Trojan Horse *you* suggested, Odysseus," Lin satirically commented.

Kev nodded. "The wrecking crew will get us past the walls. And when they do, we'll have you and Briar to thank for it. So, really, you've already locked you in as the undisputed hero."

"We can't count on anything-"

"Five minutes!" called Jacob Cole from outside the truck, accompanied by knuckles rapping the metal supporting the canvas roof. My breath hitched. The pounding rain, an incessant haze of white noise, only added to the cacophony blaring in my head.

Did this mean they could see the tree giants? Were they that close? And Briar… I fought myself between wanting to peer around the flap at the back of the truck or continue existing in blissful ignorance for a little while longer. Unable to hold back any longer, I grabbed the tarp and stuck my head out, only to find…

Nothing.

The ground shook, the earth turned up in the distance under what could be nothing other than heavy footfalls. Even from this distance, I could see the rain spattering off invisible entities, of a size beyond what I had ever thought possible for living organisms, and I remembered what they'd said at the assembly. Invisible, until they were close enough that spotting the tree giants would be no boon to our enemies, but rather a detrimental shock.

Several trucks full of magikiers chased along after the sources of these earthquakes, the spray of rain washing over them as they maintained this shield of invisibility around what creatures Briar had roped into our war.

Falling back in my seat with the flap fluttering closed once more, I choked for breath. "Five minutes!" I squeaked.

"You're really stressed out," Lin observed like it was a surprise, pulling her scarf back up over her nose as she spoke.

"Oh, am I?!"

"Well this is certainly a new side of you."

"Trust me, it's not new. It's just, somewhere along the line, I forgot how to act like everything's okay."

Kev and Lin shared a doubtful look between themselves, a silent conversation passing between their eyes. I had to wonder if Kev had known about Lin's eyes. He hardly seemed fazed as he shared in this silent conversation with her. The longer it went on, the more I found myself fuming in between them.

"What?" I finally burst, indignant.

"You? Act?" Kev mused, smirking and leaning back, "I've never heard a convincing lie leave your mouth."

My jaw dropped, brow furrowing in offense at the slight. "How would you know? If it's convincing, you wouldn't notice."

He folded his arms, turning his nose up with eyes closed and confidence in his roguish expression. "Nope. The only person you're lying to is yourself. And are *you* convinced?"

"I- huh?" Bunching my fists on my knees, I frowned up at him. "Convinced of what?"

"That you're not the badass you've proven yourself to be on more than one occasion," Lin matter-of-factly answered, bringing me to whip my head back around and turn my scrunched-up expression at her.

"I don't know what proof you're talking about-"

As if on cue, both Lin and Kev leaned forward, peering around me at each other, and heaved a great, dramatic gasp with their hands covering their mouths. "Don't tell me, you really did fool yourself?" Lin teased.

"Your first convincing lie!" Kev theatrically wailed, clutching both hands over his heart, "I'm so proud! This must be what it's like to be a father!"

Smushing my hands over his face to stop his theatrics at the source, I cried, "Oh, shut up!"

There was no hope for me when Lin started clapping, the most sarcastic clapping I had ever heard. That was the last straw.

Jabbing my elbows out to either side of me, I struck them both simultaneously between the ribs. They doubled over, cackling like hyenas, and I couldn't help my own bubble of laughter, like a helium balloon inflating in my ribcage.

Whether it was the lack of sleep or the breaking of a dam holding back all my stress, a hiccupping laugh escaped me, soon followed by a burst of hysterics to join their own, losing all control of our laughter until we were holding ourselves up on each other. We probably sounded like we'd lost our minds to anyone outside the truck, but I didn't care, relishing in the absurd buzz of the moment.

As my stomach muscles began to ache and my lungs felt about ready to shrivel up into raisins, I steeled my nerves, calmed some by this release. There was no doubt about it, I had Kev and Lin to thank for giving me a blade with which I could cut through the net of despair that had been entangling me day by day in a suffocating coil. Nothing had changed, not really, but their company was truly healing. Even in the face of what was to come.

When the last bouts of hiccupping hysterics finally subsided, Lin poked my cheek, forcing eye contact while her goggles still sat just above her hairline, dark brown roots spilling out under the iron rims. "You're not going anywhere alone, so stop acting like it. We have your back."

Kev nodded, interlocking his hands over his stomach and leaning back once more. "Mhm, and the three of us together positively amount to one whole legionary. Trained and all."

"Sure we do," I chuckled with a roll of my eyes, but my tone was light and my face ached from all the smiling. The muscles must have been out of practice.

Another triple beat of knuckles rapping on the metal frame cut through the lightness in the air, the signal that our five minutes were up. Lin snapped her goggles back over her eyes, letting her bangs fall over her forehead once more, and Jacob Cole and his team loaded back into the truck with us. Somehow, in those five minutes, the world had become a little brighter. The horizon a little clearer. Together, we would do what we had to, to get the job done. Seth, Cerenthior, Arillia. We would strive to take them all back, together.

"I'm the bounce back queen," I grumbled under my breath as the truck rumbled to life, jumping with another colossal footfall, ground lurching. Talk about bouncing back. Judging by the magnitude of this tremor, they couldn't be far from us.

"Yes, you are," Lin chuckled, patting my shoulder as Kev pulled his ukulele from his pack with a grin. The six others seated in this tight space looked warily to Jacob Cole at the sight of the instrument, but he beamed his smile – if smiles could be loud, his would bellow – and stomped his feet to the uplifting tune Kev plucked.

The drive to the trenches wasn't long, and by then, the atmosphere in the back of the truck had changed to one of keen determination, nurtured by Jacob Cole's booming singing voice as he converted the stories I'd heard last night to something more akin to shanties. He sang completely off-key and had some trouble keeping up with Kev's notably steady beat, but he had a knack for making up catchy choruses on the fly. Three of the legionaries with us even joined in once they'd learned the lines.

With the wrecking crew's irregular footfalls acting his chaotic drum beat, doffing the mantle of doom they'd symbolized for me just minutes ago, it was easy to see why so many would answer this man's call and follow him into battle, no matter the odds. An aura of greatness enwreathed him, extending to all those in his vicinity.

Shouts of "Pull them back!" and "Clear the way!" met us as we approached the trenches. The first phase. We couldn't have our own in the path of the giants. The truck skidded to a halt at the border between grassy valley and scorched plains, coming up to the rear of the trenches where legionaries and armoured bison had been gathered in preparation for the assault.

Jacob Cole stepped out of the truck first, immediately taken into the fray of legionaries awaiting his command. His team jumped out after him, taking up rigid stances to his rear, at the ready behind their leader.

His voice boomed across the scorched plains, calling all eyes upon him if they weren't already. "All troops, attention! I'm about to announce our final mission! Final, for today is the day we take back our city!"

The ground shook, a small outcry escaped some, and the vast array of legionaries glanced between each other uncertainly, but all fell into line, an automatic response to his absolute authority. I approached the opening at the back of the truck but froze as the side of his face came into view, revealing to me the darkness cast over his eyes, the resolution in the set of his jaw.

"We're going to mount a cavalry charge, rushing the forces at the tunnel directly! In three separate divisions, we'll ensure the giants reach their mark, and topple any enemies who would topple them! These giants are not our allies, but our tools! They will not hesitate to crush us if we should get in their way! Do *not* approach within fifty yards of any giant!"

There came an uproar of screams, shouts, and shock. The truck bucked under me, and I leapt out if only to catch myself on solid ground.

It almost felt natural, as I splashed into the ankle-deep flooding, to look up and find Jacob Cole silhouetted against the light of a catapulting fireball. In the distance behind him, the grey skies shimmered with the last of the invisibility magic, pulling back like unseen curtains to reveal three massive shadows. At the peak of the fireball's arc, this warm yellow luminance suddenly vanished, eclipsed by the looming silhouette of a mountainous giant, vaguely humanoid in shape but god-like in size.

Not a tree giant, but water-streaked stone and unruly moss, as tall as the two hundred-foot tall wall itself, with two others flanking it on either side, and a speck of gold flashing out ahead of them. The two on its flanks were smaller, one only ranging up to the stone giant's middle and the other barely skimming the round barrel of its stony chest. They shared more of a likeness with the tree giant at the Khuloces Base, more flexible than the stone giant and reaching out for Briar with writhing tendrils and monstrous boughs. These spasmodic limbs whipped every which way in a frayed imitation of hands.

Each of these goliaths towered over us ant-like folk, traipsing skyscrapers with their heads lost in the lowest of the smoke from the city, dragging through the thick, white-grey fluff.

The colossal stone giant crossed the trenches in one stride, swinging a long, pockmarked arm like a pitcher's throw to catch the dot of gold ahead of it, but Briar zipped between its bus-length fingers, shimmering in the light. Ropey strips of pinkish grey flesh and sinew flexed between the cracks in its stony joints, heaving and contracting grotesquely with its every move.

A whip of lightning snaked across the sky, aiming straight for the stone giant. No, not lightning.

Booming off the landscape like deafening cannon fire, a cloud of flame and smoke collided with the giant's torso, from which bloomed an inferno that curled up around it as dust and debris ricocheted off its body. I heard more than saw the bulleting shrapnel spatter the ground. Those in the trenches just up ahead couldn't react fast enough, catching only some of the shrapnel on the invisible wall of force they threw out in their defense.

There was a brief moment of calm, of silence in the wake of thunder, before the clamour of earth rumbled through my ribcage and heaved underfoot, throwing me back against the truck. The giant had dug its heel deep in the scorched plain, catching its balance, but my ears were sharp on the voices calling for medics, sobs and screams filling the sections of trenches unlucky enough to have caught the hailing shrapnel.

The stone giant swiped an arm through the smoke and dust, rearing forward again as the two to either side of it bolted suddenly for the wall in a deranged sprint, full of too many limbs and moving parts.

"A direct hit," Jacob Cole breathed and clapped my shoulder triumphantly before turning to the legionaries once more. He bellowed, "A direct hit did nothing to it! Now that is a sight to behold, but we're not here to feast our eyes, are we? Just our blades on the blood of those who would take from us all that we have! Who would steal away our very lives! Those traitors'll regret ever testing our nerve!"

The legion shouted their ravenous agreement, fury in their voices.

"March on Cerenthior one last time and fortify your will! To the end of all things! To the smoke and the fire! To war! For Arillia!"

"For Arillia!" the legion chanted. His team shouted their support among the sea of voices, reinvigorated by the colossal giant's enduring approach. Beyond their deafening cheers, my attention zeroed in on their own comrades, being rushed to the medic tent beyond our enemies' range.

There were so many voices, more than the audience within earshot of Jacob Cole. Their fury rang in my ears. Not a single soul in the trenches missed this opportunity to lend their enraged shouts to the heart-stopping outcry, until I could feel the deafening cheer of the united Arhillin vibrating in my bones.

I ducked my head, allowing the Y shape of my helmet to act the blinders I so desperately needed with all that was happening. Briar had brought the wrecking crew. Next up on Lin's jot notes, the wall had to come down. I couldn't help wondering, would three giants even be enough.

A rain-spattered mass of grey bodies poured out from the train tunnel across the distance of scorched plains, white mists splashing out around them, clouding their lower halves as they rushed through the rising deluge. One of the leaders at the assembly had mentioned something about the heavy rain making a mud trap of the scorched plains, but there were magikiers capable of solidifying sediment underfoot, and I was sure the Liberation Front had no shortage of likewise abilities.

"That's our cue," Kev noted under his breath, squeezing his hands into fists at his sides and furrowing his brow. The trucks could go no further for the mud, but the Arhillin had other means of crossing the scorched plains, more easily maneuverable and reliable means.

The armoured bison had been led to the trenches over the course of the day, a much slower trudge than the time it took to drive out by truck. Jacob Cole's own loyal mount came plodding through the mud and rain to him, having apparently wrestled out of its handler's grip at the sound of his voice. Equipped with tack and barding, even the animals were ready to go to war.

I couldn't help but shy away from his looming steed, snuffling loudly against his shoulder. He stroked its snout, urging me forward to do the same. "You're with me," he was saying as I hesitantly patted the sturdy animal. "She's easy to ride, no need to worry about falling off."

"Oh?" My voice cracked, and he turned a knowing smile my way.

"You'll just have to trust her."

"Well, you know, I do and I don't."

I watched Kev help Lin onto another mount behind a woman on Jacob Cole's team who'd taken the time to talk to me. It hadn't seemed a real conversation at the time. She was a locator magikier who'd hammered me for information about Seth so as to find him. By the end, she said she had everything she needed from me, but she wouldn't be able to pinpoint whatever signal his magic gave off until we were closer. I had already shut down with the thought she might not pick up anything at all.

Steeling my already frayed nerves, I clambered up onto Jacob Cole's armoured bison behind him, stifling the squeamish response unfurling in my chest. Seated here behind him, I couldn't see anything ahead for the size of him, but adjacent to us, Kev hopped up behind the team's force manipulator whose magic acted an umbrella shield for our unit. The other four on the team were gifted magikiers as well, but if I'd been told their abilities, I hadn't been paying close enough attention to remember now.

I clung to Jacob Cole's back, knotting my fists in the royal blue cloak swathing the neckline of his glossy black breastplate and falling in heavy folds out around him, a flag of hope and leadership for the Arhillin. He'd taken up his shout once more, a decree of strength and fellowship, of unbreakable bonds and unshakeable will, but I could only focus on not falling off. The armoured bison moved faster than I expected, jolting me against Jacob Cole's back with each galloping step.

With the locator and Lin galloping on our right, and the shield and Kev on our left, we led the first division in the charge. Mud flew up around the stampeding force, casting wet droplets up my legs and over the hems of Jacob Cole's flapping cloak, his brilliant blue wings opening wide out to either side of him among the downpour of ash-stained rain and flickering embers.

A cacophony of shouts and drumming hooves, schlepping mud and roaring fireballs burning bright across the sky, haloing his head. With my vision blocked, it was all noise, a tumult of everything happening at once. Of everything, everywhere, coming together into my ear canals and funneling into the stew of my mind. Together as one, we rode for the city.

"This is it," I whispered to myself, a noiseless breath amid the clamour. "The heart of Arillia."

35

Advantage, What Advantage?

THE LIBERATION FRONT SPILLED OUT FROM THE TUNNEL, A SIZABLE force of pora and kirranites so dense, they more closely resembled a mercurial shag carpet coating the world at the base of the wall.

Whether out of fearlessness or sheer loyalty to their cause, a company of hundreds ignored our charge, instead making a break for the legs of the nearest tree giant, smallest of the trio. Metal prongs and shiny hooks helicoptered through the air, wedging high in the jagged bark near the forty, maybe fifty-foot apex of the smallest giant.

Jacob Cole shouted to his legion, giving short commands they seemed to understand with utmost clarity. At his slightest shift, they shifted. At his barest acceleration, they accelerated. They moved as one cohesive unit, trajectory curving on a wide arc. The armoured bison brushed and bumped the sides of their saddles, squeezing our legs between them, but fearlessly rushed the teeming mass of pora swarming around the feet of the smallest tree giant. With grappling hooks and harpoons, they pinned it wherever they could, but how they hoped to overpower something so huge, the weight of which caused the very earth to shake, I couldn't fathom. Not even with the fabled strength of a hundred pora could they bring down a monstrosity like this, and certainly not with such simple weapons.

The distance shrank between us and them, the charge splashing relentlessly across the scorched plains. We had broken from the main force, intent on this section, and they were prepared to face us head on.

Peering around Jacob Cole, I found a teeming phalanx awaiting us. A line of kirranites dug high shields composed of their own fortified hide into the mud, side-by-side like a wall of prickly black carapace. There was only enough space between them through which to poke barbed spear points and pikes of the same tough material, aimed perfectly to skewer our mounts and, at this speed, carry through to impale their riders. With kirranites and pora buttressing these pikes on the other side of the shield wall, I didn't doubt their notorious strength on this front.

And Kev, Lin, and I were at the helm of this unyielding charge.

Time seemed to slow as the distance between our two sides vanished, at once taking too unbearably long to happen, and happening all too suddenly.

I held my breath for the plunge, feeling all the warmth in my body retreat to the safety of my pounding heart, as we clashed against the face of their phalanx, our force attempting to spear through like an arrowhead. For a split second, I expected our mount to buckle and stop dead in its tracks for the seeming wall we had ridden into, but the armoured bison simply reared its head, catching the hook of a pike on the prong of its horn, and brushed the danger aside.

No spears or shields could stop it bulldozing through the ranks of the helplessly grounded with a heart-stuttering disharmony of splint barding rattling and clanking off our enemies' failed defense. Sucking back breath, I peered around Jacob Cole's broad shoulders and fluttering cloak, eyes wide on the devastation we laid in our path. The charge pushed through, forcing a divide through the center of the phalanx and curling out to either side behind them as we began our assault in earnest. Jacob Cole had the reins of his goring war beast in one hand and wielded his war hammer in the other, shattering skulls and cracking bones with each swing.

I glanced down to the hefty weapon clasped in my own hands, too heavy for me to wield unless in both, even as I clung to Jacob Cole's rain-drenched cloak. A shadow flitted overhead, passing momentarily over the head of my hammer, and casting a bright glare into my eyes once gone. Another shadow caught in the corner of my eye, and a third, racing every which way and drawing my gaze skyward.

Through the wind and rain, it was difficult to make out the cables attached to each hook, entangling the smallest giant's many thrashing limbs dangerously nearby. Bodies made to look miniscule simply by comparison had launched themselves onto the tree giant by these hooks and cables, rain and firelight glinting off axe heads as they carved deep into the giant's bark, deeper than should have been possible had they not been inhumanly strong pora. They moved fast, too fast, chopping out thick slices of bark and the fleshier bits hidden beneath. In our distraction with the formidable force on the ground, these ostensible lumberjacks were making fast headway on the narrow midriff of the wailing giant.

Steam escaped its mouth as it grabbed at the pora, catching some which it voraciously shoved down its gullet like a baby bird receiving its first meal, but most were swift with their grappling gear, reacting to the giant faster than my eyes could keep up. Rather than avoid the tree giant's massive hands, they found their footing on whatever came near, using the giant's attempts to thwart them rather as steppingstones to ascend higher upon it.

I could see where they were headed. The narrowest part of its body, the neck, would make a faster kill than splitting the massive creature at the waist. They must have realized, while we scourged the ground below, timeliness was key if they intended to get the job done.

Then I would have to be just as quick.

Raking my eyes over the flailing monstrosity lashing out in every which direction to get a handle on any of the pora ascending its mind-boggling height, I searched out the telltale glints of their metallic hooks, and the sheen of the wire cables to which they were attached.

"Okay, Evelyn," I hissed, "You really butted in where you weren't wanted last night, so I think you owe me this one. Just bear with me."

If I didn't force it, if I let the magic flow through her, if I could just do this right, then I wouldn't have to worry. The pora wouldn't sniff me out, and I could finally call myself *the shonte.* I repeated this like a mantra in my mind, but the echo that reverberated through my head presented a different chant. If I messed this up, it was all over for me. For Jacob Cole and the Arhillin. For Arillia. For magikiers. And for the centions.

"I won't mess this up," I growled, and closed my eyes, holding tight to Jacob Cole's cloak. Releasing a shaky breath, I convinced myself I trusted him not to get me bucked out of the saddle, and buried my face in the sodden material, blocking out all distractions.

It was difficult to say the least, feeling for that connection to the earth while on the back of a beast currently rampaging through throngs of unmovable kirranites as the man in front of me batted the heads of pora clean off their shoulders.

So I moved through the rain instead.

Pounding down all around us, it beckoned to me while my eyes held firmly shut. I could feel it sopping and soaking through the material of his cloak under my face, traveling through the heavy threads down to the mud-caked hems, where it stuck, plastered by the mud and rain, to the bison's belly sharing in this thick layer of turned up muck.

A tug deep in my chest alerted me to the magic seeking an exit, wanting to be expulsed, expelled, but I didn't let it go. Not like I would have all those weeks ago when I understood nothing of this magic. When I had thrust it out of me, pushing it from my very veins to do my bidding. Tempestuous as the very nature it manipulated, it had a mind of its own once it escaped me, and would pour out of me, emptying me along with it, at the first chance.

But not when I channeled it through Evelyn. That part of her still alive in me, so powerful within me. She was the balance. And it was through that measure of calm, of effortless control, which she brought to the magic, that I found myself traveling through the mud spattering out around the hooves of armoured bison, encasing kirranite shell shields wedged in the waterlogged wastes, consuming the bodies of fallen riders stuck in its mud trap. I felt it all happening around me, within me, but I stayed on task, finally aware of the constant pull of the magic to explore and escape.

This branching consciousness of the magic swam through the earth and rain, a vessel through which I found the roots of the tree giant, its tendrils burrowing deep in the dead earth with each step so as to steady itself, grounding itself against its own impressive height and confounding stature.

I followed the path of its roots, climbing through the bark as if it were any other tree. Water and life filled this ginormous creature to the brim, an easy pathway for my magic even inside this conscious entity. I started in surprise with the realization I could control it.

I stopped myself on the verge of giving into this tantalizing notion, recognizing the magic's temptations. Rather, I focused myself on the outer shell of the tree giant, the bark on which sixteen separate hooks and harpoons had been secured.

On a single whim, less than a thought, my imagination took effect upon reality. The bark shifted under each of these metal pegs and became smooth like the interior of the tree fort where the tree-shaper had worked her magic. I didn't allow myself to linger in the magic, pulling back slowly and gently along the path my mind had taken.

When I opened my eyes again, pora were falling from the sky, and my hands were bereft of blood.

A wide smile cut into my cheeks – a premature celebration.

Sure, it wasn't by any fault of my own magic, but it all went to hell within a matter of seconds. I barely had time to register what I was seeing before the brief triumph I had felt snuffed suddenly out.

The moment the pora swung violently out of control, having lost their security when the hooks came undone, the tree giant's multitude of limbs had snaked out, snatching their cables in midair. Before the pora could scramble to escape their tethers, the tree giant flicked its many wrists in a speedy swinging motion, sending these weighted tethers in whistling circles, spinning so fast the pora on their ends blurred into formless shapes.

The whistling became a series of shrill screams, soon joined by the sickening sound of bones shattering under the g-force, their insides turning to sludge inside the durable bags of impenetrable flesh. I was soon to find out, they weren't totally impenetrable.

The tree giant swung several of these playthings into the cavern of its mouth, catching their sloshing, boneless cadavers on the ridge of its flat, beak-like underbite, reinforced with articulated armoured plates of ancient bark and stone. It bit down like a hydraulic press, exhibiting an incredible jaw strength powerful enough to pop the flesh and release the gore bottled up inside.

Most below didn't even notice the rain turn suddenly red, splattering down over us all.

Jacob Cole did. He must have had an eye on the sky, for he shielded me under his cloak just before the gory deluge struck, splashing over all in a moderate radius of the tree giant.

"You didn't get any in your eyes or mouth, did you?" Jacob Cole rasped over the sudden outcry of shrieks. There was a terrible worry in his voice, haggard and disturbed. Only then did I realize the extent of contagion that now drenched the landscape.

I made my mouth a tight line with nervous consideration, struggling to differentiate between the feel of blood and rain when both might have hit my face at the same time, but I'd felt the thick pellets of blood splatter before, and this wasn't it. "No, you covered me in time."

He released a shaky breath. "Good. Good..."

I peered out from under his cloak, searching his face for any hint of red. If there was any, the rain would have already washed it away. "What about you?"

He must not have heard me, signalling his troops and veering again into the fray. I caught a glimpse of Lin on the back of the locator's mount as he did, and for once, I was thankful for her choice of attire, the goggles and scarf each affording their own protection from pora infection. As for Kev…

I whipped around in my seat, searching him out among the cavalry to no avail. A fleeting thought struck horror in my mind, replacing memory with imagination as I couldn't help but consider that he might have been among the riders I'd felt in the mud, dead or still begging for their lives, pleas which fell upon deaf ears. Pulled from their saddles and ripped to pieces or devoured or trampled by their own kin.

No, I had to trust in him, and in the shielding magikier who rode with him. Now was no time to count the survivors – the colossal stone giant had yet to reach the wall, and until it did, the battle was hardly underway.

Petty reassurances played on repeat in my head like prayers, but I resituated myself in my seat and grasped my allotted war hammer in both hands, clamping my thighs around the saddle to keep from falling off. Swinging this hefty thing around would only throw me off balance – how Jacob Cole made it look so easy simply astounded me. But I had to contribute. I had to do more. Otherwise, more riders would fall, and the next might be Lin or Kev, if Kev hadn't fallen already.

I clamped my hands tighter around the long grip, the wet leather of my gloves squeaking a sullen complaint in my ears. One good hit to the head with something like this might even have the power to take out a kirranite, let alone a pora.

So why was I hesitating?

Did I even have to remind myself what they were, what they had done, what they would do? Monsters, each and every one. What chance of atonement did I think they had? Even if they had chosen the Liberation Front's cause of their own volition and weren't just put up to it by the Kaipracan, their cause hinged on the deaths of countless civilians. The rabid force swarming around us weren't magikiers, they were the dogs of the Liberation Front, the pawns of the Kaipracan. Even their own allies considered them expendable, evidenced by the fact they were here at all, the frontline dispatched to face monolithic giants capable of such mindless cruelty as what we all just witnessed.

So why wasn't I swinging?

The universe didn't wait for my answer. Instead, a dark shape soared into my peripherals, headed straight for Jacob Cole ahead of me. By the flapping of his cloak, I doubted he could see this fast-moving projectile launching after him, but I did, and I reacted instinctively.

Grabbing the long handle of my hammer in both hands, more than shoulder-width apart, I barred the creature's path and intercepted its assault.

I hardly had time to register just what I was seeing amid the haze of the pouring rain. A thick, black shell coated the horse-sized body of some strange, winged creature – or rather, all but the blue and green feathered wings sported that armoured carapace – with thorny barbs rippling out from a small peacock-like head and neck to the deep-breasted body of a startlingly large feline. Enclosed between each of its primary feathers, bulbous purple eyes peered forth, but they were wide and panicked, still belonging to the host sheathed within the carapace.

My mind lit up with this information in my split-second observation, and with it, I came to realize, this was a kirranite attached to the body of some griffin-like beast native to Cellana.

In that same instant, glossy black talons clasped the length of the handle in the space between my hands. It caught itself a moment from clotheslining itself on my defence. It mustn't have seen me riding behind Jacob Cole, but now, those countless, bulging eyes zeroed in on me. Namely, the line of beady black eyes curved over its pointed beak.

Locking my grip on the long handle, I twisted at the waist, relying on my core strength against the sheer heft of this beast-host kirranite. It leaned into my attempted resistance, still clutching the pole in its talons, and snaked its long, thick neck past my weak barricade, beak parting in anticipation of a well-placed pecking.

I recoiled but there was nowhere to go from the back of this barrelling bison, and nothing to do against an attack I couldn't block. Not while I white-knuckled the handle of my war hammer in both hands.

I heard the wood snap before I realized what had happened.

My frantic eyes raked in the fast-paced scene all around me, showing Jacob Cole twisted in the saddle, a shortsword gripped in his off hand and plunged into the shoulder joint where wing met body. The beast-host kirranite reared backwards from this injury with a shrill screech, and in doing so, its powerful grip shattered the handle of my weapon.

Reflexively, I battered the hammer's head across the face of this monstrous creature in its backwards flinch. To my surprise, the attack landed, sending the kirranite not only backwards, but down under the hooves of our mount. A strangled squawk escaped its body, soon lost to our speed and distance, but the weight of the hammerhead pulled against my single-handed grip as I followed through the swing. The broken weapon slipped from my grasp, chasing after the injured creature into the slew of mud and bodies on the ground in our wake.

Our armoured bison didn't slow, nor did those to our rear – quick to trample this toppled foe. And here I was, empty-handed save the broken handle leftover in my other hand.

"Careful, now, Anelisha!" I felt rather than heard Jacob Cole shout over his shoulder at me, a language of vibrations from his back to my chest. "Keep your eyes on the sky!"

Dropping the useless handle, I fumbled for some other weapon – mace or sabre? Would either be enough in a battle of this magnitude?

What weakness you accept in yourself! You forget what it is to borrow my strength. Forget those ridiculous weapons! Let me loose in a way that matters!

"Shut up," I hissed, too quiet to be heard by any save the unwelcome voice in my head.

And sure, the voice didn't return, but I felt her there, listening with my ears, watching through my eyes. The captive audience in my head, unable to escape me just as I was unable to escape her.

The blinding light of a fireball cut through the swift dissociation of my mind, calling me back to the present beyond my fretting and fears. With a deafening roar, this ball of furious flames soared overhead and crashed against the leg of the giant our division was in the effort of defending. The rain was quick to dowse most of the fire, but some of it caught, licking stubbornly up the giant's side.

Such powerful flames couldn't be natural in this rain, indisputably the work of magikiers. Judging by their control over it from this distance, they must have made the magic-freeing bond with Valencia. Although I supposed it was safe to assume every magikier in Liberation Front-occupied Cerenthior had done the same.

I wondered if my magic could overpower theirs even when channeled through Evelyn. I hardly had the chance to think it before her anger surged through me at the very notion of testing this theory. An echo of her thoughts leaked in among my own, infuriated that I would use her as a tool.

I caught myself a moment from arguing with the stream of consciousness buried deep within me. She would just have to help me – and by proxy, the Arhillin – whether she liked it or not.

The magic flowed out from my mind, finding the flames and squandering them with a blanketing force until, with one final flicker – a last effort on behalf of the magikiers fighting me for control – the spiralling reds and oranges succumbed to the rain.

With that, I called the magic back to me without wasting a second. I felt it return, gathering in my body once more through that open channel Evelyn provided. Checking my hands for any sign I had pushed the magic too far, I found not a scratch nor a nick. No scars, and no reaction from the pora all around me save their surprise at the giant's recovery. They couldn't trace the magic back to me.

"I have it," I breathed, incredulity in my tone. "I really have it-"

A brief glimpse of the colossal stone giant rearing its leg back for a kick was all the warning I had.

A shockwave of explosive sound and impossible upheaval reverberated through the very air, pushing out from the walls until it choked in my lungs. The armoured bison, fearless in battle, shuddered against the sudden shock, bucking and rearing in the rippling mud as the scorched plains cracked and flew every which way with the violent tremor.

I snapped my head in the stone giant's direction, finding it encased in a cloud of smoke and dust at the wall, from whence large rocks and boulders sailed outward from the place its foot made such disastrous contact with the weakest point in the wall, the tunnel.

"Take cover!" Jacob Cole's voice bellowed beyond the ringing in my ears. The rocks and rubble hailed overhead, flung from the destruction wrought by the stone giant.

The ground thundered, and I recoiled into myself on mere reaction as the tree giant our division protected suddenly bolted for the wall, tearing through pora and kirranites unhampered. Its massive feet kicked up the muddy bedding of the scorched plains, dowsing all in its wake and flooring them heavily to the ground.

It hardly noticed, making a beeline for the wall's vulnerability. Across the scorched plains, the other tree giant, the larger one, sprinted for the wall as well, shaking the earth with each titanic footfall.

I could only watch in awe as the stone giant, with its hands clasped on the top edge of the wall for balance, swung its leg back through the massive plume of smoke and dust for another kick. From the cloud emerged a blackened leg, coated in some strange substance smelling terribly of burnt rubber, dark like a shadow and clinging to the rock. As I watched, this strange discolouration climbed ever higher.

"No-" I choked out the moment I realized what it was, but by then, it was already too late.

The thick gloss of deepest black shadow raced up the stone giant's leg, too thick, too many, to be anything but an entire kirranite slurry. It ate up the stone giant's leg in one leap, swallowing ever higher, up the giant's narrow midriff, devouring its barrel-chested upper torso, its shoulders and arms, all the way to its head, and encased the two hundred-foot monstrosity entirely.

A wailing shriek pierced the heavens, blowing a hole in the clouds as the stone giant staggered back from the wall, flinging its arms and shaking its head to be rid of the shadows clinging to its body. This had to be the largest kirranite slurry in existence, able to span the colossal giant's entire surface area, and sink into it in a contest of wills. This kirranite slurry, colossal as the giant itself, had been hidden in the dark of the train tunnel. No army we could have summoned would ever have made it through such an ambush.

The tree giants to either side of their colossal compatriot slowed to a halt, unable to do anything but watch like all the rest of us as the stone giant curled in on itself, ripping and tearing at the shadows to no avail. I could see Briar sweeping around it, blowing plumes of fire over the stone giant, but her meagre attempts did nothing against the sheer size of her foe, rather calling strands of darkness out from the colossal giant in attempt to latch onto her as well.

I watched as she was forced to retreat, and the stone giant became no more than a colossal host. Two hundred feet high and encased in that glossy black, unbreakable shell from whence razor-sharp spikes more like lances protruded.

A colossal kirranite.

With an arm as long as its overstretched body, it lashed out across the plains in an instant, enclosing the tree giant our division had protected in one spidery hand. The tree giant struggled and flailed against the hand, impaling its catch several times over in the mere act of closing. Each spiny finger had so many knuckles, they wound three times around the smallest of the three giants, and such incredible strength, they squeezed, and crushed it with a booming sound in one flex.

The tree giant hardly had a moment to release its terrible wail before its body folded in half over the colossal kirranite's grip and popped much like the pora had popped between its jaws.

The top half of the tree giant dangled from the colossal kirranite's hand, limp as a doll. No one could move. I could hardly think for the terror taken up in me.

The colossal kirranite sat low on its haunches and swung its head on a neck like an earthworm, turning its bizarre face, cut in the middle with a star-shaped mouth filled with countless stony fangs, toward the half still clamped in its hand. Crouched like this, it almost looked like a child playing with insects. Until it peeled back the strange flaps of that cavernous maw, releasing a piercing noise that vibrated the very air, blurring everything in the cone of its clamour, and redirecting raindrops, now more akin to bulleting pellets capable of piercing through flesh. I could feel my body rattling, threatening to break apart as stars popped across my vision.

A sonic bloom joined into the cacophony as the colossal kirranite swung the upper half of its kill across the plains, plowing through the masses no matter their affiliations. In an instant, hundreds perished, flung into the low storm clouds or cast deep into the earth. Countless legionaries burst into stains against the cloven body of the tree giant.

The smoke and dust had cleared at the wall, rain sieving through the cloud. If I had hoped this was all for something, I saw now that I was wrong. A long crack in the stone ranged up to the top of the wall from the caved-in tunnel, but no opening had been made that our army could use. No hope of entering the city, least of all now that two of our three giants were dead or rogue.

No hope, period.

"Pull back! Scatter-!" Jacob Cole was shouting but cut himself off as he parried an attack by a pora who had come up next to us. I recoiled from their brief skirmish, the audible bludgeoning of the pora's skull reverberating in my own.

The colossal kirranite dropped the slack upper half of the tree giant, which had lost any sense of rigidity after the g-force of that sound barrier-shattering swing. The mangled cadaver fell in a seeming slow motion, crashing over the plains and crushing anyone unlucky enough to be caught beneath it.

A flood of mud and water splashed up around its body, forming a small tsunami that washed against the sides of our division's armoured bison, slopping into my knee-high boots and soaking my feet uncomfortably. The armoured bison kicked and plodded against the waves, spooked into a frenzy, but their riders reacted just as swiftly to calm them back into obedience.

My attention was fixed on the colossal kirranite. It pushed up from its knees into a monolithic stand, swinging its grotesque head toward the third and final giant, which stood a good measure taller than the one that had been ripped in half. Even so, the second tree giant only ranged up to the colossal kirranite's chest, about eighty feet tall at a glance.

The colossal kirranite's arm whipped out like it had with the last tree giant, snaking after its new prey, but this one reacted faster, ducking out of the way and swatting aside the arm with its tangle of limbs. It turned on its heel, fluidly shifting into a runner's stance aiming for the Khuloces Forest. A retreat.

This couldn't be it. The doom of our assault, an end before its beginning, with nothing but spider-webbing cracks and a sizable dent in the wall to show for it. In an instant, I could see only failure laid out before us. The colossal kirranite had taken out hundreds in a single attack, including a giant – there was nothing stopping it decimating not only our forces on the scorched plains, but the entire camp behind us.

"No," I growled, knotting my fists in Jacob Cole's cloak. "No!"

Shutting my eyes tight, I envisioned the very thing I had felt myself capable of not mere minutes ago. The tree giant, a conduit for my magic like any other tree, any other facet of nature which answered to a shonte bound to this element. I imagined myself becoming one with it, the way I had inadvertently pulled a root from the ground to trip Brett oh so long ago. The way I had explored the Khuloces Forest, hopping from tree to tree. I imagined it, an avatar for my being.

The magic flexed easily within me, already warmed up and following the flow of my desires without distraction for the magnitude of what I was about to do. Like a pent-up excitement within the very essence of the magic, it leapt from raindrop to raindrop, puddle to mud, ground to bark, and pooled in the limbs of the tree giant.

"Sorry big fella, but my friends are on the line here and we're not about to lose," I heard myself mutter, distant and near imperceptible for the creaking of wood and thundering of rain on the shell of my being – the tree giant, now a suit my magic wore.

There was no contest of wills to be had. No resilience from the tree giant's consciousness within this seeming conduit for magical energy, an avatar that I could control as well as my own body. It accepted my influence without a fuss, and I found myself sheathed inside it, locked in and sharing its own strange sensory perceptions.

The same way I had become one with the river, one with the fire, one with the forest, I was now one with this eighty-foot-tall tree giant, and the colossal kirranite had its sights set on me.

36

Maybe Mecha-Weaponizing the Trees Wasn't the Best Idea

MY ACTUAL BODY FELT A DISTANT BLUR, PUSHED TO THE BACK OF MY mind while I occupied the tree giant in its entirety. With my magic coursing all throughout, I melded with this surprisingly sublime conduit of magic on a level it didn't even possess in itself.

With this sheer domination, I controlled the tree giant's body as if it were my own and sprang back, crossing leagues of distance in one leap. Chasing my retreat, the colossal kirranite snaked another reaching hand after me on an uncannily long and winding arm.

I landed with my back – the tree giant's back – against the wall, and a hand crunching the flat top of it. All the immense weight of this giant body hung off this arm. In what had to be the largest scale game of the-floor-is-lava in existence, I had my legs pulled up to my chest and feet dug into the vertical stone.

No matter the plethora of limbs this tree giant had at its disposal, I found myself relying on two sturdy legs and two powerful arms, falling back on my own familiar physiology.

The wall supported my immense weight while below, tiny people scurried and scuttled like ants to escape my path. They had yet to realize the shift in the tree giant's actions, the shift toward my interests, now intent on staying off the ground so as not to step on any allies. For as long as I was in control, I would provide nothing short of protection for them.

No matter the wall's resilience to my weight, my shoulder creaked and cracked against gravity's insatiable pull. Damnit, I had no pain receptors, no signals to alert me when I pushed this body too far. I quickly threw my other hand onto the wall as well, sharing the weight, but the damage was already done. For now, all I could do was send a surge of magic to the wounded area, knitting the bark back together in a band-aid solution.

Fighting larger opponents was nothing new to me, of comparable proportions even on this scale. I had speed and agility on my side, but one hit from this thing and I'd be crushed like the last tree giant.

Bounding off the wall with a shower of rubble and dust mushrooming in my wake, I launched myself at the colossal kirranite, a disturbing banshee's wail escaping my avatar like a siren as I did. I crashed against its chest, entangling my many, rooting legs around its middle in a strange extrapolation of a maneuver I'd learned in Blackano. Harnessing the colossal kirranite's shoulders and arms in a pretzel of my own, I forced it into an uncomfortable position incapable of much mobility. The impaling spikes of the kirranite's shell dug into the bark of my own, but this only succeeded in fixing me against it, locking us both in place so as to keep the colossal kirranite from sweeping another devastating attack through the forces below.

Before the colossal kirranite could recollect itself, I clamped its neck between my powerful jaws in a contest of my bite strength against the durability of its shell. An animalistic fury native to this avatar released another shrill scream, deafening and powerful. The kirranite's shell vibrated between my jaws, splintering small chips through this section of its armour, but not enough for my jaws to cut through.

Swinging my weight against its center of balance, I forced the colossal kirranite to stumble and sway out of the stance that had supported us, bashing us both against the wall where the crack made it vulnerable. Another opaque cloud of dust flew up around us, invading what bizarre sensory perceptions were available to me in this body – like an awareness of what was around me without either eyesight or hearing, an echolocation of sorts through the vibrations in the ground and air – but the wall didn't give like I wanted it to.

"Shonte…" thundered the colossal kirranite beneath me, quaking the earth in the low rumble of its impossibly deep voice and rattling my jaws clamped around the muscled column of its neck. The single word seemed comprised of a multitude of speakers, all deafeningly loud and derived from the same mouth, the same lungs. The entire slurry amalgamated into one entity. "Is that you in there?"

I couldn't answer even if I wanted to, the avatar of my will simply raving that lunatic screech as I clawed uselessly at the unbreaking shell of the colossal kirranite. Beneath the shell, I knew I would only find the stony hide of the host body within, a double-layered protection, but I had to take it down somehow. I had to believe I could.

It struggled against my encircling limbs, ever-tightening, constricting, fighting to stay in control of the fight, but my own effort was my undoing as the barbed shell sawed into me. With no means of registering pain, I couldn't have known how my constricting limbs tore against each of these razor-sharp spikes. Not until the colossal kirranite ripped straight through not one, not two, but several of these snaking tendrils, the thinnest of the lot.

They burst like wires strung too taught, hanging on by fleshy threads and pliable sinews much like the pinkish grey material I had seen at the junctures between the largest giant's stony plates. Readjusting my hold on the colossal kirranite, I lit up with an idea.

The pinkish grey sinews connecting the joints had seemed a weakness, a chink in the stone giant's armour. My fingers, less like branches and more like entire trees, scrabbled at those regions, desperate to get anywhere with this attack while I still had the kirranite pinned down, albeit in a swiftly loosening hold for the damage its shell did to me the longer I restrained it.

"Where is your little body, shonte? It must be near," rumbled the colossal kirranite, freeing a leg to send a kick across the plains. Another sonic blast sounded off behind me with this kick, striking through a section of poorly positioned individuals. Whether they were my allies or the kirranite's, I couldn't tell, and it didn't seem to care. "You've learned to disguise your magic, but I need only exterminate each of these insects to find you."

It swept another kick across the plains, digging out a trench on the shovel of its foot and spraying a field of mud and stone over the battle, burying pora, kirranites, and magikiers alike. "*Stop it!*" I wanted to shout, but this body had no voice, only an animal scream.

Settling for action instead, I struggled to restrain this wild leg, but my limbs pulled taut, bark splitting under the sawing effect of the colossal kirranite's spikes. I couldn't afford to attach myself to it any longer, lest I dismember myself – the tree giant – against it.

I didn't have the chance to leap away.

Not when the colossal kirranite broke an arm free from my constraints, in the same motion fraying the bark of the limb I had considered like my right arm. I couldn't react fast enough. It clamped a hand around my waist, but I was larger than the last tree giant, and one creepily spindly hand wasn't enough to completely encircle my middle. Still, its grip was uncontestable.

The colossal kirranite pried me from it, giving me no choice but to release if I didn't want to shred myself against it, and slammed me facedown into the earth and the people below, sending shockwaves from the crater my body carved out of the scorched plains. Not my body, the tree giant's body – fast deteriorating the longer this seriously one-sided fight dragged on.

I aimed a kick out behind me, colliding with the colossal kirranite's jaw, and carried through in a distancing throw. The shell and the stone pierced deep into my foot, but the colossal kirranite succumbed to my power, sailing backwards. It didn't release me as it went, rather dragging me up from the sludge and the mud, to bash me against the wall and crash its other fist against the side of my head.

The tree giant's animal wail died in its mouth, body buckling as it sank against the wall. But my magic wasn't expelled from its body. There was life yet, coursing weakly in the bark and boughs. Just enough for me to manipulate.

It barely registered in the back of my mind that the colossal kirranite was laughing, manic and derisive. A hyena's cackle from the mouth of a behemoth. Then its foot came down on me, cracking through the leg I'd used to kick it. Looking down, I found the leg severed completely off from the rest of my body as the colossal kirranite raised its foot for another clipping strike.

I had to move fast. I was running out of options.

My hand snaked out like a viper, catching the colossal kirranite under its knee, and my other hand grappled its foot, pushing forward with my full weight. I had but one leg to rely on, and with it, I pushed off from the wall, taking the colossal kirranite down with me, under me. We landed adjacent to the ongoing battle. I was only thankful the Arhillin had pulled back, leaving me alone in this battle.

The colossal kirranite gave a powerful, skyward kick, blasting through the sound barrier once again with an echoing *boom!* and half-hidden crackle of stone shattering beneath the shell, but I'd already removed my hands, going instead for the throat. Pressure, I told myself. Pressure would crack the shell where the tree giant's wailing pitch had already weakened it.

Changing gears, the colossal kirranite turned its attention again toward the Arhillin, like I was a mere pest incapable of doing any real harm to it. Rather, took to spraying fields of mud over the army like a dog burying a bone. I knew what this was. Emotional leverage, an attempt to weaken my resolve and make me reckless, but I'd already tried restraining its limbs, to no effect but my own plummeting chances of success.

"*Please... please!*" I raved internally, hands wrapping around the colossal kirranite's throat and squeezing against the perfect rigidity of the shell and stone, skewering on the spikes that covered it.

Who do you plead with? Certainly not the centions, who've long forgotten your plight?

I started in surprise. Evelyn again? Her little drop-ins were becoming more frequent.

Or have you turned to me for help? Accepting, finally, my supremacy.

If tree giants could roll their eyes, this one would've. Still, she'd piqued my intrigue – that she would even think to help me was never something I'd considered. But my hands tightened around the colossal kirranite's throat, adamant to do this myself. It was like trying to open a jar whose lid refused to budge.

Wretch, am I not allowed to enjoy in this? To experience what fun you fail to note in this battle of truly epic proportions? This is the first mildly interesting thing you've done in your detestable lust for mediocrity.

Ugh... Still insufferable, even at a time like this. But what was most concerning was the apparent conversation she was maintaining with my own inner monologue. Not like I could answer her out loud right now, even if I wanted to.

You've succumbed to distraction, weakling.

Oh goddamnit-

Before I could brace myself, the colossal kirranite clamped its hands on my shoulders and squared its feet on my hips, tearing my hands free of its throat as it sent me flying skyward with a powerful kick. Air rushed around me. It was a moment before I realized I was sailing through the low hanging clouds, leaving a trail of shattered bark and splintered limbs across the sky.

I flew, spinning out, over the scorched plains, over the trenches, even over the camp, and crashed down skipping and skidding in the barley field, unable to control my rolling momentum in the catastrophic landing. A mountainous mound of dirt piled up behind me, catching my mangled body. Shattered limbs lay spread-eagled and limp, head lolling on a twisted neck.

The edges of my magic frayed and pulled away, the anchor I had placed in the body of the tree giant slipping. At such a distance, the finnicky magic threatened to snap back to my actual body, leagues out from where I had landed, but I was acutely aware of what would happen if it did.

An elastic return like that – like the one I'd experienced in the Khuloces Forest when carving out that path – would force the magic back into my body through the cuts I had endeavoured to avoid, but from this distance, it had the potential to lacerate all the way to my heart and stop it for good.

It was a hassle just to sit up from the deep crater of my final landing spot, the last in a long line of craters where I'd hit and bounced off the face of the world. From here, I could only watch as my failure manifested before my eyes.

I had a perfect view as the colossal kirranite tore savagely through the Arhillin on the horizon, only slightly misted by the enduring rainfall. It towered over all things, a black shadow against the grey walls of the city.

And here I lay, unable to move this broken body.

For all my trouble, the one thing I had left in me was a resounding feeling of rotten uselessness.

"*What am I doing here…?*'

The tree giant had scarce little life left in it, kept alive by my magic in its skin hankering to escape. Even if I somehow managed to hobble back into the fray, I stood no chance of defeating the colossal kirranite. No chance of breaching the impregnable walls of Cerenthior. No chance of saving Seth…

The Captain of the Arillian Spire's words returned to me, "What are you dying for?"

I'd dragged Lin and Kev into a mess I couldn't fix. To die alongside me and all the Arhillin I'd given hope. And hope, truly, was a dangerous thing.

At least I sent Faith and Brett back to the City of Gates when I had the chance. I had to believe they would meet up with Dorian in Schevon, Dorian who promised me he would send for the Empress. It was the only thing I could believe in, that they would warn the Empress and all magikierkind of Valencia's coming before it was too late.

They stood a chance without me. Hell, maybe they never needed me at all. I'd done all that I could, and if this was to be my end, at least I would die knowing my choices made a difference. Even if, when all was said and done, I did nothing but fail upwards.

Mind yourself. Your fatalism is showing. And it's attracting unwanted attention.

Attention? Oh!

At her mention of it, I noticed a slight pitter-patter of movement trampling the upturned ground around me, so minuscule in comparison to the sheer size of my avatar, I nearly missed it entirely.

Remarkably dense footsteps – with human-sized feet, at that – alerted me to the company of creatures investigating the tree giant. Not kirranites, and not magikiers, either. It was unmistakable, these were pora from the Khuloces Forest. Likely, I considered it, the very same pora who would have picked up the scent of my magic when I carved out that path through the forest, and likelier still, those cruel pursuers who'd been fast on my trail since leaving the City of Gates, who defected from the Khuloces Base in favour of chasing after a delectable meal – namely, me.

Well, here I was, but they seemed hesitant to approach any closer. I doubted they knew I was occupying this strange vessel, but who could blame them. I'd mecha-weaponized a giant, animate tree for crying out loud, and even then, my opponent hit a homerun with me as the baseball and this entire valley, the baseball diamond. Not even I could've anticipated my own present circumstances.

Slowly, this company of pora called from the Khuloces Forest by the signal *I* set off gained their confidence. Apparently, they deemed my immobility a sign of harmlessness, and began toward the smoke and fires with their backs to me. In such rough shape as I was, I supposed their judgement wasn't totally off. Even so, they made a wide berth around the tree giant on their way to the besieged city – no, not the city; to the Arhillin war camp bordering the scorched plains.

I could see it now, clear as day. They would hit it from the rear, and with a majority of the Arhillin off fighting in the effort to breach the city, a force of this many pora – no less than fifty if my estimates were correct – would bring about an infectious end to the fighting.

Whether they targeted the water supply or the wounded receiving care in what was meant to be relative safety, these pora were enough to inflict mass contagion. They would pincer our forces from the rear as the Liberation Front pouring out from Cerenthior routed the Arhillin on the battlefield. Any who returned from battle would be met with further death and would face the threat of infection in themselves.

Lin, Kev, Jacob Cole, and all the Arhillin would be lost.

Damnit.

Damnit!

I couldn't let these pora reach camp, but I could hardly move this broken body. For all the expectations thrust upon me, I couldn't figure what I was supposed to do.

And what can you do? A vermin stowaway on a ship destined for greatness. Incapable of hiding her hand, nor of closing her fist, your pacifism has no place here. So what can you do, when the walls you build up are scaled or crumble to your foes, if you refuse to take their lives?

"*Oh, not you, too!*" I groaned internally, feeling the panic arise tenfold in my mind.

Granted, what you are *doing is wallowing-*

"*Would you shut up?*"

She went silent, as if compelled by my rejection, but I could feel her fury simmering at the back of my mind; a connection that couldn't be severed while I used this shonte magic. I couldn't reject her completely, or I'd reject the magic itself.

But she brought up a good point. What could I hope to do that would keep these pora from devastating the people who took me in, who took up my cause, who were out there right now, fighting for their capital?

With a groan of exhaustion, I found the places where their feet struck the soil, homing in on the feel of this swift invasion. There were too many to focus on all at once, and too widespread to cut off with a simple wall.

I had to blockade them, it was the only thing on my mind – ironic, I supposed, while my main prerogative was to breach the barricade entombing Cerenthior. But I couldn't figure how.

They tortured and slaughtered your kin. Like animals, they pursued you. What life do they deserve?

Evelyn's poisonous voice dripped into the whirlpool of my mind, tainting the thrashing waters of my indecision. With it, a flash of fury struck in the eye of the storm churning within me. And the magic decided for me.

Reading the rush of internal pleas for my own action, it simply reacted, an extension of my mind borne of my panic, of my fury, of the ugly little monster demanding retribution for the terrible things these pora had knowingly done.

With a sound like a felled tree crashing down, one of the tree giant's legs whipped out at the company of pora to crash through them.

A wave of dirt and bodies crested over the massive appendage, sending the pora into immediate graves or casting them into the air, back toward the Khuloces Forest. But I doubted, after a bulldozing hit like that, any of them would be getting up again.

Ice-cold realization seethed through me. "*What did you make me do?*"

You think me capable of force? Dear parasite, if I had any agency in this body, I would have taken what's mine a very long time ago.

She paused, impressed. I could feel how the unwelcome sentiment settled so viciously in the borderlands between our consciousnesses.

You've surprised me. Although it took pushing you to the brink, you did what had to be done, and so you see what must *be done, given the circumstances. Weakling that you are, you would have watched your people perish before taking action had I not intervened.*

"*So you did-*"

Only insofar as my words. The brains behind your aimless brawn. So, am I to understand you'll want to hear my idea?

"*This is all just a game to you!*"

I do so relish the notion of having an impact on the real world once more. Of having a presence. Tangible. Unquestionable. You are my vessel, after all, now carry out my will.

"*Ugh, I'm cringing in the astral realm.*"

I care not. Perish, having done nothing to thwart your demise and the doom of your kind. But will you die satisfied in your pathetic efforts?

I groaned internally. "*Are you gonna share your idea or what?*"

If you insist. First, break off the sturdiest, straightest branch from your host.

The magic responded to her words as it would to my thoughts, without my input. The tree giant's arm slung across its body, snapping off a sizable limb and clearing it of all its twigs and branching bits. My control over the magic slipped between my fingers, transferring completely to Evelyn's looming presence in my head.

"*Wait-*"

Then split one of the more pliable limbs to string the branch like an arrow.

Again, the magic obeyed her command. As if of its own volition, the tree giant dug its fingers into one of its many fractured arms, from which the snaking fingers pried one of the greyish pink sinews from the crack in its bark, the bowstring. With the two burliest arms I had been using, the right – the one which the colossal kirranite damaged – braced the bow, and the left notched the arrow, pulling back in an archer's pose.

"*No! No, stop!*"

If you fight me, my magic will only lash out at you. Is that how you wish to die?

Was this her plan? To let me channel the magic through her so she could control it completely? That *snake*! She'd lulled me into a false sense of security, just like her sister…

Paranoia is unflattering on you.

The body of the tree giant shuddered violently in the effort of maintaining its archer's pose, caught a moment from release as Evelyn tested me. Waiting for me to make my move, whatever it would be. No matter what happened, whether it be my death upon rejecting the channel she made for my magic, or my death at the hands of the colossal kirranite, or even my acceptance of her idea, her will, her use of the magic, there was no outcome that didn't benefit her.

What was that song you were obsessed with as a child? The one you played over and over, to which I can ascribe a great measure of my utter loathing for you? Ah, yes, take a chance on me.

Only a truly evil entity would bring up my Mamma Mia phase at a time like this. Furious beyond words, a half-baked argument poured out of me on vitriol and spite, "*Like one arrow-shaped branch would even pierce that thing's shell! And from this distance? No way our magic could guide the shot with enough accuracy!*" Not unless…

She waited, savouring the moment of her genius, realized. Her pride spilled over, tainting my own mind. Her presence in my head was nothing like the echo of my own thoughts which alerted me to Briar's mind connections, but rather, a sense of proximity. Like when someone hovers too close over your shoulder or sits right next to you on an otherwise empty city bus. There she was, loitering too near to the forefront of my mind, ever encroaching and eager to take over.

Well? This body splinters as you lay here, and when it eventually dies, the magic will snap back and end your life, too. Is that it? Is your pride so great, your ego an unmoving eclipse upon all logic? Would you rather die than heed me? Or do you stall to remove the choice from your inert hands? Her tone mocked me, finding some sick amusement in my confusion, my hesitation.

"*Fine! But keep your hands off* my *magic or I'm turning this mecha-weaponized tree around!*"

Again with this. Do you think me blind? That I can't see what you hide behind this pathetic excuse for humour? You rent out my headspace and think me an unwitting landlord.

"*Shut up!*" The barbed thought merged into a strange sound swathing my head with noise, ringing across the valley with the tree giant's final cry, animalistic, agonized, monstrous. Even so far from my own body, I felt a shiver run down my spine for the wailing echo of it.

The tree giant had been through enough. I'd pushed its body to the last dregs of life, completely spent. Gathering the magic now in the boughs holding the makeshift bow and arrow, I pooled myself in the arrowhead. The limbs fell dead and weak in the wake of my magic. I had to work fast.

With one final exertion of strength, I lined up the shot, needing only to set a course for the colossal kirranite. I didn't need precision, I needed power.

My magic pulled the tree giant's arm back, testing the flexibility of the improvised bowstring, and released. A thunderous snap of sinews and hardwood boomed across the sky with this release, power and speed sending shocks of dust and force in the arrow's wake.

I only had a moment to suck the rest of my magic into the projectile, gathering myself there as it shot off with a speed unparalleled, whistling between the raindrops. Evelyn might've helped this measure of withdrawing the magic for the ease I felt in its execution, but there was anger in her looming presence.

I couldn't let her distract me.

Course-correcting through the air with small bursts of magic manipulating the arrow and the winds, I found myself riding this bulleting branch back over the valley, the camp, the trenches, a wicked fast transportation leaving the rest of the tree giant behind. All of me centered on this object, a kernel of magic and energy sheathed in this rocketing bullet.

The colossal kirranite's towering shadow loomed, fast approaching.

We caught our target by surprise.

Striking exactly where I intended, the arrow needled into a chink in the colossal kirranite's armour, where the shell over its neck had fractured. The needle-point collision blasted through the kirranite's armour, lancing it with enough force to send the entire, monolithic creature backwards off its feet and skewer through it to the wall behind.

Still, the kirranite flailed and latched its overstretched fingers around its throat, stymying the perforation and pinching the long splinter to wrench me out of its neck. Quickly, I moved the fluid magic, exactly how I assumed Evelyn had intended. Again, I sensed her fury.

The kirranite's shell was of a material foreign to my magic, but not the giant's. Beneath the cracks in the glossy black, there was stone and living tissue receptive to my magic. Like a syringe in the colossal kirranite's neck, I slithered from the wood of the arrow into the stony host.

It roared as my infection spread, and with both hands ripping at the wood lodged in its neck, it yanked the arrow out, but I had already pooled my magic in the stone.

"*What now?*"

Oh, do you wish to consult me? To refer back to the plan I had wrought, stolen out from under me?

"*What are you whining about?*"

Shoving distraction aside, I focused on what little I had to work with. The colossal kirranite was still in control of its host, a parasitic organism built to succeed in contests of will and bodily control. I didn't want to think what would happen if it amalgamated me – my magic – with its host body. I had to act fast, before the colossal kirranite found its bearings.

First order of business: I pushed against the kirranite's shell, lashing spikes of stone against this tough encasing. Here and there, stone protrusions jutted out through splinters in the armour.

My attempt to push against the cracks using the stone beneath, to widen the holes and shirk off the shell, had Evelyn laughing at me in my head, an uninvited heckler in the theatre of my mind. The glossy black shell seemed not only to fight the stone, but also my magic, an elastic restraint.

Better think fast. And, I should remind one such as you, smart.

"*You unhelpful-!*"

Tick tock goes the clock, with a squish and a crunch where we walk.

"*Wha-? You're cryptic enough without the rhyming. Here's an idea! Why don't you practice nonexistence! And here's a hint; that starts with silence.*"

Then I'm to understand you care nothing for your allies underfoot?

"*What!*"

The stone giant's head turned with a grating sound of rock scraping rock and a high-pitched wail raking off the glossy, black shell encasing it. Through the colossal kirranite's eyes, I scoured the ground below for any sign that I had, as Evelyn implied, partaken in the squashing of the Arhillin. A vision of red rivers flowing from the colossal kirranite's feet, of broken bodies piled high between its toes, of the Arhillin crushed into a carpet of gore filled my head, but my eyes found no such travesty underfoot.

Bodies littered the scorched plains, half-submerged in upturned mud and deep puddles, but the Arhillin kept their distance from the colossal kirranite, focusing their efforts on the Liberation Front routing them back against the trenches.

Made you look.

"*What the hell, Evelyn? I thought-! Why would you make me think-? What the hell is wrong with you!*" The magic reacted to an intrusive thought amid the boiling stupor of anger seething within me. I felt the buzz of my own warm, golden magic course through the stone giant's arm as a barbed fist with mountainous knuckles swung upwards toward the colossal kirranite's jaw, my jaw. The assault landed with a deafening blast, powerful enough to send the sky-scraping monster sailing back against the wall once again. The sharp elbow of its other arm burrowed deep in the stone of the wall, catching itself a moment from collapsing to the ground.

I bashed the same fist against my jaw again, fingers digging deep into the cracks in the colossal kirranite's armour along our shared throat. With myself, Evelyn, and the colossal kirranite all contained in the vessel of the stone giant, fighting each other through one shared body, we must have looked a confused mess to the Liberation Front and the Arhillin fighting all around us. I didn't care, tearing at the vulnerable chinks in the kirranite's armour. My awkwardly long fingers tunnelled into the holes, ripping and shredding and yanking at the flesh connecting head to body. Thick, black, tar-like fluid spewed out, caking my hand and fossilizing against the shell casing. There, it congealed and braced against my movements, slowing my efforts.

Not enough.

Nothing I tried was enough.

The colossal kirranite's other arm struck out, viper-swift, and caught my wrist in a stone-shattering grip. From an outsider's view, it might have been comical. A monster of this size fighting its own limbs. A typical stop-hitting-yourself bit. Not from my perspective. Just like that, I was out the one limb I could control.

But not out of options.

I'd created a larger opening in the shell, and with the colossal kirranite draped against the wall to support itself, I had more than enough stone to work with.

Like dough, I rolled the stone giant's neck out through the gaping chips in the kirranite's shell, until it pressed the stone wall, and pushed in to mix among it. The brownish grey of the stone giant swirled into the bluish grey of the wall, siphoning faster with the draw of my magic.

Yes, yes! The colossal kirranite grew hollow, the whipping winds whistling through the cracks in its shell and cushioned on the fleshier interior of its fast-depleting host. I drew the stone of the giant up from its toes to its knees to its hips to its chest to its neck, pushing fat and bulbous against the shell like a snake whose meal was twice as wide as its own body. The stone poured out from its neck, fluid like a river emptying into the ocean of the wall.

There, the stone twitched and jumped wildly, making room for itself in perfect imitation of the image building in my head. An arch comprised of shattered kirranite shell and stone giant plating. The colossal kirranite's body ripped to pieces, rebuilt in formation of a two hundred-foot opening in Cerenthior's encircling wall. An entrance fit for the battle at my feet, to usher in the Arhillin's reclamation of their capital city.

The wall disappeared out from under the colossal kirranite, and with it, so too did I, moving my magic rather into the archway itself.

The colossal kirranite wailed its dying shriek, a once mighty roar now guttural and wet with the skin-crawling slop of its host's flesh gurgling and gushing inside the otherwise empty shell. What remained shuddered and creaked against an impossible weight levied against the shell, new cracks chasing up its legs and buckling where the knees were meant to be. Without a solid frame to support this towering height, the shell curled inward grotesquely, bending unnaturally and shattering outward under the pressure. Shards of kirranite shell showered the ground as the colossal exoskeleton swung, devoid of musculature to sustain its standing posture, and toppled backwards one final time through the archway.

It crashed down over Cerenthior and all the Liberation Front who had gathered on the other side of the wall. When the dust cleared, the exoskeletal torso had caved in, shattered and revealing only a goop of pinkish grey guts.

The colossal kirranite, an entire kirranite slurry, was dead.

And you nearly accepted defeat. Weakling.

37

I Did That?

PANIC STIRRED IN ME, FLUTTERING HIGH IN MY CHEST – MY CHEST? – FOR the strange disparity of floating so far from myself. I had never felt so disconnected from my own body. So disengaged, I couldn't even be sure where in the mess of this battle my real body had gotten off to.

Rather, I was the stone and the rain. My magic surged through the wall, slipping down into the moat of rainwater swathing its base. Hooves and feet splashed through me, racing for the open archway. What ground the Arhillin had lost was fast made up in the chaos of all that I'd done.

I must have gone too far, spent too long outside of myself. I'd chased the fight, indulged the magic, and lost myself quite literally. But I hadn't let the magic run wild, instead channeling it through Evelyn. There was no doubting that, for the nuisance she'd proven herself to be as she rode sidecar to my plight.

You're so sure you still have a body to return to. Mm, but I suppose a corpse is still a body.

"*Would you just quit it? God, you're like my own personal Clippy! I'm sick of you-*"

Are you unaware what you've done? Blind to the fruits of your labour? I do wonder, if you've destroyed my body along with everything else that's mine, whether I'm to be stuck with your incessant jabbering as a shadow attached to my ghost.

"*What's your problem? Even if I did overuse the magic, I didn't lose control of it. It was my own doing, all of it.*"

Not hardly, ingrate! This self-preserving nonsense you cultivate in yourself is all to erase me from that which garners you respect!

"*Uh-huh. Keep making mazes with words; it makes ignoring you that much easier.*"

You would have satisfied yourself with death! Placated by the delusion of best effort! You're nothing, not a speck, next to me!

"*Oh stop! You just want what I have-*"

You stole what was always mine! What I have always deserved! And for what? So you can die alongside a legion of nobodies? So you can steal the worthiness of their hopeless plight for yourself, a testament to your false heroism? Thievery is your identity, and me your mask. My face, my magic, which you would use as mere tools to send thousands to their deaths!

"*I didn't-*"

The only credit due to you is the mortality rate of those who would follow you. Every corpse your burden, each casualty a stain on your conscience. Fooled by the mask you wear, beguiled by the serpent's tongue you waggle from it. The anguish of the broken is tribute to you, and you alone!

"*Why are you-? I'm not some villainous snake out to kill the innocent!*"

How many have wiped themselves off the record of the living just so you can play the hero? How many have died for your made-up idol.

"*What made-up idol? I'm not doing this for Dyval-*"

Forget that vile witch. She's not the one I mean.

Then… "*Seth?*"

Do you think you've done a good thing? That freeing him will redeem you of your sins? Of the river of blood at your feet? How many more will you sacrifice for him?

"*I'm not sacrificing anyone-*"

You cross this red river over a bridge of corpses and remain oblivious to your own selfish endeavours. Let them die, that you might keep yourself from sharing in the fate you feed them. You're no better than a cention. Certainly no better than me. And once you've reached your limit, how indeed will you convince yourself to stop?

At her words, an old debate struck up in me like a flame on a wick. How many had I spared with the same reasoning? That I hadn't struck Levi Videl down when I had the chance, nor Clayton when I compared their two evils. How could I spare one but not the other? An unforgiveable double standard. The same line of thinking had followed me here, ridden on my back across Arillia. I wouldn't kill the carmavi who'd cursed Kev, nor even the teleporter who'd stolen Seth away from me either time she had posed a genuine threat. Harmlessness on a harmful scale.

You create new excuses for each one. Bigger, grander, enough to excuse the next. Pushing the limits of your deformed mercy, until you yourself are complicit in the deeds of the spared.

And now… Well now I had taken part in this bloodbath, and even if the circumstances were different, if I wasn't the reason the Arhillin made this last-ditch effort, it was *my* idea to bring in the wrecking crew. It was because of *me* we'd involved giants, and, as it was, because of *me* one of them was taken over by a colossal kirranite, dealing devastation in its wake.

You stand upon your bloated bridge that you might never wet your feet in red. But if freeing one monster redeems another, then free me.

I snapped back to reason with a new fury brimming over the edges of what loose constraints held together my disjointed consciousness. "*Okay, I'll admit, you got me for a moment there, but that's crossing a line. Seth isn't a monster.*"

That's news to me.

"*Everything is news to you. You're a ghost on the outskirts of reality, Evelyn, and only homicidal maniacs want you back. But more importantly, stop screwing with me! I can see right through you, phantom!*"

You say you see through me but fail to discern your own patterns. You spit in my face now as a last resort to action. A desire to do something *as you wander a battlefield in search of a body you will not find. You may have won the day for the Arhillin, but you've lost-*

"*I haven't lost anything yet-*"

Lie to yourself all you like, but never disrespect me with such starry-eyed folly when I can so plainly see the starless night in your soul. You don't believe in a tomorrow. From the day you arrived in Blackano, you've followed the tracks laid bare at your feet, simply because it was easier to continue than to stop. Whether you return to my body or not, there's nothing at the end of this long, dark tunnel for you, and you're starkly aware of it. Whether your Seth has already taken his life, whether your efforts prove futile, whether you face the champion with success or failure, there is no future that will satisfy you.

"*Shut up-!*"

You speak with the menace of one who would act. A pretty mask, pretending as though you hold any agency in yourself whatsoever. You're no better than a pebble snowballing down a mountainside, my dearly detested. What snow you gather, what achievements you claim for yourself, are but the muck amassed from your involuntary path. A path designated by gravity's indifference. A path you make no effort to change. But I am the mountain, and the paths my streams carve from the snow are the branches of my boundless potential.

"*Nobody asked for a demeaning metaphor-*"

I cut myself off with a start, and for once, Evelyn wasn't the interruptive party. Rather, it was the sensation of a golden gleam beaming across the peripherals of my strange, out-of-body senses.

Briar!

Instinctively, I chased the golden glow slicing through the downpour, myself zipping from raindrop to raindrop in pursuit of her. Not that I had any idea what I would do once I caught up. She was my lifeline, a sense of stability in this aimless meandering, an anchor grounding me against the pull of Evelyn's whispers.

Speaking of Evelyn, her presence had all but disappeared. That looming weight, a constrictive shadow cast over my mind and entrapping me within its boundaries, had dissipated the moment my attention shifted to Briar. Just like that, the ghost in my head had been removed to a backburner once more.

Like the lifesaver she was, Briar led me with the uncanny accuracy of someone who knew me to be following her, speeding us along to a familiar mass storming through the mud. Armoured bison thundered over cobblestone and waste, shouldering past bodies, and trampling yet more underfoot. A glow of recognition warmed me up inside as I chased Briar through the raindrops, passing over the heads of not one but two familiar sparks of elemental magic. A fire-shaper and a stone-crafter, riding side-by-side on the backs of speeding mounts. And there, just ahead of them, was unmistakeably Jacob Cole's own armoured bison. Unmistakeable for the body seated in the saddle just behind him, still clinging to him as if I had any measure of control over myself.

The moment I perceived my body through the muck and the noise, something clicked back into place in the core of my disembodied being. A cord anchored in the center of my magic latched swiftly onto my body and reeled me in toward it. I ziplined back into myself, watching from dissociated eyes as I flew back toward this body I had grown into. Wild curls of auburnish red, darkened and flattened by the rain, matted in places with days of unkempt travel. Golden brown eyes shut firmly, a line of heavy eyelashes, dark and unremarkable for the lack of make-up in the wildernesses of Arillia. A body petite and yet athletic, tight with musculature trained in Blackano.

A body no different from soil in which I had germinated, myself a seed of Evelyn's fractured consciousness. How much of her existed inside me? How much of this body was *me*? Was it the dirt of my travels, the athleticism of my training? Was that me, or Evelyn?

Could I ever consider this body truly my own?

For so many years, I had looked in the mirror and seen myself, unquestioning that it was me I was seeing, but now, staring in at myself from the outside, it was like looking at a stranger I felt I should know. Was I in the face hidden from me, buried in the cloak of the rider alongside her, or was I the consciousness floating just outside?

Who was she? What was she? This form that was meant to be me…

In this mess of existence, where did *I* belong? I'd followed the magic, I'd escaped that body on the tides of it, and felt myself as one with it. Shonte magic. Which had ripped and torn through that body, always seeking to escape it. Until I channeled the magic through Evelyn. Through the part of me that wasn't me at all. And in doing so, I, myself, had escaped the body we shared. This magic awoken in me by Evelyn herself, a mere suggestion in my mind which had clicked something into place within me… Something unknowable and yet ever present. Dark and looming in the back of my very being, the shadow that clung to me.

Shonte magic, awoken by and channeled through Evelyn. Shonte magic, like a reclamation of the domenth in me's great power. What did it mean to be a shonte?

This spiraling train of thought cut suddenly short as the universe felt as if to realign. I gasped against the bone-deep chill I hadn't realized had taken over my body, finding myself swathed in the darkness and stiff all over.

My frazzled mind hastened to catch up with the many complaints my body had waiting for me, somehow still awash with relief through it all, simply to be back where I was meant to be.

Only then did I fully register the sensation of cloth on my skin and the hard leather saddle rubbing and bumping uncomfortably under me. I still had my face buried in Jacob Cole's cloak, blocking out all light with my fists knotted tightly in the material – what could very well have been a mild case of carpal tunnel ached in the joints of my fingers and wrists for the non-stop intensity of my grip.

Rearing back with a shaky breath, I opened my eyes only to squint against the glare of firelight swirling high up above.

None of the discomfort mattered.

I was back, and we were racing through the streets of Cerenthior, the impregnable city I had helped the Arhillin breach. The two-hundred-foot archway gaped behind us, carved from the stone of the giant with black flecks of kirranite carapace sheathed in the grey, and Briar soared on wings like golden brushstrokes just overhead.

She blew another bold stream of fire down ahead of us, clearing our path without so much as a nod in my direction, but there wasn't a doubt in my mind, she had spotted my wandering magic and led me back to my body intentionally.

She must have seen the subtle essence of consciousness I had become, my very magic visible to her draconic eyes. I wondered if it looked the same to her as it did to me in that fleeting moment so long ago when I touched the centions' magic, letting it fill and empower me with shonte magic. When I had gazed up at Valencia Lupei and seen a radiant star, and noticed, too, the brilliance sheathed within Briar. I wondered if she always saw magic like this, and why that was, but now wasn't the time for fanciful musings.

A quick glance to either side of me brought another surge of relief, finding both Lin and Kev still mounted behind Jacob Cole's elites on their own armoured bison. Together as one unit, the Arhillin drove the Liberation Front back under the golden banner of Briar's flames, spearing deep into the city.

I had just one final check to make. Testing for pain in my palm, I opened and closed a gloved hand. Nothing. Not a pinch, nor a sting.

The magic hadn't left a single mark on my skin, not even after I'd used it on such a massive scale. That wasn't to say a deep, mental exhaustion hadn't taken hold in me, nor the debilitating wooziness or fatigued trembling in the muscles my body must have kept clenched for all that time.

Even so, I couldn't help my radiant grin as I wriggled joyously in my seat. For all Evelyn's discouragement and reproach, an airy lightness filled my chest in the face of genuine improvement. Finally, *finally*, I was acting the shonte everyone expected me to be.

38

Friend of A Friend

THE ARHILLIN SLIPPED INTO A PRACTICED FORMATION DIVIDED BY UTILity, tearing through the Liberation Front's defenses in tiers separated by magical ability. Hastily built camps in defensible locations provided easier fallback points should the tides be turned again, where those unfit to carry on fighting mounted barricades and medic tents. The Clan Leaders fell back behind an elite force of frontline magikiers whose magic was best suited to storming these streets. Command of the respective divisions fell to trusted subordinates, and together, the Clan Leaders planned the next step of the siege on Cerenthior.

I, meanwhile, rejoiced the part I played in getting us this far.

What had been anxiety and paranoia at the start of the day had slowly morphed into a strange, new confidence with the use of my magic – the proper use, I should say. To have applied it on such a massive scale without any major complications… I could do it again. I *would* do it again.

I only hoped it would be enough for Valencia's champion.

As Jacob Cole and I rode into the central camp not ten minutes out from the heart of the city, the once-pounding rain finally lessened, coming down as a fine mist which clung to my skin and did nothing to dry my soaking hair and clothes. The ground was mud and rainwater, but the fires of war sputtered to life even through the deep-seated moisture soaked into the city. But worst of all was the smell. Now that the downpour of rain no longer sieved the air, my nostrils filled with the sickly odour of blood clinging to everything, made pungent with the earthier stench of turned up mud and a fetid burning rubber smell I had come to associate with kirranite slurries.

Here, surrounded by jogging men and women sorting out the relentless affairs of directing the Arhillin armies while holding this camp, among several others spattered across the water-logged map, Jacob Cole reined his trusty beast to a halt beside the command tent. He was the first to dismount, one leg swinging easily over the armoured bison's side to stand at almost the same height he was in the saddle, before lending me a helping hand, half-carrying me off the saddle.

I splashed both feet on the ground, feet sinking deep into brackish mud, and found myself once again dwarfed by my looming company. Willing the strength back into my wobbly knees, I sucked back breath and turned to find a shadow of movement caught in the corner of my eye. The rider who'd accompanied Lin strode up to us. Not far from them, Kev stumbled off his own mount, looking as shaken and pale as I felt, and Lin hurried along just behind her co-rider.

Seeing me, she broke into a run, splashing mud with each step. She took my hands in hers the moment she was near enough, pulling the hem of my gloves back to reveal... nothing. No wounds, no blood. She met me with a look of utmost confusion, but I didn't let her dwell in it.

Rather, I swept both Lin and Kev into an embrace, barraging them with questions of injury or infection before they could do the same to me. By some miracle – or by the apt riding of their chaperons – they were unharmed.

"Kev? The blood storm... Did you-?" I rushed out, but he shook his head. A rush of relief choked the words in my throat.

"I had my eyes closed when it happened. I didn't even realize it was blood until I saw everyone else..." His voice was thick with dismay or perhaps disgust at the memory. I couldn't blame him, recalling the gruesome sight, myself.

To my right, the locator from Jacob Cole's team who had accompanied Lin spoke quickly and factually. She'd pinpointed Seth's location. I pulled out of the hug to give my full attention, but I could hear Lin and Kev whispering between themselves, whether it was about this new revelation or the fact I'd unmistakably used my magic. There was no denying my hand in the creation of an archway two hundred feet high, but pora hadn't swarmed me. Still, I strained to catch the locator's every word.

Jacob Cole dropped his head in his hand as the battle-worn woman continued her assessment, her words clobbering me over the head, leaving me dazed and quiet. My mind ran in circles to keep up, stuck in orbit around the one thing that mattered. When she finished her report, he dismissed her with a curt nod, only to immediately pull me aside, asking that I not act rashly, to which I could only nod. Everything seemed to be happening just slightly off-kilter, like I was a mere observer, watching from the theatre of my mind.

It was enough just to keep quiet, feign comprehension and do as I was told. Whether Lin and Kev were doing the same or had some inkling of the battle plan, I couldn't tell, but they held their heads high as we were escorted to a small tent and told to wait there, where we were out of the way but easy to find.

In the silence of the tent, I registered the facts I'd been told in waves, moving in and out of my head. Seth was in the exact place Jacob Cole and his team had assumed a man of his stature and value would be kept. Easy to guard, but not so easy to move in a jam. He was high up in the Arillian Spire, surrounded by powerful, overshadowing magical energy.

He was so close, I could practically feel him within my reach. And yet, I could do nothing but pace, awaiting Jacob Cole's signal to move deeper into the city, from this makeshift camp established at this most defensible site, a high-priority target marked by these Arillian commanders prior to the assault. There was no going anywhere while the fighting persisted.

Soon, I could no longer force my legs to move under me and dropped onto a cot at the back of the small tent. Once I was seated, Lin stepped in close, drawing my attention.

"Okay, no more being polite. How the hell did you do that?" she demanded, calling me back to reality. She gestured emphatically to my hands, silently begging the question of how they weren't torn to shreds from the day's exploits with magic.

"I, uh... I figured it out. The magic." I knew I owed them both an explanation – or several – but I couldn't conceive the words to put it all together. How much had I kept to myself, and for how long? They would only be angry with me for leaving them out of the loop.

"When?" Kev curiously asked, as Lin repeated, "But *how*?"

"After that kirranite slurry, when I controlled the fire without trying to, Evelyn spoke to me. She said it was hers, and I realized, I could use it *through* her. Through whatever part of her hasn't left me..."

Finally, I had opened the floodgates, and I told them everything that had been festering in my head between us, that she had been speaking to me while I was conscious and undermining me the more I used the magic.

Appraising my expression – I wasn't even sure what I looked like as I revealed this – Lin hesitated to ask, "She's been speaking to you? Outside your dreams, whenever she wants?"

"Well, no. She pops in and out."

"Is she speaking to you right now?" Kev asked.

"She's not some inner voice – well, she's not a *constant* inner voice. She only ever sticks her nose in when I'm firing off shonte magic."

"When you're using it through her," Lin reworded, "This sounds like some deal with the devil bull. She practically *told* you to use it through her."

"So, what, the magic feeds her?" Kev contemplated.

Lin paced the tent, like a conspiracist deep in a rabbit hole. "She's a split domenth, a being of pure magic who's been cracked down the middle into some half-entity lacking the very thing she's made of. If Valencia can absorb and use the magic of magikiers who bond to her, imagine what Evelyn's doing when you channel your magic through her."

I had to give her credit; she was making more sense than I would have liked.

"How often does she speak to you?" Kev asked.

I ducked my head between my shoulders, seeing where they were going with this. "It's been getting more frequent-"

"-the more you rely on her?" Lin guessed.

"I don't know, maybe." With great hesitancy, I footnoted the stance Evelyn took while I struggled to find my body again. They listened quietly, absorbing all that I said, and before I knew it, I was spouting everything, a flood of words escaping me as I fell back into that panic and anxiety of failure, of never returning to my body, of truly losing myself. So fresh in my mind, any attempt I could have made at a subtle footnote became a detailed outline the more they let me speak. And they let me, never once interrupting.

When all the words I could muster were spent, and all the bottled anxieties had electrified my nerves to the very tips of my numbed fingers, I forced my knee to stop bouncing and huffed a soothing exhale. Kev sat on the tarp floor in front of me, an arm bent over his knee, as Lin shifted and fidgeted uneasily, her chin caught between thumb and forefinger.

In their pensive silence, I felt the weight of my own words like a two-tonne block on my back. The only escape was a change of subject, a welcome change after that anxiety-riddled tirade.

"As if it's not enough that I'm being manipulated by the voice in my head, even Bojack wants something from me."

Kev blinked in surprise and leaned forward with both elbows propped up on his knees. "Whatever he wants, I'd say it's a safe bet not giving it to him."

"Yeah, especially when what he wants is the weapon of achaion-" I paused for dramatic effect. "-to add to his collection." There, that piqued their interest.

Lin stopped her pacing, rounding back on me. "His *collection*? He has more than one of those things?"

"He said something about bringing them all back together. I don't know what for, and I don't know where, but he has five of them hidden in some secret vault." My heart rate levelled out the more I let this new, more tangible problem consume me, a distraction from the inescapability of Evelyn. From panic to confidence to new anxiety all in one day; nothing was ever straight-forward when it came to Evelyn's influence on my magic. I was happy to let it go for now.

Kev tilted his head to one side. "He has to be bluffing. The champion used one, just *one* weapon of achaion to subjugate all of Arillia, and Bojack's been stockpiling five of those mega-weapons, what, just for funsies?"

"If it's true, it's no wonder the whole world's after him. He's been sitting on nukes for who knows how long." Lin rubbed her chin in contemplation. "What'll happen when they're all back together? *Will* something happen?"

"He was being intentionally cryptic and vague."

"No surprise there," she huffed, "But this is a lead. If we have something he wants, he might show us his collection."

"Well, I don't trust him," Kev grumbled, "He's the last person I'd give anything of tactical value."

"Ditto," I huffed, but it felt more like a sigh of relief. Finally, the atmosphere had calmed some, at least for me. Kev and Lin must have noticed the paleness of my face, the white-knuckled grip of my hands on my knees, the shortness of my breath as I spoke of Evelyn. They let the subject drop, and we carried on as if I hadn't said a word about it.

Before long, the exhaustion of the day swept over us, and we took what chance we could to rest. Like cats piled atop each other, our eyes drooped, and dreamless sleep took me far away.

Late evening darkened the world beyond the tent flap by the time Jacob Cole strode in, his heavy footsteps jarring us from fickle sleep. Blood-spattered and smudged with scorch marks, Briar rode atop his broad shoulders, better suited than mine to accommodate her noticeable size growth.

With the tent door flapping back into place behind them, Briar leapt from his shoulders and caught the air on her wings, gliding onto my lap. He stumbled slightly from her take-off, a hint of exhaustion creeping into the lines of his face in that fleeting moment but steadied himself and resituated the mask of focus he wore.

"It's time?" Lin asked, for once straining to keep her naturally flat voice level.

"We've cleared the market district, a direct line to the Spire. Are you ready?"

"Oh, I've *been* ready," I growled, catching Briar in both arms as I came to a stand. My voice betrayed me, however, cracking through the rugged intonation I'd attempted.

Giving a pensive nod, his clever eyes assessed my conviction. "Good, get passionate, but leave room for caution. A scouting team of sensors have confirmed the power level of the champion skulking up top with Commander Knox. The same champion who single-handedly won the day for the Liberation Front in the City of Gates. There's no question he must be waiting for the shonte to come to him. If not, he would be down here, decimating our forces with uncontested ease."

"All the better," I decided, although my insides screamed the opposite, "I'll kill two birds with one stone."

He furrowed his brows, a tinge of concern flickering over his regard. "And the weapon he took from the City of Gates? Unseen for centuries, sheathed in myth and legend, extension of the old dragons' might?"

Lin, Kev and I shared a fleeting glance, wariness in our eyes as Bojack's request flashed through each of our minds. Could I really take it from Valencia's champion? The Kaipracan himself, as far as I was concerned.

"Mhm, good point. Three birds."

"So, uh," Kev murmured, "Now would be a great time to reveal you've had a plan for this all along."

"*Besides* running in guns blazing," Lin tacked on.

"When has that ever *not* been the plan?" I noted, hoisting Briar up in a better position. Her long body draped down to the floor like a cat reluctant to be held. "Better question; how can we even begin to plan for someone like him? Do we have any idea the extent of what he can do? What the weapon of achaion is capable of in his hands?"

"Do we?" Lin asked, returning her gaze to Jacob Cole.

"No one whose gotten close enough to observe his abilities has survived him. For which reason, I am *heavily* advising you exercise caution."

"I think you'll find my middle name is exercise. Heh, you know, like... that old joke... with a twist," I meekly riffed, but a tremble had begun in my fingers at his words and now embarrassment had my face burning red to boot.

"Annie," Kev groaned even as he stifled a chuckle at my lacking delivery, but at least his nerves seemed to have settled some.

Clearing my throat, I shook off some of my own nerves and centered myself back on what was important. "All I'm saying is improvising is as good a *plan*-" I drew air quotes around the word, juggling Briar as I did. "-as any. He can't surprise us if we're expecting to be surprised."

I could practically hear Brett's disdaining sigh. If he were here, I was sure he would've said something along the lines of, "That's not how that works," and I would have mocked him for it, knowing full well he was right. Damnit. At what point along the way did *he* become my voice of reason?

"At the very least we'll have an Arillian Clan Leader to help us out. I mean really, that's about as good as it gets, isn't it?" Lin considered.

"No, unfortunately, I won't be joining you." A strange note of reluctance entered Jacob Cole's voice. "But rest assured, you'll have my entire team at your disposal. They've already secured a ring around the Spire and have catapultiers and stone-crafters at the ready to launch the assault."

"Oh. You're needed here?" Kev guessed, unable to help his pout.

"No, I..." He released a breath, furrowing his brow. When he spoke next, his voice was measured. Serene with a sort of resignation. "I have nothing left to offer the Arhillin but my life."

Confusion knitted my brows as I quirked my head to one side, but his tone was too reminiscent of Seth's just last night. For that reason, my heart skipped a beat, blighting my gut with a sensation of white noise.

Our silence pushed him to explain. "I tasted the blood shower from those pora. I'm sure I wasn't the only one, and I doubt all those who'd been infected will come forward, but I mean to take responsibility for my life and what becomes of it. The infection will spread fastest in these final hours-" He cut himself off with a dark chuckle. "It's almost better that you'll be tucked away in the Spire as the infection renovates the playing field."

"So what? You're just giving up?" I growled, my voice wavering. Not again. Not another goodbye. "I can heal you! I've used my magic to heal others!" Minor wounds and bodily harm, never pora infection.

My enthusiasm slipped off him like oil on water as he shook his head, wearing a dejected expression. "It's been tried before. Any measure of magic driving out the infection will only make a half-pora of me as it eats up your attempts. The moment their pollution entered my system, I was compromised. I could feel my magic slipping between my fingers the more I grasped for it."

"Well why can't you just be half?"

He turned a quizzical eye on me. "Imposters get by on halves, whether they mean to or not. Half magic, half bloodlust. Still contagious. Half-pora are the ruin of their own communities."

Looking to Kev, then to Lin, I flailed my hands in search of *something*. Some reason to bring him back from the edge.

They wouldn't meet my eyes.

Losing traction, I rounded back on him. "But full pora have been working alongside magikiers! The Liberation Front proves it-"

"What you're speaking of is treasonous-"

"Is it treason to give yourself a second chance at life?"

"By the Empress' laws-"

"You didn't care about those when you let Dorian leave with Bojack!"

Knowing eyes met my indignant regard. His voice was calm on the words, "I trust in the Second Clan Leader of Schevon to make judgements and personal sacrifices, the same way I accepted that I would make my own for this war. I could have led the Arhillin in a northern retreat and become a leader of refugees in Schevon, but I *chose* to stand at Cerenthior's gates and *fight*, unafraid to die for what I believe in. I won't go back on myself. I won't become a distortion of everything I believe in."

"But this isn't..." *Fair*, I wanted to say. But what was fairness in times like these?

"I'm only fortunate I got to see my city under our banner one last time. Because of you."

The white noise traveled up my body, ringing between my ears. I was left speechless and contrite, bogged down by the same helplessness I had felt in the dream with Seth. A push to resist, to stave off his surrender, but it was like shoving air. My words could do nothing to overturn his decision.

"Annie," Lin murmured, her voice politely quieted but poignant with unspoken meaning. When I met her attempted consolation with desperation in my stare, she insisted, "We have to go."

Jacob Cole dipped his head in a nod, turning a gracious smile toward her. I could tell by the lines around his mouth, it was forced. "I'll take you to your escort and you'll be on your way."

We hardly walked more than twenty feet from the tent, so why did it feel so much like a walk down death row. Not just for me, and not just for

Jacob Cole. All those who bustled through the mud, carried atop stretchers and gurneys, were marked for death in my eyes. Even here, so close to victory. Especially here.

We were too close. Close to the end. But whose end was it?

As we walked, Jacob Cole signalled his team with a beckoning pair of fingers. "We've routed their forces back to the outlying city districts. The champion hiding in his tower won't have any reinforcements except those already holed up inside with him."

A surprising number of legionaries bustled around the base of the sky-scraping Spire, the apex of which vanished into the ceiling of clouds. They marched past us, staggering themselves in groups of six around the circumference of the cylindrical tower.

"As for the Spire itself, we've cleared most of the lower floors, but found ourselves jammed at the midway point. It's undoubtedly the champion's doing, unmatched in magical ability. It'd take more force-wielders and stone-crafters than we have at our disposal to burrow through his defenses, but we have another use for them. Monica, here, is in charge of the blitz."

He gestured to a bespectacled and ruby-haired woman on his team, a catapultier rossicar now that I recalled – even so, I had no clue what that meant for her magical ability. The dampness of the rain had frazzled her hair, lending a mad scientist aspect to her already high-energy demeanour.

I gave a meek wave, having hoped to avoid learning any names, but she sprang forward, shaking Kev's hand, then Lin's, and finally mine with an animated fervour. Her eyes crinkled with a wide, toothy smile, happier than I thought possible on the battlements surrounding the Spire.

"Perfect timing!" she crowed, "We were just running out of stone-crafters. And it'll certainly help you to have the sails on this one." She plucked the tips of Briar's membranous wings between thumb and forefinger, scrutinising her closely until she hissed and swatted the woman's intrusive hands away.

"It's an unorthodox plan," Jacob Cole noted in thoughtful consideration, rubbing the back of his neck uncertainly, "But I take it you're no stranger to unorthodox."

"That's an understatement," Kev mused.

Grinning wider, Monica bounced on her heels, glasses slipping down her straight nose, and pulled Kev and Lin along by their wrists. They dragged me between them by our linked arms.

"My thinking is, he wants to fight the shonte. To see the shonte in action, close-up and firsthand, otherwise he would have sniped you from a distance without a second thought." She glanced backwards over her shoulder, meeting my eyes. "He's one to do that. But you won't be going alone, not really. Eleven other breach groups will launch simultaneously, not quite decoys but… Well, that's not for you to concern yourselves with! They'll tackle whatever's hidden inside those walls once they're in, and you three and a half will focus on finding the champion and putting an end to him. Got it? Good. Now, you…" She pulled Lin in close at her side, giving a rundown of what she had to do as our stone-crafter, and my mind began to wander.

I couldn't help a cursory glance over my shoulder, finding Jacob Cole's sad gaze as he watched us go. I hadn't said enough, not nearly. Even now, I hardly had time to think what to say as I was drawn away. What words had been left unsaid, what goodbye could hold enough respect for this frontrunning Clan Leader of Arillia.

Legionaries hustled and bustled in our wake, blocking my view save the head of height he had over everyone. Amid all the commotion, I saw him turn, and with that, he was gone.

"You're unlikely to be shot out of the air, especially with a dragon's wings guiding your flight, but your window of opportunity won't stay open forever. You'll have to act fast," Monica was saying, the punctuation at the end of her exuberant spiel. A spiel I had almost entirely missed. "Think you can do it?"

"Of course I can," Lin answered, but she sounded as if deep in thought. Meanwhile, I internally scolded myself for succumbing to distraction yet again. Really, how scatter-brained could I get, failing to pay attention for *two* seconds?

Monica ushered us forward, something about having found the perfect positioning for us, and Briar's coils tightened around my waist, anchoring herself to me.

It was like I'd skipped ahead in time and suddenly everything was rushing around me. Whatever I missed, it certainly seemed dire.

"Launch in three!" a distant voice shouted.

"Wait-" I choked out, a last-ditch effort to understand my situation.

"Two!"

"You're *long* past the time for waiting!" chimed Monica, "Ready?"

Determination shone in Lin's eyes behind her goggles and she answered with a curt, "Mhm." Although she spoke for herself, Monica accepted her green light as the group standard.

"One!"

With a quick wink for me, perhaps meant to be encouraging, Monica stuck out her hands and made a grand, sweeping motion like she was throwing an invisible table. And yet, as she swung upwards, it became dreadfully clear to me that this was no mime act.

The ground disappeared beneath my feet, the very world launching suddenly away from me. Whistling winds choked my screams, carrying them off behind me.

I held onto Kev and Lin for dear life as Briar's wings sliced the air above us, guiding our swift ascension. All around the Spire, groups just like ours soared through the air toward the top – the other breachers.

I hardly had time to register what Lin was doing at my side, nor even that I could hardly distinguish her beyond the invisible shimmer wrapped around my friends, before the stone wall of the Spire tore open in front of us. Through the widening rift in the stone, a corridor beckoned our flight.

Well-coordinated in a way I just couldn't hope to be, Briar reflexively redirected our course to crash through the breach in the building, slowing our pace as we slipped through the tight gap.

Luck wasn't on my side.

I landed on my shoulder, crying out as I rolled over uneven tiling across the narrow corridor and finally hit the opposite wall. Here, several stories up the Spire with a spinning head and aching shoulder, I realized what a catapultier magikier could do.

Gasping for breath, I splayed both hands over the cold, tile floor, propping myself up from the blues and greys of the cracked marble tiling swimming before my eyes. It was a moment before I realized these splashes of colour composed a coherent mosaic – albeit one left in disrepair – beneath my hands and knees, then I was moving again, hastily helped to my feet by both Lin and Kev.

Briar slinked off my back as I came to a stand and scuttled to the middle of the corridor, a curved passage which I could only assume looped around this level's circumference.

"Did I miss a warning, or was that as uncalled for as it feels-?" I wheezed, but Kev interrupted with an awkward sound halfway between a shush and a whimper. "What?"

He gestured toward Briar, or perhaps to whatever lay around the corridor's bend.

"Psh, there's always time to hide," Lin said as if in response to someone else, sounding vaguely flabbergasted but more so troubled. With a flick of her tail, Briar's telltale sign of irritation, I begrudgingly acknowledged the conversation taking place outside my senses.

"Someone's coming?" I guessed, internally cussing out Evelyn's mental interference.

"You betcha," Kev worriedly muttered, pulling Lin and I toward a door on the inner length of the corridor. An uneven tile caught the toe of my boot, tripping me up as we all fell toward the unremarkable doorway. "Briar's taking care of it."

"Alone?"

"It's just one pora," Lin reported, a hasty interpretation.

"Then why aren't we helping? It's just one pora," I echoed back to her on a harsh whisper of breath.

"Faith must have gotten to her," Lin considered, her words painting confusion on my face as Kev nudged the door open with his foot. A janitorial closet awaited us on the other side, filled to the brim with cleaning products. As far as hiding went, we would just have to make do with the meagre indent of the doorway.

"Well, she made some good points after what happened this morning. You know, with the, uh..." He mimed the ripping of the pora the way the tree giant had done it.

"Briar told her about that?" I groaned between gritted teeth.

"Briar tells her everything. And Brett. She's kept us all in pretty frequent contact." A note of surprise coloured her tone to find me so out of the loop. She pulled in breath, fresh understanding in the sound of it. "No wonder you couldn't join the mental group chats. It's because of Evelyn, isn't it?"

"Yeah, I haven't been able to speak to Briar, or her to me. Not at all." What a stupid time for my heart to sink. Here, in the Arillian Spire, as the enemy bore down upon us.

With a sidelong glance, Kev shot me an apologetic smile. "You haven't missed much. They're just worried about you, that's all."

And what a time to find out, after laying bare all my grievances in the tent. I couldn't help wondering if they had already reported everything I said back to Briar. Hell, they could've been feeding her a live broadcast as I spoke, and I never would have known.

"You haven't missed much besides Brett airing his frustrations over a general lack of planning," Lin offhandedly put in, "Actually, you haven't missed anything."

"At least he's consistent," I groaned, momentarily forgetting my petty miseries.

The sound of clattering footsteps, not too dissimilar from the click of stiletto heels or the snap of something like hard plastic clashing with the tile flooring, rang out down the corridor Briar safeguarded. It was a moment before it clicked in my mind. What could have made such a strange sound, at once clacking sharply with each step and dragging across the floor like nails on chalkboard.

The prickly carapace of a kirranite. No, not just one. Too many feet clamoured down the corridor toward us, too many for Briar to handle on her own.

Bursting out from hiding, much to Kev and Lin's shock, I leapt into view just in time to spot a confusing amalgamation of lumbering forms, a mind-boggling arrangement of legs and arms, wings and tails, barrelling toward Briar. Not humanoid in the least, and yet familiar for the thick, black shell encasing their many-limbed bodies.

Kirranite parasites infecting animal host bodies, and for all the footsteps I had heard, there were only three of them. The slowest of them scuttled along the wall, eight barbed legs whipping its wolfish body forward. The other two had a confusing shape, at first grinding my mind to a halt in attempt to place what they could have been. They spread large, bat-like wings as they bounded the length of the corridor.

Briar thrashed her tail as one bore down upon her, slapping the larger creature into the wall, but she wasn't fast enough to evade the other as it slammed into her.

It latched long talons around the folds of her wings, grappling her, as the first got its legs under it once again. In another rush of frantic movement, the first launched itself at Briar, still with the second holding her down.

The monster rammed them both, sweeping Briar up between them.

In the blink of an eye, all three rushed suddenly out through the hole in the wall that Lin had created. Gravity stole them away as Briar's panicked growl echoed off the walls of the corridor back into my ears. A plume of hot fire illuminated the opening in their wake, but the sounds of struggles remained the same.

"Annie!" Lin shouted, breaking through the shock blanketing my mind. I turned toward the sound of her voice, just in time to see a black mass of limbs and spikes launch itself off the wall, directly at me. The third kirranite with a scuttlepup host body had avoided my line of sight in its crawl across the wall to get to me.

I reacted before thinking, throwing both arms in front of my face as an image of the two-hundred-foot archway flashed through my mind. A split second of thought, no, memory of an idea, shifted the stone grit of the tiles underfoot to slide me swiftly out of harm's way. The stone walls to either side of me reacted in tandem, an extension of my magic oozing into my surroundings.

I felt the walls pull away from their shape, drawn into sharp-tipped spears, and felt the rush of movement like it was my own as these makeshift weapons jutted suddenly to the place I had been not a moment prior. The tips of my spears clattered against the kirranite's hard shell, a contest of force, but the stone chipped, and the kirranite expertly rebounded off.

If it hit the ground, I would surely lose it. This thing was too fast.

"No!" The shout ripped up from my chest, and I threw my hands out, launching another flurry of spears from the walls. This time, I had an idea where to aim them, recalling the chinks in the colossal kirranite's armour.

My stone spears caught the joints where spindly legs met agile body and pierced through the weakness there, weakness I had become gravely familiar with since this morning.

I felt the shell crack more than I heard it. I felt the kirranite squealing by the vibrations of its shuddering death, enveloping my spears. Felt the heat of its blood trickle down the smooth lengths of my stony offense.

Only then did I open my eyes to it.

Some other sense had guided me, that same out-of-body sense I had felt as I leapt between the raindrops this morning. Now, all I could do was watch the animalistic kirranite slump in front of me with one final, convulsive exhale. Eight jerking legs suddenly went still and sagged loosely at its sides without touching the floor for the quintuple-pronged assault of stone pikes impaling its thorax several feet off the ground, jabbing deep through the joints.

This outcome, a reflex. A sign that Evelyn was always there, reacting right along with me whether she meant to or not. I had let her in, and the magic had followed.

"Not a single drop of blood, huh? I don't know whether to be impressed or disappointed," came a disillusioned voice from the other end of the hall. My head snapped up to find this new competitor, but my heart sank.

Now that those kirranites had taken Briar and their battle to the skies, leaving Lin, Kev, and I to handle this ourselves, could I repeat what I had just done? Could I skewer a *person* without hesitation?

It was a moment before I fully registered the man's appearance. A pora through and through, just as Briar said, but familiar for reasons I couldn't quite place. Pale hair. Paler complexion threaded with stark purple veins. Eyes like a dollop of brown amid a sea of red. He shouldn't have been so familiar.

And then he smiled, baring long canines for teeth. How could I be expected to recognize anyone so utterly transformed by pora infection.

"I don't think we've formally met," he continued when I simply gaped at him wordlessly, "No need to introduce yourself, I know who you are, but me? The name's Simon Beckett. Pleasure to finally make your acquaintance."

39

Long Overdue Introductions

OF ALL THE WAYS I COULD HAVE MET SIMON BECKETT, I SURE DIDN'T expect to find out the mimicry magikier who helped Valencia ruin my life in Blackano was no longer a magikier at all. And yet here we were.

Lin and Kev leapt out of hiding, taking up positions to my left and right but I couldn't bring myself to glance sideways and see the looks of shock and disgust I could only imagine on their faces. The horror, that I could react so violently, a split-second thought resulting in a split-second kill.

But even this unspoken anxiety was stifled at the source when Kev whispered, "Do you hear her voice?"

I knew what he meant. Evelyn.

Rifling through my own mind in search of her looming presence, already so difficult to discern even when she made herself apparent, I came up empty handed.

"Not a peep," I muttered, but for all my relief to have my headspace to myself, I couldn't help but wonder why she would keep so uncharacteristically quiet, and at a time like this, no less.

Rather than dwell on it, I pulled the stone from the floor, a hasty source of cover. Not only for us, but to conceal the shameful corpse in front of me.

The stone jumped up from below and swallowed the kirranite whole, covering legs, thorax, and all, until naught but the tips of the stone pikes remained, drenched with the wicked creature's inky black blood.

"Valencia said you'd be blood shy," teased Simon from the other end of the hall. He threw his voice with such expert ease, he sounded like he could have been right beside me, but I did my best to shake off the shivers running down my spine and steel myself against his tricks.

"She share anything else about me?"

"A few things. The way she put it, I expected you'd be more predictable." I could hear the grin in his voice. "You have a strange way of doing things, I'll give you that, but in the end, you're just some girl unlucky enough to have found herself in the middle of a feud between gods. And as strange as your methods in getting here were, you did exactly what she said once we had your Seth Knox."

"Where is he?" I growled and observed over the block of stone as Simon's chin tilted upwards. Top floor. Of course. "The Kaipracan really made *you* his last line of defense?"

He tilted his head to one side, a wide smile curling in the corners. "The Kaipracan, huh?" He paused, rolling this infamous title over his tongue, but gave me neither confirmation nor denial. "Tenebret can handle himself, it's all he's ever done. I just figured I'd take the chance to introduce myself, offer you some closure in your final moments."

The sheer arrogance of his words, reflected in his tone, left a sour taste in my mouth. "You call it closure; I call it insufferable. You're in my way."

"I'm curious," he mused as if I hadn't said a word, letting heavy eyelids droop over shrewd eyes, "Can the shonte hold her own against one measly pora? I have my doubts, you know, watching you stall here with me." His eyes glittered with intrigue. "You're not a pacifist, are you?"

"Why don't we ask your little kirranite buddies?" Lin chipped in, "Oh, but where'd they all scamper off to? That's right-" She patted the block of stone. "You better start running, pora."

He simply shrugged, never once glancing away from me. "Tsk, tsk. Taking all the credit? Two out of three served their purpose getting rid of that dragon of yours."

"They're nothing to her." My voice shook, betraying emotion.

"Scared to lose another?" A coy note danced on his tone, like he knew something I didn't. "Is he even worth it, your Seth?"

"What kind of question is that? Of course he is! I wouldn't be here otherwise!" I shot back, but his grin only widened, baring a long-toothed smile. Jagged fangs.

"It's unfortunate to die with regrets. But you'll wish you never came all this way-" He paused, theatrical in the performance. "-when you see him."

Fury boiled up in my chest, but Lin's hand pressed mine at my side, and Kev stepped ahead of me. "Did you miss the part where she speared your buddy here like it was nothing?" he interjected, throwing both arms out to the slab of stone encasing the beast-host kirranite, so animated in his gesture as if Simon were hard of hearing.

"No, as a matter of fact. I didn't. But you must have realized I've made a disgustingly easy target of myself. It's no accident. Go ahead. Take a stab at it," Simon mused, opening his arms wide.

He stood at the other end of the corridor, presuming to know me, and all I could do was stare. Maybe I should, I thought. If I could slay that kirranite so easily, so quickly, maybe I *could*.

Tilting his head to one side so his pale locks fell over one ear, he met my unease with a triumphant smile. "Come on, shonte! You're the pawn who travelled across the board against all odds and became a queen! You can pierce the shell of a kirranite, you can break the skin of a pora, but can you take my life like it's nothing?"

"Big talk for a dead man," Lin noted, and punctuated her words with a flick of her wrist. With that, the stone of the floor beneath Simon Beckett's feet opened wide.

Except, he wasn't falling. He bolted forward, landing expertly on a hand just ahead of this gaping pit, and sprang forward. Twisting through the air, the mere strength in one arm seemed enough to propel him the entire length of the hallway.

In an instant, he was right there atop the makeshift cover I had pulled from the floor, elbows resting on his squatting knees, beaming down at us from red eyes intent on Lin.

"Dead man? Funny, I've never felt so alive."

None of us could move fast enough. Not faster than the inhuman speed of a pora. He swiped down at her with one hand, nails as black as night, thick and curved to a point like talons tipping each finger, and with the other, reached behind his back to grasp the hilt of some weapon concealed there.

Time seemed to slow as I touched the residual magic leftover in the block of stone acting our cover, the meagre failsafe I'd planted. It was easy enough to re-establish my claim over the stone with my magic already nestled therein.

Finding my bearings within it, I bolted the stone upward, catching him in the chest so the air knocked clean from his lungs.

With a guttural noise stuck halfway between a wheeze and a gasp, he soared toward the ceiling on this platform of stone. This didn't block his attack, only veered it off course. His clawed hand swept down with a speed so fast, his entire arm seemed to blur, whizzing just above Lin's head.

The disturbance from the force of his swing shoved into me, nearly knocking me off my feet. Lin fell backwards on her elbows, taking the brunt of this power like a tidal wave of air. I only managed to catch my balance with a foot thrown backwards, and only then grabbed both Kev and Lin by their wrists, bolting off around the stone.

With that kind of force, Simon could have taken Lin's head clean off had the hit landed. This, the unbelievable strength of pora.

He was an unstoppable force, an impenetrable demon.

Leaning into the magic still possessing the slab of stone, I reanimated this makeshift hand to grapple Simon's body as he rebounded off the ceiling. Instead, his feet met the stone, springing off and maneuvering around my attack.

Through the blur of speed hiding his finer movements, I was able to make out the strange fluidity he possessed in himself.

He moved in mid-air like a cat, twisting his body and angling his core so his feet always landed exactly where he meant them to, and the moment I registered his feather-light step on the stone face, he was already using it like a springboard to launch himself after us, twisting and slipping between the fingers of rock. He was just too fast.

We wouldn't stand a chance against him in close-quarters combat.

I could feel Simon's feet pounding the tiles behind us, fast approaching. My magic followed him underfoot, shifting tiles like a sliding puzzle this way and that on the grit they were laid into to trip him up. It was the only thing slowing his unstoppable pursuit.

We couldn't outrun him, but I could block him. Pulling my magic ahead of Simon, I dragged a stone wall from the floor to the ceiling, stretching the floor thin to either side of it in its creation.

"What do we do?" I demanded on a harsh breath. The wall behind us wouldn't hold forever. There wasn't enough stone to pool into it from the surrounding floor.

"Well, for starters, turning your back on pora is a bad move in general," Kev feebly noted.

At his timid words, we three slid to a halt. I spun on my heel to face the wall I'd made, only to watch as a spiderweb of cracks splintered out from the center. Faster than I'd anticipated.

Kev double-fisted an iron grip on the hilt of his war hammer, prepared for the inevitable breach. This, the weapon best suited to make up for any lacking strength with sheer weight.

He was a scout, I had to remind myself, and had been for a handful of weeks in the City of Gates. While that wasn't enough time to master much, he must have faced pora at some point, and surely knew better than I how to handle one. Even when he could access his magic, there was never a point at which he could have benefitted from it – the fire-resistant oils on pora skin made them especially hard to barbeque. So even now, barred from his magic, he was at no less of a disadvantage.

"And in the same vein, you should probably have your mace out," he continued, nodding down to the weapons sheathed on my hips.

I fumbled for the mace on my hip, palm slick with sweat and numb fingers slipping off the grip. "Okay?" I prompted uneasily, holding my mace up in front of me with both hands, although it hardly required both.

Lin readjusted my stance without a word, as natural as it had been back in Blackano when it was no more than training.

Kev jumped slightly, as if in realization I was waiting on his command, and he tapped a finger to his chin, like he was rifling through an old memory bank. Finally, he said, "Spread out and use triple sequence. Jump in and out, two at a time, one person always circling to intercept or parry his counterattacks. Keep him guessing where the next attack will come from. The three-combatants formation we learned in Blackano, remember?"

"Triple sequence," Lin echoed, eyes shining in recollection of the pattern we were meant to use for three-on-one combat dealing with pora.

Triple sequence ensured two of the three would always be flanking, keeping the pora busy – a majority of pora experienced hyperactivity, it was how they could move and react so fast – as the third scouted an opening, but the roles varied at intermittent speeds. Always moving, always circling, overloading the pora's hyperactive mind. It required full concentration not just on the enemy, but on allies as well. Make too many mistakes, and you risked tripping them up. I would know. I came dangerously close to failing this section of the exam. Hell, I never pulled off triple sequence without someone counting the actions out loud, not once.

Sure, it was a basic formation, but we hardly had time to learn the basics, let alone master them. Granted, if we were up against a kirranite, Kev and I would be completely useless – we had only just begun that unit when the Liberation Front made their big move.

A grating destruction shrieked in my ears, and the rock in the dead center of the wall shredded to the floor, revealing a sliver of Simon's face beyond his clawing fingers.

"You think you can put me down with tactics as uninspired as triple sequence?" he snarled, joined by the clatter of stone chipping off to the marble floor as his resilient fingers chiselled through, widening the breach. "Are you trying to insult me? I took all the same courses. Hell, I graduated with flying colours; the Key-Keeper himself even called me a savant of the advanced classes."

So he took advanced classes, too. Damnit. I supposed he had to; it wasn't like mimicry would do him any favours on the battlefield. And now, with superhuman strength and speed on his side, I couldn't even count all the ways he outmatched us.

"If you graduated top of your class, how'd you end up a pora?" Lin shot back, keen to keep him talking, to slow him down in any way she could. With another flick of her wrist, she pulled a chunk of stone down from the ceiling to block the gap in the middle of the barricade.

An avalanche of stone collapsed with a puff of dust and flying debris, and in that same flurry of motion, Kev took advantage of the hindrance to Simon's line of sight, ducking behind cover just adjacent to the weakness dug out of the wall.

Lin's rockfall settled against it just off base, leaving a section of the aperture unimpeded. Her magic could only control the break in the ceiling, not the gravity that wrenched this rock, slate, and sediment down.

Completely unfazed by this latest attempt to block him, Simon answered, "I'd chalk it up to numbers. I was separated from my team, and I was surrounded by magikiers with that little something you just can't learn in a classroom." By his lacklustre tone and unimpressed stare, intent on me, I wondered if he even noticed Kev was no longer by my side. He simply shoved an arm through to push the rock away with that phenomenal pora strength of his. "You'd think all that training would have helped, but in the end, it's all just chaos and chance."

"Magikiers? I asked how you became a pora," Lin egged him on, and in that same moment, Kev swung his hammer down on Simon's arm protruding through the opening.

Simon snapped his arm back faster than Kev could bring his hammer down, but he couldn't escape the unexpected attack entirely. The twenty-pound, steel ball on the head of the hammerhead clipped Simon's knuckles with a sickening crunch, and he howled on the other side of the wall, disappearing from view through the opening.

Fast as I could, I reformed the stone from all that Lin had dropped to the floor, clogging what progress Simon had made.

"Of course they were magikiers!" Simon shouted from the other side, a feral note in the snarl of it. Even so, he threw his voice with an almost expert precision.

Although I knew him to be on the other side of the wall, I had to fight my instincts not to flinch as his voice sounded right behind my ear. With it, he told his story, apparently determined to garner our pity.

"I couldn't have survived disembowelment as a magikier. They left me there dying, I couldn't move, I couldn't even scream as I struggled for breath!"

"So you drank pora blood," Lin guessed, touching a hand to floor at the foot of the barricade where she carved a gaping maw out of the foundation. After I'd used so much of the stone to create the barricade, she was able to use her magic to dig straight through. A pitfall trap to the level below. Clever.

"To the rest of the world, I must have looked like a corpse. I couldn't damn well move for the pain of it, but I was lucky. I wasn't the only corpse around. Bodies caked the streets under me, an unlikely banquet, the bedding for my open coffin. Even stale as it was, the rotten blood healed me. The traces of magic still alive in it *became* me. It closed the second mouth carved out of my body; it gave me strength to walk again. I'd never realized just how fundamentally outmatched we were as magikiers, not until I stopped being one. Now I know, they're just fodder. For centions, for kirranites, for pora. For me. Magikiers were created to be fodder."

"Now that's a new level of hypocrisy I wouldn't have expected from Valencia's eyes and ears on Cellana," I egged him on, sending my feelers through the stone to gauge where he was on the other side of the wall.

"Careful, dove. Keep trying to use my conscience against me and you might discover I don't have one."

There, the pressure of feet, and a third pressure point. Likely a knee. He was crouched.

I started in surprise when a clawed hand raked through the section of floor I'd pooled my magic into, digging out a large chunk as easily as a knife cutting through butter. His deft hands turned tiles and hard stone over like it was nothing, working faster than I would've thought possible.

Too late, I realized what he was doing.

"Get back!" I cried, throwing my hands out to Kev and Lin as Simon bolted down the hole he'd dug out on the other side, only to rebound off the floor below and leap up through Lin's pitfall trap on this side. I barely kept pace with his movements in the stone.

Ignoring Lin and Kev to either side of him, each bookending the failed trap, Simon simply followed through. His eyes, the sclera filling red with the bloodlust of pora, were fixed on me.

I couldn't react fast enough.

His knees collided with my chest, sending me rocketing backwards. I hardly had time to process the world moving around me before my back struck the floor, then my head, and my vision flashed white for the sudden pain threatening to split my skull.

The air rushed from my lungs, squeezed out of me like the last remnants of toothpaste pushed up from the bottom. It was all I could do just to gasp for breath, straining to get even a mouthful down past the blockade his weight made upon my chest, stifling what faint remnants of breath still filled in my lungs.

It was a moment before I realized he'd drawn my own sabre against me, pressed to my throat, and had a dagger of his own held out behind him. A threat. Through my hazy vision, I could see Lin and Kev over either of his shoulders, each hesitant to make a move.

"If I could bottle the fear in your eyes," he purred, his deranged stare raising the hair on my arms.

I couldn't bring myself to move, frozen under his blade – *my* blade – as a roster of trained maneuvers raced through my mind, too fast to focus on any single one. Beyond the ringing in my ears and the panic rushing through my veins, I barely caught his whispered words, spoken as if to himself, "A taste will have to do."

He slid the edge of the blade across my cheek, tracing a vibrant sting of pain down to the curve of my upper lip. His nostrils flared, discoloured tongue wetting his peeling lips, but he set his jaw and sucked back breath between his fangs. This, a not even remotely concealed attempt to compose himself against the scent of my blood.

A bone-rattling shudder coursed down my spine, leaving tremors in its wake.

"Hey, dumbass, Valencia doesn't want her sister turned!" I heard Lin shout from behind him, a hidden plea for mercy, but I couldn't wrench my eyes from his, hovering mere inches above my face.

Not until a flash of movement collided against him, breaking over his back. In the blink of an eye, the weight on my chest disappeared. *He* disappeared, and Kev stood defensively over me. In the rush of it all, I only glimpsed the follow through of Kev's powerful swing, hammer like a wrecking ball – the blow that had knocked Simon away from me.

He must have taken advantage of Simon's fixation on my blood to duck around the defensive dagger held between them.

Simon moved with the force of Kev's walloping attack, ducking into a roll, and in the same fluid motion, got his feet under him, one hand raking through the stone to slow his momentum, and flung back up into a stand as his back hit the leftmost wall.

His chest heaved with breath, body shaking noticeably as his own blood dripped from the ragged fingernails of his left hand, but his wild-eyed stare held fast to the sabre, my sabre, gripped in his right hand.

He raised my sabre to his mouth and traced his tongue along the line of red coating its edge. Pupils blown in satisfaction, he lapped up every last drop.

Lin rushed to my side.

"It's fine, he barely sliced me-" I was saying, but a flash of ice raced through my veins, stiffening in my muscles and contorting what control I had over my own movement. I felt my heartbeat in every twitching extremity, every tightening muscle, and nearly choked for the sudden tightness winding around my lungs. The words wedged themselves in my throat on a hitch of breath.

This ice in my blood, like a hand inside a puppet, rushed to my arms and seemed to fill them on the inside. They were moving. How strange a sight, to see my own limbs acting out against me. What resistance I posed against this involuntary motion only tore at my shoulders, like the blood itself was moving my arms and nothing else.

This unwelcome thrust of movement sent a powerful blow sailing into Lin beside me. There was no maneuver to it, no center of balance nor any proper technique, just the force itself. My rampant arms knocked her clean off her feet, unexpected as it was to have come from me.

"Annie?" Kev uncertainly asked, glancing back at me over his shoulder, but I could hardly hear him for the deafening heartbeat in my ears. Blood, blood, everything in me centered on the virulent ice that had become of my blood.

"What's going on?" I hacked out through the tightness in my windpipe, "What did you do!"

"I'll take that to mean I'm your first," Simon mocked, an almost giddy mania in the singsong of his voice, "Unsurprising. I doubt most other pora would be able to stop themselves after just a taste. It really is..." An involuntary sound slipped out of him. "Delectable. Indescribable." The red of his sclera leaked into the last slivers of his irises, light brown rings around void-black pupils squeezing out to nothing, until the red intermingled with the black in his eyes like unmixed dyes. "Addictive."

A visible shudder ran down his spine, and he curled his fingers at his side. In his other hand, my sabre's poor hilt bent under the pressure of his clenched fist.

By the unrelenting pull of the blood within, my body flew through the air, feet dragging on the uneven floor beneath me. With this sudden motion, I felt the cool air on my skin, moist with sweat. Beads of it dripped along the side of my face, a pleasant cooling sensation in the rush of air against my skin. Sweat, I realized, not shivers or numbness, but a hot and dry sweat.

This sweeping cold flash wasn't cold at all. A downward glance proved it, showing my red-hot skin, blotchy and rash-like. A heat so severe, I mistook it for cold. This scorching flash of pain – simple as that, it was pain – would boil my blood, and cook my brain in my skull. Even now, a headache was growing, beginning its shrill scream between my pounding ears as a deep and terrible squeezing sensation took root all throughout my body. A widespread ache, an intensifying pressure.

Not good, not good at all.

A fever like this would kill me before long, whether Simon meant to or not.

My legs buckled under me and I lost all the strength in my knees, but I hardly needed to stand on my own. Something else held me up. Something deeper, at once light as air and heavier, stuffier, which defied the pull of gravity.

My body was nothing more than a blood puppet for Simon.

He flung my body sideways with a flick of his index finger. I, myself, was neither running nor jumping, but simply moving with the invisible force dragging at my blood and wrenching my body along with it.

My vision swam, a feverish contortion of my environment. Warped and wobbly, my perceptions failed me for the extreme heat cooking my mind.

You see now what it is to be auxiliary to a body under a parasite's control.

"Shut up, Evelyn," I puffed, feeling my breath as steam escaping my oven-like lungs. The taste of blood hit the back of my throat, hot and coppery over my tongue. Damnit, I dreaded to think what this was doing to the delicate blood vessels in my body.

"Evelyn?" Simon's voice echoed strangely in my ears, somehow less real than the voice in my head. "Do we have a visitor?"

I couldn't answer him, could hardly think with any measure of clarity. The heat in my blood stifled all cognizance at the source, leaving my extremities numb and puffy, and my head feeling as if it floated two feet above my body. Stars popped before my hazy vision, and I forced my eyes shut.

I had to escape.

It was a last resort, but the only option I could see laid out before me, here on the verge of losing consciousness.

Homing in on Evelyn's voice, I pulled the magic back into my body enough to let it all flow through her, and then out once more on my scorching-hot breath.

It was all I could do to stay in the fight.

I could see no other option but to risk, no, *sacrifice* my commandeered body and rely entirely on my magic. I didn't have time to think up an alternative. I didn't have time to stall or try to talk my way out of this. There was no leaving Kev and Lin to face him on their own. There was no other choice.

A flicker of light flared against my closed eyelids; a split-second spark chased by a plume of fire. The leaping inferno snaked into the air on my seething exhale, and *I* went with it.

Out from my mouth poured an avatar of flame. A pseudo-body my magic and my consciousness could inhabit. Behind me, my body wilted, insentient and vacant. Simon's blood puppetry had my body under absolute control, but not my magic.

The flames and I were as one, and there, nestled in among the burning hot radiance, I felt Evelyn's presence stir powerfully at the hems of my being. Waiting and watching.

I hovered outside the blood puppet that had been made of my body, an astral projection of roaring flames. This fire had no anchor, fuelled only by shonte magic. It wouldn't last long while my body suffered such severe conditions, but I'd have to make do with what I had.

I sensed my environment with the strange, extra-sensory perception of the elements that came with these out-of-body experiences, and judged the whereabouts of Kev, Lin, and even Simon by the disturbance their breaths made in the air.

Simon's was barely perceptible, unlike the adrenaline-fuelled pumping of my friends' lungs, but even if there was no change in the air around him at all, while the heat of my flame avatar masked the heat from their bodies, I could at the very least track the feel of everyone's feet on the stone floor and the pumping of the fluids in their bodies.

Yes, there!

Directing my magic, I streaked toward Simon, scorching everything in my path. Right there. He stood with his back to the wall, an easy target-

My magic leapt in response to my thoughts, so fast I nearly missed all sensory perceptions of the body he flung directly in my path: his blood puppet, my own body, breathing so shallowly and suspended just high enough off the floor, I nearly missed the signs.

To either side of my flame avatar, Lin and Kev flanked around the blood puppet, truly a meat shield Simon had thrown out in front, and assumed triple sequence just as discussed. They bounded into combat with their quarry, taking advantage while his blood puppet blocked his line of sight. Even so, he flung his blood puppet every which way, not at all beholden to gravity or even, it seemed, the laws of physics. He could stop the momentum on a dime, altering direction in the blink of an eye, but he could only move his blood puppet so fast, and certainly not as fast as his own body could move.

For the first time, *I* moved faster.

The flames of my being raced across the marble, swirling to the left of Simon's blood puppet to take up Lin's place in triple sequence, striking with a lick of fire. My heat merely glanced off his skin, soaked with the strange oils unique to pora which made their exterior so fire-resistant, but the ends of his pale hair lit up with bright embers, and his clothes blackened where I made my flimsy contact.

This flame avatar had no physical strength, nor even any advantage against his fireproof exterior. But Simon flinched, shielding his eyes against my brightness, and Kev took advantage of the opening with a swing of his hammer.

Simon blocked the head of it with an outstretched hand, and though there was a sickening crunch, he managed to clench it with white-knuckled fingers, and with his other hand, wrested the weapon from Kev's grasp.

With a jerk of Simon's chin, the blood puppet flung full force into Kev, knocking him back against the wall and forcing his grip to slacken on the handle enough for Simon to wrench it free entirely, disarming him.

In the same motion, Simon used his momentum to swing the hammer back around, one-handed for all the immense strength he wielded as a pora.

I could see the path of the swing, the wide arc which would bring the hammer head back against Kev and demolish him in one strike if he didn't get out of the way in time. But Kev was still recovering from Simon's last attack, unaware where the next would come from.

I steeled myself. How could I be so useless against one pora but still expect to face Valencia's champion with any hope of victory? No. If Briar's flames could char pora to the bone, surely the fire of a shonte could do the same.

Rushing forward, I moved my flames faster than Simon could move the hammer, becoming a wall of fire between them as my heat made a wavering mirage of the air all around me. Until I reached whatever temperature Briar could achieve with her breath, my flames would do nothing to stop Simon swinging right through me.

But I wasn't the only one intent on action.

The moment I moved my flames between them like sprawling wings of fire and a wall of overpowering heat, Kev reached out to me. I felt my flames sear his fingertips, tasted the last chippings of his nail polish in the chemical smoke, and with these senses, felt his magic prodding into mine.

Without a second thought, I let him through.

Kev's finnicky magic snapped against the connection between us, sharp and forceful.

He was like a bolt of lightning, crackling energy popping and fizzling through me in contest not only with my magic, but the carmavi curse mark restraining his own. I surrendered my flames to his control, the lightning bolt of Kev's magic making what limited use of my flames it could.

Powerful sparks popped everywhere his cursed magic touched, and he ran with it. All the way to the center of my being, where a sudden burst of his cursed magic lashed out against him, a blast of destructive power in all directions.

The explosion – because that's what it was, an explosion – bashed into Simon, Kev, and my own semi-conscious body like a tidal wave of fiery force, interrupting Simon's swing and ramming everything away from me. Before the carmavi curse mark, I had only ever seen Kev use his magic to tame and shape fire to his will, but this was something different entirely. He had pushed against the restraints of the carmavi curse until it pushed back, setting off a volatile blast.

Catching the brunt of the explosion, Simon lost his grip on the hammer which went clattering down the hall, but he caught himself several steps back. Kev had no such luck, nor the strength to do anything but shield his face with raised forearms and suffer his own attack.

Lin reacted instantaneously, causing a fissure to break the stone and clamp down on the left arm and shoulder of my physical body when the force of the explosion sent it careening into the wall.

Though he still had his puppeteer's fingers in my arterial system, Simon could no longer use my body, his blood puppet, like a blunt force weapon.

With a small, triumphant sound, Lin took Kev's place in our triple sequence formation, allowing him a moment's rest on the outskirts of combat. Simon must have noticed her satisfaction, for an expression of realization dawned on his face that she was the one to confiscate his blood puppet.

And fury boiled in his eyes.

The way he singled his focus on her, it was like my flame avatar wasn't even there – although I supposed, for all the injury my fire could do him, or lack thereof, it came as no surprise. Somehow, it still felt like an insult, further kindling the protective rage popping off blue sparks in my unsettled flames.

But I couldn't get between them like with Kev. My flames would only burn Lin, never help.

Simon's nimble feet hit the ground at break-neck speed as he danced around her defensive attacks. He skipped easily over the shallow cracks her magic blew out of the floor to trip him up, but this at least kept him at a distance.

"Annie!" Kev's haggard voice reverberated through the air, catching my senses beyond mere hearing, but rather feeling. I understood the intention behind his shout, a signal to get into position, but I couldn't help noticing the stifled pain in his voice.

No time to worry about that, now.

Placing my flames so as to hit Simon, whose body would shield Lin, I felt the crackle and pop of Kev's magic erupting from within me once more, taking my flames along with it in explosive bursts.

This time, there was no holding back. A haze of purple enshrouded my flames, a feeling of vertigo hitting me hard the moment I felt his magic and the carnavi curse's stopper reach into me, but Kev got his desired effect.

Simon flew off his feet, a lucky hit for the chaotic trajectory of the blast. Behind him, Lin crouched low to the ground, fingers digging into strategic cracks carved from the stone. Like this, she held on against the intense wave of force which hurdled out from me with a thunderous boom.

The world shook all around us, precipitous dust and stone raining from the ceiling as cracks burst across the walls to either side of me. Simon's feet hit the quaking floor, angled against the force of the blast, and from this position, he launched himself forward once more so his knee rammed Lin's back, a hand shoving her face into the rubble.

In the wake of this cacophony, there was only the pitter-patter of raining sediment joined by the low roar of my flames. I felt the magic slipping out of my grasp, hasty to retreat to my insentient body slumped against the wall, one arm encased in stone, as the dying spark in the center of my being clung to life, nearly blown out by the blast.

Not yet.

I forced the magic to hold, finding its strange senses limited now, merely framing the world around me as if my perceptions were a plastic wrap vacuum sealed to my surroundings. I could only focus on gathering my flames back to me, taking what heat I could from the very air around me.

I couldn't afford to bow out now, not with Simon's knee pressed into Lin's back, fist knotted in the material of her scarf. If I gave in, if I withdrew to my overheating body, Simon would have every advantage over both Lin and Kev.

Not that he didn't have the advantage right this instant as he wrenched Lin up by her scarf, the loop of it catching around her neck, still with his knee planted heavily against the base of her spine. Like this, the lower half of her face was exposed, and Simon's wide eyes gave away his surprise to note the markings on her skin.

In one smooth motion, he ripped the iron-rimmed goggles from her face with his injured hand, tossing them aside to reveal the state of her eyes.

"Well would ya look at that." He let loose a low whistle, jerking her scarf back yet more so she was forced to dig her fingers between the cloth and her throat. Anything to keep it from strangling her. "Wouldn't you rather a drop of pora blood to complete the look? As you are now, it's a little misleading."

"So now you're a pora pusher?" she growled through the pain, maintaining an illusion of composure even as tears beaded on her eyelashes.

A long, curled grin stretched across his face, making the uncanny veins pop around his discoloured eyes. "In a way."

Before I could think what to do, so limited in my options by my half-dowsed flames, Simon struck at her uncovered mouth with the blood-coated fingers of his injured hand, the one which had been crushed by Kev's hammer.

In the same moment, Lin released her grip on the scarf, allowing it to wrench her backwards by her neck as her hand splayed over the stone of the floor, further breaking down the already broken up stone shards into a fine, powdery sand.

She scooped up a fistful, quick as a striking viper, and threw the grit backwards. The cloud flew past Simon's open-handed strike – aimed to force his blood down her throat – and mushroomed around his arm, obscuring everything it contained from my weakened senses.

He's faster.

Evelyn's unmistakable voice rang too clearly, too impressively through me, a lawnmower cutting through the weeds of my overgrown mind. I knew she was right.

For a moment, the world stood perfectly still.

Then Lin hit the ground, coughing and wheezing. Simon had automatically let go of her scarf as a fistful of sand shot into his eyes, blinding him.

The cloud began to clear, allowing my perceptions through as Simon crouched forward, tucking his head and frantically rubbing at his eyes with both hands.

From behind, where the cloud of dust offered a measure of cover, Kev leapt into view with rivulets of blood flinging out from the dark of his sweat-dampened and flapping hair. He had his hammer in hand again, and a clear shot to the back of Simon's head, but his arms trembled against the hammer's weight. White-knuckled fingers clung desperately to the grip, putting everything he had behind this last-ditch attack.

Moving faster than I thought possible, my sputtering flames raced across the floor, positioning myself to propel the hammer forward, and Kev caught onto my plan immediately.

He called forth a final blast from the fast-fading remnants of my fire, enough to propel his hammer and send it caving into Simon's skull and spinal column.

Simon didn't even see it coming.

Dowsed by this latest blast, my flames went out and I felt myself jolt backwards as if tugged by a wire connected to the center of my being. My body, my true body, wrenched me back with nauseating insistence, like an inverted tackle. In the blink of an eye, my flame avatar dissipated into wisps of smoke, and I could do nothing to combat the pull on my magic.

A snapback.

The magic that had consumed me now rushed back into my body through fresh gashes ripped open on my palms, up a latticework of slits opening upon my arms and over my shoulders until, finally, the magic pooled and reintegrated into my body without ripping its way in. I had never been so consciously aware of just what was happening when the cuts opened on my palms, not until now. And I was back, clinging to conscious, but myself once more.

A moment of calm, of bleary readjustment was all I was afforded. Then followed pain.

Excruciation like a hundred lashings ravaged my arms, blood pooling in my gloves. My knees wobbled traitorously as I struggled to get my feet under me, barely able to carry my own weight. But I had to stand, to alleviate the pain in my arm lest the jagged stone clamped around it rip at the open wounds.

Carefully, I wriggled out of the uneven crack holding my arm in the wall and fell to my knees once free, quaking uncontrollably.

In front of me, Simon's body twitched in the effort to hold onto life, a grotesque shape deforming the back of his head. His greedy eyes slid down to the spreading pool of red leaking out from the seams of my gloves.

With hands shaking as tremulously as my own, he reached for the red between us.

"Stop!" I choked out, guttural and broken. I hadn't forgotten what he said about his transformation into a pora. How quickly blood had healed him as he lay dying on the battlefield. But I didn't have eyes on Lin and Kev, and my body was sapped and slow, seeming yet more so in comparison to the flame avatar I had so swiftly become accustomed to.

I launched myself forward, determined to stop him anyway. It didn't cross my mind that in doing this, I was only throwing food at a wild animal.

His hand shifted trajectory, his eyes landing square on my blood-soaked sleeve. I felt his fist clamp around my wrist before I saw him cross the distance to me, striking too fast to dodge. But just as suddenly as he had me in his grasp, a boot crashed down on his elbow, stomping his arm down into the floor with enough force to invert the joint.

Not that I was an expert on the footwear of my friends, but I didn't recognize this boot. Not hardly. And when my gaze trailed up, curious to see to whom it belonged, I most certainly didn't recognize the incredible height, powerful build, or raven black hair of the man standing over us.

Without a doubt, this man was the Liberation Front's exalted Tenebret, Valencia's champion on Cellana, and the centions' age-old enemy, the Kaipracan. Come to face me at last.

40

Lost and Found

BEFORE I COULD REACT, CHAOS STEPPED IN TO SHAKE THE WORLD. AND I mean that in a painfully literal sense.

I couldn't see where the sudden upheaval came from, but the entire building bucked with an earthquake. The entire corridor shook, rattled, and then the ground seemed to jump. My feet left the floor or was it that the floor disappeared out from under me. The very ground itself, the foundation of the Spire, plummeted downwards as if into a sinkhole.

With no sense of spatial awareness, I didn't know which way to twist so as to hit the ground without injury. Vertigo struck my dizzy head, a violent juddering sensation taking hold in me as everything was shaken out of place. And for a split second, rock shards, dust, and debris hung suspended in the air all around me as the momentum shifted again.

Before I could fix my position for the inevitable crash down, gravity got its unrelenting hook around me and yanked me back to the ground.

New pains registered across my body, zeroing my focus back in upon myself – a single point. My wrist.

I heard the crack a moment before I felt it as my body crunched against hard marble flooring. I almost couldn't hear the city of screams funnelling into my ears over my own pained outcry.

Tears sprang to my eyes, spilling onto my cheeks to wash the dust and grime from my face.

The sounds of catastrophe were too loud, too vast, for me to register my own fall. A titanic roar of toppling buildings rang out across the city of

Cerenthior, a sound like thousands of Kev's explosions going off in a massive radius centered on the Spire. And destruction. Like the wailing cacophony of hell, I heard the destruction of Cerenthior singing harmony with the agony screaming in my wounds.

Fighting through the blinding pain in my wrist, I simply focused on taking back control of my hyperventilating lungs.

Like a worm, I wriggled on the floor until I lay on my back with my forearm clutched to my chest. Shuddering, shaky breaths raked in through my open mouth, tasting of copper and heavy with dust.

My eyes fluttered open. Well, one did. I hadn't noticed the cascade of blood which gushed down from my forehead and pooled in the lines of my left eyelid, forcing that eye closed.

I nearly believed the other had stopped working entirely when I finally got my bearings.

What I saw only confused me.

My vision swam as I took in the gold trimmings on fantastic colouration making a reeling nebula of the high ceiling. Nestled in among the spinning colours, dead center and the focal point of my gaze, my own face stared back at me.

For a moment, I figured I was looking in a mirror, but for the graceful ferocity in my reflection's eyes, the triumphant tilt of her chin, the sea of wavy, red hair cascading all around her, and her body, entombed in a sarcophagus of colossal wings. There was no mistaking it. This was a depiction of Evelyn Lupei in her prime.

Finally, I registered the bigger picture. A gold-embossed mural decorated the high, arched ceiling, illustrating a baroque battle scene. Chunks of ceiling and the masterpiece wrought upon it had fallen away, but I could make out the gist of the story it told. A gargantuan monstrosity with shining, crimson scales, a gullet, chest, and belly which glowed like hot embers, and wings like a red dawn, strewn haphazardly across a corpse-littered battlefield. Legions of dead piled up beneath the dragon's body, but a familiar figure stood over it, raising the dragon's severed head, which should have been too heavy to hold, up to the sky and to the golden light of the centions. Here she was, glorious and terrifying – Valencia, accompanied by her sister whose body I inhabited.

Even half-destroyed and further muddied by my own failing vision, I realized the weight behind this illustrated retelling of Arillian history. The Lupei sisters, Valencia and Evelyn, had decapitated the mythical dragon, the crimson emberbreast, Fiamme.

I tore my eyes from the mesmerizing artwork overhead, gathering myself back in the present moment.

The corridor had been replaced with a large, open room – Lin, Kev, even Simon were nowhere to be seen. An archway along the far wall opened to a view of the ravaged city, beset by smoke and rubble. To see it all from this vantage point, I must have been transported to a room at the peak of the Spire, but how could that be? I hadn't felt the embrace of magic like I had when the teleporting magikier grabbed me. It was like I hadn't moved an inch, and yet here I was, with chunks of ceiling littering the floor all around me.

Breathing sharply, I moved as if to pull myself up to a stand, but a voice stayed me. "No need to burden yourself, I just want to talk." His voice was so soft, I was sure I shouldn't have been able to catch his words as clearly as I did, more whispered into my mind than my ears.

Words escaped me on a gravelly grunt, slurred and practically inaudible, but I was sure he heard me. "Where are my friends?"

"Where you left them. Likely deciding whether to come to your rescue or end the life of my handler." Standing against the stone half-wall blocking the open archway, the man with raven-black hair gazed out over the ruined city.

I saw beyond him the devastation wrought by this colossal earthquake, for the first time understanding why it looked like a bomb went off in the City of Gates, but his daylight-outlined silhouette blocked the view.

Tenebret held a polearm in his hands, draped across his shoulders. The shaft was thin, weightless in his grasp, and bone-white. The long, single-edged blade at one end looked to be welded from a strange metal fashioned in the aspect of gold and garnet dragon scales, glinting under the light of the ring across the sky. Like the eye of a needle, the middle of the hooked blade was hollow, perfectly shaped to trap, block, and disarm weapon attacks at range. At the other end of the six-foot pole was a flurry of crimson red and golden-threaded silks floating gracefully to the floor where they slithered, whispering softly over the marble, with his every movement. I imagined them ribboning out mid-battle, feather-light, in an elegant dance.

The weapon of achaion looked nothing like I expected – something grislier, scarier, perhaps? – but as far as expectations went, neither did Tenebret.

The gravity that drew me into orbit around him had disappeared, and that aura of inscrutable power which he wore like a mantle – a silent alarm denoting the unmistakable might of Valencia's champion – now faded out to a background noise.

This silhouette of a man at the window was no monster of gigantic proportions, not like I had envisioned him in my classes. Granted, my Blackano teachings showed evidence to the contrary – that the Kaipracan could assume a monstrous form like a force of nature.

But now, staring up at him, he didn't even loom over me – he hardly cast a shadow in comparison to the daunting figure which had stood over Simon and I not seconds ago. He simply gazed back from tired eyes, listless and unconcerned.

The thing was, the raven-haired man standing before me was so unremarkably human. Pockmarks blemished his face. Heavy-set eyes peered out from a world-weary expression. Thin lips tucked into deep, downturned dimples on either side of his mouth.

He carried a certain melancholy about him, like a splash of grey beneath a canvas of colour. Such meticulously crafted ordinariness, I could have walked past him on a normal day without batting an eyelash in his direction.

And he had shaken the city, brought it to the ground, with a thought.

"Simon Beckett's your *handler*?" I groaned, my tone half-mocking, half-confounded. "How does that make sense?"

"You're not wrong to be surprised. He's harmless to me, but Valencia insists we maintain contact and I'd be a fool to forfeit the last sanctuary of my mind. So, she has her loyal mouthpieces follow me around like lost little ducklings. Her eyes and ears, each and every one."

Shifting uncomfortably, I blew a stray curl out of my face only for it to stick to the blood pooling around my eye. Begrudging my dishevelment, I grumbled, "Ah, there's the sense."

He tilted his head to one side, seeming to truly register the sorry state I was in for the first time, and a glint of surprise entered his eyes. "You're injured?"

"You noticed?" I peeled off the disgusting mess of my gloves too wet and tight around the swelling in my wrist for comfort. A small surge of blood released with the shucked leathers, painting the clothes on my chest where I held my wrist still.

"How the great Evelyn has fallen. What a dismal reunion."

Scraping back the breath to speak through gritted teeth, I indicated with an index finger toward my head. "Sorry to break it to you, but you're not talking to Evelyn right now."

He raised a shoulder in a lethargic shrug. "And you, the imposter under her mask, it's about time we met. But you're not here for me, are you?" He drew the glaive across his shoulders, a gentle gliding gesture turning my attention toward the back of the room. "You've come all this way, razed a path through Arillia, for him."

I didn't turn my head, wary to lose my peripheral view of this notorious monster for a single moment, but I glanced down the path of his point.

The room was in shambles, chunks of the ornate ceiling shaken loose from the calamitous tremors now littering the floor, but I hardly noticed the careless wreckage when my eyes fell upon the target of his gesture.

"Seth!" The word escaped me on a broken breath. He sat slumped against the back wall, wrists held up by iron manacles bolted to the stone, with sweat-soaked hair hanging down around his face. The regal overcoat I had once admired was now draped over his shuddering body in tattered rags.

I barely registered that Tenebret was still speaking over the rage ringing in my head, tinging my vision red. "Ironic. You would blaze a trail through Arillia for him, and she would tear it all down for her. I suppose it pays, having nothing left to go to war over. To be the last relic of ancient times."

My eyes snapped back to Tenebret. He hadn't moved an inch from the window, still poised with a casual air for conversation, not a fight, but I didn't let my guard down because of it. Not that I could take him if he were to attack. Here I lay, unarmed, wrist broken, body still reeling from the effects of Simon's control. To engage in a fight would be futile. Senseless.

I had no intention to egg him on. Nor, it seemed, was he interested in fighting me.

"Let him go," I rasped through the pain forcing intrusive words into my brain – pain, wrist, *pain* – while my entire being was centered on the radiant agony in the break. "He was the bait and I bit. Now let him go."

"Bait?" Tenebret mused on a soft breath, a tinge of exasperation colouring his tone. Like an adult talking down to a child. "He's the last true Knox. His blood carried ancient magic descended from the prototypical magikier."

"Carried?" I echoed, emphasizing the past tense he had used, but Tenebret talked over me as if I hadn't opened my mouth at all.

"Or is it that you think the centions – notorious for their failures in creation – made the first magikier without error? Complete. Flawless. *Stable.* Setting aside the fact of what Reuven Knox became, he was nonetheless the index case of impurity in the blood of born magikiers."

"Maybe *you're* unfamiliar with the centions' omissions-" I growled, only to catch myself on a hiss of breath as pain speared through my wrist, rerouting my attention back to that point.

I didn't realize I'd shut my eyes against the pain until they blinked open, finding Tenebret stooped directly over me. He peered down at me from pitch black eyes, like an owl over a mouse.

He held the weapon of achaion in one hand behind his back, touching the tip of the blade to the floor. No wind blew through the open window, but the ribbons at the glaive's end stirred of their own accord, unbeholden to gravity and reaching as if for my hand.

I didn't have time to think about it. He crouched low over me, drawing my gaze back up to his face.

Neither of us dared to blink.

So close, his meticulously crafted ordinariness fell away like a doffed cloak. What I had assumed to be a sickly pale and pockmarked complexion was rather rough, white scarring from hundreds, no, thousands of long-healed lashings. A handsomely warm complexion peaked through the tight-knitted latticework of scar tissue.

Recognition struck me, deeper than my own awareness, and a single word filled my mind. Vincladimhús. The voice that followed was mine but not my own.

Yes, the stains of Vincladimhús. Mortals would undergo such tremendous destruction of the self, they break apart into nothing, but see here how an immortal is merely tarnished. You're no match.

Evelyn's interruption reawakened in me memory of my studies. The dungeon of old, reserved for the centions' greatest foes. Not a physical place one could reach by travel across land or sea, but rather, an abyss where they tossed their greatest mistakes, be they former allies or age-old enemies. The Kaipracan spent longer than any other in that inconceivable prison, and Valencia helped him escape it.

And what, I wonder, did he offer her in return?

"There she is," Tenebret whispered, slipping in close with a hand reaching toward me.

Nimble fingertips brushed my hair aside, but I didn't feel his touch. In fact, when his thumb and index clamped my cheekbones just under my eyes, I didn't feel anything at all. Not the pain in my wrist, nor the dizziness still swathing my head. I couldn't feel my body as I collapsed into a dream.

There was only Tenebret, enshrouded in the haze of mist that hemmed the edges of dreams as he chased me into the depths of my subconscious. His face loomed over mine, behind it, a tail of smoke and shadow. He pushed me deeper and deeper, until I found myself in a vast expanse of floating rivers, twisting and swirling in the open air of this subconscious place, each shimmering with flashes of memory beyond my recollection. Memories not my own.

And then I felt *her.* Evelyn scratched and clawed at my back from within, fingers pressing out of my skin, then hands and arms, to grab onto my ribs and hoist herself forward, until she'd emerged all the way to her hips. Like a disturbing rendition of the Roman two-faced god, she reached out from within me, striving for a body of her own, only to stick out from my back where her skin was the same as mine, her limp, dead hair not just tangled with the red curls of mine but the very same as it, tethering the backs of our heads to one another. There was no breaking away from me, nor me from her.

Still, she refused to yield.

I toppled under her struggles, losing my balance in the strange, flowing atmosphere of the dream, and gripped the distorted ground – at once grass, rock, gravel, cobblestone, and more – against her relentless pulling. She wrenched my head back by my hair – our hair – and elbowed into my side to escape me, but there was only futility in her increasingly pathetic efforts. All I could do was wince against the pain, curling in around myself on the ground as the sounds of her struggles encased me like a bubble, warbling and muffled as if underwater. She stole the breath from my lungs with each animal yell, forcing me into silence.

Only Tenebret's voice rang clear and true, though the face that had followed me into this wretched nightmare did little more than stare down at me – at us – with mouth unmoving. His voice had no discernible source but was nonetheless booming, all surrounding, and inescapable. "So this is the pitiful creature they've reduced you to. Half-formed with no more room in your being for anything but this rabid desperation. You cannot escape her as you are, Evelyn. You know this."

"Then help me!" she raved with that warbling quality of voice. Spittle flew from lips so chapped, so starved, that broken lines carved the flesh of her mouth and the skin surrounding, even up to the famished hollows of her cheeks.

"Why should I?" Tenebret simply answered, wearing a disillusioned tone, "Valencia sang your praises as a visionary warrior. Noble and ingenious. Benevolent and composed. But most of all, strong. The person you once were, who even I knew you to be. I trusted Valencia's word that you were still that person, but I see nothing of your former self in this… this caricature they've made of you."

"The parasite in my body, only. That's what you see! Too weak to best *one* pora! Too spineless to steel nerves perpetually frayed! Laughable! Insignificant!" Evelyn thundered, shaking our entire body with the fury heaving in her emaciated chest, "Rid me of the parasite in my skin and see what I truly am! Now! Now, now, now-!"

"Enough." Though his tone was sharp, Tenebret's tactile voice seemed rather a swaddling blanket enfolding the both of us into one.

Under the potent pressure of his sound, the separation between Evelyn's back and mine stitched closed, sewing us together until we were two halves of one whole body. And slowly, ever so slowly, Evelyn's heaving breath stabilized. Her body stopped twitching, her frenzied voice calmed into low, inaudible grumblings, and her struggles passed over to tranquility.

My forearms were still pressed to the ground, propped under me along with my knees, but I had no more need of this cowering posture. I pushed myself up until I was seated on my knees, a strange fluidity of movement coordinating with Evelyn's as she faced out from my back. And there was peace in the space between our minds.

Tenebret's colourless voice returned. "You can't wrench yourself free by force alone, nor should you try. Take responsibility for the garden you've sown, but know, the flowers are their own."

"That's weird. It almost sounds like you're vouching for me." The biting thought slipped out of me on a whisper of breath taken back from Evelyn's lungs.

I couldn't read him at all. He was at once my enemy and yet simultaneously on my side, lecturing Evelyn on the same arguments I had repeatedly failed to convince her of? How did that make sense?

"You?" He pondered over the word, heralding a silence over this continually shifting dreamscape. "No, not just you."

"And what am I in this allegory you've crafted?" Evelyn hissed from behind me, voice seething with rage now buried, calmer than she was mere moments ago. "A stand-in for the centions who did to me what you now imply I do to this worm growing on my back?"

"Are you blind to all that you do? All that you say? Can you not see the cycle you've become a part of?" Tenebret mused, "And is that no different from the centions' own blindness to their own misconducts?"

She spat at the effigy of him still hovering over us, a thick globule dashing across his unmoving face. It had no reaction. It didn't even blink.

"You disappoint me." His voice resounded through the cage of our ribs. "You want so badly for me to see things as you do, and I would try, but sensory perceptions are to reality what memory is to history, and perspective is to truth. Understanding is an illusion."

"Don't you talk down to me," she hissed, a shudder taking root in our combined form. "Not you, beast."

A jaded sigh breezed through the dream, sorrowful and yet warm on my skin.

"As pora before you, and kirranites before they, and the dragons and my own kin, the aethuri, now you, too, have become the very demon their propaganda claimed you to be, baseless accusations of past sins and amplified mistakes now realized in this twisted creature begging and spitting before me. Demonized, in more ways than one. And every time, the centions have rallied their soldiers against the demons their words create. Unshade your eyes, Evelyn. The cycle continued with domenths, and if the loudmouths of the Liberation Front keep up their shtick, the same will come to magikiers."

"Let it! Let them see what faithless gods they worship! And let us rise in their stead. Me, Tenebret, let me rise from this body-snatcher!"

"The ever-marching clock will strike twelve forevermore. Always ticking, an endless loop. But evil people are much rarer than evil choices, evil actions, evil ignorance. When these back even a good person into a corner, the world will look upon them and carve Evil into their skin. Here and now, the clock chimes twelve again." A note of melancholy dripped from his tone, weeping in my heart. "But I pry my own hand from the face of this clock. Whether you reclaim your body or perish within your host, I withdraw from these theatrics."

"You dare insinuate-?" Evelyn raged, fury spitting fire from our lungs, but she choked on burdened breath, losing her voice.

The mute face slid its unblinking gaze to me, locking eyes with mine. "There remains the problem of you."

"Me?" I squeaked through a throat too tight even to breathe.

"You should be no more than a body, stripped of its soul, empty on the inside, and yet here you are. A living thing. A sentient thing. You oppose the one from whom you've derived yourself, capable of your own choices, with agency to do as you will. And what do you do with it? Fight for the centions?"

I swallowed back saliva, a loud gulp, and opened my now too-dry mouth to speak. "I'm here to save Seth and help the Arhillin take back their city-"

"Then you're here for magikiers."

"I... Yes? I don't know what you're asking."

Distraction entered his tone, speaking more to himself than to me. "How peculiar a pattern."

Furrowing my brows in confusion, I glanced around the infinitely open space. "What pattern?"

He ignored my repetition like one ignores a cave's echo, still speaking to himself. "How long spent studying those like you with so few answers. Do you follow in the footsteps of your forebears knowingly?"

I started in surprise, head dizzying with the concept I couldn't help but parrot aloud, "Back it up a sec. There are others like me?"

"You are, of course, the first in modern times to make contact with your counterpart. Second only to Herren's first reincarnation in the time of the Great Dragons. Evelyn should know something of this." A cruel intonation entered his tone, and I felt Evelyn fuming on my back, but I spoke before she could steal the breath from my lungs again.

"Wait, wait, wait," I rasped, unable to think, but he didn't seem to hear me. "You mean the original shonte?"

A condescending chuckle bounced through the air. "Shonte, you call yourselves, but this terminology is only a key by which to unlock the powerful being bound to your mortal form, and centions themselves, the lock. Are you not aware of what you are?"

"Evidently not! But how can I be when the only ones who know anything speak a language of cryptic half-phrases?" I clenched my hands into fists on my thighs, working to tone down my frustration.

"Pity. Perhaps one day, when the domenth to whom you're tethered poses less of a problem, I can study you."

Irate heat spread over my chest and up my neck at the repugnant notion. "I'm not some lab rat."

"Not yet." He paused, the gravity of his silence swathing my buzzing head. "Yes, I've decided. I won't kill you; I won't even capture you lest Valencia get her hands on you. For the time being, I want nothing to do with you."

"Wha-? Why do you work for her if you hate her so much!" I spluttered, my heightening indignation warming me up to the tips of my ears.

"What a vexingly common misconception," he groaned, and I could practically hear him palming his tired eyes in frustration. "Granted, many who sheltered themselves under the refuge of my banner have taken up arms in her name and joined the Liberation Front. But let it be known, my only role in this was my leniency."

"You leveled the City of Gates and took the weapon of achaion!"

"Should I have left it for Valencia, who slayed the brilliant creature from whose bones it was made? My Collector was apprehended on his way to the City of Gates, and Liberation Front forces had already captured the city. What choice did I have?"

My head was spinning, but a light flicked on in sudden understanding. "You teleported there to get it. Like just now when you took me from Simon. *That's* what leveled the City of Gates."

"My unfortunate footprint."

"And Seth? Why did the Liberation Front bring him to you if not for some great, big, evil scheme, courtesy of Valencia?"

"He passed through her hands before mine."

"But you wanted him, and the Liberation Front handed him over," I persisted, "It wouldn't be the first time they've handed magikiers over to you, would it? You've been stockpiling carmavi magikiers."

His eyes glistened at my words, the first inkling of consciousness in the haunting face before me. "I have."

"If you wanted Seth for the same reason, he isn't carmavi."

"No, that he is not, but I haven't forgotten the significance of the Knox lineage. Valencia yields to my competence in unearthing the old magic buried deep in the recesses of his genetics. And so, it's unfortunate, there's nothing I can do with this broken magikier."

With furrowed brows in confusion, I opened my mouth to demand an explanation, but he wasn't done.

"Now she tries to placate me with promise of two others, both from an offshoot of the Knox bloodline, but I know where their loyalties lie. I know what will happen if I awaken the old magic in them. It was for that reason she had this one sent to her first. To beguile him as she did them."

"Then my sister freed you for nothing," Evelyn snarled, derailing my train of thought as she stole the breath from my lungs, "You do everything for yourself. First a coward among your kind, now a traitor to your only allies–"

"Allies?" he barked, voice like the crack of a whip, "You were the ones who destroyed all that I loved in the names of those you now seek to ruin!"

"Do you not want the same?" A hint of satisfaction, of triumph, coloured Evelyn's gloating tone. She had finally gotten a rise out of him. "Have our interests not aligned?"

"The time is long gone for me to claim my vengeance, for who is left to find solace in peace times with me but enemies of ages past, tainted by foul pretences and fouler deeds? Butchers, every last one of you."

"So you're more like…" I considered it, finding the breath in my lungs once more to speak, "Tentative associates?"

He scoffed. "More or less."

I knew it was a long shot – and highly controversial – but I took a deep breath, raised my chin, and with voice as soft as snowfall, offered, "You have more options than you're letting yourself see. Tenebret… you can join me. We can stop the Liberation Front before they make everything worse for all magikierkind and… And we can hold the centions accountable for their failures. I know where your Collector is being taken, and through him, I know where the other weapons of achaion will be. They'll go back to the centions if we don't do something about it."

All was silent. Even Evelyn held her breath – our breath – in suspense, awaiting Tenebret's response.

"Are you, the centions' champion, now a separatist, too?" he finally mused, a dry, almost mocking tone tainted by hidden darkness. "Wishing for a new empire removed from your despots? To do peacefully, through discourse, negotiations, and an arms race of incomparable weapons, what the Liberation Front strives to achieve through strife and confrontation?"

"Isn't that the better way? The system they built is so broken, it *needs* to be rebuilt. *Without* throwing armies at each other until one side runs out of bodies."

"You're not the first to think so. Look to my alleged empire and see the warpaint branded onto the faces of the disparaged, appointed the savage enemies of civilized folk. Look to your own Empress of magikierkind, a front posing as autonomy, and see the marks of centions on more than just her banners. How do you expect to hold immortals to account when those who make up the oppressed are finite?"

"They'll have to listen if we-"

"They won't," he simply said, "They can't be reasoned with unless threatened, and if you threaten them with the weapons of achaion as you're implying, you'll just become another defector for their dutiful loyalists to rally against." A glint of cunning entered his eyes. "If you were to bring the weapons to me, you would have little to worry about. With those weapons, I am still the Kaipracan, the greatest evil on Cellana, the ancient enemy of centions and all their children, but the magic of dragons will be out of the centions' reach and in better hands."

"Capable hands, I think you mean. What's stopping you from decimating everyone who opposes you with an arsenal like that? You're as untrustworthy as the centions, and just as caught up in their webs and wars."

"So you think the arms of achaion are better left to you? And for what? Leverage and pretty words?"

"Just give me a chance!"

"What chance do you have? You're as blinded by hope as you are ever hopeless. I don't fight for Valencia or her Liberation Front, but I will not hinder her efforts to dispatch those who've long deserved death, especially now that the weapons are on their way back to the centions. Let her perish or succeed by whatever efforts she puts forth. Nothing will change for me."

"But what about everyone else! Are you really so stuck in their ways you'd rather actively do nothing than give help to the people who need it most?" I demanded, only to feel the breath suck back through my lungs on the cusp of Evelyn's tirade.

"You won't even repay those who helped you before anyone else would have dared? My sister, who freed you from eternal torment, and who suffered the centions' wrath just as you have? You could free me from my *enduring* sufferance, recompense for her trouble-!"

"Enough!" A sharp clap of thunder roiled through the dream, shaking the floating rivers from their winding paths, and moving through the ground like a static shock. The moment this frenetic energy hit my knees, I felt a tug in the core of my being, sucking Evelyn back inside me so sharply that a sting came with it, slicing pain on the tops of my cheeks just below my eyes. I didn't have time to think about it before I was wrenched backwards through my own eyes, deep and deeper still, until I awoke.

My good eye flashed open, the blood-caked one struggling just to squint, and that strange stinging sensation just below them returned, carried over from the dream. There was too much to focus on, the bodily pains I had left behind now groaning all over, albeit muted for the numb sensation of magical sedation humming under my skin.

Tenebret leaned back from me, dropping his thumb and forefinger from my face where the stinging sensations persisted, but his listless gaze caught on something beyond me.

I heard their hobbling footsteps and heavy breathing before I turned my head to see them. My eyes passed over Seth, still wilted against the wall, and found the double doors just as Kev and Lin burst into the room, wielding weapons and propping each other up as if they could pose any sort of threat to someone like Tenebret. They couldn't, not even in their prime.

But for all their weaknesses, there wasn't an ounce of hesitation in their fervent eyes.

Misplaced determination.

With a flick of his finger, Tenebret drew a line through the air, reflected in the ornate ceiling, across which a massive fissure ripped open above their heads.

41

From the Ashes

"STOP!" I CROAKED AS THE CEILING SPLIT IN HALF, HEAVY CHUNKS OF DEbris raining through. Throwing my good arm forward, I rushed to summon the magic without thinking of the consequence, but even this slight jostling motion was enough to have me biting back breath as a blast of pain shot through my ostensibly *not* good arm, firing off warning bells around my head and disrupting all thought. I lost the thread, the magic feeling further from me than it had in weeks.

My entire body recoiled, my outstretched hand clamping shut against the pain in my opposite wrist, but my fingers closed around something solid. Porous and so dry, it seemed to suck the blood from my wounds and the moisture from my skin. And yet, this thing felt natural in my grasp, like my fingers and palm had slotted into a perfect handprint.

When I glanced up from under my eyelashes, wet with pained tears, I startled in surprise to see what had found my hand just as I closed my fist.

The weapon of achaion, its bone-white handle clenched in my fist, had sought out my grasp seemingly of its own accord. And here in my hand, it did what I couldn't, modifying itself by whatever intrinsic magic was sheathed within it.

The length of the glaive extended in my grip, doubling, no, tripling in size and span, as the hook along the blade's dull edge became more prominent, until it was flat against Lin and Kev's bodies.

Jerking my wrist, I swept the two caught on its hook aside, out of the way of the clamouring avalanche of stone, for this had all happened as fast as a thought.

Brushed to the farthest wall where Seth sat slumped and unconscious in his bindings, they evaded the brunt of the demolition, but even so, Lin had to burst the closest barrage of stone, shattering whole chunks into pebble showers before their heads would be caved in.

Beyond the semi-deafened ringing in my ears, I heard Tenebret suck in breath between his teeth, a note of surprise colouring the sound. I rounded on him with a snarl.

"You said you want nothing to do with me!" This furious reminder felt as if to lodge in my throat for the wrath compressing my lungs. "You could have killed them!"

My words flew over him, entirely unheard for the expression of shock waking his tired eyes. He stared down at Fiamme clasped in my grip, the epitome of disbelief etched on his pale features. My own sharp words rang in my ears, the small sounds of settling dust seeming rather to crash through the imposing silence of the room.

Most of the ceiling had collapsed, the sky now peeking through, and for a moment, all was still. And all eyes were on me.

After all this time and all my worries, this legendary weapon of achaion, the glaive carved from the bones of a dragon, had chosen *me*. Deemed me worthy to wield it, even over the most powerful creature on Cellana himself.

It retracted to regular size in my hand, shorter now than it had been in Tenebret's grasp so as to better complement my height, and somehow… different.

I couldn't put a finger on why, but the glaive itself held a warmer glow in the reds and golds of the blade, now even less like a blade with rounded edges, a sizable oval eye, and a broad, fishhook shape. In my hands, it had become a tool for disarming and manipulating a fight, capable of incredible extension and reduction in the blink of an eye. And it was alive, a hidden sentience sheathed in the bones of the ancient dragon it was made from. In my hand was the spirit of the crimson emberbreast herself, Fiamme.

A spark of kinship blazed in my chest, binding me to the tool clenched in my fist. The centions had remade her into a weapon, but in my hands, she would save lives.

"She would choose the same hands that helped slay her in another life?" Tenebret's voice shook, rippling through the air like waves of force shoving against my skull. His fury slopped off him, a suffocating heat. "Matching two halves of separate wholes together, incompatible puzzle pieces forced to fit. This imposter's hands, bloodied by someone else, are no more fit to wield Fiamme than Evelyn herself."

"Leave her alone!" Lin shouted from the other side of the room, but I didn't dare break eye contact with Tenebret, sensing the volatility of his wrath like waves sloshing over me.

"Fiamme wouldn't accept this," he hissed, reaching for the staff in my hand. There was nowhere for me to go while he crouched over me, no room for me to evade him or strength in my body for me to try, but I didn't have to.

A whistling of wind was our only warning before a streak of gold bulleted in through the crack in the ceiling, and Briar extended her long wings into a spiralling swoop following the walls, gaining speed in her descent.

Quiet joy filled me at her appearance. She'd been gone so long, I had almost started to believe Simon's taunting words.

And then she landed, striking with all the force of her swift descent directly onto my stomach with wings unfurled, curtaining me off from Tenebret's view.

I doubled forward upon impact, winded by the force of her landing and gasping for breath. And that's when Fiamme made contact with Briar's scales.

What came next, no one was expecting.

There was no sound, no real impact to be felt, no true way of knowing it had happened besides the shift in the balance of the room, the weight of the world, the kilter of magic itself.

The moment Briar brushed against the weapon of achaion crafted from the bones of her kin, a burst of blinding light bloomed out from the point of contact, carrying absolute silence on blazing emptiness.

I couldn't be sure how vast the radiant burst grew to be, but my eyes didn't recover for a good thirty seconds – feeling more like a lifetime with everything that was going on. When my vision finally readjusted, Briar had disappeared. Or rather, Briar was no longer the Briar I had come to recognize.

Consumed by the radiance now captured in her scales as swirling flames of red, green, blue, and purple lined with metallic ribbons of gold and bronze, Briar was undergoing a rapid transformation. The growth spurt of these past few weeks, now accelerating at a phenomenal rate.

She leapt into the air on a whirlwind of colours, sieving off of her like dust, as her body changed. With each burst of colour, she grew into a mightier form. When once I would have called her serpentine, now she was unmistakeably dragonesque. The growth spurt of the past few weeks took only seconds to double, then triple, and flourish exponentially beyond even that.

Sheathed in this pulsating veil of radiance and wheeling colours, Briar was reawakening into the form the centions had stripped from her when they first confined her to the tiny, inanimate vessel they had made of her – an inanimate vessel not unlike the one into which the centions had suppressed Evelyn's domenth magic, only a sliver of which had returned to our shared body, bringing with it her consciousness.

Briar was returning to her former glory, and as she did, I could feel Evelyn rising to the surface to watch.

The tops of my cheeks tickled, the muscles twitching where I had felt that stinging sensation in the dream we shared with Tenebret, but more than that, Evelyn's dark cloud of envy brewed like a storm over my own consciousness.

Why her? They wouldn't have chosen her to be reborn. Not after all that she did, all that she was… Why her?

Briar must have realized she would outgrow the room, for she barreled out the window, shedding light and indescribable colour over everything in her wake. Just as quickly as she had appeared, she was gone again, fleeing the room before her size could bring the entire ceiling down on us.

"Briar?" Tenebret breathed, an odd note painting his tone, but I didn't have time to register the spark of recognition in his eyes, nor decipher the unreadable expression furrowing his brow. Not while his distraction offered a rare opening, and the window behind him, an improvised doorway.

With a flourish of my hand, I twirled Fiamme over my knuckles until the hooked end struck Tenebret's side, momentarily winding him. I heard Briar's voice in the back of my head, or rather, felt a flood of protest pour into me through the buzzing connection she tried to open between our minds, but now wasn't the time for distraction.

Fiamme maneuvered so naturally in my grip, the dull knob of the staff pressing Tenebret's navel while the deepened curve of the hook snagged his waist. I had him right where I wanted him. I only had to think the word, "*Extend!*" and Fiamme complied.

The staff shoved Tenebret backwards, his boot heels dragging on the marble floor, until the window ledge caught the backs of his knees.

I twisted the pole in my hand as he lost his balance over the ledge, and the hook rotated so as not to catch his back. Over he went with naught but a reactive shout and grasping hands, too swept up in the distraction Briar had involuntarily provided to fight back.

For a moment, I thought maybe he would latch onto Fiamme to stabilize himself, until the staff shortened back to its normal length in response to this very thought, and he was gone, toppling out the same exit Briar had taken.

I froze, staring at the open window he had so unceremoniously tumbled through.

Surely, he wouldn't be *the* Kaipracan if a measly fall from the peak of the Arillian Spire could do him in. Right? God, I sure hoped not. What would that make me?

A hypocrite most unworthy of the praise you would receive.

"Shut up, Evelyn," I hissed under my breath in the hush that had fallen over the room in the wake of all that had happened, and all so fast. Tenebret's shout still reverberated off the walls, or maybe it was just in my ears.

"What just happened?" Kev's shaken voice crossed the room to me, uncertain celebration wavering over his tone. "Did Briar…? Is he…? He can't be *dead*, can he?"

"No shot," Lin answered, but even she sounded doubtful of this, "After all the Liberation Front's big talk about their *champion*? After whatever the hell earthquake he pulled on us just now and everything Brett said he did in the City of Gates? No way someone like that just stumbles out a window and dies."

And she was right.

As if to punctuate Lin's words, the entire room shook with the weight of some colossal thing clinging to the side of the building, and in through the window rocketed a plum-coloured arm as wide around the wrist as the window was tall.

Besides the astral colouration and gargantuan size of this appendage, this arm had the same general shape and proportions of a human arm, but that hardly seemed to matter when the pinky finger alone measured my full height from head to toe, tipped with a pointed nail as black as night.

"Return what was stolen from me!" boomed the voice of the Kaipracan in his true form, his volume alone shattering the stone surrounding the window. The intrusive hand slammed down on the floor, searching me out, but I clutched the weapon of achaion close to my chest and crawled backwards on one elbow.

With a series of boney snaps, the staff retracted into itself like a set of Russian nesting dolls until it wasn't much longer than a baton in my grasp and tipped with the hook and eyelet my influence had made of its blade. Like this, it looked more like a dull sickle, duller still when the silk ribbons on its end flew up and around itself. These thick layers of silk wrapped the bone and metal like a tightfitting sleeve, rounding all edges.

Another room-shaking collision crashed down on the ceiling, shaking dust and rubble loose from the already fractured stone. Through the open hole, a colossal shadow blocked out the light of day, glinting with the gold of dragon scales each the size of an average car's windshield.

Only then did it truly hit me. I had instigated the wrath of titans.

The shadow over the hole in the ceiling disappeared, and the plum-coloured hand jerked suddenly backwards as if the giant it belonged to had been wrenched away from the Spire. Through the destroyed window, I could finally make out the full forms of these battling behemoths.

The first thing I saw were wings larger than ship sails, a gold and white patterned wingspan encompassing the entire Spire, attached like a bat's wings from shoulders to the very tip of a long tail. Beneath the radiant canvas they painted across the sky, a confusing jumble of gold and purple at once amazed and confounded me.

Briar no longer possessed that slinky form I had come to associate with her, now broad, deep-chested, and powerful, with a mane of white frills trailing the length of her narrow, fox-like face down her long and winding neck. Flying like this, her body whipped around like a ribbon through the air as her four legs, proportioned for a feline gait, ensnared and grappled her prey. The antlers that had crowned her head now branched out like a magnificent headdress of white-tipped spears, and the stubs along her jawline had grown into expressive golden frills lined with white spines. Magnificent in the regal arches of her features and yet ferocious in the palpable power of her form; just beholding her grandeur shook me to my core.

And she had the Kaipracan ensnared in her formidable talons – yes, talons. Even from here, I could see the difference in her front digits, no longer cloven hooves but lethal talons. Just another restraint I hadn't realized the centions forced on her.

The Kaipracan himself was an eyeful, not exactly digestible in a single glance, and it wasn't just because of the iridescent purples of his complexion, like looking at a nebula painted across the night sky, nor his cascading raven black hair as long as he was tall.

Ignoring the sheer size of him – practically on par with Briar – he was for the most part human-shaped, so it wasn't a complete shock to my system when taking in the less human factors, like the quartet of curled, jet-black tusks protruding from his upper and lower jaws, nor the four arms in pairs on either side of his muscular torso, nor even the black-furred hindquarters befitting of a goat ranging from his waist to cloven hooves where his feet should have been. His hoofprint alone could have flattened the City of Gates. Even with all that, he wasn't exactly the bestial monstrosity I had been anticipating after everything I'd heard about the fabled Kaipracan.

And Briar was holding her own against him, refusing to release him from her talons for the sheer devastation that would wreak upon the city below. Rather, with the Kaipracan grappled in her claws, she pounded her rippling wings, driving the both of them higher and higher into the overcast sky until the heavy cloud coverage gobbled them up, out of view.

Whether she was thinking of the city or obtaining privacy, I couldn't tell, but a weaseling conspiracy had entered my mind. After all, Tenebret had recognized Briar the moment she transformed, and there wasn't an ounce of hostility in his regard. That much, I was certain of.

It was enough to make me wonder if Briar had known exactly what would come over her upon touching the weapon of achaion. If she had known, all along, the restraints it would unshackle from her, and not just the advantage it would give me.

Wobbling to an unsteady stand, I got my feet under me with Fiamme sheathed on my hip and my broken wrist clutched to my chest in my other hand. Whatever Tenebret had done to get into my head, it had lessened the pain upon waking, enough for me to gather enough strength in my legs to hobble across the trashed room.

I fell to my knees beside Kev and Lin, the stopper placed on my pain acting my mask, and yet there was no hiding the damage done. They busied themselves with removing Seth's chains, leaving me with nothing to do but watch through tear-blurred eyes, catching on the marks of abuse written into Seth's body after only five days of Liberation Front captivity and Tenebret's experimentations – whatever that implied.

Lin made quick work of the stone, releasing Seth from his bindings to the wall so he spilled limply into Kev's ready arms, but the metal cuffs themselves held fast to his bruised and scabbing wrists, fastened tight. Still, he was as good as…

"He's not-?" I rasped, choking on the emotion in my throat.

"He's holding on," Kev answered, as if he'd read my thoughts, "But he needs medical attention, fast. I mean, we're all in the same boat, but he's-"

"You said your magic can heal," Lin cut in, all business as she glanced sidelong at me, "Do you still have the strength to do it?"

Determination struck a match behind my eyes, and I dipped my chin in a curt nod. "Even if I don't, I have to try."

"Well now, hang on a second," Kev hastily leapt in, "Try, but still be careful. You're in about as rough shape as him, and everything you said about Evelyn, with your magic-"

Bumping his side, I flashed an encouraging smile, brightened my eyes, and lightened my tone on the words, "It's okay. I'll be fine."

Judging by his doubtful expression, he still felt he could argue that point, but he let it drop with hands flapping in gesture for me to take it away, and so that, I did.

"Hear that, Evelyn? Work with me, here," I muttered under my breath.

Kev and Lin's sidelong glance between each other, brimming with concern, tipped me off to this slight faux pas. Okay, admittedly I could have aimed the thought at Evelyn rather than speak my crazy aloud, but times were tough, and I wasn't exactly at the top of my game in the way of *reducing* concerns about me. When was I ever?

"*I know you're listening,*" I continued in the privacy of our shared mind, "*Just, keep the channel open for me. Okay?*"

You speak as though I am not slave to your will.

"There you are," I breathed, closing my eyes to home in on the warmth of magic aglow behind her voice. Just like that, it flooded to the surface of my skin, hot on my palms already thick with the coagulating blood of my last failure.

The magic flowed out of me in pulses, washing over Kev, Lin, and Seth. I found their wounds immediately, gathering the waves of healing magic in the broken parts of them I was determined to fix. As for my own, well, the magic only poured out of me, not into me.

That was enough for me. To fix them, to heal the wounds they only received because of me, because I led them here and because he took the hit for me.

The rips, gashes, and scrapes were the first to knit back together with fluids carrying away infection, and scar tissue growing in the place of skin. Then went the bruises, the misplaced blood beneath the surface returning to repaired blood vessels. Damaged muscles, injured bone, my magic delved deeper and deeper, fixing all in its path with each wave of healing energy pulsing out from my hands and washing through my friends.

And yet, while the life returned to Kev and Lin's haggard complexions with the reparations my magic worked, Seth didn't stir. He showed no signs of improvement, and for the first time, I realized just how uninjured he was – on the surface. Something was wrong, that much was certain, but I just couldn't see it, and no matter how I pushed, my magic wasn't touching him.

No, that wasn't quite right. My magic was pouring into him, just as it was with Kev and Lin, but in Seth, it simply had nowhere to go, sifting away into his body without actually changing anything. Whatever the problem was, my efforts had no impact on it.

Unacceptable.

After everything, I *had* to be able to save him. To wake him. To bring him back.

Shutting my eyes tighter, I scrunched up my face and followed the flow of magic crashing out from me now in tidal waves. The skin under my eyes seemed to shift, a slight discomfort, but I ignored it. Instead, I searched on the riptide of my magic, soaking deeper into Seth on its hunt for something to mend, only to feel the healing energy pool as if caught in an eddy, churning as a waterspout over a tub drain, and sink away to nothing. It wasn't soaking into his body at all but getting swallowed up by some abyssal emptiness beneath his skin.

Only then did I notice the sucking sensation drawing my magic in, siphoning it into this insatiable abyss. I felt it first in my chest, like I'd had the wind knocked out of me. Then in the numbness prickling down my arms, the chill biting into my fingertips. It wasn't painful, not in the usual way, but it was draining.

I noted Lin's voice distantly. "What's that?"

"Wha-? Annie!" Kev's voice rocked me from my concentration, the urgency – no, it was outright panic – calling me out of my own mind. "Annie, stop! Your face-!" He lost the words, beyond comprehension.

What about my face? That was the question I wanted to ask, but distraction lifted it from the tip of my tongue when I tried to open my eyes – emphasis on *tried.* The thin line of separation between my eyelids felt as though it had grown over on both eyes, as if sewn shut by my very eyelashes.

Rather, that strange tickling sensation renewed itself with new vigour on the tops of my cheeks, just beneath my disobedient eyelids. The shift I had felt now more of a deepening wrinkle, a fold under each eye.

A sound like a dry chuckle found my ears on tones too familiar, the breath escaping my own lungs. The very sound raised the hairs on my arms, my heart stuttering a beat, only to break into an excitable gallop.

"That egotistical fool." My voice spoke these snide words with a flavour of triumph. That was all it took.

Something snapped within me, then. Something deep and indescribable. A centering sensation always there and yet imperceptible – until broken.

All in an instant, a dark shroud consumed not only my vision, but my entire being as the magic cut suddenly short, dying in my hands to cease its healing flow. The last thing I felt were the arms of my friends looping around me, catching me as I fell forward.

A wall. I had hit a wall, not just from the overuse of my magic – of pouring it like a faucet into Seth only for the darkness within him to eat it up – but in that moment, I was only grateful, for on the brink of my collapse, another had awoken.

With my eyes sewn shut, Evelyn had surfaced beyond mind alone, unto perception, voice, and our shared body; my worst fears, confirmed.

Shonte – the word itself, a catalyst, an evocation, to take powerful, untamed magic into my hands. The raw magic of the being locked within me. Tenebret had said so himself, cryptic and vague as he'd been.

Now I was sure of it. The more I used this magic Evelyn facilitated in me, the more she emerged from within. Her reawakening.

42

Long Train Running

Day 25

A SEEMING ETERNITY PASSED IN IMMEMORABLE OBSCURITY, TRAPPING me in half-dreams never quite lucid enough to stick. Fleeting moments of clarity brought about snippets of consciousness, counting days through swift-forgotten encounters with unrecognizable silhouettes, hazy around the edges. Until finally, I opened my eyes to a train compartment – no, not my actual eyes, I soon realized.

This was just another dream. And as had become troublingly standard, I wasn't alone here in the shuddering train car, seated on a brown leather bench seat rough with wear and tear, facing my cerebral guest.

Yes, guest. Rare though it was, this time, the intruder in my head was a welcome visitor.

Seth sat on the leather bench seat across from mine, his chin resting in his palm and elbow propped up on the windowsill. With legs crossed, thigh over thigh, the toe of his dress shoe nearly brushed my knee for the intimacy of the train compartment.

To see him here, whole again and in front of me, no matter that it was a dream, seemed a soothing balm to the anxiety I had carried with me for so long. For just this moment, I indulged myself, simply taking him in.

Sunlight showered over him from the frosted windowpane, catching in the dark strands of hair falling into his cornflower blue eyes and dancing over his rich complexion, highlighting the burgundy undertones of his dark skin.

He hardly looked the haggard mess I had last seen of him, but he was also the one constructing this dream and all that I saw within it.

"Seth," I breathed, unable to tear my thoughts from the subjects most pressing on my mind, most recent, most disturbing. The fact that I couldn't heal him, and before even that, our last interaction – the kiss that had almost become so much more, and more pressing, the confession that he had meant to end his life that night. Was he thinking about it, too? Was he beset by a flood of muddled emotions like I was, knocking into me in bafflingly convoluted and destabilizing waves?

He spoke with measured intonation, fixing his distant gaze on the window. "You've been out of commission for a few days, now, but we're all aboard the northbound train to Schevon." Ah, so we were back to strict formality, the easiest out by which to forego more difficult conversations. A twinge of disappointment settled low in my gut.

"A train? Like, on the same tracks taken over by the Liberation Front?"

A muscle twitched in the corner of his mouth, threatening a smile. "Yes and no. It wasn't long after the Arhillin drove the Liberation Front out of their city that they reclaimed the tracks, too."

"They won…?" A flash of gold and purple sparred in my mind's eye. "What about the Kaipracan?"

"Though he had taken on his more vulnerable and more destructive form near the end of the battle, Briar lost him in the smoke and fire."

"*Lost* him? How'd she manage that? He was a hundred-foot-tall monster last I checked, and *purple*!"

"Few were as ready to believe Valencia's champion could be the Kaipracan and that he was in Arillia as you were. When they saw what he was, who he was, the Arhillin broke rank. They nearly lost the day, until Briar broke off from her battle and focused instead on routing the Liberation Front on the ground."

Against myself, a childish grin picked up the corners of my mouth. "Would it be in bad taste to say I called it? I knew, I *knew* he was the Kaipracan."

"You did," he smirked, "Even as his prisoner, I refused to believe it. He was so…"

"Plain?" I offered, cupping my elbow in one hand, and raising my index finger on the other. "You have to admit, he was pretty drab for an ancient, god-like being. Unimpressive, if I'm being honest."

The smirk on his lips ranged up to his eyes, crinkling with a genuine smile as he tilted his head in his hand. Still, he kept his regard glued to the world speeding by beyond the window. "I can give you the rest of the recap if you'd like. You *did* knock yourself out just in time to miss the big finale."

I snapped my mouth shut, gesturing for him to continue with an animated nod.

"Once the Kaipracan fled the battle, the Liberation Front's morale plummeted. With Briar raining fire down on them from overhead, they were forced to retreat and run out by the Arhillin, corralled north where they were pincered by the people of the City of Gates bolstering Schevon's border forces. I don't know if you planned this, but when you positioned our people there, you ensured the surrender of the Liberation Front and a resounding victory for all of Arillia."

Betraying my surprise – and evident lack of planning – I sputtered, "They were already there?"

"They'd arrived by train because of your friends from the Khuloces Base."

"So we got the Liberation Front, all of them?"

"Most. Any who weren't slain on the battlefield or taken prisoner along the border are being weeded out by the Arhillin in Arillia and the Schevorlain in Schevon. We won, Anelisha. You did the impossible, you're finally safe. So won't you sleep?"

I quirked my head to one side, painting confusion plain on my face. "Is that not…?" With a glance down at myself, I tried to decipher his meaning only to come up empty handed. "I was under the impression that's what I was doing. I'm certainly not *awake* right now."

"No. No, you aren't."

"Wha-? Well, if I'm not sleeping either, then what's all this?" I gestured to the warm-hued compartment, the wooden sliding doors boxing us in, the clinking of the decorative crystal chandelier quivering over our heads.

"One degree off from a daydream," he answered, following my gesture with his eyes to take in our surroundings. "I didn't build this dream, it's just your surroundings. Some part of you is aware enough to fill in the gaps where my magic can't reach. Limited by the part of you that's still conscious."

I glanced around the space with new appreciation, rubbing the worn leather to either side of my thighs. "Huh. You'd think they'd scrape the bottom of the barrel for the coma patient, but this place is downright swanky."

"Anelisha," he sighed, a hitch of soft laughter in his voice sending a jolt straight to my heart, "I thought hearing the outcome of the battle would settle it. That you accomplished everything you set out to, did such incredible things to get to where you are, to bring everyone to Schevon, *including* me. You need to rest."

"Hey, you're preaching to the choir, but I don't control the finer workings of my, what is it, melatonin production?"

"That's not the issue."

"There's an issue?"

Still without meeting my eyes directly, he brought a hand to the nape of his neck, blowing air. "Only a small one, I'm sure. Since you've been in this half-sleeping state, your body's been conscious. Sort of. Someone else is awake inside, but it's like you're in a trance."

A stroke of fear, white and paralyzing, burned through my gut.

"What?" It was all I could think to say for the maelstrom of thoughts churning in my head. "Ev-"

"Don't say her name," he interrupted, landing his eyes on mine, "It's better if we don't draw her attention."

"But she's awake?"

"Not quite. Like you were for so long, she was just present. But when you sank into waking dreams, she rose to the surface. If you just sleep, if you turn off your mind, she'll go away, too, and your body will be able to rest and recover."

"But... *how*? Tenebret said he wouldn't help her."

He flinched at the name, a spark of something like fear glinting in the gem-like blue of his eyes, but he shook off his reaction and brought a hand to his chin in contemplation. "He did?"

"Word for word, he wanted nothing to do with either her *or* me." I paused, recalling Tenebret's contrite attitude toward the footprint of his magic, and the strange sensation borne in my skin beneath the press of his fingers. "But he drew her out to speak to her. His magic still touched her. God! He's like the Elephant's Foot of magical radiation!"

"Elephant's Foot-?"

"He's the Kaipracan! Of course he's gonna leave a mark on my psyche after forcing his way in! All to have a chat with the nefarious celebrity in my brain. He's gotta be some humble if he thought he wasn't dropping a bomb with that stunt-"

"But no more of her essence is in you than there was before," Seth reminded me, quelling my hysterics before I could lose myself to raving. "She's still just a fragment of herself, probably the only reason she can't do much more than sit, stare, and shut you out."

"Well at least there's that, huh?" Sarcasm dripped from my tone, but I worked to calm myself, crossing my arms over my chest as I leaned back in my seat. "He said something when he was in my head that got me thinking, and maybe this just goes to confirm it. That shonte magic is just domenth magic through a funnel. A very specific funnel, a magikier funnel."

Surprise etched itself plain on his face. "The first shonte was made long before there were magikiers."

"Seth, I know this might come as a shock to you, but I don't think the centions gave an accurate representation of the original shonte. Or the origin of magikiers. Why should they if they have everything to hide?"

He shook his head, furrowing his brows in confusion and even mild insult. "Don't speak like that-"

"But things are finally starting to add up. Why the Kaipracan abducts the rarest of all magikiers, and why he says he studies others like me. Because carmavi magikiers and domenth reincarnations are the same! These taboo magikiers who the centions seem to hate but make anyway, whose magic pulls directly from them, who I was one of, pre-shonte-ification. They're all unawakened reincarnations of halved domenths, just like I was before I got a pinch of Evelyn's essence in me-"

"Don't say her name-"

"Every single carmavi magikier, all with the potential to become shontes, just like me. All they'd have to do is take the essence of the domenth they're bound to and tap into cention magic with that word, that key. No wonder Valencia's collecting carmavi like they're her golden ticket. They are!"

"That can't be right."

"Point out the fault in my logic, then," I challenged him, a twinge of anger coiling in my chest for his close-mindedness, so rare from him. "How can't you see what I'm seeing? That the very first carmavi magikier was this *Herren* guy's reincarnation. That he was the original shonte. I can't be crazy for putting it all together like this."

"You're completely ignoring everything the centions have taught us."

"Because they've repeatedly taught us lies! Seth, if I'm right, you could have the blood of the first magikier *and* the first shonte, but you're not a carmavi, not a reincarnation. Whatever genealogy is so unique to you, these facts alone are worthy enough causes for both Valencia and the Kaipracan to try to get their hands on you-"

"The way you're speaking could get you thrown in jail, or worse-"

"But you're the only one I'm saying this to. Seth..." Quieting my temper, I put a dampener on my excitement and leaned forward, shortening the distance between us in this already small compartment. "You were the head archivist in Blackano. You know the numbers. So how many carmavi magikiers are there at a time? How many are there now, and how many domenths were there?"

He shook his head, refusing to meet my imploring eyes. "I came here to push Evelyn back into the recesses of your mind, not pass dissenting ideas around like they're nothing."

"They're not nothing-"

"Then what are they?" His low, heavy tone shoved me back against my seat, his steely regard dragging me down with the weight of his severity. "When you say these things, it sounds like an argument in favour of treason. It *sounds* like you'd rather join the Liberation Front."

"What? No, of course I wouldn't-"

"Then what's your argument? That everything we fight for is a lie? That the soldiers I led and the lives they lost were all in vain? Their sacrifices, in defense of an unworthy cause?"

"No! I-" While he glared at me, eyes like chips of ice, I wasn't sure what I meant for him to feel, to think, in my telling him any of this. While my heart pounded and my fingertips numbed, while TV static filled my body and white noise buzzed between my ears, I simply wasn't sure of anything. "I'm sorry, I... I don't know. I just thought I was piecing the puzzle together-"

"What's said is said," he breathed, catching his temples between thumb and middle finger, "But I just can't hear this right now. With everything that's... Now that I'm..." His tone turned inward, unfinished thoughts pouring out of him, but I could just as well have not been there. "I can't keep doing this."

My voice came out small. Meek. "No, no, I should've thought about what I was saying. I just, I got excited-"

"It's not that." New resolution burned in his eyes, but there was something deeper behind it, something he couldn't hide, like the determination was no more than a mask for his fear, for his shame. "There's something I haven't been telling you, and it's been making everything, all of this, just *that* much harder to..." He ran a hand up through his hair, letting soft locks slide between his long fingers and fall back into his eyes avoiding mine. A shudder ran through me as I noticed his smoky-eyed gaze on my neck, my gut swirling with the memory of when he kissed me there.

"Tell me," I whispered, barely audible over my heart's thunderous rattling in the cage of my ribs. Leaning forward, I placed a hand on his knee, rubbing my thumb over the woolen material of his dress pants, but he flinched from my touch, his back straight against the seat.

"Even if I say nothing, I have no doubts you'll find out. I was stupid to let it go on this long." He sounded so broken, so renounced, but something else distracted me. His eyes were on mine, and I could swear I saw the blue pull back in wisps to reveal a vibrant red beneath, like drops of red dye overcoming water's gentler hue. "I'd just rather you hear it from me-"

"That so?" a third voice interrupted, dark and moody with dissatisfaction, "You've been hiding it all this time, and *now* you want to ruin the surprise? Where's your showmanship?"

As this familiar voice filled the confines of the train compartment, a glare of light flashed in through the frosted panes and caught in my eyes, blinding me momentarily. When I blinked my vision back to normal, Seth was gone, not even an indent in the seat across from mine hinting at his having been there. There was only a long, red feather, mocking me.

A groan escaped my tightened lungs, and I rocked forward, clenching my hands on the edge of my seat with locked elbows. "Goddamnit, Evelyn, we talked about your interruptions."

"Did we? As I remember it, you yelled your complaints into the void, and I had a hearty chuckle at your expense."

"You couldn't just enjoy having a body?"

"To what end? My grip was waning, and it's not like I could do much with it, anyway. Not as I am now." I could hear the disinterested shrug in her blasé tone, hiding deeper frustrations. "I figured, if I must return to my shackles, I might as well get the timing right. Make a spectacle of it, as it were."

"Make a nuisance of it, actually," I huffed, but my mind was elsewhere, chasing the trail of Seth's unfinished confession.

"Whine all you like, I'm sick of you fawning over him. See, now, my rightful place stifling you to the background where all along I had been, though you know not the sufferance it is to exist on the true outskirts of being. The way it shreds you down to nothing while simultaneously, unconsciously, you cannot help but rebuild yourself forevermore. Caught in the excruciation of the in-between."

"Oh, shut up, Sisyphus. I don't want to hear it."

A beat of silence, and the very walls of the train compartment wept with Evelyn's pervasive malice. "I could show you." Tracks of light contoured the edges and corners of the ornate wood, tearing away sliver by sliver to fill the empty space with long, threatening splinters. The rest of the train compartment fell away, until I sat alone on a disseminating bench seat, innumerable shining splinters dancing around me in the endless abyss.

"You can't hurt me."

"You misunderstand. I can't *kill* you. What I do here won't harm our physical body. But you? This morsel of consciousness only now passing to sleep?" A shard of wood shot forward, pinning straight through the back of my hand to the seat beneath. And there was pain – the pain of wounds I couldn't recognize in my own memories, drawn to the surface by Evelyn's cruel intent. "This fabrication of self you parade around is my plaything here in this headspace we share. This mindscape I command."

I couldn't help the pitiful sound of struggle which escaped me as I pulled my hand from the wooden stake. Had the splinter expanded while I wasn't looking?

When I raised my hand before my eyes, a hole the size of a golf ball had been carved out of my palm to the back of my hand, leaking rivulets of red from both sides down my arm. Pain washed through the gaping wound in clusters of mix-and-matched memories, decimating my resolve in the purple swelling around it.

It felt so real, so painful – how could this be a dream?

"Time has a funny way of warping itself in the unconscious mind, you know," Evelyn whispered into my ear beyond the pain shrieking in my head, shrill and insistent, "Moments might pass in the real world, mere seconds, but I could have you here for what feels like days, weeks, months, unto time immemorial. No more than a blink of an eye in the context of my long life, but an eternity for you, leech."

"Why even bother? There's no point to it, you won't affect anything. Not really." For all my fury, my voice still trembled.

"That may be true once you wake up, but why not have a little fun while I can?"

"But it's not real," I heaved through the agony insisting it's importance in my head, setting off alarm bells throughout my body.

"How long, I wonder, before you'll believe it is? Before you forget your life outside the hell I create for you? The hell you've long deserved." I could hear the leering grin in her voice. "It's not like I have anything better to do, is it?"

Another shard flung forward, spearing the hollow of my wrist to the leather cushion supporting my back, then another, and a third, a fourth, catching my shoulder, nestling between my ribs, plunging deep beneath my collarbone. A flurry of wooden nails rushed into me, lengthening within the case of my flesh. They affixed me to the seat at my back like pins spreading a butterfly, until I sagged between these elongating spikes, sobbing from aching lungs.

"What have I to gain? What have I to lose? Nothing, always nothing, already stolen out from under me by your very being. You, who thieved the breath from my lungs just to spit nonsense in Tenebret's face."

A hiccup of breath, trembling and gasping wetly in my throat, carried the weak words, "I didn't-"

"Had it been me, *just* me, I would have stricken him down until he knelt shuddering and weeping at my feet, but the worm that you are, grovelled at his instead. Begged for mercy, for *help*. Pathetic thing that you are as to beseech a beast and in doing so, lower me to your level."

Another stab of pain coursed through my abdomen, forcing a shuddering breath up from punctured lungs. "Don't pretend you didn't beg for something, just like me. And you got it. He released you, whether he meant to or not."

"Wrong." That familiar tingle on my skin returned to the tops of my cheekbones just beneath my eyes. With some clarity, I registered a hint of familiarity in the sensation, like blinking. "He didn't release me; he only woke what was sleeping in this body. What you've been poking and prodding at to control *my* magic."

"Funny, I almost wish he was still here, just to shut you up-"

Amidst the fog of confusion muddling my thoughts, I mistook the whistling air for a hiss of breath forced out between gritted teeth. This chilling sound ushered in another javelin thrown with Olympic force, filling my mouth to puncture through the back of my skull.

I could feel Evelyn rifling through my memories in search of a pain on this level, something to pair with the context of this forever worsening dream.

"Oh, continue your impudence if you'd like. All the better to carve it out of that unseemly temperament you went and developed," Evelyn mused somewhere beyond the shrill ringing in my head, an amalgamation of old headaches now revitalized all at once, "You've given me an arsenal of hurt, little parasite. I'd quite like to make use of it."

As with the gaping holes in my lungs having no bearing on my capacity for breath or speech, so too the spike skewering down my throat posed no greater blockage to my words than to bring discomfort to my jaws as I spoke around it, muffled and gagging but no less distinct in this absurd dreamscape.

"So now you're going to condition me like one of Pavlov's dogs-?" I caught myself on a hitched breath, a spike of pain shearing through all coherent thought. This, the only true interruption for my words.

"Your willingness to lay down your life, to fight the centions' battles and suffer your mortal peril in their immortal stead; all your self-sacrificing tendencies have only manufactured weapons catered to your own suffering, fitted perfectly to my hands. And how can I refuse such a splendid gift, after all the abuse you've put my body through?"

A scream ripped from my throat.

"You'll pay in pain for all that you've cost me."

I couldn't say how much time passed in the throes of this unending nightmare, but it did truly feel an eternity, blurring together over a bridge of torment and derision. Evelyn never tired, never stopped, not for a single instant, but my exhaustion was soon written into the lines she'd carved from my withering body, rebuilt again and again only to be picked apart once more, flayed into bits. The first to go was my voice – not because of any physical aspects of the dream, no. I had nothing more to say, nor even would Evelyn respond to me, lost to her own glee in doing to me what had been done to her in ages past. Then went my presence of mind. This, she endeavoured to draw back to the foreground of my mind, wanting me present, craving my awareness of all that she did to me.

When I woke, I was surprised.

There had been no warning. No lead-up to freedom. Hell, for a moment, I expected to look down at my hands and see the same blood that had stained into my skin, forever slick and spilling. Only once the haze of sleep had begun to clear was I surprised at the absence of wrinkles. The lack of aging. For surely, after everything, I couldn't be the same girl in the same body as before. Young. Unhurt. Alive.

It was a moment before I realized, I *should* have been injured – the fiasco at the Spire came back to me distantly, as tidal waves against a flat horizon. My throat was hoarse, scratchy and uncomfortable as if I'd been screaming, as I pushed up from a plush bed warm with duvet and quilt coverings – the air in the room was cold and dry, worse on my throat, but decorated extravagantly, dizzyingly, with silver trimmings on the furnishings and rich green wallpaper pressing in all around me from high-ceilinged walls. My unfocused stare landed on a mirror near the tall, white door, and suddenly, nothing else mattered.

I rushed forward, stumbling over an ottoman at the end of the bed and only barely catching myself on sleep-heavy arms, my hands planted on the wall to either side of the mirror. Shaky breaths escaped me as I stared at my reflection, the face that loomed over me in my nightmares – but there was something so subtly different about it.

My heart stuttered in my chest at what I saw, and resumed again, pounding awfully against my ribcage.

It was just as I thought. Along the tired lines beneath my eyes were folds that had never been there before. Exactly where Tenebret had placed his thumb and finger upon entering my head, to wake what morsel of Evelyn lived on in this body and see for himself the sister Valencia would go to war over.

Tentatively, I brought a hand to the slight, almost indiscernible line under my right eye, but hesitation gripped me. Tightening a fist against the tremble in my fingers, I pushed an exhale from my squeezing lungs and leaned more securely against my other arm, braced against the wall. Slowly and ever so carefully, I released my right fist and pressed my thumb beneath the fold.

The mirror's reflection donned an aspect of horror as the skin under the eye tented, the underlid of the fold tucking up under the top lid. There was no pain, none at all, only that mild sensation of skin in the wrong position.

Slowly, I pressed my thumb downward, dragging the underlid of the slit just enough to reveal a sliver of what lay beneath.

Nausea roiled low in my gut as stars popped across my field of view, tunneled in on this fingerprint-sized spot on my face. There, beneath the slit in my skin, was an eye just like the one above, but narrower, smaller, half-moon shaped and rolled back as if deep in sleep.

Evelyn's eyes, there on the tops of my cheekbones.

Tenebret hadn't just woken her within me but provided her with a measure of control over our body. His mere touch grew a new pair of eyes through which she could see, appendages only she could control. Rather than erase me to make space for her, his magic had merged us just that much more.

I felt the scream rip from my already damaged throat more than I heard it, but saw my fingers pressing in against the unwanted eyes more than I felt them.

In an instant, another pair of hands had me by my shoulders, and a third set took solid hold of my wrists, wrenching them away from my face.

I hadn't even noticed the door open beside me, but within seconds, I was being dragged back to the ottoman and wrestled down by all these hands fixed so firmly to my arms.

Only faintly did I register the familiarity of the voices talking over me.

"Annie! Calm down!" a less-than-calm voice shouted down at me, but I recognized it. I recognized *him.* And although his abrasive tone wasn't quite as effective in de-escalation as he might have intended, the mere sound of him was enough to snap me back to awareness.

My struggles ceased like a cold wind had swept over and frozen me. My empty stare ranged up the silhouette pressing me down, and I found those familiar turquoise eyes above mine. "Brett?" I whimpered, voice breaking over his name, "I- My face- It's Evelyn-"

The truly calming voice of my sister found me then, stifling the tendrils of panic coiling tight around my lungs. "Shh, Annie, it's okay. You're safe."

"Safe?" I repeated, finding myself shaking my head. "No. Where am I? How long-?"

"It's been five days since the Spire," Lin joined in, and I finally noticed her pink hair over by the back wall where she busied herself investigating the mirror I had been fixated upon. "But we only just arrived in the Cobblestone City of Schevon a few hours ago."

"By train," I whispered, fresh understanding abuzz behind my eyes. It hadn't even been a day since Seth visited my dream – since Evelyn took it over. At the thought, a hollow shudder began in my shoulders, wracking my body.

Brett's hands loosened on my upper arms, a spark of concern glinting in his eyes and furrowing his brows. "You're shaking. Are you cold?" He pulled the quilt from the end of the bed, wrapping it about my shoulders, but the convulsive tremors showed no sign of stopping.

Only then did I notice the intense chill of the room, and the intricate patterns of frost adorning the edges of the windowpanes making up a large portion of the wall adjacent to my bed, beside which stood Kev. Schevon, the country to the north of Arillia. Just how far north were we?

"Was it Evelyn?" Kev whispered, loud amid the silence of the room, "On the train? In your dreams?"

I snapped my eyes to his. "How'd you…?"

An uneasy smile tightened the curve of his mouth as he rubbed a hand over the back of his neck. "Oh, uh, she showed up. In the Spire. You passed out and she…"

"Woke up," Lin stiffly finished for him, shooting Kev a rude gesture in the absence of a glare – her usual goggles and mask had been replaced with a porcelain mask, featureless save the reflective circular lenses hiding her eyes, and decorated with silver floral embellishments the likes of which decorated the room's furniture. "She couldn't do much except talk, but boy, she sure does love to talk. I don't envy you rooming with her up top." She tapped a gloved finger to the mask's temple in gesture.

"So you asked Seth to get me back?" And just look how that turned out.

"Well, when Briar tried, she couldn't get past Evelyn," Kev noted, pulling his hand down from the nape of his neck to his collarbone as he studied the high ceiling, "Wherever you were in there, you weren't conscious, but Seth, his area of expertise is in the unconscious. Problem was, he's been a... *difficult* man to reach?"

"To say the least," Lin huffed. Above me, Brett and Faith shared a disapproving look I couldn't decipher.

"But at least with him, Briar could be our go-between. And when you finally started dreaming, he jumped in."

"Why'd you need a go-between? You were right there with him-" Memory struck, resurfacing from the haze of everything that had happened before Evelyn's absolute subjugation. I rounded a hard look on Brett and Faith, pulling the quilt tighter around myself. "Where is he?"

The disapproval in their eyes passed over to unease, silence filling the space between our words. "He..." Faith began, "He's busy with the Schevonian Clan Leaders."

It was almost obnoxiously clear to me there was more to this story, I'd have to be an idiot not to see it in the way Brett, Lin, and Kev stared at her, or hear it in the uncertain lilt of her voice, but I didn't push it. Seth had said, after all, he wanted to be the one to tell me – whatever the hell it was they weren't telling me.

"Fine," I said, voice flat, "So where can I find them?" Focusing on this, on him... anything would be easier than giving myself back over to the darkness in my head, to the horror in my reflection. I needed something to focus on, and I'd been focused on this for so long, it was practically second nature.

"We don't even get a hello?" Faith snapped, matching the severity of my tone, "We haven't seen you since the Khuloces Forest. I was worried about you!"

Heart clenching, I recoiled back from the vulnerability in her eyes. "It's not over yet. Not until I see with my own eyes… Not until I know everything we did wasn't for nothing." I would fix whatever was afflicting him, which they all seemed to know about and figured I was better off not knowing. Hell, even Evelyn had seemed to know, and that was just unacceptable!

Letting the quilt fall from my quaking shoulders, I swung my legs over the ottoman and came to a stand, ignoring the headrush which bloomed with darkness before my eyes. I had to look strong, or they would never let me go.

"Annie," Lin began, extending a hand to me as I passed, moving for the door. I could swear she'd gotten taller while I wasn't paying attention. "You won't find him if you go looking by yourself-"

"So, you're coming with me?" I entreated as I wrenched the door open, only to stand back in shock as a sound of stumbling and general cries of alarm filled the staircase in the hall beyond.

I hardly had a chance to register what I was seeing as Dorian stumbled down the stairs, falling headlong back into my life. He must have lost his footing on the landing and come tumbling down the moment I whipped open the door.

With arms flinging ahead to catch himself should he fall, he barely managed to fix his hasty footing the entire way down as gravity kept the stunt going, falling ever forward, until he crashed down into a roll, caught himself on one hand, and pulled off a last-second handspring to set himself back on his feet at the base of the stairs. And there I stood, eyes wide and astounded, in the doorway just in front of him.

Standing straight and impossibly unhurt, he glanced behind himself, as if surprised he hadn't broken his neck in that barely saved fall – and honestly, same – before meeting my eyes with a greeting smile. "Hi!"

"Oh my god," I groaned, striding past him for the stairs. Where they led, I had no clue, but anywhere was better than this fast-overcrowding space.

Leaping to keep stride with me, Dorian held a finger out ahead of himself to announce, "Now isn't the time for a tour of the palace, you've been invited to dinner."

"Dinner?" I echoed as the footsteps of my friends joined ours in the stairwell.

"A secret meeting with the powers of Blackano, Arillia, and Schevon," Dorian explained, "Master Hamish asked me to get you all."

"Seth, too? I'm sorta looking for him."

"Well..." he muttered, raising a hand to the back of his neck with averted gaze.

"How'd your Master know she was awake?" Brett interrupted from behind, and I could hear the clear accusation of secret surveillance in his tone.

"He'd be a poor Clan Leader if he didn't have even one seer in his entourage." Finding my sidelong glance, Dorian closed his eyes in that infectious, full-faced smile of his. "You'll be happy to hear, the Empress will be there."

My feet froze on the stairs, nearly bringing Lin to crash into me from behind, and I rounded to face Dorian fully. "The Empress? Like, of magikiers?"

"The one and only." He beamed now with a shining pride in himself. "Said I'd reach out to her for you, didn't I?"

"So she's here?"

"Arrived in Schevon only yesterday, but no one's seen her, fear of a Liberation Front attack on her Imperial Majesty being a valid concern and all. That's why-" He cut himself off, producing from the satchel on his hip a lavish gown and mask. "-this secret meeting with the Eastern Leaders has become something of an event."

43

Masquerade the Dread!

WHO THE HELL THOUGHT I COULD PULL OFF AN EVENING GOWN FIT FOR a world-class gala event? A weaver magikier, apparently, but more importantly, no one who knew me! This presumptuous weaver who'd been tasked with designing my outfit obviously mistook me for some kind of regal and confident hero-type, the *achaion* as they'd started calling me. Just a fancier word for champion. It was humiliating!

This designer, bane of my fragile self-esteem, had me in a rich scarlet and sheer, plunging V-neck dress with golden lace in floral patterns running down the deep neckline, and even included a leg sheath for the weapon of achaion – reduced to a silk-wrapped sickle at the moment – visible through the maxi slit skirts. As if wearing such a beautiful and delicate garment wasn't bad enough, it was now plastered to my skin from the clammy drizzle misting off sun-stained clouds, a light rain just cold enough to cover me with goosebumps beneath the thin material of my shawl.

It might have been an acceptable turn of events if I wasn't the *only* one in a dress.

Faith and Lin got to wear fitted, sacramento green suits like Brett, Kev, and Dorian, each of them disguised behind gorgeous Schevonian masks made pretty with silver designs. And here I was, pulling my gold and red shawl tighter around my shoulders as the wild tresses of my hair stuck wetly to the sides of my own golden half-mask, designed with inspiration from Briar's new form, dragonesque from the tip of my nose to the spiked crown. At the very least, this mask hid the slits under my eyes.

We approached the glass dome of the ballroom on the roof of the sprawling palace of Schevon built into the northern mountain range. Truly, a beautiful sight Dorian happily described for me in greater detail than the surrounding mists offered, but here I was trudging through the rooftop garden as panic gripped my lungs, staring down at my T-strap stilettos.

It would be here that the lavish meeting took place – how could Dorian even think to call it secret? – with more than a hundred patrons and an equal number of staff. Through frost-stamped windows, the dandelion fluffs of white dresses swung and floated around rich green suits, a mesmerizing waltz partaken by innumerable ballroom dancers inside.

I dropped both arms at my sides and stooped my shoulders with a whine. "Remind me again why I have to go in there? Isn't there a back entrance?"

Dorian watched me contritely, catching the hem of my shawl as it slipped down my arms. "I would have taken you that way, but it's reserved for the Empress when she arrives."

"Of course it is."

"I mean, she *is* the Empress," Kev considered with a hand on his chin, "She's sorta earned the special treatment."

Earned it... Tenebret's words returned to me, brief though they were, of the centions' involvement in the Empress' reign. Just how far from their control had she removed herself? Just how autonomous had the centions allowed her regime to be? And just how much credence could I give to the words of one so antithetical and reviled as the Kaipracan?

"I think I'm gonna be sick," I croaked, stopping again, "Granted, if I were alone out here, I'd be face down in the dirt, sobbing uncontrollably."

"Silver linings, Annie. Silver linings," Lin mused, picking a dewdrop flower in full bloom from the trimmed shrubbery to her right and bringing it to her mask to smell.

"Is it optimism to be aware of just how close I am to keeling over?"

"Sure, why not?" Kev chuckled.

Peering around Faith who had taken up the lead of our little group, I pushed my damp hair from the eyeholes of my porcelain mask to catch another glimpse of the dancers in their perfect form.

A desperate groan escaped me, and I wrenched my shawl around my shoulders as if I could squeeze myself out of time and space within its folds. "Do they expect me to dance, too?"

"*That's* what you're so worried about?" Brett sighed from my other side, where he stood with one hand on his hip, the other pinching the bridge of his nose. "Annie, you're a fine dancer."

"Okay, one, if that was even remotely true before, you just jinxed it. And two, that's an outright lie! I mean, it's like high society in there! Everyone is gorgeous and elegant and– and *refined*–!"

"You can be those things," he mused, but a dubious crease cut between his brows as he spoke.

I rounded on him, incredulity in my eyes. "Do I need to remind you of The Incident?"

"You were prepared with that," Dorian noted, quietly observing our exchange with a glint of fascination lighting up his lively regard. But Brett knew immediately what I was talking about, evident in the way he tugged at the collar of his dress shirt and averted his eyes.

"That's a bad example, and hard to replicate–"

"What about the *Other* Incident? Or the time the ends of my hair caught fire and I panicked and slapped a lit candle at your bare skin? Hm? We had *such* fun picking the wax out of your chest hair, didn't we?"

By the expression drawing his mouth down in the corners, this had just graduated to a shove-his-face-into-both-hands moment, and that he did, hiding a beet red blush. "I can't believe you're willingly bringing that up."

"Exactly! And I wasn't even dancing that time!"

"If it helps any, the ball's just a front," Dorian put in, amusement colouring his tone. "With everyone inside wearing these masks, any Liberation Front rogues who do manage to weasel their way in will be too busy figuring out who's who in the fancy festivities to realize the ones they're looking for aren't there at all."

"That's... mildly comforting. I guess," I huffed, and shut my eyes tight with a big inhale.

Disconnecting my senses from the outside world only went to tune me into my own nerve-wracked body, to feel the nausea roiling over in my gut twofold. My eyes flashed open again.

"Ooh, no, no, no. I should *not* be listening to my body right now, there's definitely some sorta problem in there."

Kev tapped a pensive finger to his chin. "Doesn't that mean you *should* be listening–?"

"Nuh-uh. Ignoring it is the only way I'll be able to stand with any dignity in front of the Eastern Leaders, let alone the *Empress*–" My voice became a squeak, choked high in my throat, and the gush of words cut out to nothing.

"Who needs dignity, anyway? We've gotten this far without it," Lin remarked, already scrapping all bets on my fight to scrounge up whatever it took to keep myself together.

Pursing my lips, I shot her a glare she could hardly see for the half-mask hiding the set of my brows. "You know what, no!"

"No, you need dignity, or…?" Kev warily guessed, as if fearing I was about to turn us around and ditch the meeting entirely.

Shaking off my trepidations, I pounded a fist on my palm and marched forward through the rain. "Dignified or not, there's no point to me panicking in the rain if I'll be panicking inside, too. No more wasting time!"

"Finally," Faith quietly sighed from the front, where she held an arm over her head to keep the rain from slicking her hair flat along the sides of her face and down her neck – at least, no more than it already had, made messier with flyaways jutting errantly from the middle parting. Hah, it wasn't often *she* was the one with unruly hair. In this, at least, I could find the teeniest, tiniest morsel of satisfaction to get me by.

At the path's end, a man wearing a sacramento green tailcoat jacket with light-catching silver buttons opened the high, crystal glass doors to us, through which we entered the crystalline ballroom as a group. A gorgeous chandelier the size of a small boat hung from a high, domed ceiling, and polished marble flooring befitting of an ice palace swept us into the large, open space where the music sounded as though it could have been played on a million crystal glasses, chiming beautifully on the crisp air captured within this seeming snow globe of dandelion dancers.

Upon striding into the spacious room on clicking, gold-tipped heels, I was thankful for the rain, now disguising that I was sweating bullets. I could swear everyone was looking at me, the only one among my company wearing such eye-catching regalia – my outfitter must have missed the memo, because everyone else was wearing some shade of green or silver. I was half-tempted to call out Dorian's empty reassurances – did he really think these extravagant measures would keep unwanted eyes off of me, or was I just the distraction keeping eyes off the Empress?

Brett's hand brushed my waist, sending an electric bolt through me in surprise, and I realized I'd fallen behind Dorian's lead in favour of sticking to the walls and shrinking into shadow.

Brett's lips came to my ear as he gestured toward the others making their way through the crowd, and on his breath, the words, "We're trying *not* to look suspicious, remember?"

"What's so suspicious about social anxiety?" I grumbled back, but nevertheless followed his guiding hand to join the masses of flourishing dancers.

In a strange, almost disassociated way, letting him steer me like this brought to mind all those times we would go to parties and clubs back in Blackano, a surplus of excuses to drink and forget the changes and disasters taking place all around us. When the crowds became too much for me, he would take the edge off by navigating me through to the other side, and always, whether we were dating or not, his touch was an unparalleled comfort. He never let me lose my way back then, nor did he now.

A warm feeling poured through me, stifling some of the nervousness still coating my internal organs like tar. "Thanks."

"Hm?" A note of genuine confusion picked up his voice, and I couldn't help but give a light chuckle. It was so second-nature to him, he didn't even know the extent of his assistance.

"You're looking at me funny," he noted, and I could only smile up at him. He was my first relationship. He knew me better than most ever had or ever would, and he was one of my best friends. But only now was I beginning to realize, I loved him in a way I would never love anyone else. These powerful sentiments carried over from romantic love, only heightened now as we took care of each other through this messed up world and our messy lives.

Breaking my gaze from his, I ducked my head in a shrug. "I was just thinking about how much I appreciate all the things you do for me."

"Oh?" he smirked, a note of pleasant surprise playing over his lowered voice.

"I don't always say it, and we don't always see eye to eye, but it doesn't hurt to get sappy every now and then." My eyes turned downward, watching the pirouetting feet all around us, but it was Seth's face which I saw in my mind's eye, painted with pain, despair, confusion.

In Blackano, he always had his partner to shoulder the burden of responsibility alongside him. He had always had it together, so much so, it was easy to forget just how young Seth was for a man of his position. Then his world had come crashing down around him, and we found ourselves here on Cellana, where he had assumed the role of commander by merit of his lineage, his name, and played the part accordingly.

In just one month, he had fallen into so deep a darkness and hadn't said a word of it, not until he said his goodbyes to me. Twice he had tried, but I hadn't really felt the weight of it until he made it abundantly clear for me. Such unrelenting darkness, that which I still didn't fully understand, but it was enough to consume him, enough to guide him to the edge. And it was enough to open my eyes to the sea of uncertainty laid out before me; that I never *really* knew what was going on in the minds of those closest to me.

Raising my gaze back up to Brett's, I pushed a smile through my bleak expression. "I'd rather be sappy than regret never saying anything. So, you can just call me a spile for all the sap I'll be tapping from this tree of camaraderie-"

"Okay, enough of that particular metaphor." He squeezed my side comfortingly, dipping his head closer to mine. "You know you don't have to be a *spile* with me. I'm not going anywhere."

"Well, y'know… we can't always predict what the future holds," I murmured, leaning into his side. "If I've learned anything since becoming a magikier, it's that."

A hint of a smile nestled in the corner of his mouth, fondness in his regard. "And just look at you now."

"A mess? That much I could've predicted," I joked, and plucked the soaked skirts of my dress up between my thumbs and forefingers in a mock curtsy. "Granted, the dress is a surprise."

He rolled his eyes, but the glimmer of a smile was there, hidden in the shape of his eyes and the curve of his lips. A wide grin stretched across my face.

"I'll always have your back, Annie, that's no surprise. We can fight and argue and bicker till the cows come home, and it sucks, but you can count on me."

I bumped his side, beaming up at him. "I know."

"Good. Then come on." There was a playful lightness to his tone as he planted his hands on my shoulders and steered me after the others, ignoring my curtsy. "Wouldn't want you accidentally becoming the life of the party."

"Ah yes, because *that's* something I'm prone to," I teased, striding along ahead of him under his hands.

With a snort and a deadpan tone, he informed me, "With enough drinks in you, it is."

The smile slid from my face, only fleetingly, but I teased in a tone laden with underlying severity, "Well don't say *that*."

I could practically hear Val's voice in the back of my mind encouraging the use of a little liquid confidence. My eyes strayed to the ample staff roving around the place carrying trays of colourful beverages in fancy flutes. It would certainly ease the anxiety – I shook off this dangerous notion, reminding myself of everything this line of thinking had led to last time.

Dorian took us through a beautifully carved stone arch at the far end of the ballroom. The spectacular corridor was lined with floor-to-ceiling mirrors leading to an iron-railed spiral stairwell to the grand hall below, but Dorian stopped us halfway down the length of this bizarre passage where none ventured.

He gestured grandly to Lin and had her crack the stone of some strange machination buried in the wall behind the mirrors, causing a sliver of the reflective glass to sink into the floor with a churning and chugging of mechanical engineering. There behind it was revealed a short vestibule where a dark-haired young woman in a sacramento green suit stood guard, leading into the chamber where I figured the secret meeting was to take place.

With a familiar nod to the young woman, Dorian ushered us through, and the secret door snapped back up into place behind us, calling a startled noise out of Kev. Dorian made sure to head the troupe beside me through this narrow passage which permitted only two to walk shoulder-to-shoulder.

"Ready to make your entrance?" he jauntily asked.

I parted my lips to speak, but my mouth was too dry.

He quirked me an encouraging smile. "If it takes any weight off your shoulders, you won't have to worry too much about first impressions. They've heard all about you."

"And would have already made up their minds about you," Faith spoke softly, "Keep your head up, Annie."

"Mm, great," I muttered, but gritted my teeth and shook out my shoulders, fixing the feather-light mask fitted comfortably on my face.

"Trust me, your actions across Arillia speak louder than anything you could say here," Dorian blithely noted.

"You underestimate my propensity for saying the wrong thing," I facetiously teased, catching his eye with an attempt at a smile of my own, and strode forward.

A hush fell over the room the moment I stepped in, but I hardly had the chance to burn up under the stares of these notable men and women seated around the heavy, round table in the center of this carousel-looking chamber. I recognized a handful of them, but my eyes were drawn to something else.

Reflective surfaces broke up the continued theme of silvers and greens so favoured in this lavish palace, giving the impression this smoky room could accommodate more than the ten already seated at this massive table fit for twenty. With gilded mirrors adorning the walls and five glass displays adorning the table, the teardrop lights on the silver chandelier overhead seemed rather a spattering of starlight twinkling all throughout the room. But even this elegance was diminished by the presence of what was contained in each of those glass displays.

My breath caught in my throat.

"No way," I heard Lin whisper from behind me, unable to help herself.

There, displayed on the round table before all, were five bone-white artefacts. In the glass case at the forefront, a rippled greatsword with an ornate, gold hilt. To its right, a pair of curved twin swords, edged with razor-sharp blades of polished bronze. To the left, a composite longbow wrapped with purple silks. Beyond that, a sizable war hammer, the head of which could have doubled as an anvil. And finally, in the glass case at the other end of the table, a circular, emerald-encrusted shield engraved with imagery I couldn't discern from this angle. I didn't have to ask to know, these were the other weapons of achaion. Bojack's collection.

It came as no surprise, then, that Bojack was seated at the far back of the round table. There, he slumped in his antique, velveteen chair with an elbow propped on the arm and his mouth pressed to his knuckles, deep in thought with a crease drawn between furrowed brows. Unlike the other richly dressed men and women seated around the table, he had no mask concealing his shrewd expression, and his gaze hadn't snapped to me at my entrance but rather held firm on the display cases in front of him, as if watching for something.

What he'd asked of me the last time we spoke resurfaced in my mind, and I wondered if something really was going to happen now that all the weapons of achaion were gathered together in one room. Judging by the look on his face, he didn't know what to expect, but he'd readied himself for anything. Surely, he knew best out of all of us the dangers associated with these mystical and powerful artefacts.

And on that topic, I wondered which of these weapons was responsible for the continuous deterioration of his body, the white half of his hair, the life-or-death dependence on his magic. Here it was, his morbid curiosity and his life's work laid out before a gathering of Eastern Leaders.

My eyes passed over the others at the table, my curiosity getting the better of me. Would I recognize the Empress for what she was when I saw her? Was she already here?

A finely manicured man wearing a black frockcoat draped over his shoulders with a plum and orange silk lining on the inside and bronze plates in a lacework design on the lapels and breast pocket sat on Bojack's right. He carried a cool confidence in his posture as he raised two purple and black fingers – tipped with glossy, plum violet nail polish as if to counteract the body horror of their crooked deformity – and beckoned us into the room. Dorian obligingly stepped forward, giving my arm one last reassuring squeeze as he went, and took the available seat to the man's right.

"Welcome," spoke this deep-voiced man whom I could only assume to be Dorian's master, the Second Clan Leader of Schevon, Grimshaw Hamish. His powerful, rumbling voice carried a distinguishable and calming quality, raising the hair on my arms.

He was hard to look away from once ensnared in his meditative regard, exceptionally pale to the point his lips stood out as a stark contrast of rose petal pink, with thick, ash blond hair falling over smoky, long lashed, purplish brown puce eyes. His bronze mask covered the left half of his face, adorned with dark purple designs outlining and accentuating his features rather than hiding them.

Something about this gentleman caught me off-guard, discreetly familiar like someone I'd encountered in a dream, and yet I was sure I didn't know him. My mind blanked and I almost forgot what I was doing here, until Faith nudged me forward and I leapt to the nearest available seat at the table.

There, I found myself situated beside two men I did recognize, representing the asylum seekers of Blackano while Seth was once again unavailable. Dorian had given me a rundown of names, ranks, and brief descriptions on our way over, and I'd been more than a little relieved to learn Brigadier General Lyovin, who'd set us upon our mission from the bastion at the City of Gates, was now General Lyovin, promoted since his near career ending tribunal. And so here he sat, greeting me with a smile, and on his other side sat his colleague, the man who'd stepped up in Seth's absence, General Griffith. Of everyone here, they spoke the least, a respectful quietness in their comportment as displaced leaders with no land to their claim.

Between the trio we three made and the trio of Grimshaw, Dorian, and Bojack were two others whom I recognized immediately, even with the silvered half-masks they wore. In the seat beside Dorian was the catapultier magikier who had led Jacob Cole's team, Monica her name was, now standing in as de facto Clan Leader of County Chthial in Arillia. She dipped her head in a greeting nod, and I smiled back at her, but I was loath to admit how my heart sank at the sight of her if only because I knew what her being here meant for Jacob Cole. It should have been him seated here at this council of Eastern Leaders. Hers was the place he had so merrily spoken of in the command tent behind the frontlines when he and Dorian were reminiscing on older days. The stories he'd told over dinner refurnished themselves in the stage of my mind, fitting the scenes he'd described to this a place where he would never again step foot.

Careful to squash these desolate thoughts before they could discolour the world around me and leach out all the light, I focused myself on the present. This quiet endeavour was made yet more difficult while, a couple chairs to Monica's left, there sat none other than the curmudgeonly Captain of the Arillian Spire. In the time since I'd last seen her, she'd ascended the ranks, chosen as Clan Leader of Cerenthior in the wake of all that had happened, and I'd had to clamp my mouth shut to stop myself vocalizing my critical reaction.

A tremble began in my fingertips, but I focused on my breathing and calmed the anxiety that came with having all these nerve-wracking individuals I'd been sufficiently intimidated by when it was just the two of us now eclipsing me in a group setting. Three others sat across from Monica and the Captain of the Arillian Spire whom I didn't recognize, and somehow that made them even more daunting.

I wracked my brain to recall the finer points of Dorian's debriefing. The First Clan Leader of Schevon, Harrison Ithast, unmistakeably sat between the Second and Third Clan Leaders of Trime, Elise Anspeth and Bella Fausswir, but I wasn't quite sure who was who. The three of them scrutinized me so blatantly, so unabashedly unafraid to catch my eye, I could feel a clammy sweat starting on my palms.

No sign of the Empress yet, that much was clear, and this realization brought a slight relief. The illusion of procrastinating my judgement, even while the table busied themselves sizing me up with cunning eyes and secret hearts. It was as Faith had said. They'd already made their judgements about me; I could see it plain on their half-masked faces and in the rigidity of their postures. But that was the extent of the read I got off of them.

Only Grimshaw sat with any manner of genuine comfort or perhaps it would be more correct to call it a seeming neutrality. He leaned back in his velveteen armchair with legs crossed thigh over thigh, and for it, he was utterly indecipherable. "All here are welcome at our table. Please, sit," he continued, speaking now to Faith, Brett, Kev, and Lin, and gestured widely to the available seats on my left. And so, they sat, situating themselves as close to me as the seating arrangements allowed.

With that, Grimshaw gave Bojack a pointed nod, and heaving a world-weary sigh, Bojack complied with the tacit request.

He came to a stand at the other end of the table, the rattle of metal chains slithering over stone tiles accompanying his movement. I realized with a start; his ankles were shackled. Still a prisoner, then. I supposed I shouldn't have been surprised.

"Let's get this started before the Empress steals the show, then, shall we?" Bojack huffed, glancing around the circle of masks as eyes trailed from me to him, and then to the display cases gathered here before all, "Not like I have much choice."

Dorian coughed pointedly into his hand, and Bojack rolled his eyes with a bitter nod of his head. I could only imagine all the hassle Dorian endured in coercing even an ounce of Bojack's compliance.

And so, with a lethargic arm extended in gesture to the display cases, Bojack put on a listless if not outright bored intonation and presented, "Behold, the arms of achaion." He sent a sidelong glance over his shoulder to Grimshaw, an unaired question in his eyes asking if he could return to his thoughtful silence now, but Grimshaw circled a hand, urging him on, and he dryly whinged, "Lot of trouble for a fancy knickknack collection if you ask me."

"These aren't *knickknacks*," hissed the man I'd never met before, laying the disdain on thick. The silver mask covering the bottom half of his face to the bridge of his beak-like nose muffled his voice and further detracted from the nasally quality of his speech with its distracting elegance, decorated with green gems in floral patterns along the curves of his nose, cheekbones, and jaw. As a First Clan Leader, Dorian had made it abundantly clear, this Harrison Ithast fellow was the highest-ranking Eastern Leader present.

"Unless you can use them, I think you'll find there's little difference between these pretty things and paperweights." Bojack flashed a wicked grin at the man. "Or do you want a go at the trial of achaion?"

"Bojack," Grimshaw warned, but there was only disapproving exasperation in his tone as, on his other side, Dorian dropped his face in his hands.

"Then what are they doing here?" the elder of the Trime Clan Leaders spoke up, scrunching her nose behind her quarter-mask like she'd tasted something sour. Her eagle-eyed glare was fixed on Grimshaw. "They should be kept apart, hidden, *protected*. Lest the Kaipracan catch wind of their location."

"They were already going to the Kaipracan," Grimshaw coolly explained, his eyes sliding to Bojack's back, "Isn't that right?"

"They were going to the highest bidder," Bojack corrected him as if that made a difference.

"But my bounty hunter intercepted the transaction," Grimshaw continued, returning his tepid gaze to the disgruntled woman. "And now, we have reason to believe they can be used."

A hush fell over the table as eyes shifted and postures straightened. Distrust and suspicion pervaded the heavy air like an immutable stench.

"By who?" the Captain of the Arillian Spire spoke up, speaking with a slow and measured intonation made spine-chilling by that harsh voice of hers. She made it clear by tone alone, there were few present she would entrust with such powerful weapons, but her eyes were on me.

"As the keepers of the land bridge to the West, Trime has the most need-" the younger of the Trime Clan Leaders began, only to immediately find herself spoken over by the man beside her.

"The Liberation Front devastated Schevon's border forces and continues to pose a threat from the south. If any Clan should have these weapons-"

"You can't intend to take them all for yourself," Monica puttered, "Arillia can't be rebuilt without sound defenses-"

"And leave Schevon unfortified? If the Liberation Front were to combine forces with the Orange Sages of the northern isles-" heatedly continued the man, but he cut himself off when Grimshaw made a low noise in his throat, disillusionment captured in the sound.

Grimshaw made no comment, nor did his nonchalant comportment diminish in the slightest, but he didn't have to say anything. The other Schevonian Clan Leader let it go, lowering his gaze respectfully.

Vaguely, I recalled something Dorian had said when I first heard him mention his master. That Grimshaw had led the Orange Sages of the Schevonian Isles, his clan, but they'd disappeared. Now, I wasn't so sure they hadn't simply defected.

"And again we see the Ego of Schevon," the Captain of the Arillian Spire scoffed, "Unwilling to lend aid to those who need it."

"And where was Arillia when the north fell?" Harrison Ithast challenged her, speaking as though the question was mere harmless illumination on an understated matter.

"If Schevon had reached out for help, we would have answered, but you *knew* the threat Arillia faced." The Captain launched up from her seat, slamming her fists down on the table's edge. "All of you! While Trime kept airborne on floating cities, far out of reach of the threat below, and Schevon dug underground in these sprawling mountain ranges, we in Arillia were run out of our homes and slaughtered! Those of us who survived, driven to barbarism in sequestered camps! *That's* where we were! You don't know what it is to feel weak, and yet you demand these weapons for yourselves."

"It's true," Grimshaw began, the gravity of his voice calling all eyes on him, "It's been a long time since we've all sat here together. Longer still since we've stood as one. We didn't notice as we fell into the trap of division. Of rejecting each other in favour of ourselves, our own borders, our own turfs. But this new threat, this Valencia Lupei and her infectious ideas, is a common enemy unbeholden to the bounds of our made-up borders. It's for that reason these weapons must be wielded by those willing to fight for each and every one of us."

"Noble words," the Captain of the Arillian Spire hissed, unmoved, "But your actions tell a different story. I didn't see you standing against the Liberation Front on the battlefield that had become of my country."

"My title is just that, a title in memoriam. I was the last Clan Leader of the Schevonian Isles before my domain fell to a plague of pora, not unlike Arillia. If I had reinforcements to offer, I would have sent them."

The elder of the Trime Clan Leaders turned a disdaining eye on the Captain of the Arillian Spire. "Sit down, Helena."

"Yes, sit, won't you," Bojack tacked on with groaning stretch, "There's no point fighting over the arms, anyway." He thought about it. "Besides my amusement, but even that's running thin."

Monica quirked her head to the side. "What do you mean?"

"Look to your Uniter and tell me what you see," Bojack said around a yawn, gesturing vaguely in my direction, and I bolted upright in my seat, unsure what he wanted from me.

All eyes were once again on me. No, not me, the weapon of achaion already holstered on my thigh. It was hardly new information that the Captain of the Arillian Spire didn't think much of me, but her cold regard made it starkly evident, she would have already confiscated Fiamme from me if she could.

Only then did she seat herself, moving slowly without removing her eyes from me, such that she reminded me of a viper preparing to strike. The table fell silent, and across from me, Bojack met my gaze with a Cheshire Cat grin.

"Beginning to grasp the reality, are we?" he carried on, like a lecturer in front of his class, "The best and possibly only candidates for harnessing these arms have just entered the room."

At his words, a surge of whispers and disagreements passed around the table, and I looked to my friends in confusion. They were just as bewildered as I.

"I see you're dubious," Bojack offhandedly remarked, "But, if any of you were capable of kinship, you might realize the weapons of achaion are each kin, connected as brethren and drawn to the hands of those who share deep bonds. Now that one has made its choice, the rest have… biases, I guess you could call it."

"You can't mean…?" General Griffith breathed, casting an astute eye over my speechless entourage.

No wonder Dorian had permitted them to attend a secret meeting of this calibre; they were the guinea pigs. Unaffiliated with Arillia, Schevon, or Trime, they were the perfect candidates not just because of our existing fellowship, but because they could operate outside of biased jurisdictions. But only if the weapons of achaion accepted them, I reminded myself.

It was this reminder which brought me to the realization, my heart didn't race with fear at the thought of putting them to the test like I would have expected, nor did my mind buzz with dark imaginings of what would happen if they failed the trial of achaion. Even with an example of exactly that outcome seated directly across from me, my immediate reaction wasn't one of concern. Rather, a spark of confidence unfurled in my chest, light and promising.

"You think it'll work?" I asked in a quiet voice, gaze locked with Bojack's.

"Capricious things, these weapons," he mused, and ran a hand through the white of his hair in gesture, "If this isn't evidence enough that I've been wrong before, then for liability's sake, take everything I've said and my decades of studies in devotion to these ancient relics with a grain of salt. Any unforeseen deaths this day won't stain my conscience, or my record." He looked to Grimshaw, whose measured expression neither confirmed nor denied this statement, so he sighed and continued, "That said, if I were a gambling man, and I am, my money's on you lot," before sinking back into his seat, hand waving in a circle and elbow propped on the arm with an air of utter disinterest. "So, who'd like to place some bets?"

"Stop that," Grimshaw dryly chided, hardly paying him any mind, but something about the familiarity of his tone told me he was accustomed to Bojack's bad behaviour.

Peering sidelong toward Faith on my left, I was surprised to note the pensive consideration in the squint of her eyes, enraptured upon the dual blades in their glass case. Beyond her, Brett's eyes met mine, and I could see the uncertainty in them. A question of worth, of whether he belonged in this line-up of candidates. My smiling encouragement came as an innate response, doubtless and authentic.

On his other side, Lin and Kev were locked in silent conversation, a language of looks shared between them. She reached a wandering hand to the glass case exhibiting the sizable hammer, but he pawed her hand away with a shake of his head.

"The weapons call to you?" guessed Monica as she watched them, voice breathy and eyes sparkling with transparent fascination. Unlike the other leaders, she had seen how Lin and Kev handled themselves in the theatre of war, having fought alongside them while I rode with Jacob Cole. There was no trepidation to be found in her expressive features, only unrestrained excitement.

"It's... bizarre," Faith said, and looked to General Griffith for permission to speak. With his nod, she continued, "It's sort of like when Briar makes her presence known in my mind without speaking. I know she's there, but there's no real sign that she's in my head besides a feeling. From the moment I stepped into this room, that unspoken presence has been in the back of my mind, and I think it's coming from those." She raised a pointed finger to the twin swords.

"Really?" Lin interjected, glancing up from the hammer. "I figured it was this hunk of dragon-bone."

Kev shook his head. "I don't know what you're talking about. It's gotta be the bow."

Leaning his temple against his knuckles, Brett reasoned, "And for me, it's the greatsword. So I take it, the arms of achaion have already made their choices?"

From the other end of the table, Bojack's eyes glimmered with intrigue. "Must be nice to have that little reassurance, but just because they call to you doesn't guarantee they'll accept you as achaion."

"Should we really be deciding this while the Empress isn't present?" tsked the younger of the Trime Clan Leaders, but something in the way she said it made me think the Empress would ensure the weapons of achaion went to Trime. It was, after all, the land bridge to the West where the Empress held greater domain.

"It wouldn't change matters," Grimshaw noted, a hint of annoyance entering his tone.

"Have I miscounted or does this leave the dragon-bone shield without a wielder?" the elder of the two Trime Clan Leaders spoke up, giving rise to the earlier tensions in the room.

"Actually," I chimed in, "As far as bonds go, I know someone who fits the bill. Seth Knox, the man we rescued from the Arillian Spire..." The words died on my tongue as faces fell and expressions turned sour around the table. Even the Generals averted their eyes, mouths turning down in distaste or embarrassment – I couldn't figure which.

Bojack cast a sullen glance over the shield in front of him. "It'd be a death sentence."

I was taken aback, a crease drawn between my brows in disdain. "Why? If anyone would be worthy-"

"The magic in him isn't compatible. Why do you think the Kaipracan sent a magikier to collect these treasures and not his most loyal kirranites or pora? Dragon-bone is like poison to them. It's a clash of pure magic and the magical decay that oozes off those parasites. They can't exist together, so it follows that a pora could never wield a weapon of achaion. It would only register the pora's magic as a threat and eliminate it with the trial."

"Okay, but why is that relevant to Seth?" I demanded, but he gave me a pitying look as if I should have known the answer.

"When we found him in the Spire, it was clear," Monica began in a gentle tone, "The last descendent of the Knox lineage had been infected with the pora disease some time ago. I'm sorry."

I barely registered her words, flashes of the blood shower spattering the hollows of my mind with horrific red, and an image of Jacob Cole resurfaced from the murky depths, the despair of his confession painted in his expression. "No." My voice cracked on the word. "He's not pora. He's used his magic to visit my dreams."

"You're not wrong. He admits he's half-pora," General Lyovin explained to me in his thick-accented voice. "That he had healing in time to stop pora disease completely eradicating magic, but he is just as infectious."

On his other side, General Griffith dipped his chin in a sage nod. "It's the reason he let himself be taken from the bastion in your place. If he'd explained his condition to his advisors, I'm sure you wouldn't have been sent out after a lost cause like him."

I caught the tinge of disapproval in his voice, directed not at me nor even this talk of Seth, but rather, to the man who'd assigned me the task of retrieving him in the first place. And yet, General Griffith's evident hang-ups with General Lyovin's choices hardly mattered to me, not while all the scattered puzzle pieces I hadn't wanted to address clicked together in my head. The secret Seth wanted to be the one to tell me, the Kaipracan's cryptic hints toward his broken magic, his hopeless despair in the belief that death was his only option, all the way back to the night in the City of Gates when I'd healed his bloody wound. All along, he'd kept it from me – that he'd been infected from the start, and my magic had made a half-pora of him.

"Where is he?" My voice shook.

Jacob Cole's relentless sense of duty returned to me, a grim reminder of the lengths all were expected to go to keep the impossibly fast-spreading pora infection out of magikier cities.

Searing hot tears sprung to my eyes, and I clenched my fists on my thighs, so tight, I felt my nails dig into the meat of my palms. "He's not... He can't be...?"

"He's okay," Faith leapt in, and found my wrist with a consoling squeeze.

"He's been taken into custody as a healed pora with the opportunity to prove his enduring fidelity," Grimshaw said when all the rest held silent, "After standing witness to the cooperation of pora and magikiers in the Liberation Front, it stands to reason, the same may be possible for those who've shown true devotion to the centions."

"It's beyond reason," the First Clan Leader of Schevon disdained. "He still poses the risk of infecting magikiers like any other pora."

"He's been remarkably compliant," Dorian optimistically spoke up.

"You can thank your friends here-" The Captain of the Arillian Spire motioned to Lin and Kev. "-for shielding him the moment he was found and proving their hard-headedness in demanding an audience with the Third Clan Leader of Arillia."

"Jacob Cole?" I gasped, sitting upright in my seat, "How is he?"

It was Monica who spoke up, hastening to clarify the story. "When we heard what had become of Seth Knox, and that he'd continued to serve as Commander of the City of Gates for weeks while afflicted with the infection, I felt it necessary to put your theories to the test. I'd overheard your conversation with Jacob Cole, and so, I took matters into my own hands. I had him healed. He'd already lost the majority of his magic to the infection, but the transformation was halted before completion. Like these Schevonian clansmen are doing for your commander, my team is evaluating him closely to better understand the half-pora transformation."

The beak-nosed man shook his head with a reproachful harrumph, shooting a glare toward Grimshaw. "How can you stand for this after everything you've seen? The slaughter of your people–"

"I'm no stranger to half-pora," Grimshaw reminded him, the rumbling depth of his voice shaking my very bones and snapping the man's mouth shut in humbled respect. "Droves of them, no, of good men and women, sent over sea cliffs with cinderblocks on their feet at the mere accusation of hidden infection. If it took the events witnessed in Arillia for us to start reconsidering the execution of half-pora, then I'll gladly stick my neck out for the man under my charge."

I stared back and forth between them like I was watching a tennis match, made all the more dizzying with the surge of questions roiling around in my brain. So, Dorian's master had defended Seth upon his arrival in Schevon. I had to admit, it was the little things like this that really worked wonders in the way of first impressions.

"Can I…" I knew it was a long shot, but I wrung my hands on my lap and continued, "Can I see him?"

Grimshaw turned a contrite eye on me. "It wouldn't be advisable for the time being. Magic like yours, it could break his will. And if that were to happen, we'd risk losing our shonte."

"I understand." A bold-faced lie. Sure, I grasped the rationale – temptation, infection, plague – but what I couldn't comprehend was the unfairness of it all. That this had happened to Seth, had *been* happening to Seth under my nose. And that, after everything, I couldn't go to him.

"Might I remind you," the elder of the Trime Clan Leaders croaked from a throat withered with age, "We haven't solved the problem of the dragon-bone shield and who it'll go to."

"Sir," a voice interrupted, and all eyes turned to the girl in sacramento green guarding the secret entrance. Her eyes were on Grimshaw. "The Empress will be here shortly."

"Perfect timing. Thank you, Jennifer," Grimshaw remarked, and turned his gaze back onto me. "You may want to leave the talking to us when the Empress arrives."

I couldn't help but glance over my shoulder to be sure he was talking to me. "Well, she knows about the Liberation Front? About Valencia?"

"She's been informed," the beak-nosed man nodded, to a chorus of inscrutable reactions from his other colleagues. "But it's on the topic of you she's expressed her... misgivings."

"Me?"

"You're the shonte, Champion of Blackano, Champion of Arillia, and Uniter of the East," Grimshaw explained, "It's like I said. The Eastern Leaders haven't gathered like this in a *very* long time. Not until you came along."

"It wasn't my intention..." Hell, rerouting everyone to Schevon wasn't even my idea, I was just the mouthpiece.

"Like I've always said," Bojack drawled from his casual position sprawled across the arms of his armchair, "A genius by accident is still a genius."

"Huh, now there's a surprise. Was that a compliment?"

"I usually say it about myself," he offhandedly remarked, peering unfazed at his fingernails.

"Ah, there it is."

Dorian fixed a disapproving look on the spread-eagled man seated across Grimshaw from him. "Bojack, we've been over this."

"Oh?" He gave more attention to the study of his nails. "I so rarely listen to you."

"Remind me again why I allowed you at this meeting," Grimshaw mused, a mild inflection of threat captured in the gravity of his voice.

"Because I'm a delight," Bojack deadpanned, unmoved, "Nay, a paragon of moral support, as you just witnessed. Oh, and I'm the only expert on this side of the war."

"Quit your boasting," Grimshaw sighed, a fitting tone for the annoyance this incorrigible nuisance of a man brought out in anyone who kept his company for any length of time. Including, it appeared, this highly spoken of and noble-minded Clan Leader of Schevon.

The click of pointed heels registered in the back of my mind, but it was the deafening silence as the room went quiet that alerted me to the new addition to our secret gathering. Not even Bojack dared challenge the sudden rush of this suffocating hush, sinking deeper in his seat as if he meant to disappear into the cushions. Craning my neck, I nearly leapt out of my seat at the sight of a tall woman gliding into the room.

She emerged with an understated flourish from the mirrors themselves. I hadn't even noticed a panel whisper open across the floor, revealing a narrow, arched corridor leading deeper into the labyrinthine maze of the lower palace floors, dug straight out of the mountainside. But there she was. The Empress in all her glory.

44

A Little Late for Ultimatums

THE FIRST THING I NOTICED WAS THE MASK SHE WORE, OR MORE ACCURATELY, the exquisite headdress which crowned her golden head of hair and spiraled down the curves of her face as if the gold had melted in the shape of delicate floral outlines and diamond-encrusted starbursts. It did little to hide the majesty of her features, regal and sharp. This elaborate accessory trailed down from her fine jawline in thin, jewel-encrusted chains and connected to a golden mantle around her neckline, affixed with one, large gem in the center of her chest.

I recognized what it was the moment it caught my eye. This translucent gem, multi-faceted and iridescent with a rainbow of colours caught in the refractions, could be nothing other than the timeless essence of pure domenth magic crystallized into an inanimate jewel. I'd seen something like this only once before, but the one I saw had been missing a sliver – a sliver which had found its way into my body and brought Evelyn in with it. This one, I was positive, couldn't have been Evelyn's essence, which Valencia had taken off of Dyval when they clashed in battle. I was sure of it, this gem adorning the Empress of magikierkind was the essence of some other domenth who'd been halved just like Evelyn had.

Before I knew it, I'd flown to my feet, sending my chair screeching out backwards from me. I was sure everyone was staring, but it was the Empress's measured gaze, seething with a disrespected glare and emanating an aura of absolute power that had me shaking to my core.

In her glare, I felt the monumental weight of a cention's disdain, that which I'd felt when Dyval herself had berated me in the space between worlds. As I'd passed through the gate to Cellana and endured the slights and insults of an enraged cention, that was the only other time I ever felt what this woman's gaze carried in it so effortlessly.

"Dyval?" I whispered, barely audible over the blood rushing in my ears.

The Kaipracan's words returned to me, and I finally understood. The Empress was a façade. Magikiers on Cellana had never grown out of the rule of centions like they were told. Just as it was in Blackano, the magikiers of this world answered to a cention sovereign masked under a guise they could trust. The Kaipracan knew it, and, it seemed, so did the Eastern Leaders, for none of them wore the looks of shock and disbelief that the Generals now gazed upon the Empress with, nor the flabbergasted awe captured in Faith and Brett's eyes as they studied the sight standing there before them, nor Kev and Lin's incredulity, nor even Dorian's wide-eyed astonishment.

"Just as insolent as you've always been, Anelisha," acknowledged the Empress in a smoky voice, and I was sure of it. Although she sounded more human than the last time I'd heard her, less of an invasion into my mind which threatened to capsize my sanity with every word, I recognized her voice for who she really was.

I wanted to scream. To shout at this latest betrayal of what I'd thought was the reality. Instead, I fell back in my seat, breathless and, for whatever reason I couldn't place, gutted. Maybe I'd banked on the hope that the Empress was someone I could believe in. Maybe, I was only just realizing how little I believed in the centions themselves. And there, sheathed within that desolate sentiment, I found a kernel of truth.

Dyval knew all along what was happening in Arillia and what was coming from Blackano. All the urgency I had felt to warn the Empress of the coming war was misplaced. I just wanted the people to be prepared, and I had thought, misguidedly, that if the Empress knew, she would have done something, anything.

How many countless hours had Seth and I spent mulling over how to send this message to the Empress, to force her to see what was happening so she would take the initiative and send reinforcements, but she already knew. From the very beginning, before we'd ever set foot on Cellana soil, she was well aware of the situation, and just like the centions had always done, she let the fires grow and eat away at everything until there was nothing left to fuel it. Or, she would have let it get to that point. I didn't.

No wonder she had her misgivings about me.

The expression slid from my face, becoming cold and empty, and I raised my chin in an indicative nod to the gem decorating her golden mantle. "Which domenth was that?"

Everyone else seemed to fall away, and just like that, no matter all the eyes I could feel watching us like a spectacle laid out before them, it could very well have been just her and me in this room of mirrors. Our eyes locked onto one another, and nothing else mattered.

A snake-like grin contorted her face, mirthless and boastful. "Are you familiar with the name Reuven Knox?" She spoke slowly, every word a scrupulous choice, like she had all the time in the world. I supposed she did.

"The Kaipracan mentioned him," I answered, working to conceal the whirlwind of theories that came with the name she'd so unceremoniously dropped at my feet. "He was the first shonte, and before that, the first magikier. Wasn't he?"

"He was the first reincarnation of the domenth, Herren." At the name, a shiver coursed up my spine, and an itch sank into the tops of my cheeks where I knew those unsettling eye slits to be. I could feel Evelyn's loathed presence rousing in the back of my mind, raising her unsolicited head in interest, but I shoved her down. Not here. Not now.

Flickers of second-hand memories flashed through my mind in retaliation against my pushing. A face that was oddly recognizable, captured in still images from ages long past. For a moment, I nearly let my jaw drop as the realization struck me. The man in these memories, although quite obviously captured at an older age with an unrecognizable hair style and distinctive scars, shared the face of the young man seated across from me. He even had Dorian's smile.

I stared across the table at Dorian, now unmistakeable to me as the modern reincarnation of the domenth, Herren. In these unwelcome memories, Evelyn had called him Ren. A flash of heat, of tenderness, of joy – a lover. A flash of fury, of hurt, of betrayal – a rebel on the opposing side. And a flash of pure devastation – a loss.

Herren was the first domenth to have his magic sheered from his body, even before Evelyn, and they had called it death. These echoes of long-lost context swirled in the haze of reminiscing Evelyn had apparently taken to in this moment, and I had to work to separate myself from her thoughts, returning myself to my present.

Sure, I had put together that carmavi magikiers were the result of domenth reincarnations, just like me, but I hadn't given much consideration to what it meant that Dorian was a carmavi. And now, to have the ice-bucket realization splashed upon me that the domenth he'd been reincarnated from had some relation to the squatter in my head, it was almost too much to rationalize.

Dyval thumbed the dazzling gem, a thoughtful expression coming over her as she paced the circumference of the table behind all those seated around it. I wondered if she was remembering him like Evelyn was remembering him as I followed her with my eyes. The sharp clicks of her heels with each step came muffled by the skirts of her gossamer gown slithering over the tile behind her and filling the room with this soft sound.

"And?" I finally demanded, earning a kick under the table from Faith.

"It was my mother's idea to awaken the magic in his mortal reincarnation," she mused, "She brought my sisters and I together, and we bound the magic of halved domenths to a word, *shonte.* Words have power, you see, and once she fed the reincarnation the sweet nectar of Herren's magic, the ritual was complete. A mortal who'd devoted his life in service to us could wield the magic of a domenth." She leveled her gaze with mine, narrowing her gold-lined eyes. "It was a mistake. When you took this power for yourself, you summoned Evelyn's magic through that bond, that word, having already infused a piece of her with the body you now share. I take it, that was her doing."

I held my tongue. She was right, Evelyn was the one to kickstart that little transformation sequence, but what did it matter now? What's done was done.

She traced a finger over the glass case of the dragon-bone shield, staring into the designs engraved upon the face of the large artefact. A compendium of untold histories passed behind her eyes, so unfathomably vast and deep, I nearly lost myself in them. "By now, you must recognize what it is to possess power. The first shonte understood right away."

A beat of pensive silence passed, and my overburdened mind could only draw blanks. "Enlighten me."

She raised an eyebrow at me but carried on with a casual air. "It's the domain of the powerful to make choices. We cast our stones over the rippling waters of time and space and peoples, and the ripples we make are as tsunamis to the weak. Power is relevance, but it's comparative. So it goes that power is measured by conflict to escape obsoletion. The powerful fight to maintain our place or to ascend ever higher up the ladder of relevance, and the weak flock to the victors as they burn the effigies of those they once professed to love. These contests between the powerful few to sate the desperate savagery of the ample weak. You are not exempt from this, Champion. Surely, you've already witnessed what I speak of."

"I've witnessed a lot of people making powerful choices, people you might consider weak, who banded together and overcame something bigger than themselves. What's your point?" I demanded.

"You see only what you wish to see."

"You think you're any different?" I scoffed, but she ignored me.

"What is *your* choice, Champion?" She swept around the table, letting her fingertips ghost over the glass displays, until she stood directly over me and placed a hand on my shoulder. My friends recoiled back from her, and though I tensed, I did my best not to flinch at her touch. Against myself, a slight tremble took root in my fingers as she watched me down the length of her nose, her expression unreadable. "If power begets conflict, I'd like to know with certainty that you're an extension of my hand and not a knife in my back."

"Do I have a choice?"

"Always. You have, before you, two options. You will choose to accept me as your sovereign, your Empress, and you will be my champion, a warrior at my disposal, or you will choose to forfeit all power and waste away in the dungeons of Vincladimhús until your body is broken and your life is spent. So make your choice."

I'd always hated ultimatums. Something about them felt so despicable to me, I never really understood why.

Dyval took a step back and offered the back of her hand to me, prompting me to seal my unwavering loyalty with a kiss to the gold-embroidered silk of her glove.

An oath of fealty to a cention carries powerful magic.

The words rattled in my head, unmistakably Evelyn, but I didn't need to hear it to feel the waves of magic rolling off of Dyval. I wondered if this was anything like the bond Valencia made with her loyalists.

I glanced to Dorian, then to Grimshaw, but their expressions were equally indecipherable. For once, Dorian wasn't smiling, but rather watching the scene unfold intently with his elbows propped up on the table and his hands interlocked in front of his mouth. Grimshaw was a blank wall, entirely devoid of emotion. Then there was Bojack, avoiding all eye contact and feigning like he wasn't even here. I supposed I couldn't blame him. It was the Empress who set the bounty for his head and only his head, after all.

Beside me, the furrow of Faith's brow was like an open book. I knew, if the roles were reversed, she would have accepted in an instant. The worst part was I understood her confusion. After all, I was opposed to the Liberation Front – hell, Valencia needed me dead more than any of her true enemies; getting rid of me was the only way she could get her sister back. Not to mention, everything I'd done in all this time was in favour of the centions' side. So why was I hesitating?

"As your champion, what would you have me do?" I asked, leaning back from her offered hand.

"That will be for me to decide and you to obey." Her tone shifted, almost imperceptibly, with a hint of triumphant accusation. "Do you distrust me?"

"Okay, I have a question for you. Did that sound like an appealing answer in your head, or can you just not hear yourself?"

Faith kicked me harder this time, and I probably deserved it, but Dyval only flashed that slimy grin down at me as a collective inhale stole the air out of the room, inviting the kind of silence that itched under my skin and made me want to bounce a knee under the table. I could practically feel the Captain of the Arillian Spire's disbelieving glare, astounded that I would take this tone with a cention – I liked to think it made her feel a little better about the tone I took with her the last time we spoke.

"Look, Dyval," I tried again, "If I'm being completely honest with you, which I have been every time we've had these obscenely stress-inducing chats, I don't like how you run things. And then I look around me, and I see great leaders I would follow into battle, to the end of hope and beyond." My gaze found General Lyovin to my right, and the corners of my mouth raised into an involuntary smile. "Individuals who've risked everything to set things back to the way they should be. Who've believed so deeply in something, they were willing to put their trust in me and suffer the consequence whether I succeeded or failed." I shot the Captain of the Arillian Spire a smirk. "They may not have been nice to me, and I can't exactly blame them – I mean, you know what I'm like – but they listened to me. They went out on a limb to help me when I needed them." I glanced to Monica, an image of Jacob Cole taking the center stage of my mind. "They gave me hope when I couldn't see the light at the end of the tunnel, and they stood side by side with me at what looked like the end of all things." I returned my gaze to Dyval, but it was Tenebret who occupied my thoughts. For a moment, in my mind, I was back there at the height of the Spire, staring into the face of futility. "I've seen the devastation you've wrought upon your enemies, so deep they'll never heal. I've seen the lengths they feel they have to go in the pursuit of peace. And I've seen them forsake all hope for peace, so entrenched in your wars that they don't see any future on the other side of it. I've seen a lot, Dyval, and after all that, I'm not too stoked about handing all my agency over to you."

"You know the alternative," she reminded me, that spine-chilling grin still staring me in the face, eyes unblinking and mouth just slightly too big for my comfort. The longer I looked at her, the less human she appeared.

That was when I made the colossal mistake of glancing at Brett. I'd never seen such a blatantly distraught look on his face. He made no effort to hide the distress under his eyes, too focused on conveying a desperate message through them. He met my glance with a lecture clear in his own, pleading with me to just suck it up and agree to whatever Dyval was asking. He knew exactly where my mind was, and I could plainly see the terror this incited in him.

My eyes found the hand still offered in front of me.

She's backed you into a corner.

Loyalty or death.

Not just death.

Not helping.

"You don't know how badly I wanted to believe in you," I finally said, voice as hollow as the feeling in my chest, "How hopeful I was that things would be different after Blackano, that you'd be less… you." I choked on a self-deprecating laugh and spoke my next words around a derisive smile. "But you're the Empress! You had all the opportunity in the world to show that anything I said or did got through to you, and it's just so glaringly obvious, not a single thing has. The one person I really thought I made a difference in, and you're still just as absent, unfeeling, selfish… I wouldn't hesitate to give my life for magikiers, but I can't pledge myself to someone I don't believe in." My eyes trailed up to hers, the empty smile still plastered on my disillusioned face. "Frankly, I think I hate you."

That sickening smile of hers widened somehow higher on her cheeks, turning my stomach over at the sight. "You've made your choice clear."

"You're just glad to be rid of me," I sassed back, only to immediately lose whatever cool points the backtalk might've gained me as I winced at the sudden blur of movement in front of me.

In my defense, I thought she was going to end me right then and there. To be fair, I had no idea how imprisonment in the dungeon of old worked. For all I knew, one measly bop on the head would blip me over there to be locked up for all eternity. But she didn't touch me. In fact, she'd staggered back from me.

Opening my eyes out of the mortifying wince that had left me entirely at her nonexistent mercy, I came to the sudden and truly horrifying realization, I had inadvertently started a brand-new conflict.

The source of the commotion became immediately clear to me, for there in front of me was the dragon-bone shield, no longer contained to its case and jutting out of the broken mirror between Dyval and I. At the other end of the table stood Dorian, caught in a pitcher's pose for having thrown the shield between us, and looking simultaneously appalled at himself and proud of his handiwork.

Only then did I realize what this all meant. The dragon-bone shield had chosen him. And he had chosen me over the centions.

Bojack cowered back in his seat, making himself small in Dorian's shadow as he stared up at him from eyes as round as pennies. Beside him, Grimshaw set his jaw, fury evident in his expression. Welp, it seemed not a single person had expected this from Dorian, not even himself.

Dyval righted herself from the readied stance she had so seamlessly slipped into. Her seething glare swept over the room, dropping the temperature below zero. "It appears you'll have fitting company in your confinement, Evelyn."

I snapped to face her, curling my lip, but the voice that escaped me in a furious growl was hardly my own. "Leave Ren out of this."

A clatter of toppled chairs and scraping chair legs clamoured behind me as Kev and Lin dove for the weapons which had called to them and Faith and Brett followed suit, foregoing all fear of the trial of achaion in favour of taking up arms in defense of me. Faith took my wrist, Brett pressed a hand to my side, and before I knew it, they'd blocked me off from Dyval, forming a circle around me.

So it was on them that Dyval focused her attention, and if it were a fair fight, I was sure she would have easily stamped us out in an instant, but it wasn't a fair fight. No, it was hardly a fight at all.

From behind Dyval, a doorway of light ripped open through the very air itself. I recognized the rectangular tear through space, but it didn't register with me right away what I was seeing. When it did, the breath escaped me in one big whoosh as the coherent thought began to form in my mind that this was a gateway born of the gate key. Before I could finish the thought, it was over.

I couldn't exactly fathom *what* was over. In a way, it felt like everything was over. Game over. Because there behind Dyval stood someone I had wished never to see again.

I recognized her immediately, faster than I could register what I was seeing.

Valencia Lupei.

She stepped through the gateway of light like she owned the place, emerging directly behind Dyval, and in the next instant, her hand was protruding through Dyval's chest, gripped around the gem embedded in her mantle and dowsed in the red of her blood.

A shockwave of darkness burst from Valencia's fist, sending a blast of force through the room which had the mirrors rippling and the chandelier chiming above our heads, but the necrotic cloud never left Dyval's body. Rather, it stained into her opened chest, and the momentary shock captured in the cention's wild-eyed stare was dowsed along with the lights, overtaken by shadow and a fast-spreading decay.

All I could do was stare. It was all any of us could do, for we had just witnessed Valencia do the impossible.

She yanked her hand back with an awful squelching sound and let Dyval's body drop, left with a gaping hole through her chest now oozing with the festering darkness that had leapt off Valencia's arm. And there she stood, Valencia, flipping the gate key over her knuckles with all the casual bravado of one who just dispatched a *cention* without so much as breaking a sweat, and she met our slack-jawed stares in open horror with a roguish grin.

"One down. You made that easy for me," she practically purred, giddy with her entrance, and she passed a radiant smile over the audience to her spectacle, landing razor-sharp eyes on me. Her breath left her on a satisfied sigh. "Long time no see, my little Eve."

About The Author

Julia T. Lye is a writer and lover of stories living and working in Ottawa, Ontario, and is a self-proclaimed geek. Her published stories, ranging from fantasy to science fiction and the macabre, have been featured in numerous collections and anthologies. When Julia isn't writing, she can be found drawing and illustrating characters from her stories, Dungeons and Dragons, movies and TV shows. You can read about Julia's writing journey at www.julialye.com and engage with her via social media. Julia is a graduate of Carleton University.

www.julialye.com
www.anelisha-knight.tumblr.com
@juliatlye

www.ingramcontent.com/pod-product-compliance
Lightning Source LLC
LaVergne TN
LVHW041052080826
845145LV00007B/1542

* 9 7 8 1 8 9 6 7 9 4 5 5 6 *